A Text Book Of

ADVANCED MANUFACTURING PROCESSES

For
Semester - V
Third Year Diploma Course in
Mechanical Engineering Group

As Per MSBTE's 'G' Scheme Syllabus

Prashant K. Ambadekar

M.E., LMISTE, AMIE
Assistant Professor in Mechanical Department,
South Indian Education Society,
Graduate School of Technology
Nerul, Navi Mumbai.

S. S. Agarwal

H.O.D.
Department of Production Engg.
V.B.V. Polytechnic
Vasai Road (W), Dist. Thane

NIRALI ™
PRAKASHAN
ADVANCEMENT OF KNOWLEDGE

N3112

Advanced Manufacturing Process   **ISBN 978-93-83971-62-6**

Fourth Edition   :   **June 2017**

©   :   **Authors**

Published By :   Polyplate

NIRALI PRAKASHAN

Abhyudaya Pragati, 1312, Shivaji Nagar,
Off J.M. Road, Pune – 411005
Tel - (020) 25512336/37/39, Fax - (020) 25511379
Email : niralipune@pragationline.com

☞ **DISTRIBUTION CENTRES**

PUNE

Nirali Prakashan : 119, Budhwar Peth, Jogeshwari Mandir Lane, Pune 411002, Maharashtra
Tel : (020) 2445 2044, 66022708, Fax : (020) 2445 1538
Email : bookorder@pragationline.com, niralilocal@pragationline.com

Nirali Prakashan : S. No. 28/27, Dhyari, Near Pari Company, Pune 411041
Tel : (020) 24690204 Fax : (020) 24690316
Email : dhyari@pragationline.com, bookorder@pragationline.com

MUMBAI

Nirali Prakashan : 385, S.V.P. Road, Rasdhara Co-op. Hsg. Society Ltd.,
Girgaum, Mumbai 400004, Maharashtra
Tel : (022) 2385 6339 / 2386 9976, Fax : (022) 2386 9976
Email : niralimumbai@pragationline.com

☞ **DISTRIBUTION BRANCHES**

JALGAON

Nirali Prakashan : 34, V. V. Golani Market, Navi Peth, Jalgaon 425001,
Maharashtra, Tel : (0257) 222 0395, Mob : 94234 91860

KOLHAPUR

Nirali Prakashan : New Mahadvar Road, Kedar Plaza, 1st Floor Opp. IDBI Bank
Kolhapur 416 012, Maharashtra. Mob : 9850046155

NAGPUR

Pratibha Book Distributors : Above Maratha Mandir, Shop No. 3, First Floor,
Rani Jhanshi Square, Sitabuldi, Nagpur 440012, Maharashtra
Tel : (0712) 254 7129

DELHI

Nirali Prakashan : 4593/21, Basement, Aggarwal Lane 15, Ansari Road, Daryaganj
Near Times of India Building, New Delhi 110002
Mob : 08505972553

BENGALURU

Pragati Book House : House No. 1, Sanjeevappa Lane, Avenue Road Cross,
Opp. Rice Church, Bengaluru – 560002.
Tel : (080) 64513344, 64513355,Mob : 9880582331, 9845021552
Email:bharatsavla@yahoo.com

CHENNAI

Pragati Books : 9/1, Montieth Road, Behind Taas Mahal, Egmore,
Chennai 600008 Tamil Nadu, Tel : (044) 6518 3535,
Mob : 94440 01782 / 98450 21552 / 98805 82331,
Email : bharatsavla@yahoo.com

niralipune@pragationline.com | www.pragationline.com

Also find us on 🅕 www.facebook.com/niralibooks

Preface ...

We are glad to present this book entitled "ADVANCED MANUFACTURING PROCESSES" for fifth semester students of ME/ PG/ PT course. While writing this book, we had continuously kept in mind to give the students more than the examination point of view. The book is written in a simple language so that the students can understand it easily. The meaning of important terms has been given at the end of chapters wherever applicable. Also, the summary of each chapter is given for the students to have a quick review during the examination.

Many contents have been introduced for the first time in this subject. The curriculum is such that it is not possible for the students to cover the syllabus from one reference book. This book provides the required syllabus in detail.

The basic manufacturing methods like casting, forging, extrusion etc. are well understood by the students in the lower semester. But students should also be aware of the processes like boring, broaching, milling and gear cutting which are performed on the workpiece. So these topics are newly added in the syllabus and forms Chapter 3 and 4.

The non-traditional manufacturing processes are now used mostly in manufacturing industry. These methods are explained with their process characteristics in Chapter 1.

The surface finishing methods which are necessary to be performed for many reasons are detailed in Chapter 5.

Any machine cannot function properly without maintenance. The importance of maintenance and how it should be done is elaborated in Chapter 6.

From student's point of view, C.N.C. programming is a hard nut to cut. Every care has been taken to make this treatise as self explanatory as possible with the use of tool path, co-ordinates table and program explanation in Chapter 2.

Answers to MSBTE questions are given at the end of Chapters. Chapters 3, 4 and 5 are newly added in this revised syllabus. So there are no MSBTE questions for these chapters.

We like to take this opportunity to thanks Mr. Pradeep Furia, Mr. Jignesh Bhai, Mr. Shashikant Patel and Mr. Akbar Shaikh (D.T.P.), Mrs. Anagha Kaware (Proof Reading), Miss Chaitali Takle (Fig. Drawing) and all the staff of Nirali Prakashan for their co-operation in making this book.

We offer thanks from the bottom of our heart to our family members for always giving us moral support and inspiration to write this book.

Finally, there was, is and always will be the love of our students whom we always taught as well as our friends and our well-wishers.

While every care is taken to eliminate errors, but they make creep in. Any valuable suggestions and further guidelines to improve this book will be highly appreciated, and can be send to prashantambadekar@gmail.com.

Author

Syllabus ...

Topic 1 : Non Traditional Machining   **[Hrs. 10, Marks 20]**

  1.1 Need and Importance, Classification.   **[04 Marks]**

  1.2 AJM, WJM, EDM, W-EDM - Setup, Working, Process Parameters, Advantages, Disadvantages and Applications.   **[08 Marks]**

  1.3 PAM, LBM - Setup, Working, Process parameters, Advantages, Disadvantages and Applications.   **[08 Marks]**

Topic 2: Introduction to CNC   **[Hrs. 08, Marks 16]**

  2.1 Introduction, Advantages of CNC, Open Loop and Closed Loop Control, Axis Identification, Absolute and Incremental Co-ordinate System - G Codes and M Codes.   **[08 Marks]**

  2.2 Fundamental Part Programming - Simple Lathe and Milling Programmes. Dry run, Jog Mode, Block by Block execution, Safety Procedures, Adaptive controls, Displays and Indicators.   **[08 Marks]**

Topic 3: Other Machining Methods   **[Hrs. 08, Marks 16]**

  3.1 Introduction, Classification of Broaching Machines, Basic parts of Horizontal Broaching Machine and their Functions, Applications, Advantages and Limitations of Broaching Machine.   **[08 Marks]**

  3.2 Capstan, Turret Lathe and Automats, Planer and Planomiller function of parts and Operations.   **[04 Marks]**

  3.3 Boring Machines – Types, Tools and Operations.   **[04 Marks]**

Topic 4: Milling and Gear Cutting   **[Hrs. 10, Marks 22]**

  4.1 Milling: Introduction, Classification, Basic parts of Column and Knee type Milling Machine and their Functions, Standard Milling Cutters, Milling Operations like Plain Milling, Side Milling, Straddle Milling, Gang Milling, Face Milling - Slot Milling, Slitting. Up Milling and down Milling, Cutting Parameters.   **[10 Marks]**

  4.2 Gear Cutting: Introduction, Gear Manufacturing Methods, Universal Dividing Head and Indexing Methods, Gear Shaping and Gear Hobbing - Setup, Working, Advantages, Disadvantages, Applications, Gear Finishing Methods - Grinding, Shaving, Burnishing.   **[12 Marks]**

Topic 5: Surface Finishing   **[Hrs. 06, Marks 14]**

  5.1 Grinding Machines: Classification and Working of Grinding Machine - Surface, Cylindrical, Centreless, Grinding Wheel Specifications, Grinding Wheel Dressing and Truing. Selection Criteria for Grinding Wheel. Balancing of Grinding Wheels, Safety Precautions.   **[08 Marks]**

  5.2 Super Finishing: Methods of Surface Finishing like Honing, Lapping, Burnishing, Polishing and Buffing - Setup, Working, Advantages, Limitations and Applications.   **[06 Marks]**

Topic 6: Maintenance of Machine Tools   **[Hrs. 06, Marks 12]**

Need and Importance of Maintenance Activity, Types of Maintenance, Basic Maintenance Practices for Simple Machine Elements, viz. Bearing, Coupling, Shaft and Pulley, Gears, Chains, Machine Belts. Repair Cycle Analysis, Repair Complexity, Maintenance Manual, Maintenance Records.

Contents ...

NON-TRADITIONAL MACHINING

At the end of this chapter students will be able to:

➲ Identify various non-traditional processes.

➲ Describe the various processes.

➲ Distinguish between the various processes.

➲ Decide on which process to use.

1.1 NON-TRADITIONAL MACHINING PROCESSES [W-11]

1.1.1 Introduction

- Machining process removes certain parts of the work piece to change them to final product. Traditional, also termed conventional, machining requires the presence of a tool that is harder than the workpiece to be machined. This tool should be penetrated in the workpiece to a certain depth. Moreover, a relative motion between the tool and workpiece is responsible for forming or generating the required shape.

- The end of Second World War brought a new revolution in the Engineering industry. Many new materials were developed to fulfill the needs of aircraft industry, missile technology, space research equipment and nuclear industry. These materials like carbides, tungsten, ceramics, tantalum, beryllium, uranium, nitro-alloy etc. are extremely hard and sometimes unmachinable by traditional machining processes.

- Also, these materials possess high strength to weight ratio, hardness and heat resisting qualities making it sometimes impossible for machining. When conventional methods are tried, it is difficult, time consuming and uneconomical to machine the work piece material. This adds to the fact that during conventional machining processes an increase in hardness of work piece material results in a decrease in economic cutting speed. This needed the development of improved cutting tool material.

- The newer machining processes, so developed are often called 'Modern Machining Methods' or non-traditional machining processes or unconventional machining processes. These are unconventional in the sense that conventional tools are not utilized for cutting the material. It employs some form of energy like mechanical, chemical, thermal, electro-chemical etc. for cutting the material. Also the absence of tool-workpiece contact or relative motion, makes the process a non-traditional one.

- *Non-traditional manufacturing processes* is defined as a group of processes that cut material by utilizing mechanical, thermal, electrical or chemical energy or combinations of these energies but do not use a sharp and hard cutting tools as required for traditional manufacturing processes.   [S-12; W-14]

1.1.2 Characteristics of Traditional Machining Processes

- The traditional machining processes has the following characteristics:
    (i)   Material removal takes place due to application of cutting forces.
    (ii)   Energy domain is mechanical energy.
    (iii)   Macroscopic chips formation takes place.
    (iv)   Formation of chip takes place due to shear deformation.
    (v)   Cutting tool is required and should be harder than the material to cut.

1.1.3 Limitations of the Traditional Methods

- The traditional machining processes have the following limitations:
    (i)   Harder materials cannot be machined.
    (ii)   Tool should be harder than the material to be cut.
    (iii)   Higher tool forces are required to cut harder material.
    (iv)   Very minute holes cannot be produced.
    (v)   Difficult to produce complex shapes in harder material.
    (vi)   Sometimes requirements for surface finish and tolerances are very high.
    (vii)   Temperature rise or residual stresses are undesirable or unacceptable.
    (viii) Sometimes workpiece is too flexible to resist cutting forces or too difficult to clamp.

1.1.4 Need of Non-Traditional Machining Processes

[S-12, 17, W-15]

- The need of non-traditional processes is justified by the following points:
  - (i) To machine the exotic material those were difficult to machine by conventional machining processes.
  - (ii) To fulfill the requirements of new age like innovative design, tighter tolerances, micromachining and economy.
  - (iii) To obtain intricate shapes. For example, a square blind hole of 15 mm × 15 mm with a depth of 30 mm.
  - (iv) Overcome difficulty to machine the material. For example, Inconel, Ti alloy, carbide, ceramics.
  - (v) To fulfill the requirement of low stress grinding. (if done by conventional then it reduce productivity).
  - (vi) Drilling deep hole with small hole diameter (For example, 15 mm diameter hole with l:d ratio of 20).
  - (vii) Machining of composites.

1.1.5 Characteristics of Non-Traditional Machining Processes

[S-12]

- The non-traditional processes has the following points characteristics:
  - (i) Material removal takes place either by chip formation (AJM) or by non-chip formation (ECM).
  - (ii) Physical tool may be present (EDM, ECM) or absent (LBM-beam, WJM-water).
  - (iii) Tool need not be harder than the workpiece.
  - (iv) Energy domain is not necessary mechanical as in USM, AJM, WJM, but can be electro-thermal (EDM) or electro-chemical (ECM).

1.1.6 Advantages of Non-Traditional Machining Processes

[W-11, S-12]

- The non-traditional machining processes has the advantages like:
  - (i) Any material can be machined irrespective of its hardness.
  - (ii) Any complicated shape can be produced on the work piece.
  - (iii) Very fine holes can be easily drilled.
  - (iv) The parts produced are burr-free.
  - (v) No mechanical force is exerted on the work piece, so fragile work piece can be machined.
  - (vi) Drilling of tapered holes is possible.
  - (vii) Through cutting of any material.

1.1.7 Classification of Non-Traditional Machining Processes

[W-11, S-13, 15, 16]

- Depending upon the type of energy used, the non-traditional processes are classified as:

  (i) Thermal

      (a) Electric Discharge Machining (EDM)

      (b) Wire cut EDM (WEDM)

      (c) Laser Beam Machining (LBM)

      (d) Ion Beam Machining (IBM)

      (e) Electron Beam Machining (EBM)

      (f) Electric Discharge Grinding (EDG)

      (g) Plasma arc Machining (PAM)

  (ii) Mechanical

      (a) Abrasive Jet Machining (AJM)

      (b) Ultrasonic Machining (USM)

      (c) Water Jet Machining (WJM)

  (iii) Electro-chemical

      (a) Electro-Chemical Machining (ECM)

      (b) Electro-Chemical Grinding (ECG)

  (iv) Chemical

      (a) Chemical Machining (CHM)

1.1.8 Comparison between Traditional and Non-Traditional Machining Process

[W-13, W-14]

Sr. No.	Parameters	Traditional Machining Process	Non-traditional Machining Process
1.	Tool geometry	It uses a physical cutting tool of fixed geometry.	It uses some sort of energy along with a tool which doesn't have a fixed geometry.
2.	Tool hardness	Tool material should be harder than the metal to be cut.	Hardness of tool is independent of the material hardness.
3.	Cutting ability	Hard metals are difficult to cut and sometimes impossible.	Almost any known hard material can be cut.
4.	Complex profile	Difficult to produce complex shapes.	Complex profiles can easily be obtained.

contd. ...

5.	Metal removal rate	Metal removal rate is comparatively high.	Metal removal rate is low.
6.	Metal removal method	Metal is removed in the form of chips.	Metal is removed by melting, vapourization, electrochemical reaction etc.
7.	Tool force and tool life	Higher tool forces are required to cut harder material and so less tool life.	Tool force is independent of the material hardness and so more tool life.
8.	Application	Very minute holes cannot be produced.	Very fine or minute holes can be easily drilled.
9.	Example	Turning, Milling, Shaping, Drilling etc.	EDM, LBM, USM, EBM, PAM, ECM etc.
10.	Accuracy and surface finish	Lower accuracy and surface finish.	Higher accuracy and surface finish in most of the cases.
11.	Suitability	Suitable for every type of material.	Has limitations for certain materials.

1.1.9 Process Selection [W-12]

- Following parameters are taken into consideration while selecting a particular non-traditional process.

    (i)   Physical properties of the work piece.

    (ii) Type of operation required. For example, cutting, hole making.

    (iii) Shape and size required to be produced.

    (iv) Process capabilities such as tolerance required, surface finish, metal removal rate, power requirement etc.

    (v)   Economic considerations.

1.1.10 Importance of Non-Traditional Machining Processes

[W-11, S-12, S-13]

(i)   Any material can be machined irrespective of its hardness.

(ii) To machine complex part geometries that are not possible to machine by conventional machining. For example, square shaped blind holes.

(iii) To avoid damage to the surface that often accompanies conventional machining.

(iv) To machine deep hole with small diameter. For example, ϕ 1.2 mm hold with 25 mm depth.

(v)   To machine composites.

1.2 ABRASIVE JET MACHINING   [S-12]

1.2.1 Principle of AJM   [W-12, 14]

- Abrasive jet machining is a process that removes material from a workpiece with the help of abrasive particles.
- The process differs from sand blasting is that in AJM the abrasive particles has much smaller diameter of about 0.025 mm.
- The process consists of mixture of fine abrasive particles and gas at high pressure.
- This stream of mixture is directed through a nozzle on to the surface of the workpiece as shown in Fig. 1.1.
- The abrasive particles impinge on the workpiece at high speed.
- As the particle impacts the surface, it causes a small fracture of the work surface which results in removal of metal.
- The gas stream carries both the abrasive particles and the fractured (wear) particles way.

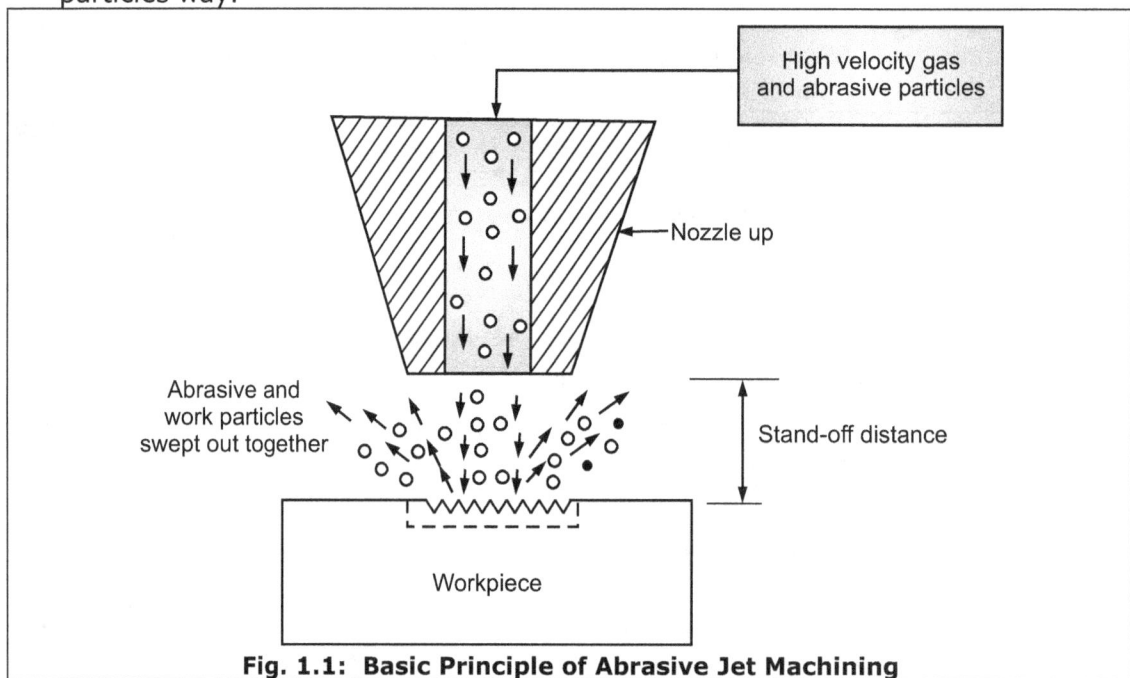

Fig. 1.1: Basic Principle of Abrasive Jet Machining

1.2.2 Characteristics of AJM

- Used for machining delicate or very hard materials.
- Produces no heat damage to workpiece surface.
- Produces a taper in deep cuts
- The process is used mainly to cut materials that are heat-sensitive, brittle, thin or hard.
- Intricate shapes and cuts are performed easily.

1.2.3 Abrasive Used

- Abrasive material used is aluminium oxide (preferred) or silicon carbide or sodium bicarbonate etc.
- The grains should have sharp edges.
- The grain size should be of 10-50 micro m.
- Grains should not be reused as the sharp edges are worn down and smaller particles can clog nozzle.

1.2.4 Gas

- Mass flow rate of abrasive is proportional to gas pressure and gas flow.
- Gas pressure typically ranges from 0.2 N/mm^2 to 1 N/mm^2.
- Typically used gas is air or nitrogen or Carbon-di-oxide.
- Gas composition effects pressure flow relationship.

1.2.5 Nozzle

- Must be hard material to reduce wear by abrasives: Tungsten Carbide (lasts 12 to 30 hr) or Sapphire (lasts 300 hr).
- Cross-sectional area of orifice should be around 0.05-0.2 mm^2.
- Orifice can be round or rectangular.
- Head can be straight, or at a right angle.

1.2.6 Process Set-up   [S-12, W-12]

- A typical set-up of abrasive jet machining is shown in Fig. 1.20.
- The abrasive particles are held in the hopper 7 through which it is fed into the mixing chamber 11.
- A regulator 8 controls the flow of abrasive particles.
- Gas at high pressure is supplied to the mixing chamber through a pipe line as shown in Fig. 1.2.
- A pressure gauge 9 and a regulator 10 is incorporated in the pipeline to control the gas flow and its pressure.
- The mixing chamber, carrying the abrasive particles is vibrated by the device 12 and the amplitude of these vibrations controls the flow of abrasive particles.
- These abrasive particles travel through the hose 4 and enter into the nozzle 3.
- The control valve 5 and pressure gauge 6 controls the flow of abrasive particles.
- This outgoing high speed steam that comes out of the nozzle is known as abrasive jet 2.
- When such jet impinges on the workpiece 1, the erosion caused by their impact enables the removal of metal.

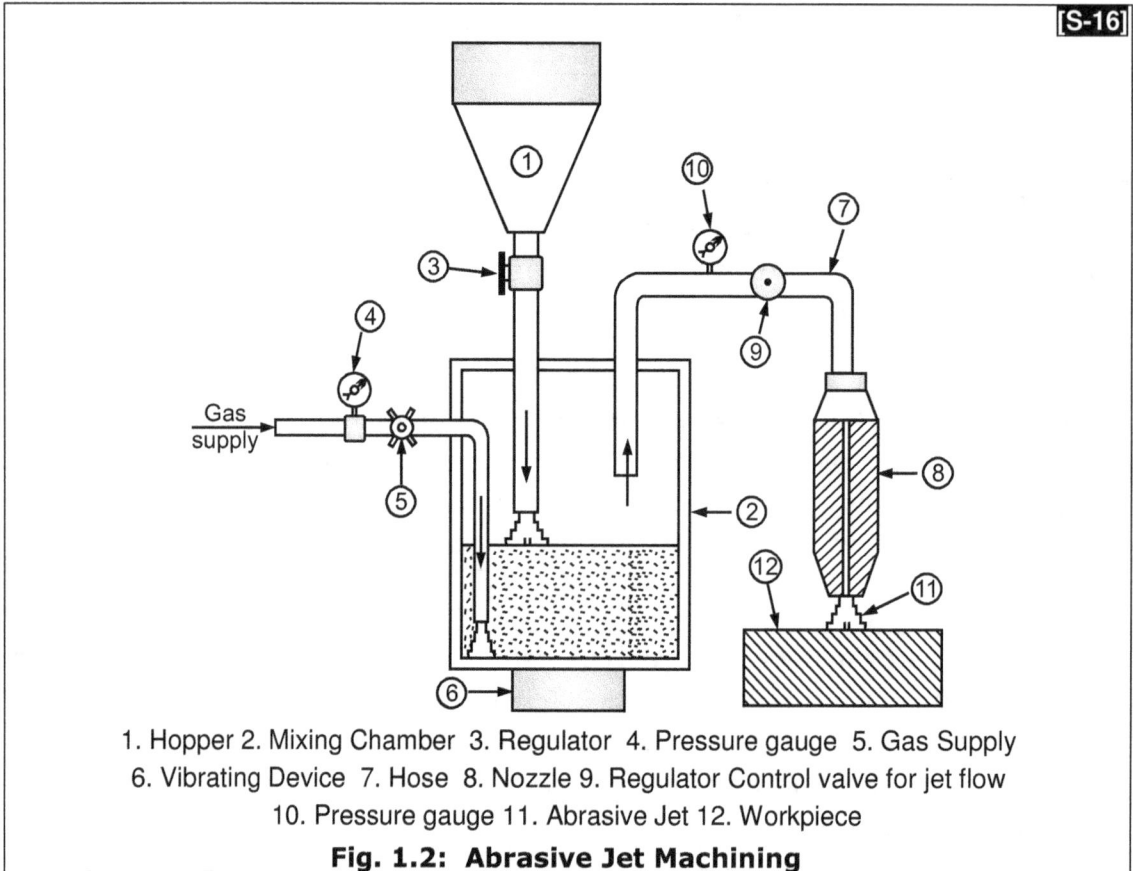

1. Hopper 2. Mixing Chamber 3. Regulator 4. Pressure gauge 5. Gas Supply
6. Vibrating Device 7. Hose 8. Nozzle 9. Regulator Control valve for jet flow
10. Pressure gauge 11. Abrasive Jet 12. Workpiece

Fig. 1.2: Abrasive Jet Machining

1.2.7 Process Characteristics of AJM

The important process parameters are:

1. Abrasives

- The abrasive material used is Al_2O_3 or SiC.
- The grain size is around 25 μm.
- The shape of abrasive is generally spherical.
- The mass Flow rate is 3–20 g/min.

2. Gas carrier

- The type of gas used is Air, N_2 or CO_2.
- The air density is 1.3 kg/m^3, Velocity 150–300 m/s and pressure 2–8 bar.
- The flow rate is around 30 L/min.

3. Nozzle

- The nozzle is made of Tungsten carbide or sapphire.
- Its shape is circular, 0.3–0.5 mm internal diameter or rectangular (0.08 mm 0.51 mm to 6.61 mm, 0.51 mm).

○   The tip distance is 0.25–15 mm.

○   The life of WC is 12–30 hour and sapphire is 300 hours.

○   The operating angle is 60° to 90° to the surface.

○   Stand-off distance – 0.5 to 5 mm.

1.2.8 Advantages of AJM   [W-14]

(i)   Intricate cavities and holes of any shapes can be easily machines.

(ii)   Brittle material of thin section can be easily machined.

(iii) Low initial investment is required.

(iv) No direct contact of tool and workpiece.

(v)   Amount of heat generated is not appreciable.

(vi) Normally inaccessible portions can be machined with fairly good accuracy.

1.2.9 Disadvantages of AJM   [W-14]

(i)   Low metal removal rate.

(ii)   Once used, abrasive particles cannot be reused.

(iii) Not suitable for machining of ductile material.

(iv) Relatively poor machining accuracy.

(v)   There is possibility of abrasive particle getting embedded in the work material, hence cleaning needs to be necessarily done after the operation.

1.2.10 Applications of AJM   [W-11, 12, 14, 16; S-15, 16]

(i)   Fine drilling and micro welding.

(ii)   Machining of semi conductors.

(iii) Frosting and abrading of glass articles.

(iv) Machining of intricate profile on hard and fragile materials.

(v)   Cleaning and cutting operations on materiel like germanium, silicon, quartz, mica.

(vi) Machining of brittle materials like glass, ceramics, refractories etc.

1.3 WATER JET MACHINING (WJM)

1.3.1 Introduction

- If we want to clean the area outside the home/office/school we throw water with high pressure so that the dirt gets washed away. A stream of water generated through a pipe that flows with high pressure washes away the mud.

- Similarly a jet of water may be used to cut a sheet of metal. If the jet of water is directed on the metal sheet in such a way that on striking on the surface, the high velocity flow is virtually stopped, then most of the kinetic energy of the water is converted into pressure energy that induces high stresses in the material.

- As soon as the jet impacts on the sheet, a transient pressure as much as three times the normal stagnation pressure may be generated. Erosion occurs if the fluid pressure exceeds the ultimate strength of the material.

- The key element in water jet machining (WJM) is a water jet, which travels at velocities as high as 900 m/s. When the stream strikes a workpiece surface, the erosive force of water removes the material rapidly. The water, in this case, acts like a saw and cuts a narrow groove in the workpiece material.

- Water jet cutting can reduce the costs and speed up the processes by eliminating or reducing expensive secondary machining process. Since no heat is applied on the materials, cut edges are clean with minimal burr. Problems such as cracked edge defects, crystalisation, hardening, reduced wealdability and machinability are reduced in this process.

- Water jet technology uses the principle of pressurising water to extremely high pressures, and allowing the water to escape through a very small opening called "orifice" or "jewel". Water jet cutting uses the beam of water exiting the orifice to cut soft materials. This method is not suitable for cutting hard materials. The inlet water is typically pressurised between 1300 – 4000 bars. This high pressure is forced through a tiny hole in the jewel, which is typically 0.18 to 0.4 mm in diameter.

- WJM is suitable for cutting plastics, foods, rubber insulation, automotive carpeting and headliners, and most textiles.

1.3.2 Principle of Working

- The process filters water to remove contaminants larger than 0.50 microns approximately.

- This water is then compressed a pressure of about 420 MPa, after which it moves through reinforced hoses to the cutting head.

- The nozzle converts the high pressure liquid to a high velocity jet.

- This jet is then directed on to the workpiece which removes material through the erosion effect caused by a high velocity, small jet of water.

1.3.3 Set-up or Equipments of WJM Process [W-15]

- The apparatus of water jet machining consists of the following components:

  - **Reservoir:** It is used for storing water that is to be used in the machining operation.

  - **Hydraulic Pump:** The hydraulic pump is powered from a electric motor and supplies the water from the reservouir.

  - **Intensifier:** It is connected to the pump. It pressurizes the water acquired from the pump to a desired level.

  - **Accumulator:** The accumulator maintains the continuous flow of the high-pressure water and eliminates pressure fluctuations. It is used for temporarily storing the pressurized water. It is connected to the flow regulator through a control valve.

  - **Control Valve:** It controls the direction and pressure of pressurized water that is to be supplied to the nozzle.

  - **Flow regulator:** It is used to regulate the flow of water.

  - **Nozzle:** It renders the pressurized water as a water jet at high velocity. The nozzle provides a coherent water jet stream for optimum cutting of low-density material that is considered unmachinable by conventional methods.

  - Nozzles are normally made from synthetic sapphire which is wear resistant and easily machinable.

  - The nozzle gets damaged by particles of dirt and the accumulation of mineral deposits on the orifice due to erosive water hardness.

  - Nozzle internal diameter varies from 0.07 mm to 0.5 mm.

  - **High-pressure tubing.** High-pressure tubing transports pressurized water to the cutting head. Typical tube diameters are 6 to 14 mm. and is made from stainless steel.

  - The equipment allows for flexible movement of the cutting head.

  - The cutting action is controlled either manually or through a valve specially designed for this purpose.

  - **Catcher.** The catcher acts as a reservoir for collecting the machining debris entrained in the water jet. Moreover, it reduces the noise levels associated with the reduction in the velocity of the water jet.

1.3.4 Working Process

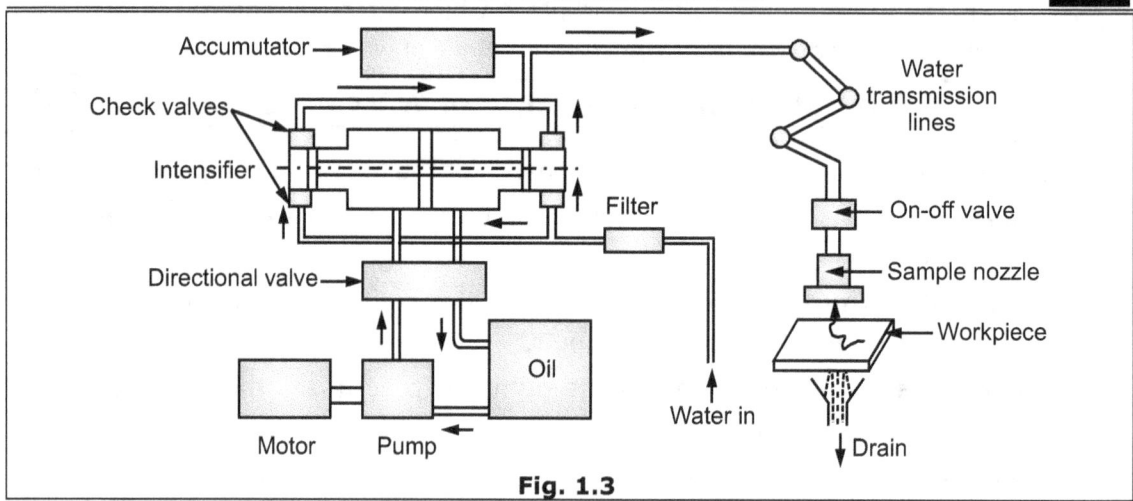

Fig. 1.3

- AS shown in Fig. 1.3, water from the reservoir is pumped to the intensifier using a hydraulic pump.
- The intensifier accepts the water at low pressure and pressurizes it to around 400 MPa.
- Pressurized water is then sent to the accumulator. The accumulator temporarily stores the pressurized water during the idle period and given out during cutting.
- Pressurized water then enters the nozzle by passing through the control valve and flow regulator.
- Control valve controls the direction of water and limits the pressure of water under permissible limits.
- Flow regulator regulates and controls the flow rate of water.
- Pressurized water finally enters the nozzle. Here, it expands with a tremendous increase in its kinetic energy. High velocity water jet is produced by the nozzle.
- The jet stream coming out of the nozzle strikes the workpiece and induces stresses. These stresses are used to cuts the workpiece.
- The water is then collected in a drain system.

1.3.5 Process Parameters

(a) The stand-off distance:

1. It is the gap between the jet nozzle and the workpiece.
2. MRR increases with the increase of stand-off distance upto a certain limit after which it remains unchanged for a certain tip distances and then falls gradually.

(b) Wear rate of the nozzle:

1. It depends on the hardness of the nozzle material, pressure (hence, velocity) of the jet and nozzle design.

(c) Fluid Pressure:

1. The increase in pressure allows more power to be used in the machining process, which in turn increases the depth of the cut.

2. The quality of cutting improves at higher pressures by widening the diameter of the jet and by lowering

3. the traverse speed. Moreover, the larger the pump pressure, the greater will be the depth of the cut.

(d) Jet Fluid:

1. The fluid used must possess low viscosity to minimize the energy losses and be non-corrosive, non-toxic, common, and inexpensive.

2. Water is commonly used for cutting alloy steels.

(e) Target material:

1. Brittle materials will fracture, while ductile ones will cut well.

2. Material thicknesses range from 0.8 to 25 mm or more.

1.3.6 Advantages of WJM

- Any contour can be obtained and gives a clean and sharp cut.
- It has multidirectional cutting capacity.
- No heat is produced.
- Cuts can be started at any location without the need for predrilled holes.
- There is no deflection to the rest of the workpiece.
- The tool does not wear and, therefore, does not need sharpening.
- The process is environmentally safe.
- Grinding and polishing are eliminated, reducing secondary operation
- It allows for more accurate cutting of soft material.

1.3.7 Disadvantages of WJM

- Hourly rates are relatively high.
- It is not suitable for mass production because of high maintenance requirements.
- Only a limited number of materials can be cut economically.
- Thick parts cannot be cut by this process economically and accurately.
- Taper is also a problem with water jet cutting in very thick materials. Taper is when the jet exits the part at different angle than it enters the part, and cause dimensional inaccuracy.
- Initial cost of the set-up is high.

1.3.8 Applications of WJM   [S-15, W-16]

- Water jet machining is used to cut thin non-metallic sheets.
- It is used to cut rubber, wood, ceramics and many other soft materials.
- It is used for machining circuit boards.
- It is used in food industry.

1.4 ELECTRIC DISCHARGE MACHINING (EDM)

1.4.1 Introduction

- Whenever sparking takes place between two electrical contacts, a small amount of material is removed from each of the contact. This fact is used to produce sparks between the tool and work piece in EDM.
- It is also known as spark erosion, electro-erosion or spark machining.

1.4.2 Principle of Working   [S-11, 15, 16; W-11, W-13, 14]

- EDM works on the principle that heat energy generated by a spark is used to remove material from the work piece.
- In this process an electric spark gap is generated to machine the workpiece to produce the desired shape.
- The tool and work piece are separated by a small gap called as spark gap. The gap varies from 0.01 mm to 0.5 mm. The tool and work piece both are immersed in the dielectric fluid.
- When supply is made 'ON', thousands of sparks are produced per second. The duration of each spark is very short.
- When the spark comes in contact with the dielectric fluid in the spark gap, the fluid gets ionized. It allows current to flow between the tool and work piece as shown in Fig. 1.4.
- A very high temperature of around 10000°C is generated in the spark region. As a result, the material gets melted and is removed from the work piece.
- These melted particles of the metal are then driven away by the dielectric fluid.

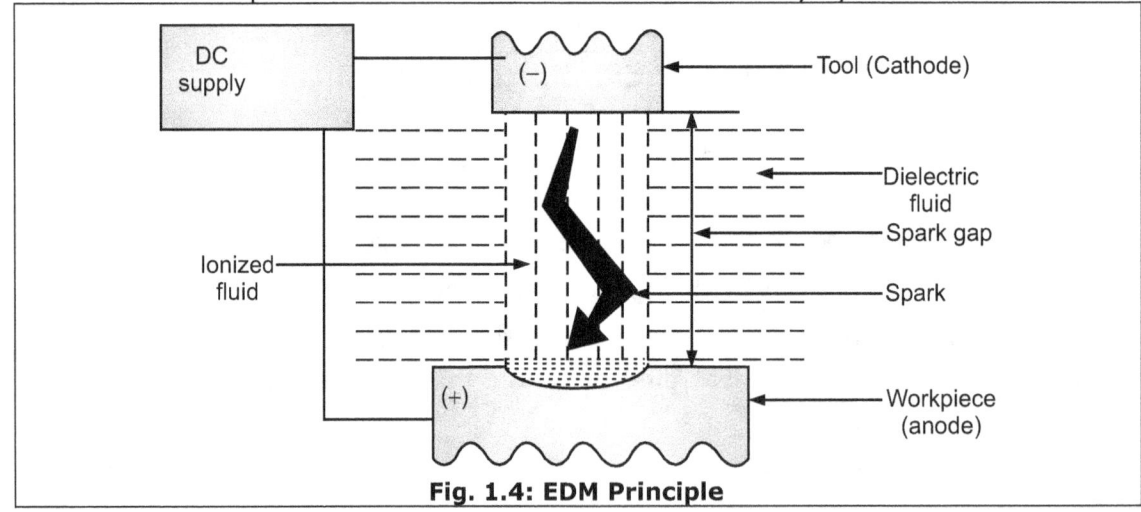

Fig. 1.4: EDM Principle

1.4.3 Set-up of EDM

- A set-up for EDM is shown in Fig. 1.5.
- It consists of the four major components:
  (i)   Tool and work piece.
  (ii) Dielectric fluid system.
  (iii) R-C circuit and power supply unit.
  (iv) Tool feed mechanism.

[W-11]

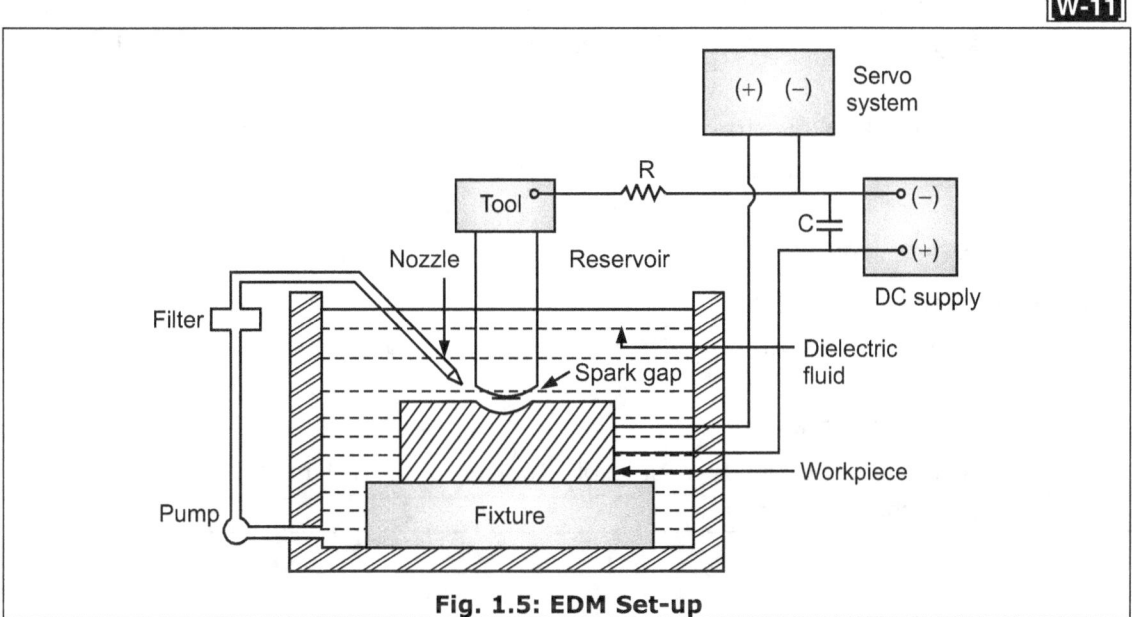

Fig. 1.5: EDM Set-up

(i) Tool and work piece:

- The tool and work piece is kept in a reservouir and is connected to a DC power supply.
- The tool is connected to negative terminal, so that it becomes cathode, while work piece is connected to positive terminal and become anode.
- Work piece can be mounted on the machine table with any suitable work holding device like magnetic table, chuck, vice etc.

(ii) A dielectric system:

- The reservoir is filled with dielectric fluid such that the spark gap is immersed in it.
- Dielectric is continuously flushed into the spark gap. The used dielectric is filtered and recirculated in to the reservoir.
- The dielectric fluid is pumped at a pressure of 2 kg/cm^2 or less.

(iii) A R-C circuit: (Relaxation Circuit)

- A R-C circuit is shown in Fig. 1.6. A resistor R is connected in series and a capacitor C is connected in parallel.

- When the supply is made 'ON' the capacitor voltage starts rising continuously.

- When the capacitor voltage equals the breakdown voltage, (of dielectric fluid) a spark discharge will occur in the spark gap.

- The spark persists until the capacitor voltage falls below that which is required to maintain sparking.

- After the capacitor discharge, sparking ceases and the dielectric fluid in the spark gap gets deionized. The capacitor is then recharged and the cycle repeats itself.

- The time taken by the capacitor to recharge upto the breakdown voltage should be sufficient to allow the dielectric to deionize.

- Resistor R in the circuit prevents the charging of capacitor before the spark gap is deionized.

(iv) Tool feed mechanism:

- Since during operation both the tool and work piece are eroded, it is necessary to feed the tool continuously towards the work piece so as to maintain the spark gap.

- This can be achieved by a suitable tool feed control mechanism along with servo mechanism system.

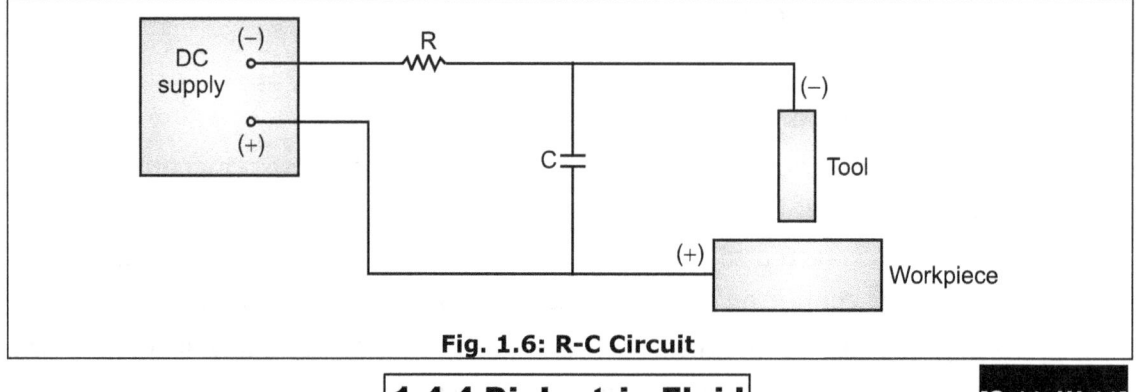

Fig. 1.6: R-C Circuit

1.4.4 Dielectric Fluid   [S-11, W-11]

- A dielectric fluid is a liquid which acts as an insulator between consecutive spark discharge and as a conductor during the spark discharge.

- It has dielectric properties, to act as an insulator at one time and to act as a conductor at other time.

- The dielectric fluid used is paraffin oil, transformer oil, lubricating oils, kerosene, distilled water etc.

1.4.5 Functions of Dielectric Fluid

[W-11, S-12, W-12, W-13]

- A dielectric fluid should possess the following functions:
  (i) It should act as an insulator until the required breakdown voltage is attained.
  (ii) It should act as a conductor, once the breakdown voltage is reached.
  (iii) It should clean the spark gap by carrying away the molten metal.
  (iv) It should deionize the spark gap rapidly after the discharge has occurred.
  (v) It should cool the tool, work piece and the spark region.

1.4.6 Characteristics of Dielectric Fluid   [S-11, S-12]

- The following characteristics are required by the dielectric fluid:
  (i) It should have low viscosity.
  (ii) It should have high flash point.
  (iii) It should have controlled level of toxicity.
  (iv) It should have freedom from acid and alkaline products.
  (v) It should have high dielectric strength (i.e. remain electrically non-conductive until the required breakdown voltage is attained).
  (vi) It should be cheap and easily available.
  (vii) It should have high fluidity.

1.4.7 Flushing of the Dielectric Fluid

- Flushing is defined as providing a fresh dielectric fluid between the tool and work piece.
- Due to successive spark discharge, the particles eroded from the tool and work piece contaminates the dielectric.
- This reduces its insulation strength and hence spark may occur easily.
- To prevent this premature occurrence of discharge, due to the eroded particles, flushing is necessary.
- The various methods of flushing are:
  (i) Injection Flushing: Dielectric fluid is injected through the hollow tool or hollow work piece.
  (ii) Side Flushing: Dielectric fluid is flushed from side of the tool.
  (iii) Suction Flushing: Dielectric fluid is sucked either through work piece or tool.

1.4.8 Tool used in EDM : (Electrode)

- The tool used in EDM is in the form of an electrode.

- The tool is made slightly undersize for inside machining and oversize for outside machining as shown in Fig. 1.7.

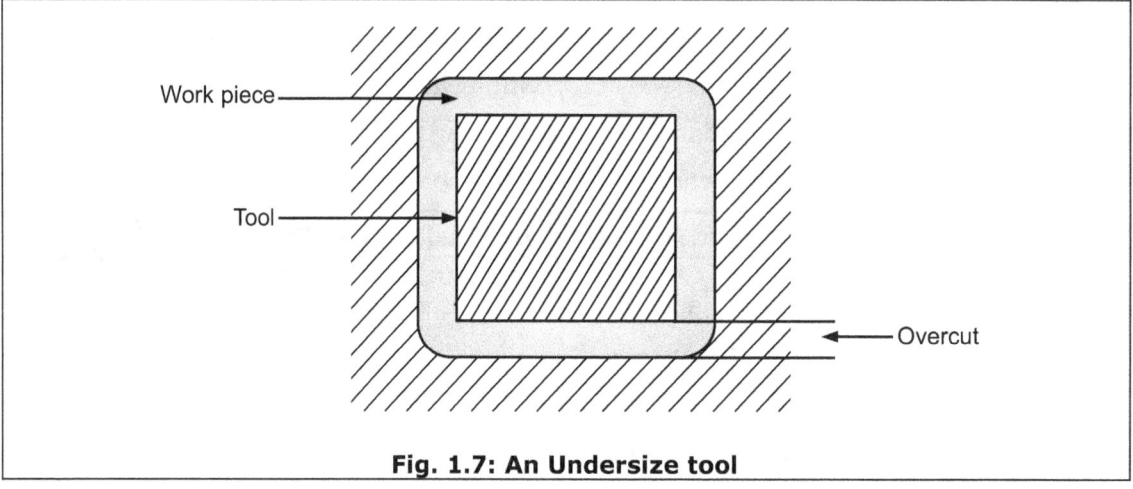

Fig. 1.7: An Undersize tool

- The tool has reverse profile (mirror image) of what is to be produced on the work piece as shown in Fig. 1.8.

- The tool or electrode material is broadly classified into two groups:

  (i) Metallic group.

  (ii) Non-metallic group.

- The metallic group includes materials like copper, brass, aluminium, steel, zinc, tungsten alloy etc.

- The most popular non-metallic material used in EDM is graphite because it is inexpensive and easily machinable. A graphite electrode with finer grains results in lower tool wear, better surface finish and higher metal removal rate.

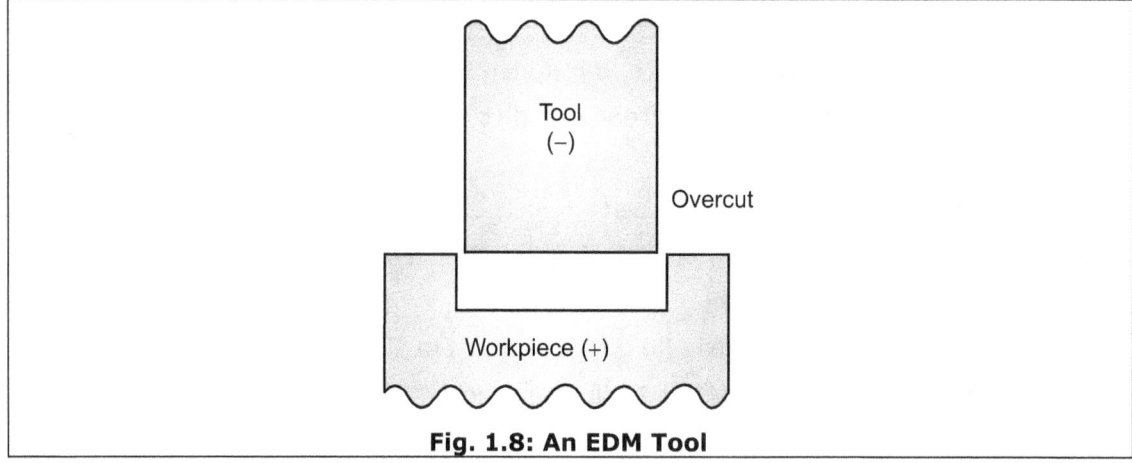

Fig. 1.8: An EDM Tool

1.4.9 Requirement of Tool Material [S-10, 13, 16, W-12]

- The tool used in EDM is electrode and should have some ideal characteristics as mentioned below:

  (i)   It should be a good conductor of electricity.

  (ii) It should have high thermal conductivity.

  (iii) It should be cheap and readily available.

  (iv) It should have low wear (erosion) rate.

  (v)   It should have low electric resistance.

  (vi) It should have good machinability.

  (vii) It should have high melting point.

1.4.10 Process Parameters [W-11, S-12, W-13]

- The main process parameters or controlling parameters in EDM are:

  (i)   Supply voltage.

  (ii)   Break down voltage.

  (iii) Resistance and Capacitance.

  (iv)   Spark gap setting.

  (v)   Pulse duration.

  (vi)   Spark frequency.

(i)   Supply voltage:

- It is the voltage which is provided by the power supply system.
- It ranges between 50 V to 400 V DC supply.

(ii) Break down voltage:

- It is the voltage at which the dielectric breakdown.
- Increase in breakdown voltage results in increase of spark energy.
- Consequently the metal removal rate increases which results in poor surface finish.

(iii) Resistance and Capacitance:

- Increase in capacitance will result in increase of metal removal rate.
- Decrease in resistance will result in increase of metal removal rate.

(iv) Spark gap setting:

- Decrease in spark gap results in lower metal removal rate.
- This results in better surface finish and high accuracy.

(v)   Pulse duration:

- The pulse duration ranges from 2 to 2000 μsec.
- Decrease in pulse duration will result in high tool wear.
- Increase in pulse duration results in lower metal removal rate.

(vi) Spark frequency:

- It is about 1000 sparks/sec.
- The increase in spark frequency results in improved surface finish.
- Because the spark energy is shared by more number of sparks, this decreases the crater size.
- The effect of various process parameters on metal removal rate is shown in Fig. 1.9.

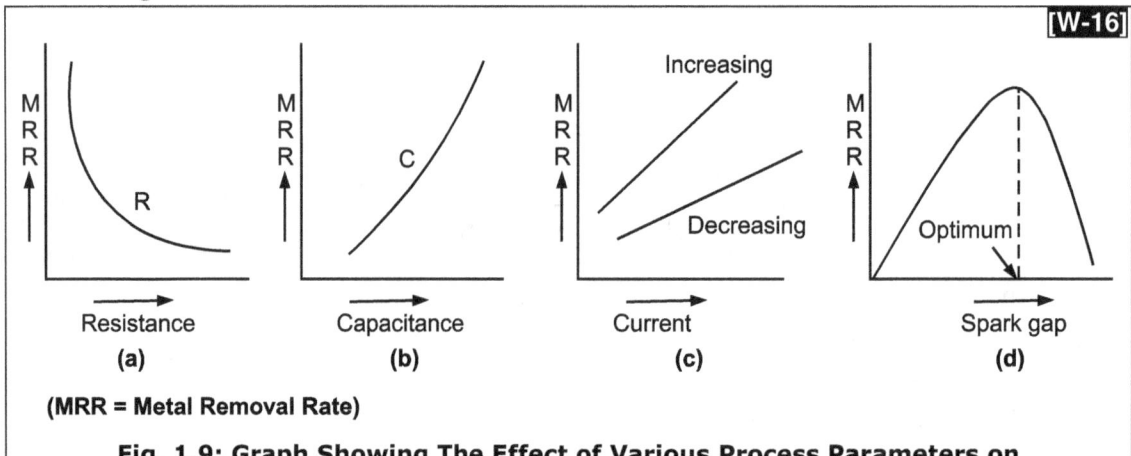

(MRR = Metal Removal Rate)

Fig. 1.9: Graph Showing The Effect of Various Process Parameters on Metal Removal Rate (a) Resistance (b) Capacitance (c) Current (d) Spark Gap

1.4.11 Output Characteristics   [W-11, S-13]

- The process characteristics (output characteristics) which are affected by the controlling parameter are:
  - (i) Metal removal rate.
  - (ii) Tool wear.
  - (iii) Surface finish.
  - (iv) Accuracy.

(i) Metal removal rate:

- o It is the volume of metal removed from the work piece per unit time.
- o The metal removal rate depends upon the current density.
- o It increases with increase in the current.
- o The metal removal rate in EDM is 5 to 80 mm^3/sec, which is very low as compared to conventional machining rate.

(ii) Tool wear:

- o As sparking takes place, tool wear is inevitable.
- o Increase in pulse duration decreases tool wear.
- o It depends upon metal removal rate, current and the spark gap.

(iii) Surface finish:

- Surface finish depends on the metal removal rate.
- High metal removal rate produces poor surface finish.
- For rough cuts heavy current is used and for finish cuts less current is used.
- Increase in spark frequency results in improved surface finish.

(iv) Accuracy:

- Tolerance value of ± 0.05 could be easily achieved in EDM.
- By close control of several variables, a tolerance of ± 0.003 mm can be obtained.
- An overcut of minimum of 100 micron is produced.
- The overcut increases with high current.

1.4.12 Advantages of EDM [W-11]

(i) Any material can be machined irrespective of its hardness.

(ii) Any complicated shape can be produced on the work piece.

(iii) There is no physical contact between the tool and the work piece; therefore no stresses are produced in the work piece.

(iv) Delicate work piece (small electronic parts) which cannot withstand cutting forces can be machined.

(v) Very fine holes can be easily drilled.

(vi) A very good surface finish can be obtained.

1.4.13 Disadvantages of EDM [S-15]

(i) Metal removal rate is slow.

(ii) Taper holes are produced.

(iii) Overcut is formed.

(iv) Cannot produce very sharp corners.

(v) Excessive tool wear occurs during machining.

(vi) Power consumption is high.

(vii) Unable to machine electrically non-conductive material.

1.4.14 Applications of EDM [S-12, 15; W-12, W-13]

(i) It is used in making stamping tools, wire drawing and extrusion dies, header dies, forging dies etc.

(ii) Internal threads can be produced in harder material by using a rotary spindle.

(iii) In machining delicate work piece like copper parts are used for fitting in vacuum tubes.

(iv) For machining of exotic materials used in aerospace industries.

(v) In resharpening of cutting tools and broaches.

(vi) In microhole drilling, curve hole drilling.

1.5 WIRE CUT ELECTRIC DISCHARGE MACHINING (WEDM)

[S-12, 17]

1.5.1 Introduction

- The fundamental principle of metal removal in wire cut EDM is the same as that of EDM.

- It employs electrical energy to remove metal from the work piece without touching it.

- The process can be used only when the workpiece to be cut has a through hole in it or the cut is to be taken from the outer edge into the workpiece as shown in Fig. 1.10.

- It uses a wire of about 0.3 mm diameter as a tool.

- The wire (electrode) is made-up of copper or tungsten.

- Deionized water is used as dielectric fluid.

Fig. 1.10: A WEDM Tool

1.5.2 Principle of Working   [W-10]

- WEDM works on the principle that the heat energy generated by a spark is used to remove material from the work piece. Fig. 1.10

- It uses a wire of about 0.3 mm diameter as an electrode or tool.

- A constant gap of 0.5 mm is maintained between the wire and work piece with the help of control system as shown in Fig. 1.11.

- The wire is continuously moved at a constant speed through the work piece.

- A dielectric fluid is constantly flushed in the area of machining.

- When the machine tool is switched 'ON', sparks are generated between the tool and work piece.

- When the spark comes in contact with the dielectric fluid in the gap, the fluid gets ionized and it allows the current to flow between the tool and work piece.
- Heat generated during the sparking process results in melting of the work piece.
- These melted particles of the metal are then driven away by the dielectric field.
- In order to create the desired shape on the work piece the table motions are controlled by the positioning unit (control system).

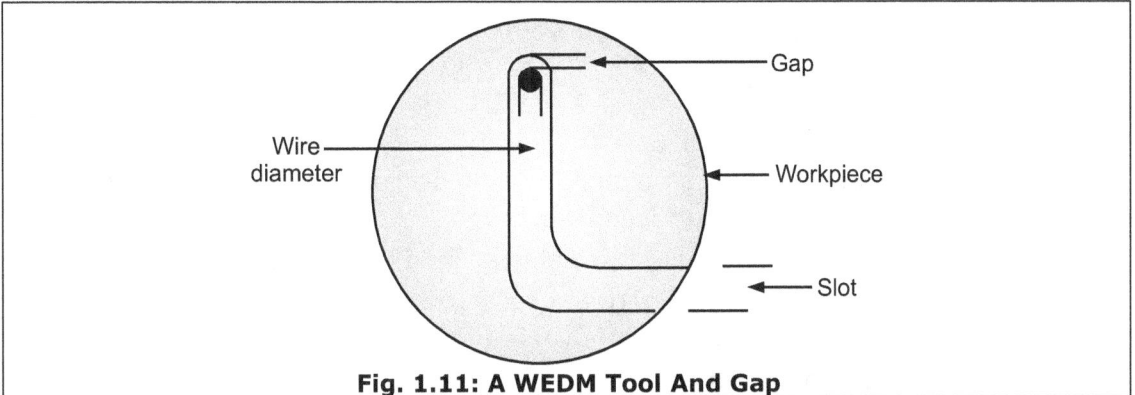

Fig. 1.11: A WEDM Tool And Gap

1.5.3 Set-up of WEDM   [S-12]

- The basic elements in a WEDM process, as shown in Fig. 1.12 are given below:
  (i)   Power supply system.
  (ii) Di-electric system.
  (iii) A CNC control system (work piece positioning unit).
  (iv) Wire drive system.

(i) Power supply system:

[W-11]

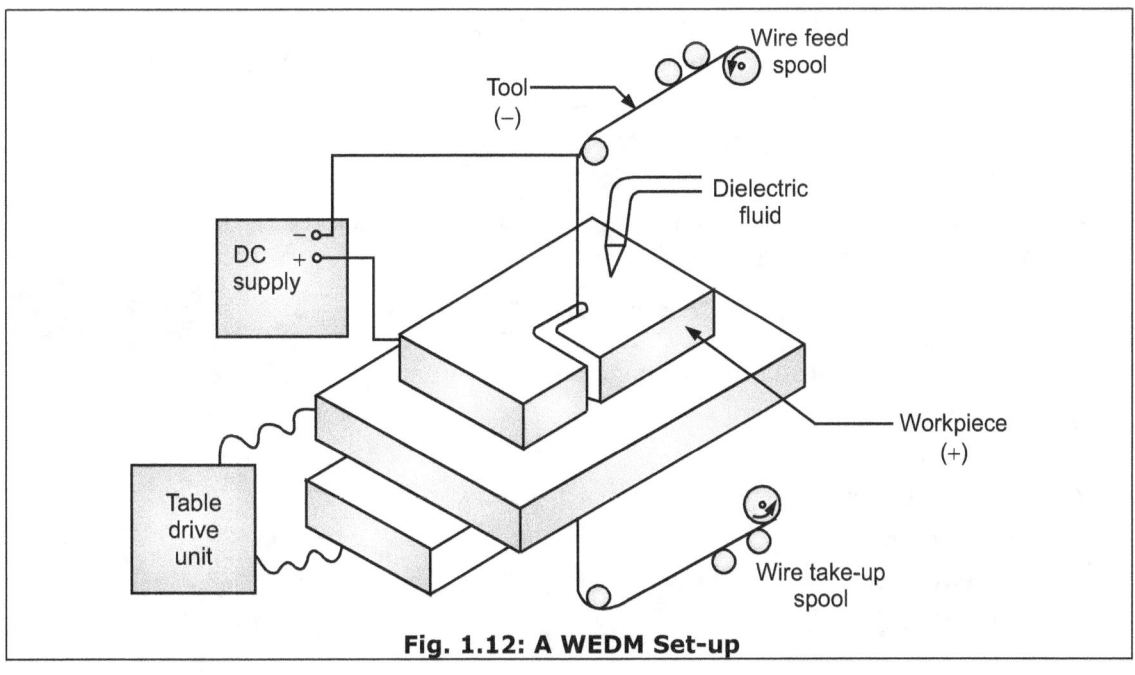

Fig. 1.12: A WEDM Set-up

o The work piece is mounted on the table.

o The tool is connected to negative terminal, so that it becomes cathode, while work piece is connected to positive terminal and become anode.

o The tool and work piece is connected to a DC power supply.

o The supply is in the form of a pulse. A voltage of about 50 V is applied to the system.

o However because of very small wire size, it cannot carry current more than 30 A.

(ii) A dielectric system:

o Deionized water is used as a dielectric fluid in WEDM. It gives high metal removal rate and better surface finish.

o A nozzle is employed to inject the dielectric fluid in the machining area.

o Both the work piece and the wire are constantly flushed with dielectric fluid at the area being machined.

o The dielectric also serves as a coolant.

(iii) A CNC control system:

o A CNC control system is used for the movement of work table.

o The table has movement in two axis (direction).

o The table can also be moved in both the directions simultaneously for taking contouring cuts.

(iv) Wire drive system:

o This system performs three functions:

    (i) to feed the fresh wire for machining (wire feed mechanism).

    (ii) to take-up the used wire (wire take-up mechanism).

    (iii) to keep the wire under appropriate tension so that it moves in the machining area as a straight wire.

o The wire is used only once because due to sparking which takes place at the surface of the wire, the wire no longer remains round.

o During operation when the supply is made 'ON' the dielectric fluid gets ionized and results in melting of work piece.

1.5.4 Controlling Parameters   [W-13, 15, S-15]

• The main process parameters or controlling parameters in WEDM are:

    (i) Discharge current.

    (ii) Pulse duration.

    (iii) Pulse frequency.

    (iv) Wire speed.

    (v) Wire tension.

    (vi) Dielectric flow.

(i) Discharge current:

- o Material removal rate increases with current.

- o Increasing the current increases the crater depth up to a certain value, beyond which increasing these parameters yield a smoother surface.

- o The wire being small cannot carry current more than 30 A.

(ii) Pulse duration:

- o Increase in pulse duration results in more removal of material.

- o Increasing the pulse duration results in reduced surface roughness.

(iii) Pulse frequency:

- o Material removal rate increases with pulse frequency.

- o The pulse frequency is about 1 MHz.

- o This results in reduced crater size or better surface finish.

(iv) Cutting rate:

- o The wire speed is in the range of 2.5 to 150 mm/sec.

- o The cutting rate depends upon the thickness of the work piece.

- o The maximum depth of material that can be machined is about 90 mm.

- o The average machining rate of 10-15 mm^2/min is generally achieved.

(v) Wire tension:

- o The appropriate wire tension should be maintained in order to keep the wire straight.

- o A series of tension rollers is provided to keep the required tension.

- o The wire tension is 50 % to 60 % of its tensile strength.

(vi) Dielectric flow:

- o A nozzle is employed to inject the dielectric fluid in the machining area.

- o The supply of dielectric should be continuous and enough to allow the sparking.

- o The dielectric fluid can be reused, but only after filtration.

1.5.5 Advantages of WEDM

(i)   Straight holes can be produced to close tolerances.

(ii) As a NC unit is used, the machine can be operated unattended for longer period of time.

(iii) High degree of accuracy and good surface finish can be obtained.

(iv) Very sharp angles can be cut with almost no radius.

(v)   EDM eliminates the need for post-machining heat treating and possible part distortion.

(vi) The parts produced are burr-free.

1.5.6 Disadvantages of WEDM

(i) Wire cannot be reused, because due to sparking the wire no longer remains round.

(ii) If proper tension in wire is not maintained, the surface finish will be poor.

(iii) Only electrically conductive material can be machined.

(iv) Residual stresses are induced in the work piece during machining.

(v) The maximum depth of work piece which can be machined is around 90 mm.

(vi) A hole is necessary in the work piece for machining of surface which are not at the edges.

1.5.7 Applications of WEDM

(i) Punches and dies used in press tools can be made.

(ii) For the production of moulds and dies.

(iii) Used to cut out complex contours in electrically conductive work pieces.

(iv) Simple, flat shapes, which usually would be stamped, may be a job for wire EDM when they require a superior quality edge.

(v) Cylindrical pins as small as 5 mm in diameter can be machined.

1.6 PLASMA ARC MACHINING [W-16, S-17]

1.6.1 Introduction

- The three states of matter are solid, liquid and gases. The fourth state of matter is obtained when gases are heated to temperatures about 5500°C.

- At this temperature, the gases are partially ionized and exist in the form of a mixture of free electrons, positively charged ions and neutral atoms. This mixture is termed as plasma.

- When a gas is heated, then the number of collisions between the atoms increases. Due to this the gas ionizes, (i.e. the atoms are stripped-off their outer electrons) which results in electrons and ions. The electrons thus produced, in turn, collide with atoms, increase their kinetic energy and ionize them so that more electrons and ions are produced. Thus, the plasma has an ability to conduct electricity due to the presence of electrons.

- When the gas is completely ionized, then the temperature of the central part of the plasma is between 11000°C to 28000°C.

- When such an ionized gas is directed on the workpiece through a high velocity jet, the metal is removed by melting.

1.6.2 Principle of PAM

- When a high velocity jet of plasma is directed on the workpiece surface by means of a plasma arc cutting torch, the metal from the workpiece melts which results in to the machining of the workpiece.

- The continuous attack of electrons on the workpiece which transfer the heat energy of plasma on the workpiece causes the workpiece to melt.

1.6.3 Set-up of the Process   [S-15, W-16]

- The set-up of the process consists of:

  (i) Plasma cutting torch.

  (ii) Tool and workpiece.

  (iii) Gas supply unit.

  (iv) Cooling system.

  (v) Power supply.

(i) Plasma cutting torch:

  o A plasma cutting torch is shown in Fig. 1.13. It carries a tungsten electrode fitted in a small chamber.

  o At other end of the torch is a small converging orifice called as nozzle.

  o One side of the torch provides a passage for supply of gas into the torch.

(ii) Tool and workpiece:

  o The electrode is connected to negative terminal of a D.C. power supply and therefore acts as a cathode.

  o The nozzle is made anode by connecting to the positive terminal of the power supply through a suitable resistor. This resistor limits the current through the nozzle to about 50 A.

  o The workpiece to be machined is also connected to the positive terminal of the supply.

  o The anode and cathode are separated by an insulator.

(iii) Gas supply unit:

  o It consists of gas cylinder, regulators and gas supply hoses.

  o The commonly used gases are argon or nitrogen or the mixture of two. For certain useful purposes, a percentage of hydrogen may be added.

  o The choice of the gas depends upon the material to be cut, economics and the quality of the cut edge desired.

  o The flow rate of the gas varies directly with the thickness of the workpiece. Typical gas flow rate is 2 to 11 m^3/hr.

(iv) Cooling system:

- o A provision is made for circulating the water around the torch so that the electrodes and the nozzle both remains water cooled.

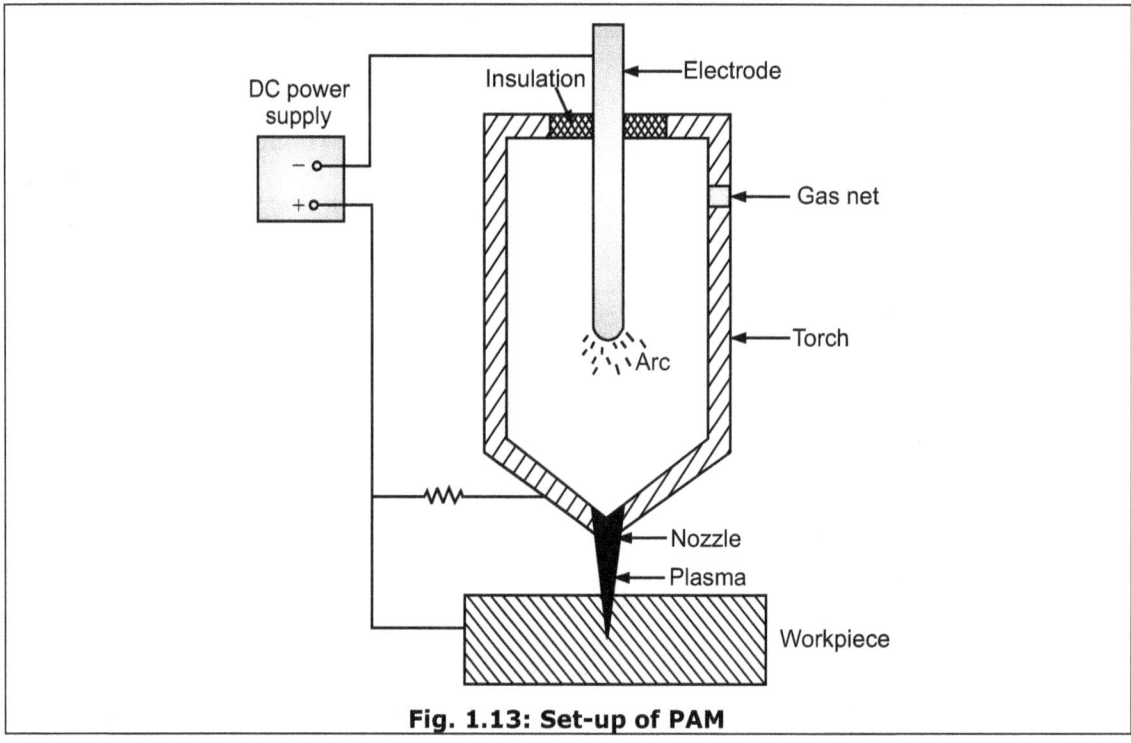

Fig. 1.13: Set-up of PAM

(v) Power supply:

- o A D.C. power supply of 400 V, 200 KW and upto 1000 A is supplied to the nozzle.
- o When supply is made ON, a strong arc is struck between the electrode and the nozzle and the gas is forced into the chamber.
- o When the gas molecules collide with the high velocity electrons of the arc, plasma is formed. This plasma is forced through the nozzle (anode) onto the workpiece.
- o The heat produced from this jet of plasma is sufficient to raise the workpiece temperature above its melting point and the high velocity gas stream effectively blows the molten metal away.

1.6.4 Controlling Parameters

(i) Stand-off distance:

- o Increase in the stand-off distance reduces the depth of penetration and hence narrows the cut width at the bottom.
- o The stand-off distance depends on the thickness of the metal to cut. The typical value of the stand-off distance varies from 5 mm to 10 mm.

(ii) Cutting speed:

  o Increase in the cutting speed reduces the depth of immersion of the plasma jet, leading to narrowing of the cut in the lower portion.

  o Decrease in the cutting speed will cause the opening of the cut at the bottom of the workpiece.

  o For example, the typical cutting speed for aluminium at 80 KW power and 4 mm orifice diameter is 8 mm/sec.

(iii) Gas:

  o The gas flow rate is directly proportional to the thickness of the material.

  o The selection of a particular gas depends on the quality of cut and the economics.

1.6.5 Advantages of PAM   [S-15, 16, W-16]

(i)   The rate of cutting is high.

(ii) It is used to cut any metal irrespective of its hardness and even to non-conducting material like concrete.

(iii) It can cut carbon steel-up to 10 times faster than oxy-fuel cutting.

(iv) The process is finding ever increasing applications because it gives the highest temperature available for many practical sources.

1.6.6 Disadvantages of PAM   [S-16, W-16]

(i)   Protection of noise is necessary.

(ii) Heat affected zone is more.

(iii) High initial cost of the equipment.

(iv) Safety precautions are necessary for the operator and those in the nearby area.

1.6.7 Applications of PAM   [W-11, 14; S-12, 15]

(i)   For stock cutting, plate beveling, shape cutting and piercing.

(ii) In manufacture of automotive and rail road components.

(iii) It can cut hot extrusions to desired length.

(iv) For removal of gates and riser from casting in foundary.

1.7 LASER BEAM MACHINING (LBM)

1.7.1 Introduction

• LASER is an abbreviation for **L**ight **A**mplification by **S**timulated **E**mission of **R**adiation.

• It is a device for producing a narrow beam of light, capable of travelling over vast distances without dispersion.

• It is also capable of being focused to give enormous power densities (10^8 watts per cm^2 for high-energy lasers).

• A laser converts electrical energy into a highly coherent light beam.

1.7.2 Characteristics of Laser

- A laser beam has the following properties:
  (i) A laser beam is highly monochromatic.
  (ii) Laser ray is highly pure beam of light.
  (iii) It is an intense beam of light.
  (iv) Highly directional.
  (v) Highly collimated.
  (vi) The light produced by Laser is coherent.
- These properties allow laser light to be focused, using optical lens, onto a very small spot with resulting high power densities.

1.7.3 Physical Principle of Laser [S-12; W-14]

- The process of generation of laser beam i.e. lasing action is explained through the physical principal of laser.
- Consider an atom of a solid laser medium.
- If the atom or molecule of a solid medium does not emit energy; it is said to be in a low-energy state or ground state. See Fig. 1.14 (a).
- All the electrons of such an atom occupy orbit that have lowest potential energy. At $0°K$ all the electrons are in ground state.
- The electrons at the ground state can be excited to higher energy state by absorbing energy of various forms. See Fig. 1.14 (b).
- The energy can be absorbed through vibrations at higher temperature by chemical reactions with other atoms, by collision with other atoms, by absorption of photons etc.
- When energy from a light source is made to fall on a solid medium, the atoms of the medium absorbs radiations.
- As a result, the electrons of the atoms of the medium jump to higher energy level.
- These atoms which have absorbed high energy are said to be in an excited state.
- This excited state atom spontaneously returns to the ground state energy by emitting a photon with a frequency proportional to the energy difference between the excited state and the lower state. See Fig. 1.14 (c).
- In the simplest case, the substance will return directly to the ground state, emitting a single photon with the same frequency as the absorbed photon.
- In a laser, the atoms or molecules are excited so that more of them are at higher energy levels than at lower energy levels. This condition is known as an inverted population.
- Once the atoms or molecules are in this excited state, they readily emit radiation.
- If a photon whose frequency corresponds to the energy difference between the excited state and the ground state strikes an excited atom, the atom is stimulated to emit a second photon of the same characteristics.

- The bombarding photon and the emitted photon each may then strike other excited atoms, stimulating further emissions of photons, all of the same frequency and all in phase.
- As all the excited atoms releases photon in the form of a chain, this produces a steady beam of coherent light called as a LASER beam. See Fig. 1.14 (d).

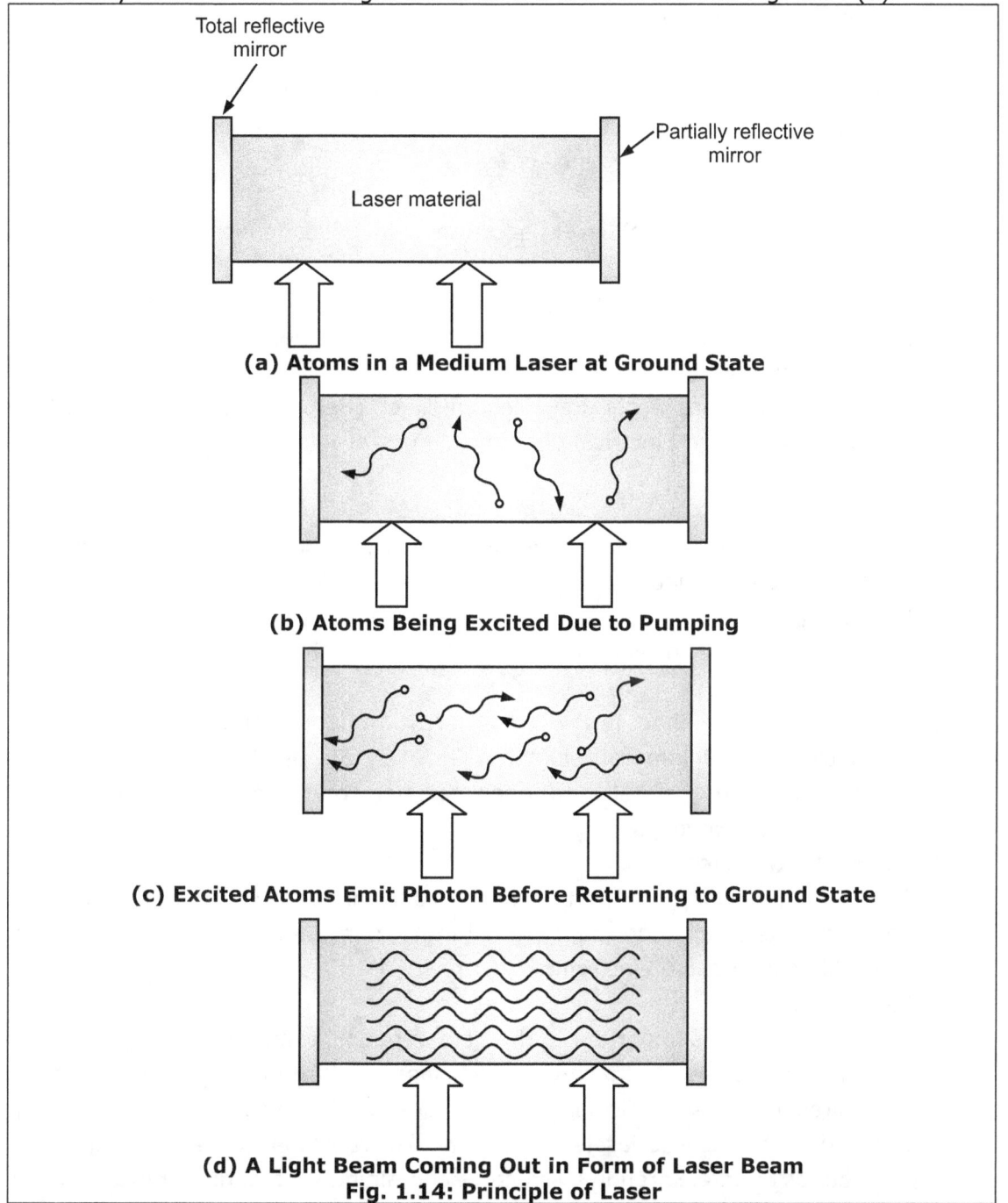

Total reflective mirror

Partially reflective mirror

Laser material

(a) Atoms in a Medium Laser at Ground State

(b) Atoms Being Excited Due to Pumping

(c) Excited Atoms Emit Photon Before Returning to Ground State

(d) A Light Beam Coming Out in Form of Laser Beam
Fig. 1.14: Principle of Laser

1.7.4 Types of Laser

* According to the materials used to produce laser light, laser is classified as:
  (i)   Gas Lasers.
  (ii) Crystal Lasers (solid lasers).
  (iii) Semiconductor Lasers.

(i) Gas Laser:
  o Gas lasers generally have a wide variety of characteristics.
  o Gas lasers using many gases have been built and used for many purposes.
  o They are one of the oldest types of laser.
  o For example,
    (i)   Helium-neon (HeNe) laser is common in education because of its low cost.
    (ii) Carbon dioxide lasers are often used in industry for cutting and welding.
    (iii) Metal ion lasers are gas lasers that generate deep ultraviolet wavelengths.
  o Other examples are Argon-ion, Helium-silver (HeAg), neon-copper (NeCu), nitrogen **T**ransverse **E**lectrical discharge in gas at **A**tmospheric pressure (TEA) laser etc.

(ii) Solid Laser:
  o A solid state laser is one in which the atoms that emit light are fixed within a crystal or a glassy material.
  o For example,
    (i)   Ruby rod (the chromium atoms embedded in the ruby's aluminium oxide crystal).
    (ii) Yttrium orthovanadate (Nd:YVO4), Yttrium lithium fluoride (Nd:YLF) and Yttrium aluminium garnet (Nd:YAG). They are used for cutting, welding and marking of metals and other materials, and also in spectroscopy and for pumping dye lasers.

(iii) Semiconductor Laser:
  o It is a unique, and perhaps the most important, type of laser. It is unique because of its small dimensions (mm × mm × mm), and its natural integration capabilities with micro electronic circuitry.
  o For example,
    (i)   Silicon laser is important in the field of optical computing.
    (ii) Vertical cavity surface-emitting lasers, (VCSELs) whose emission direction is perpendicular to the surface of the wafer.
    (iii) Quantum cascade lasers have an active transition between energy sub-bands of an electron in a structure containing several quantum wells.

1.7.5 Laser Action in Ruby Rod

- The ruby rod laser material is in the form of crystal of aluminium oxide that contains about 0.05 % chromium. The ruby rod is in the form of a cylindrical crystal of 10 mm diameter and 100 mm length.

- The ends of ruby rod are made reflective by mirrors as shown in Fig. 1.15.

- Two mirrors parallel to each other are provided at each end to reflect the incoming light.

- One of these mirrors is fully reflective while the other is partially reflective to allow the light to pass through it.

- When light is thrown by the flash lamp on the ruby rod, the chromium atoms inside it get excited to higher energy level.

- The excited atoms emit photons before it returns to its normal state. The photons come out from the transparent mirror in the form of laser beam.

- When it is focused through the lens, this laser beam falls on the work piece. As a result the beam melts the work piece, vapourizes it and penetrates into it.

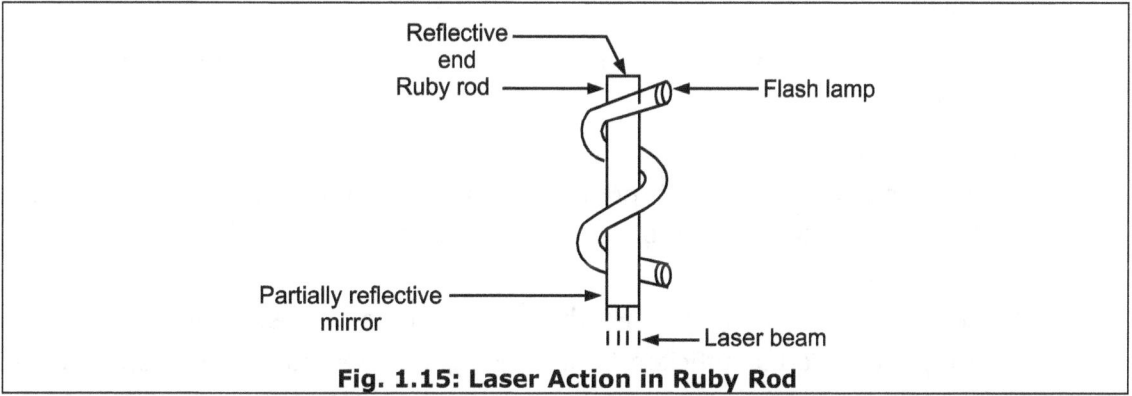

Fig. 1.15: Laser Action in Ruby Rod

1.7.6 Set-up of Laser Beam Machining

[W-11, 13, S-12, 15, 17]

- The set-up of laser beam machining is shown in the Fig. 1.16 and it consist of:

(i) Ruby rod with reflecting mirror.

(ii) Flash lamp.

(iii) Cooling arrangement.

(iv) Lens.

(v) Power supply.

(i) Ruby Rod with Reflecting Mirror:

- o It is crystalline aluminium oxide which is about 10 mm in diameter and 100 mm in length.
- o The ends of a ruby rod are made reflective by two parallel mirrors.
- o One of these mirrors is fully reflective while the other is partially reflective (partially transparent) to allow the beam to pass through it.

(ii) Flash lamp:

- o A flash lamp is filled with gas like Xenon, Argon, krypton etc.
- o The flash lamp surrounds the ruby rod.
- o When the flash lamp is charged, it starts emitting high intense flashes of light.
- o The ruby rod and flash lamp both are kept in a highly reflecting cylinder.

(iii) Cooling arrangement:

- o The efficiency of ruby rod reduces at higher temperature. It is therefore necessary to continuously cool the ruby rod. For this purpose liquid nitrogen at $-196°C$ is supplied to the ruby.
- o The flash lamp operates best when it is warm. Hence, hot air is circulated around it.
- o A vacuum chamber is provided between the two to maintain the temperature difference between them.

(iv) Lens:

- o The laser beam is passed through the lens on to the work piece. The focal length should be accurate in order to machine the work piece.

(v) Power supply:

- o When power supply is made 'ON', the flash lamp emits flashes of light.
- o The ruby rod absorbs sufficient light. This light travels to and fro between the two parallel mirrors.
- o This amplified stream of light comes out through partially transparent mirror and is focused on the lens.
- o The lens converge the laser beam on the work piece.
- o This melts the work piece and vapourizes it which results in machining of the work piece.
  - During operation, the work piece to be cut is placed on the aluminium work table.
  - The motion can be given either to work piece or to the beam or both depending upon the requirement.
  - The operator visually inspects the process and accordingly adjusts the motion.

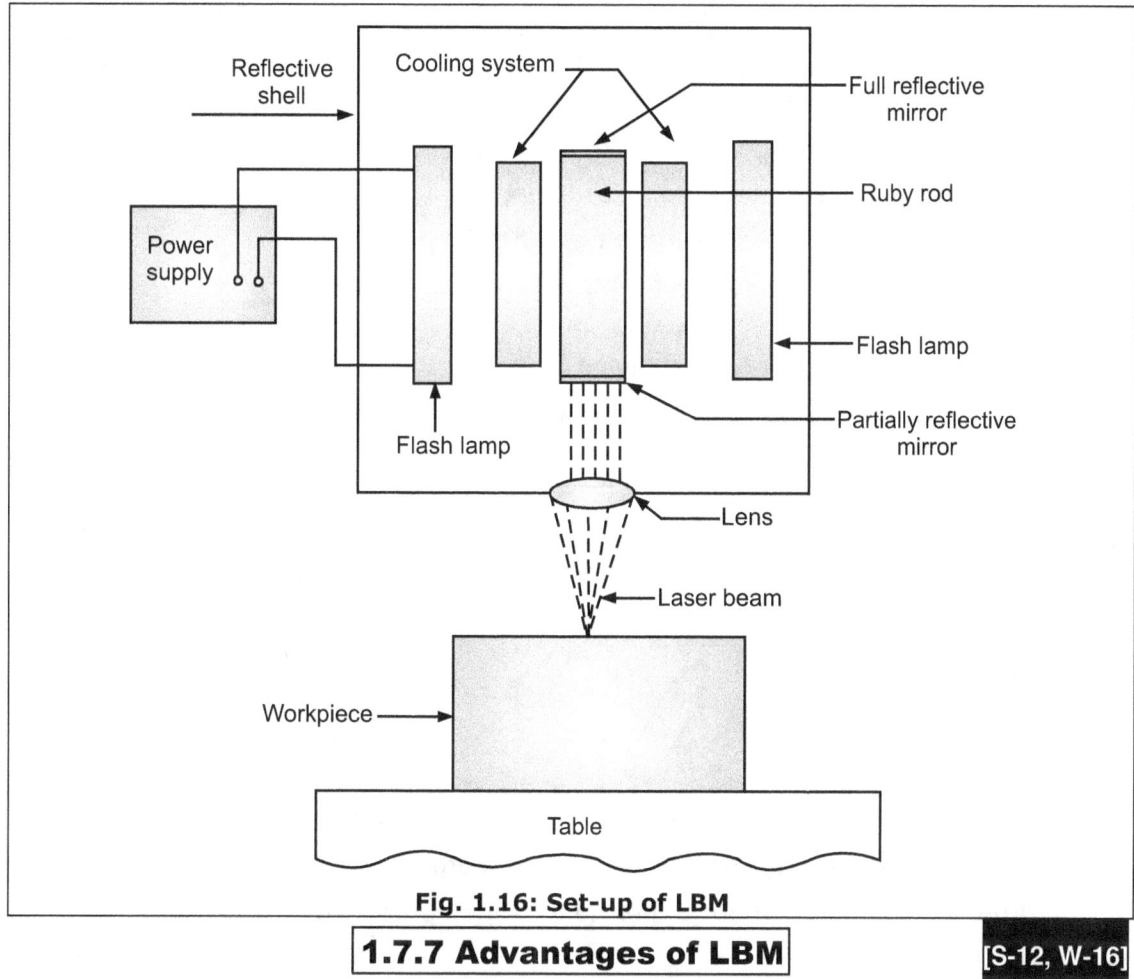

Fig. 1.16: Set-up of LBM

1.7.7 Advantages of LBM   [S-12, W-16]

(i)   As there is no tool, there is no question of tool wear.

(ii) Extremely small holes can be drilled.

(iii) It can cut through air, gas, vacuum and even through liquid.

(iv) Angular drilling or cutting can be obtained by tilting the work piece.

(v) The process can be used for cutting, drilling and welding.

(vi) No mechanical force is exerted on the work piece, so fragile work piece can be machined.

1.7.8 Disadvantages of LBM   [W-16]

(i)   High capital and operating cost.

(ii) It cannot cut highly conductive and reflective material. (For example, Al, Co and their alloys).

(iii) Life of flash lamp is short.

(iv) Skilled operator is required for controlling the process.

(v) Only small amount of material can be removed.

1.7.9 Applications of LBM [W-11, 12; S-12, 15]

- Drilling holes in surgical needles, diamond wire drawing dies, nylon buttons etc.
  - (i)   Cutting or engraving patterns on thin films.
  - (ii)   Trimming of sheet metal and plastic parts.
  - (iii) Non-circular holes can be machined with the aid of CNC.
  - (iv)   It is also used for welding of metals.
  - (v)   Laser is also used in communications (a laser beam can carry much more information than can radio waves).
  - (vi)   Lasers are also used as entertainment in theatres, concerts, and light shows.

1.7.10 Controlling Parameters   [S-16]

- The main process parameters or controlling parameters in LBM are:
  - (i)   Focal Length.
  - (ii)   Flash Lamp.
  - (iii) Power Density.

(i) Focal Length:
  - o   The work piece should be placed close to the lens for machining.
  - o   If focal length is less, straight holes will be produced.
  - o   If the focal length is more, taper holes will be produced.

(ii) Flash lamp:
  - o   It operates at a rate of 12 flashes every single minute.
  - o   It should be kept warm to obtain maximum efficiency.

(iii) Power density:
  - o   The power density of the beam determines whether the beam will perform the function of cutting or welding.
  - o   For machining operation, the power density should be higher i.e. around 1.5×10^7 W/cm^2.

1.7.11 Application of Laser Beam For Welding [W-12]

- Laser beam welding (LBW) is a welding technique used to join metals and alloys through the use of a laser.
- It can be used to weld dissimilar metals which do not exhibit excessive hardenability.

- The beam provides a concentrated heat source, allowing for narrow, deep welds and high welding rates.

- The process is frequently used in high volume applications, such as in the automotive industry.

- LBW is a versatile process, capable of welding carbon steels, HSLA steels, stainless steel, aluminium, and titanium.

- The speed of welding is proportional to the amount of power supplied but also depends on the type and thickness of the workpiece.

1.7.12 Laser Beam Welding   [W-15]

- The beam is targeted on the workpiece surface which is to be welded.

  o At the surface, the large concentration of light energy is converted into thermal energy.

  o The surface of the workpiece starts melting and progresses through it by surface conductance.

  o For welding, the beam energy is maintained below the vapourization temperature of the workpiece material.

  o Concentrated energy produces melting and coalescence before a heat affected zone is developed.

  o The role of focusing lenses in this process is really important because it concentrates the beam energy into a focal spot as small as 0.005 in diameters or even less.

  o Because the penetration of the workpiece depends on conducted heat, the thickness of the materials to be welded is generally less than 0.80 inches.

  o When the materials to be welded are thick and have high thermal conductivity like for example aluminium the advantage of having a minimal heat affected zone can be seriously affected.

  o Because the heat source in this type of welding process is the energy of light, the workpiece will be welded purely which means the fatigue strength of the welded joint will be excellent.

  o The function of all laser beam welding processes whether they be gas (carbon dioxide, helium, neon etc.) or other lasing sources is based on the principles of the excitation of atoms using intense light, electricity, electron beams, chemicals etc., and the spontaneous and stimulated release of photons.

1.7.13 Difference Between EDM and LBM [W-14, S-16]

Sr. No.	Parameters	EDM	LBM
1.	Working principle	It works on the principle of spark erosion.	It works on the principle of LASER.
2.	Tools used	Tool made of some soft material is used.	Laser material is used as a tool.
3.	Accuracy	Accuracy is less as compared to LBM.	Accuracy is comparatively more.
4.	Metal removal rate	High metal removal rate.	Metal removal rate is low.
5.	Tool wear	More wear of tool due to sparks.	It uses a beam as a tool which does not wear.
6.	Material	It cannot be applied to non-conducting material.	It can be applied to non-conducting material.
7.	Heat affected zone	HAZ is high.	HAZ is small.
8.	Power consumption	Power consumed is less.	High power consumption of around 2700 kW/cm^3/min.

1.8 ELECTRO CHEMICAL MACHINING (ECM)

1.8.1 Introduction

- Consider two electrodes placed in a tank containing conductive solution. One electrode is made cathode and the other is made anode. When current is switched 'ON', the positive ions move towards the cathode and the negative ions move towards the anode. Electrochemical reaction takes place and metal is removed from the anode and plated on the cathode.

- This process is known as electroplating.

1.8.2 Principle of Working [W-12]

- ECM utilizes the principle of reverse of electroplating.

- Here the tool is made cathode and the work piece the anode. *(The work piece is used as the anode, so the metal ions are removed from the work piece, forming ions in the electrolyte. The ions are not allowed to deposit onto the tool.)*

- The electrolyte is so selected that after electrolysis there is no decomposition of metal on the tool.
- A close gap of about 0.5 mm is maintained between the tool and work piece.
- An electrolyte is continuously pumped into the gap and a D.C. voltage is applied.
- Due to the applied voltage the current flows in the electrolyte.
- Due to this the positively charged ions are attracted towards the cathode and the negatively charged ions are attracted towards the anode.
- The metal from anode is removed atom by atom by removing negative charges that bind the surface atoms to their neighbours.
- The ionized atoms are then positively charged and can be attracted away from the work piece.
- Thus, electrochemical reaction takes place in presence of the electrolyte which results in removal of metal from the work piece.

1.8.3 Set-Up Of ECM (Working of ECM)

- A typical set-up of ECM is shown in the Fig. 1.17. It consists of the following systems.
  - (i) A D.C. power supply unit.
  - (ii) Work piece and work holding system.
  - (iii) Tool and tool feed system.
  - (iv) Electrolyte supply system.

(i) A D.C. Power Supply Unit:
  - o In ECM, the current of about 40,000 A is applied across a D.C. voltage of 5 to 30 volts.

(ii) Work Piece and Work Holding System:
  - o The work piece is made anode. The work piece is placed on a table in a tank.
  - o The table material is non-conductive and have good thermal stability.

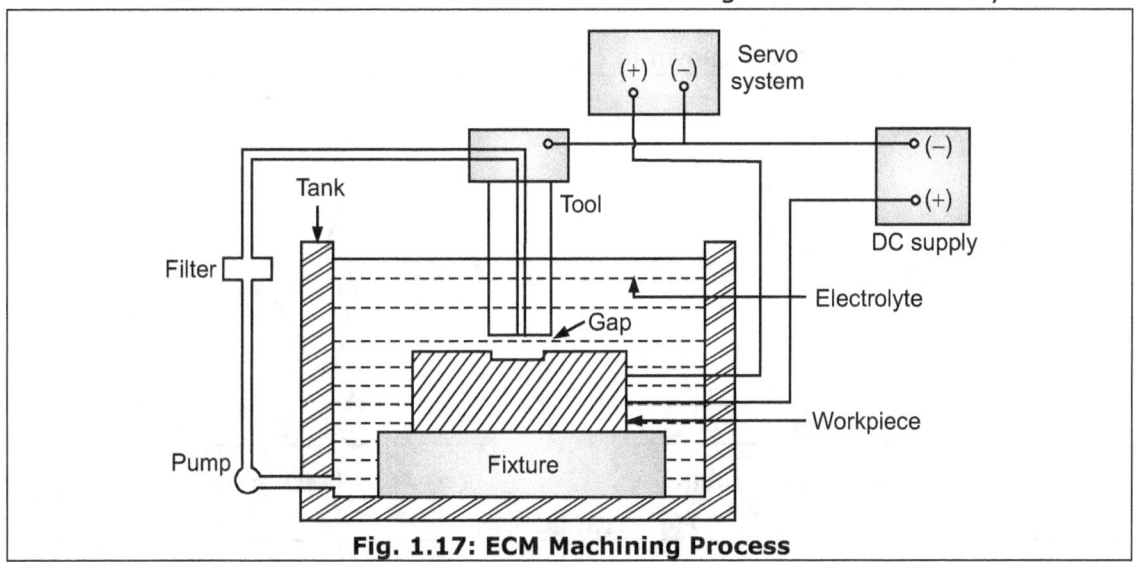

Fig. 1.17: ECM Machining Process

(iii) Tool and tool feed system

- o The tool is made cathode.
- o A small gap is maintained between the tool and work piece.
- o In order to maintain the gap during machining, the tool is continuously feed towards the work piece by servo mechanism.
- o The tool used is hollow to provide passage for the electrolyte.
- o The tool has reverse profile of that to be produced on the work piece.

(iv) Electrolyte supply system

- o An electrolyte is continuously pumped in to the gap between the tool and the work piece.
- o The electrolyte selected is such that it will not plate material on the tool.
- o When a D.C. voltage is applied, current flows through the equipment and electrochemical reaction takes place.
- o This results in removal of material from the work piece. The metal removal rate is proportional to the current intensity.

1.8.4 Tool Material for ECM

- • The general requirements of tool material are as follows:
  - (i) It should be a good conductor of electricity.
  - (ii) It should have good machinability.
  - (iii) It should be chemically inert to the electrolyte (i.e. it should not react with the electrolyte).
  - (iv) It should have high thermal conductivity.
  - (v) It should be anti-corrosive in nature.
- • The commonly used tool materials are copper, brass, stainless steel, aluminium, graphite, bronze, tungsten.
- • The shape of a ECM tool is shown in Fig. 1.18.

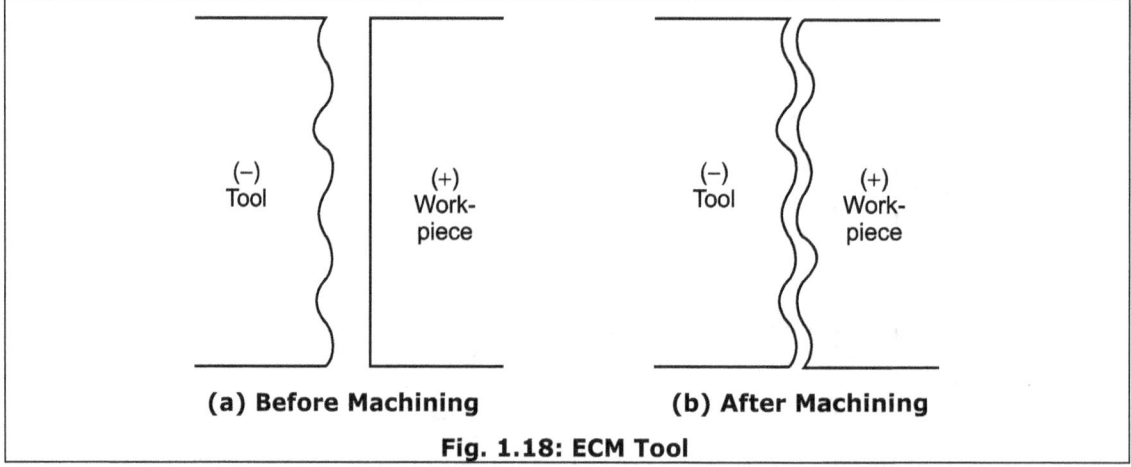

(a) Before Machining   (b) After Machining

Fig. 1.18: ECM Tool

1.8.5 Electrolyte

- The functions of electrolyte are:
  - (i)   It should carry current between the tool and work piece.
  - (ii) It should dissipate the heat produced in the process.
  - (iii) It should carry away the products of reaction away from the machining area.
  - (iv) It should flow with high velocity.
  - (v)   It should allow the electrochemical reaction to occur.
- The commonly used electrolytes are sodium nitrate, sodium chloride, sodium hydroxide, sodium sulphate, sodium fluoride, potassium nitrate, potassium chloride etc.

1.8.6 Properties of Electrolyte

- The electrolyte should possess the following properties:
  - (i)   High electrical conductivity.
  - (ii) Non-corrrosive and non-toxic in nature.
  - (iii) Low viscosity and high specific heat.
  - (iv) Chemically stable.
  - (v)   Inexpensive and readily available.

1.8.7 Advantages of ECM

- (i)   The process has no tool wear, so tool life is high.
- (ii) It generates a burr free surface.
- (iii) The metal removal rate is high.
- (iv) It is used for profiling and contouring of complex shapes.

1.8.8 Disadvantages of ECM

- (i)   Heavy initial investment.
- (ii) High power consumption.
- (iii) It cannot produce sharp corner and edges.
- (iv) Only electrically conductive material can be machined.
- (v)   Floor space area required is more.

1.8.9 Applications of ECM   [W-11, S-12, W-13]

- (i)   It can be used for die-sinking operations.
- (ii) Drilling a jet engine turbine blade.
- (iii) Multiple hole drilling.
- (iv) Steam turbine blades can be machined within close limits.

1.8.10 Similarities between EDM and ECM

(i)   Tool and work piece are separated by a small gap.

(ii) Tool used should be a conductor of electricity.

(iii) High capital investment.

(iv) High power consumption.

(v) Only electrically conductive material can be machined.

(vi) A fluid is used as a conducting medium between the tool and work piece.

(vii)Tool is fed continuously towards the work piece to maintain a constant gap between them.

1.8.11 Difference between EDM and ECM

Sr. No.	Parameters	EDM	ECM
1.	Conducting fluid	Uses dielectric fluid as a conducting medium between tool and work piece.	Uses electrolyte as a conducting medium between tool and work piece.
2.	Tool wear	Wear of tool takes place during the process. So more electrodes are needed.	There is no wear of tool during the process, so tool life is high.
3.	Heat generated	Heat is generated during the process.	No heat is generated during the process.
4.	Metal removal rate	Low metal removal rate. (about 1000 mm^3/min)	Metal removal rate is high. (about 15000 mm^3/min)
5.	Working principle	It works on the principle of spark erosion.	It works on the principle of faraday's law of electrolysis.
6.	Machining action	Metal is removed by melting and vapourization.	Metal is removed by electrochemical reaction.
7.	Power supply	Pulsed DC, high voltage, low current. (400 V, 500 A)	DC, low voltage, high current. (50 V, 40000 A).
8.	Tools used	Tools used are oversize for machining inside surfaces and undersize for machining outside surfaces.	Tools used are of the required size of the workpiece.
9.	Power consumption	Less (2 kW/cm^3/min.).	More (7 kW/cm^3/min.).

1.8.12 Difference Between Dielectric Fluid And Electrolyte

[S-15]

Sr. No.	Dielectric Fluid	Electrolyte
1.	It is used as a conducting medium in EDM process.	It is used as a conducting medium in ECM process.
2.	It acts as conductor and insulator both.	It always provides a passage for supply of electricity.
3.	Tool wear takes place because of the dielectric fluid.	The electrolyte selected is such that there is no wear of tool.
4.	Dielectric fluid may or may not be corrosive in nature.	It should be non-corrosive in nature.

1.9 ELECTRON BEAM MACHINING (EBM)

1.9.1 Introduction

- When the electrons are focused and concentrated on a small spot on the metal, the kinetic energy of the electrons is converted into heat energy which is sufficient to melt the workpiece.

- When this technique is used on the metal, it is called as electron beam machining.

- In EBM, electrons emitted from the hot source are accelerated and focused on a very small area of the workpiece. These beams of electrons travel at about 50% to 80% of the velocity of sound.

- When such a high velocity of electrons strikes the workpiece, it results in melting of the workpiece.

- But the process should be performed in vacuum to prevent scattering of electrons and to obtain maximum efficiency (i.e. greater depth to width ratio).

- The maximum distance between the electron gun and the workpiece is usually 100 mm.

- The process uses an electric current of 0.001 A and a power of 25 KW.

- The metal removal rate is upto 40 mm^3/sec.

- The process is particularly useful for materials with high melting point and low thermal conductivity.

- The process is also applied successfully for welding of parts.

1.9.2 Principle of Working of EBM [W-12, W-13]

- When a high velocity beam of electron is focused on a workpiece, the electrons strikes on the workpiece and their kinetic energy is converted into heat energy.

- This heat results in removal of material from the workpiece by vapourization and melting.

1.9.3 Set-up of Electron Beam Machining [S-11, W-12]

- The set-up of EBM consists of six basic units as shown in Fig. 1.19.

  (i)   Electron gun.

  (ii) Magnetic lens.

  (iii) Magnetic deflection coil.

  (iv) Movable table.

  (v)   Monitoring instrument.

  (vi) Vacuum chamber.

(i) Electron Gun:

- o   An electron gun consists of a cathode, a grid cup and an anode.

- o   A cathode is a tungsten filament which is heated by a low voltage current.

- o   A grid cup is negatively biased with respect to the filament.

- o   An anode is in the form of a ring. It is kept at a ground potential.

- o   When the cathode is heated it emits electrons by thermionic emission.

- o   As there is a high potential difference between anode and cathode, the electrons are accelerated towards the anode by a high velocity. The accelerating voltage is about 50 to 200 KV.

- o   The grid helps in narrowing the beam.

(ii) Magnetic Lens:

- o   A magnetic lens further converges the beam into a narrow spot on the workpiece.

(iii) Magnetic Deflection Coil:

- o   A magnetic deflection coil (beam deflection coil) is used to deflect the beam further either onto a different spots on the workpiece or for moving it along a contour.

(iv) Movable Table:

- o   A table which is used to mount the workpiece is kept in the vacuum chamber.

- o   The table is numerically controlled to move under the beam. Thus, the machining of workpiece is done by either moving the table or by deflecting the beam.

(v) Monitoring Instrument:

- o A light microscope is kept to monitor the complete process. The operator can adjust the position of the workpiece as per the requirement and observe the actual machining process.
- o Generally the beam remains stationary and the workpiece is moved.

(vi) Vacuum Chamber:

- o A vacuum of 10^{-6} torr (mm of Hg) is kept in the chamber. The vacuum helps in the following:
- o The beam retains its narrow configuration over a long distance.
- o The electrons do not lose energy by collision with air molecules.
- o The electrons emitted from the gun maintain their high velocity until they strike the workpiece.

[S-10]

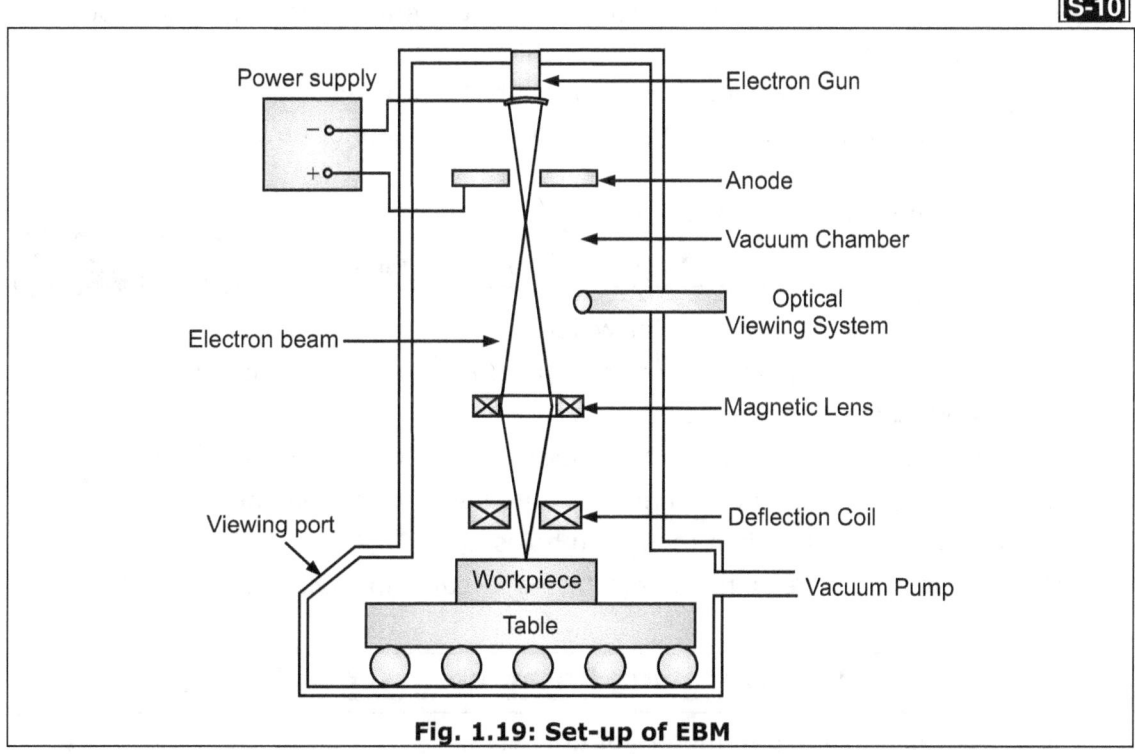

Fig. 1.19: Set-up of EBM

1.9.4 Working of EBM

- • The electrons which come out of the electron gun and pass through the magnetic lens posses a very high energy.
- • When this narrow stream of electrons strike the workpiece, the kinetic energy of electrons is converted into the heat energy and this heat melts the workpiece.

1.9.5 Advantages of EBM

(i)   As beam is used as a tool, there is no wear of the tool.

(ii)   Drilling of tapered holes is possible.

(iii) High speed perforation of any kind of material.

(iv) The process is suitable for automatic machining.

(v)   Holes, slots, orifices etc. which cannot be made by any other method can be produced by EBM.

(vi) The size of heat affected zone can be held within 10% of the cut width.

(vii) Through cutting of any material.

1.9.6 Disadvantages of EBM

(i)   Very high cost of equipment.

(ii)   Size of workpiece is limited to size of the vacuum.

(iii) The process results in X-ray emission which retards the production rate and limits the size of the parts to be machined.

(iv) Skilled operators are required to operate the process.

(v)   Exact straight edges or right angles or corners cannot be cut.

(vi) The process can be operated only in vacuum.

(vii) Metal removal rate is low.

1.9.7 Applications of EBM   [W-11, S-12, W-13]

(i)   The process is mainly used for welding.

(ii)   Micromachining operations on thin materials like drilling, scribing etc.

(iii) Engraving of metals and ceramics.

(iv) Drilling of micro holes in turbine blades, metering or flow orifice etc.

(v)   Producing metering holes in injector nozzles of diesel engines.

(vi) To remove small broken taps from holes.

(vii) Welding of connections in electronic circuits involving small and precise connections.

1.9.8 Controlling Parameters for EBM

- The various controlling parameters of EBM are:

(i) Beam current.

(ii) Spot diameter.

(i) Beam current:

    o   The beam current depends on the grid voltage.

    o   If the grid voltage is more negative with respect to the cathode, then the more it restricts the emission of electrons.

(ii) Beam diameter:

- o The beam diameter depends on the beam current, the accelerating voltage, the magnetic lens and distance between gun and the workpiece.

1.9.9 Differentiation Between EBM and LBM

Sr. No.	Parameters	EBM	LBM
1.	Working principle	When a high velocity beam of electron strikes the workpiece its kinetic energy is converted into heat energy.	When the excited atoms releases photon in the form of a chain, a laser beam is generated which when strikes on the workpiece melts it.
2.	Tools used	Electron gun is used as a tool.	Laser material is used as a tool.
3.	Accuracy	Accuracy is good.	Accuracy is comparatively more.
4.	Metal removal rate	Metal removal rate is low.	Metal removal rate is high.
5.	Environment or process requirement	The complete process should be kept in vacuum.	Vacuum is required between flash lamp and ruby rod.
6.	Workpiece material	Usually only metals.	Any material, but not very suitable for plastics.

1.10 ULTRASONIC MACHINING

1.10.1 Introduction

- Sonic waves are produced by rarefaction and compression of a medium such as air. These are the waves which are audible to human ear. The frequency of sonic waves ranges from 20 to 16 kHz.

- This is a very wide range and all human beings are not capable of hearing through the whole range. It varies from person to person but the limits are as given above.

- The waves which have a frequency above 16 KHz are not sonic (or above sonic) and are called as ultra-sonic waves. These waves have frequency above that of the upper frequency limit of the human ear and are not audible to human ear.

- Due to their high frequency they have high energy and penetration in a number of media and are useful for a number of industrial processes in medical, engineering and defense field.

1.10.2 Principle of Working   [W-11, S-13]

- The term ultrasonic refers to waves of high frequency, generally above the hearing range of a normal human ear, i.e. generally above 20 kHz. In this process, a cutting tool is given mechanical vibration so that it oscillates axially at high frequency in abrasive slurry against the stationary workpiece.

- The tool has the same shape as the shape to be machined. The impact of the abrasive causes the metal removal from the workpiece. This method is generally used to machine hard and brittle materials.

- Every abrasive grain is hammered into the work surface by a high-frequency oscillating tool that cause chipping of fine particles from the workpiece resulting in the removal of material.

- The most appropriate frequencies in this case are 20,000-30,000 cps (cycle per second) with amplitude of 0.2 mm.

- The electronics oscillator and amplifier, also known as generator, convert the electrical energy at low frequency to high frequency. The transducer works on the principle of magnetostriction. The magnetostriction effect is the one in which the material changes in dimension in response to an electric field.

- The vibrations thus produced are focused on the cutting point by means of a horn or a tuned vibration concentrator. The abrasive used in the process is supplied in the form of slurry suspended in a carrier fluid and the tool feed is achieved by means of static loading of the vibrator head that transmits vibrations to the tool.

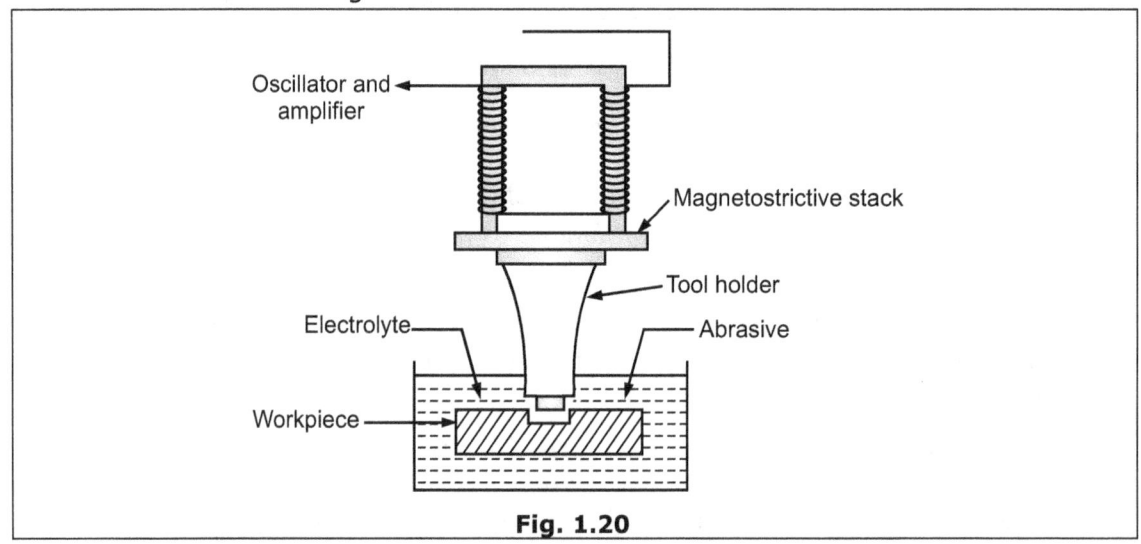

Fig. 1.20

1.10.3 Tool Description

- The tool is made of relatively soft material that should have high strength and ductility.

- Stainless steel and low carbon steel are commonly used tool materials.

- It has a shape of mirror image of the cavity desired on the workpiece.

- The tool is connected to the tool holder by brazing, soldering or by mechanical fastening.

- The tool feed rate is about 0.1 mm/sec.

1.10.4 Process Description or Set-up

[W-11, 12; S-12, 13, W-13]

- The set-up of the process is shown in Fig. 1.21 and the elements of the process are:

  (i) Transducer.

  (ii) Tool.

  (iii) Abrasive slurry.

  (iv) Tool feed mechanism.

(i)   Transducer:

  o   The transducer is made of magnetostrictive material like nickel, iron-cobalt, iron-Al etc. A generator converts the available electrical energy of low frequency to high frequency and is supplied to the transducer.

  o   Due to this the longitudinal strains are produced in the transducer.

(ii) Tool:

  o   It consists of two parts i.e. the tool holder and the tool tip. The tool holder is connected to the transducer and it transmits the vibratory energy from the transducer to the tool tip.

  o   This causes linear oscillatory motion of the tool when the workpiece comes in contact with the tool.

(iii) Abrasive slurry:

  o   The mixture of abrasive particles and water is used as abrasive slurry. This slurry is continuously fed at the tool workpiece contact.

  o   When the supply is made ON, the abrasive grains are hammered by the high frequency oscillatory tool into the workpiece. This results in removal of material from the workpiece.

  o   Because of this impact of the tool, the process is also known as impact grinding.

  o   The grain size of an abrasive has a marked effect on the MRR and surface finish.

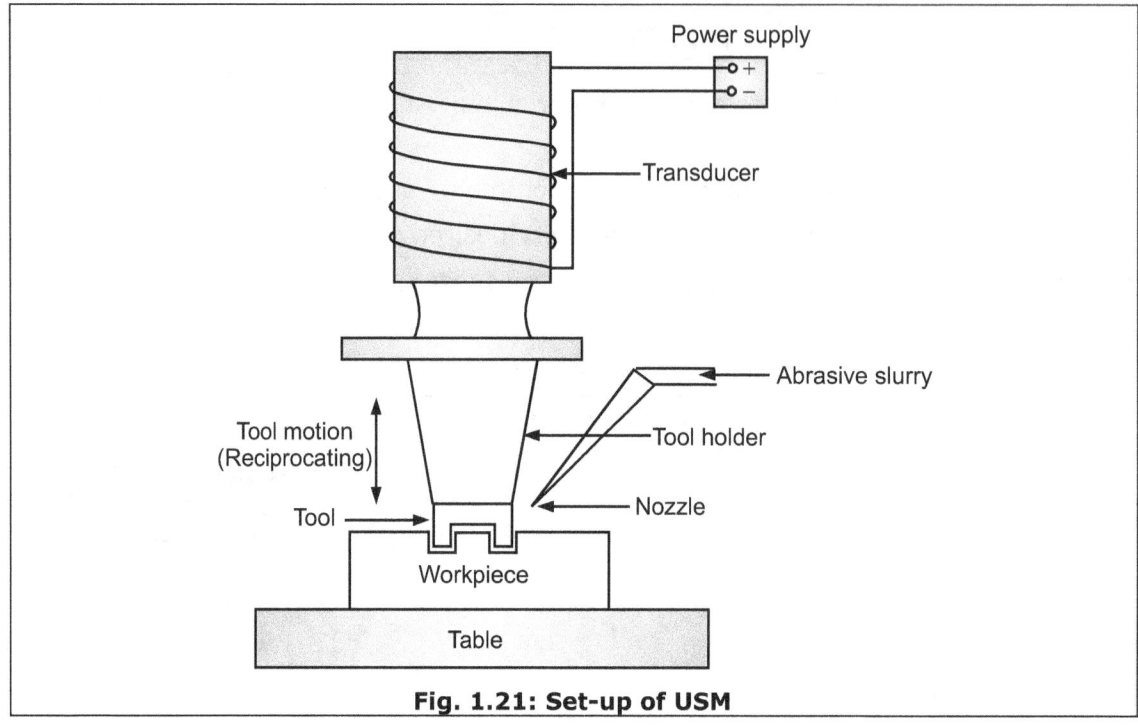

Fig. 1.21: Set-up of USM

(iv) Tool feed mechanism:

- ○ As the tool machines the workpiece, the gap between the two increases. Thus, for machining action the tool must be fed continuously into the workpiece.

- ○ This is done by a tool feed mechanism which uses counter weights for the purpose.

- ○ The tool is pressed against the workpiece with a load of few kilograms and fed downwards continuously as the cavity is cut in the workpiece.

1.10.5 Advantages of USM

(i) Any known hard material can be easily machined.

(ii) It can be used for machining of both conductive and non-conductive material.

(iii) The process is noiseless.

(iv) Complex shapes with good accuracy and reasonable surface finish can be obtained.

(v) No heat is generated in the process, so the physical properties of the workpiece remain unchanged.

(vi) As there are no high speed moving parts, the working on machine is not hazardous.

1.10.6 Disadvantages of USM

(i)   The abrasive slurry has to be periodically replaced.

(ii)   The metal removal rate is low.

(iii) It is not suitable for heavy stock removal.

(iv)   The initial equipment cost and the tooling cost is high.

(v)   The slurry has to be replaced periodically for better machining action.

(vi)   Power consumption is quite high.

1.10.7 Applications of USM

(i)   Cutting internal threads in ceramics and glasses by rotating the workpiece.

(ii)   Cutting of industrial diamonds.

(iii) Manufacturing of wire drawing, punching and blanking dies.

(iv)   In dentistry work to drill holes in teeth.

(v)   In making holes of any shape for which the tool can be made.

(vi)   Coining of glass and ceramics.

1.11 CHEMICAL MACHINING

1.11.1 Introduction

- Chemical machining is the oldest of the non-traditional processes. It was based on the observation that chemicals attack metals and etch them, thereby removing small amount of materials from the workpiece.

- This process is carried out by using reagents or etchants, such as acids and alkaline solutions.

- The mechanism is to use chemical reaction between the material of the workpiece and some chemical reagent, so that the products of the reaction can be removed easily. Thus, the surface of the workpiece is etched away, exposing the lower layers, and the process is continued until the desired amount of material is removed.

- The time of immersion or exposure depends upon the amount of material to be removed by the chemical action.

- For aluminium the etchant is sodium hydroxide, for mild steel it is hydrochloride acid and nitric acid, for stainless steel it is iron chloride etc.

- The etchant, its concentration, operating temperature and the etch rate (in mm/min) depends on the material to be etched.

- This process is also called etching or chemical milling.

1.11.2 Procedure of Chemical Machining

- The Chemical Machining Process is shown in Fig. 1.22.

- Residual stresses (due to prior processing) should be relieved in order to prevent warping of the workpiece after chemical machining.

- The surfaces are thoroughly degreased and cleaned to ensure good adhesion of the masking material and uniform material removal.

- Those regions of the workpiece that must not undergo chemical machining are covered by a non-reacting material, called a mask (tapes, paints, elastomers and plastics). The masking material should not react with the chemical reagent.

- The masking is peeled-off by scribe and peel technique from the various regions that requires etching.

- The exposed surfaces are etched with etchants like NaOH, $FeCl_2$, HNO_3 etc.

- After machining the parts are thoroughly washed to prevent further reactions with any etchant residues.

- The rest of the masking material is removed and the part is cleaned and inspected.

- Additional finishing operations may be performed on chemically milled parts.

- This sequence may be repeated to produce stepped cavities and various contours.

- Metal removal rates in CHM are generally indicated as penetration rates, mm/min. Since rate of chemical attack of the work material by the etchant is directed into the surface.

- The penetration rate is unaffected by surface area.

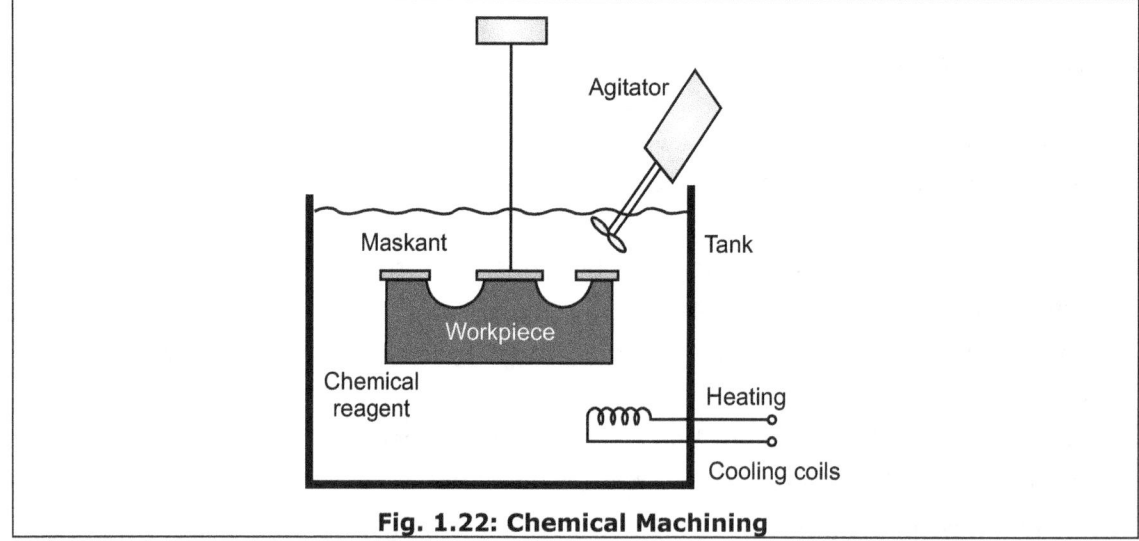

Fig. 1.22: Chemical Machining

1.11.3 Advantages of Chemical Machining

(i)   Complex shapes can be produced.

(ii)   No stresses are induced in the material.

(iii)   Parts of minimum thickness such as foil can be easily machined.

(iv)   The process can be applied to any metal of any shape.

(v)   The parts produced are free of burrs.

(vi)   All faces of the workpiece can be machined simultaneously.

1.11.4 Disadvantages of Chemical Machining

(i)   Slow metal removal rate.

(ii)   Sharp corner cannot be produced.

(iii)   The maskant, etchants and other chemicals used in the process are corrosive and toxic, so due care must be taken for the protection of the operator.

(iv)   It requires very long time to machine thick material.

(v)   Considerable undercut takes place below the edges protected by the maskant.

(vi)   Skilled operator is required to machine the workpiece.

1.11.5 Applications of Chemical Machining

(i)   Shallow cavities produced on plates, sheets, forgings, and extrusions.

(ii)   Chemical milling used in the aerospace industry for parts like wings.

(iii)   To produce decorative surfaces on elevator doors, ashtrays, panels, instrument dials etc.

(iv)   Process is also used for microelectronic devices like computers, television, electric motors, telephone system, medical instruments etc.

(v)   To produce special geometric shapes on radar reflectors, heat exchangers etc.

Important Points

- **Anode:** The positive terminal in an electrolytic cell or battery. In EDM, it is applied to the workpiece.

- **Breakdown:** When the molecules of atom split into ions and electrons, it is said as breakdown.

- **Breakdown voltage:** The voltage at which the dielectric fluid splits into ions and electrons is said as breakdown voltage.

- **Capacitor:** An electrical component that stores an electric charge. The current for the spark comes directly from the capacitors when they are discharged.

- **Coherent light:** It is made-up of waves of the same wavelength; ordinary light contains many different wavelengths.
- **Collimated light:** The light rays of collimated light are almost perfectly parallel and headed in almost exactly the same direction.
- **Cathode:** The negative terminal in an electrolytic cell or battery. In EDM it is applied to the tool.
- **Conductor:** A material that allows the flow of electric current through it is known as conductor.
- **Contamination:** The accumulation of debris in the dielectric fluid, causing a decrease in the fluid's dielectric strength. This is called as contamination.
- **Crater:** The small cavities left on the EDM surface of the workpiece by the EDM sparks. It is also known as pits.
- **Deionization:** A return of the condition of the dielectric fluid to a non-conductive state. It is opposite of ionization.
- **Dielectric strength:** The voltage at which the insulating qualities of a material break down. In EDM, it is applied to dielectric fluid.
- **Discharge:** It is the EDM spark.
- **Discharge channel:** The conductive path formed by ionized dielectric fluid between the electrode and workpiece is known as discharge channel.
- **Electrochemical reaction:** The reaction between metals in the presence of chemicals and electric current.
- **Electrolyte:** A normally conductive liquid or gas.
- **Exotics**: The third group of metallic used as EDM electrode materials. Includes all rarely used metals such as tantalum, nickel, molybdenum etc.
- **Eroded:** The material is removed from the workpiece because of wear.
- **Flashpoint:** The temperature at which any flammable material will burst into flame. A factor in selecting dielectric fluid for EDM.
- **Gap voltage:** This can be measured as two different values during one complete cycle. The voltage which can be read across the electrode and workpiece gap before the spark current begins to flow is called the open gap voltage. The voltage which can be read across the gap during the spark current discharge is the working gap voltage.
- **Ionized:** The molecules of atom gets split into ions and electrons.
- **Insulator:** A material that is a poor conductor of electric current is known as insulator.
- **Intense beam of light**: It's divergence is very small.
- **Magnetostriction:**
- The property because of which material exhibits change in dimension (expands and contracts in each cycle) when they are magnetized is called as magnetostriction or piezomagnetism.
- **Magnetostrictive material:**
- The material which shows the property of magnetostriction is called as magnetostrictive material.

- **Metal Removal Rate (MRR):** The rate at which material is removed from the workpiece by EDM. It is expressed in mm^3/sec.
- **Monochromatic:** The beam has single wave length.
- **Non-toxic:** Non-poisonous.
- **Overcut:** An EDM cavity is always larger than the electrode used to machine it. The difference between the size of the electrode and the size of the cavity (or hole) being machined is called the overcut.
- **Photon:** It is the particle composing light and other forms of electromagnetic radiation.
- **Pulsed supply:** A supply of such variations having a regular waveform in which the variable quantity rises sharply from a base value to a maximum value and then falls back to the base value in a relatively short time.
- **Pure beam of light:** All the light rays in the beam are nearly of the same colour.
- **Resistance:** Resistance is the property of a component which restricts the flow of electric current.
- **Resistor:** A resistor is a component of an electrical circuit that resists the flow of electrical current. A resistor has two terminals across which electricity must pass, and is designed to drop the voltage of the current as it flows from one terminal to the next.
- **Spark:** An electrical discharge of very short duration between two conducting materials.
- **Surface roughness:** Surface irregularities on a machined surface.
- **Transducer:** The transducer is a device that converts the electrical energy to mechanical vibration whose frequency corresponds to the electrical supply frequency.
- **Stand-off distance:** The distance between the nozzle tip (in case of AJM and WJM) or the lens (in case of EBM) and the workpiece surface is called as stand-off distance.

Non-Traditional Processes
- Any hard material can be machined.
- Complex profiles can be obtained.

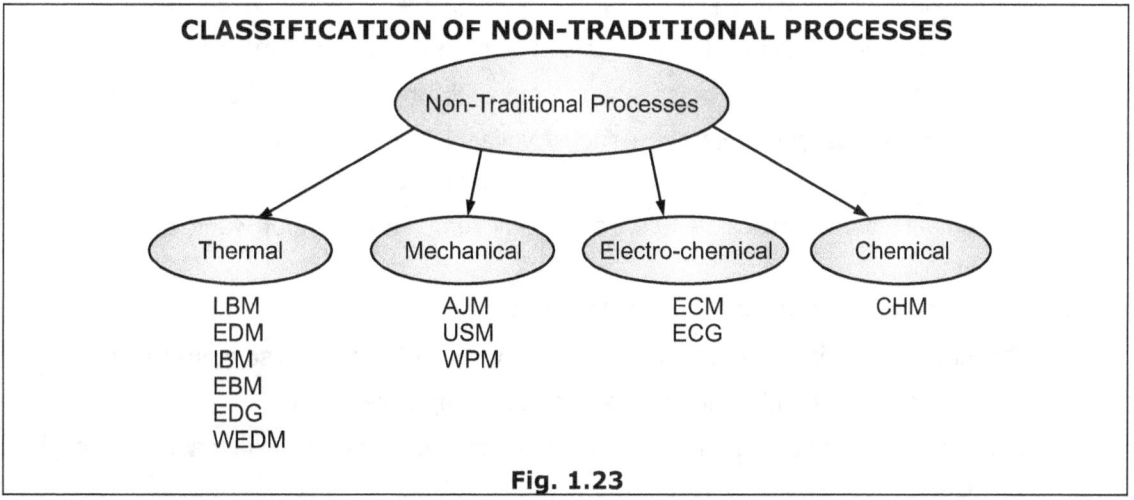

CLASSIFICATION OF NON-TRADITIONAL PROCESSES

Non-Traditional Processes

Thermal	Mechanical	Electro-chemical	Chemical
LBM	AJM	ECM	CHM
EDM	USM	ECG	
IBM	WPM		
EBM			
EDG			
WEDM			

Fig. 1.23

Abrasive Jet Machining

- The process consists of mixture of fine abrasive particles, usually about 0.025 mm in diameter and gas at high pressure.
- This stream of mixture is directed through a nozzle on to the surface of the workpiece.
- The abrasive particles impinge on the workpiece at high speed.
- As the particle impacts the surface, it causes a small fracture of the work surface which results in removal of metal.
- The gas stream carries both the abrasive particles and the fractured (wear) particles way.

Water Jet Machining

- A jet of water is used to cut a metal.
- Water from the reservoir is pumped to the intensifier.
- Water is then sent to the accumulator.
- Pressurized water finally enters the nozzle.
- The jet induce stresses and machining of material by erosion occurs.

Electric Discharge Machining (EDM)

- Heat energy generated by a spark is used to remove material from the work piece.
- The tool and work piece are separated by a small gap called as spark gap.
- The tool is made cathode, while work piece is made anode.
- When sparking occur the dielectric fluid gets ionized and results in machining of work piece.
- A dielectric fluid is a liquid which acts as an insulator between consecutive spark discharge and as a conductor during the spark discharge.
- The dielectric fluid used is paraffin oil, transformer oil, lubricating oil, kerosene, distilled water etc
- Flushing is providing a fresh dielectric fluid between the tool and work piece.
- The tool has the reverse profile of what is to be produced on the work piece.
- The tool material is copper, brass, aluminium, steel, zinc, tungsten alloy, graphite etc.
- The main process parameters are supply voltage, break down voltage, resistance and capacitance, spark gap setting, pulse duration, spark frequency.
- The output characteristics in EDM are metal removal rate, tool wear, surface finish, accuracy.

Wire Cut Electric Discharge Machining (WEDM)

- The fundamental principle of metal removal in wire cut EDM is the same as that of EDM.
- The process is used only when part is to be cut completely through.
- It uses a wire of about 0.3 mm diameter as a tool (electrode) which is made-up of copper or tungsten.

- The wire is continuously moved at a constant speed through the work piece.
- In order to create the desired shape on the work piece the table motions are controlled by the positioning unit (control system).
- The tool is made cathode, while work piece is made anode.
- Both the work piece and the wire are constantly flushed with a dielectric fluid at the area being machined.

Plasma Arc Machining (PAM)

- Plasma, the fourth state of matter, is obtained when gases are heated to temperatures about $5500^{\circ}C$.
- At this temperature, the gases are partially ionized and exist in the form of a mixture of free electrons, positively charged ions and neutral atoms.
- When a high velocity jet of plasma is directed on the workpiece surface by means of a plasma arc cutting torch, the metal from the workpiece melts which results in to the machining of the workpiece.

Laser Beam Machining (LBM)

- LASER is a acronym for **L**ight **A**mplification by **S**timulated **E**mission of **R**adiation.
- If the atom or molecule of a solid medium does not emit energy; it is said to be in a ground state.
- The electrons in ruby rod which are in the ground state can be excited to higher energy state by absorbing energy of various forms.
- These atoms which have absorbed higher energy spontaneously returns to the ground state energy by emitting a photon.
- The photons in the form of a chain produce a steady beam of coherent light called as a LASER beam.
- When the Laser beam is focused through the lens on the work piece, it melts the work piece, vapourizes it and machining takes place.
- Laser materials are classified as gas lasers, solid lasers and semiconductors lasers.

Electro Chemical Machining (ECM)

- ECM utilizes the principle of reverse of electroplating.
- Here the tool is made cathode and the work piece is made anode.
- The tool has reverse profile of that to be produced on the work piece.
- The tool material is copper, brass, stainless steel, aluminium, graphite, bronze, tungsten.
- A close gap of about 0.5 mm is maintained between the tool and the work piece.
- During the process electrochemical reaction takes place in presence of the electrolyte which results in removal of metal from the work piece.

- The electrolytes used are sodium nitrate, sodium chloride, sodium hydroxide, sodium sulphate, sodium fluoride, potassium nitrate, potassium chloride etc.
- The tool is continuously feed towards the work piece by servo mechanism.
- The tool used is hollow to provide passage for the electrolyte.

Electron Beam Machining (EBM)

- When a high velocity beam of electron is focused on a workpiece, the electrons strikes on the workpiece and their kinetic energy is converted into heat energy.
- This heat results in removal of material from the workpiece by vapourization and melting.
- The set-up of EBM consists of electron gun, magnetic lens, magnetic deflection coil, movable table, monitoring instrument.
- The entire process is carried out in vacuum to prevent the scattering of electrons by collision with the molecules in the atmosphere.
- The important controlling parameters of EBM are beam current and spot diameter.

Ultrasonic Machining (USM)

- Ultrasonic waves of frequency above 16 kHz are used to machine the workpiece.
- It uses abrasive slurry to remove the material from the workpiece.
- A shaped tool is given a mechanical vibration against the stationary workpiece. This causes the removal of material from the workpiece by the abrasive action of the tool.
- As the tool machines the workpiece, the gap between the two increases. Thus, for machining action the tool must be fed continuously into the workpiece.

Chemical Machining (CHM)

- Chemical machining is the oldest of the non-traditional processes.
- Chemical reaction between the material of the workpiece along with some chemical reagent removes material from the workpiece.
- The time of immersion or exposure depends upon the amount of material to be removed by the chemical action.
- The etchant, its concentration, operating temperature and the etch rate (in mm/min) depends on the material to be etched.

Practice Questions

1.	State the characteristics of traditional machining processes.	**[Refer Section 1.1.2]**
2.	What are the limitations of the traditional machining processes?	**[Refer Section 1.1.3]**
3.	State the need of non-traditional machining processes.	**[Refer Section 1.1.4]**
4.	State the characteristics of non-traditional machining processes.	**[Refer Section 1.1.5]**
5.	State the advantages of non-traditional machining processes.	**[Refer Section 1.1.6]**
6.	Classify non-traditional machining processes in brief.	**[Refer Section 1.1.7]**

7.   Differentiate between traditional and non-traditional machining processes.

[Refer Section 1.1.8]

8.   What are the main parameters to be considered while selecting a particular non-traditional process?   **[Refer Section 1.1.9]**

9.   Explain the importance of non-traditional machining process.   **[Refer Section 1.1.10]**

10. Describe the set-up of AJM with neat sketch.   **[Refer Section 1.2.6]**

11. Describe the set-up of WJM with neat sketch.   **[Refer Section 1.3.4]**

12. Explain the working principle of EDM.   **[Refer Section 1.4.2]**

13. Explain R-C circuit in EDM with a neat sketch.   **[Refer Section 1.4.3]**

14. Explain the set-up of a EDM process. Draw a labelled sketch.   **[Refer Section 1.4.3]**

15. Draw a diagram of EDM setup and label it.   **[Refer Section 1.4.3]**

16. What are the main components in EDM machining process?   **[Refer Section 1.4.3]**

17. Explain the machining action in EDM.   **[Refer Section 1.4.3]**

18. Explain the R-C mechanism used in EDM with suitable sketch.   **[Refer Section 1.4.3]**

19. Enlist the functions of a dielectric fluid.   **[Refer Section 1.4.5]**

20. State the characteristics of a dielectric fluid.   **[Refer Section 1.4.6]**

21. What is flushing of a dielectric fluid?   **[Refer Section 1.4.7]**

22. What materials are used for making a EDM tool?   **[Refer Section 1.4.8]**

23. What is the requirement of EDM tool material?   **[Refer Section 1.4.9]**

24. What is the effect of process parameters on metal removal rate? **[Refer Section 1.4.11]**

25. Which parameters control the EDM process?   **[Refer Section 1.4.10]**

26. Show by graph the effect of control parameters on MRR.   **[Refer Section 1.4.10]**

27. Explain the working principle of WEDM.   **[Refer Section 1.5.2]**

28. Explain WEDM machining process.   **[Refer Section 1.5.3]**

29. What are the controlling parameters in WEDM?   **[Refer Section 1.5.4]**

30. Describe the set-up of PAM with neat sketch.   **[Refer Section 1.6.3]**

31. What are the controlling parameters in PAM?   **[Refer Section 1.6.4]**

32. What are the characteristics of laser?   **[Refer Section 1.7.2]**

33. Explain the physical principal of laser.   **[Refer Section 1.7.3]]**

34. How are Laser classified?   **[Refer Section 1.7.4]**

35. Explain Laser action in ruby rod.   **[Refer Section 1.7.5]**

36. Explain LBM with a sketch.   **[Refer Section 1.7.6]**

37. Which parameters control the LBM process?   **[Refer Section 1.7.10]**

38. How is Laser beam used for welding?   **[Refer Section 1.7.12]**

39. Differentiate between EDM and LBM.   **[Refer Section 1.7.13]**

40. Explain the working principle of ECM.   **[Refer Section 1.8.2]**

41. Explain the working mechanism of ECM.   **[Refer Section 1.8.3]**

42. List the tool materials and dielectric used in ECM?   **[Refer Section 1.8.4 & 1.8.5]**

43. What are the requirements of tool material used in ECM?   **[Refer Section 1.8.4]**

44. Enlist are the functions of electrolyte.   **[Refer Section 1.8.5]**

45. Differentiate between EDM and ECM.   **[Refer Section 1.8.11]**

46. Differentiate between dielectric fluid and electrolyte   **[Refer Section 1.8.12]**

47. Describe the set-up of EBM.   **[Refer Section 1.9.3]**

48. What are the controlling parameters in EBM?   **[Refer Section 1.9.8]**

49. Differentiate between EBM and LBM.   **[Refer Section 1.9.9]**

50. Describe the set-up of USM with neat sketch.   **[Refer Section 1.10.4]**

51. Describe the process of chemical machining.   **[Refer Section 1.11.2]**

Exercise

1. Which of the following processes use mechanical energy as the principal energy source:

    (a) ECG (b) LBM (c) Conventional milling (d) USM (e) WJM (f) WEDM

2. Ultrasonic machining can be used to machine both metallic and non-metallic materials:

    (a) True (b) False

3. Applications of electron beam machining are limited to metallic work materials due to the need for the work to be electrically conductive:

    (a) True (b) False

4. Which one of the following is closest to the temperatures used in plasma arc cutting?

    (a) $2750^{\circ}C$ (b) $5500^{\circ}C$ (c) $8300^{\circ}C$ (d) $11,000^{\circ}C$ (e) $16,500^{\circ}C$

5. Chemical milling is used in which of the following applications (two best answers):

    (a) drilling holes with high depth-to- diameter ratio (b) making intricate patterns in thin sheet metal (c) removing material to make shallow pockets in metal (d) removing metal from aircraft wing panels (e) cutting of plastic sheets.

6. Of the following processes, which one is noted for the highest material removal rates:

    (a) Electric discharge machining

    (b) Electrochemical machining

    (c) Laser beam machining

    (d) Oxyfuel cutting

    (e) Plasma arc cutting

    (f) Ultrasonic machining

    (g) Water jet cutting.

7. Which of the following processes would be best to drill a hole with a square cross-section, 0.25 inch on a side and 1-inch deep in a steel workpiece?

    (a) AJM   (b) CHM   (c) EDM   (d) LBM   (e) WEDM

8. Which of the following processes would be best for cutting a narrow slot, less than 0.015 inch wide, in a 3/8 inch thick sheet of fiber-reinforced plastic.

    (a) AJM   (b) CHM   (c) EDM   (d) LBM   (e) WEDM

9. Which of the following processes would be best for cutting a hole of 0.003 inch diameter through a plate of aluminum that is 1/16-inch thick

    (a) AJM   (b) CHM   (c) EDM   (d) LBM   (e) WEDM

10. Which of the following processes could be used to cut a large piece of 1/2-inch plate steel into two sections?

    (a) AJM   (b) CHM   (c) EDM   (d) LBM   (e) WEDM

11. For the following application, identify one or more non-traditional machining processes that might be used and present arguments to support your selection. Assume that either the part geometry or the work material (or both) preclude the use of conventional machining. The application is a matrix of 0.1 mm diameter holes in a plate of 3.2 mm thick hardened tool steel. The matrix is rectangular, 75 by 125 mm

12. Identify the process for machining a through-hole in the shape of the letter L in a 12.5 mm thick plate of glass. The size of the "L" is 25 by 15 mm and the width of the hole is 3 mm.

13. For the following application, identify one or more non-traditional machining processes that might be used. The application is a blind-hole in the shape of the letter G in a 50 mm cube of steel. The overall size of the "G" is 25 by 19 mm, the depth of the hole is 3.8 mm and its width is 3 mm.

14. A Company involves cutting and forming of flat sheets of fiber-glass for the pleasure boat industry. Manual methods based on portable saws are currently used to perform the cutting operation, but production is slow and scrap rates are high. The foreman says the company should invest in a plasma arc cutting machine, but the plant manager thinks it would be too expensive. What do you think? Justify your answer by indicating the characteristics of the process that make PAM attractive or unattractive in this application.

15. Suggest a suitable non-traditional process for cutting glass plate in 2 pieces.

16. Suggest a suitable non-traditional process for making a hole in M.S. plate

17. Suggest suitable non-traditional machining process for performing following operations. Give reason.

    (a) To prepare complex contour.

    (b) To prepare surgical needle.

    (c) For cutting cavities to forging dies.

    (d) Making small diameter hole in fuel injection nozzle.

18. Following are the machining requirements. Select appropriate non-traditional machining process for each with justification:

    (i) Machining profile of glass

    (ii) Cutting of hot extrusion components

    (iii) Cutting internal threads in hard material

    (iv) Cutting and engraving pattern in thin films.

Answers

1. (c), (d), and (e)   2. (a)
3. (b)   4. (d)
5. (c) and (d)   6. (e)
7. (c)   8. (d) and (f)
9. (d)   10. (e)
11. **EBM** and **LBM** can make holes of this size with depth-to-diameter ratios as large as 3.2/0.1 = 32
12. USM works on glass and other brittle non-metallic materials. This is probably the best process. LBM might also work.
13. **ECM** and **EDM** would be useful for pocketing operations such as this.
14. In PAM, the workpart must be an electrically conductive material. Fiber glass is not electrically conductive. PAM is therefore not an appropriate process for this application.
15. AJM and USM
16. ECM and EDM
17. WEDM, LBM, EDM, EBM.

MSBTE Questions & Answers as Per 'G' Scheme

Winter 2014

1. State the principles of EDM. With a neat sketch explain the process of metal removal. **(4 M)**
Ans. Refer Section 1.4.2.
2. Give any four applications of PAM. **(4 M)**
Ans. Refer Section 1.6.7.
3. What are non-traditional machining processes? Compare traditional and non-traditional machining process. **(6 M)**
Ans. Refer Section 1.1.1 and 1.1.8.
4. What is Lasing action? Differentiate between EDM and LBM. **(6 M)**
Ans. Refer Section 1.7.3 and 1.7.13.
5. Explain the working principle of AJM. State the advantages, limitations and applications of AJM. **(8 M)**
Ans. Refer Section 1.2.1, 1.2.8, 1.2.9 and 1.2.10.

Summer 2015

1. Give classification of non-traditional machining processes. **(4 M)**
Ans. Refer Section 1.1.7.
2. Draw neat labelled diagram of EDM and explain the processes w.r.t. its principle, applications and limitations. **(6 M)**
Ans. Refer Section 1.4.2, 1.4.3, 1.4.13 and 1.4.14.
3. Draw neat labelled sketch of PAM. Explain its working. Also state its advantages and applications. **(6 M)**
Ans. Refer Section 1.6.3, 1.6.5 and 1.6.7.

4. State difference between dielectric, fluid and electrolyte. **(4 M)**
Ans. Refer Section 1.8.12.
5. Give any two applications of AJM, LBM, WEDM and WJM. **(4 M)**
Ans. Refer Section 1.2.10, 1.7.9, 1.5.7 and 1.3.8.
6. State and explain controlling parameters in WEDM. **(4 M)**
Ans. Refer Section 1.5.4.
7. With neat sketch explain LBM. **(4 M)**
Ans. Refer Section 1.7.6.

Winter 2015

1. Describe set-up of WJM with neat sketch. **(4 M)**
Ans. Refer Section 1.3.3 and Fig. 1.3.
2. State need of non-traditional machining processes. **(4 M)**
Ans. Refer Section 1.1.4.
3. Explain controlling parameters in WEDM. **(6 M)**
Ans. Refer Section 1.5.4.
4. How laser beam is used for welding? **(4 M)**
Ans. Refer Section 1.7.12.
5. Following are the machining requirements. Select appropriate non-traditional machining process for each with justification: (i) Machining profile of glass, (ii) Cutting of hot extrusion components, (iii) Cutting internal threads in hard material, (iv) Cutting and engraving pattern in thin films.
Ans. **(i)** **Machining profile of glass:** Abrasive water jet machining is most appropriate as glass is brittle and with AWJM the doing perfect machining with the help of sharp edges of abrasive metal particles.
    (ii) **Cutting of hot extrusion components:** Electric discharge machining is used for cutting of hot extrusion components and dies.
    (iii) **Cutting internal threads in hard material:** Internal threads can be done with electrical discharge machined (EDM) into hard materials by complexity of components.
    (iv) **Cutting and engraving pattern in thin films:** Film-Laser beam machining is most suitable to engrave the patterns in the thin films which is done by focusing all the energy with the help of laser.

Summer 2016

1. List the ideal characteristics of electrode materials used in EDM. **(4 M)**
Ans. Refer Section 1.4.9.
2. Explain the principles and working of EDM with neat sketch. **(6 M)**
Ans. Refer Section 1.4.2.
3. Explain the process parameters of laser beam machining. **(6 M)**
Ans. Refer Section 1.7.10.
4. Draw a neat sketch of abrasive jet machining and list any four applications of AJM. **(4 M)**
Ans. Refer Fig. 1.2 and Section 1.2.10.
5. State the advantages and disadvantages of plasma arc machining. **(4 M)**
Ans. Refer Sections 1.6.5 and 1.6.6.
6. Differentiate between EDM and LBM process. **(4 M)**
Ans. Refer Section 1.7.13.
7. Classify non-traditional machining process on the basis of type of energy used. **(4 M)**
Ans. Refer Section 1.1.7.

Winter 2016

1. State four needs of non-traditional machining processes.   **(4 M)**
Ans. Refer Section 1.1.4.
2. Differentiate between EDM and W-EDM.   **(4 M)**
Ans.

Sr. No.	EDM	W-EDM
1.	Complicated cutout cannot be easily machined. Mirror shaped tool is used to produce desired shape.	Complicated cutout can be easily machined. Small diameter thin wire is used to cut desired profile
2.	Hole or cut in workpiece is not needed.	Hole or cut in workpiece is needed if surface to be machined is not in contact with periphery of workpiece.
3.	Surface roughness is more due to heat generated.	Surface roughness of machined part is less
4.	Surface micro structure may be distorted	No distortion in surface micro structure
5.	Sharp corners or edges cannot be produced.	Sharp corner can be produce.

3. Sketch output characteristics of EDM.   **(6 M)**
Ans. Refer Fig. 1.9.
  • The process characteristics (output characteristics) which are affected by the controlling parameter are:
  (i) Metal removal rate. (ii) Tool wear. (iii) Surface finish. (iv) Accuracy.

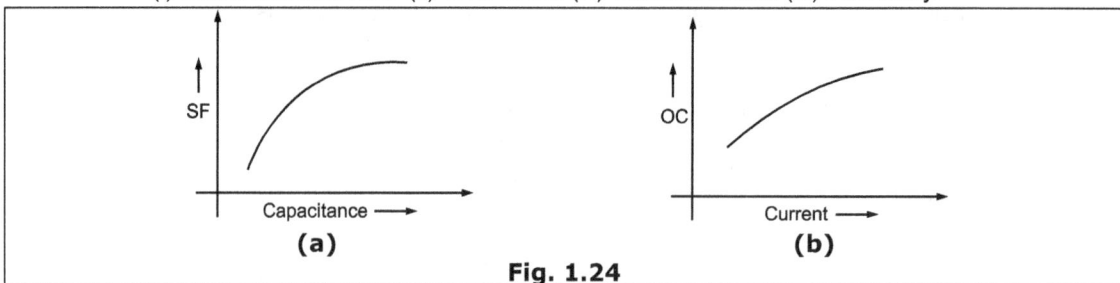

Fig. 1.24

4. List advantages & disadvantages of LBM.   **(4 M)**
Ans. Refer Sections 1.7.7 and 1.7.8.
5. List applications of AJM & WJM process.   **(4 M)**
Ans. Refer Sections 1.2.10 and 1.3.8.
6. Explain PAM process with sketch alongwith advantages & disadvantages.   **(8 M)**
Ans. Refer Section 1.6, 1.6.2, 1.6.3, 1.6.5 and 1.6.6.

Summer 2017

1. State any four needs for non-traditional machining process.   **(4 M)**
Ans. Refer Section 1.1.4.
2. Explain LBM with suitable neat sketch.   **(4 M)**
Ans. Refer Section 1.7.6.
3. Following are the machining requirements, select non-traditional machining process for each with justification:
  1. Machining profile of glass.2. Cutting internal threads in hard materials.3. Cutting of hot extrusion components.   **(4 M)**
Ans. Refer to Exercise of Chapter 1.
4. Define: (i) PAM, (ii) WEDM   **(4 M)**
Ans. Refer Sections 1.5 and 1.6.

■■■

INTRODUCTION TO CNC

At the end of this chapter students will be able to:

⊃ Understand the features of CNC machine.

⊃ Identify different axes on the CNC machine.

⊃ Able to develop a part program for CNC machine.

2.1 INTRODUCTION TO CNC MACHINE

- CNC stands for Computer Numerically Controlled. CNC machines can perform various functions, which can be performed on conventional machines.

  It is a machine that is usually programmed and controlled by a computer so as to offer very short set-up times and also the flexibility to run batches.

  A CNC machine is a type of industrial tool that performs commands based on the numeric code that is entered into the machine.

- CNC machines are traditionally programmed using a set of commands known as G-codes and M-codes.

- Basically CNC machine is a cutting process in which material is removed form a work-piece by a tool. Cutting tools of various profiles (shapes) are available including round, square and angled. A wide variety of part shapes and geometries are possible with these machines.

- CNC machine is one of the common machine tools in machinery industry that can perform those repetitive tasks of drilling and turning that used to be human jobs long time ago.

- The movements of the work pieces and cutters are accurately controlled, usually via the precision ground slides along with the lead-screw or with analogous technology.

- CNC machines are usually programmed by using a series of standard commands that we named it as G-codes to represent specific CNC tasks in alpha-numeric form.
- There are many different sizes for a CNC machine based on the purpose and location of usage, as well as the materials that need to be cut.
- Normally, materials like plastic and wood are the easiest things to cut, unlike steel that need more stronger milling machine and longer time.
- With CNC machine, we can improve the speed of cut compared to manual operation.
- It also reduced the rejection when rigidity results increased. Thus, in long run business, it will indeed save a lot of time and overhead due to less wastage happened.
- In production line, it is very important to have all the parts produced exactly the same. However, nothing is perfect. CNC machine may also have a possibility of fault lies in the operator due to a mill can cut with absolute precision as close as 0.0001 of an inch.
- Lastly, with the automated cooling systems, CNC machines are able to maintain the quality of raw material by spraying or blasting the hot metal or even tooling with specially formulated coolant.

2.2 FEATURES OF CNC MACHINE

- Computer NC systems include additional features beyond what is feasible with conventional hard-wired NC. These features include the following:
- **Storage of more than one part program:** CNC controller can store many programs in its memory unit.
- **Various forms of program input:** The part program can be feed to a CNC controllers through multiple capabilities, such as punched tape, magnetic tape, floppy diskettes, RS-232 communications with external computers, and manual data input.
- **Program editing at the machine tool:** The part program in the controller's memory can be edited and used for similar work piece.
- **Fixed cycles and programming subroutines:** If same operation is to be performed repeatedly, then the programmer need not have to write the blocks every time. He can call the already saved cycles number of times.
- **Cutter length and size compensation:** A program written for particular diameter of a tool can also execute properly for different tool diameters. Similarly same program can be used for varying lengths of tool by entering the proper dimensions into the MCU.

- **Acceleration and deceleration calculations:** When the cutter moves at high feed rates, it generates tool marks on the work surface when the cutter changes its path abruptly. This feature decelerates the feed rate where the tool path change and then accelerated back-up to the programmed feed rate after the direction change.
- **Communications interface:** Most CNC controllers are equipped with a standard RS-232 or other communications interface to link the machine to other computers and computer driven devices.
- **Diagnostics:** Many modern CNC systems possess a diagnostics capability that monitors certain aspects of the machine tool to detect malfunctions or signs of impending malfunctions or to diagnose system breakdowns.

2.3 MAIN COMPONENTS OF CNC MACHINE

- Any CNC will consists of the following basic elements:
  - Program of instruction.
  - Machine control unit
  - Machine tool
- These basic components of any CNC machine are shown in Fig. 2.1.

2.3.1 Program of instruction

- The part program is called as program of instruction.
- It is prepared by the part programmer.
- It is the detail step-by-step set of instructions which tells the machine tool what to do.
- The part program is a combination of numbers and letters and is fed to the controller.
- It is generally input to through the keyboard manually.

2.3.2 The Machine Control Unit (MCU)

- The MCU is the hardware that distinguishes CNC from conventional NC.
- The MCU consists of the following components and subsystems:
  1. Central Processing Unit,
  2. Memory,
  3. Input/Output Interface.
- **Central Processing Unit:**
  - The central processing unit (CPU) is the brain of the MCU.
  - It manages the other components in the MCU based on software contained in main memory.

- o   The CPU can be divided into three sections:

   (a) Control section: The control section retrieves commands and data from memory and generates signals to activate other components in the MCU. In short, it sequences, co-ordinates, and regulates all the activities of the MCU computer.

   (b) Arithmetic-logic unit: The arithmetic-logic unit (ALU) consists of the circuitry to perform various calculations (addition, subtraction, and multiplication), counting, and logical functions required by software residing in memory.

   (c) Immediate access memory: The immediate access memory provides a temporary storage of data being processed by the CPU. It is connected to main memory of the system data bus.

- **Memory:**
  - o   The immediate access memory in the CPU is not intended for storing CNC software.
  - o   A much greater storage capacity is required for the various programs and data needed to operate the CNC system.
  - o   CNC memory can be divided into two categories:

   (a) Primary memory: Primary memory consists of ROM (read-only memory) and RAM (random access memory) devices. Operating system software and machine interface programs are generally stored in ROM. These programs are usually installed by the manufacturer of the MCU. Numerical control part programs are stored in RAM devices. Current programs in RAM can be erased and replaced by new programs as jobs are changed.

   (b) Secondary memory: High-capacity secondary memory devices are used to store large programs and data files, which are transferred to main memory as needed.

- **Input/Output Interface:**
  - o   The I/O interface provides communication software between the various components of the CNC system, other computer systems, and the machine operator.
  - o   As its name suggests, the I/O interface transmits and receives data and signals to and from external devices.
  - o   The I/O interface also includes a display (CRT or LED) for communication of data and information from the MCU to the machine operator.
  - o   The display is used to indicate current status of the program as it is being executed and to warn the operator of any malfunctions in the CNC system.

2.3.3 Machine Tool

- The third basic element of an CNC system is the equipment that processes the work piece. Such a component that performs useful work is called as *machine tool*.
- It performs the sequence of operations to transform the raw material into a finished product which is further useful.
- The machine tool receives signal from the MCU. The signals are understood by the machine spindle, table and other parts like motors and controls.
- The program of instruction directs the MCU which in turn makes the processing element work.

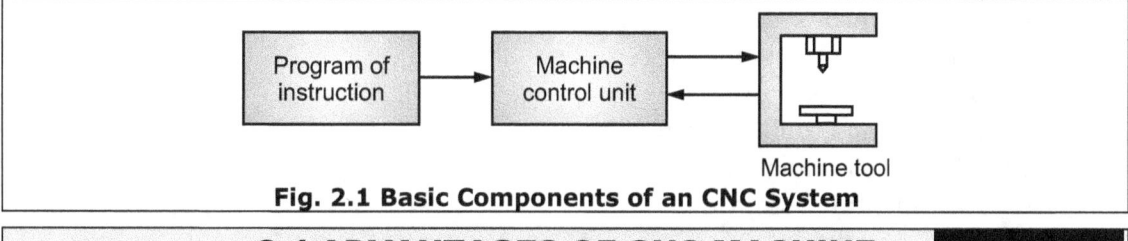

Fig. 2.1 Basic Components of an CNC System

2.4 ADVANTAGES OF CNC MACHINE   [W-14, 16, S-16]

- CNC machines have many advantages. But a few important are listed below:
  - Greater accuracy of job is achieved.
  - Higher repeatability and improved product quality.
  - Less operator skill is required to run CNC machine.
  - Better machine utilization hence reduced idle time.
  - High production rate as speed, feed, depth of cut are optimum for best quality.
  - Lower tooling cost, per piece in mass production.
  - Jigs and fixtures cost can be reduced.
  - Reduced cycle time.
  - Better tool life and machineability.
  - Less scrap due to consistent accuracy, less errors.
  - Excellent reliability as dimensions are based on programes.
  - Reduced in-process inventory of parts in process.
  - Design changes are possible. Any change in design is feasible at lowest cost.
  - Productivity can be improved to great extent.
  - Tool set-up time can be reduced.
  - Most suitable for continuous and better production.
  - Program can be stored and used again when required.
  - Optimum speed and feed for best surface finish can be used.

2.5 DISADVANTAGES OF CNC MACHINE

- A few disadvantages of CNC Machines are:
  - o CNC machines are more expensive than manually operated machines, although costs are slowly coming down.
  - o CNC machines are more complex machines.
  - o Cost of control systems used is high.
  - o Maintenance cost is high.
  - o The CNC machine operator needs basic training and skills, enough to supervise several machines.

2.6 CLASSIFICATION OF CNC MACHINES

- The classification of CNC machine tool can be done in four ways.
  - o Based on control system characteristics
    - Point to point position system.
    - Straight line system.
    - Contouring (continuous path).
  - o Based on positioning co-ordinates:
    - Incremental system.
    - Absolute system.
  - o Based on feedback or type of control system
    - Open loop system.
    - Closed loop system.
  - o According to the structure of control circuits:
    - Analogue system.
    - Digital system.

2.6.1 Based on Control System Characteristics

(a) Point to Point System:

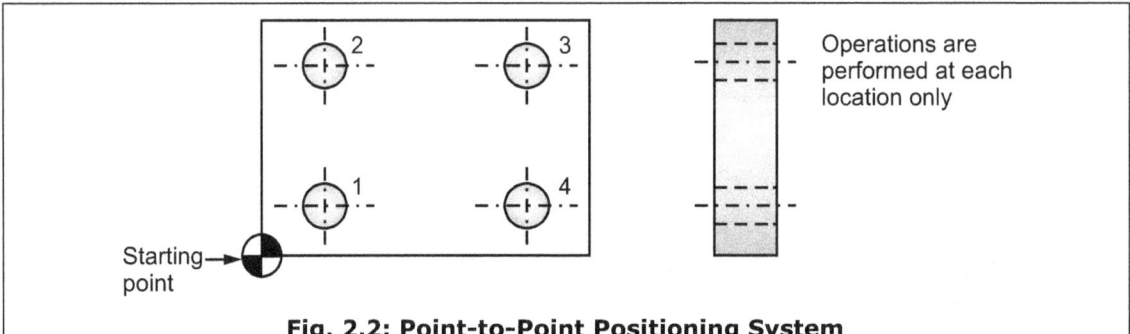

Fig. 2.2: Point-to-Point Positioning System

- In this method, the cutting tool (or the table) moves from one point to another point.

- Machining is done only at desired points. No machining is done when the spindle moves from one point to another point.

- This system is suitable for drilling, reaming, counter boring, tapping, spot welding and similar operation. The tool movement from one location to another is very fast.
- The speed or the path accomplished is not important in such system.
- As shown in Fig. 2.2 the tool will drill hole at point 1, then it will have idle movement till point 2. At point 2 it will again drill hole and move idle to point 3 and so on.
- In these machine system, each axis is driven separately.
- In a point-to-point control system, the dimensional information that must be given to the machine tool will be a series of required position of the two slides.
- Servo systems can be used to move the slides and no attempt is made to move the slide until the cutter has been retracted back.

(b) Straight Line System:

- In this system, the cutting tool moves in a straight line during machining operation as shown in Fig. 2.3. The tool feed is controlled in such systems.
- This system is used in milling of slots or cutting of grooves.
- Straight line cuts parallel to the horizontal axes can only be programmed.
- Angular cuts are not possible with such system because the tool motion along both the axes needs to be controlled simultaneously.
- The system which can perform straight line cuts can also perform point-to-point movement.

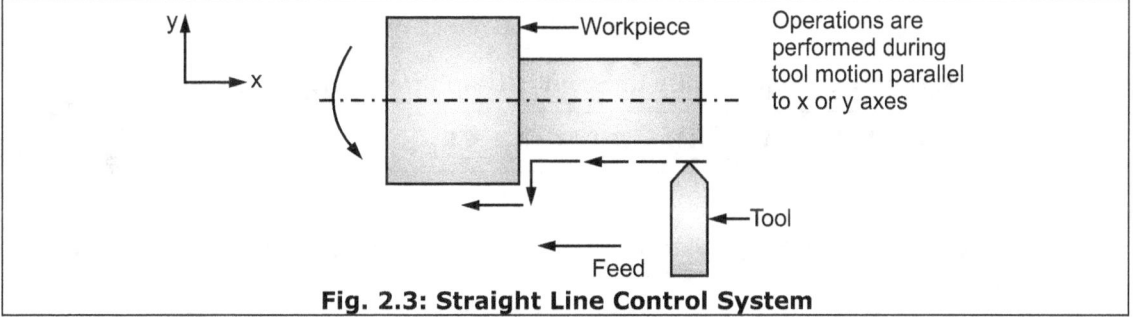

Fig. 2.3: Straight Line Control System

(c) Contouring System:

- This is a most complex, most flexible and expensive system. It enables the machining of profiles, contours and curved surfaces.
- In this system, the motion of the tool and the work piece are controlled along many axes, simultaneously and this facilitates machining of different types of curved surfaces, profiles and taper or angular cuts.
- The feed of the tool is very closely controlled so as to move the tool simultaneously in required directions by synchroning movement in both directions.
- The machining of curved profile is accomplished by breaking into short straight lines that approximate the curve. Because for machining a curved path as shown in Fig. 2.4, the direction of feed rate must continuously be changed so as to follow the path.

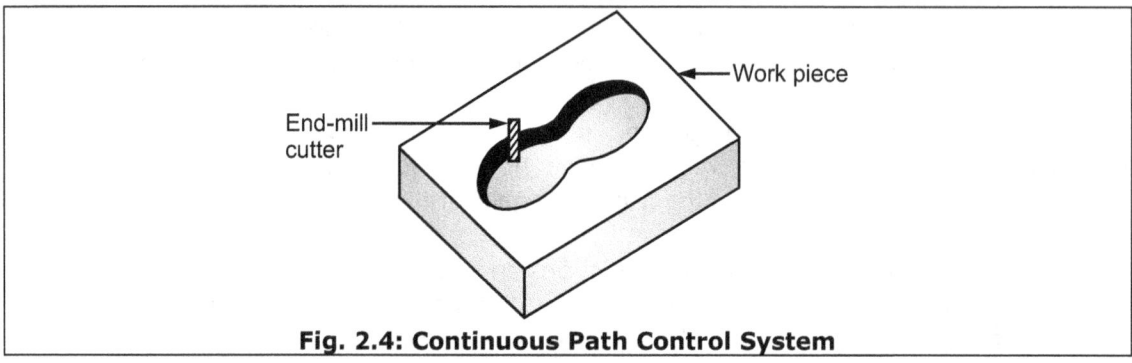

Fig. 2.4: Continuous Path Control System

- The cutter path for the three systems is shown in Fig. 2.5.

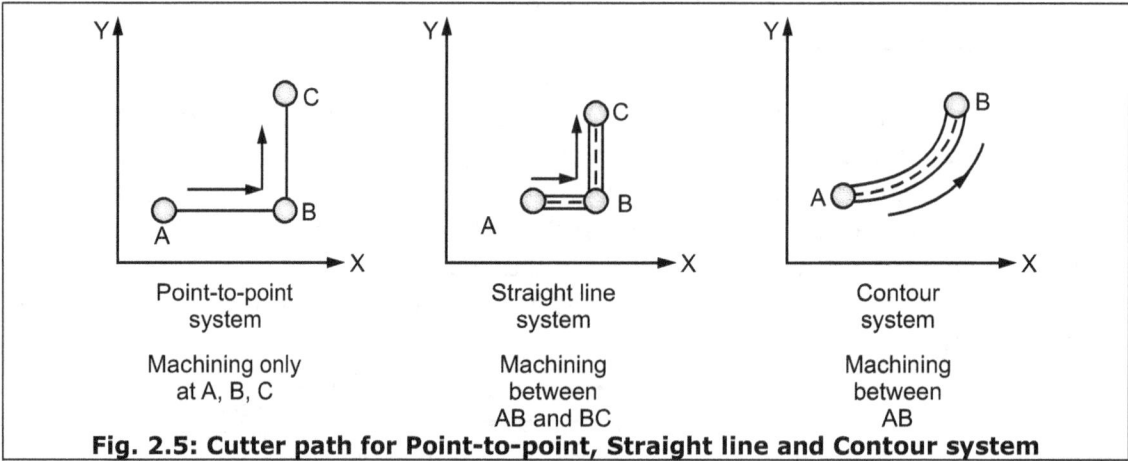

Fig. 2.5: Cutter path for Point-to-point, Straight line and Contour system

2.6.2 Based on Positioning Co-ordinates [S-15, 17]

(a) Absolute System:

- In absolute dimensioning system the co-ordinates of points are always taken from a fixed point.

- The fixed point is generally the south west corner of the table for milling and the workpiece center point on the other end of the chuck for lathe machines.

- It has an advantage to write the program easily.

- It is also easy to check and edit a program.

- Consider a Fig. 2.6. The coordinates of the points P_1, P_2, P_3, P_4 in absolute system is taken as given below:

Point	Co-ordinates
P_1	1,4
P_2	2,1
P_3	7,6
P_4	3,2

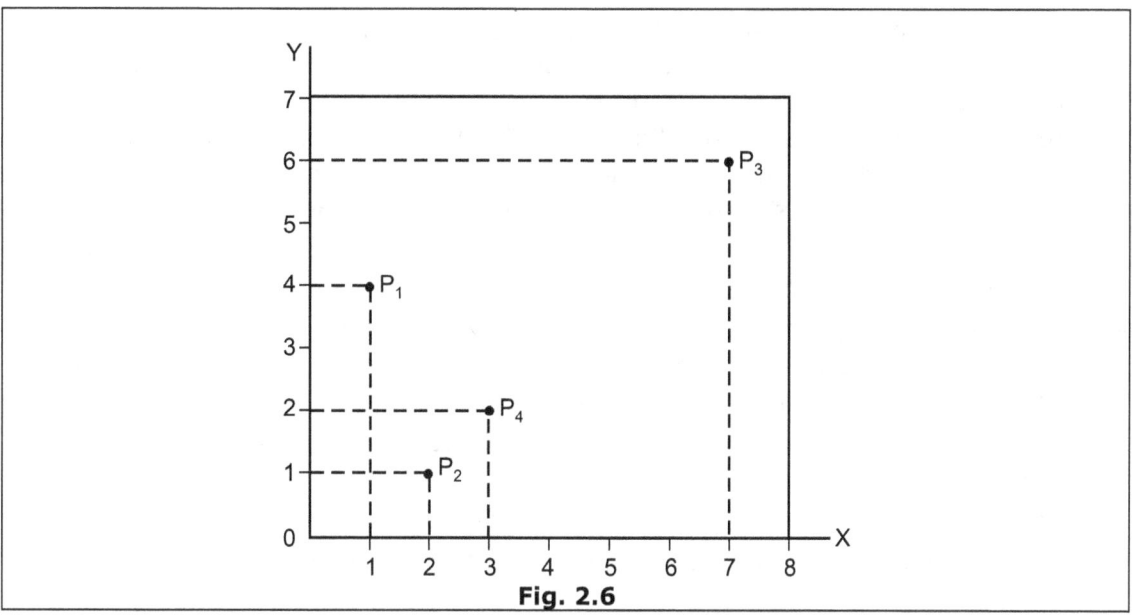

Fig. 2.6

(b) Incremental System:

- In incremental system the co-ordinates of any points are calculated with reference to the previous position of the tool.

- It becomes difficult to edit the program written in incremental mode.

- Its special use is in writing subroutine programs.

- Consider a Fig. 2.6. The coordinates of the points P_1, P_2, P_3, P_4 in incremental system is taken as given below:

Point	Co-ordinates
P_1	1, 4
P_2	1, −3
P_3	5, 5
P_4	−4, −4

2.6.3 Based on Feedback or Type of Control System   [S-17]

- It is sometimes also referred to as electronic control system. It is based on the presence or absence of a feedback device. It sends and receives electronic information from the drive motors. The two types of loop system are:

(a) Open loop control system

- As shown in the Fig. 2.7 (a), it consists of an input device which loads the program in the machine. The program is decoded in the machine understandable format and the required signals are send to the control unit (MCU). The MCU sends the series of electrical pulses to the drive unit (stepper motor). This results in the motion of the slides through a desired distance.

- The stepper motor is used to drive the worktable of the machine. The output shaft of a stepper motor rotates through a fixed angle in response to an input pulse. Thus the stepper motor converts the digital electrical signal into proportional movement of the slide. However there is no provision to ensure that the slide has actually moved through the desired distance only and that it has actually acquired the desired portion as a result of this movement.

- The actual movement of the slide may vary with change in external conditions, wear of the drive components, backlash error in lead screw etc.

- As the name suggests, open loop control system has no loop (or the loop is open), since there is no feedback device. It is simple to design, less expensive and less accurate as compared to closed loop control system.

- The stepping motor is driven by a series of electrical pulses generated by the MCU.

- Each pulse causes the motor to rotate a fraction of one revolution.

- The fraction is expressed in terms of the step angle, α, given by

$$\alpha = 360/N, \text{ degrees}$$

where,   N = Number of pulses required for one revolution.

  o   If the motor receives "n" number of pulses then the total angle,

  o   In terms of the number of revolutions, it would be (n/N),

- If there is a 1 : 1 gear ratio between the motor and the leadscrew, then the leadscrew has (n/N) revolutions.

- If the pitch of leadscrew is p (mm/rev), then the distance travelled axially, say x, can be used to achieve a specified x-increment in a point-to-point system.

- The pulse frequency, f, in pulses/sec determines the travel speed of the tool or the workpiece.

$$60\, f = N\ (\text{RPM})$$

where,   N = Number of pulses per revolution,

          RPM = RPM of the lead screw

- The travel speed, V, is then given by V = p (RPM)

where, p pitch in mm/rev

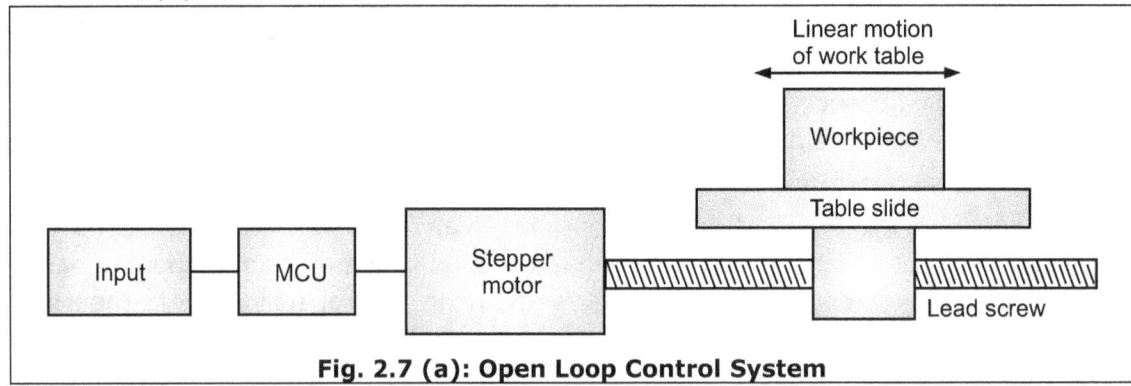

Fig. 2.7 (a): Open Loop Control System

(b) Closed Loop Control System [S-10, 15, W-15]

- The name indicates that the closed loop control system has a loop that is closed as shown in Fig. 2.7 (b). A feedback device is used for this purpose. This makes the design of closed loop a little complicated and expensive. But a very high degree of accuracy is achieved in the movement of slide.
- This system is similar to open loop control system. But it consists of two additional devices in the form of feedback transducer and a comparator as shown in the Fig.
- The transducer feedbacks the actual slide displacement to the comparator. The comparator compares the actually achieved slide movement with the command signal. If there is any error then it is feedback to the MCU.
- The MCU then sends the corrective commands to the drive unit and the cycle repeats until there is no error signal from the comparator.

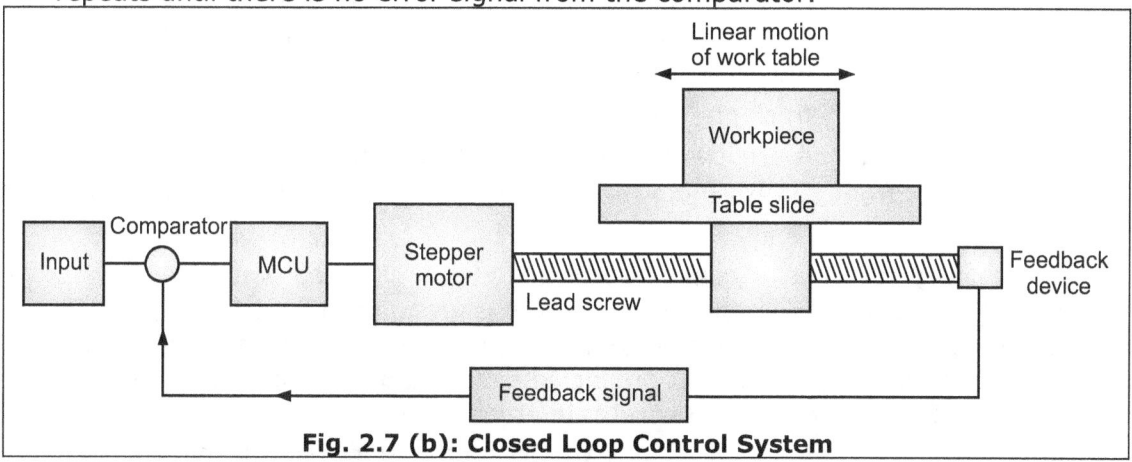

Fig. 2.7 (b): Closed Loop Control System

2.6.4 Based on Structure of Control System

Analogue and Digital Control:

- Control system may be divided into analogue and digital system. In an analogue control system the quantities may be varied continuously. In digital system, they are varied as per presence or absence of a quantity.
- In digital system of machine tool, each cycle of information provides a voltage pulse where each pulse represents a basic length unit which determines the system resolution. Therefore, the digital system is of fine accuracy while the analogue information can accept any value.
- The accuracy achieved in an analogue system depends on the accuracy of various components used to construct the electronic circuit and on the precision of sensor which is used practically in a digital system it is easier to obtain high accuracies.
- Both analogue and digital system are used in CNC machine tools. The input of the numerical control system is always digital, as the dimensions that are from the drawing are given in numbers which are in digital form.

- The output of numerical control system is always analogue as the slides of the machine tools are moving in a continuous and straight path. Therefore, each one of system type contain analogue and digital information unit.
- The type of control, digital or analogue is called by type of information appearing at the control loop input.
- Whenever a control loop sequence of pulses is applied, the control is digital and if the input is continuously variable, the control is analogue.

2.7 MACHINING CENTER

- Each machine tool, regardless of how well it is automated, is designed to perform basically one type of operation. But in manufacturing operations most parts require a number of different cutting operations on their various surfaces.
- For example, consider a diesel engine block. All surfaces on this engine block require different types of machining operations, such as turning, facing, milling, drilling, boring and threading. The traditional way to perform these operations is by moving the part from one machine tool to the another machine tool until all machining operations are completed. This will consume a considerable time in moving parts from one machine to machine, clamping them and then removing them from machine table.
- A machining center is a computer-controlled machine tool with automatic tool changing capability. The machining center is designed to perform a variety of cutting operations on different surfaces of the workpiece. Any machining center is capable of carrying out milling, drilling, reaming, tapping, boring, facing, turning and other operations without operator intervention for change of tools.
- In a machining center, after a particular operation, say turning has been completed, the workpiece does not have to be moved to another machine for additional operations, say drilling, boring etc. In other words, the tool and the machine are brought to the workpiece.
- Most of the machining centers are provided with two work tables called as pallets. While the workpiece on one pallet is being machined, the operator set-up the next workpiece on the free pallet. When the workpiece is machined, the automatic pallet changer (APC) moves the pallet with the finished workpiece away from the working area and moves the other pallet with the new workpiece to the working area. The operator can then unload the finished workpiece from the first pallet and set-up a new workpiece on it while the operation on second pallet is being carried out.
- Machining centers with several pallets are also available where machine can be programmed to accept new pallet when the work on the previous pallet is completed.
- Thus, on machining center, the non-productive time is reduced to a great extent. A typical machining center is shown in Fig. 2.8.

Fig. 2.8: A Machining Center

2.8 COMPARISON

2.8.1 Absolute System of Incremental System [W-15]

Sr. No.	Absolute System	Incremental System
1.	In absolute system the tool locations are always defined in relation to the workpiece zero.	In incremental system, the tool locations are defined with reference to the previous tool location.
2.	It is easy to check and edit the program.	It is difficult to check and edit the program.
3.	The main advantage of the absolute system as compared with the incremental system, is in the cases of interruption that force the operator to stop the machine.	In incremental system, any time the work is interrupted, before switching on again, the operator must bring the tool manually to the exact place of the last operation in which the interruption occurred.
4.	Almost all point-to-point positioning systems use absolute systems.	Incremental systems are not often used for controlling point-to-point machine tools.
5.	Absolute system is used for general program.	Incremental system is used for Canned cycle, Do loop and Sub program.

2.8.2 CNC and Conventional Milling Machine

Sr. No.	Parameters	CNC milling machines	Conventional milling machines
1.	Tools used	The carbide tip tools are used for faster cutting speeds.	Cutting speeds of the tools is comparatively less.
2.	Control system	Computer is used for controlling the table movements.	Table movements can be made automatic without the use of computer.
3.	Constructional features	It contains stepper motor for table movement.	It is rigid in construction.
4.	Accuracy of job	Higher accuracy with closed tolerance can be obtained.	Comparatively less accuracy is obtained.

2.8.3 Open Loop and Closed Loop System [W-14]

Parameter	Open Loop Control System	Closed Loop Control System
1. Design	It is simple in design.	It is complex in design.
2. Feedback	There is no feedback element.	A feedback element is present in this system.
3. Input	The input is directly given to the MCU.	The input and feedback signal is given to the comparator which sends the required signal to the MCU.
4. Processing time	Time required for processing is less.	Time required for processing is more.
5. Output	The output may not be as desired.	The output given is exactly as desired.
6. Output	The output cannot be controlled.	It provides a controlled output.
7. Cost	It is cheaper as compared.	It is expensive as compared.

2.9 AXIS IDENTIFICATION IN MILLING   [W-13, 14]

- Most of the machines have two or more slideways, arranged perpendicular to one another. Each slide is fitted with a control system and for the purpose of giving commands to the control system the axes should be properly identified. Therefore the part programmer must be familiar with the axes on the machining centers. He should be aware of the axes in order to formulate the movement of slide in the various directions for writing the program.

- The axes on the machining centers are divided into two types.

  (i) Linear axes: X, Y and Z axes are identified as linear axes as shown in Fig. 2.9 (a).

  (ii) Rotary axes: A, B and C axes are identified as rotary axes as shown in Fig. 2.9 (b).

Z-axis:

- First the Z-axis is fixed for the machine tool. It is the main spindle axis.

- In a vertical milling machine, the vertical axis of the machine spindle is set as the Z-axis.

- The positive Z-axis is taken in the direction that causes the cutting tool to move away from the workpiece. (i.e. it increases the distance between the workpiece and the tool).

- It means that movement of the cutter in upward direction is positive Z-axis. The movement of the tool in downward direction i.e. towards the workpiece is set as negative Z-axis.

- On vertical machining centers Z-axis is vertical and on horizontal machining centers Z-axis is horizontal.

X-axis:

- It is always horizontal and parallel to the workpiece/holding surface.

- It indicates the longitudinal travel of the work table.

- When looking from the tool spindle to the column, the positive X direction is identified as being to the right in vertical milling machine.

Y-axis:

- It is perpendicular to both X and Z-axes.

- It is also horizontal and indicates the cross travel of the table.

- The positive Y direction is the direction which completes with the +X and +Z motions a right hand cartesian co-ordinate system as shown in Fig. 2.9 (b).

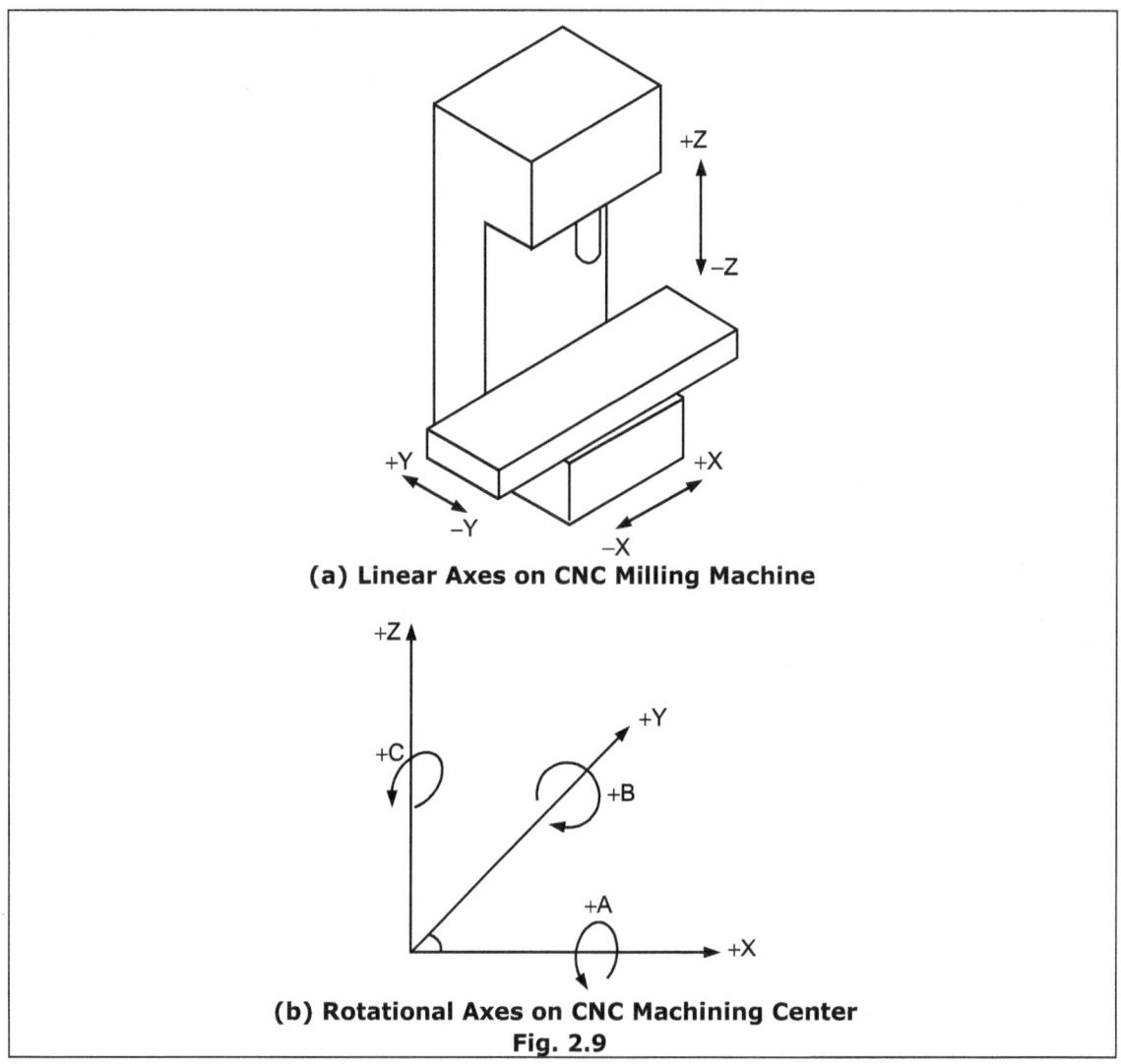

(a) Linear Axes on CNC Milling Machine

(b) Rotational Axes on CNC Machining Center
Fig. 2.9

A-axis:

- It is the axis of rotary motion of a tool along X-axis.
- Clockwise rotation is considered as positive movement and is identified by looking in +X direction.

B-axis:

- It is the axis of rotary motion of a tool along Y-axis.
- Clockwise rotation is considered as positive movement and is identified by looking in +Y direction.

C-axis:

- It is the axis of rotary motion of a tool along Z-axis.
- Clockwise rotation is considered as positive movement and is identified by looking in +Z direction.

2.9.1 Thumb Rule for Axis Identification

- The axes can also be identified by using a right hand and is known as right hand thumb rule for axis identification as shown in Fig. 2.10.
- But the Z-axis is to be fixed first before using the rule.
- The Z-axis is fixed as the main spindle axis.
- It is indicated by the middle finger of the right hand.
- The X-axis is then identified as horizontal and parallel to the workpiece surface.
- The X-axis is always indicated by the thumb.
- After the X and Z-axes have been identified, the Y-axis is perpendicular to the X and Z-axes.
- The Y-axis is then indicated by the index finger of the right hand.
- The positive direction of all the three axes is along the outward direction of the fingers (away from the palm).
- The negative direction of all the three axes is along the fingers pointing towards the palm.

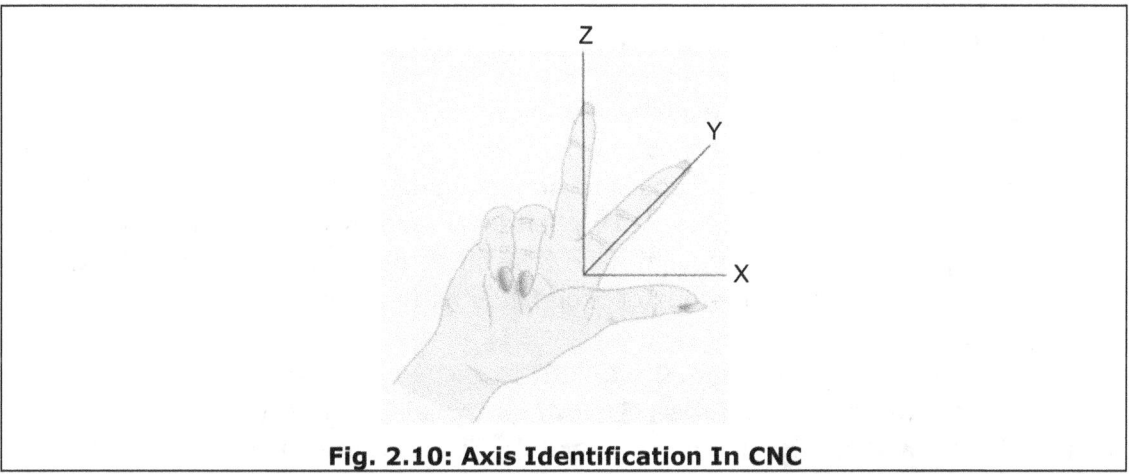

Fig. 2.10: Axis Identification In CNC

2.10 AUTOMATIC TOOL CHANGER
[W-09, W-11, S-12, S-13]

- In a machining center, several different cutting tools are used to produce a part.
- To improve the utilization of machining center, it is necessary to minimize the idle motion of the tool.
- The tool must be replaced quickly for the next machining operation.
- In such case ATC plays a very important role.
- ATC are used on machines where number of tools are used for machining operations.
- They allow tool changing without the intervention of the operator.
- The tool is automatically selected and changed by the T-word and use of miscellaneous function (M06).

- Typically, an ATC grips the tool in the spindle, pulls it out and replaces it with another tool. An ATC is provided to pick-up the programmed tool from the tool magazine and mount it on the spindle. The removed tool is put back in the magazine and the ATC picks-up the next tool.
- The ATC is thus ready with the tool for the next operation and awaits the current operation to be over to replace the tool.
- Several machining centers can perform tool change operation in less than 4 seconds.
- An ATC consists of a tool magazine for storing the tools and a tool change unit for transferring the tool from tool magazine to machine spindle.

2.11 NC WORDS

- The most important component in the CNC system is the part programming.
- Even a slight error in the program can change the dimensions of the final component.
- The part programming uses various words like G-words, N-words etc. to write a CNC program.
- These words are called as NC words. A NC word is a collection of characters used to form an instruction.
- The different NC words are explained below:

  (i) Sequence Number (N-Words): The first word in every block is the sequence number. The sequence number is used to identify the block. The sequence number is preceded by letter 'N' and is written N001, N002 etc. The program is executed from lowest block number to highest block. The block may proceed in steps of 5 or 10 so as to insert the accidently omitted blocks.

  (ii) Preparatory functions (G words): Explained in Section 2.12.

  (iii) Miscellaneous functions (M-words): Explained in Section 2.13.

  (iv) Co-ordinates (X, Y and Z words): These words give final co-ordinate positions for X, Y, Z motions. In CNC lathe there are only two linear axes X and Z. X is perpendicular to the spindle axis and Z is along the spindle axis. In CNC milling there are three linear axes X, Y and Z. X and Y are horizontal axes while Z is vertical axis.

  To specify angular positions around these linear axes, I, J and K axes are used.

  (v) Feed Function (F-word): The feed function is used to specify the feed rate in the machining operation. The feed rate is expressed in mm/min or mm/rev.

  For example, If feed is 120 then it will be represented as F120. But appropriate G code should be specified to instruct the machine whether the feed value is in mm/min or mm/rev i.e. (G94 or G95).

(vi) Spindle Speed Function (Sword): The spindle speed is specified in revolutions per minutes (r.p.m.). if the machine runs at 1200 rpm then the speed will be specified as S1200.

(vii) Tool Selection Function (T-word): The T-word is needed only for machines with automatic tool changer. The ATC keeps a records of which tool is kept at what location.

For example, if tool no. 06 is drilling tool then the command will prompt T 06, i.e. tool number 06 should be used next.

2.12 PREPARATORY FUNCTIONS (G-CODES)   [W-14]

- The preparatory word prepares the control unit to execute the instructions given in the part program.
- The G codes directs the CNC machine to process the co-ordinate data in a particular manner.
- The preparatory code is represented in two digits preceded by the letter G.
- More than one G-code can be programmed in a block, such as G90 G21 G94 but they must be from the different groups.
- If two G-codes from the same group are programmed in the same block, then they cancel each other.
- Also in this case the last programmed G-code will be executed. For example, if the block is written like N90 G00 G01 X35 Y10 F100 EOB then the G01 code will be executed.
- All G-codes are either modal or non-modal. Modal codes stay in effect until they are cancelled by another code of the same group. For example, G90 is cancelled by G91, G21 is cancelled by G20.
- Non-modal codes stay in effect only for the blocks for which they are programmed. After execution of that block their function is automatically turned-off. For example, G04 is a non-modal code for dwell which remains active in that block only.
- The various G-codes used on machining center/milling machine are given in Table 2.1.

Table 2.1: G-codes for Machining Center   [W-15, S-17]

Group	G-code	Meaning
01	G00	Rapid positioning.
	G01	Linear interpolation.
	G02	Circular interpolation (Clockwise).
	G03	Circular interpolation (Counter Clockwise).
00	G04	Dwell.
	G10	Tool length offset value.
02	G17	XY plane selection.
	G18	ZX plane selection.
	G19	YZ plane selection.
06	G20	Programming in inch units.
	G21	Programming in metric units.

	G27	Reference point return check.
00	G28	Automatic return to reference point.
	G29	Automatic return from reference point.
	G30	Return to 2nd, 3rd or 4th reference point.
07	G40	Cutter diameter compensation cancel.
	G41	Cutter diameter compensation left.
	G42	Cutter diameter compensation right.
08	G43	Tool length compensation in positive (+) direction.
	G44	Tool length compensation in negative (−) direction.
00	G45	Tool offset increase.
	G46	Tool offset decrease.
08	G49	Tool length offset cancel.
0.4	G70	Finishing cycle
	G71	Multiply turning cycle
0.0	G72	Multiply facing cycle
	G76	Thread cutting cycle
	G73	Pattern repeating cycle
	G74	Drilling cycle (in Z-direction)
	G75	Grooving cycle
09	G80	Canned cycle cancel.
	G81	Drilling cycle (canned).
	G82	Counter boring cycle (canned).
	G83	Peck drilling cycle (canned).
	G84	Tapping cycle (canned).
	G85	Boring cycle (canned).
	G87	Back boring cycle (canned).
03	G90	Absolute Positioning.
	G91	Incremental Positioning.
00	G92	Zero preset.
05	G94	Feed rate in mm/min.
	G95	Feed rate in mm/rev.
02	G96	Constant surface speed control.
	G97	Constant surface speed control cancel.

2.13 MISCELLANEOUS FUNCTIONS (M-CODES)   [W-14]

- The miscellaneous functions are used to specify certain miscellaneous functions like spindle start and stop, coolant on and off etc.
- The miscellaneous functions are those functions which are not related to the dimensional movement of the machine. These functions operate some control on the machine.
- The miscellaneous function is represented in two digits preceded by the letter M.
- Only one M-code can be programmed in a block.
- All M-codes are modal.

Table 2.2: M-codes for Machining Center   [W-15, S-17]

M-code	Meaning
M00	Program Stop
M01	Optional Stop
M02	Program End
M03	Spindle Start (Clockwise)
M04	Spindle Start (Counter Clockwise)
M05	Spindle Stop
M06	Tool Change
M07	Thru Spindle Coolant ON
M08	Coolant ON
M09	Coolant OFF
M30	End Program
M98	Call Subroutine
M99	End of subroutine

2.14 PROGRAMMING FORMATS

- Format is the method of writing the words in a block of instruction.

- Various NC words are used to write one block of instruction.

- Each block of instruction is separated by an end of block (EOB) or enter symbol.

- Until the controller executes the current block, it does not jump to the next block of instruction.

- The set of various blocks of instructions which tells the machine tool about the steps to be performed to manufacture a component is known as part programming.

- In general the blocks of instruction looks as shown below:

    N10 G90 G21 G94 G40 EOB

    N20 M03 S1100 M08 EOB

- The following are the three program formats being used for part programming.

2.14.1 Fixed Block Format

- In fixed block format, instructions are always given in same sequence. All the instructions must be given in every block, including those instructions which remain unchanged from the preceding blocks.

- For example, If some co-ordinate values (i.e. x, y, z values) remain constant from one to next block, these values have to be specified in the next block also.

- In this system, only data is provided in the program and the identifying address letters are not given, but the data must be input in a specified sequence and the characters within each word must be of same length.

- For the work piece shown in Fig. 2.11, the blocks of instructions will be written as:

N	G	X	Y	Z	F	S	EOB
0050	00	20	30	00	150	1000	EOB
0060	00	90	30	00	150	1000	EOB

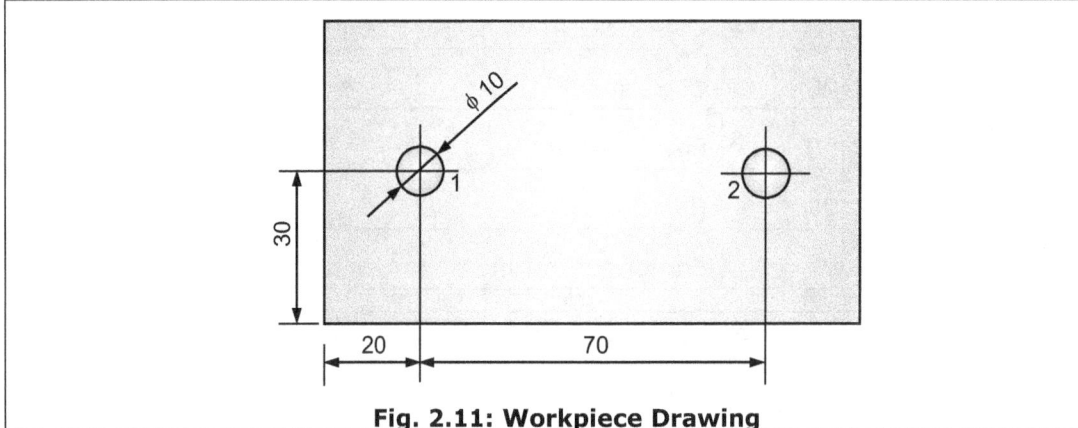

Fig. 2.11: Workpiece Drawing

2.14.2 Tab Sequential Format

- In this programming format, instructions in a block are always given in the same sequence similar to fixed block format.

- But each word is separated by the TAB character.

- It has one advantage over the earlier format that if a word remains the same as in preceding block, it need not be written again. But to maintain sequence of words, TAB only should be written in the succeeding block.

- For the work piece shown in Fig., the blocks of instructions will be written as:

N	G	X	Y	Z	F	S	EOB
0050TAB	00TAB	20TAB	30TAB	00TAB	150TAB	100	EOB
0060TAB	00TAB	90TAB	TAB	TAB	TAB		EOB

2.14.3 Word Address Format

* This format is standardized by EIA and is most widely used.

* In this format, each data is preceded by a word called as NC word.

* Each such alphabet has been standardized to represent a particular axial co-ordinate or function.

* It has one advantage over the earlier format that if a word remains the same as in preceding block, it need not be written again.

* As such, the program shortens because only those words are required to be written which change from one block to other.

* For the work piece shown in figure, the blocks of instructions will be written as:

| N0050 | G00 | X20 | Y30 | Z00 | F150 | S 1000 | EOB |
| N0060 | X90 | EOB | | | | | |

2.15 PART PROGRAMMING

* Part programming is defined as the procedure by which the sequence of processing steps to be performed on a C.N.C. machine is planned or documented.

* Part programming can also be defined as the way in which the blocks of instructions are planned (written) such that after its execution on the C.N.C. machine the required shape is obtained on the workpiece in minimum possible time. **[W-14]**

* Part programming is an important feature of a CNC system. It is a complete set of instructions for machining a component on CNC machine.

* A program consists of a number of lines or blocks each of which is command for a specific operation, such as moving the tool, starting and stopping the spindle, specifying feed rates etc. Each line or block in turn consists of a series of words or codes.

* The shape, size and dimensional accuracy of desired component depends mainly on how accurately the program is prepared.

* The part program is actually a set of directions about the processing steps to be sequentially performed on the work piece.

* The part program is preceded by the design/development procedures viz. designing of component, detailed drawing and process planning. Process planning is the procedure of deciding as to what operations are required to be done on the work piece and in what sequence.

* Thus, even though a programer may not be a skilled machinist, he should posses thorough knowledge of relevant machining operations.

2.15.1 Part Program For Drilling Holes

- A number of holes can be drilled in the workpiece using the vertical machining centre.

- For this purpose the linear interpolation (G01 code) is used.

- G01 should always follow by feed rate.

- The two axes (X and Y) are horizontal axes similar to the number line. The third axis is the Z axis which is perpendicular to the two axes. The Z axis is spindle axis and is vertical. The tool movement away from the workpiece is positive Z axis and the tool movement towards the workpiece is referred as negative Z axis.

- Generally the surface of the workpiece is taken as zero, above which is positive Z and below it is negative Z.

- Sometimes the zero is located at some distance above the workpiece surface. This position is called as reference position.

2.15.2 Procedure To Write A Part Program

- The part program varies from controller to controller. Also the program written for the same controller by different programmer may differ.

- But in general the following procedure can be followed to write a part program.

    (i)   Study the given component carefully.

    (ii)   Assume suitable data if it is not mentioned in the question.

    (iii)   Decide the path to be followed by the cutter.

    (iv)   Write the co-ordinates of all the points in a separate table.

    (v)   Then start writing the program.

    (vi)   The first four blocks can be kept common for almost all the programs.

    (vii)   In the next block bring the tool to position number 1 but above the workpiece surface. Use G00.

    (viii) Then move the tool inside the workpiece. Use G01.

    (ix)   Then move the tool to earlier position.

    (x)   Then move the tool to next position by referring the table.

    (xi)   After the last tool position bring the tool above the workpiece surface. Use G01.

    (xii)   Again the last blocks can be common for all the programs.

2.16 PART PROGRAM FOR DRILLING OPERATION

Program 2.1: *Write a program to drill the two holes as shown in the Fig 2.12. The plate thickness is 10 mm.*

Assume: The cutting tool diameter is 10 mm. Reference plane is at the top surface of the plate.

- The X and Y co-ordinates of various tool positions are shown in Table 2.3.

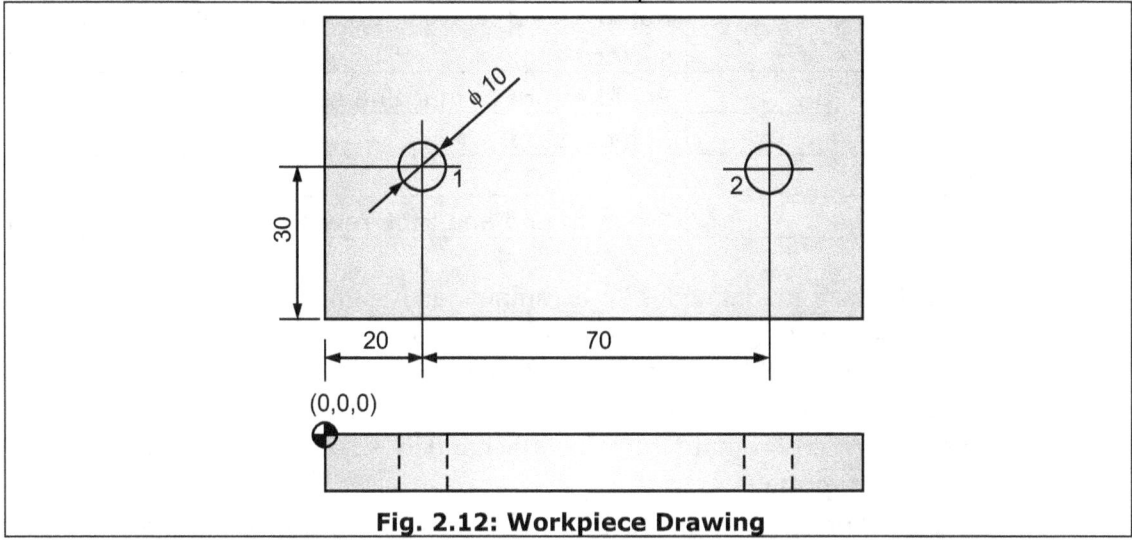

Fig. 2.12: Workpiece Drawing

Table 2.3: X and Y Co-ordinates of various Tool Positions

Position No.	X and Y Co-ordinates	Position No.	X and Y Co-ordinates
1	20, 30	2	90, 30

Part program:

Program	Description
01214	Program Number
N110 G90 G21 G94 G40 EOB	Absolute mode, input in mm, feed in mm/min, tool diameter compensation cancel.
N120 M03 S1100 M08 EOB	Spindle start clockwise direction, spindle speed, coolant on.
N130 G00 Z5 EOB	Rapid travel of tool to 5 mm above the plate surface.
N140 G00 X20 Y30 EOB	Rapid travel of tool to position 1 (20, 30).
N150 G01 Z-10 F90 EOB	Movement of tool 10 mm inside the workpiece. (drilling) [Total tool movement is 15 mm in Z direction].

contd. ...

N160 G00 Z5 EOB	Rapid travel of tool to 5 mm above the plate surface.
N170 G00 X90 EOB	Rapid travel of tool to position 2 (90, 30).
N180 G01 Z-10 F90 EOB	Movement of tool 10 mm inside the workpiece. (drilling)
N190 G00 Z5 EOB	Rapid travel of tool to 5 mm above the plate surface.
N200 G28 EOB	Rapid return to machine reference position.
N210 M05 EOB	Spindle stop.
N220 M09 EOB	Coolant-off.
N230 M30 EOB	Program end and tape rewind.

Note:
1. G00 and G01 is a modal code. So it remains active until cancelled by the code of same group. Therefore it is not necessary to write G00 from block number N 140 and N170. Still it is written for students in this example.
2. Even if G01 is written in above blocks, it is not incorrect.
3. In N170, as Y co-ordinate remains unchanged so no need to write Y 30. (Word address format)

Program 2.2: *Write a program to drill the two holes as shown in the Fig 2.13. The plate thickness is 10 mm. Use **incremental mode** of programming.*

Assume: The cutting tool diameter is 10 mm. Reference plane is at the top surface of the plate.

- The X and Y co-ordinates of various tool positions are shown in Table 2.4.
- **Note:** For incremental mode spindle is manually positioned to the tool change position. In this case it is (−10, −10, 5)

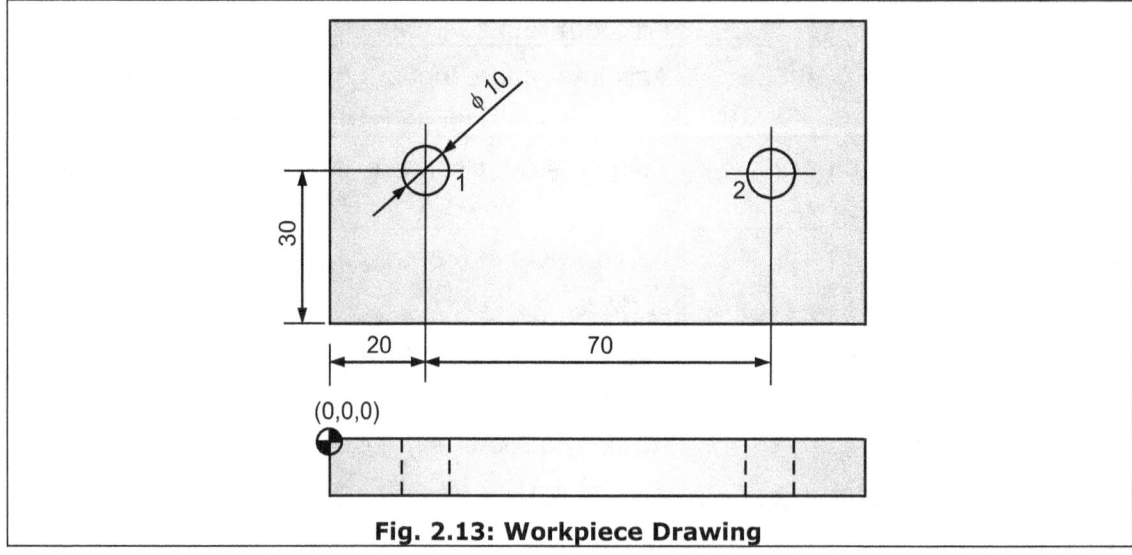

Fig. 2.13: Workpiece Drawing

Table 2.4: X and Y Co-ordinates of various Tool Positions

Position No.	X and Y Co-ordinates	Position No.	X and Y Co-ordinates
1	30, 40	2	70, 00

Part program:

Program	Description
02215	
N110 G91 G21 G94 G40 EOB	Incremental mode, input in mm, feed in mm/min, tool diameter compensation cancel.
N120 M03 S1100 M08 EOB	Spindle start clockwise direction, spindle speed, coolant on.
N130 G00 X30 Y40 Z5 EOB	Tool travel to position 1 (30, 40) and 5 mm above the workpiece.
N140 G01 Z15 F90 EOB	Movement of tool 10 mm inside the workpiece. (drilling) [Total tool movement is 15 mm in Z direction]
N150 G00 Z15 EOB	Rapid travel of tool to 5 mm above the plate surface.
N160 G00 X70 EOB	Rapid travel of tool to position 2 (70, 00).
N170 G01 Z-15 F90 EOB	Movement of tool 10 mm inside the workpiece. (drilling)
N180 G00 Z15 EOB	Rapid travel of tool to 5 mm above the plate surface.
N190 G28 EOB	Rapid return to machine reference position.
N200 M05 EOB	Spindle stop.
N210 M09 EOB	Coolant-off.
N220 M30 EOB	Program end and tape rewind.

Program 2.3: *Write the program to drill the holes for the job shown in Fig. 2.14.*

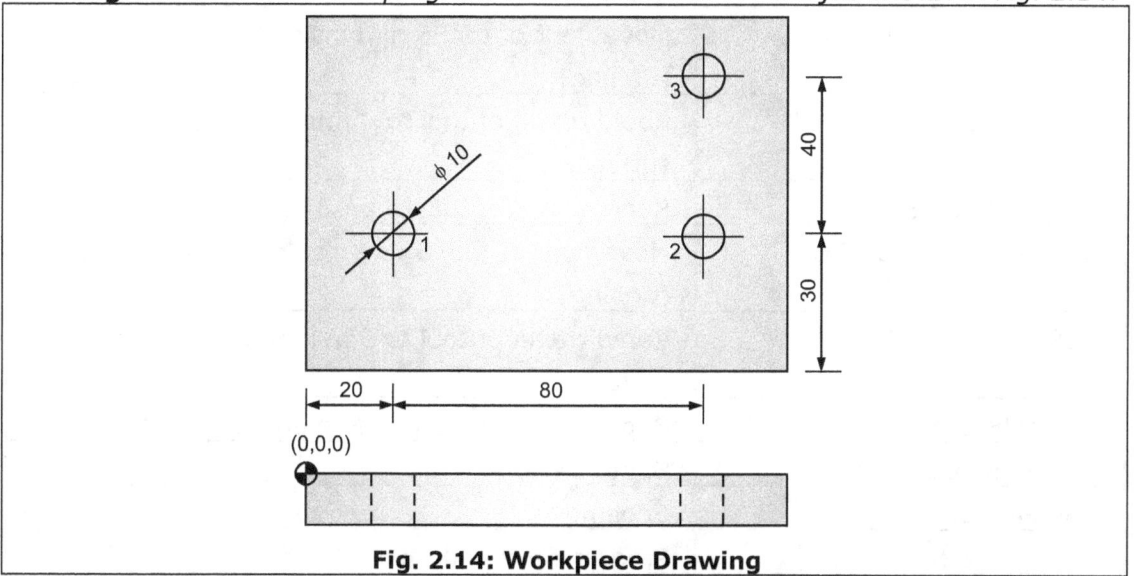

Fig. 2.14: Workpiece Drawing

Assume: The depth of workpiece is 5 mm. The workpiece reference surface is at the lower left corner of the workpiece.

- The X and Y co-ordinates of various tool positions are shown in Table 2.5.

Table 2.5: X and Y Co-ordinates of various Tool Positions

Position No.	X and Y Co-ordinates	Position No.	X and Y Co-ordinates
1	20, 30	3	100, 70
2	100, 30		

Part program:

Program	Description
03216	Program number
N10 G90 G21 G94 EOB	Absolute mode, input in mm, feed in mm/min.
N15 M03 S1100 M08 EOB	Spindle starts clockwise direction, spindle speed, coolant on.
N20 G00 Z4 EOB	Rapid travel of tool to 4 mm above the plate surface.
N25 G00 X20 Y20 EOB	Rapid travel of tool to position 1 (20, 30).
N30 G01 Z-5 F90 EOB	Movement of tool 5 mm inside the workpiece. (drilling) [Total tool movement is 9 mm in Z direction]
N35 G00 Z4 EOB	Rapid travel of tool to 4 mm above the plate surface.
N40 G00 X10 Y20 EOB	Rapid travel of tool to position 2 (100, 30).
N45 G01 Z-5 F90 EOB	Movement of tool 5 mm inside the workpiece. (drilling)
N50 G00 Z4 EOB	Rapid travel of tool to 4 mm above the plate surface.
N55 G00 Y60 EOB	Rapid travel of tool to position 3 (100, 70).
N60 G01 Z-5 F90 EOB	Movement of tool 5 mm inside the workpiece. (drilling).
N65 G00 Z5 EOB	Rapid travel of tool to 5 mm above the plate surface.
N70 G28 EOB	Rapid return to machine reference position.
N75 M05 EOB	Spindle stop.
N80 M09 EOB	Coolant-off.
N85 M30 EOB	Program end and tape rewind.

Program 2.4: *Write a program to drill the 5 holes of 08 mm diameter in a 150×150 mm workpiece as shown in the Fig 2.15. The plate thickness is 10 mm. Z reference is 5 mm above the workpiece surface.*

Assume: The cutting tool diameter is 08 mm.

- The X and Y co-ordinates of various tool positions are shown in Table 2.6.

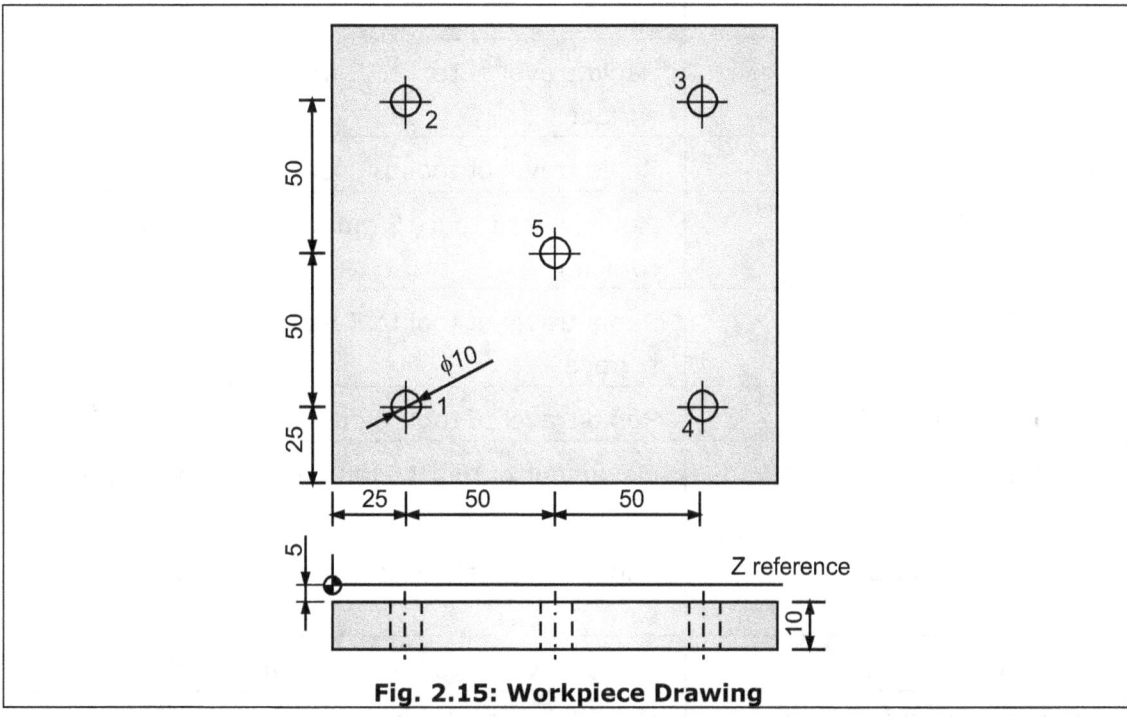

Fig. 2.15: Workpiece Drawing

Table 2.6: X and Y Co-ordinates of various Tool Positions

Position No.	X and Y Co-ordinates	Position No.	X and Y Co-ordinates
1	25, 25	4	100, 25
2	25, 125	5	75, 75
3	100, 125		

Part Program:

Program	Description
04217	
N110 G90 G21 G94 G40 EOB	Absolute mode, input in mm, feed in mm/min, tool diameter compensation cancel.
N120 M03 S1100 M08 EOB	Spindle start clockwise direction, spindle speed, coolant on.

contd. ...

N130 G00 Z0 EOB	Rapid travel of tool to 5 mm above the plate surface. [As Z zero is 5 mm above the plate)
N140 G00 X25 Y25 EOB	Rapid travel of tool to position 1 (25, 25).
N150 G01 Z-15 F90 EOB	Movement of tool 15 mm inside the workpiece. (drilling)
N160 G00 Z0 EOB	Rapid travel of tool to 5 mm above the plate surface.
N170 G00 Y125 EOB	Rapid travel of tool to position 2 (25, 125).
N180 G01 Z-15 F90 EOB	Movement of tool 15 mm inside the workpiece. (drilling)
N190 G00 Z0 EOB	Rapid travel of tool to 5 mm above the plate surface.
N200 G00 X100 EOB	Rapid travel of tool to position 3 (100, 125).
N210 G01 Z-15 F90 EOB	Movement of tool 15 mm inside the workpiece. (drilling)
N220 G00 Z0 EOB	Rapid travel of tool to 5 mm above the plate surface.
N230 G00 X100 Y25 EOB	Rapid travel of tool to position 4 (100, 25).
N240 G01 Z-15 F90 EOB	Movement of tool 15 mm inside the workpiece. (drilling)
N250 G00 Z0 EOB	Rapid travel of tool to 5 mm above the plate surface.
N260 G00 X75 Y75 EOB	Rapid travel of tool to position 5 (75, 75).
N270 G01 Z-15 F90 EOB	Movement of tool 15 mm inside the workpiece. (drilling)
N280 G00 Z0 EOB	Rapid travel of tool to 5 mm above the plate surface.
N290 G28 EOB	Rapid return to machine reference position.
N300 M05 EOB	Spindle stop.
N310 M09 EOB	Coolant-off.
N320 M30 EOB	Program end and tape rewind.

Program 2.5: *Write a program to drill the 4 holes in the workpiece as shown in the Fig 2.16. The depth of plate is 6 mm.*

Assume: Z = 00 is at the top surface of the workpiece.

- The X and Y co-ordinates of various tool positions are shown in Table 2.7.

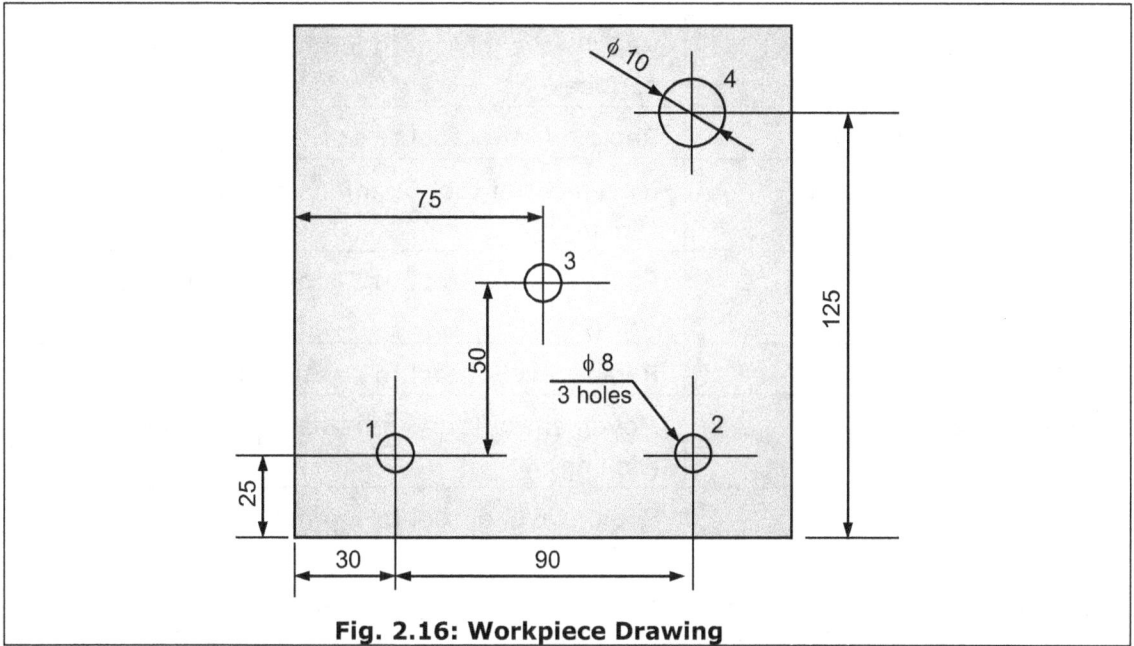

Fig. 2.16: Workpiece Drawing

Table 2.7: X and Y Co-ordinates of various Tool Positions

Position No.	X and Y Co-ordinates	Position No.	X and Y Co-ordinates
1	30, 25	3	75, 75
2	120, 25	4	120, 125

Part Program:

Program	Description
05218	
N110 M06 T01 EOB	Tool change to tool at position no. 1 (ϕ 8 mm)
N120 G90 G21 G94 G40 EOB	Absolute mode, input in mm, feed in mm/min, tool diameter compensation cancel.
N130 M03 S1100 M08 EOB	Spindle starts clockwise direction, spindle speed, coolant on.
N140 G00 Z5 EOB	Rapid travel of tool to 5 mm above the plate surface.

contd. ...

N150 G00 X30 Y25 EOB	Rapid travel of tool to position 1 (30, 25).
N160 G01 Z-6 F90 EOB	Movement of tool 6 mm inside the workpiece. (drilling) [Total tool movement is 11 mm in Z direction]
N170 G00 Z5 EOB	Rapid travel of tool to 5 mm above the plate surface.
N180 G00 X120 EOB	Rapid travel of tool to position 2 (120, 25).
N190 G01 Z-6 F90 EOB	Movement of tool 6 mm inside the workpiece. (drilling)
N200 G00 Z5 EOB	Rapid travel of tool to 5 mm above the plate surface.
N210 G00 X75 Y75 EOB	Rapid travel of tool to position 3 (75, 75).
N220 G01 Z-6 F90 EOB	Movement of tool 6 mm inside the workpiece. (drilling)
N230 G00 Z5 M09 EOB	Rapid travel of tool to 5 mm above the plate surface, coolant off.
N240 G28 EOB	Rapid return to machine reference position.
N250 M05 EOB	Spindle stop.
N260 M06 T02 EOB	Tool change to tool at position no. 2 (Φ10 mm)
N270 M03 S1100 M08 EOB	Spindle starts clockwise direction, spindle speed, coolant on.
N280 G00 Z5 EOB	Rapid travel of tool to 5 mm above the plate surface.
N290 G00 X120 Y125 EOB	Rapid travel of tool to position 4 (120, 125).
N300 G01 Z-6 F90 EOB	Movement of tool 6 mm inside the workpiece. (drilling)
N310 G00 Z5 EOB	Rapid travel of tool to 5 mm above the plate surface.
N320 G28 EOB	Rapid return to machine reference position.
N330 M05 EOB	Spindle stop.
N340 M09 EOB	Coolant-off.
N350 M30 EOB	Program end and tape rewind.

Program 2.6: *Write the program for the job shown in Fig 2.17. Holes are to be drilled in a sequence shown in Fig. 2.17.* [W-08]

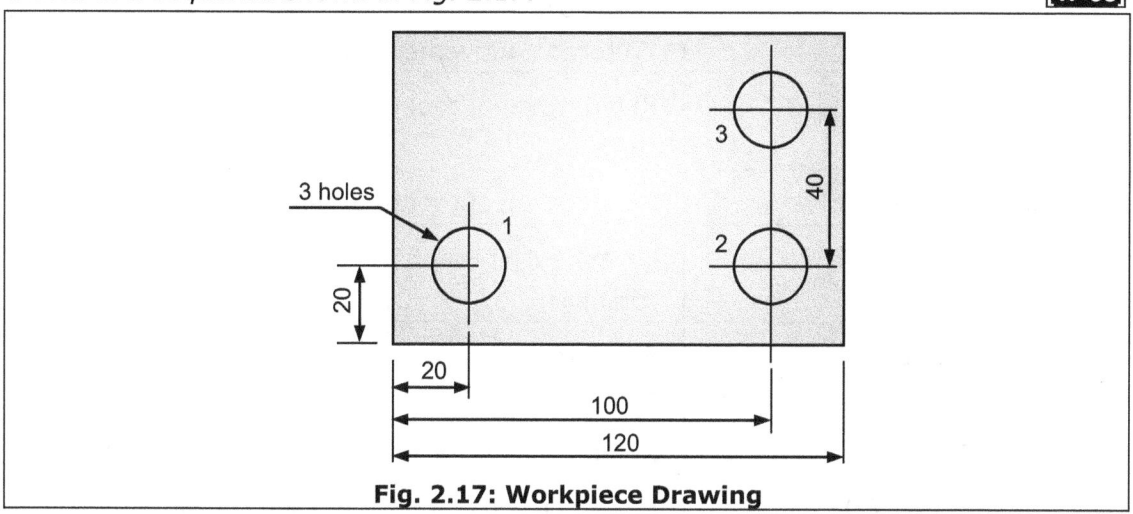

Fig. 2.17: Workpiece Drawing

Assume: The depth of workpiece is 5 mm. The workpiece reference surface is at the lower left corner of the workpiece.

* The X and Y co-ordinates of various tool positions are shown in Table 2.8.

Table 2.8: X and Y Co-ordinates of various Tool Positions

Position No.	X and Y Co-ordinates	Position No.	X and Y Co-ordinates
1	20, 20	3	100, 60
2	100, 20		

Part Program:

Program	Description
06219	Program number.
	Return to machine reference position.
N10 G90 G21 G94 EOB	Absolute mode, input in mm, feed in mm/min.
N15 M03 S1100 M08 EOB	Spindle starts clockwise direction, spindle speed, coolant on.
N20 G00 Z4 EOB	Rapid travel of tool to 4 mm above the plate surface.
N25 G00 X20 Y20 EOB	Rapid travel of tool to position 1 (20, 20).

contd. ...

N30 G01 Z-5 F90 EOB	Movement of tool 5 mm inside the workpiece. (drilling). [Total tool movement in Z direction is 9 mm]
N35 G00 Z4 EOB	Rapid travel of tool to 4 mm above the plate surface.
N40 G00 X10 Y20 EOB	Rapid travel of tool to position 2 (100, 20).
N45 G01 Z-5 F90 EOB	Movement of tool 5 mm inside the workpiece. (drilling).
N50 G00 Z4 EOB	Rapid travel of tool to 4 mm above the plate surface.
N55 G00 Y60 EOB	Rapid travel of tool to position 3 (100, 60).
N60 G01 Z-5 F90 EOB	Movement of tool 5 mm inside the workpiece. (drilling).
N65 G00 Z5 EOB	Rapid travel of tool to 5 mm above the plate surface.
N70 G00 X100 Y25 EOB	Rapid travel of tool to position 4 (100, 25).
N75 G01 Z-5 F90 EOB	Movement of tool 5 mm inside the workpiece. (drilling).
N80 G00 Z4 EOB	Rapid travel of tool to 4 mm above the plate surface.
N85 G28 EOB	Rapid return to machine reference position.
N90 M05 EOB	Spindle stop.
N95 M09 EOB	Coolant-off.
N100 M30 EOB	Program end and tape rewind.

2.17 PART PROGRAM ON SLOT MILLING [S-12]

Program 2.7: *Write a part program to machine the 10 mm slot inside the workpiece as shown in the Fig. 2.18 (a). Use a 10 mm diameter end mill. The part depth is 10 mm and the slot depth is 5 mm. Use a depth of cut of 2.5 mm.*

Assume: Z datum is at lower left corner of the plate.

- The tool path is shown in Fig. 2.18 (b).
- The X and Y co-ordinates of various tool positions are shown in Table 2.9.

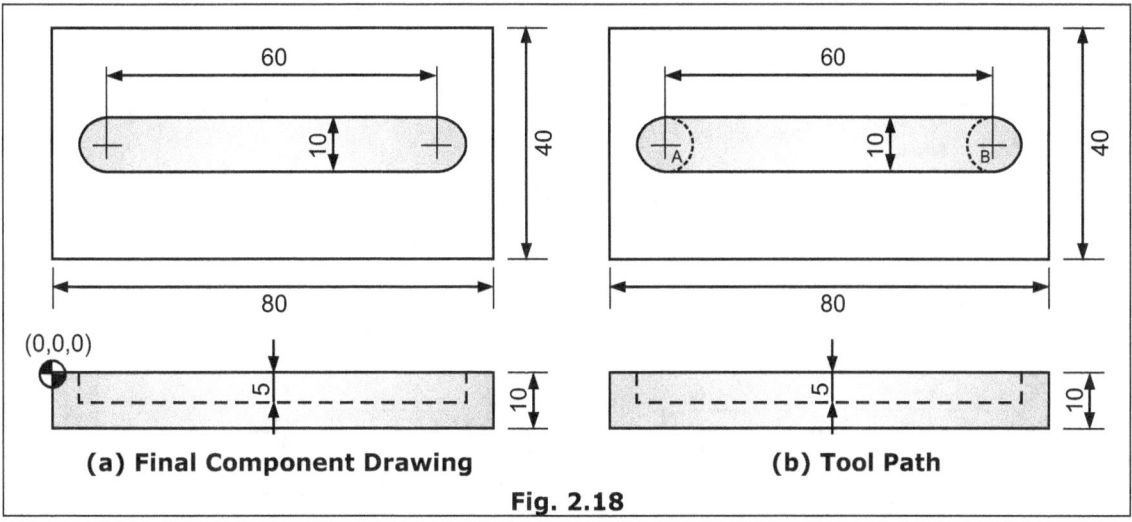

(a) Final Component Drawing   (b) Tool Path

Fig. 2.18

Table 2.9: X and Y Co-ordinates of Various Tool Position

Position No.	X and Y Co-ordinates	Position No.	X and Y Co-ordinates
A	10, 20	B	70, 20

Part Program:

Program	Description
07220	Program number.
N110 G90 G21 G94 EOB	Absolute mode, input in mm, feed in mm/min.
N120 M06 T01 EOB	Tool change, tool at tool position number 1 of 10 mm diameter in the tool magazine.
N130 M03 S900 EOB	Spindle start clockwise direction, spindle speed.
N140 G00 Z5 M08 EOB	Rapid travel of cutter to 5 mm (reference position) above the workpiece surface, coolant on.
N150 G00 X10 Y20 EOB	Rapid travel of cutter to position A (10, 20).
N160 G01 Z-2.5 F50 EOB	Take required depth of cut of 2.5 mm with the given feed, so G01.
N170 X70 Y20 EOB	Cutter travel to position number B (70, 20).
N180 Z-5 EOB	Take a depth of cut of another 2.5 mm.
N190 X10 EOB	Cutter travel to position number A (10, 20).
N200 G00 Z5 EOB	Rapid travel of cutter 5 mm above the workpiece surface.
N210 G28 EOB	Rapid return to machine reference position.
N220 M05 EOB	Spindle stop.
N230 M09 EOB	Coolant-off.
N240 M30 EOB	Program end and tape rewind.

Program 2.8: *Write a part program to machine the 5 mm slot inside the workpiece as shown in the Fig. 2.19 (a). Use a 5 mm diameter end mill. The part depth is 8 mm and the slot depth is 2 mm. The Z reference is 7 mm above the workpiece surface.*

- The tool path is shown in Fig. 2.19 (b).
- The X and Y co-ordinates of various tool positions are shown in Table 2.10.

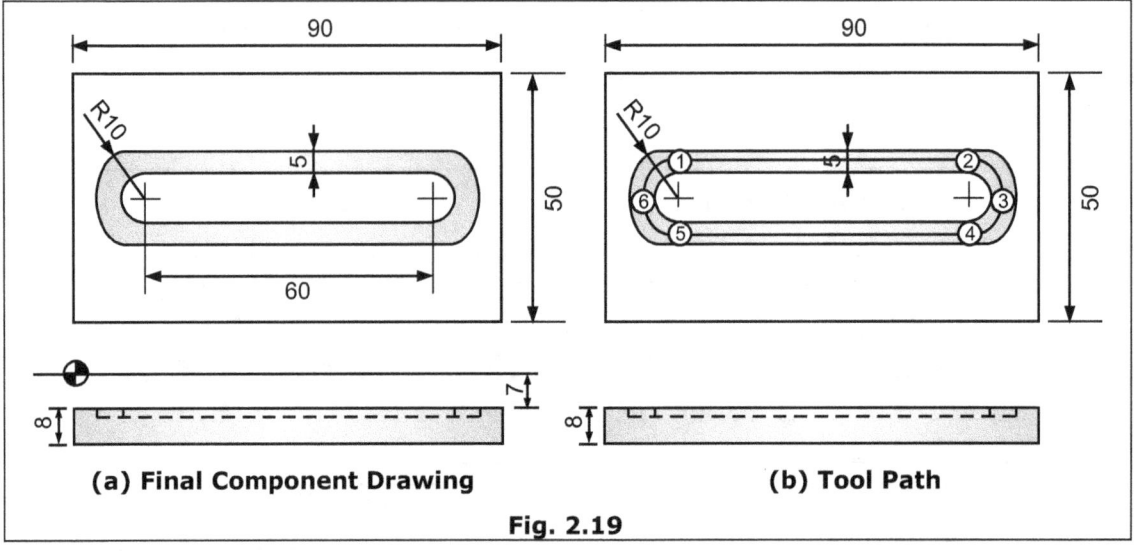

(a) Final Component Drawing   **(b) Tool Path**

Fig. 2.19

Table 2.10: X and Y Co-ordinates of Various Tool Position

Position No.	X and Y Co-ordinates	Position No.	X and Y Co-ordinates
1.	15, 32.5	4	75, 17.5
2.	75, 32.5	5	15, 17.5
3.	82.5, 25	6	7.5, 25

Part Program:

Program	Description
08220	Program number.
N110 G90 G21 G94 EOB	Absolute mode, input in mm, feed in mm/min.
N120 M06 T03 EOB	Tool change, end mill of 5 mm diameter at tool position number 3 in the tool magazine.
N130 M03 S800 EOB	Spindle start clockwise direction, spindle speed.
N140 G00 Z0 M08 EOB	Rapid travel of cutter to 7 mm above the workpiece surface, coolant on.

contd. ...

N150 G00 X15 Y-32.5 EOB	Rapid travel of cutter to position 1 (15,–32.5).
N160 G01 Z-9 F55 EOB	Take required depth of cut of 2 mm with the given feed, so G01. (7 mm + 2 mm = 9 mm)
N170 X75 EOB	Cutter travel to position number 2 (75,–32.5).
N180 G02 X82.5 Y25 R5 F55 EOB	Cutter travel to position number 3 (82.5, 25). The inside radius of the slot is 5 mm.
N190 G02 X75 Y17.5 R5 F55 EOB	Cutter travel to position number 4 (75, 17.5).
N200 G01 X15 F55 EOB	Cutter travel to position number 5 (15, 17.5).
N210 G02 X7.5 Y25 R5 F55 EOB	Cutter travel to position number 6 (7.5, 25).
N220 G02 X15 Y-32.5 R5 F55 EOB	Cutter travel to position number 1 (15, –32.5).
N230 G00 Z0 EOB	Rapid travel of cutter 7 mm above the workpiece surface.
N240 G28 EOB	Rapid return to machine reference position.
N250 M05 EOB	Spindle stop.
N260 M09 EOB	Coolant-off.
N270 M30 EOB	Program end and tape rewind.

2.18 PART PROGRAM FOR MACHINING ALONG STRAIGHT LINE

* A straight line is horizontal, vertical or inclined at an angle in any direction. In order to machine along a straight line, linear interpolation (G01 code) is used.

* While machining along a straight line, the tool is first taken to the required depth outside the workpiece and then G01 code is used.

* G01 is a modal code and feed should be specified with G01.

* The two axes (X and Y) are horizontal axes similar to the number line. The third axis is the Z-axis which is perpendicular to the two axes. The Z-axis is spindle axis and is vertical. The tool movement away from the workpiece is positive Z-axis and the tool movement towards the workpiece is referred as negative Z-axis.

* Generally the surface of the workpiece is taken as zero, above which is positive Z and below it is negative Z.

2.18.1 Procedure To Write A Part Program

* The part program varies from controller to controller. Also the program written for the same controller by different programmer may differ.

* But in general the following procedure can be followed to write a part program.

    (i)   Study the given component carefully.

    (ii) Assume suitable data if it is not mentioned in the question.

(iii) Decide the path to be followed by the cutter.

(iv) Mark the tool path on a separate dimensionless drawing as shown in Fig. 2.20 (b).

(v) Number the various points along the path.

(vi) Number the starting and end position of the tool which should be outside and slightly away from the component.

(vii) Write the co-ordinates of all the points in a separate table.

(viii) Then start writing the program.

(ix) The first four blocks can be kept common for almost all the programs.

(x) In the next block bring the tool to position number 1 but above the workpiece surface. Use G00.

(xi) Then obtain the required depth of cut in the next block. Use G00.

(xii) Then move the tool to position number 2 i.e. touch the workpiece using G01.

(xiii) Then move the tool from position number 2 till the last position of the tool by referring the table and using G01 or G02 or G03 code.

(xiv) After the last tool position bring the tool above the workpiece surface. Use G01.

(xv) Again the last blocks can be common for all the programs.

Program 2.9: *Write a part program to machine around the outside of the part as shown in the Fig. 2.20 (a). Use a 6 mm diameter end mill. The part depth is 3 mm. Use a feed rate of 90 mm/min.*   [S-13]

- The Z zero (Z0) is at the workpiece top surface.
- The tool path is shown in Fig. 2.20 (b).
- The X and Y co-ordinates of various tool positions are shown in Table 2.11.

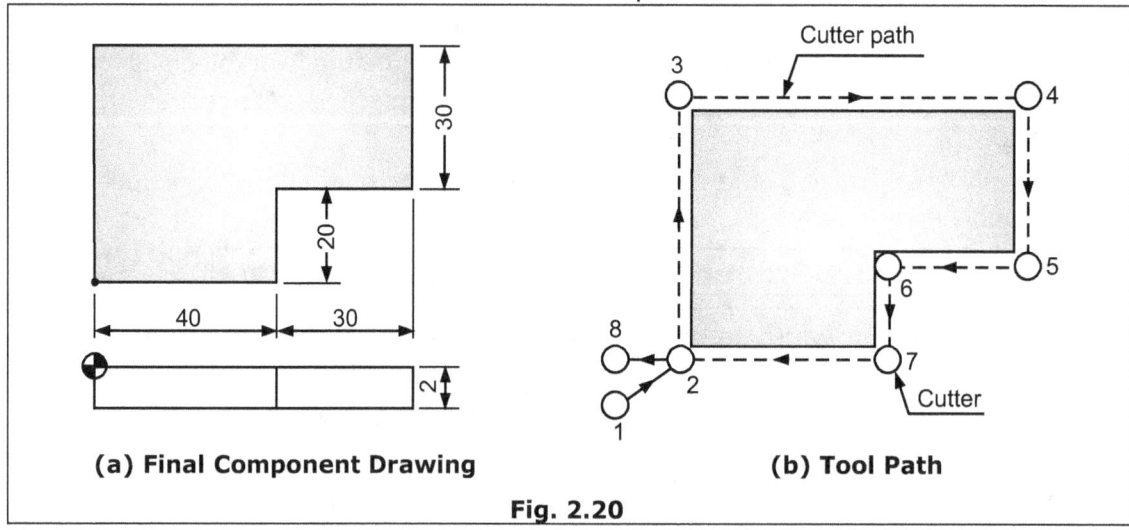

(a) Final Component Drawing   **(b) Tool Path**

Fig. 2.20

Table 2.11: X and Y Co-ordinates of various Tool Position

Position No.	X and Y Co-ordinates	Position No.	X and Y Co-ordinates
1	(−10, −10)	5	(73, 17)
2	(−3, −3)	6	(43, 17)
3	(−3, 53)	7	(43,−3)
4	(73, 53)	8	(−10,−3)

Part Program:

Program	Description
09222	Program number.
N110 G90 G21 G94 EOB	Absolute mode, input in mm, feed in mm/min.
N120 M06 T01 EOB	Tool change, tool at tool position number 1 in the tool magazine.
N130 M03 S800 EOB	Spindle start clockwise direction, spindle speed.
N140 G00 X-10 Y-10 EOB	Rapid travel of cutter to position 1 (−10, −10).
N150 G00 Z5 M08 EOB	Rapid travel of cutter to 5 mm above the workpiece surface, coolant on.
N160 G01 Z-3 F90 EOB	Take required depth of cut with the given feed, so G01.
N170 G01 X-3 Y-3 EOB	Cutter travel to position number 2 (−3, −3).
N180 G01 Y53 EOB	Cutter travel to position number 3 (−3, 53).
N190 G01 X73 EOB	Cutter travel to position number 4 (73, 53).
N200 G01 Y17 EOB	Cutter travel to position number 5 (73, 17).
N210 G01 X43 EOB	Cutter travel to position number 6 (43, 17).
N220 G01 Y-3 EOB	Cutter travel to position number 7 (43, −3).
N230 G01 X-10 EOB	Cutter travel to position number 8 (−10, −3).
N240 G00 Z5 EOB	Rapid travel of cutter 5 mm above the workpiece surface.
N250 G28 EOB	Rapid return to machine reference position.
N260 M05 EOB	Spindle stop.
N270 M09 EOB	Coolant-off.
N280 M30 EOB	Program end and tape rewind.

Note:

1. G01 is a modal code. So it remains active until cancelled. Therefore it is not necessary to write G01 from block number N170 to N230. It is written for students in this example.

2. Even if G01 is written in above blocks, it is not incorrect.

3. In N180, as X co-ordinate remains unchanged, so no need to write X-3. (Word address format)

Program 2.10: *Write a part program for the component shown in the Fig. 2.21 (a). Use a 6 mm diameter end mill. The part depth is 3 mm.* [W-12]

- The Z zero (Z0) is at the workpiece top surface.
- The tool path is shown in Fig. 2.21 (b).
- The X and Y co-ordinates of various tool positions are shown in Table 2.12.

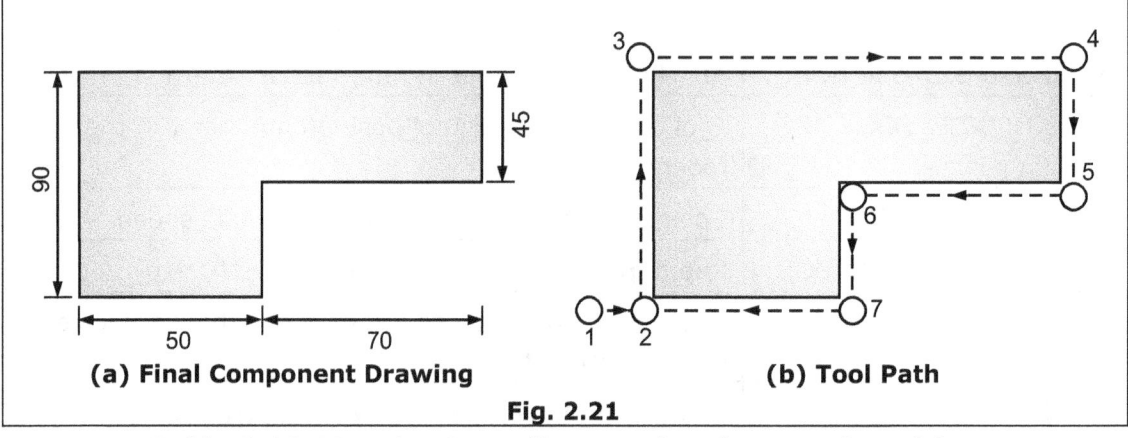

(a) Final Component Drawing   **(b) Tool Path**

Fig. 2.21

Table 2.12: X and Y Co-ordinates of various Tool Position

Position No.	X and Y Co-ordinates	Position No.	X and Y Co-ordinates
1	(−10, −10)	5	(123, 42)
2	(−3, −3)	6	(53, 42)
3	(−3, 93)	7	(53, −3)
4	(123, 93)		

Part Program:

Program	Description
10223	Program number.
N110 G90 G21 G94 EOB	Absolute mode, input in mm, feed in mm/min.
N120 M06 T03 EOB	Tool change, tool at tool position number 3 in the tool magazine.
N130 M03 S800 EOB	Spindle start clockwise direction, spindle speed.
N140 G00 X-10 Y-10 EOB	Rapid travel of cutter to position 1 (−10,−10).

contd. ...

N150 G00 Z5 M08 EOB	Rapid travel of cutter to 5 mm above the workpiece surface, coolant on.
N160 G01 Z-3 F90 EOB	Take required depth of cut with the given feed, so G01.
N170 X-3 Y-3 EOB	Cutter travel to position number 2 (-3,-3).
N180 Y 93 EOB	Cutter travel to position number 3 (-3, 93).
N190 X 123 EOB	Cutter travel to position number 4 (123, 93).
N200 Y42 EOB	Cutter travel to position number 5 (123, 42).
N210 X53 EOB	Cutter travel to position number 6 (53, 42).
N220 Y-3 EOB	Cutter travel to position number 7 (53,-3).
N230 G00 Z5 EOB	Rapid travel of cutter 5 mm above the workpiece surface.
N240 G28 EOB	Rapid return to machine reference position.
N250 M05 EOB	Spindle stop.
N260 M09 EOB	Coolant-off.
N270 M30 EOB	Program end and tape rewind.

Program 2.11: *Write a part program to machine around the outside of the part as shown in the Fig. 2.22 (a). Use a 6 mm diameter end mill. The part depth is 3 mm. Use a feed rate of 120 mm/min.*

Assume: Z datum is at lower left corner of the plate.

- The tool path is shown in Fig. 2.22 (b).
- The X and Y co-ordinates of various tool positions are shown in Table 2.13.

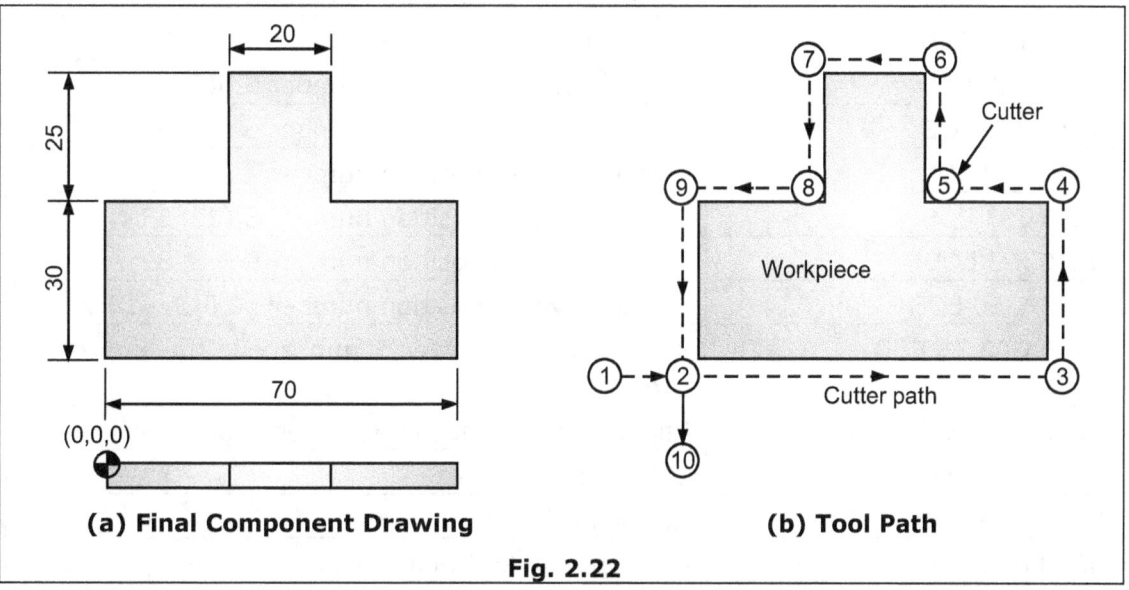

(a) Final Component Drawing   **(b) Tool Path**

Fig. 2.22

Table 2.13: X and Y Co-ordinates of various Tool Position

Position No.	X and Y Co-ordinates	Position No.	X and Y Co-ordinates
1	−10, −3	6	48, 58
2	−3, −3	7	22, 58
3	73, −3	8	22, 33
4	73, 33	9	−3, 33
5	48, 33	10	−3, −10

Part Program:

Program	Description
11224	Program number.
N110 G90 G21 G94 G40 EOB	Absolute mode, input in mm, feed in mm/min, cutter diameter compensation cancel.
N120 M06 T01 EOB	Tool change, tool at tool position number 1 in the tool magazine.
N130 M03 S900 EOB	Spindle start clockwise direction, spindle speed.
N140 G00 Z5 M08 EOB	Rapid travel of cutter to 5 mm (reference position) above the workpiece surface, coolant-on.
N150 G00 X-10 Y-3 EOB	Rapid travel of cutter to position 1 (−10,−3).
N160 G01 Z-3 F120 EOB	Take required depth of cut with the given feed, so G01.
N170 X-3 EOB	Cutter travel to position number 2 (−3, −3).
N180 X73 EOB	Cutter travel to position number 3 (73, −3).
N190 Y33 EOB	Cutter travel to position number 4 (73, 33).
N200 X48 EOB	Cutter travel to position number 5 (48, 33).
N210 Y58 EOB	Cutter travel to position number 6 (48, 58).
N220 X22 EOB	Cutter travel to position number 7 (22, 58).
N230 Y33 EOB	Cutter travel to position number 8 (22, 33).
N240 X-3 EOB	Cutter travel to position number 9 (−3, 33).
N250 Y-10 EOB	Cutter travel to position number 10 (−3, −10).
N260 G00 Z5 EOB	Rapid travel of cutter 5 mm above the workpiece surface.
N270 G28 EOB	Rapid return to machine reference position.
N280 M05 EOB	Spindle stop.
N290 M09 EOB	Coolant-off.
N300 M30 EOB	Program end and tape rewind.

Program 2.12: *Write a part program to machine around the outside of the part as shown in the Fig. 2.23 (a). Use a 4 mm diameter end mill. The part depth is 5 mm.*

Assume: The reference point is 10 mm above the workpiece surface.
* The tool path is shown in Fig. 2.23 (b).
* The X and Y co-ordinates of various tool positions are shown in Table 2.14.

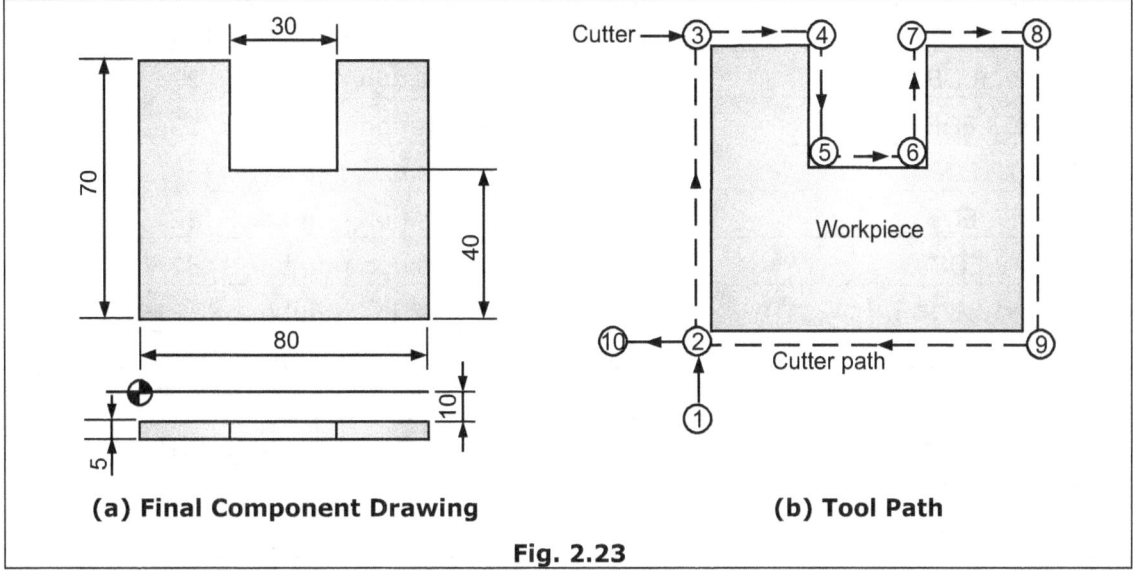

(a) Final Component Drawing   **(b) Tool Path**

Fig. 2.23

Table 2.14: X and Y Co-ordinates of Various Tool Position

Position No.	X and Y Co-ordinates	Position No.	X and Y Co-ordinates
1	−2, −10	6	53, 42
2	−2, −2	7	53, 72
3	−2, 72	8	82, 72
4	27, 72	9	82, −2
5	27, 42	10	−10, −2

Part Program:

Program	Description
12225	Program number.
N110 G90 G21 G94 G40 EOB	Absolute mode, input in mm, feed in mm/min, cutter diameter compensation cancel.
N120 M06 T04 EOB	Tool change, end mill tool at tool position number 4 in the tool magazine.
N130 M03 S800 EOB	Spindle start clockwise direction, spindle speed.
N140 G00 Z0 M08 EOB	Rapid travel of cutter to 10 mm above the workpiece surface, coolant on.

contd. ...

N150 G00 X-2 Y-10 EOB	Rapid travel of cutter to position 1 (−2,−10).
N160 G00 Z-5 F95 EOB	Take required depth of cut of 5 mm.
N170 Y-2 EOB	Cutter travel to position number 2 (−2,−2) with the given feed, so G01.
N180 Y72 EOB	Cutter travel to position number 3 (−2, 72).
N190 X27 EOB	Cutter travel to position number 4 (27, 72).
N200 Y42 EOB	Cutter travel to position number 5 (27, 42).
N210 X53 EOB	Cutter travel to position number 6 (53, 42).
N220 Y72 EOB	Cutter travel to position number 7 (53, 72).
N230 X82 EOB	Cutter travel to position number 8 (82, 72).
N240 Y-2 EOB	Cutter travel to position number 9 (82,−2).
N250 X-10 EOB	Cutter travel to position number 10 (−10, −2).
N260 G00 Z10 EOB	Rapid travel of cutter 10 mm above the work-piece surface.
N270 G28 EOB	Rapid return to machine reference position.
N280 M05 EOB	Spindle stop.
N290 M09 EOB	Coolant-off.
N300 M30 EOB	Program end and tape rewind.

Program 2.13: *Write a part program for the job shown in Fig. 2.24 (a).*

Data: The reference point is at the top surface of the workpiece surface. A 4 mm diameter end mill is used. The part depth is 3 mm. The tool path is shown in Fig. 2.24 (b). The X and Y co-ordinates of various tool positions are shown in Table 2.15.

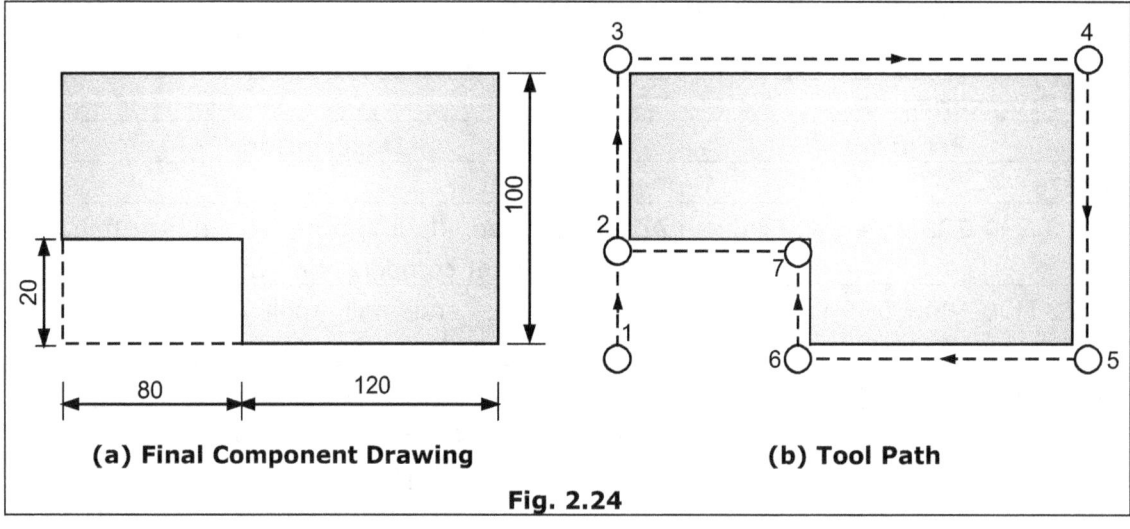

(a) Final Component Drawing   **(b) Tool Path**

Fig. 2.24

Table 2.15: X and Y Co-ordinates of Various Tool Position

Position No.	X and Y Co-ordinates	Position No.	X and Y Co-ordinates
1	−2, −10	5	202, −2
2	−2, 18	6	78, −2
3	−2, 102	7	78, 18
4	202, 102		

Part Program:

Program	Description
13226	Program number.
N110 G90 G21 G94 G40 EOB	Absolute mode, input in mm, feed in mm/min, cutter diameter compensation cancel.
N120 M06 T08 EOB	Tool change, end mill tool at tool position number 8 in the tool magazine.
N130 M03 S900 EOB	Spindle start clockwise direction, spindle speed.
N140 G00 Z5 M08 EOB	Rapid travel of cutter to 5 mm above the workpiece surface, coolant on.
N150 G00 X-2 Y-10 EOB	Rapid travel of cutter to position 1 (−2, −10).
N160 G00 Z-3 F95 EOB	Take required depth of cut of 3 mm.
N170 Y18 EOB	Cutter travel to position number 2 (−2, 18) with the given feed, so G01.
N180 Y102 EOB	Cutter travel to position number 3 (−2, 102).
N190 X202 EOB	Cutter travel to position number 4 (202, 102).
N200 Y-2 EOB	Cutter travel to position number 5 (202, −2).
N210 X78 EOB	Cutter travel to position number 6 (78, −2).
N220 Y18 EOB	Cutter travel to position number 7 (78, 18).
N230 X-2 EOB	Cutter travel to position number 2(−2, 18).
N240 G00 Z5 EOB	Rapid travel of cutter 5 mm above the workpiece surface.
N250 G28 EOB	Rapid return to machine reference position.
N260 M05 EOB	Spindle stop.
N270 M09 EOB	Coolant-off.
N280 M30 EOB	Program end and tape rewind.

2.19 PART PROGRAM FOR MACHINING ALONG CURVED SURFACE

- When curved surfaces are to be machined then the preparatory codes G02 and G03 are used. There are two basic methods used to program circular path.
  - Center point programming (I J method). (Arc Vector method).
  - Radius programming.

2.19.1 Center Point Programming

- When circular interpolation is performed, the following information is necessary.
  - (i) Arc direction or direction of cutter travel.
  - (ii) Arc start point.
  - (iii) Arc center point.
  - (iv) Arc end point.

(i) Arc Direction or Direction of Cutter Travel:

- Based on whether G02 or G03 code is used, the arc direction will be clockwise or counterclockwise respectively as shown in the Fig 2.25 (a).

- Both G02 and G03 are modal codes and are controlled by a feed rate function (F-word), just like G01.

- These codes must be programmed in the block of information where circular interpolation starts.

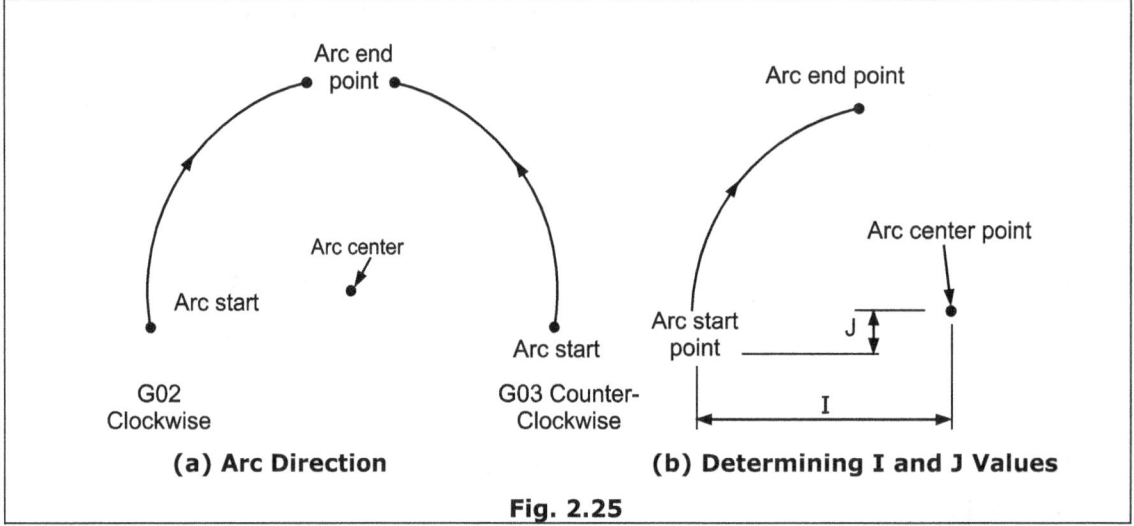

(a) Arc Direction   **(b) Determining I and J Values**

Fig. 2.25

(ii) Arc Start Point:

- The start point of the arc is usually the end point of linear line or the end point of a previous arc. The cutting tool starts machining from the start point.

(iii) Arc Center Point:

- The center point of the arc is the center of the circle or arc. The center point is described by I, J and K words. These words are incremental values regardless of whether they have been programmed in the absolute or incremental mode.
- The I, J and K values are taken as shown in Fig 2.25 (b).

  > I value = Horizontal distance (X-co-ordinate) from the arc start point to the arc center point.

  > J value = Vertical distance (Y-co-ordinate) from the arc start point to the arc center point.

- As in milling, the arc is machined (cut) along two axes (X and Y) only, therefore K value is not required.
- The distance and direction for I and J values is always taken **from the start** of the arc **to the center** of the arc.
- If the arc center point is located above (+J) or to the right (+I) of the start point, a positive sign must be used for I and J values.
- If the arc center point is located below (−J) or to the left (−I) of the start point, a negative sign (−) must be used for I and J values.
- The method to determine the I and J values and their sign is shown in Fig. 2.26.
- In Fig. 2.26 (a) center point is to the right of start point so I is +10 and as center point is below the start point so J is − 4. Similarly Figs. 2.26 (b) to (f) are self explanatory.

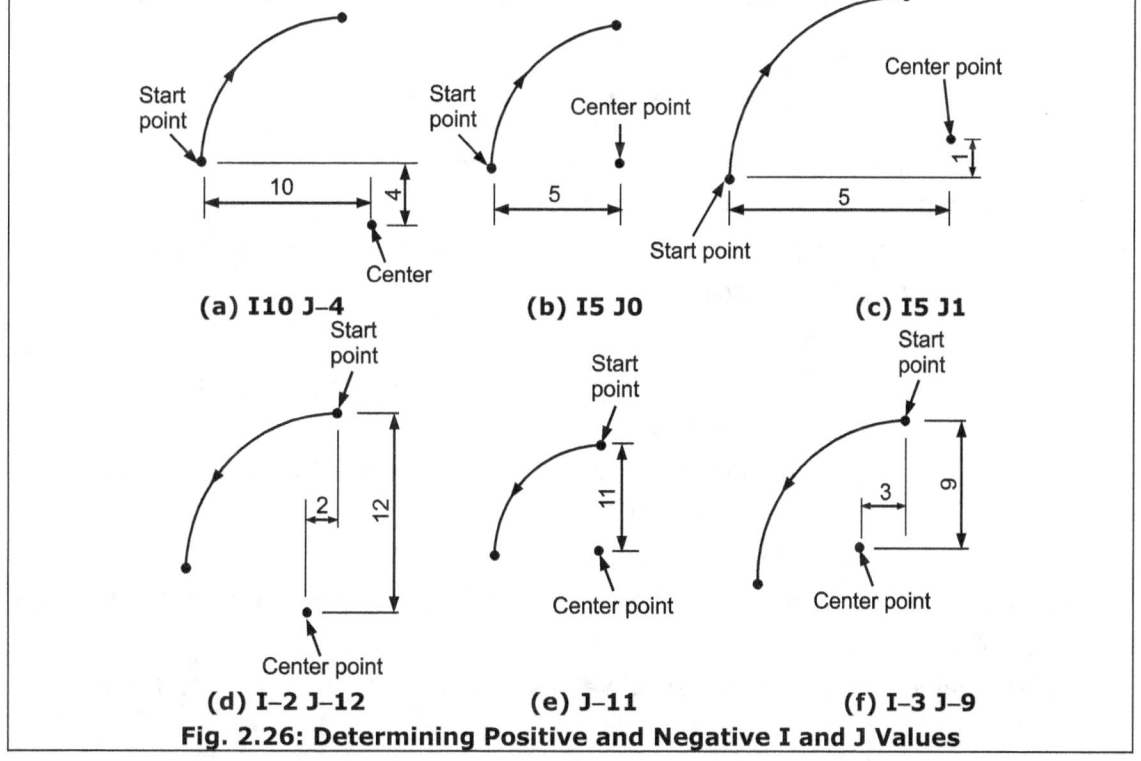

Fig. 2.26: Determining Positive and Negative I and J Values

(iv) Arc End Point:

- o It is the co-ordinate position for the end point of the arc. When machining is carried out, then with G02 or G03 code the arc end point is given and not the start point.
- o The G02 or G03 block is shown in the Fig. 2.27 and is written as below:

  For example,   N110 G02 X_F Y_F I_ J_ F_ EOB

  For example,   N210 G03 X_F Y_F I_ J_ F_ EOB

  X_F = X-co-ordinate of the arc end point.

  Y_F = Y-co-ordinate of the arc end point.

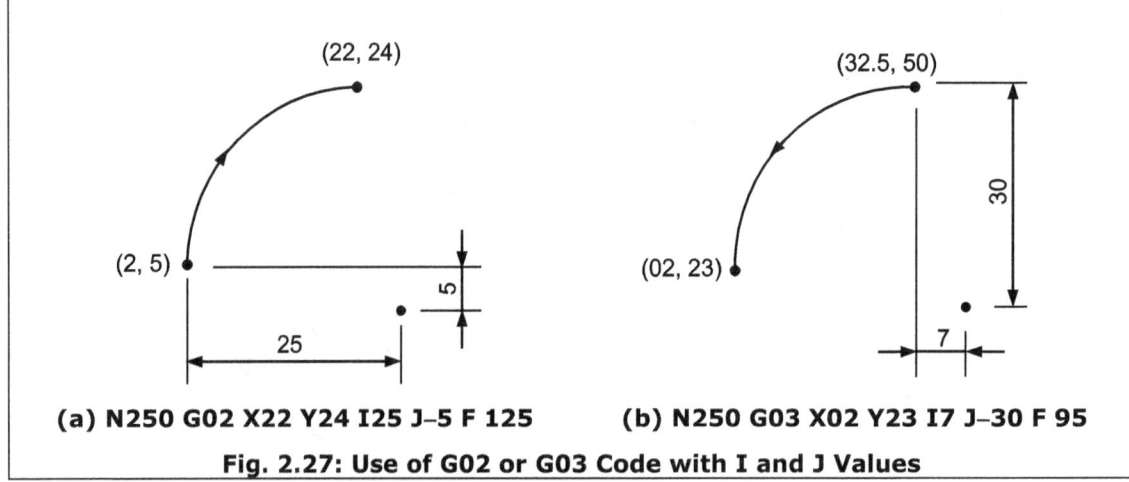

(a) N250 G02 X22 Y24 I25 J–5 F 125   **(b) N250 G03 X02 Y23 I7 J–30 F 95**

Fig. 2.27: Use of G02 or G03 Code with I and J Values

2.19.2 Radius Programming

- If circular interpolation is programmed using radius value, the value of radius is required to be given with G02 or G03 code.
- The format for radius programming is shown in Fig. 2.28 and is written as:

  N50 G02 X_ Y_ R_ F_ EOB

  N100 G03 X_ Y_ R_ F_ EOB

  X = Distance from start point of the arc to the end point of the arc in X direction.

  Y = Distance from start point of the arc to the end point of the arc in Y direction.

  R = Value of radius of the arc.

Note: If arc is more than 180° then R is positive and if arc is less than 180° then R is negative.

X and Y values are the incremental values from the arc start point to the arc end point.

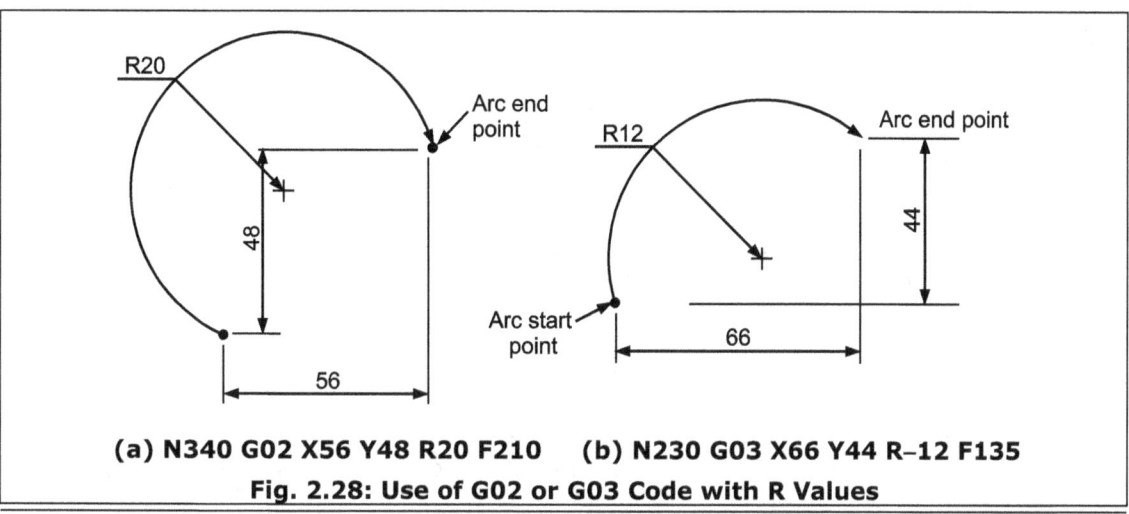

(a) N340 G02 X56 Y48 R20 F210   (b) N230 G03 X66 Y44 R–12 F135

Fig. 2.28: Use of G02 or G03 Code with R Values

Program 2.14: *Write a part program to machine around the outside of the part as shown in the Fig. 2.29 (a). Use a 5 mm diameter end mill. The part depth is 3 mm. Use a feed rate of 100 mm/min.*

Assume: The Z reference is 5 mm above the workpiece surface.

- The tool path is shown in Fig. 2.29 (b).
- The X and Y co-ordinates of various tool positions are shown in Table 2.16.

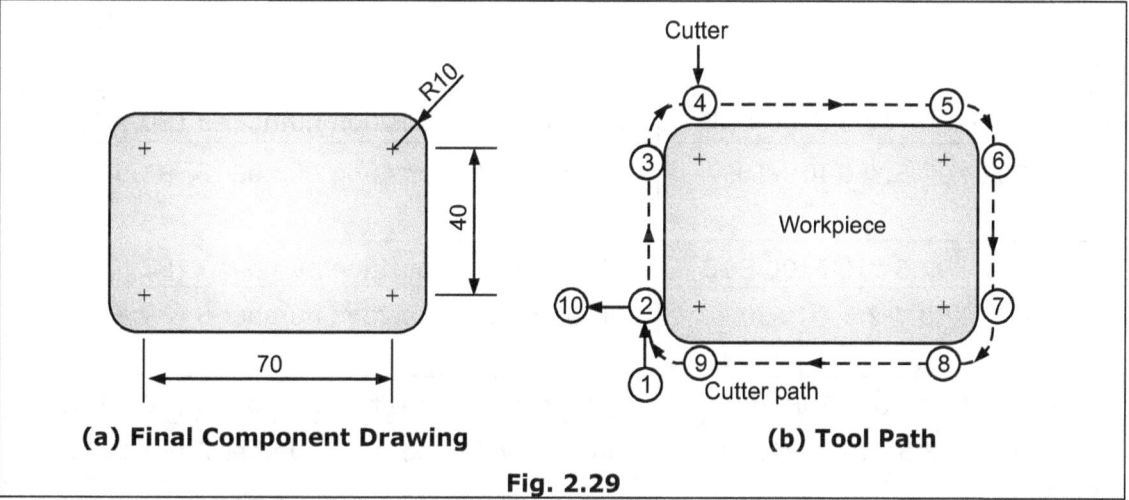

(a) Final Component Drawing   **(b) Tool Path**

Fig. 2.29

Table 2.16: X and Y Co-ordinates of Various Tool Position

Position No.	X and Y Co-ordinates	Position No.	X and Y Co-ordinates
1	−2.5, −10	6	92.5, 50
2	−2.5, 10	7	92.5, 10
3	−2.5, 50	8	80, −2.5
4	10, 62.5	9	10, −2.5
5	80, 62.5	10	−20, 10

Part Program:

Program	Description
14232	Program number.
N10 G90 G21 G94 G40 EOB	Absolute mode, input in mm, feed in mm/min, cutter diameter compensation cancel.
N20 M06 T01 EOB	Tool change, tool at tool position number 1 in the tool magazine.
N30 M03 S800 EOB	Spindle start clockwise direction, spindle speed.
N40 G00 X-2.5 Y-10 EOB	Rapid travel of cutter to position 1 (−2.5,−10).
N50 M08 EOB	Coolant-on.
N60 G00 Z-3 EOB	Take required depth of cut of 3 mm.
N70 G01X-2.5 Y10 F100 EOB	Cutter travel to position number 2 (−2.5, 10) with the given feed, so G01.
N80 Y50 EOB	Cutter travel to position number 3 (−2.5, 50).
N90 G02 X10 Y62.5 I10 J0 F90 EOB	Cutter travel to position number 4 (10, 62.5).
N100 G01 X80 Y62.5 F100 EOB	Cutter travel to position number 5 (80, 62.5).
N110 G02 X92.5 Y50 I0 J-10 F90 EOB	Cutter travel to position number 6 (92.5, 50).
N120 G01 X92.5 Y10 F100 EOB	Cutter travel to position number 7 (92.5, 10).
N130 G02 X80 Y-2.5 I-10 J0 F90 EOB	Cutter travel to position number 8 (80,−2.5).
N140 G01 X10 F100 EOB	Cutter travel to position number 9 (10,−2.5).
N150 G02 X-2.5 Y10 I0 J10 F90 EOB	Cutter travel to position number 2 (−2.5, 10).
N160 G00 X-20 Y5 EOB	Rapid travel to position number 10 (−20, 10).
N170 G00 Z5 EOB	Rapid travel of cutter 5 mm above the workpiece surface.
N180 G28 EOB	Rapid return to machine reference position.
N190 M05 EOB	Spindle stop.
N200 M09 EOB	Coolant-off.
N210 M30 EOB	Program end and tape rewind.

Program 2.15: *Write a part program to machine around the outside of the part as shown in the Fig. 2.30 (a). The part depth is 3 mm. The Z reference is at the workpiece surface.*

Assume: Use a 5 mm diameter end mill.

o The tool path is shown in Fig. 2.30 (b).

o The X and Y co-ordinates of various tool positions are shown in Table 2.17.

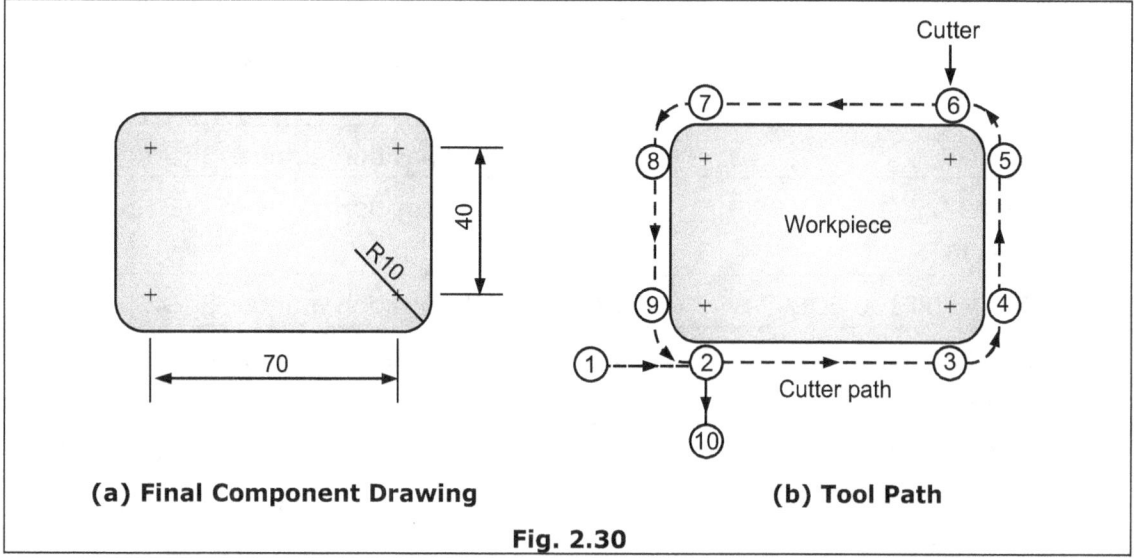

(a) Final Component Drawing   **(b) Tool Path**

Fig. 2.30

Table 2.17: X and Y Co-ordinates of Various Tool Position

Position No.	X and Y Co-ordinates	Position No.	X and Y Co-ordinates
1	−20, −2.5	6	80, 62.5
2	10, −2.5	7	10, 62.5
3	80, −2.5	8	−2.5, 50
4	92.5, 10	9	−2.5, 10
5	92.5, 50	10	10, −20

Part Program:

Program	Description
15233	Program number.
N10 G90 G21 G94 G40 EOB	Absolute mode, input in mm, feed in mm/min, cutter diameter compensation cancel.
N20 M06 T02 EOB	Tool change, tool at tool position number 2 in the tool magazine.

***contd.* ...**

N30 M03 S800 EOB	Spindle start clockwise direction, spindle speed.
N40 G00 X-20 Y-2.5 EOB	Rapid travel of cutter to position 1 (−20, −2.5).
N50 G00 Z-3 EOB	Rapid travel of cutter to −3 mm as depth of cut.
N60 M08 EOB	Coolant-on.
N70 G01 X10 Y-2. F100 EOB	Cutter travel to position number 2 (10, −2.5) with the given feed, so G01.
N80 X80 EOB	Cutter travel to position number 3 (80, −2.5).
N90 G03 X92.5 Y10 I0 J10 F90 EOB	Cutter travel to position number 4 (92.5, 10).
N100 G01 Y50 F100 EOB	Cutter travel to position number 5 (92.5, 50).
N110 G03 X80 Y62.5 I-10 J0 F90 EOB	Cutter travel to position number 6 (80, 62.5).
N120 G01 X10 F100 EOB	Cutter travel to position number 7 (10, 62.5).
N130 G03 X-2.5 Y50 I0 J-10 F90 EOB	Cutter travel to position number 8 (−2.5, 50).
N140 G01 Y10 F100 EOB	Cutter travel to position number 9 (−2.5, 10).
N150 G03 X10 Y-2.5 I10 J0 F90 EOB	Cutter travel to position number 2 (10, −2.5).
N160 G00 X10 Y-20 EOB	Rapid travel to position number 10 (10, −20).
N170 G00 Z5 EOB	Rapid travel of cutter 5 mm above the workpiece surface.
N180 G28 EOB	Rapid return to machine reference position.
N190 M05 EOB	Spindle stop.
N200 M09 EOB	Coolant-off.
N210 M30 EOB	Program end and tape rewind.

Program 2.16: *Prepare a part program for the given job as shown in Fig 2.31. Use following machining data:*

Speed = 800 rpm
Feed = 10 mm/min
Depth of cut = 3 mm
Thickness of job = 3 mm

Assume: Use a 6 mm diameter end mill. The Z reference is at the workpiece surface. The tool path is shown in Fig. 2.31. The X and Y co-ordinates of various tool positions are shown in Table 2.18.

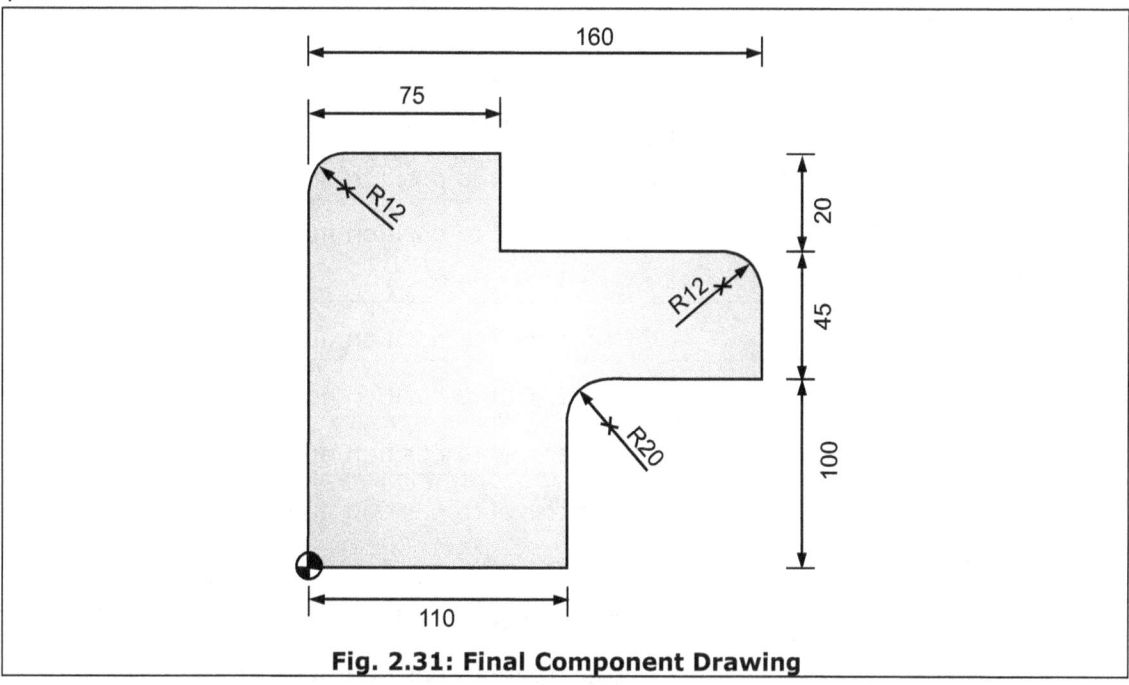

Fig. 2.31: Final Component Drawing

Table 2.18: X and Y Co-ordinates of Various Tool Position

Position No.	X and Y Co-ordinates	Position No.	X and Y Co-ordinates
1	−10, −3	7	148, 148
2	−3, −3	8	163, 142
3	−3, 145	9	163, 97
4	12, 168	10	133, 97
5	78, 168	11	113, 80
6	78, 148	12	113, −3

Part Program:

Program	Description
16234	Program number.
N20 G90 G21 G9 EOB	Absolute mode, input in mm, feed in mm/min.
N30 M06 T01 EOB	Tool change, tool at tool position number 1 in the tool magazine.
N40 M03 S800 EOB	Spindle start clockwise direction, spindle speed.

contd. ...

N50 G00 X-10 Y-3 EOB	Rapid travel of cutter to position 1 (−10, −3).
N60 G00 Z-3 EOB	Rapid travel of cutter to −3 mm as depth of cut.
N70 M08 EOB	Coolant-on.
N80 G01 X-3 F10 EOB	Cutter travel to position number 2 (−3, −3) with the given feed, so G01.
N90 Y145 EOB	Cutter travel to position number 3 (−3, 145).
N100 G02 X12 Y168 I10 J0 F10 EOB	Cutter travel to position number 4 (12, 168).
N110 G01 X78 F10 EOB	Cutter travel to position number 5 (78, 168).
N120 Y148 EOB	Cutter travel to position number 6 (78, 148).
N130 X148 EOB	Cutter travel to position number 7 (148, 148).
N140 G02 X163 Y142 I0 J-10 F10 EOB	Cutter travel to position number 8 (163, 142).
N150 G01 Y97 F100 EOB	Cutter travel to position number 9 (163, 97).
N160 X133 EOB	Cutter travel to position number 10 (133, 97).
N170 G02 X113 Y80 I0 J-10 EOB	Cutter travel to position number 11 (113, 80).
N 180 G01 Y-3 F10 EOB	Cutter travel to position number 12 (113, −3).
N 190 X113 F10 EOB	Cutter travel to position number 2 (−3, −3).
N200 G00 Z5 EOB	Rapid travel of cutter 5 mm above the workpiece surface.
N210 G28 EOB	Rapid return to machine reference position.
N220 M05 EOB	Spindle stop.
N230 M09 EOB	Coolant-off.
N240 M30 EOB	Program end and tape rewind.

Program 2.17: *Calculate the co-ordinates for various points and complete the program for the Fig. 2.32 (a) milling part. Workpiece size is X 100 Y 110 Z6. Use a 12.5 mm end mill.*

Assume: Feed rate of 110 mm/min for linear interpolation and 90 mm/min for circular interpolation. The tool path is shown in Fig. 2.32 (b). The X and Y co-ordinates of various tool positions are shown in Table 2.19.

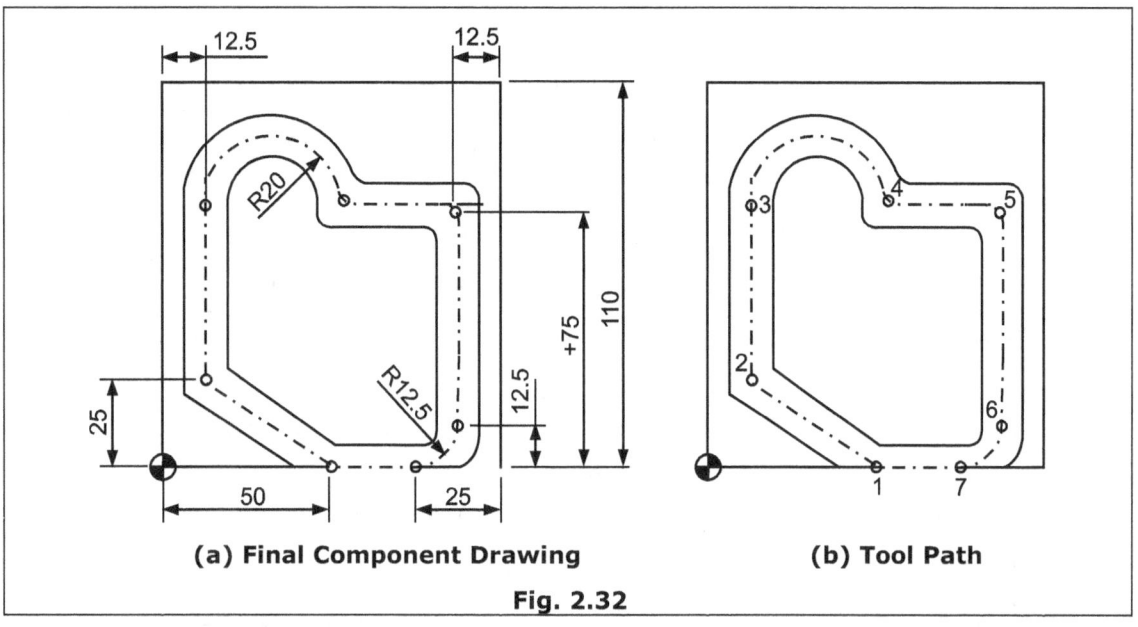

(a) Final Component Drawing   (b) Tool Path

Fig. 2.32

Table 2.19: X and Y Co-ordinates of Various Tool Position

Position No.	X and Y Co-ordinates	Position No.	X and Y Co-ordinates
1	50, 0	5	87.5, 75
2	12.5, 25	6	87.5, 12.5
3	12.5, 75	7	75, 0
4	62.5, 75		

Program	Description
17235	Program number.
N20 G90 G21 G94 G40 EOB	Absolute mode, input in mm, feed in mm/min, cutter diameter compensation cancel.
N30 M06 T08 EOB	Tool change, tool at tool position number 8 in the tool magazine.
N40 M03 S950 EOB	Spindle start clockwise direction, spindle speed.
N50 G00 X50 Y0 EOB	Cutter moved to position 1 (50, 0).
N60 G00 Z3 M08 EOB	Rapid travel of cutter to 3 mm above the workpiece surface, coolant on.
N70 G01 Z-6 F80 EOB	Take required depth of cut with the given feed, so G01.

contd. ...

N80 G01 X12.5 Y25 F110 EOB	Cutter travel to position number 2 (12.5, 25).
N90 G01 Y75 EOB	Cutter travel to position number 3 (12.5, 75).
N100 G02 X162.5 Y75 I20 J0 F90 EOB	Cutter travel to position number 4 (62.5, 75).
N110 G01 X87.5 F110 EOB	Cutter travel to position number 5 (87.5, 75).
N120 G01 Y12.5 EOB	Cutter travel to position number 6 (87.5, 12.5).
N130 G02 X75 Y0 I-12.5 J0 F90 EOB	Cutter travel to position number 7 (75, 0).
N140 G00 Z5 EOB	Rapid travel of cutter 5 mm above the workpiece surface.
N150 G28 EOB	Rapid return to machine reference position.
N160 M05 EOB	Spindle stop.
N170 M09 EOB	Coolant-off.
N180 M30 EOB	Program end and tape rewind.

2.20 CUTTER RADIUS COMPENSATION

[S-10, W-10, W-12, S-13]

- It is also called as cutter offset by some controller manufacturer.
- A workpiece is machined by the periphery of the cutting tool and not by the center of the cutter (tool tip).
- A part program has to be developed for the exact size of the cutter to be used on the machine.
- But during actual machining, if a smaller diameter cutter is selected, it will result in a larger workpiece.
- Similarly a larger diameter cutter will result in smaller workpiece.
- It is therefore necessary to compensate for the different diameter cutter by using cutter radius compensation.
- When cutter compensation is used, the cutter diameter can be ignored and the tool path can be developed for the center line of the tool rather than the point on the periphery.
- Compensation is done by offsetting the tool path by the distance equal to the radius of the cutter.
- This value is entered into the memory of the control system under the address D01 or D02 etc.
- When the offset file is called, the tool path will automatically be offset by the tool radius.

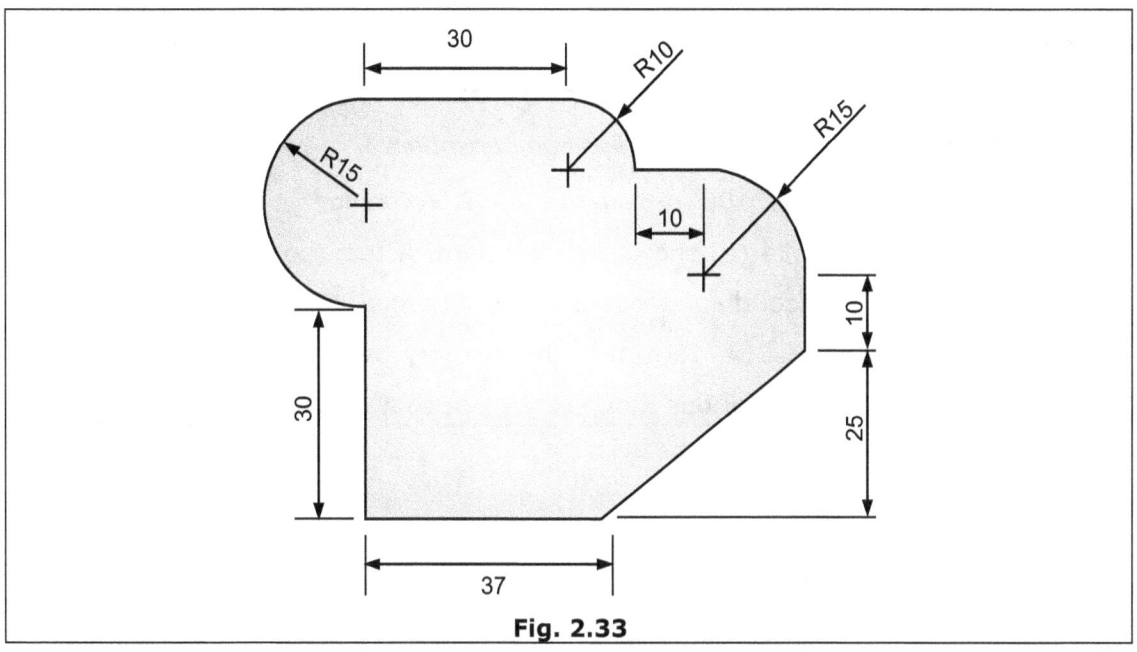

Fig. 2.33

- For any change in the cutter diameter, this offset can be changed. There is no need to make any change in the part program.

- Cutter compensation can be made to the right or to the left of the part to be machined. The direction in which the cutter path has to be shifted is decided by the direction of cut. For example in Fig. 2.33, the direction of cut is clockwise so compensation should be provided to shift the cutter path towards left. Because shifting the cutter path towards right would result in a small size workpiece.

- Similarly, if the direction of cut is counterclockwise, the compensation should be applied to shift the center path towards right from the part profile.

- Cutter compensation direction is controlled by G-code. The following three G-codes are used for cutter radius compensation.

    o G-40 Cutter compensation cancel.

    o G-41 Compensation applied to shift the programmed cutter path to left.

    o G-42 Compensation applied to shift the programmed cutter path to right.

- The format of cutter compensation will look like -- N050 G41 D01 EOB.

2.20.1 Advantages of Cutter Radius Compensation

(i) Cutter path need not be calculated mathematically.

(ii) The same program can be used for cutter of any diameter.

(iii) The part program can be developed using the cutter radius as zero i.e. on the actual drawing dimensions of the component.

(iv) The programmer job is simplified.

Program 2.18: *Write the co-ordinates for various points and complete a part program to machine around the outside of the part as shown in the Fig. 2.34 (a). The part depth is 3 mm. Use cutter radius compensation.*

Assume: Feed rate is 100 mm/min. The Z reference is 5 mm above the workpiece surface. Fig. 2.34 (b) shows the tool path. Actual tool (end mill) diameter is 10 mm. Programmed tool diameter is 0. i.e. programming is done as per the part drawing. Store D01 = 0 – 5 = – 5 mm in the memory before running the program. The X and Y co-ordinates of various tool position are shown in table 2.20.

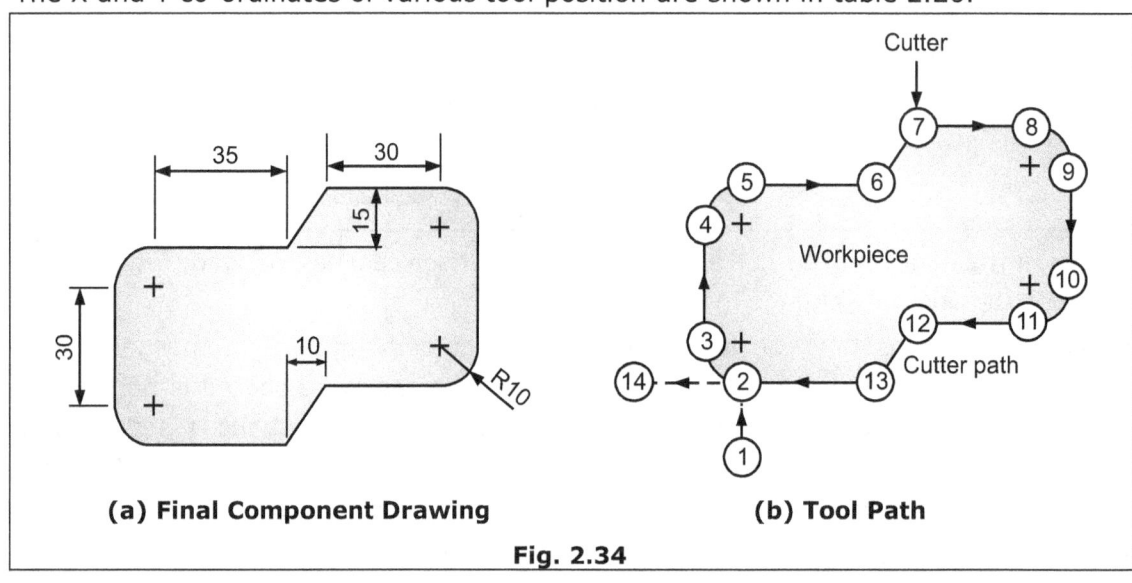

(a) **Final Component Drawing**   (b) **Tool Path**

Fig. 2.34

Table 2.20: X and Y Co-ordinates of various Tool Position

Position No.	X and Y Co-ordinates	Position No.	X and Y Co-ordinates
1	10, –20	8	85, 65
2	10, 0	9	95, 55
3	0, 10	10	95, 25
4	0, 40	11	85, 10
5	10, 50	12	55, 10
6	45, 50	13	45, 0
7	55, 65	14	–15, 0

Part Program:

Program	Description
21241	Program number.
N20 G90 G21 G94 G40 EOB	Absolute mode, input in mm, feed in mm/min, cutter diameter compensation cancel.
N30 M06 T03 EOB	Tool change, tool at tool position number 3 in the tool magazine.
N40 M03 S1100 EOB	Spindle start clockwise direction, spindle speed.
N50 G41 D01 EOB	Cutter diameter compensation left by amount found in D01.
N60 G00 X10 Y–20 EOB	Rapid travel of cutter to position 1 (10, –20).
N70 Z0 M08 EOB	Rapid travel of cutter to 5 mm above the workpiece surface, coolant on.
N80 G01 Z–3 F100 EOB	Take required depth of cut with the given feed, so G01.
N90 G01 X10 Y0 F100 EOB	Cutter travel to position number 2 (10, 0).
N100 G02 X–5 Y10 I0 J10 F90 EOB	Cutter travel to position number 3 (0, 10).
N110 G01 Y40 F100 EOB	Cutter travel to position number 4 (0, 40).
N120 G02 X10 Y55 I10 J0 F90 EOB	Cutter travel to position number 5 (10, 50).
N130 G01 X45 F100 EOB	Cutter travel to position number 6 (45, 50).
N140 X55 Y70 F95 EOB	Cutter travel to position number 7 (55, 65).
N150 X8 F100 EOB	Cutter travel to position number 8 (85, 65).
N160 G02 X100 Y55 I0 J–10 F90 EOB	Cutter travel to position number 9 (95, 55).
N170 G01 Y25 F100 EOB	Cutter travel to position number 10 (95, 25)
N180 G02 X85 Y10 I–10 J0 F90 EOB	Cutter travel to position number 11 (85, 10).
N190 G01 X55 F100 EOB	Cutter travel to position number 12 (55, 10).
N200 X45 Y–5 F100 EOB	Cutter travel to position number 13 (45, 0).

***contd.* ...**

N210 X–15 EOB	Cutter travel to position number 14 (–15, 0).
N220 G00 Z10 EOB	Rapid travel of cutter 10 mm above the workpiece surface.
N230 G40 EOB	Cutter compensation cancel.
N240 G28 EOB	Rapid return to machine reference position.
N250 M05 EOB	Spindle stop.
N260 M09 EOB	Coolant-off.
N270 M30 EOB	Program end and tape rewind.

Program 2.19: *Write a part program to machine around the outside of the part as shown in the Fig. 2.35 (a). Use an 8 mm diameter end mill. The part depth is 4 mm. Use a feed rate of 110 mm/min. Use cutter radius compensation. The Z 0 is at the top of the workpiece surface.*

Assume: Actual tool (end mill) diameter is 08 mm. Programmed tool diameter is 0. i.e. programming is done as per the part drawing. Store D01 = 0 – 4 = – 4 mm in the memory before running the program. The tool path is shown in Fig. 2.35 (b) and the X and Y co-ordinates of various tool positions are shown in table 2.21.

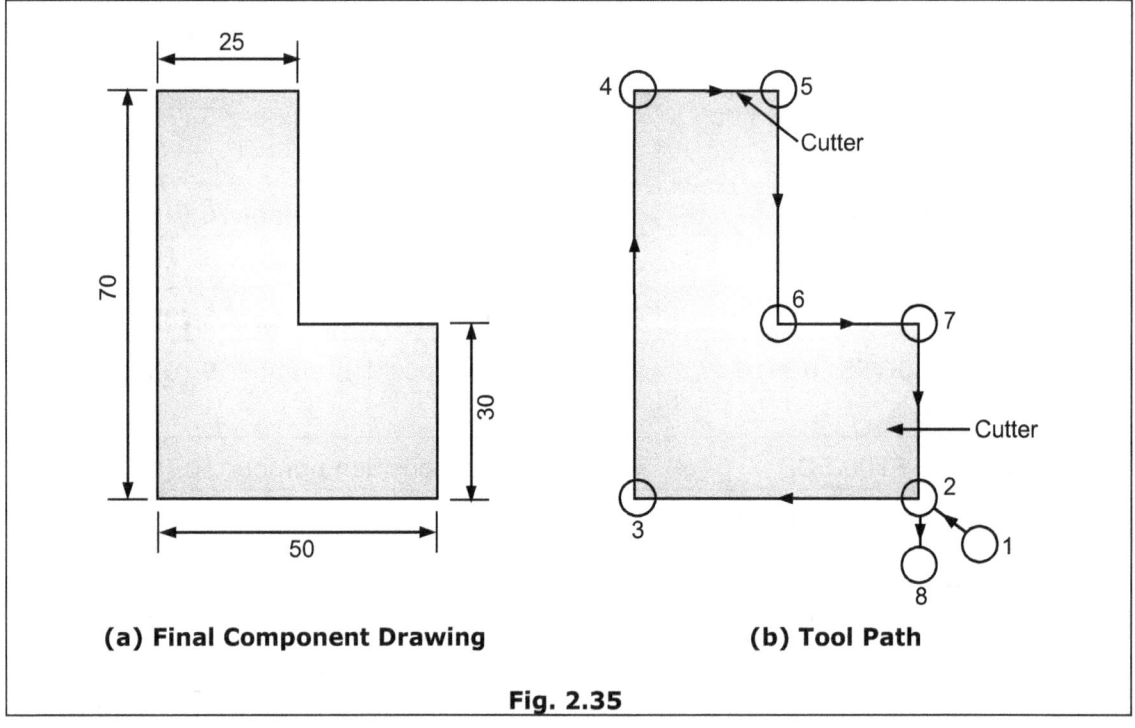

(a) Final Component Drawing   (b) Tool Path

Fig. 2.35

Table 2.21: X and Y Co-ordinates of Various Tool Positions

Position No.	X and Y Co-ordinates	Position No.	X and Y Co-ordinates
1	60, −10	5	25, 70
2	50, 0	6	25, 30
3	0, 0	7	50, 30
4	0, 70	8	50, −15

Part Program:

Program	Description
08222	Program number.
N110 G90 G21 G94 G40 EOB	Absolute mode, input in mm, feed in mm/min, cutter diameter compensation cancel.
N120 M06 T03 EOB	Tool change, tool at tool position number 3 in the tool magazine.
N130 M03 S800 EOB	Spindle start clockwise direction, spindle speed.
N140 G00 X60 Y−10 EOB	Rapid travel of cutter to position 1 (60, −10).
N150 G00 Z5 M08 EOB	Rapid travel of cutter to 5 mm above the workpiece surface, coolant-on.
N160 G00 Z-4 EOB	Take required depth of cut.
N170 G41 D01 EOB	Cutter diameter compensation left by amount found in D01.
N175 G01 X50 Y0 F110 EOB	Cutter travel to position number 2 (50, 0) with the required feed G01.
N180 X0 EOB	Cutter travel to position number 3 (0, 0).
N190 Y70 EOB	Cutter travel to position number 4 (0, 70).
N200 X25 EOB	Cutter travel to position number 5 (25, 70).
N210 Y30 EOB	Cutter travel to position number 6 (25, 30).
N220 X50 EOB	Cutter travel to position number 7 (50, 30).
N230 Y−10	Cutter travel to position number 8 (50, −15).
N240 G00 Z5	Rapid travel of cutter 5 mm above the workpiece surface.
N250 G40 EOB	Cutter compensation cancel.
N260 G28 EOB	Rapid return to machine reference position.
N270 M05 EOB	Spindle stop.
N280 M09 EOB	Coolant-off.
N290 M30 EOB	Program end and tape rewind.

Program 2.20: *Write a part program to machine around the outside of the part as shown in the Fig. 2.36 (a). Use a 5 mm diameter end mill. The part thickness is 4 mm. Use cutter radius compensation. Zero datum is at 5 mm above the workpiece surface at the lower left corner of the workpiece.*

Assume: Actual tool (end mill) diameter is 5 mm. Programmed tool diameter is 0. i.e. programming is done as per the part drawing.

Store D01 = 0 – 2.5 = – 2.5 mm in the memory before running the program. The computer generated tool path is shown in Fig. 2.36 (b) and the various tool positions of X and Y co-ordinates are given in table 2.22.

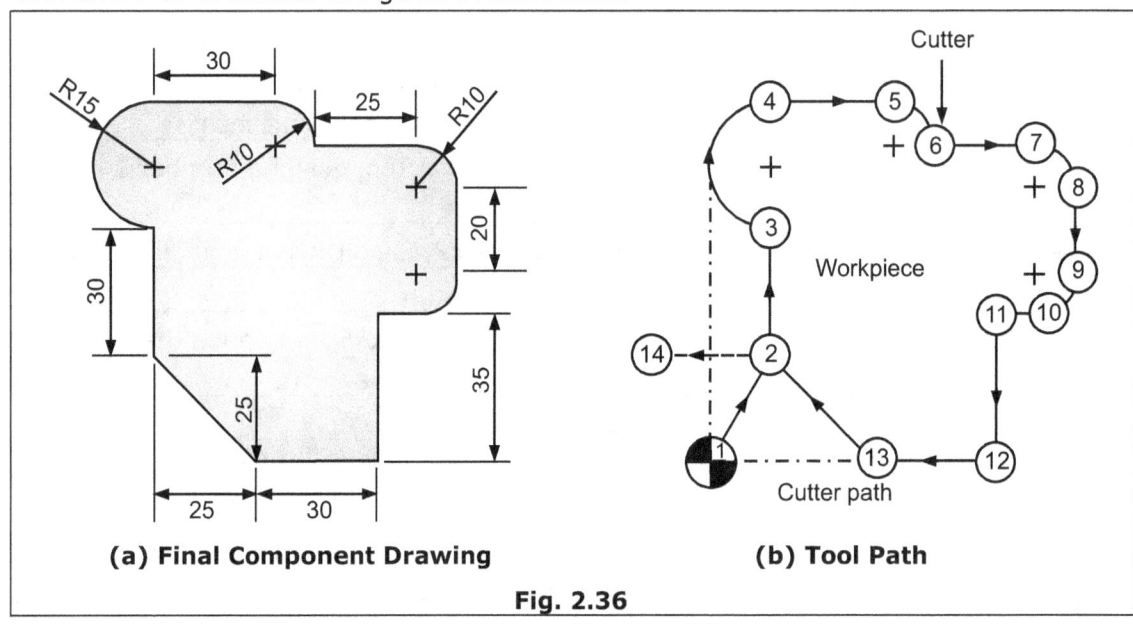

(a) Final Component Drawing   (b) Tool Path

Fig. 2.36

Table 2.22: X and Y Co-ordinates of Various Tool Position

Position No.	X and Y Co-ordinates	Position No.	X and Y Co-ordinates
1	0, 0	8	90, 65
2	15, 25	9	90, 45
3	15, 55	10	80, 35
4	15, 85	11	70, 35
5	45, 85	12	70, 00
6	55, 75	13	40, 00
7	80, 75	14	–10, 25

Part Program:

Program	Description
23243	Program number.
N110 G90 G21 G94 G40 EOB	Absolute mode, input in mm, feed in mm/min, cutter diameter compensation cancel.
N120 M06 T04 EOB	Tool change, tool at tool position number 4 in the tool magazine.
N130 M03 S800 EOB	Spindle start clockwise direction, spindle speed.
N140 G00 X0 Y0 EOB	Rapid travel of cutter to position 1 (0, 0).
N150 G00 Z0 M08 EOB	Rapid travel of cutter to 5 mm above the workpiece surface (i.e. at 0, 0, 0) coolant-on.
N160 G00 Z-4 EOB	Take required depth of cut with the rapid feed, so G00.
N170 G41 D01 G01 X15 Y25 F110 EOB	Cutter diameter compensation left by amount found in D01, cutter travel to position number 2 (15, 25).
N180 Y55 EOB	Cutter travel to position number 3 (15, 55).
N190 G02 Y85 I0 J15 EOB	Cutter travel to position number 4 (15, 85).
N200 G01 X45 EOB	Cutter travel to position number 5 (45, 85).
N210 G02 X55 Y75 I0 J–10 EOB	Cutter travel to position number 6 (55, 75).
N220 G01 X80 EOB	Cutter travel to position number 7 (80, 75).
N230 G02 X90 Y65 I0 J–10 EOB	Cutter travel to position number 8 (90, 65).
N240 G01 Y45 EOB	Cutter travel to position number 9 (90, 45).
N250 G02 X80 Y35 I–10 J0 EOB	Cutter travel to position number 10 (80, 35).
N260 G01 X40 EOB	Cutter travel to position number 11 (70, 35).
N270 G01 Y00 EOB	Cutter travel to position number 12 (70, 00).
N280 G01 X40 EOB	Cutter travel to position number 13 (40, 00).
N290 G01 X15 Y25 EOB	Cutter travel to position number 2 (15, 25).
N300 G01 X–10 EOB	Cutter travel to position number 14 (–10, 25).
N310 G00 Z5 EOB	Rapid travel of cutter 5 mm above the workpiece surface.
N320 G40 EOB	Cutter compensation cancel.
N330 G28 EOB	Rapid return to machine reference position.
N340 M05 EOB	Spindle stop.
N350 M09 EOB	Coolant-off.
N360 M30 EOB	Program end and tape rewind.

Program 2.21: *Write a part program for the job shown in Fig. 2.37 (A) (a) Using cutter radius compensation as given below. Programmed cutter diameter = 0 mm. Diameter of cutter available = 28 mm.*   [W-11]

Data: Actual tool (end mill) diameter is 28 mm. Programmed tool diameter is 0. i.e. programming is done as per the part drawing.

Store D01 = (0 – 28)/2 = – 14 mm in the memory before running the program. The computer generated tool path is shown in Fig. 2.37 (A) (b) and the various tool positions of X and Y co-ordinates are given in table 2.23.

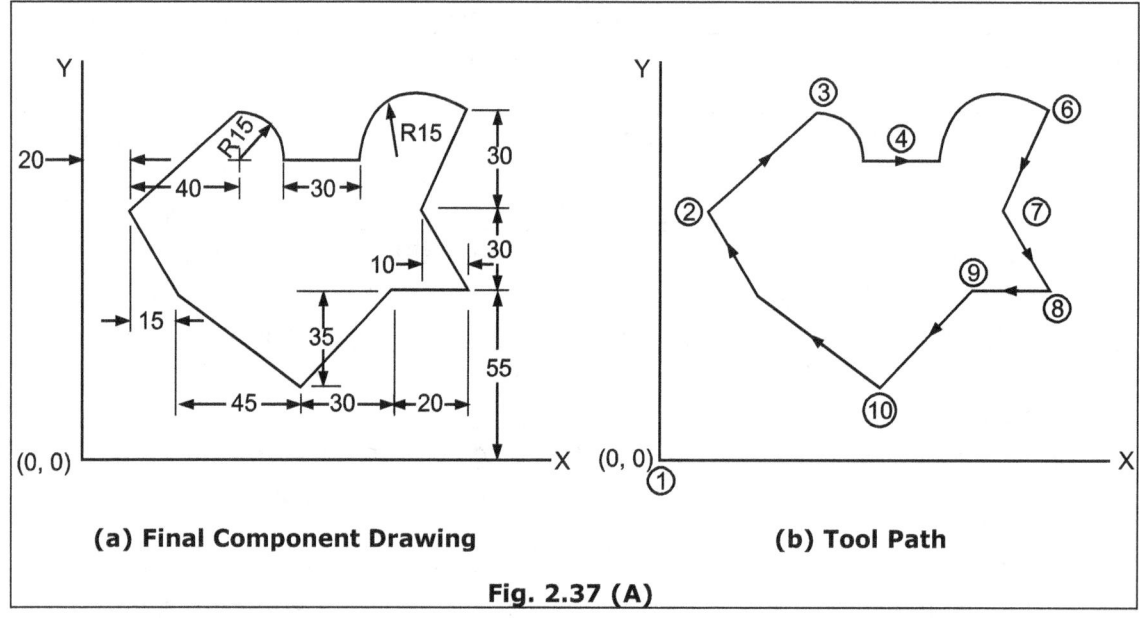

(a) Final Component Drawing   **(b) Tool Path**

Fig. 2.37 (A)

Table 2.23: X and Y Co-ordinates of Various Tool Position

Position No.	X and Y Co-ordinates	Position No.	X and Y Co-ordinates
1	0, 0	7	120, 85
2	20, 85	8	130, 55
3	60, 115	9	110, 55
4	75, 100	10	80, 20
5	105, 100	11	35, 55
6	130, 115		

Part Program:

Program	Description
29243	Program number.
N110 G90 G21 G94 G40 EOB	Absolute mode, input in mm, feed in mm/min, cutter diameter compensation cancel.
N120 M06 T04 EOB	Tool change, tool at tool position number 4 in the tool magazine.
N130 M03 S800 EOB	Spindle start clockwise direction, spindle speed.
N140 G00 X0 Y0 EOB	Rapid travel of cutter to position 1 (0, 0).
N150 G00 Z5 M08 EOB	Rapid travel of cutter to 5 mm above the workpiece surface (i.e. at 0, 0, 0) coolant on.
N160 G00 Z-4 EOB	Take required depth of cut with the rapid feed, so G00.
N170 G41 D01 G01 X20 Y85 F110 EOB	Cutter diameter compensation left by amount found in D01, cutter travel to position number 2 (20, 85).
N180 G01 X60 Y 115 EOB	Cutter travel to position number 3 (60, 115).
N190 G02 X75 Y100 I 0 J -15 EOB	Cutter travel to position number 4 (75, 100).
N200 G 01 X 105 EOB	Cutter travel to position number 5 (105, 100).
N210 G02 X 130 Y115 I15 J0 EOB	Cutter travel to position number 6 (130, 115).
N220 G01 X120 Y 85 EOB	Cutter travel to position number 7 (120, 85).
N230 G01 X130 Y55 EOB	Cutter travel to position number 8 (130, 55).
N240 G01 X110 EOB	Cutter travel to position number 9 (110, 55).
N250 G01 X80 Y20 EOB	Cutter travel to position number 10 (80, 20).
N260 G01 X35 Y55 EOB	Cutter travel to position number 11 (35, 55).
N270 G01 X20 Y85 EOB	Cutter travel to position number 1 (20, 85).
N280 G00 Z5 EOB	Rapid travel of cutter 5 mm above the workpiece surface.
N290 G40 EOB	Cutter compensation cancel.
N300 G28 EOB	Rapid return to machine reference position.
N310 M05 EOB	Spindle stop.
N320 M09 EOB	Coolant-off.
N330 M30 EOB	Program end and tape rewind.

Program 2.21 (A): *Prepare a part program for the component shown in Fig. 2.37 (B) (a) by using the following data : Use a 10 mm diameter end mill. The part depth is 4 mm. Use a feed rate of 120 mm/min and spindle speed of 800 rpm. Use cutter radius compensation. Take z=0 at top surface of job.* **[S-15]**

Data: Fig. 2.37 (B) (b) shows the tool path. Actual tool (end mill) diameter is 10 mm. Programmed tool diameter is 0. i.e. programming is done as per the part drawing. Store D01 = 0 – 5 = 5 mm in the memory before running the program. The X and Y co-ordinates of various tool position are shown in table 2.23A.

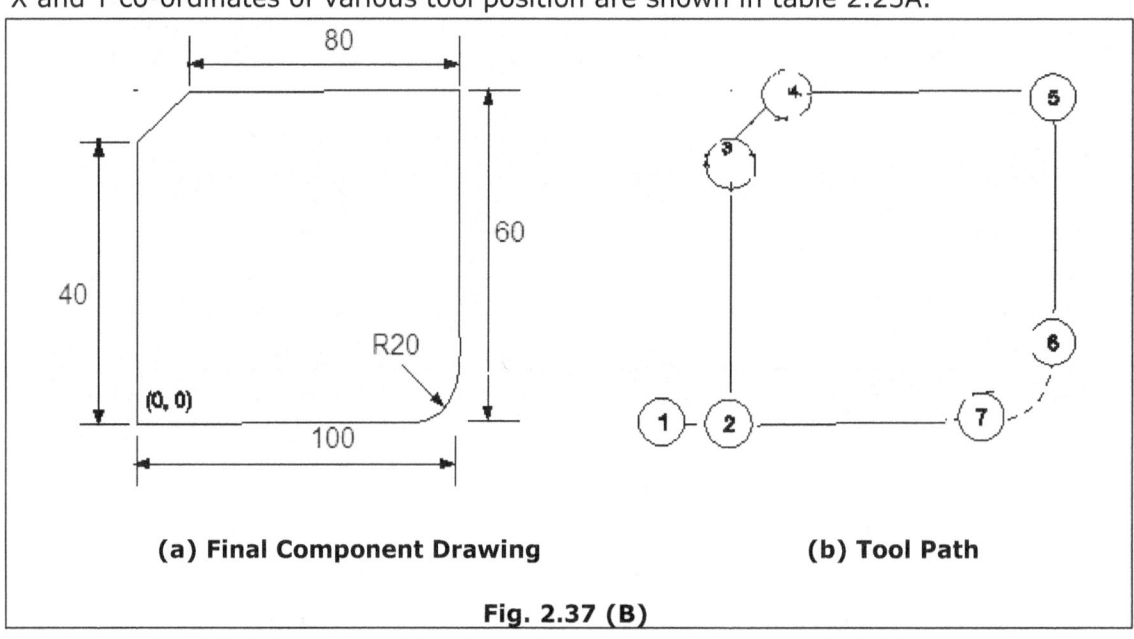

    (a) Final Component Drawing   **(b) Tool Path**

Fig. 2.37 (B)

Table 2.23 (A): X and Y Co-ordinates of Various Tool Position

Position No.	X and Y Co-ordinates	Position No.	X and Y Co-ordinates
1	−10, 0	5	100, 60
2	0, 0	6	100, 20
3	0, 40	7	80, 0
4	20, 60		

Part Program:

Program	Description
212419	Program number.
N10 G28 U00 V00 W00 EOB	Return to machine reference position.
N20 G90 G21 G94 G40 EOB	Absolute mode, input in mm, feed in mm/min, cutter diameter compensation cancel.
N30 M06 T01 EOB	Tool change, tool at tool position number 1 in the tool magazine.
N40 M03 S800 EOB	Spindle start clockwise direction, spindle speed.
N50 G41 D01 EOB	Cutter diameter compensation left by amount found in D01.
N60 G00 X10 Y-20 Z0 EOB	Rapid travel of cutter to position 1 (10, 0, 5) and 5 mm above the workpiece surface,
N70 G00 Z-4 M08 EOB	Take the required depth of cut of 4 mm, coolant ON.
N80 G01 X10 Y-0 F100 EOB	Cutter travel to position number 2 (0, 0) with the required feed.
N90 Y40 EOB	Cutter travel to position number 3 (0, 40).
N100 X20 Y60 EOB	Cutter travel to position number 4 (20, 60).
N110 X100 EOB	Cutter travel to position number 5 (100, 60).
N120 Y20 EOB	Cutter travel to position number 6 (100, 20).
N130 G02 X80 Y0 R20 F100 EOB	Cutter travel to position number 7 (80, 00).
N140 G01 X0 Y0 F120 EOB	Cutter travel to position number 2 (0,0).
N150 G00 Z10 EOB	Rapid travel of cutter 10 mm above the workpiece surface.
N160 G40 EOB	Cutter compensation cancel.
N170 G28 U00 V00 W00 EOB	Rapid return to machine reference position.
N180 M05 EOB	Spindle stop.
N190 M09 EOB	Coolant off.
N200 M30 EOB	Program end and tape rewind.

2.21 SUBROUTINE [W-08, S-09, W-09, W-11, S-12]

- When an identical machining operation is to be performed repeatedly then the general method of forming a program will be lengthy, time consuming, tedious and will use more computer memory space.

- In such case subroutine is a powerful time saving technique.

- A subroutine is an independent program similar to any usual program.

- It is stored in the computer's memory under separate program number.

- When required a subroutine can be called anywhere in the main program and for any number of times.

- After execution of subroutine the controller returns back to the main program and continues with the main program.

- In order to call the subroutine in the main program, the miscellaneous code M98 is used and the block of instruction is as shown below:

    N035 M98 P95 L1 EOB

    o   M98 instructs the controller to jump to a subroutine.

    o   P95 tells the controller that 95 (example) is the program number.

    o   L1 instructs the controller to execute the subroutine one time.

- In order to end the subroutine and to return back to the main program a miscellaneous code M99 is used.

- Generally the main program is written in absolute mode (G90) and the subroutine in incremental mode (G91) since it has to be used at different locations.

- It is therefore necessary to use the preparatory code G91 at the start of subroutine and code G90 before use of M99.

2.22 CANNED CYCLE [W-08, S-09, W-09, W-13]

- When a same operation has to be repeated for number of times then the program becomes lengthy, time consuming, tedious and uses more computer memory space.

- All these factors can be eliminated by the use of canned cycle.

- Canned cycle is written in the main program, but it reduces the length of program.

- The canned cycle may be defined as a set of instructions stored in the memory of the system, to perform a fixed sequence of operations.

- Basically, canned cycle is designed or prepared to reduce the labour space in memory of computer and time required for part programming.

- Canned cycle is used for repetitively and common used machining operations. And it is stored in the memory under the G codes.
- It is also called as fixed cycle.
- It is used for repetitive operation where material is to be cut in multiple passes.
- It reduces the length of program and its complexity.
- In canned cycle final position is fed in the block of instruction and the cutter path is automatically plotted by the controller itself.
- It can be called in the program by using G-codes.
- Canned cycles should be canceled after their use by using the code G-80.

2.23 DIFFERENCE BETWEEN SUBROUTINE AND CANNED CYCLE
[W-12, 13, S-13, 16]

Sr. No.	Subroutine	Canned cycle
1.	It is the separate program which is called in the main program.	It is not a program but part of the main program.
2.	It is called and ended by miscellaneous function.	It is called and ended by preparatory function.
3.	It is used when multiple passes are required at different locations.	It is used when multiple passes are required at the same location.
4.	One point is given in every block of instruction till the operation is completed.	Directly the final point is given in the block of instruction.
5.	The cutter path for every point is to be given by the programmer.	The cutter path for every pass is generated by the controller.

2.24 IMPORTANCE OF SUBROUTINE AND CANNED
[W-08, S-09, W-09, S-10]

Subroutine:
- When an identical machining operation is to be performed repeatedly then the normal method of writing a program is lengthy, time consuming, tedious and uses more computer memory space. In such case subroutine is a very important technique.
- Since the subroutine is written in incremental mode, it can be used at different locations for repeated operations.
- It is stored in the computer's memory and can be called in the main program for any number of times, thus reducing the memory space.

- After execution of subroutine the controller returns back to the main program and continues with the main program, thus reducing the length of the main program.

- It is easy to call subroutine in the main program by the use of miscellaneous code M98.

Canned cycle:

- When a same operation has to be repeated for number of times then the program becomes lengthy, time consuming, tedious and uses more computer memory space. All these factors can be eliminated by the use of canned cycle. Canned cycle is written in the main program, but it reduces the length of program. There are special codes for the use of canned cycle.

Example:

(i)   In order to mill the 8 slots as shown in the figure the **subroutine** can be used. Here a program is to be written for one slot only in the incremental mode and the same can be called 8 times for machining the slots.

(ii) In a turning operation if the number of pass is four or five then the same can be written in a single block with the help of **canned cycle**.

(iii) In a drilling operation if more number of holes are to be drilled as shown in the figure then **canned cycle** is very useful.

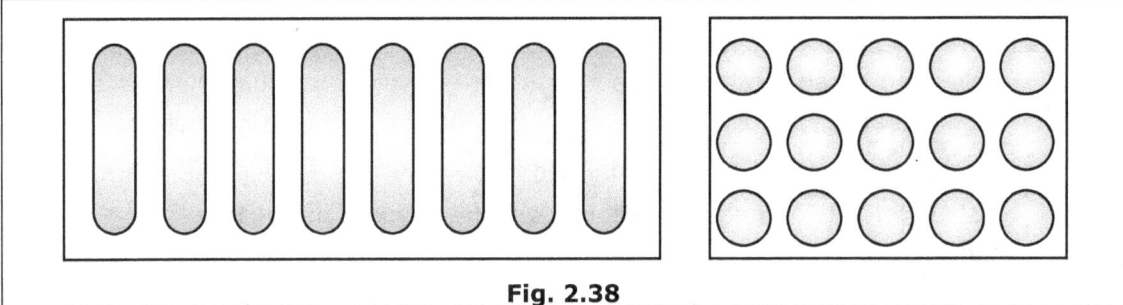

Fig. 2.38

2.25 PART PROGRAM FOR TURNING OPERATION

Program 2.22: *Prepare the NC part program to machine the work piece shown in Fig. 2.39 (a) on CNC lathe operations to be done.*

(i) Facing the workpiece

(ii) To reduce diameter of bar from 30 mm to 26 mm.   **[S-09]**

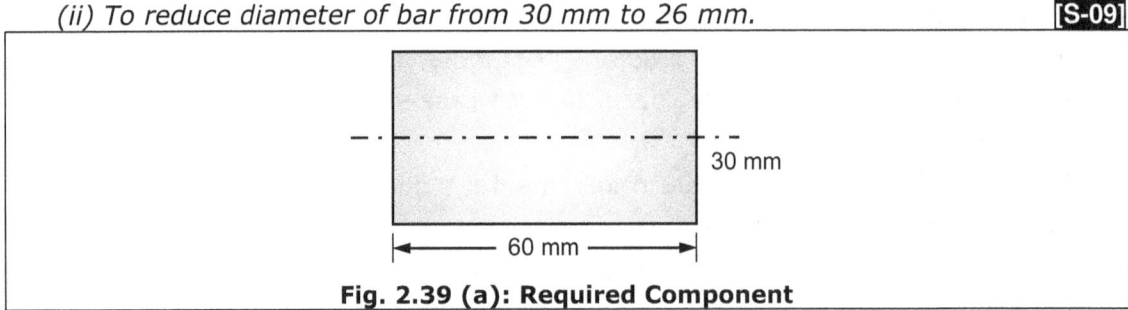

30 mm

60 mm

Fig. 2.39 (a): Required Component

The tool movements for removal of material from the work piece to obtain the required component are shown in Fig. 2.39 (b).

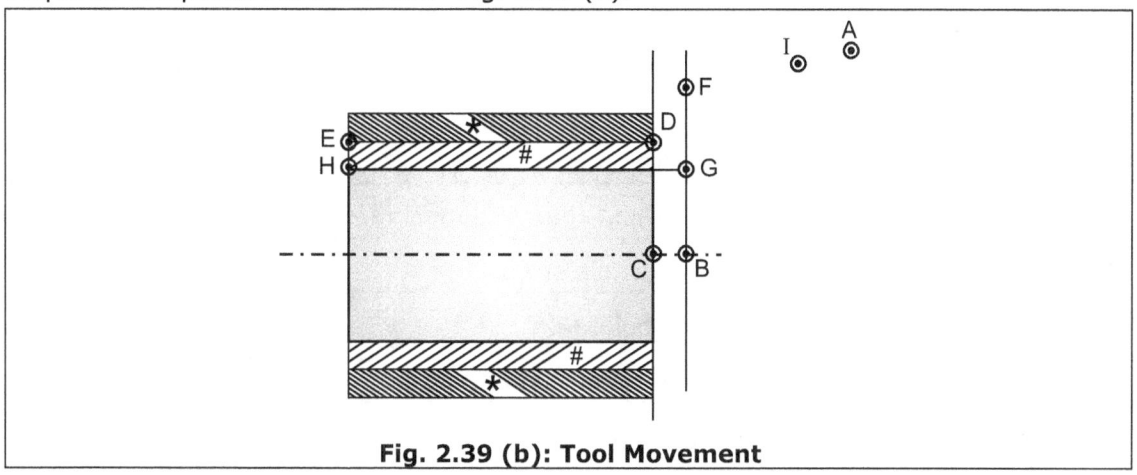

Fig. 2.39 (b): Tool Movement

Tool sequence is A-B-C-D-E-F-G-H-I

1. * sign indicates block no. N160.
2. # sign indicates block no. N190.

Table 2.24: X and Z Co-ordinates of Various Tool Position

Position No.	X and Z Co-ordinates	Position No.	X and Z Co-ordinates	Position No.	X and Z Co-ordinates
A	Machine home position	D	28, 00	G	26, 02
B	0, 02	E	28, -60	H	26, -60
C	0, 0	F	33, 02	I	80, 50

Part Program:

Program	Description
	Program Number
N110 G90 G21 G94 EOB	Absolute mode, input in mm, feed in mm/min.
N120 M03 S800 M08 EOB	Spindle start clockwise direction, spindle speed, coolant on.
N130 G00 X0 Z2 EOB	Rapid travel of tool to Position B.
N140 G01 Z 0 F 200 EOB	Movement of tool to the Position C.
N150 X28 EOB	Facing operation. Tool at Position D.
N160 Z -60 EOB	Turning to diameter 28 mm for a length of 60 mm. (Position E.)

contd. ...

N170 G00 X33 Z2 EOB	Rapid travel of tool to Position F
N180 G01 X26 F200 EOB	Movement of tool to Position G
N190 Z -60 EOB	Turning to diameter 26 mm for a length of 60 mm. (Position H)
N200 G00 X80 Z50 EOB	Rapid travel of tool away from the workpiece
N210 G28 EOB	Rapid return to machine reference position
N220 M05 EOB	Spindle stop.
N230 M09 EOB	Coolant off.
N240 M30 EOB	Program end and tape rewind.

Program 2.23: *Write a part program for plane turning of a component to reduce its diameter from 44 mm to 40 mm over length of 70 mm. State assumptions made if any.* [W-08]

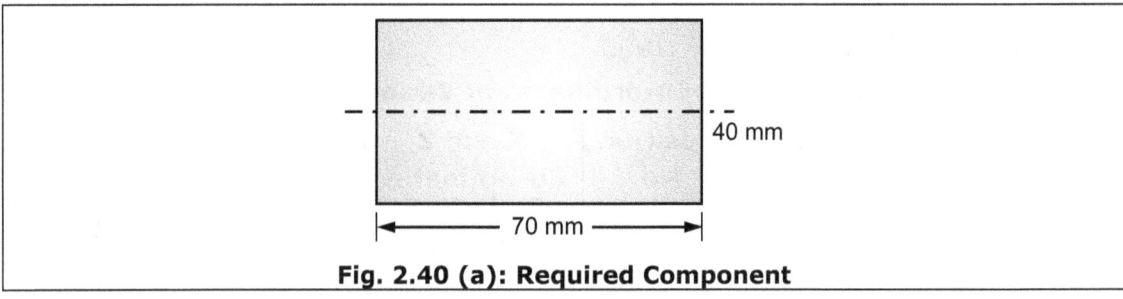

Fig. 2.40 (a): Required Component

The tool movements for removal of material from the work piece to obtain the required component are shown in Fig. 2.40 (b).

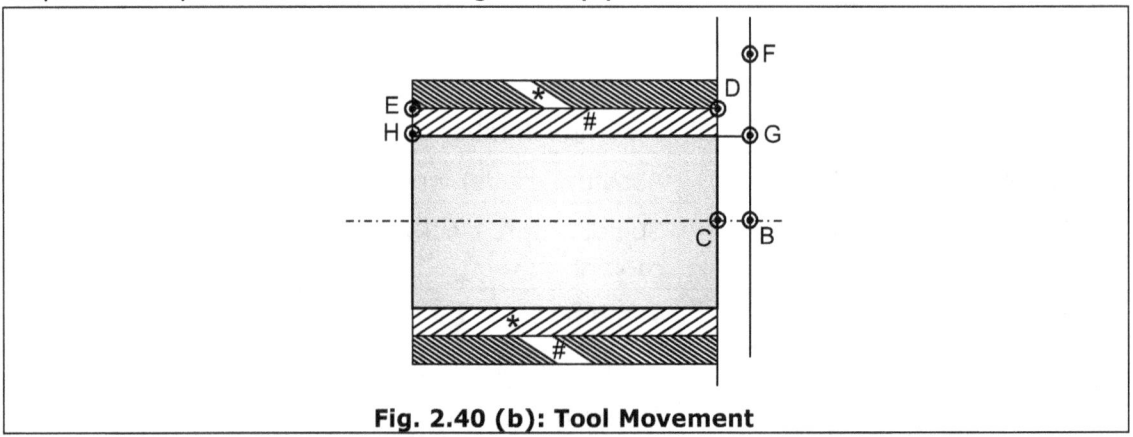

Fig. 2.40 (b): Tool Movement

Tool sequence is A-B-C-D-E-F-G-H-I

1. * sign indicates block no. N160.

2. # sign indicates block no. N190.

Table 2.25: X and Z Co-ordinates of Various Tool Position

Position No.	X and Z Co-ordinates	Position No.	X and Z Co-ordinates	Position No.	X and Z Co-ordinates
A	Machine home position	D	42, 00	G	40, 02
B	0, 02	E	42, –70	H	40, -70
C	0, 0	F	46, 02	I	80, 50

Program	Description
	Program Number
N110 G90 G21 G94 EOB	Absolute mode, input in mm, feed in mm/min.
N120 M03 S800 M08 EOB	Spindle start clockwise direction, spindle speed, coolant-on.
N130 G00 X0 Z2 EOB	Rapid travel of tool to Position B.
N140 G01 Z 0 F 200 EOB	Movement of tool to Position C.
N150 X42 EOB	Facing operation. Tool at Position D
N160 Z -70 EOB	Turning to diameter 42 mm for a length of 70 mm. (Position E)
N170 G00 X46 Z2 EOB	Rapid travel of tool to Position F
N180 G01 X40 F200 EOB	Movement of tool to Position G.
N190 Z -70 EOB	Turning to diameter 40 mm for a length of 70 mm. (Position H)
N200 G00 X80 Z50 EOB	Rapid travel of tool away from the work piece (Position I)
N210 G28 EOB	Rapid return to machine reference position.
N220 M05 EOB	Spindle stop.
N230 M09 EOB	Coolant-off.
N240 M30 EOB	Program end and tape rewind.

Program 2.24: *Write a program to reduce the diameter of the bar from 34 mm to 26 mm as shown in Fig. 2.41 (a). Assume a depth of cut of 1 mm. The length of work piece is 142 mm.*

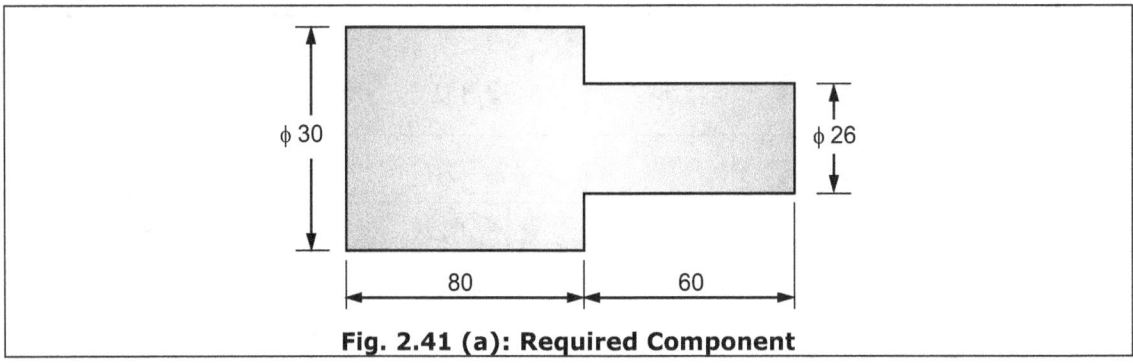

Fig. 2.41 (a): Required Component

The tool movements for removal of material from the work piece to obtain the required component are shown in Fig. 2.41 (b).

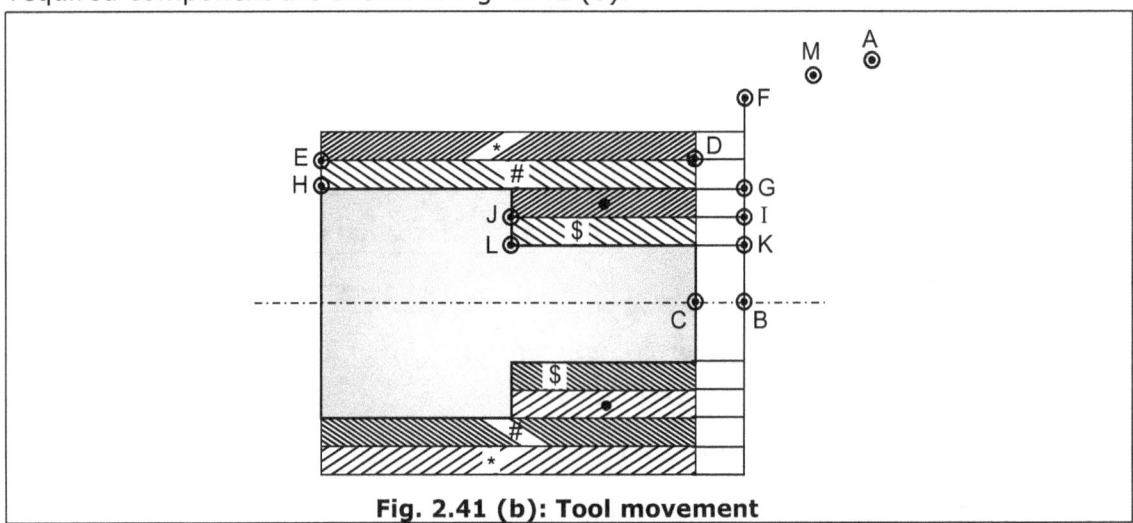

Fig. 2.41 (b): Tool movement

Table 2.26: X and Z Co-ordinates of Various Tool Position

Position No.	X and Z Co-ordinates	Position No.	X and Z Co-ordinates	Position No.	X and Z Co-ordinates
A	Machine home position	F	36, 02	K	26, 02
B	0, 2	G	30, 02	L	26, −60
C	0, 0	H	30, −140	M	85, 50
D	32, 0	I	28, 02		
E	32, −140	J	28, − 60		

Tool sequence is A-B-C-D-E-F-G-H-F-I-J-G-K-L-M-A

1. * sign indicates block no. N160
2. # sign indicates block no. N190
3. • sign indicates block no. N220
4. $ sign indicates block no. N250

Program	Description
	Program Number
N110 G90 G21 G94 EOB	Absolute mode, input in mm, feed in mm/min.
N120 M03 S800 M08 EOB	Spindle start clockwise direction, spindle speed, coolant-on.
N130 G00 X0 Z2 EOB	Rapid travel of tool to Position B.
N140 G01 Z 0 F 200 EOB	Movement of tool to the Position C.
N150 X32 EOB	Facing operation. Tool at Position D.
N160 Z -140 EOB	Turning to diameter 32 mm for a length of 140 mm. (Position E)
N170 G00 X36 Z2 EOB	Rapid travel of tool to Position F.
N180 G01 X30 F200 EOB	Movement of tool to Position G.
N190 Z -140 EOB	Turning to diameter 30 mm for a length of 140 mm. (Position H).
N200 G00 X36 Z2 EOB	Rapid travel of tool to Position F.
N210 G01 X28 F200 EOB	Movement of tool to Position I.
N220 Z-60 F200 EOB	Turning to diameter 28 mm for a length of 60 mm. (Position J.)
N230 G00 X36 Z2 EOB	Rapid travel of tool to Position F.
N240 G01 X26 F 200 EOB	Movement of tool to Position K.
N250 Z-60 F200 EOB	Turning to diameter 26 mm for a length of 60 mm. (Position L.)
N260 G00 X80 Z50 EOB	Rapid travel of tool away from the work piece. (Position M).
N270 G28 EOB	Rapid return to machine reference position.
N280 M05 EOB	Spindle stop.
N290 M09 EOB	Coolant-off.
N300 M30 EOB	Program end and tape rewind.

Program 2.25: *Write a program to reduce the diameter of the bar from 51 mm to 32 mm as shown in Fig. 2.42 (a). Assume a depth of cut of 2 mm. The length of work piece is 140 mm.*

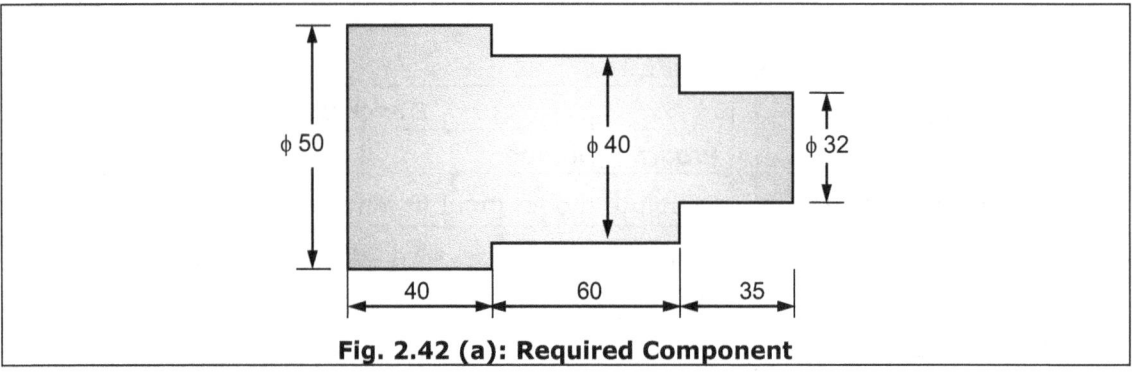

Fig. 2.42 (a): Required Component

The tool movements for removal of material from the work piece to obtain the required component are shown in Fig. 2.42 (b).

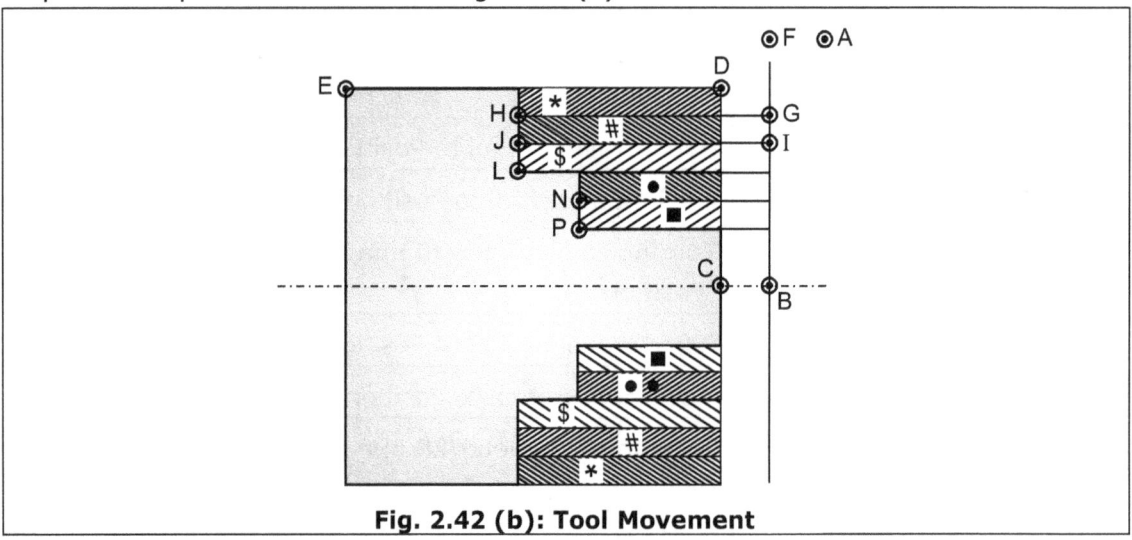

Fig. 2.42 (b): Tool Movement

Table 2.27: X and Z Co-ordinates of Various Tool Position

Position No.	X and Z Co-ordinates	Position No.	X and Z Co-ordinates	Position No.	X and Z Co-ordinates
A	Machine home position	G	46, 02	M	36, 02
B	0, 02	H	46, −95	N	36, −35
C	0, 0	I	42, 02	O	32, 02
D	50, 0	J	42, −95	P	32, −35
E	50, −135	K	40, 02	Q	80, 50
F	55, 02	L	40, −95		

Tool sequence is A-B-C-D-E-F-G-H-F-I-J-F-K-L-G-M-N-G-O-P-Q

1. * sign indicates block no. N190

2. # sign indicates block no. N220

3. • sign indicates block no. N280

4. ■ sign indicates block no. N310

Program	Description
	Program Number
N110 G90 G21 G94 EOB	Absolute mode, input in mm, feed in mm/min.
N120 M03 S800 M08 EOB	Spindlestart clockwise direction, spindle speed, coolant on.
N130 G00 X0 Z2 EOB	Rapid travel of tool to Position B.
N140 G01 Z 0 F 200 EOB	Movement of tool to the Position C.
N150 X50 EOB	Facing operation. Tool Position at D.
N160 Z -135 EOB	Turning to diameter 50 mm for a length of135 mm. (Position E).
N170 G00 X55 Z2 EOB	Rapid travel of tool to Position F.
N180 G01 X46 F200 EOB	Movement of tool to Position G
N190 Z -95 EOB	Turning to diameter 46 mm for a length of 95 mm. (Position H).
N200 G00 X50 Z2 EOB	Rapid travel of tool to Position F.
N210 G01 X42 F200 EOB	Movement of tool to Position I.
N220 Z-95 F200 EOB	Turning to diameter 42 mm for a length of 95 mm. (Position J.)
N230 G00 X45 Z2 EOB	Rapid travel of tool to Position F.
N240 G01 X40 F 200 EOB	Movement of tool to Position K.
N250 Z-95 F200 EOB	Turning to diameter 40 mm for a length of 95 mm. (Position L.)
N260 G00 X46 Z2 EOB	Rapid travel of tool to Position G.
N270 G01 X36 F 200 EOB	Movement of tool to Position M.
N280 Z-35 F200 EOB	Turning to diameter 36 mm for a length of 35 mm. (Position N)

contd. ...

N290 G00 X40 Z2 EOB	Rapid travel of tool to Position K.
N300 G01 X32 F 200 EOB	Movement of tool to Position O.
N310 Z-35 F200 EOB	Turning to diameter 32 mm for a length of 35 mm. (Position P.)
N320 G00 X80 Z50 EOB	Rapid travel of tool away from the workpiece Position Q.
N330 G28 EOB	Rapid return to machine reference position.
N340 M05 EOB	Spindle stop.
N350 M09 EOB	Coolant-off.
N360 M30 EOB	Program end and tape rewind.

Program 2.26: *Prepare a program to machine work piece as shown in Fig. below on CNC lathe.*

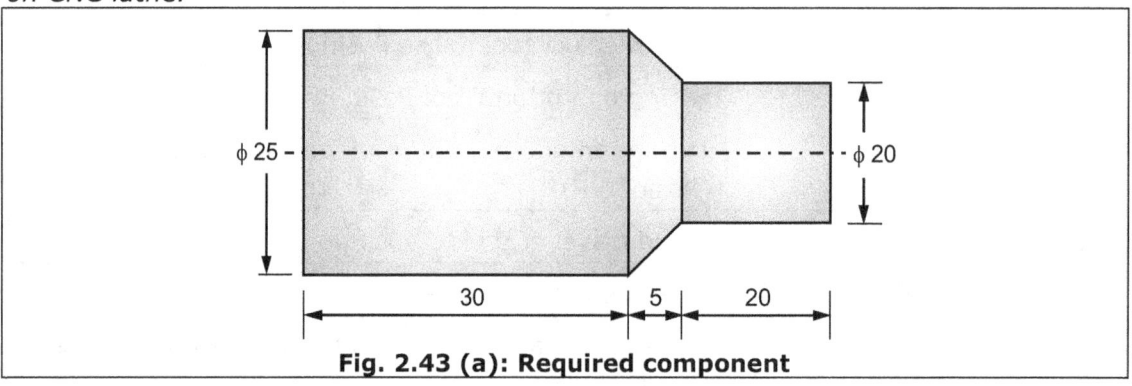

Fig. 2.43 (a): Required component

The tool movements for removal of material from the work piece to obtain the required component are shown in Fig. 2.43.

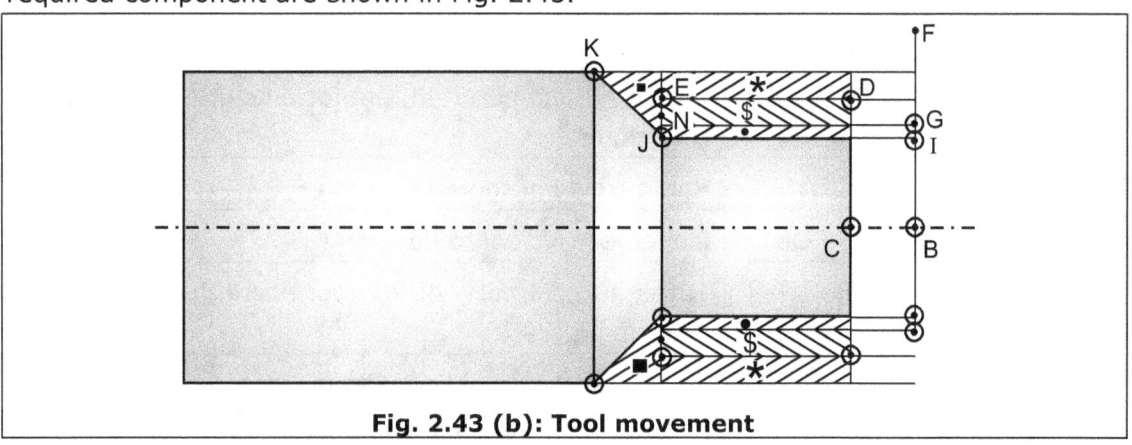

Fig. 2.43 (b): Tool movement

Tool sequence is A-B-C-D-E-F-G-H-F-I-J-K

1. * sign indicates block no. N150
2. $ sign indicates block no. N180
3. • sign indicates block no. N210
4. ■ sign indicates block no. N220

Table 2.28: X and Z Co-ordinates of Various Tool Position

Position No.	X and Z Co-ordinates	Position No.	X and Z Co-ordinates	Position No.	X and Z Co-ordinates
A	Machine home position	E	23, −20	I	20, 02
B	0, 02	F	28, 02	J	20, −20
C	0, 0	G	21, 02	K	25, −25
D	23, 0	H	21, −20	L	80, 50

Program	Description
	Program Number
N100 G90 G21 G94 EOB	Absolute mode, input in mm, feed in mm/min.
N110 M03 S800 M08 EOB	Spindle start clockwise direction, spindle speed, coolant on.
N120 G00 X0 Z2 EOB	Rapid travel of tool to Position B.
N130 G01 Z 0 F 200 EOB	Movement of tool to Position C
N140 X23 EOB	Facing operation. (Position D.)
N150 Z -20 EOB	Turning to diameter 23 mm for a length of 20 mm. (Position E.)
N160 G00 X28 Z2 EOB	Rapid travel of tool to Position F.
N170 G01 X21 F200 EOB	Movement of tool to the Position G.
N180 Z-20 EOB	Turning to diameter 21 mm for a length of 20 mm. Position H.
N190 G00 X28 Z2 EOB	Rapid travel of tool to Position F.
N200 G01 X20 F200 EOB	Movement of tool to Position I.
N210 Z-20 EOB	Turning to diameter 20 mm for a length of 20 mm. (Position J).
N220 X25 Z -25 EOB	Taper Turning for a length of 5 mm. Position K.
N230 G00 X80 Z50 EOB	Rapid travel of tool away from the work piece. Position L.
N240 G28 EOB	Rapid return to machine reference position.
N250 M05 EOB	Spindle stop.
N230 M09 EOB	Coolant-off.
N240 M30 EOB	Program end and tape rewind.

Program 2.27: *Prepare a program to machine work piece as shown in Fig. 2.44 (a) below on CNC lathe.* **[S-08, W-16]**

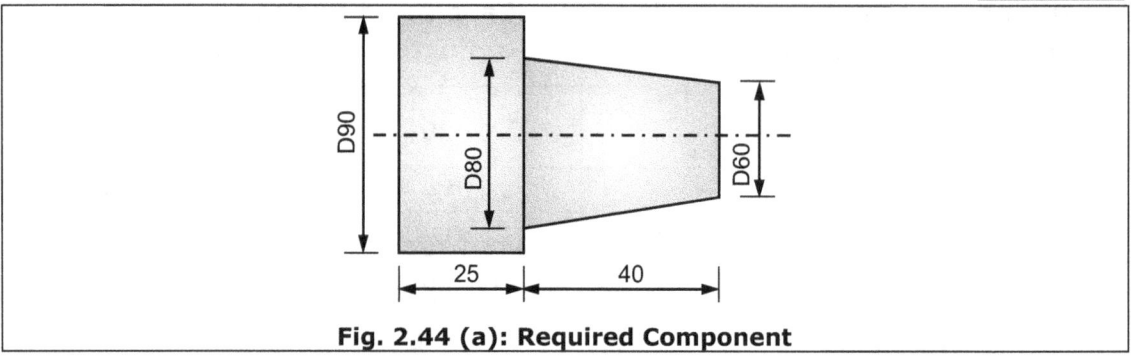

Fig. 2.44 (a): Required Component

The tool movements for removal of material from the work piece to obtain the required component are shown in Fig. 2.44.

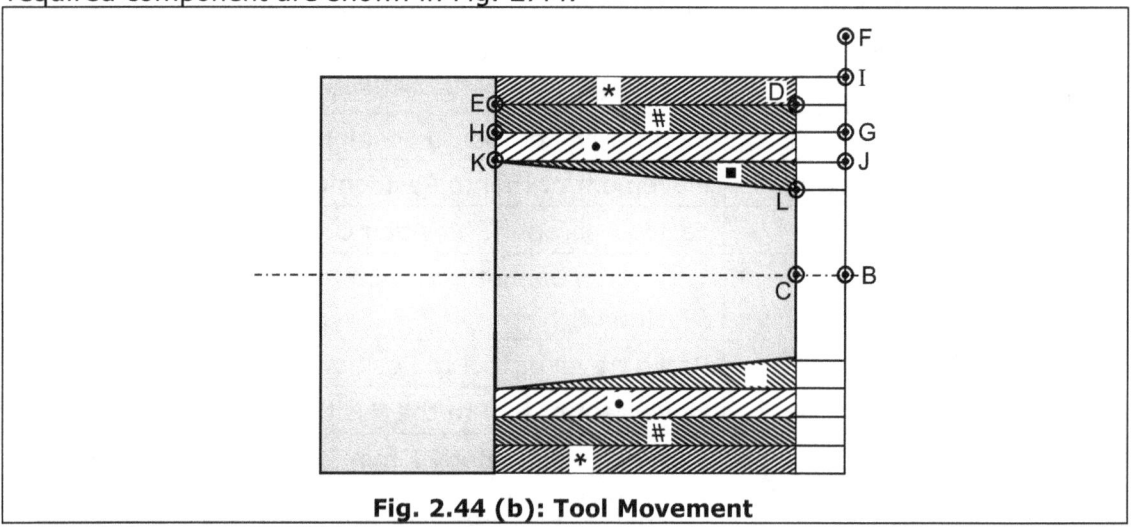

Fig. 2.44 (b): Tool Movement

Tool sequence is A-B-C-D-E-F-G-H-I-J-K-I

1. * sign indicates block no. N150
2. # sign indicates block no. N180
3. • sign indicates block no. N210
4. ■ sign indicates block no. N240

Table 2.29: X and Z Co-ordinates of Various Tool Position

Position No.	X and Z Co-ordinates	Position No.	X and Z Co-ordinates	Position No.	X and Z Co-ordinates
A	Machine home position	E	86, −40	I	90, 02
B	0, 02	F	93, 02	J	80, 02
C	0, 0	G	82, 02	K	80, −40
D	86, 0	H	82, −40	L	60, 00

Program	Description
	Program Number
N100 G90 G21 G94 EOB	Absolute mode, input in mm, feed in mm/min.
N110 M03 S800 M08 EOB	Spindle start clockwise direction, spindle speed, coolant on.
N120 G00 X0 Z2 EOB	Rapid travel of tool to Position B.
N130 G01 Z 0 F 200 EOB	Movement of tool to the Position C.
N140 X86 EOB	Facing operation. Tool at Position D.
N150 Z -40 EOB	Turning to diameter 86 mm for a length of 40 mm and depth of cut as 2 mm. (Position E).
N160 G00 X93 Z2 EOB	Rapid travel of tool to Position F.
N170 G01 X82 F200 EOB	Movement of tool to Position G.
N180 Z-40 EOB	Turning to diameter 86 mm for a length of 40 mm and depth of cut as 2 mm. (Position H).
N190 G00 X90 Z2 EOB	Rapid travel of tool to Position I.
N200 G01 X80 F200 EOB	Movement of tool to Position J.
N210 Z-40 EOB	Turning to diameter 80 mm for a length of 40 mm and depth of cut as 2 mm. (Position k).
N220 G00 X 86 Z0 EOB	Rapid travel of tool to Position D.
N230 G01 X60 Z0 F200	Tool travel to position L with linear interpolation.
N240 X80 Z -40 EOB	Taper Turning for a length of 40 mm. Position k.
N250 G00 X100 Z50 EOB	Rapid travel of tool away from the workpiece.
N260 G28 EOB	Rapid return to machine reference position.
N270 M05 EOB	Spindle stop.
N280 M09 EOB	Coolant-off.
N290 M30 EOB	Program end and tape rewind.

Program 2.28:*Prepare a program to machine work piece as shown in Fig. 2.45 on a CNC lathe.* **[S-10]**

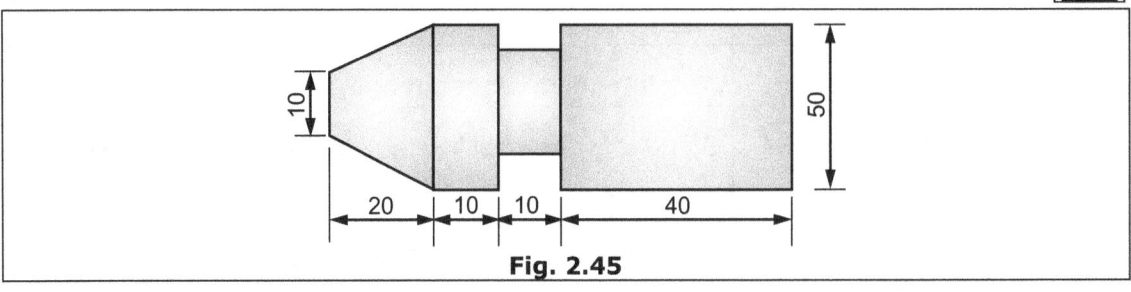

Fig. 2.45

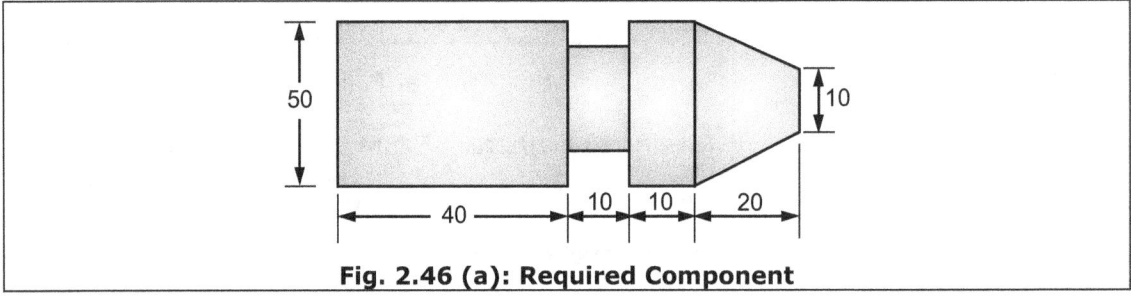

Fig. 2.46 (a): Required Component

1. Assume length of workpiece more than 80 mm.
2. The job will be reversed as shown in Fig. 2.46 (b) and then operations will be performed.

The tool movements for removal of material from the work piece to obtain the required component are shown in Fig. 2.46 (b).

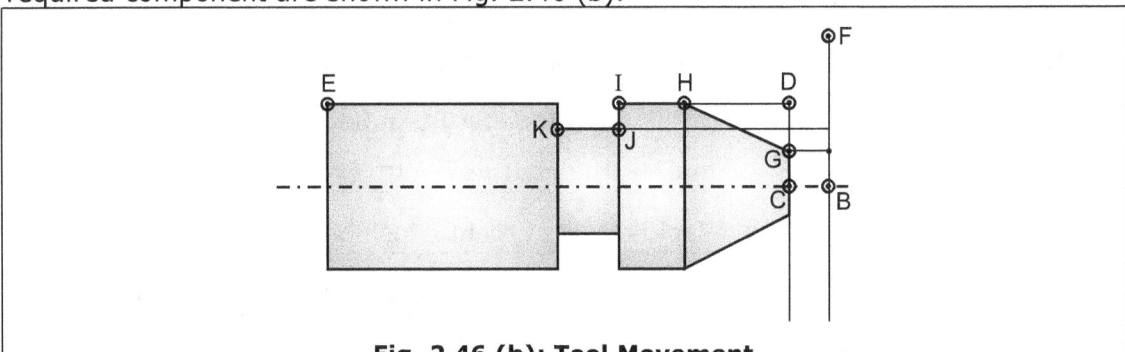

Fig. 2.46 (b): Tool Movement

Table 2.30: X and Z Co-ordinates of Various Tool Position

Position No.	X and Z Co-ordinates	Position No.	X and Z Co-ordinates	Position No.	X and Z Co-ordinates
A	Machine home position	E	50, –80	I	50, -30
B	0, 02	F	55, 00	J	45, -30
C	0, 0	G	10, 00	K	45, -40
D	50, 0	H	50, –20	L	80, 50

Program	Description
	Program Number
N100 G90 G21 G94 EOB	Absolute mode, input in mm, feed in mm/min.
N110 M03 S800 M08 EOB	Spindle start clockwise direction, spindle speed, coolant-on.
N120 G00 X0 Z2 EOB	Rapid travel of tool to position B.
N130 G01 Z 0 F 200 EOB	Movement of tool to the position C.
N140 X50 EOB	Facing operation. Tool at (Position D).
N150 Z -80 EOB	Turning to diameter 50 mm for a length of 80 mm. (Position E).
N160 G00 X55 Z0 EOB	Rapid travel of tool to the position F.
N170 G01 X10 Z0 F200 EOB	Movement of tool to the position G.
N180 G01 X 50 Z-20 EOB	Taper Turning for a length of 20 mm.(Position H).
N190 G28 EOB	Rapid travel of tool to the position A.
N200 M06 T01 EOB	TOOL change to parting tool.
N210 G00 X50 Z-30 EOB	Rapid travel of tool to the position I.
N220 G01 X 45 Z-30 EOB	Tool travel to position J with linear interpolation.
N230 G01 Z-40 F200 EOB	Grooving operation to cut 5 mm groove. (Position K)
N240 G00 X80 Z 50 EOB	Rapid travel of tool TO POSITION L.
N250 G28 EOB	Rapid return to machine reference position.
N260 M05 EOB	Spindle stop.
N270 M09 EOB	Coolant-off.
N280 M30 EOB	Program end and tape rewind.

2.26 PART PROGRAM FOR MACHINING ALONG CURVED SURFACE

- When curved surfaces are to be machined then the preparatory codes G02 and G03 are used. There are two basic methods used to program circular path.
  - Center point programming (I K method). (Arc Vector method).
  - Radius programming.

2.26.1 Center Point Programming

- When circular interpolation is performed, the following information is necessary.
    - (i)   Arc direction or direction of cutter travel.
    - (ii)   Arc start point.
    - (iii) Arc center point.
    - (iv) Arc end point.

(i) Arc direction or direction of cutter travel:

- o   Based on whether G02 or G03 code is used, the arc direction will be clockwise or counterclockwise respectively as shown in the Fig 2.47.
- o   Both G02 and G03 are modal codes and are controlled by a feed rate function (F-word), just like G01.
- o   These codes must be programmed in the block of information where circular interpolation starts.

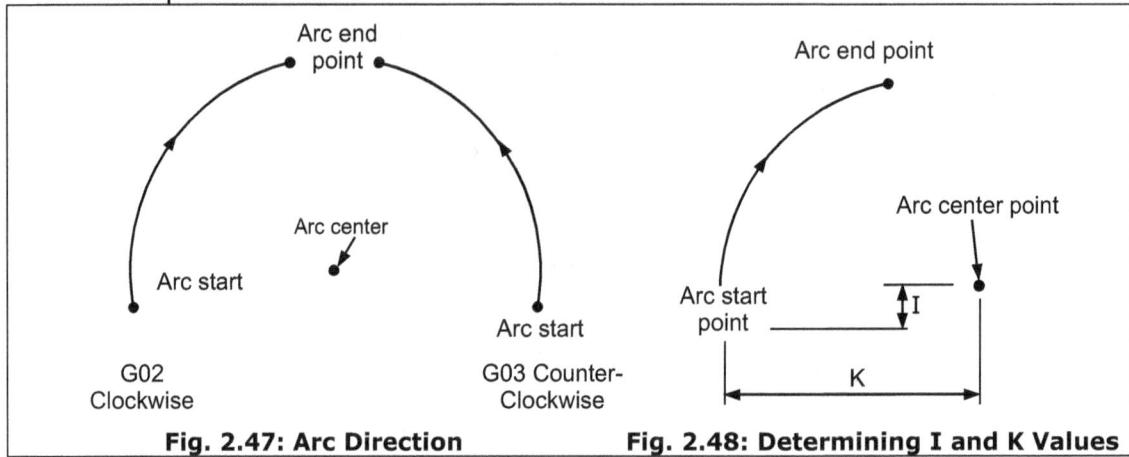

Fig. 2.47: Arc Direction   Fig. 2.48: Determining I and K Values

(ii) Arc start point:

- o   The start point of the arc is usually the end point of linear line or the end point of a previous arc. The cutting tool starts machining from the start point.

(iii) Arc center point:

- o   The center point of the arc is the center of the circle or arc. The center point is described by I and K words. These words are incremental values regardless of whether they have been programmed in the absolute or incremental mode.
- o   The I and K values are taken as shown in Fig 2.48.

  I value = Distance along X-axis from the arc start point to the arc center point.

  K value = Distance along Z-axis from the arc start point to the arc center point.

- o   The distance and direction for I and K values is always taken **from the start** of the arc **to the center** of the arc.

o   If on a drawing, the center point of arc is located above or to the right of the start point, a positive sign (+) must be used for K and I values.

o   Similarly if the arc center point is located below or to the left of the start point, a negative sign (–) must be used for K and I values.

o   The method to determine the I and K values and their sign is shown in Fig. 2.49.

o   In Fig. 2.49 (a) center point is to the right of start point so I is +10 and as center point is below the start point so K is – 4. Similarly Figs. 2.49 (b) to (f) are self explanatory.

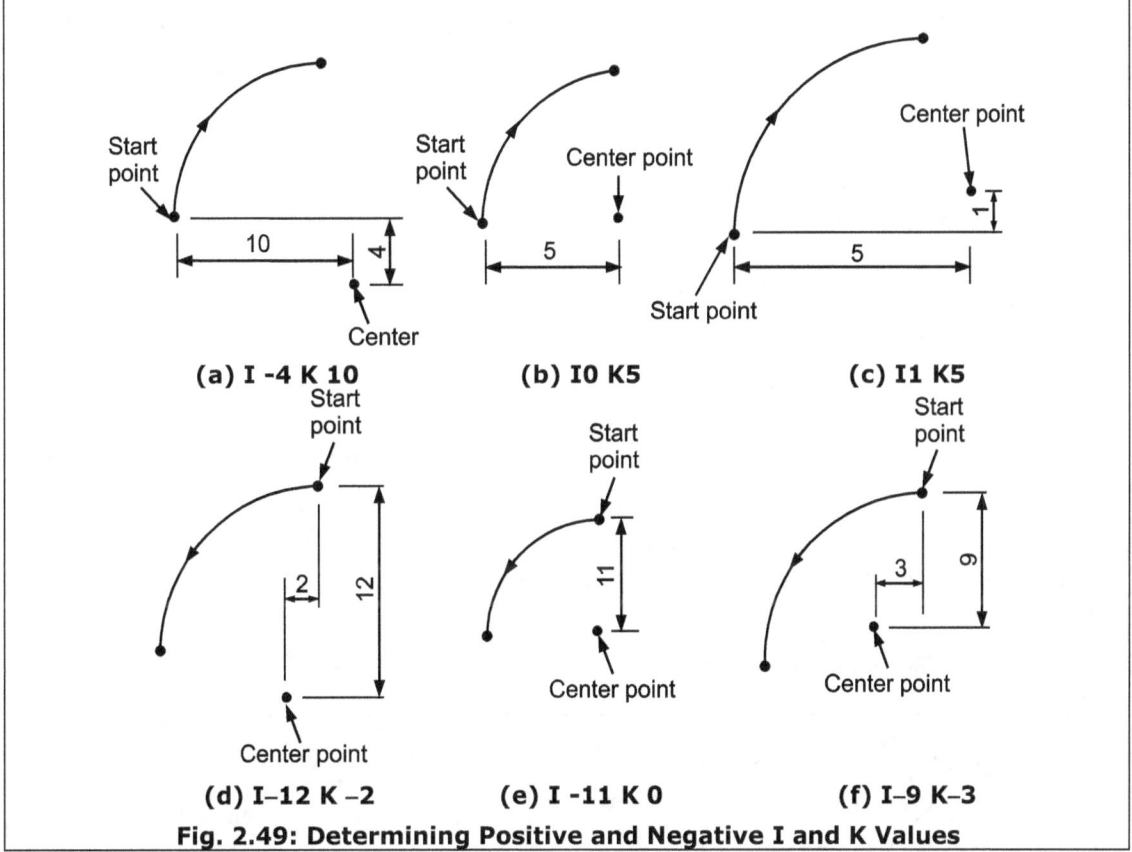

Fig. 2.49: Determining Positive and Negative I and K Values

(iv) Arc end point:

o   It is the co-ordinate position for the end point of the arc. When machining is carried out, then with G02 or G03 code the arc end point is given and not the start point.

o   The G02 or G03 block is shown in the Fig. 2.50 and is written as below:

For example, N110 G02 X_F Y_F I_ K_ F_ EOB

For example, N210 G03 X_F Y_F I_ K_ F_ EOB

X_F = X-co-ordinate of the arc end point.

Y_F = Y-co-ordinate of the arc end point.

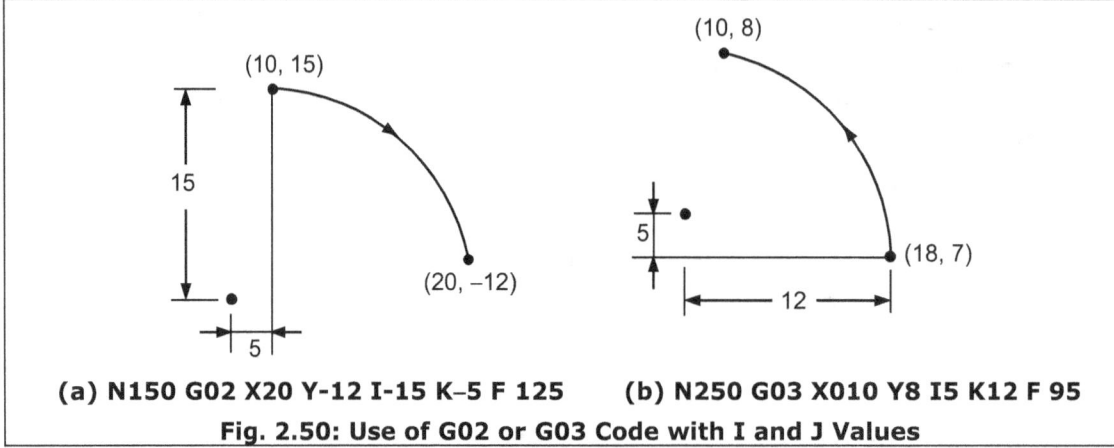

(a) N150 G02 X20 Y-12 I-15 K–5 F 125   **(b) N250 G03 X010 Y8 I5 K12 F 95**

Fig. 2.50: Use of G02 or G03 Code with I and J Values

2.26.2 Radius Programming

- If circular interpolation is programmed using radius value, the value of radius is required to be given with G02 or G03 code.
- The format for radius programming is shown in Fig. 2.51 and is written as:

     N50   G02 X_ Y_ R_ F_ EOB

     N100   G03 X_ Y_ R_ F_ EOB

             X = Distance from start point of the arc to the end point of the arc in X direction.

             Y = Distance from start point of the arc to the end point of the arc in Y direction.

             R = Value of radius of the arc.

Note: If arc is more than 180° then R is positive and if arc is less than 180° then R is negative.

X and Y values are the incremental values from the arc start point to the arc end point.

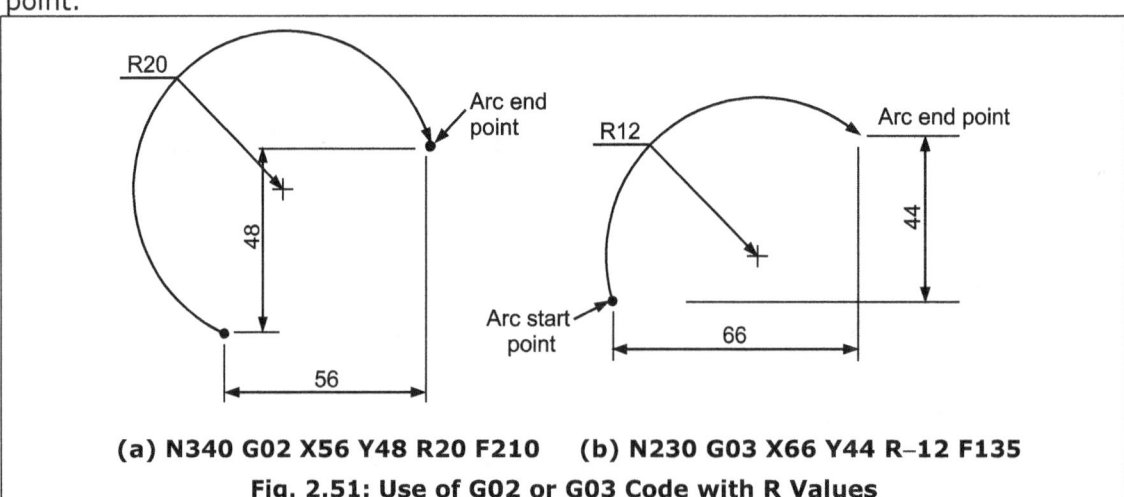

(a) N340 G02 X56 Y48 R20 F210   **(b) N230 G03 X66 Y44 R–12 F135**

Fig. 2.51: Use of G02 or G03 Code with R Values

Program 2.29: *Prepare a part program to machine the work piece shown in Fig. 2.52 (a) on the CNC lathe machine.* [W-14]

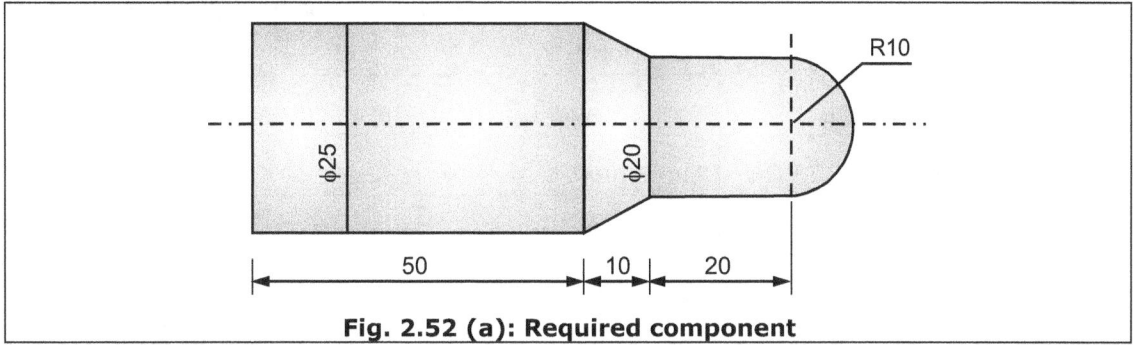

Fig. 2.52 (a): Required component

The tool movements for removal of material from the work piece to obtain the required component are shown in Fig. 2.52 (b).

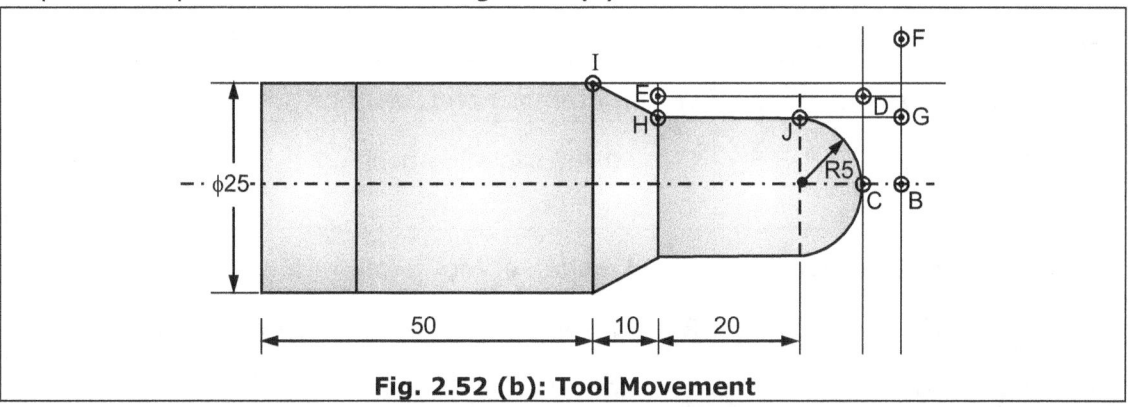

Fig. 2.52 (b): Tool Movement

Table 2.31: X and Z Co-ordinates of Various Tool Position

Position No.	X and Z Co-ordinates	Position No.	X and Z Co-ordinates	Position No.	X and Z Co-ordinates
A	Machine home position	E	22, –25	I	25, –35
B	0, 02	F	30, 02	J	20, –5
C	0, 0	G	20, 02	K	
D	22, 0	H	20, –25		

Program	Description
	Program Number
N100 G90 G21 G94 EOB	Absolute mode, input in mm, feed in mm/min.
N110 M03 S800 M08 EOB	Spindle start clockwise direction, spindle speed, coolant-on.
N120 G00 X0 Z2 EOB	Rapid travel of tool to position B.
N130 G01 Z 0 F 200 EOB	Movement of tool to the position C.

contd. ...

N140 X22 EOB	Facing operation. Tool at (Position D).
N150 Z-25 EOB	Turning to diameter 22 mm for a length of 25 mm. (Position E).
N160 G00 X30 Z2 EOB	Rapid travel of tool to the position F.
N170 G01 X20 Z2 F200 EOB	Movement of tool to the position G.
N180 Z-25 EOB	Linear interpolation (Position H).
N190 G01 X -35 Z 25 F200 EOB	Taper turning Position I.
N200 G00 X30 Z2 EOB	Rapid travel of tool to the position F.
N210 G00 X 0 Z 2 EOB	Rapid travel of tool to the position B.
N220 G01 Z0 F100 EOB	Linear interpolation (Position C).
N230 G03 X20 Z-5 I0 K-5 F 120 EOB	Circular interpolation position J.
N240 G00 X 50 Z30 EOB	Rapid motion of tool away from work piece.
N250 G28 EOB	Rapid return to machine reference position.
N260 M05 EOB	Spindle stop.
N270 M09 EOB	Coolant-off.
N280 M30 EOB	Program end and tape rewind.

Program 2.30: *Prepare a part program to machine the work piece shown in Fig. 2.53 (a) on the CNC lathe machine.* [S-15]

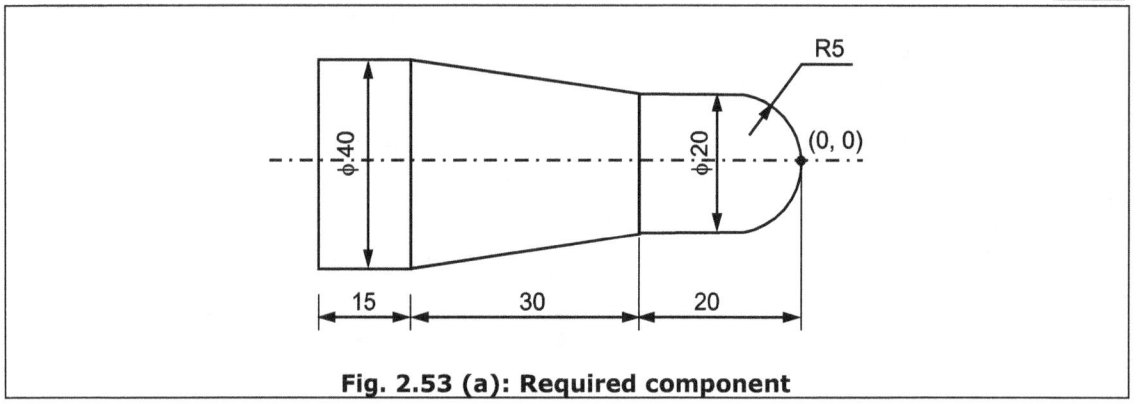

Fig. 2.53 (a): Required component

The tool movements for removal of material from the work piece to obtain the required component are shown in Fig. 2.53 (b).

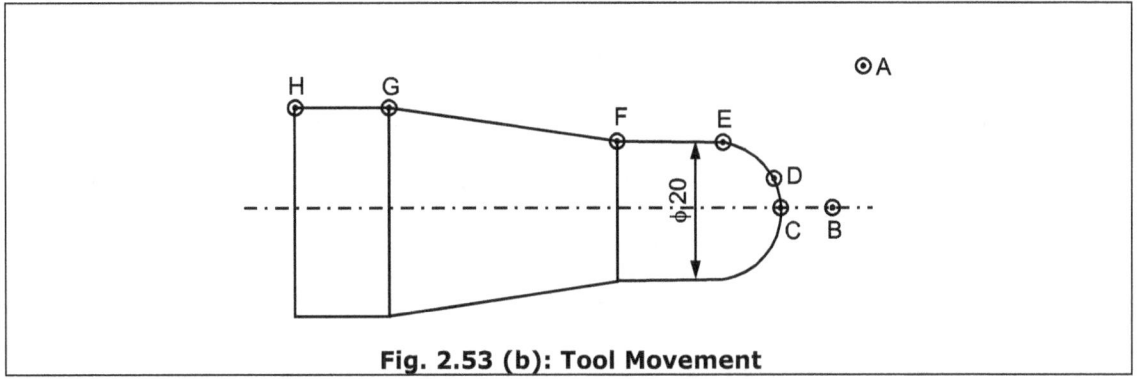

Fig. 2.53 (b): Tool Movement

Table 2.32: X and Z Co-ordinates of Various Tool Position

Position No.	X and Z Co-ordinates	Position No.	X and Z Co-ordinates
A	Machine home position	E	20, –5
B	0, 02	F	20, –20
C	0, 0	G	40, –50
D	10, 0	H	40, –65

Program	Description
	Program Number
N100 G90 G21 G94 EOB	Absolute mode, input in mm, feed in mm/min.
N110 M03 S800 M08 EOB	Spindle start clockwise direction, spindle speed, coolant-on.
N120 G00 X0 Z2 EOB	Rapid travel of tool to position B.
N130 G01 Z 0 F 150 EOB	Movement of tool to the position C.
N140 X10 EOB	Facing operation. Tool at (Position D).
N150 G02 X20 Z-5 I5 J0 F150 EOB	Circular interpolation to diameter 20 mm. (Position E).
N160 G01 X20 Z-20 F150 EOB	Rapid travel of tool to the position F.

contd. ...

N170 G01 X40 Z-50 F150 EOB	Taper turning to the position G.
N180 Z-65 EOB	Linear interpolation (Position H).
N190 G00 X 50 Z30 EOB	Rapid motion of tool away from work piece.
N200 G28 EOB	Rapid return to machine reference position.
N210 M05 EOB	Spindle stop.
N220 M09 EOB	Coolant-off.
N230 M30 EOB	Program end and tape rewind.

2.27 JOG MODE

- The mode that allows for the manual operation of tool movement via the jog buttons is called as jog mode.
- Jog mode is mostly used to travel the CNC machine table slide for movement of table along x-axis or z-axis.
- These axis movements can be via a jog mode button or through the CNC machine hand wheel. It is also called as manual mode.
- In this mode, the CNC machine behaves like a standard or conventional machine. A CNC milling machine behaves like a manual milling machine. A CNC lathe behaves like an engine lathe.
- With the jog mode, the operator of a CNC machine is allowed to press buttons, turn hand wheels, and activate switches in order to attain the desired machine function.
- The activation of each button or switch in the manual mode has an immediate response.
- For example, if the correct mode switch position is selected and if the correct button is pressed, the spindle will start. If a switch is turned-on, the coolant will come on. If a joystick is held in one direction or another, the corresponding machine axis will move.

2.28 ADAPTIVE CONTROL

- During the past two decades the number of CNC systems has grown tremendously in almost every field of manufacturing.
- A common drawback of these systems is that their machining control variables, such as speeds or feed rates, are prescribed by a part programmer.

- The determination of these operating parameters depends on the Knowledge and experience regarding the work piece, tool materials, coolant conditions and other factors.

- In order to reduce the chance of a tool failure the part programmer must consider the most adverse conditions (which in practice will seldom occur), and select conservative values for the machining variables. This practice consequently slows down the system's production.

- By contrast in adaptive control machining, there is improvement in the production rate and reduction in the machining cost as a result of calculating and setting of optimal parameters during machining.

- These systems are based on real-time control of the cutting variables with reference to measurements of the machining process state-variables.

- The adaptive control, which is a logical extension of the CNC-mechanism is basically a feedback system that treats the CNC as an internal unit and in which the machining variables automatically adapt themselves to the actual conditions of the machining process.

- Adaptive control marked as the last achievement in the NC machines is a system which is able to measure one or more process variables.

- Some of the process variables that have been used in adaptive control systems include spindle deflection or force, torque, cutting temperature, vibration amplitude and horsepower.

- With the knowledge of these process variables the system is able to regulate feed and/or speed in order to compensate for undesirable changes in the process variables.

- The final scope of this control system is to optimize the machining process.

- Adaptive control can be defined as a set of techniques for automatic adjustment of the controllers in real time, in order to achieve or to maintain a desired level of performance of the control system when the parameters of the machine tool are unknown and/or change with time.

2.28.1 Using Adaptive control

- The principal reason for using CNC machines is because it reduces non-productive time in machining operation.

- This can be achieved by reducing the tool set-up time, tool change time, work piece handling time and other delays.

- Although CNC are capable to reduce this non-productive time but it is do little to reduce actual machining time, because they cannot control the process.

- Adaptive control system determines the correct feed and speed are automatically found and it is not necessary to spend efforts on calculations of optimum feeds and speeds.

- It takes into account the variations in work-material hardness, width or depth of cut, air gaps in part geometry and so on.

- Adaptive control has the capability to respond to and compensate for these variations during process.

- By doing this the in-process time is reduced by using optimum speeds and/or feeds.

- By increasing tool life simultaneously with time saving, the adaptive control system contribute to lower operating costs, which justifies the extra price of adding AC to a conventional NC machine.

- However, adaptive control should be utilized in applications where the following conditions are met:

  1. The in-process time consumes a significant portion of the total production time

  2. There are significant sources of variability in the process for which adaptive control can compensate.

  3. The operating cost of the machine tool is high.

  4. Material like steel, titanium and high strength alloys are to be machined.

2.28.2 Benefits of Adaptive Control Machining

- There are many the potential benefits in using adaptive control system. However, there are many machining operations were adaptive control cannot be justified. The benefits from the adaptive control are laid below:

  1. **Increased production rates:** The on-line adjustments allow for variations in work geometry, material and tool wear provide the capability to achieve the highest removal rates that are consistent with the existing conditions. As a result of high removal rates more parts are produced thus the productivity increases.

  2. **Increased tool life:** In combination with the higher production rates the adaptive control will generally provide a more efficient and uniform use of the cutter throughout its life and due to the adjustments that are made as not to severe load the tool there will be less broken tools.

  3. **Greater part protection:** As the maximum allowable force is set for the cutter and spindle, on the same basis can be set for the part in order to protect it from any undesirable out-of-tolerance condition or damage.

4. **Less operator intervention:** With the application of adaptive control the control process has been moved further towards management via the part programmer.

5. **Easier part programming:** In the NC machine tools the part programmer was obliged to find the correct speeds and feeds to be used and this was coming after several trials until the part programmer felt satisfied with the part. With adaptive control this is almost done automatically and the limits that have to be set to it, can be easily determined by the system software.

2.28.3 Functions of Adaptive Control

- The three functions of adaptive control are:
- **IDENTIFICATION FUNCTIONS**
  - This involves determining the current performance of the process or system.
  - Normally, the performance quality of the system is defined by some relevant index of performance.
  - The identification function is concerned with determining the current value of this performance measure by making use of the feedback data from the process.
  - Since the environment will change overtime, the performance of the system will also change. Accordingly the identification is one that must proceed over time or less continuously.
  - Identification of the system may involve a number of possible measurements activities.
- **DECISION FUNCTION**
  - Once the system performance is determined, the next function is to decide how the control mechanism should be adjusted to improve process performance.
  - The decision procedure is carried out by means of a pre-programmed logic provided by the designer. Depending upon the logic the decision may be to change one or more of the controllable process.
- **MODIFICATION FUNCTION**
  - The third AC function is to implement the decision. While the decision function is a logic function, modification is concerned with a physical or mechanical change in the system.
  - It is a hardware function rather than a software function. The modification involves changing the system parameters or variables so as to drive the process towards a more optimal state.
  - The process is assumed to be influenced by some time varying environment. The adaptive system first identifies the current performance by taking measurements of inputs and outputs.

- o Depending on current performance, a decision procedure is carried out to determine what changes are needed to improve system performance.
- o Actual changes to the system are made in the modification function.

2.28.4 Types of Adaptive Control Systems

- The AC is basically a feedback system in which cutting speed and feed automatically adapt themselves to the actual condition of the process and are varied accordingly to the changes in the work conditions as work progresses.
- That is done by performing of the process output variables and calculating either a performance level or machine constrains.
- In practice the AC system of machine tools can be classified into two types:
- **ADAPTIVE CONTROL OPTIMIZATION (ACO)**
  - o This systems are based on a performance index specified for the system.
  - o This performance index is usually an economic function such as maximum production rate or minimum machining cost.
  - o The objective is to optimize the index of performance by controlling speeds and/or feeds.
- **ADAPTIVE CONTROL CONSTRAINT (ACC)**
  - o ACC are systems in which machining conditions such as spindle speed or feed rate are maximized within the prescribed limits of machines and tool constrains such as maximum torque, force or horse power.

2.28.5 Sources of Variability in Adaptive Control

- The following are the typical sources of variability in machining where AC can be most advantageously applied.
  1. Variable geometry of cut in the form of changing depth or width of cut: In these cases, feed rate is usually adjusted to compensate for the variability.
  2. Variable work piece hardness and Variable machinability: When hard spots or other areas of difficulty are encountered in a work piece, either speed or feed is reduced to avoid premature failure of tool.
  3. Variable work piece rigidity: if the work piece deflect as a result of insufficient rigidity in set-up, the feed rate must be reduced to maintain accuracy in the process.
  4. Tool wear: It has been observed in research that as the tool begins to dull, the cutting force increases. The adaptive controller will typically respond to tool dulling by reducing feed rate.
  5. Air gaps during cutting: the work piece geometry may contain shaped sections where no machining needs to be performed. These are called as air gaps. If the tool feed with same rate at such places, the time will be lost. The AC will increase the feed rate at such air gaps.

2.29 PROGRAM ON CUTTER OFFSET

- When the surface of the work piece to be machined is inclined, curved or not parallel to the machine axes, the movement of cutter will slightly be different than the machining of straight surfaces.

- In such cases the cutter has to be moved slightly more or slightly less so that the work piece will not be machined undercut or overcut.

- This distance moved by the cutter is called as cutter offset.

- The amount of offset can be added to or subtracted from (explained later) to arrive at the correct cutter coordinates.

- The cutter offset can be calculated by simple trigonometric relation.

- For machining the work piece shown in the Fig. 2.54 (a), the cutter cannot be positioned at point Z but must be positioned above Z by some unknown distance. This unknown distance is denoted by Y and can be obtained by solving the XYZ as shown in the Fig. 2.54(b).

- Similarly, the cutter cannot be moved to point R, but to some unknown distance short of point R. This unknown distance is denoted by X and can be obtained by solving the PQR as shown in the Fig. 2.54 (b).

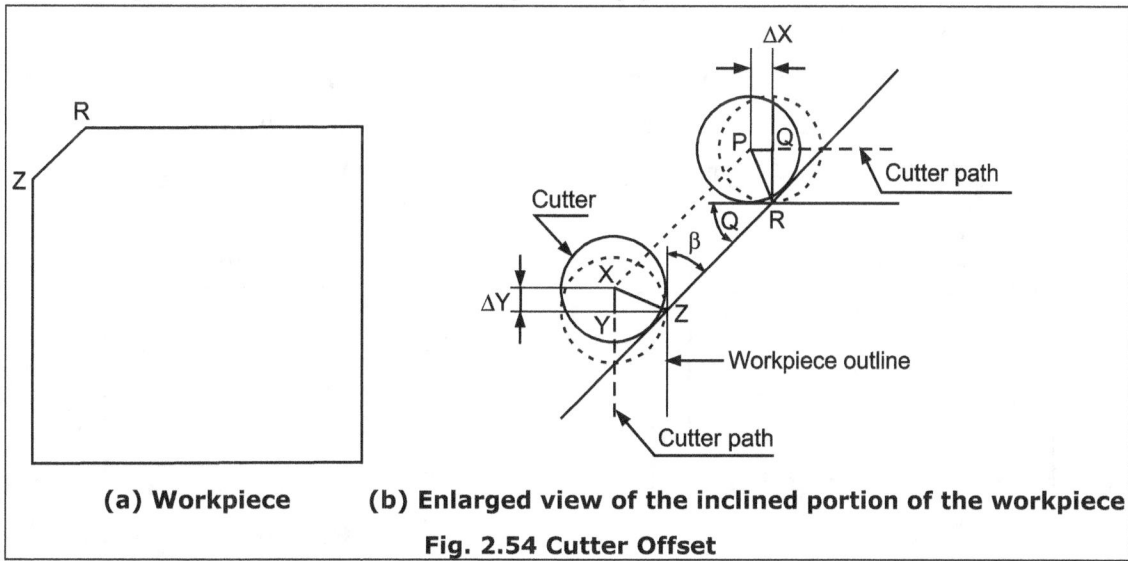

| (a) Workpiece | (b) Enlarged view of the inclined portion of the workpiece |

Fig. 2.54 Cutter Offset

Offset calculation for Y:

- In order to calculate the offset distance Y, consider the XYZ.
  - XY = Y
  - XZ = Cutter radius

- o XYZ = /2
- o Tan (/2) = XY / XZ
- o Tan (/2) = Y / Cutter radius
- o Y = Cutter radius × Tan (/2)
- Y is added to the y- coordinate of point Z.
- The x-coordinate of point Z is calculated by usual procedure.

Offset calculation for X:

- Similarly to calculate the offset distance X,
  - o X = Cutter radius × Tan (α /2)
- X is subtracted from the x-coordinate of point R.
- The y-coordinate of point R is calculated by usual procedure.

Program 2.31: *Prepare a part program for the given job as shown in Fig. 2.55 (a) by using the following data:*

Speed = 1000 rpm.

Feed = 10 mm/min.

Depth of cut = 3 mm.

Tool position from the surface of the workpiece is 10 mm above.

Thickness of job = 3 mm.

Date : Consider:

- o The tool diameter is 10 mm.
- o The Z reference is at 10 mm from the surface of the workpiece.

The actual path moved by the tool while machining is shown in the Fig. 2.55 (b). The X and Y co-ordinates of various tool positions are shown in Table 2.32.

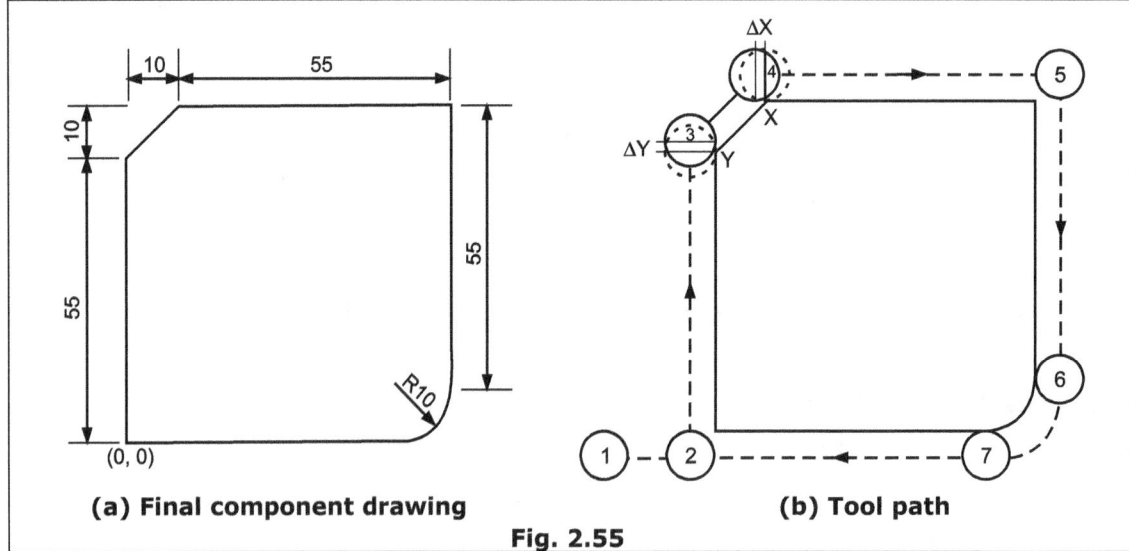

(a) Final component drawing   **(b) Tool path**

Fig. 2.55

Offset calculation:

For position 3:

$$Y = \text{Cutter radius} \times \tan(\text{/2})$$
$$= 5 \times \tan(45/2) = 4.14 \text{ mm}$$

y-coordinate of position 3 = 55 + Y = 59.14

For position 4:

$$X = \text{Cutter radius} \times \tan(\alpha/2)$$
$$= 5 \times \tan(45/2) = 4.14 \text{ mm}$$

x-coordinate of position 4 = 10 − X = 5.86

Table 2.32: X and Y Co-ordinates of Various Tool Position

Position No.	X and Y Co-ordinates	Position No.	X and Y Co-ordinates
1	−10, −5	5	70, 70
2	−5, −5	6	70, 10
3	−5, 59.14	7	55, −5
4	5.86, 70		

Part Program:

Program	Description
20809	Program number.
N100 G28 U0 V0 W0 EOB	Return to machine reference position.
N110 G90 G21 G94 G40 EOB	Absolute mode, input in mm, feed in mm/min, cutter diameter compensation cancel.
N120 M06 T01 EOB	Tool change, end mill tool at tool position number 01 in the tool magazine.
N130 M03 S1000 EOB	Spindle start clockwise direction, spindle speed.
N140 G00 Z0 M08 EOB	Rapid travel of cutter to 10 mm above the workpiece surface, coolant on.
N150 X-10 Y-5 Z-13 EOB	Rapid travel of cutter to position 1 (-10,-5) and a depth of cut of -3 mm.
N160 G01 X-5 F10 EOB	Cutter travel to position number 2 (-5,-5).
N170 Y59.14 EOB	Cutter travel to position number 3 (-5, 59.14).
N180 X5.86 Y70 EOB	Cutter travel to position number 4 (5.86, 70).
N190 X70 EOB	Cutter travel to position number 5 (70, 70).

contd. ...

N200 Y10 EOB	Cutter travel to position number 6 (70, 10).
N210 G02 X55 Y-5 R10 F10 EOB	Cutter travel to position number 7 (55, -5) Circular interpolation (clockwise)
N220 X-10 EOB	Cutter travel to position number 1 (-10, -5).
N230 G00 Z00 EOB	Rapid travel of cutter 10 mm above the workpiece surface.
N240 G28 U00 V00 W00 EOB	Rapid return to machine reference position.
N250 M05 EOB	Spindle stop.
N260 M09 EOB	Coolant off.
N 270 M30 EOB	Program end and tape rewind.

Program 2.32: *Prepare a part program for the given job as shown in Fig. 2.56 (a) by using the following data:*   **[W-15]**

Speed = 1000 rpm.

Feed = 50 mm/min.

Tool position from the surface of the workpiece is 5 mm above.

Thickness of job = 2 mm.

Data: Consider:

The tool diameter is 10 mm.

The actual path moved by the tool while machining is shown in the Fig. 2.56 (b). The X and Y co-ordinates of various tool positions are shown in Table 2.33.

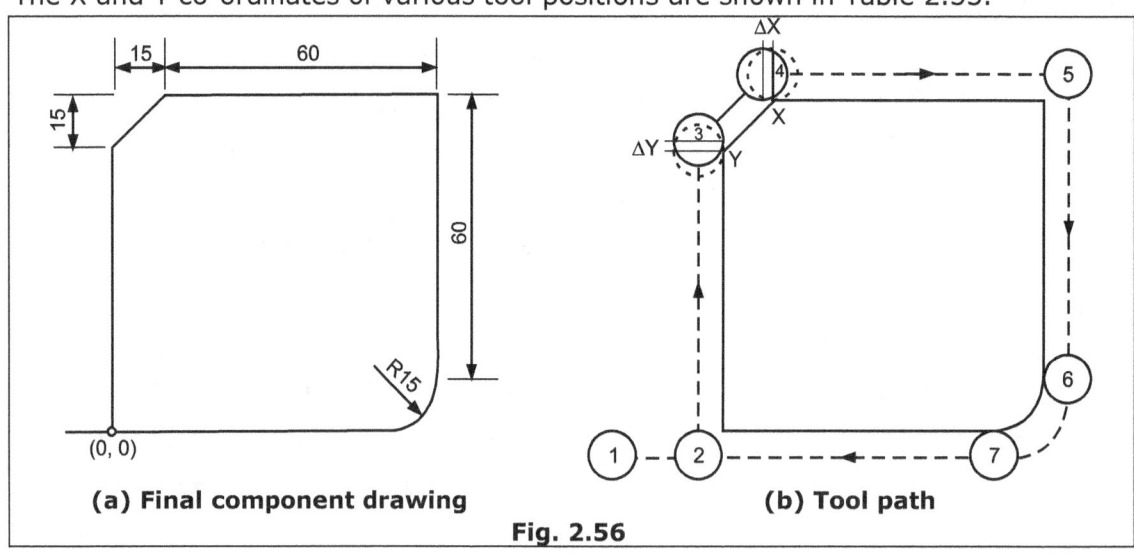

(a) Final component drawing   **(b) Tool path**

Fig. 2.56

Offset calculation:

For position 3:

$$Y = \text{Cutter radius} \times \tan(\,/2)$$
$$= 5 \times \tan(45/2) = 4.14 \text{ mm}$$

y-coordinate of position 3 = 60 + Y = 64.14

For position 4:

$$X = \text{Cutter radius} \times \tan(a/2)$$
$$= 5 \times \tan(45/2) = 4.14 \text{ mm}$$

x-coordinate of position 4 = 15 – X = 10.86

Table 2.33: X and Y Co-ordinates of Various Tool Position

Position No.	X and Y Co-ordinates	Position No.	X and Y Co-ordinates
1	–10, –5	5	80, 80
2	–5, –5	6	80, 15
3	–5, 64.14	7	60, –5
4	10.86, 80		

Part Program:

Program	Description
02356	Program number.
N100 G28 U0 V0 W0 EOB	Return to machine reference position.
N110 G90 G21 G94 EOB	Absolute mode, input in mm, feed in mm/min.
N120 M06 T01 EOB	Tool change, end mill tool at tool position number 01 in the tool magazine.
N130 M03 S1000 EOB	Spindle start clockwise direction, spindle speed.
N140 G00 Z0 M08 EOB	Rapid travel of cutter to 10 mm above the workpiece surface, coolant on.
N150 X-10 Y-5 Z-13 EOB	Rapid travel of cutter to position 1 (–10, –5) and a depth of cut of –3 mm.
N160 G01 X-5 F10 EOB	Cutter travel to position number 2 (–5, –5).
N170 Y59.14 EOB	Cutter travel to position number 3 (–5, 64.14).
N180 X5.86 Y70 EOB	Cutter travel to position number 4 (10.86, 80).

contd. ...

N190　X70 EOB	Cutter travel to position number 5 (80, 80).
N200　Y10 EOB	Cutter travel to position number 6 (80, 15).
N210　G02 X55 Y-5 R10 F10 EOB	Cutter travel to position number 7 (60, −5) Circular interpolation (clockwise)
N220　X-10 EOB	Cutter travel to position number 1 (−10, −5).
N230　G00 Z00 EOB	Rapid travel of cutter 10 mm above the workpiece surface.
N240　G28 U00 V00 W00 EOB	Rapid return to machine reference position.
N250　M05 EOB	Spindle stop.
N260　M09 EOB	Coolant off.
N 270　M30 EOB	Program end and tape rewind.

Program 2.33: *Prepare a part program for the given job as shown in Fig. 2.57 (a). The thickness of workpiece is 3 mm. The tool diameter is 10 mm.*

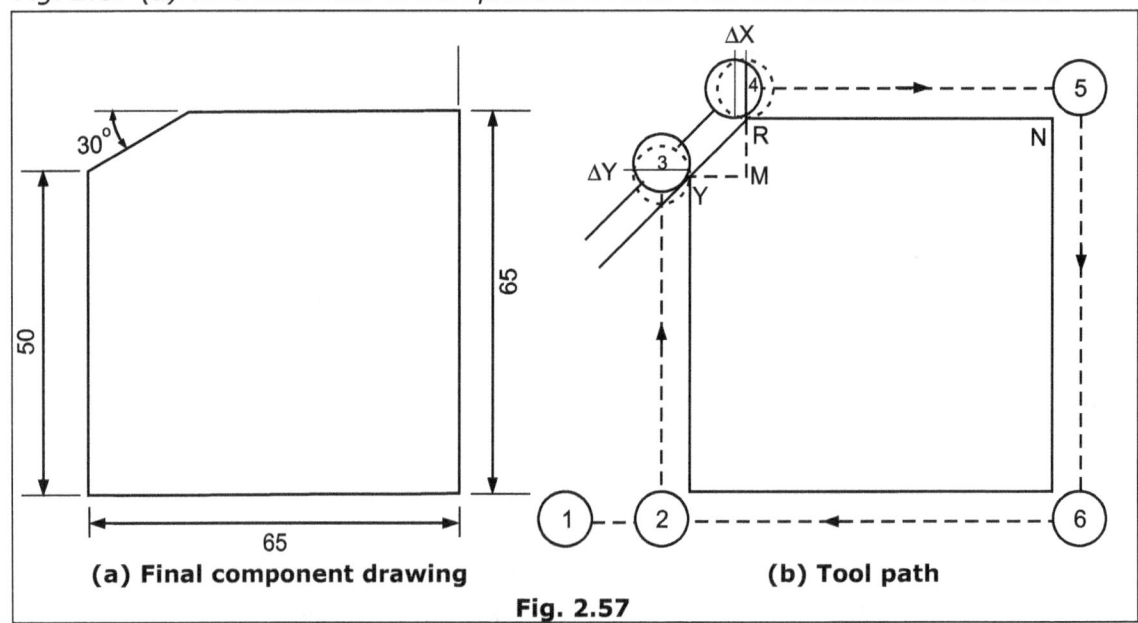

(a) Final component drawing　　　　(b) Tool path

Fig. 2.57

Data: Assume: Z datum is at lower left corner of the plate. The tool path is shown in Fig. 2.57 (b). The X and Y co-ordinates of various tool positions are shown in Table 2.34.

Offset calculation:

For position 3: The offset is in Y direction and is represented by Y. This offset has to be added to the y-coordinate of point Z. The x-coordinate of position 3 will be the same as that of position 2.

$$Y = \text{Cutter radius} \times \tan (\,/2)$$
$$= 10 \times \tan (60/2)$$
$$= 5.77 \text{ mm}$$

So,   y-coordinate of position 3 = 50 + Y

$$= 55.77$$

For position 4: The offset is in X direction and is represented by X. This offset has to be subtracted from the x-coordinate of point R. The y-coordinate of position 4 will be the same as that of position 5.

$$X = \text{Cutter radius} \times \tan(\alpha/2)$$

$$= 10 \times \tan(30/2)$$

$$= 2.67 \text{ mm}$$

In ZMR,

$$ZM = RM \times \tan(ZRM)$$

$$= 10 \times \tan 60$$

$$= 17.32$$

So,   x-coordinate of position 4 = ZM - X

$$= 17.32 - 2.67$$

$$= 14.65$$

Table 2.34: X and Y Co-ordinates of Various Tool Position

Position No.	X and Y Co-ordinates	Position No.	X and Y Co-ordinates
1	−10 , −5	4	14.65, 70
2	−5 , −5	5	70 , 70
3	−5 , 55.77	6	70 , -5

Part Program :

Program	Description
20809	Program number.
N10 G28 U0 V0 W0 EOB	Return to machine reference position.
N20 G90 G21 G94 G40 EOB	Absolute mode, input in mm, feed in mm/min, cutter diameter compensation cancel.
N30 M06 T01 EOB	Tool change, end mill tool at tool position number 01 in the tool magazine.
N40 M03 S1000 EOB	Spindle start clockwise direction, spindle speed.
N50 G00 Z5 M08 EOB	Rapid travel of cutter to 5 mm above the workpiece surface, coolant on.

contd. ...

N60 X-10 Y-5 Z-3 EOB	Rapid travel of cutter to position 1 (−10,−5) and a depth of cut of −3 mm.
N70 G01 X-5 F60 EOB	Cutter travel to position number 2 (−5,−5).
N80 Y55.77 EOB	Cutter travel to position number 3 (−5, 55.77).
N90 X14.65 Y70 EOB	Cutter travel to position number 4 (14.65, 70).
N100 X70 EOB	Cutter travel to position number 5 (70, 70).
N110 Y-5 EOB	Cutter travel to position number 6 (70, −5).
N120 X-10 EOB	Cutter travel to position number 1 (−10, −5).
N130 G00 Z10 EOB	Rapid travel of cutter 10 mm above the workpiece surface.
N140 G28 U00 V00 W00 EOB	Rapid return to machine reference position.
N150 M05 EOB	Spindle stop.
N160 M09 EOB	Coolant off.
N 170 M30 EOB	Program end and tape rewind.

Program 2.34: *Prepare a part program for the given job as shown in Fig. 2.58 (a). The thickness of workpiece is 5 mm. The tool diameter is 8 mm.*

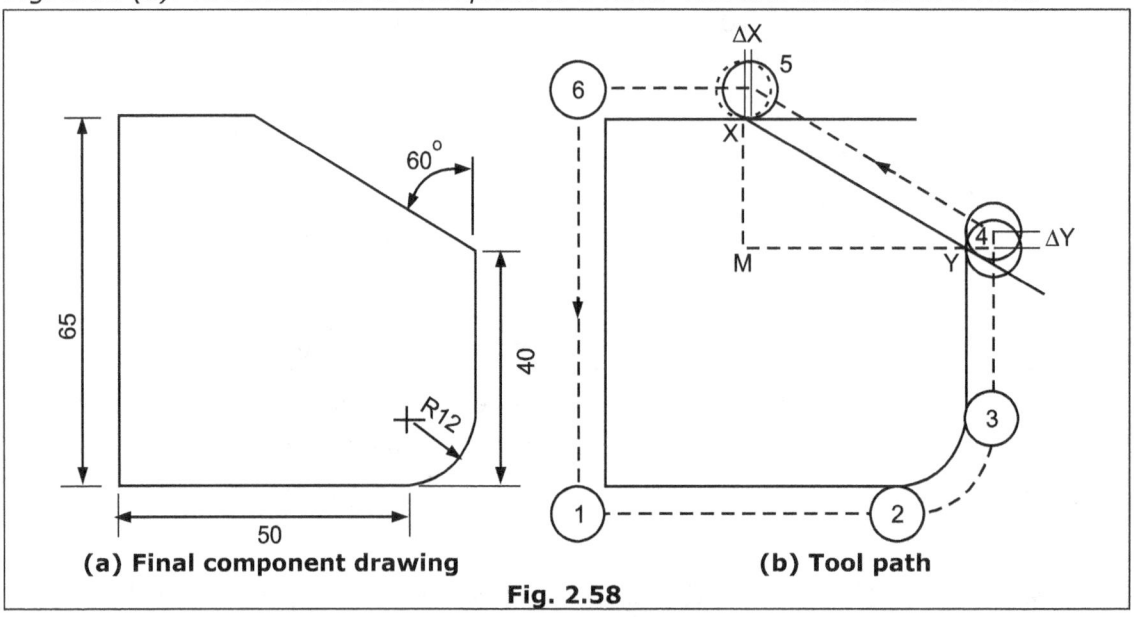

(a) Final component drawing   **(b) Tool path**

Fig. 2.58

Assume: Z datum is at lower left corner of the plate. The tool path is shown in Fig. 2.58 (b). The X and Y co-ordinates of various tool positions are shown in Table 2.35.

Offset calculation:

For position 4: The offset is in Y direction and is represented by Y. This offset has to be added to the y-coordinate of point Y. The x-coordinate of position 4 will be the same as that of position 3.

$$Y = \text{Cutter radius} \times \tan(\,/2)$$
$$= 8 \times \tan(60/2)$$
$$= 4.61 \text{ mm}$$

So,   y-coordinate of position 4 $= 40 + Y$
$$= 44.61$$

For position 5: The offset is in X direction and is represented by X. This offset has to be added to the x-coordinate of point X. The y-coordinate of position 5 will be the same as that of position 6.

$$X = \text{Cutter radius} \times \tan(a/2)$$
$$= 8 \times \tan(30/2)$$
$$= 2.14 \text{ mm}$$

In XMY,

$$MY = XM \times \tan(MXY)$$
$$= 25 \times \tan 60$$
$$= 43.30$$

So,   x-coordinate of position 5 $= 62 - MY + X$
$$= 62 - 43.30 + 2.14$$
$$= 20.84$$

Table 2.35: X and Y Co-ordinates of Various Tool Position

Position No.	X and Y Co-ordinates	Position No.	X and Y Co-ordinates
1	– 4, – 4	4	66, 44.61
2	50, –4	5	20.84, 68
3	66, 12	6	– 4, 68

Part Program :

Program	Description
20809	Program number.
N05 G28 U0 V0 W0 EOB	Return to machine reference position.
N10 G90 G21 G94 G40 EOB	Absolute mode, input in mm, feed in mm/min, cutter diameter compensation cancel.
N15 M06 T06 EOB	Tool change, end mill of 8 mm diameter at tool position number 06 in the tool magazine.
N20 M03 S1000 EOB	Spindle start clockwise direction, spindle speed.
N25 G00 Z5 M08 EOB	Rapid travel of cutter to 5 mm above the workpiece surface, coolant on.
N30 X-4 Y-4 EOB	Rapid travel of cutter to position 1 (-4,-4) and a depth of cut of -3 mm.
N35 G01 Z-5 F60 EOB	Take a 5 mm depth of cut by G01.
N40 X50 EOB	Cutter travel to position number 2 (50,-4)

contd. ...

N45 G03 X66 Y12 F50 EOB	Cutter travel to position number 3 (66 , 12).
N50 G01 Y44.61 F60 EOB	Cutter travel to position number 4 (66, 44.61).
N55 X20.84 Y68 EOB	Cutter travel to position number 5 (20.84, 68).
N60 X-4 EOB	Cutter travel to position number 6 (-4 ,68).
N65 Y-4 EOB	Cutter travel to position number 1 (-4, -4).
N70 G00 Z10 EOB	Rapid travel of cutter 10 mm above the workpiece surface.
N75 G28 U00 V00 W00 EOB	Rapid return to machine reference position.
N80 M05 EOB	Spindle stop.
N85 M09 EOB	Coolant off.
N90 M30 EOB	Program end and tape rewind.

Important Points

Machining Center

- A machining center is a computer-controlled machine tool with automatic tool changing capability.
- Any machining center is capable of carrying out milling, drilling, reaming, tapping, boring, facing, turning and other operations without operator intervention for change of tools.
- In a machining center, the workpiece does not have to be moved to another machine for additional operations. The tool and the machine are brought to the workpiece.
- On machining center, the non-productive time is reduced to a great extent.

Axis Identification

- The three linear axes identified on the machining centers are X, Y and Z axes.
- Z-axis is always the main spindle axis.
- X-axis is always horizontal and parallel to the workpiece surface.
- Y-axis is perpendicular to both X and Z axes.

Automatic Tool Changer

- ATC is used to change the tool automatically in the least possible time.
- They allow tool changing without the intervention of the operator.
- An ATC grips the tool in the spindle, pulls it out and replaces it with another tool.
- An ATC consists of a tool magazine for storing the tools and a tool change unit for transferring the tool from tool magazine to machine spindle.

Tool Magazine

- The tool magazine is used to store the tools required during the machining operation.
- The tools in the magazine are identified by the tool number.

CNC Programming

- The part programming uses various NC words to write a CNC program.
- Various NC words are used to write one block of instruction.
- The set of various blocks of instructions which tells the machine tool about the steps to be performed to manufacture a component is known as part programming.

Preparatory Functions

- The preparatory word prepares the control unit to execute the instructions given in the part program.
- More than one G-code from the different groups can be programmed in one block.
- If two G-codes from the same group are programmed in the same block, then the last programmed G-code will be executed.
- All G-codes are either modal or non-modal. Modal codes stay in effect until they are cancelled by another code of the same group.
- Non-modal codes stay in effect only for the blocks for which they are programmed.

Miscellaneous Functions
- The miscellaneous functions are used to specify certain miscellaneous functions.
- Only one M-code can be programmed in a block.
- All M-codes are modal.

Machining Along Straight Line
- While machining along a straight line, the tool is first taken to the required depth outside the workpiece and then G01 code is used.
- G01 is a modal code and feed should be specified with G01.
- Generally the workpiece surface is taken as zero, above which is positive Z and below it is negative Z.

Machining Along Curved Surface
- When curved surfaces are to be machined then the codes G02 and G03 are used.

Cutter Radius Compensation
- Using cutter compensation the tool path can be developed for the center line of the tool rather than the point on the periphery.
- The tool path is offset by the distance equal to the radius of the cutter.
- This value is stored in the control system under the address D01 or D02 etc.

Advantages of Cutter Radius Compensation
- Cutter path need not be calculated mathematically.
- The same program can be used for cutter of any diameter.
- The part program can be developed using the actual dimensions of the component.

Subroutine
- A subroutine is a program used when identical machining operation is to be performed.
- It is stored in the computer's memory under separate program number.
- A subroutine can be called anywhere and for any number of times in the main program.
- After execution of subroutine the controller returns back to the main program.
- The subroutine is always written in incremental mode.

Canned Cycle
- It is a set of instructions that perform a fixed sequence of operation.
- It is used for repetitive operation.

Practice Questions

1. Define CNC.   **(Refer Section 2.1)**
2. What are the features of CNC machine ?   **(Refer Section 2.2)**
3. Explain the main components of CNC machine.   **(Refer Section 2.3)**
4. Give advantages of CNC machine.   **(Refer Section 2.4)**
5. Give disadvantages of CNC machine.   **(Refer Section 2.5)**
6. Give the classification of CNC machines.   **(Refer Section 2.6)**
7. Classify CNC based on control system characteristics.   **(Refer Section 2.6.1)**
8. Classify CNC based on positioning co-ordinates.   **(Refer Section 2.6.3)**
9. Classify CNC based on feedback.   **(Refer Section 2.6.3)**
10. Classify CNC based on type of control system.   **(Refer Section 2.6.3)**
11. Describe electronic control system.   **(Refer Section 2.6.3)**
12. Compare between absolute and incremental system.   **(Refer Section 2.8.1)**
13. Compare between CNC milling machine and conventional milling machine?   **(Refer Section 2.8.2)**
14. Compare between open loop and closed loop control system.   **(Refer Section 2.8.3)**

15. What is meant by axis identification of CNC. **(Refer Section 2.9)**
16. How linear and rotary axes are identified (designated on CNC machines)?
 (Refer Section 2.9)
17. Explain thumb rate for axis identification in CNC. **(Refer Section 2.9.1)**
18. Explain various NC words. **(Refer Section 2.11)**
19. Explain preparatory functions. **(Refer Section 2.12)**
20. Explain Miscellaneous functions. What are preparatory functions? What are modal and non-modal codes? **(Refer Section 2.12)**
21. Explain programming formats. **(Refer Section 2.14)**
22. Define part programming. **(Refer Section 2.15)**
23. What is cutter radius compensation? **(Refer Section 2.20)**
24. Give advantages of CRC. **(Refer Section 2.20.1)**
25. Define subroutine. **(Refer Section 2.21)**
26. Define canned cycle. **(Refer Section 2.22)**
27. Compare between subroutines canned cycle. **(Refer Section 2.23)**
28. Give importance of subroutines canned cycle. **(Refer Section 2.24)**
29. Explain Jag mode. **(Refer Section 2.27)**
30. Explain adaptive control. **(Refer Section 2.28)**
31. Give benefits of ACM. **(Refer Section 2.28.2)**
32. What are the functions of Adaptive control? **(Refer Section 2.28.3)**
33. Explain the type of ACS. **(Refer Section 2.28.4)**
34. What are the sources of variability in AC? **(Refer Section 2.28.5)**

MSBTE Questions & Answers as Per 'G' Scheme

Winter 2014

1. Compare closed loop CNC system with open loop CNC system. **(4 M)**
Ans. Refer Section 2.8.3.
2. Define part program. Explain the terms 'preparatory functions' and 'miscellaneous functions' in the context of CNC programming. **(4 M)**
Ans. Refer Section 2.15, 2.12 and 2.13.
3. What are the advantages of CNC machines? **(6 M)**
Ans. Refer Section 2.4.
4. How are linear and rotary axes identified in CNC machines. **(6 M)**
Ans. Refer Section 2.9.
5. Prepare a part program to machines to workpiece shown in Fig. 1 on CNC lathe machine.
 (8 M)

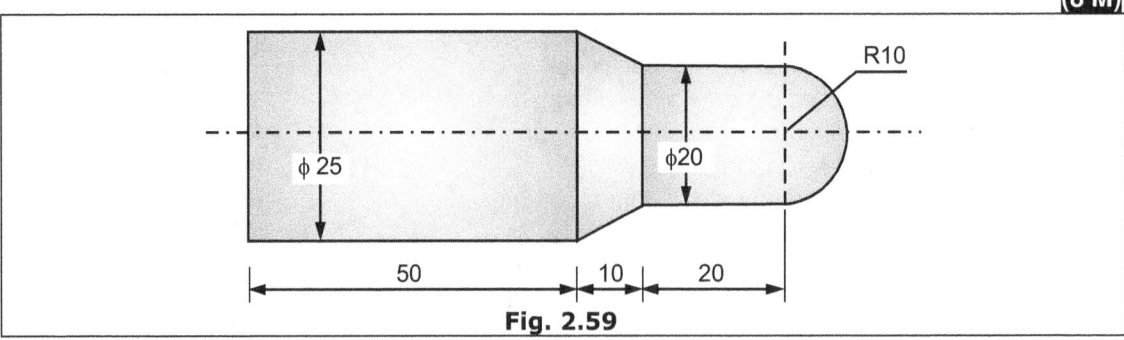

Fig. 2.59

Ans. Refer program 2.29, page 2.85.

Summer 2015

1. With neat sketch explain closed loop control system. **(4 M)**

Ans. Refer Section 2.6.3.

2. Explain absolute and incremental part programming. **(4 M)**

Ans. Refer Section 2.6.2.

3. Prepare a part program for the component shown in Fig. 2.37 (B) (a) by using the following data : Use a 10 mm diameter end mill. The part depth is 4 mm. Use a feed rate of 120 mm/min and spindle speed of 800 rpm. Use cutter radius compensation. Take z = 0 at top surface of job. **(6 M)**

Ans. Refer Program 2.21 (A).

4. Prepare a part program to machine the work piece shown in Fig. 2.53 (a) on the CNC lathe machine. **(6 M)**

Ans. Refer Program 2.30.

Winter 2015

1. Distinguish between absolute and incremental coordinate system of CNC. **(4 M)**

Ans. Refer Section 2.8.1.

2. Explain the closed loop control system with block diagram and state functions of each element. **(6 M)**

Ans. Refer Section 2.6.3 (b).

3. Explain the use of following codes in part programming G95, G41, M06, M98. **(4 M)**

Ans. Refer Table 2.1 and 2.2.

4. Prepare a part program for the given job as shown in Fig. 2.56 (a) by using the following data:

Speed = 1000 rpm.

Feed = 50 mm/min.

Tool position from the surface of the workpiece is 5 mm above.

Thickness of job = 2 mm. **(4 M)**

Ans. Refer Program 2.32.

Summer 2016

1. Differentiate between subroutine and canned cycles used in CNC part programming. **(4 M)**

Ans. Refer Section 2.23.

2. What are the advantages and disadvantages of using CNC machines for machining? **(4 M)**

Ans. Refer Sections 2.4 and 2.5.

3. Write a part program to machine the part given in figure on CNC milling machine. **(8 M)**

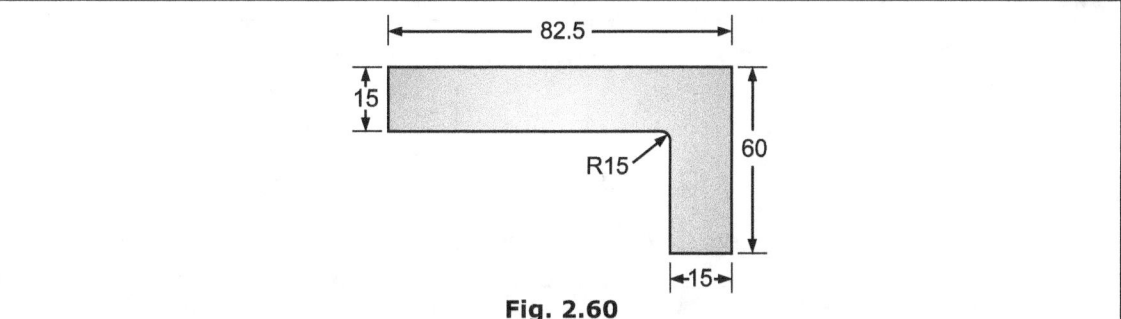

Fig. 2.60

Ans. Refer Program 2.32.

1. Sketch any two CNC tool magazines. **(4 M)**

Ans.

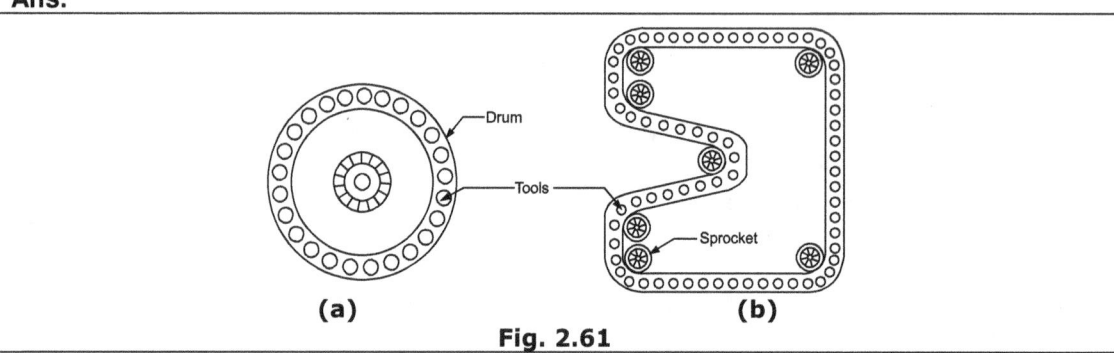

Fig. 2.61

2. Write CNC programme for turning a component shown in Fig. 2.62. Assume suitable data if necessary.

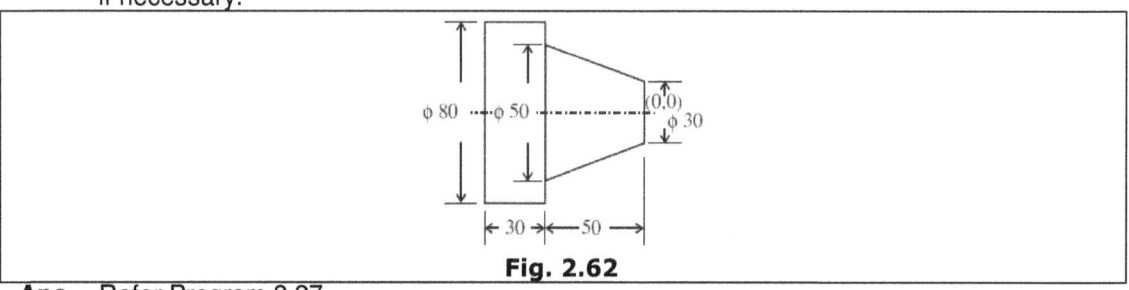

Fig. 2.62

Ans. Refer Program 2.27.

3. Write CNC programme for milling a component as shown in Fig. 2.63 with end mill of 20 mm diameter, thickness of plate 10 mm, feed 90 mm/min, spindle rpm 450. Assume suitable data if necessary.

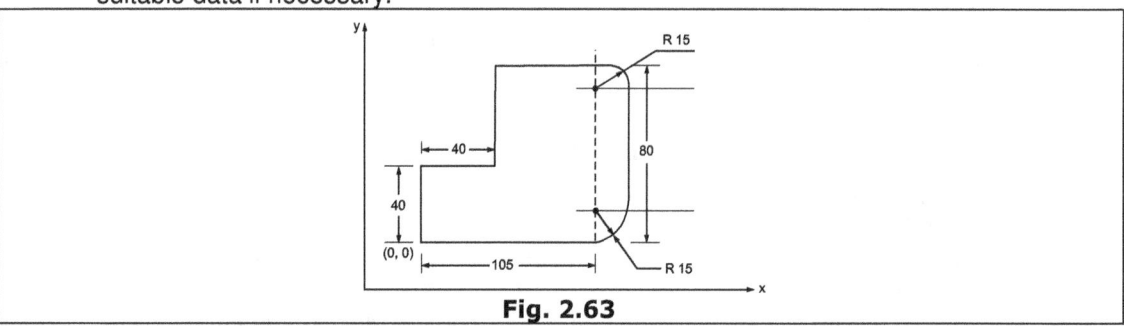

Fig. 2.63

Ans.

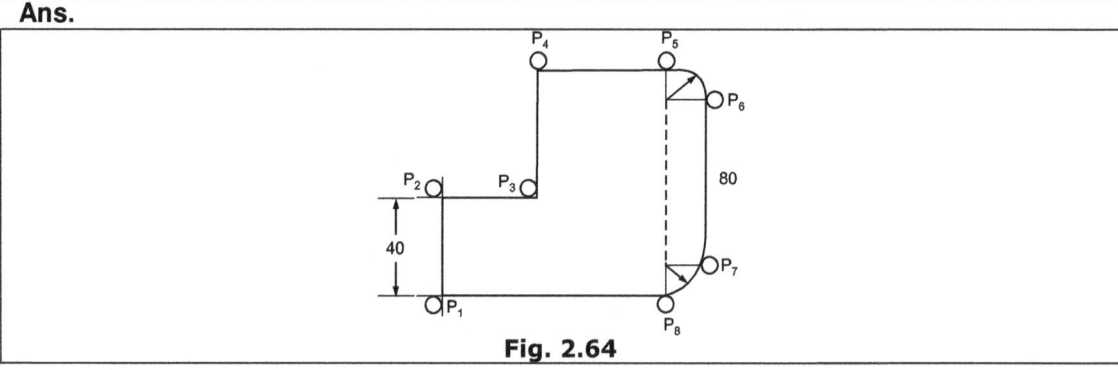

Fig. 2.64

Pt	X	Y	Z
P1	−10	− 10	
P2	−10	50	
P3	30	50	
P4	30	90	
P5	105	90	
P6	130	65	
P7	130	15	
P8	105	− 10	

N10 G90 G21   N10 G90 G21 N94 FOB
N20 T01 M06   N20 M06 TO1 FOB
N30 S1000 M03   F30 M03 S450 EOB
N40 G00 X-10 Y0   N40 G00 X-10 Y-10 EOB
N50 G00 Z5 M08   N50 G00 Z-5 FOB
N60 G01 Z-10   N60 G01 Z-10 F90 FOB
N70 G01 G42 D01 X0 Y0   N70 G01 X-10 450 F90 FOB
N120 G01 X-130 Y-15 F90 FOB   N80 X30 EOB
N130 G02 X-105 Y-10 R15 FOB   N90 Y90 EOB
N140 G01 X-10 Y-10 F90 FOB   N100 X105 FOB
N150 G00 250   N110 G02 X130 Y65 R15 EOB
N160 G2800 V0 W0 EOB
N170 M05

4. Write advantages & applications of CNC machine.
Ans. **Advantages:** Refer Section 2.4.
     Applications of CNC:
     1. CNC machines are extensively used in industries where metal removal is parts. For example, automotive industries where gears, shafts and other complex material.
     2. CNC machines are also used in the manufacturing industries for producing rounded and even threaded jobs.
     3. Fabrication industries for a number of machining operations such as plastic cutting, shearing, forming and welding to create these plates.
     4. For measuring or controlling the dimensions of product using co-ordinate.

Summer 2017

1. Explain the use of following codes in part programming G95, G41, M06, M98.
Ans. Refer Tables 2.1 and 2.2.
2. State meaning of absolute and incremental co-ordinate system.
Ans. Refer Section 2.6.2.
3. Prepare a part program for machining component as shown in Fig. 2.65. Use following data: cutting speed : 1200 rpm, feed : 60 min/min, thickness of component 3 mm, Tool reference position is 4 mm above the surface of the workpiece. Assume suitable data if any. Neglect cutter radius compensation.

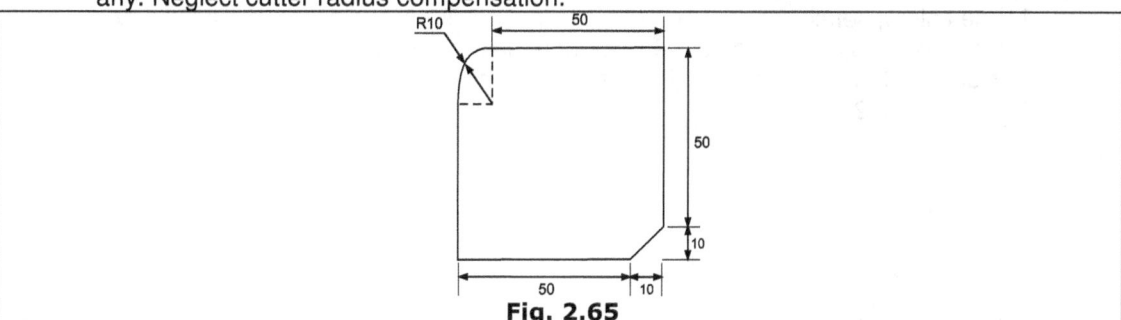

Fig. 2.65

Ans. Refer similar problem to 2.31.

4. Prepare a part program to machine the workpiece shown in Fig. 2.66 on CNC lathe.

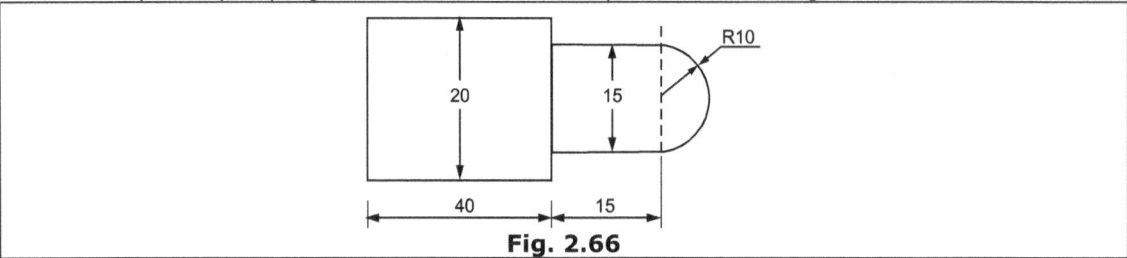

Fig. 2.66

Ans. Refer similar problem to 2.29.

5. Explain the following terms in CNC machine programming:
(i) Dry run, (ii) Jog mode, (iii) Black by Block execution

Ans. **(i) Dry run:** Setting a new component on a CNC machine may include incorrect placement of the work holding device, improper cutting tool assembly, incorrect loading of cutting tools into the machine's turret or magazine, incorrect lengths of cutting tools and incorrectly entering the offset values. When the CNC is run for the first job, it is a crucial and time consuming task. A small negligence might be cause of an accident like tool breakage.

To make the first run easy and safe the CNC machine manufacturers and CNC control manufacturers provides a way by which the tool feed can be easily controlled with feed override. In dry run mode, the tool feed can be lower manually by the operator if the tool is entering a bit danger zone and can increase the tool feed when the tool is away from the component.

Thus in dry run mode there is movement of tool only with feed control in the hands of operator.

In Dry Run all the cnc blocks whether those are starting with G00 or G01 and other G-code like G02/G03 run with the same feed, which is controlled through Feed Override. On Fanuc the feed override is controlled through Handwheel after feed override button press, and there also exists a Rapid Feed Button which if pressed during Dry Run Mode the CNC machine program block will run with Rapid Feed. The dry-run function may slow rapid motions and speed-up cutting motions, so never allow a cutting tool to machine the workpiece under the influence of dry-run.

(ii) Jog mode: Refer Section 2.27.

(iii) Black by Block execution: A CNC program block is normally written as
          N40 G01 X80 Y 20 F100 EOB
Each block consists of various NC works separated by space. Each NC word is succeeded by a numeric value. The last NC word in a block is EOB (end of a block). While execution of a CNC program the controller reads the first block of instruction. It then moves to second block only if it reads the EOB word. (It can also be replaced by Lf(line finish), semicolon (;) or enter sign). If a block does not end with this NC word, then the controller will not execute the block and the program does not continues.

6. Explain: (i) Open loop control, (ii) Closed loop control in CNC.

Ans. Refer Section 2.6.3.

■■■

Chapter **3**

OTHER MACHINING METHODS

About This Chapter

At the end of this chapter students will be able to:

➲ State and visualise the basic principle of broaching.

➲ Classify broaching machines w.r.t. configuration and use.

➲ Understand the difference between centre and capstan/turret lathe.

➲ State and visualise the basic principle of boring.

➲ Understand how boring is carried out.

3.1 INTRODUCTION TO BROACHING

- Broaching is the process of removing metal with a tool called as broach, which has "teeth" arranged in a row. Each tooth is successively higher than the previous tooth and removes more material.

- The amount of tooth rise between the successive teeth of the broach is equivalent to the infeed given in shaping.

- Thus the first few sets of teeth remove most of the material, while the last few provide a finishing cut with very small amount of material removal.

- The geometric shape of the last set of teeth is identical to the required geometry of the designed part.

- In broaching, one stroke or cycle of the machine produces a finished part.

- Broaching is used to produce both internal and external features.

- Production rates are high and tolerances of +/– 0.01 mm are possible.

- Broaching is similar to planning, competes with milling and boring, and gives turning and grinding stiff competition.

- Properly used, broaching can greatly increase productivity, hold tight tolerances, produce precision finishes, and minimize the need for highly skilled machine operators.

- Machining by broaching is preferably used for making straight through holes of various forms and sizes of section, internal and external through straight or helical slots or grooves, external surfaces of different shapes, teeth of external and internal splines and small spur gears etc.

(3.1)

3.2 CLASSIFICATION OF BROACHING MACHINES [W-14]

- A broaching machine is one of the simplest machine tool. It is designed for machining accurate external and internal surfaces. The basic principle movement used in broaching is of straight line motion. Either the broach or the work piece is moved along the straight line in order to occur the machining. [S-15]
- A broaching machine is classified as below:
  - According to the method of operation
    - (a) Pull broaching machine
    - (b) Push broaching machine
    - (c) Stationary broaching machine
    - (d) Continuous broaching machine
  - According to the kind of operation
    - (a) Internal broaching machine
    - (b) External broaching machine
  - According to their use
    - (a) Single purpose broaching machine
    - (b) Combination broaching machine
  - According to direction of broaching machine
    - (a) Horizontal BM
    - (b) Vertical BM
  - According to their construction
    - (a) Solid
    - (b) Built-up
    - (c) Progressive
    - (d) Inserted tooth
  - According to their function
    - (a) Keyway broach
    - (b) Spline broach
    - (c) Sizing broach
    - (d) Spiral broach
    - (e) surface broach

3.3 BROACHING TOOL

□ A broach is a cutting tool having multiple teeth along its length. The elements of broaching tool are shown in Fig. 3.1 and are explained as below:

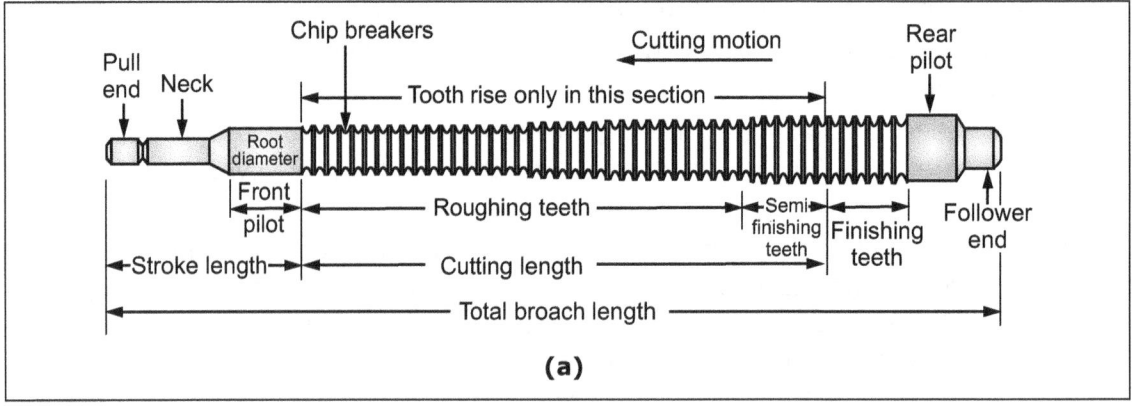

(a)

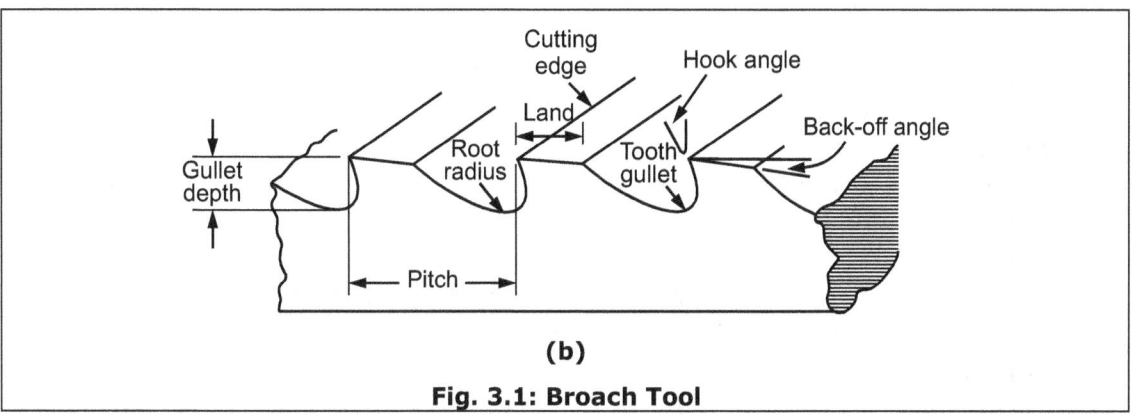

(b)
Fig. 3.1: Broach Tool

Pull End:
- o It is that end of the broach which is connected to the puller of the broaching machine.
- o Pull end occurs only in pull broach.

Front Pilot:
- o It guides the broach in to the hole of the hole of the work piece.
- o It serves as a safety check to prevent overloading of the first roughing tooth and correct axial alignment.

Roughing Teeth:
- o The teeth which take the first cuts in any broaching operation are known as roughing teeth. Generally they take heavier cuts than the semifinishing teeth. Most of the metal removal is done by the roughing teeth.

Semi-finishing teeth:
- o It follows the roughing teeth and removes small amount of material.
- o It provides smoothness to the surface of the work piece.

Finishing teeth:
- o All the finishing teeth are of the same size. They produce exact size and finish the work piece.

Rear pilot:
- o The rear pilot maintains tool alignment as the final finish teeth pass through the work piece hole.

Chip breaker:
- o Notches in the teeth of broaches which breaks-up chips, facilitating their removal is called as chip breaker.

Land:
- o The thickness of the top of the broach tooth is called as land. It gives a slight clearance and thus form the clearance angle or back-off angle.

Chip Space:
- o Space between broach teeth which accommodates chips during cut. Sometimes called the "chip gullet," it includes the face angle, face angle radius, and back-of-tooth radius.

Face Angle:

o Angle of the cutting edge of a broach tooth. Sometimes called the "hook" angle or rake angle forms one part of the cutting edge.

Face Angle Radius:

o The radius just below the cutting edge that blends into the back of tooth radius.

Rise per Tooth:

o Progressive increase in tooth height from tooth-to-tooth of a broach. Usually greater in roughing teeth than in semifinishing teeth.

Back-off angle:

o It provides relief to the tooth, to prevent excessive rubbing on the work.

3.4 COMPARISON BETWEEN PULL AND PUSH BROACH

[W-14, W-15, S-16, 17]

Sr. No.	Pull Broach	Push Broach
1.	This broach is designed to pull out of the work piece.	This broach is designed to push through the work piece.
2.	It is longer in length than push broach.	It is comparatively shorter in length.
3.	It is used where a longer surface is to be broached.	It is used where a short length is to be broached.
4.	It carries more number of teeth and more stock can be removed in one pass.	It carries less number of teeth and less material is removed in each pass.
5.	The pull broach is in tension.	The push broach is in compression.

3.5 BASIC PARTS OF HORIZONTAL BROACHING MACHINE

• The basic parts of a horizontal broaching machine are shown in Fig. 3.2.

[W-15]

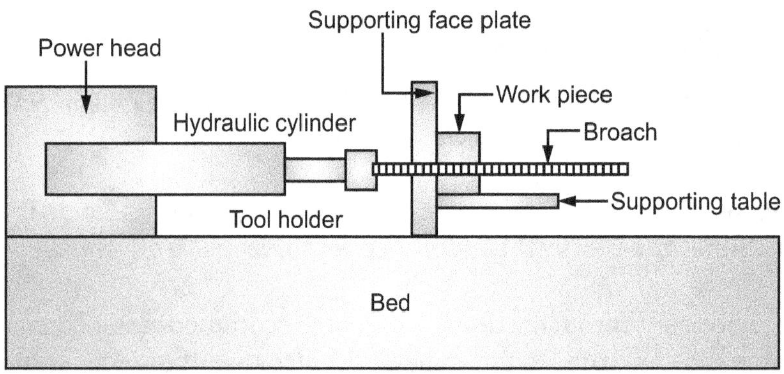

Fig. 3.2: Parts of a horizontal broaching machine

3.5.1 Functions of Parts   [W-15]

* The functions of various parts of a horizontal broaching machine are:

   (i) Power head: It provides arrangement for getting required power to run the system.

   (ii) Machine bed: It is support to all machine members. It also absorb shock and vibrations as it is made of cast iron.

   (iii) Tool holder: It is a device to hold the tool correctly in position in order to maintain precision and accuracy in all machined w/p.

   (iv) Supporting table: It gives enough support to the w/p. It provides stability to the w/p during operation.

   (v) Pulling head: It is used to transmit motion to the broach from piston rod of hydraulic cylinder.

   (vi) Drive mechanism: Used to pull or push the broach through the work piece.

3.5.2 Advantages of Broaching Machine

* The broaching machine provides following advantages:
   1. Higher production rate with unskilled worker.
   2. Longer tool life since each tooth removes less material.
   3. Roughing and finishing operations can be performed by the same tool and in one pass.
   4. Cutting fluid can be easily applied.

3.5.3 Applications of Broaching Machine

* Broaching machines are used in following area:
   1. In automotive industry for manufacturing gears, cylinder block, pistons, carburetors etc.
   2. Forming of teeth in internal and external gears, in cutting suitable grooves or splines in casting or forging.
   3. Cutting of keyways and holes square, hexagonal and other shapes very efficiently.
   4. Machining irregularly shaped holes of considerable length very economically in mass production.

3.6 ADVANTAGES OF BROACHING   [W-16, S-17]

* The advantages of broaching are listed below:
   1. The process can be done for both internal and external machining.
   2. It is simple operation, hence does not require highly skilled operator.
   3. As loading and unloading is rapid, the rate of production is high.
   4. As both roughing and finishing can be done in one pass, so broaching is fast operation.
   5. Broaching is faster than any other machining process.
   6. High accuracy and higher surface finish can be obtained.
   7. The cutting force of the broach serves to clamp the work piece and hold it firmly in position.
   8. Any form that can be produced on a broaching tool can be produced by the tool.

3.7 DISADVANTAGES OF BROACHING

- The disadvantages of broaching are as follows:
  1. It is a single purpose tool.
  2. Tool cost is very high, so the process is justified only for mass production.
  3. In some cases, it is not suited for low production rates.
  4. The parts to be broached must be strong enough to withstand high cutting forces.
  5. Surface to be broached must be accessible.
  6. Blind holes cannot be easily produced.
  7. Tool sharpening is difficult and expensive process.

3.8 APPLICATIONS OF BROACHING   [W-15, S-17]

- The applications of broaching are listed below:
  1. Machining of bearing caps.
  2. In automobile to machine cylinder block, cylinder heads, connecting rods etc.
  3. For machining of gears, sprocket teeth, etc.
  4. For machining of aircraft engine parts.
  5. For machining of turbine blades.
  6. For producing variety of shapes.
  7. For making hand tools like pliers, wrenches etc.
- The various shapes that can be machined by a branch is shown in Fig. 3.3.

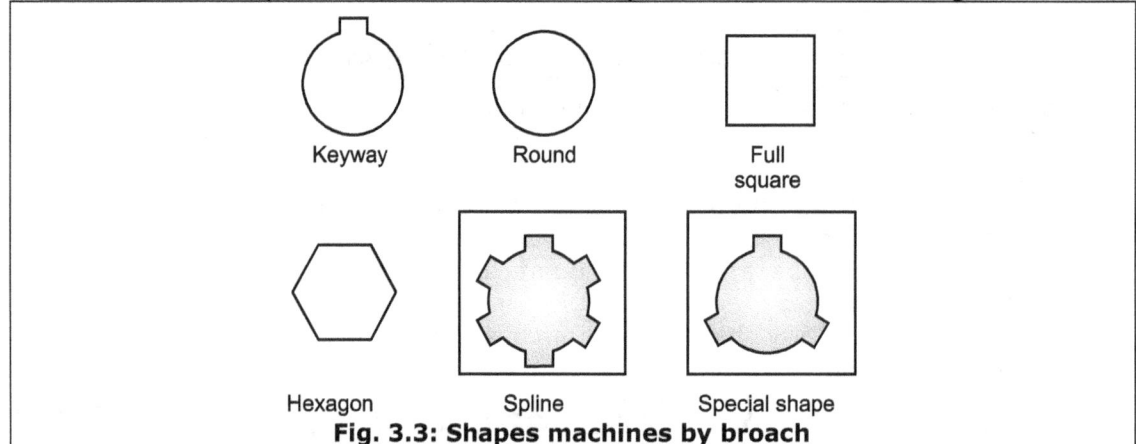

Keyway   Round   Full square

Hexagon   Spline   Special shape

Fig. 3.3: Shapes machines by broach

3.9 MATERIAL OF BROACH

- Being a cutting tool, broaches are also made of materials having the usual cutting tool material properties, i.e., high strength, hardness, toughness and good heat and wear resistance.
- For ease of manufacture and resharpening the complex shape and cutting edges, broaches are mostly made of HSS (high speed steel).
- To enhance cutting speed, productivity and product quality, now-a-days cemented carbide segments (assembled) or replaceable inserts are also used specially for stronger and harder work materials like cast irons and steels. TiN coated carbides provide much longer tool life in broaching.
- Since broaching speed (velocity) is usually quite low, ceramic tools are not used.

3.10 CAPSTAN AND TURRET LATHE

- Capstan and turret lathes are elementary special purpose machines which are useful in mass production. Both the machines are very similar in construction, operation and application.

- A capstan lathe or a turret lathe is a production lathe used to manufacture any number of identical pieces in the minimum time.

- These lathes are development of engine lathes. The capstan lathe was first developed in the United States of America by Pratt and Whitney sometimes in 1860.

- Special characteristics of a capstan or turret lathe enable it to perform a series of operations such as drilling, turning, boring, thread cutting, reaming, chamfering, cutting-off and many other operations in a regular sequence to produce a large number of identical pieces in a minimum time.

- During the process of machining a job on the centre lathe, considerable time is taken in changing and setting tools.

- In Capstan and turret lathes the tailstock is replaced by an indexable multi-station tool head called the capstan or turret respectively.

- The turret is a six sided block (like a large hexagon nut) which is mounted on the bed and to each face of which tools may be attached.

- Various types of cutting tools can be mounted on a turret. The turret can be indexed to bring the required tool in the cutting position and can be fed to the workpiece.

- This feature enables large quantities of identical turned parts to be produced in a maximum time frame.

- The capstan lathe is so called because of the hexagon shaped tool carrier the capstan, which replaces the tail stock of the centre lathe. The capstan (tool head) is mounted on the capstan slide, which in turn is mounted on a suitable rest or saddle, which is fitted on the lathe bed.

- Unlike the capstan machine which is stationary, turret machines are more versatile and mobile since it contains the turret slides that glide straight to the bed, instead of being fixed in one place.

- Although considerable skill is required to set and adjust the tools properly, but once they are set, little skill is required to operate the machine.

- Fig. 3.4 and 3.5 shows the pictorial view of capstan and turret lathe.

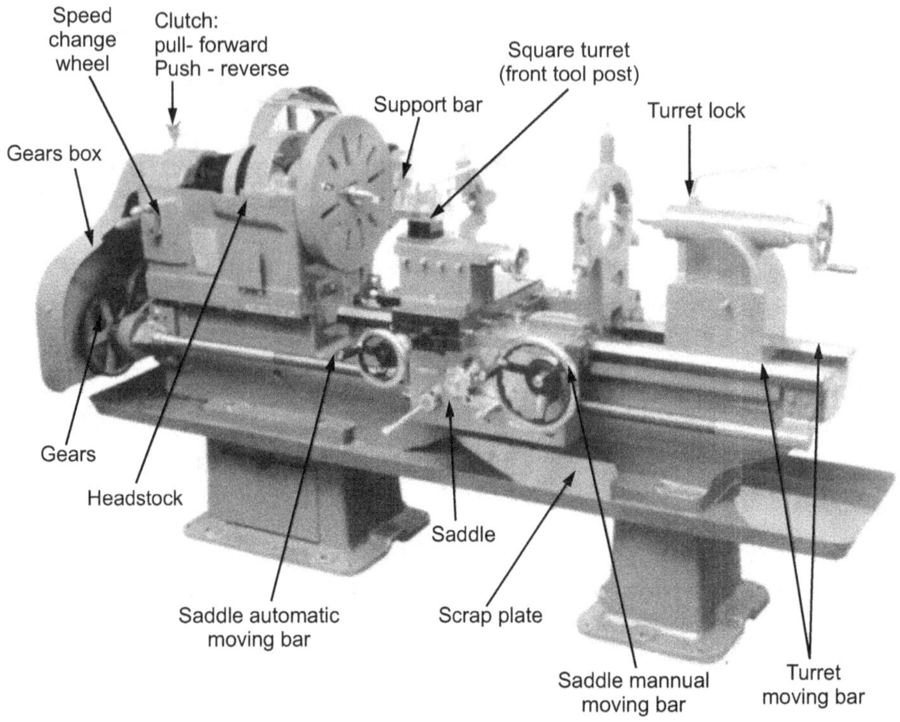

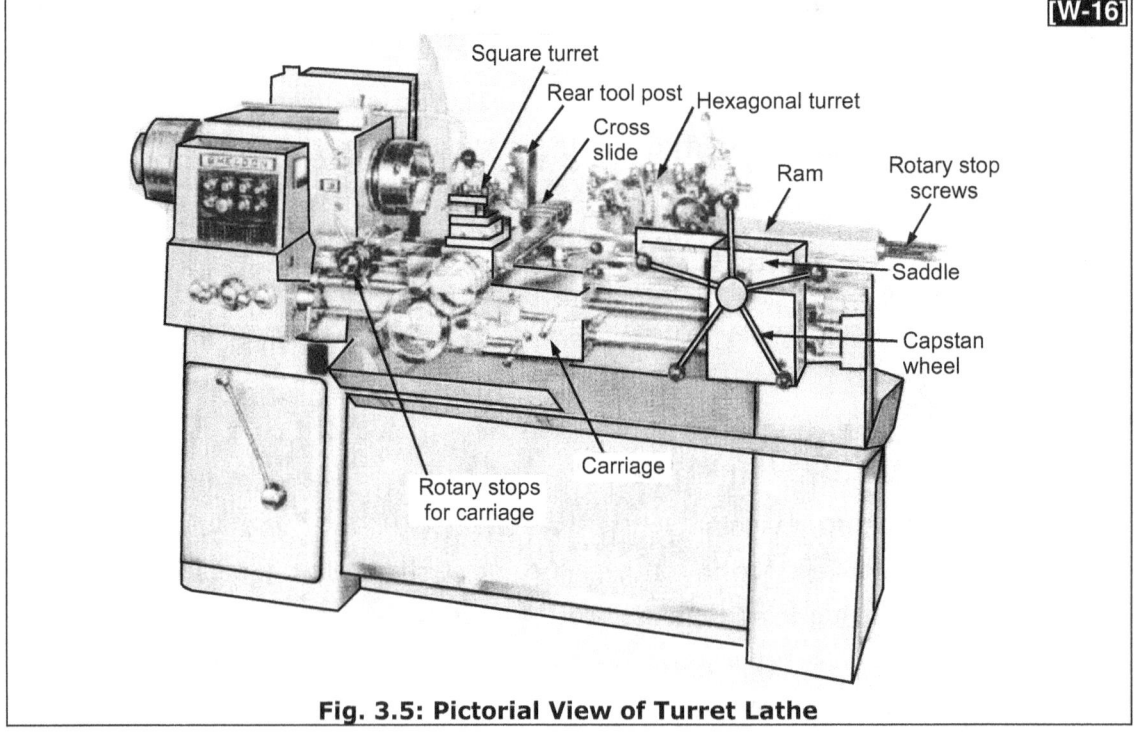

Fig. 3.4: Pictorial View of Capstan Lathe

[W-16]

Fig. 3.5: Pictorial View of Turret Lathe

3.11 PRINCIPLE PARTS OF CAPSTAN LATHE

- The capstan lathe as shown in Fig. 3.6 is similar in construction to an engine lathe and carries the following parts:

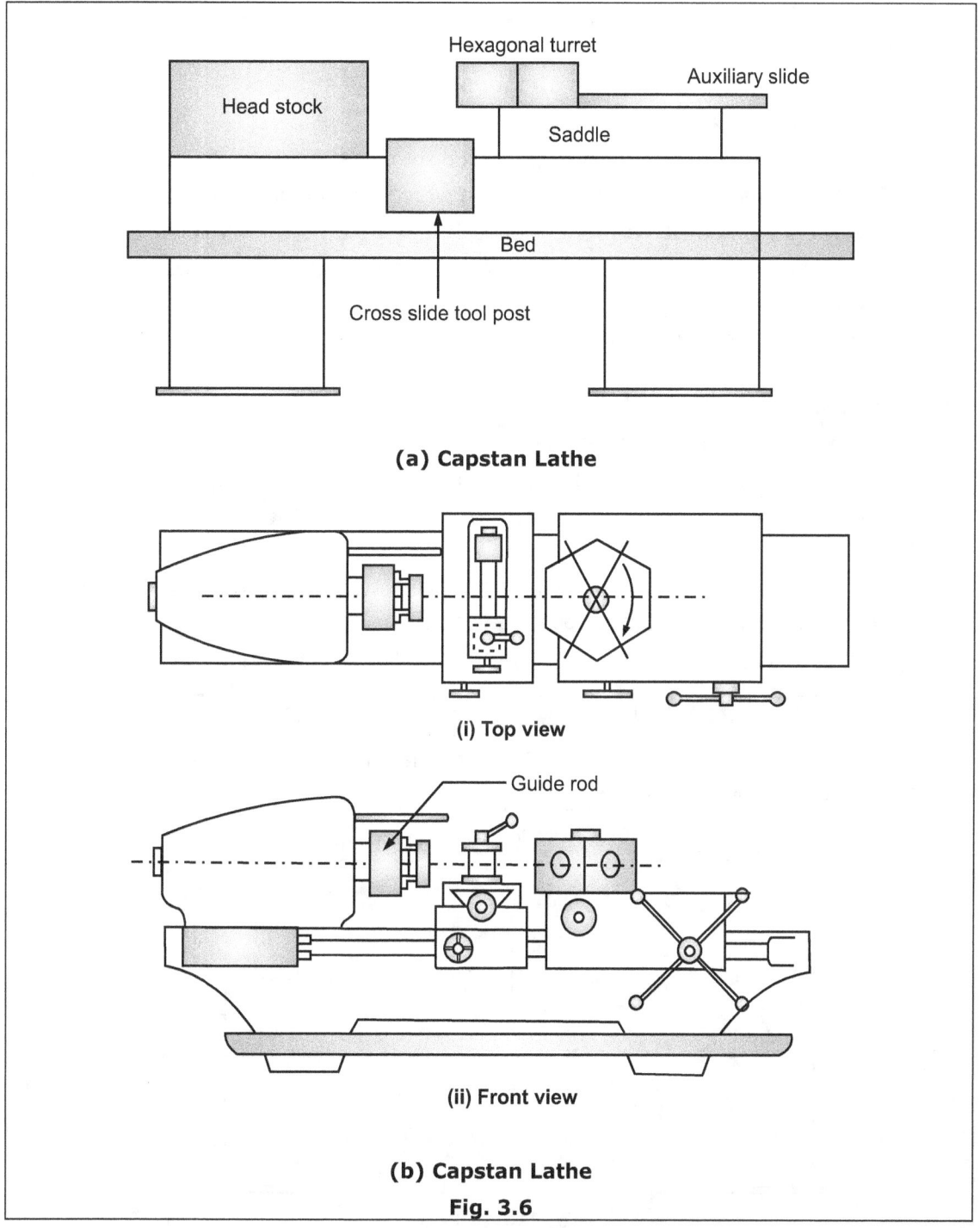

(a) Capstan Lathe

(i) Top view

(ii) Front view

(b) Capstan Lathe

Fig. 3.6

Bed

- o It is a heavy C.I. casting which supports the complete machine.

Head stock

- o It is similar to the head stock of a centre lathe. But it is larger and heavier in construction.
- o It can hold work pieces up to 60 mm diameter.

Cross slide and saddle

- o The regular tool post in lathe is replaced by cross slide tool post.
- o The cross slide is mounted on a saddle which has a transverse movement.
- o The cross slide carries a tool post which may hold up to four tools.
- o The tools may be indexed at 90° and the required tool may be brought into operation.
- o In addition the cross slide also supports a rear tool post that may carry two tools.

Capstan head

- o It is hexagonal or circular in shape.
- o It can hold 6 tools in shank through the centre of each hexagonal face.
- o The turret can be indexed to bring the required tool in position.

Auxiliary slide

- o The turret is mounted on an auxiliary slide which slides on the guideways provided on the top surface of the saddle.
- o A star wheel provides the movement of the turret towards the head stock.

3.12 PRINCIPLE PARTS OF TURRET LATHE

- • The turret lathe as shown in Fig. 3.7 is similar in construction to capstan lathe and carries the following parts:

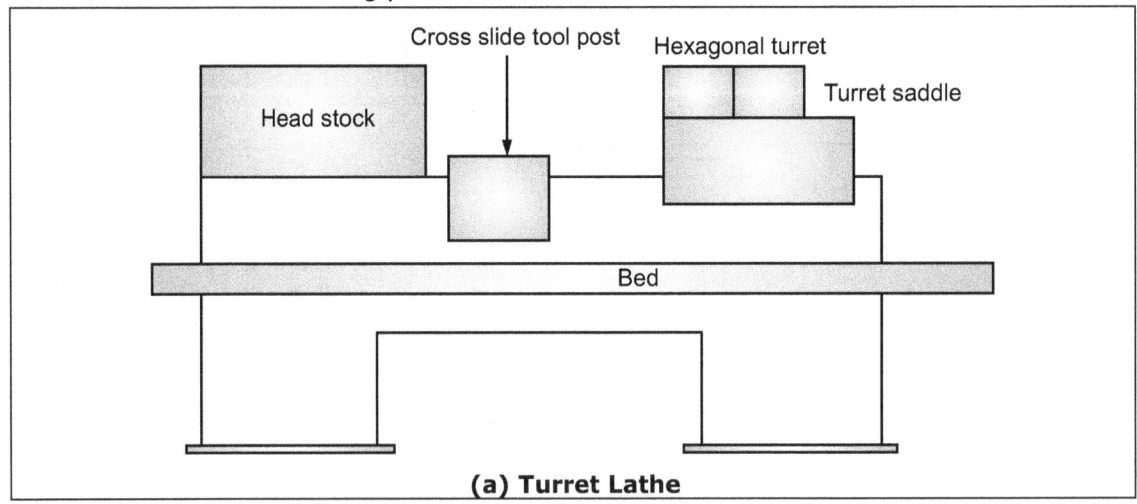

(a) Turret Lathe

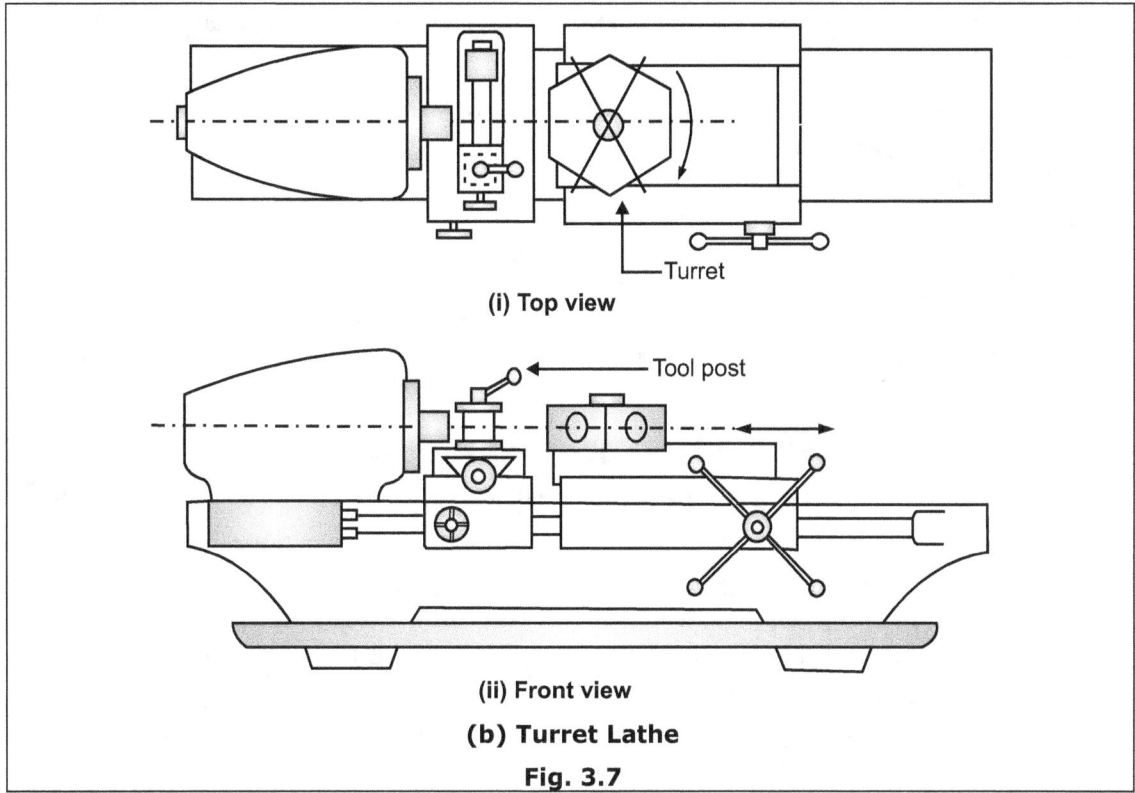

(i) Top view

(ii) Front view

(b) Turret Lathe

Fig. 3.7

Bed
- o It is a heavy C.I. casting which supports the complete machine.

Head stock
- o It is similar to the head stock of a centre lathe. But it is larger and heavier in construction.
- o It can hold work pieces up to 200 mm diameter.

Cross slide and saddle
- o The regular tool post in lathe is replaced by cross slide tool post.
- o The cross slide is mounted on a saddle which has a transverse movement.
- o The cross slide carries a tool post which may hold up to four tools.
- o The tools may be indexed at 90° and the required tool may be brought into operation.
- o In addition the cross slide also supports a rear tool post that may carry two tools.

Turret head
- o It is square, hexagonal or octagonal in shape.
- o It can hold 4, 6 or 8 tools in shank through the centre of each hexagonal face.
- o The turret can be indexed to bring the required tool in position.
- o The turret is directly mounted on the top of the saddle.
- o The turret movement is obtained by the movement of the saddle.
- o The turret slide and the saddle is fed by a star wheel towards the head stock.

3.13 IMPORTANT FEATURES OF CAPSTAN AND TURRET LATHE

[S-16]

(i)   They posses axially movable hexagonal turret in place of tailstock.

(ii)   They are semiautomatic.

(iii)   They hold large number of cutting tools (as shown in Fig. 3.3 and 3.4).

(iv)   They are costlier the centre lathes.

(v)   They are more suitable and economical for batch production.

(vi)   They require more setting time but have less cycle time.

(vii)   One additional guide rod or pilot bar is provided on the headstock of the turret lathe as shown in Fig. 3.3 to ensure rigid axial travel of the turret head.

3.14 DIFFERENCE BETWEEN CENTRE AND CAPSTAN/TURRET LATHE

[W-11]

Sr. No.	Centre lathe	Capstan and Turret lathe
1.	It is manual machine tool.	IT is semiautomatic machine tool.
2.	It possesses a tail stock to support the workpiece or to hold the tool.	It possesses an axially movable indexable turret in place of tailstock.
3.	It holds only one cutting tool at a time.	It holds large number of cutting tools. *(upto four in indexable tool post on the front slide, one in the rear slide and upto six in the turret, if hexagonal).*
4.	Rate of production is less.	Are more productive. *(for faster mounting, rapid speed change, quick engagement and overlapped functioning of the tools).*
5.	Repetitive production of same job is quite difficult.	It enables repetitive production of same job requiring less involvement, effort and attention of the operator. *(pre-setting of work–speed and feed rate and length of travel of the cutting tools is set only once).*
6.	It is cheaper as compared to semi-automatic lathes.	It is relatively costlier.
7.	It is suitable for job order production.	It is suitable and economically feasible for batch production or small lot production.

3.15 DIFFERENCE BETWEEN CAPSTAN AND TURRET LATHE

[W-11, 14; S-13, 15, 17]

Sr. No.	Capstan lathe	Turret lathe
1.	It is a light duty machine.	Turret lathes are relatively more robust and heavy duty machine.
2.	The turret head is mounted on the ram and the ram is mounted on the saddle and moves on the guideways.	The turret head is directly mounted on the saddle and the saddle slides over the bed ways.
3.	The saddle will not be moved during machining.	The saddle is moved along with the turret head during machining.
4.	The lengthwise movement of turret is less.	The lengthwise movement of turret is more.
5.	Only short workpieces can be machined.	Long work pieces can be machined.
6.	Collet is used to hold the workpiece.	Jaw chuck is used to hold the workpiece.
7.	It is easy to move the turret head as it slides over the ram.	It is difficult to move the turret head along with saddle.
8.	The turret head cannot be moved crosswise.	The turret head can be moved crosswise in some turret lathes.
9.	As the construction of lathe is not rigid, heavy cut cannot be given.	As the construction of lathe is rigid, heavy cut can be given.
10.	It is used for machining work pieces up to 60 mm diameter.	It is used for machining workpieces up to 200 mm diameter.
11.	Capstan lathes generally deal with short or long rod type blanks held in collet.	Turret lathes mostly work on chucking type jobs held in the quick acting chucks.
12.	The turret travels with limited stroke length within a saddle type guide block, called auxiliary bed, which is clamped on the main bed.	In turret lathe, the heavy turret being mounted on the saddle which directly slides with larger stroke length on the main bed.
13.	External screw threads are cut in capstan lathe using a self opening die being mounted in one face of the turret.	In turret lathes external threads are cut by a single point or multipoint chasing tool being mounted on the front slide and moved by a short leadscrew and a swing type half nut.
14.	The turret of capstan lathe is called as a capstan head which may be circular or hexagonal.	The turret of turret lathe is called as a turret head which may be square, octagonal or hexagonal.

3.16 ADVANTAGES OF CAPSTAN AND TURRET LATHE

(i) As it carry turret which carry number of tools to perform different operations simultaneously, thus enables mass production.

(ii) Less skilled operators are required as compared with engine lathe.

(iii) No need to change tools or more the tool to other machines, as many operations can be performed without the need to change tooling layout.

(iv) Elimination of set-up times between operations reduces the production time considerably.

(v) Provides the level of accuracy required for interchangeable production.

(vi) Threads are usually cut by taps and dies, making the operation easier.

3.17 DISADVANTAGES OF CAPSTAN AND TURRET LATHE

(i) Initial investment cost is high.

(ii) Initial setting time is very high.

(iii) Not suitable for small number of jobs.

3.18 SPECIFICATIONS OF CAPSTAN AND TURRET LATHE

• The following factors are necessary to specify a capstan and turret lathe:

(i) Height of centre from the lathe bed.

(ii) Distance between spindle nose and turret face.

(iii) Maximum bar diameter that can be held by the chuck.

(iv) Bore diameter in turret.

(v) Speed range.

(vi) Feed range.

(vii) Power of the main motor.

(viii) Floor space area required.

3.19 PLANOMILLER [W-14, S-16]

• As the construction of this machine is similar to a double housing planer, it is called as plano miller.

• A planomiller is shown in the Fig. 3.8 and its construction is explained below.

• The actual machine is shown in Fig. 3.9.

Construction:

1. **Bed:** A fixed bed is considered as the base of the machine.

2. **Table:** A table is mounted on the bed. The table has longitudinal movement only.

3. **Column:** Two vertical columns, one on each side of the bed are mounted on the bed.

4. **Cross-rail:** A cross rail is fitted on the column. It may be lowered or raised to suit the height of the workpiece.

5. **Milling Head:** Two vertical milling head are fitted on the cross-rail which can move towards each other. Two horizontal milling head are mounted on the column which can move vertical over it.

6. **Milling cutter:** Each milling head carries one cutter.

Working:

The workpiece can be machined in four different ways according to requirements.

(a) By moving the table and cutter rotate in its position.

(b) By keeping the table stationary and feeding the cutters by moving the milling heads.

(c) By moving the table and the milling heads simultaneously.

(d) By heaping the table stationary, moving the cross-rail downwards and the side cutter up and down.

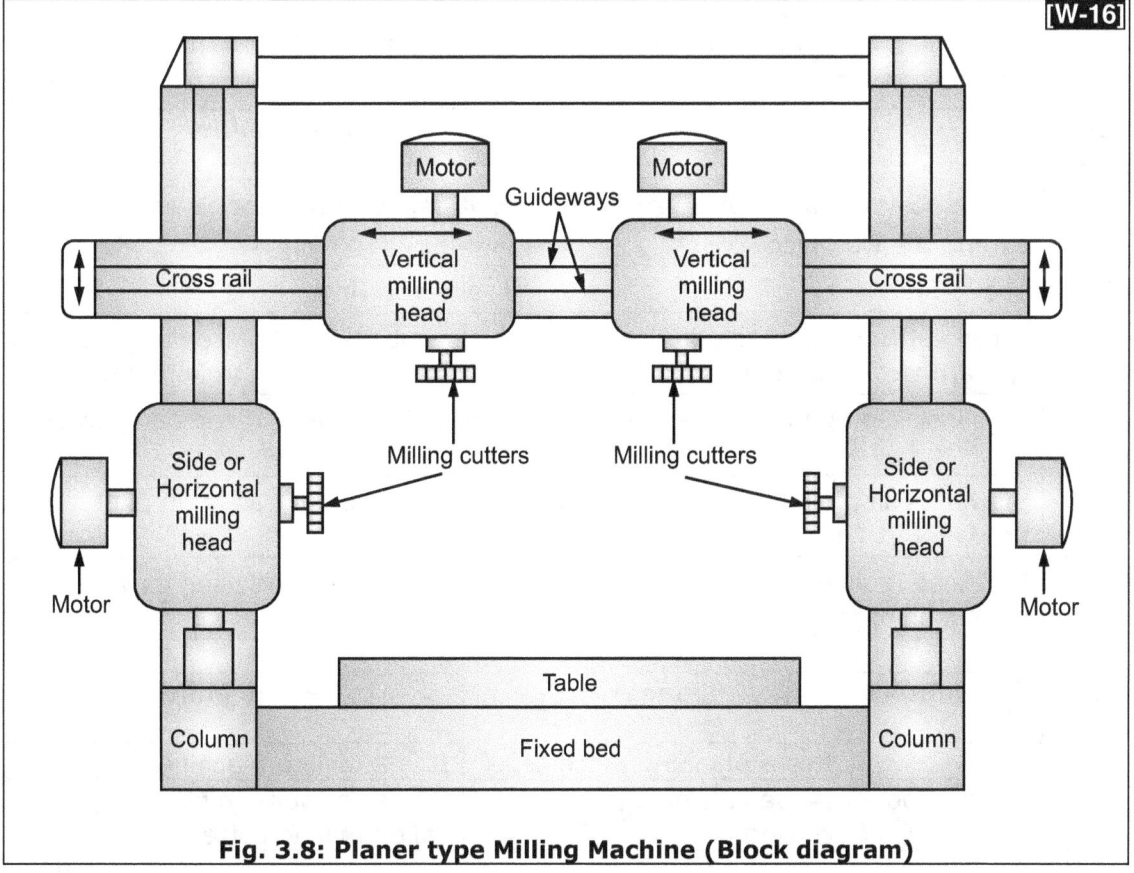

Fig. 3.8: Planer type Milling Machine (Block diagram)

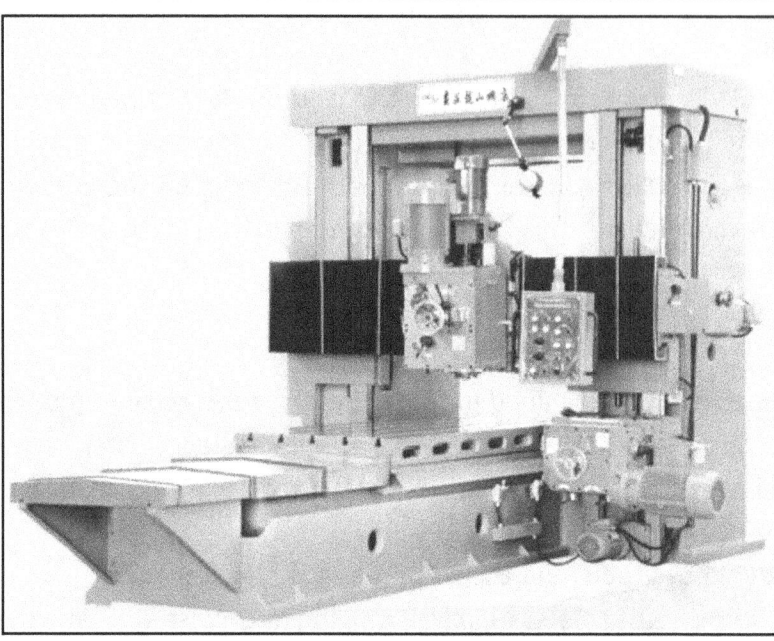

Fig. 3.9: Plano Miller (Planar type milling machine in Pictorial View)

3.19.1 Difference between Planar and Plano Miller

[S-17]

Sr. No.	Planer	Plano Miller
1.	Single point cutting tool is used for cutting the workpiece.	Multi point cutting tool is used for cutting the workpiece.
2.	Tool is stationery.	Tool is rotating.
3.	It can cut the workpiece during forward stroke of table only.	It can cut the workpiece during both, forward and return stroke of table.
4.	Highly skilled operator is required.	Semiskilled operator can be operate this machines.
5.	Slower as single point cutting tool is used.	Faster than planer as multi point cutting tool is used.
6.	Different Tools are required as per the shape of job.	Single cutter can be used for nos. of jobs.

Sr. No.	Parameters	Planer	Plano Miller
1.	Type	It is a planning machine.	It is a milling machine.
2.	Cutting tool	It uses a single point cutting tool	It uses a multi point cutting tool called milling cutter.

contd. ...

3.	Number of tools	Only one tool can be operated on the machine tool at a time.	Number of tools can be operated simultaneously on this machine tool.
4.	Motor	Only one motor is required to operate the milling tool head.	Each milling head has an individual motor to operate the tool head.
5.	Cutting speed	Cutting speed is provided to the table.	Cutting speed is provided to the spindle.
6.	Table movement	The table moves fast and provide cutting speed.	The table moves slow and provide feed.

3.20 BORING MACHINES   [S-16, 17]

- Boring is the process of enlarging the already existing hole. This existing hole can be due to casting, forging, drilling or punching.
- Boring can also be used for trueing and finishing the previously drilled holes.
- The machine used for performing the boring operation is called as boring machine.
- These are production machines and their existence is justified where boring on large scale is required.

3.21 TYPES OF BORING MACHINES   [S-17]

- Boring machines are classified as follows:
- Horizontal boring machine
    - (a)   Table type boring machine
    - (b)   Planer type boring machine
    - (c)   Floor type boring machine
    - (d)   Multiple head type boring machine
- Vertical boring machine
    - (a)   Standard vertical boring mill
    - (b)   Vertical turret lathe
- Jig boring machine

3.22 PRINCIPLE FEATURES OF HORIZONTAL BORING MACHINE
[W-16]

- The HBM is made to handle medium to very large-sized parts, but these parts are usually somewhat rectangular in shape, though they may be asymmetrical or irregular. The available cutting tools only limit the size of cut, the rigidity of the spindle, and the available horsepower.
- The principle features of horizontal boring machine are
    - **(a) Heavy and strong bed:** It has a heavy and strong bed, which carries the entire load of different parts, work piece and tools mounted over it.
    - **(b) Two vertical columns:** One column is mounted on each end of the table.
    - **(c) Head stock:** It can be moved vertically along the main column to facilitate different size work pieces.

(d) Horizontal table: It is mounted on the saddle and can be moved in longitudinal and cross directions.

(e) Horizontal spindle: It is mounted in the head stock. This spindle apart from rotating can also be fed forward or backward.

(f) Bar holder: It is also known as end support. It can be adjusted vertically over the end column.

3.23 SPECIFICATION OF THE HORIZONTAL BORING MACHINE
[W-14]

- A horizontal boring machine should be specified by the following details:

  (a) Type of machine

  (b) Maximum spindle travel

  (c) Maximum travel of table in longitudinal direction.

  (d) Maximum travel of table in cross-direction.

  (e) Spindle speeds and feeds.

  (f) Maximum travel of spindle.

  (g) Maximum allowable weight of the machine.

  (h) Heights of the column.

  (i) Horse power of the motor

  (j) Weight of the machine.

  (k) Floor space area required.

  (l) Size of the table.

3.24 TABLE TYPE HORIZONTAL BORING MACHINE   [W-16]

- A table type horizontal boring machine is shown in the Fig. 3.10 and its construction is explained below.

- The table type horizontal boring machine consists of the following parts:

  1. Bed: It is a heavy CI structure and supports the different parts of the machine. It carries longitudinal guideways machined at the top surface. On each end of the bed. A column is mounted.

  2. Main Column: The main column carries vertical guideways over which the head stock travels up and down. The headstock is balanced in the required position by counter weights, which are generally placed outside the column.

  3. Headstock: This unit mounted on the column carries a number of different mechanisms like spindle assembly, feed gear box, headstock extension, speed and feed changing mechanism, main driving mechanism etc.

  4. Table and Saddle: The machine consists of two saddle and a rotary table. The lower saddle moves longitudinally over the bed. The upper saddle moves crosswise over the top guideways on lower saddle. The table swivels over the circular guideways on the upper saddle.

5. **End support column:** It is mounted directly on the bed guideways. It carries vertical guideways along which the bar holder moves. The bar holder is used to support the overhanging (other end) boring bar.

6. **Boring bars:** It supports the cutter for boring on workpiece having larger bore diameter.

Working:

*   During operation the cutting tool rotates and the work piece remains stationary.
*   Feed is provided by moving the work piece in horizontal direction as per the requirement.

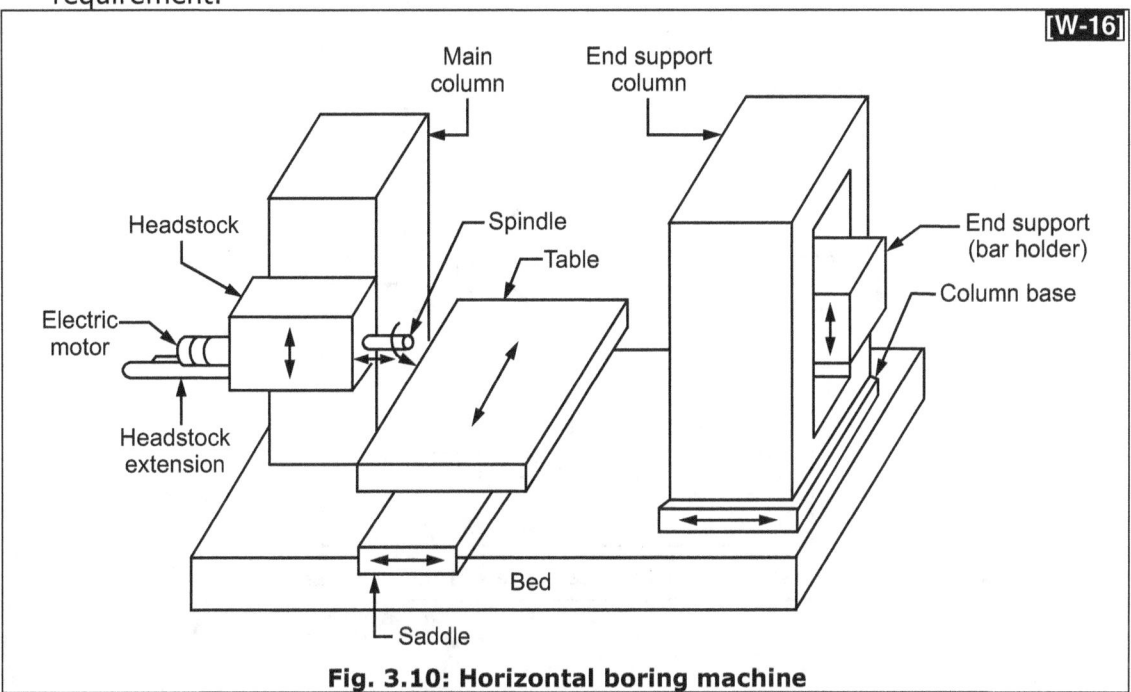

Fig. 3.10: Horizontal boring machine

3.25 STANDARD VERTICAL BORING MILL

*   The standard vertical boring mill is shown in the Fig. 3.11 and its construction is explained below.

*   The standard vertical boring mill machine consists of the following parts:

1. **Bed:** It is heavy C.I. structure which supports the complete machine. Circular guideways are provided over the top of the bed.

2. **Table:** Table is mounted over the bed and can swivel about the vertical axis. T slots are provided over the table for clamping the work.

3. **Column:** Two columns are mounted on each end of the bed. Vertical guideways are provided on the column.

4. **Cross rail:** A cross rail is mounted between the two columns. It can slide vertically over the column.

5. **Spindle head:** Two vertical spindle heads are mounted over the cross rail. They can move horizontally over the guideways machined on the cross-rail. Two horizontal spindle heads can move vertically over the column.

Working:

- The work piece is clamped on the table over which T-slots are provided.
- The rotating work piece is fed against the fixed tools, which results in cuts being taken on the job.
- For example, castings for steam turbine, tables for machine tools and pressure vessels.

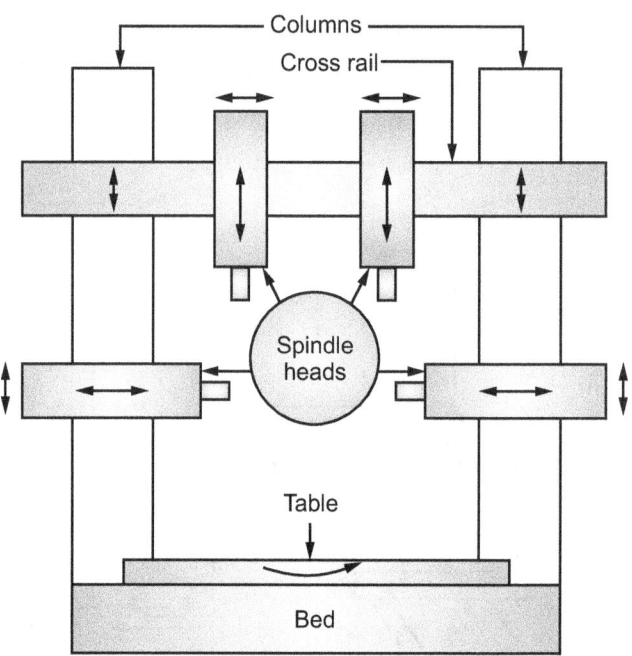

(a) Vertical boring machine (Block diagram)

(b) Pictorial view

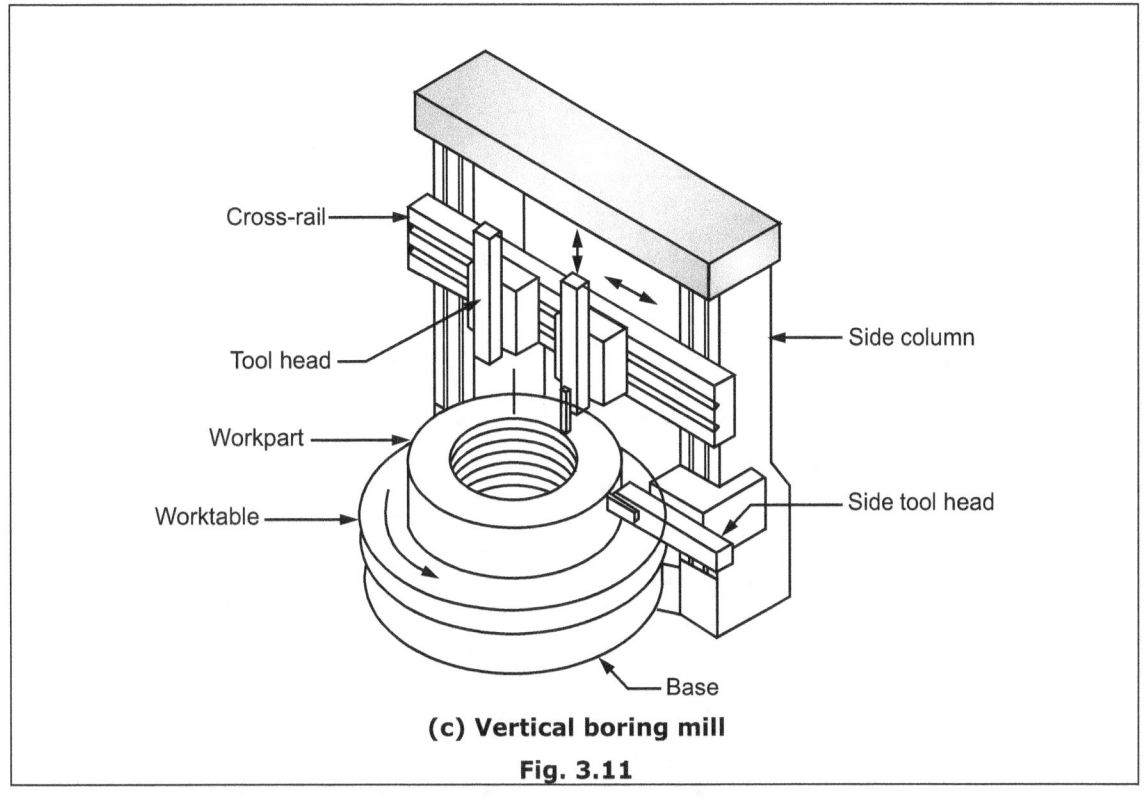

(c) Vertical boring mill

Fig. 3.11

3.26 VERTICAL TURRET LATHE

- The vertical turret lathe is shown in the Fig. 3.12 and its construction is explained below.
- The vertical turret lathe machine consists of the following parts:
  1. **Bed:** It is heavy C.I. casting which supports the complete machine.
  2. **Table:** It is mounted over the bed and rotates over the circular guideways on the bed about a vertical axis.
  3. **Column:** Two vertical columns are mounted over the bed.
  4. **Cross rail:** A cross-rail is mounted over the two columns.
  5. **Turret head:** A indexable turret head is mounted on the saddle. It carries number of tools.
  6. **Saddle:** The saddle is mounted on the cross rail and can move in horizontal or vertical direction.
  7. **Tool posts:** Two tool posts, one on each column is mounted. Each tool post can slide vertically or slideways on the column.

Working:

- The work piece is held over the table. The table rotates over the bed about a vertical axis. The turret head can be indexed after each operation to bring the proper tool in position for the next operation.

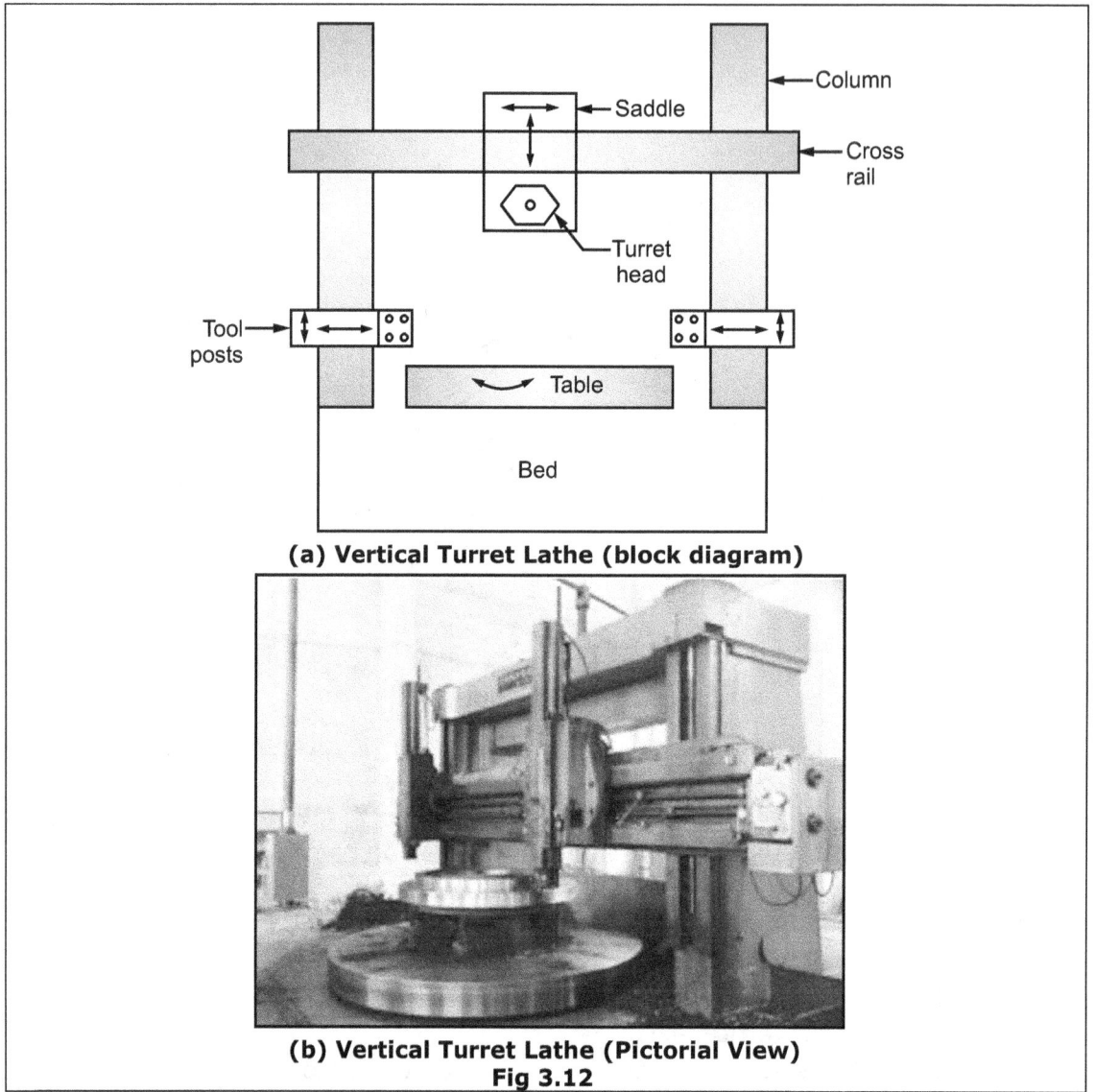

(a) Vertical Turret Lathe (block diagram)

(b) Vertical Turret Lathe (Pictorial View)
Fig 3.12

3.27 SPECIFICATION OF THE VERTICAL BORING MACHINE

[S-16]

- A vertical boring machine should be specified by the following details:
    - (a) Distance from spindle axis to spindle head.
    - (b) Distance from spindle axis to column head.
    - (c) Distance from spindle axis to face of table.
    - (d) Maximum vertical travel of the spindle head.
    - (e) Number of interchangeable spindles.
    - (f) Maximum table travel (longitudinal)
    - (g) Maximum table travel (cross)
    - (h) Number of T-slots.
    - (i) Working surface of the table.

(j) Number of spindle speeds.
(k) Range of spindle speeds.
(l) Gross weight of the machine.
(m) Overall dimensions of the machine.

3.28 JIG BORING MACHINE

* The jig boring machine is used for producing holes at exact location as needed in jigs and fixtures, templates, dies, gauges that needs very high accuracy.
* The applications of this machine includes boring holes in cylinder block, liner of automobile engines.
* The machine is designed to give an accuracy of 0.0025 mm.
* The jig boring machine is shown in the Fig. 3.13 and its construction is explained below.
* The jig boring machine consists of the following parts:
  1. **Bed:** It is a C.I. casting which supports the other members of the machine. It has cross guideways machined on its top surface.
  2. **Column:** It is vertical C.I. casting mounted on the base. Counter weights are provided inside the column for balancing the spindle head.
  3. **Spindle head:** It is mounted on the front face of the column. It can slide up and down along the vertical guideways on the front face of the column.
  4. **Table and saddle:** The saddle travels in cross direction over the bed. The table is mounted over the saddle and the same can be moved longitudinally over the guidedeways machined on the saddle.

Working:
* The work piece is mounted on the table, which can be moved in cross direction by moving the saddle and longitudinally by moving the table.
* The tool is mounted in the spindle and can be moved vertically to accommodate and machine work pieces of varying heights.

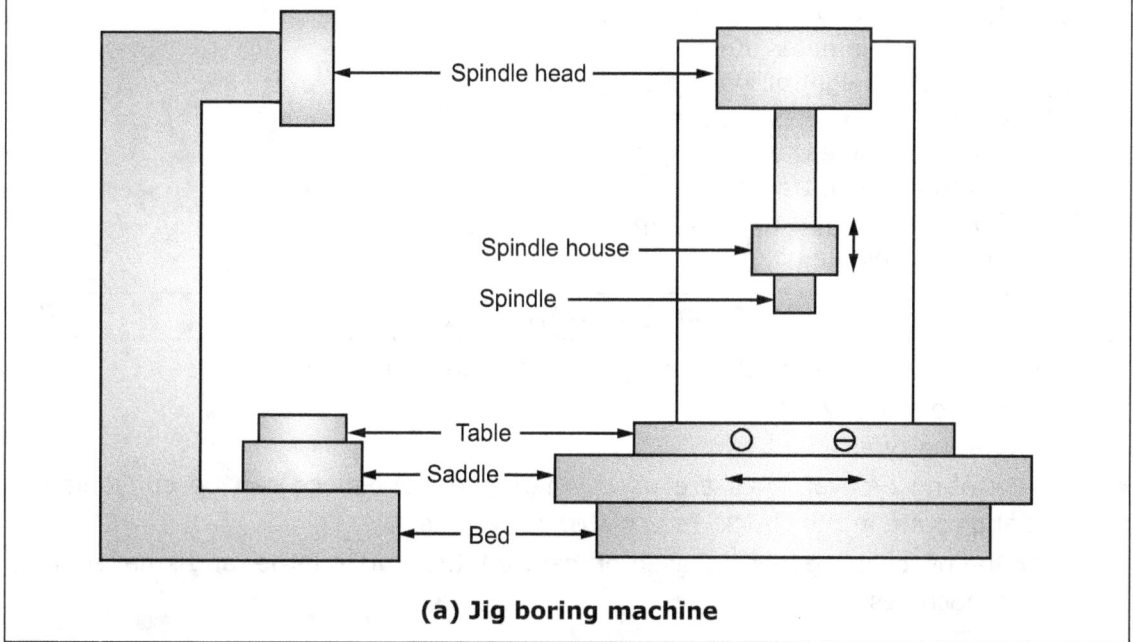

(a) Jig boring machine

(b) Jig Boring machine (Pictorial View)
Fig. 3.13

3.29 SPECIFICATION OF THE JIG BORING MACHINE

- A jig boring machine should be specified by the following details:
  (a) Distance from spindle axis from column.
  (b) Maximum diameter of hole drilled.
  (c) Maximum diameter of hole bored.
  (d) Maximum weight of work piece permissible.
  (e) Number of spindles speeds.
  (f) Maximum table travel (longitudinal).
  (g) Maximum table travel (cross).
  (h) Maximum vertical travel of spindle.
  (i) Taper in spindle hole.

3.30 BORING TOOLS [S-17]

- The boring tools used on the boring machines are of mainly two types
  (i) Non-Rotating type.
  (ii) Rotating type.
- Non-Rotating type of tools are used when, the work-piece can be conveniently held and rotate in the chuck, face plate, or fixtures.
- This type of tools is generally used on centre lathe, turret lathe, and smaller sizes boring machines.

- Because in these machines most of the boring operations use a single point cutting tool.
- They are generally forged out of tool steel and ground to correct angles.
- They are made in pairs consisting of a roughing and finishing tool.
- The Fig. 3.14 shows single point boring tools.

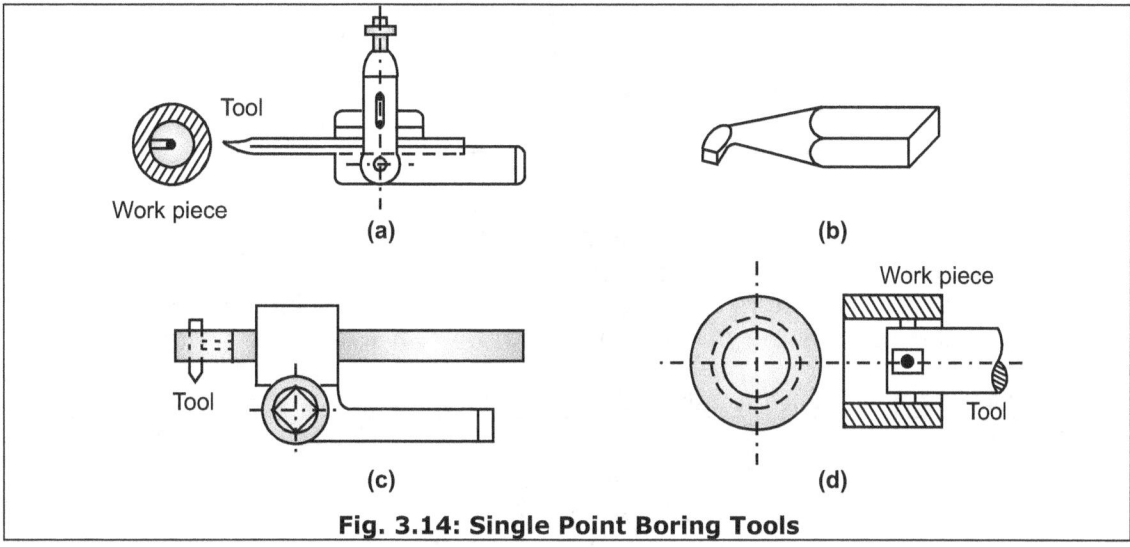

Fig. 3.14: Single Point Boring Tools

- The application of rough or finish boring tools dependents upon the grade of surface finish required. In operation these tools are held either in tool post, turret head, or tail stock.
- The work is held in chuck face plate, and revolved, the tool is fed in to the work piece by moving the slide rest, turret slide, or tail stock spindle.
- These type of tools used for boring short holes only. For boring long holes bars are used.
- When the rotation of the work-piece is inconvenient or impracticable due to its shape, rotating type of boring tools are used.
- For example fly cutters, double cutter, boring bar, and boring head.
- Fly cutter consists of a single point cutting tool mounted on a bar. The adjustment of fly cutter may be made by a micrometer dial. Fig. 3.15 and Fig. 3.16 shows a fly cutter.

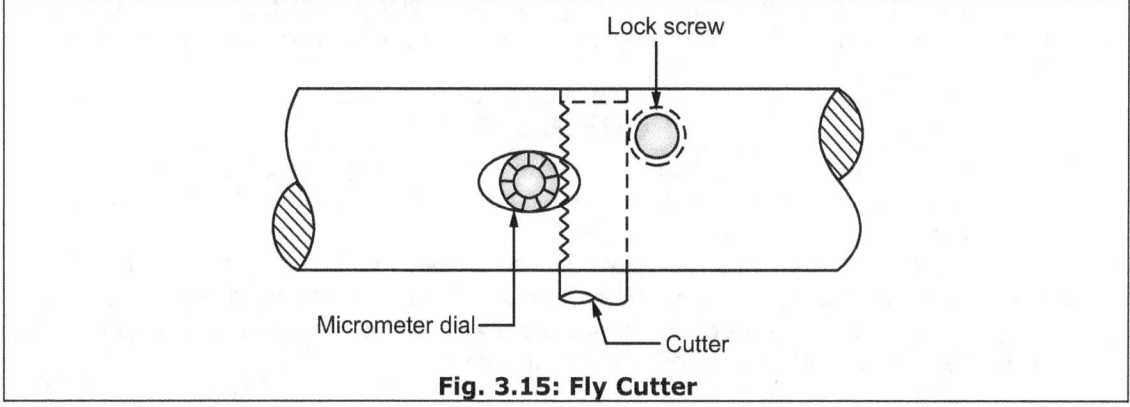

Fig. 3.15: Fly Cutter

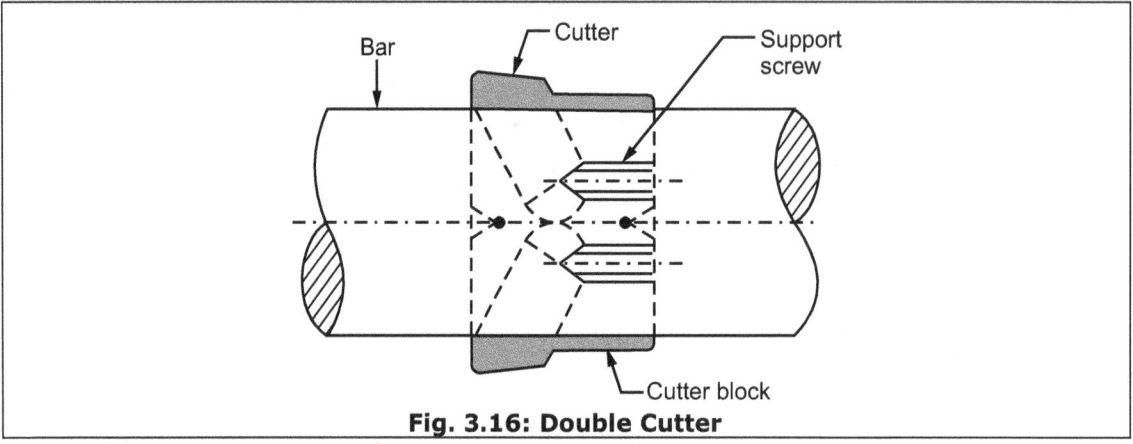

Fig. 3.16: Double Cutter

- Double cutter consists of two opposing single point cutters resting in a groove of a bar. The double cutters are widely used in a production boring. The use of double cutter reduces the machining time to a great extent as a compared to fly cutter.
- Fig. 3.17 shows a device for size adjustment of a bar tool.

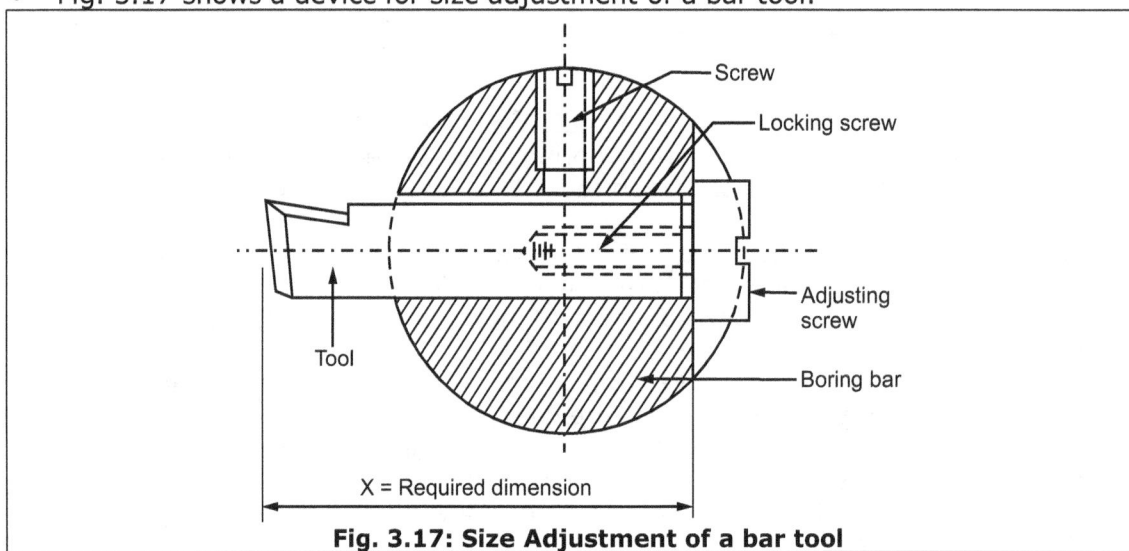

Fig. 3.17: Size Adjustment of a bar tool

- The length of the tool to obtain the required hole size is adjustment by adjusting set screw from its centre. For precision boring work, a tool having micrometer adjustment is used.

3.31 BORING BARS

- The boring bar and boring head are the tool holding devices, in a horizontal boring machine on which cutters are mounted according to the operation requirements.
- The boring bar is the simplest boring tool holder in which cutter is held in a crossed slot on the boring bar. The length of the tool from the centre of the boring bar can be adjusted by a set screw provided behind the boring tool. Fig. 3.18 shows boring bar with cutter mounted on it.

- The boring bar serves to transmit the power from boring machine spindle to the cutter as well as to hold it rigidly during the cutting operation. It also reduces vibrations during the operation provided the bar should be of maximum diameter and minimum length.
- The boring bar may be provided with two or more single point cutters to distribute the work and also equalize the thrust of the cut.
- The boring bar is supported at the ends, to minimize the vibrations of the cutters and bending of the bars.

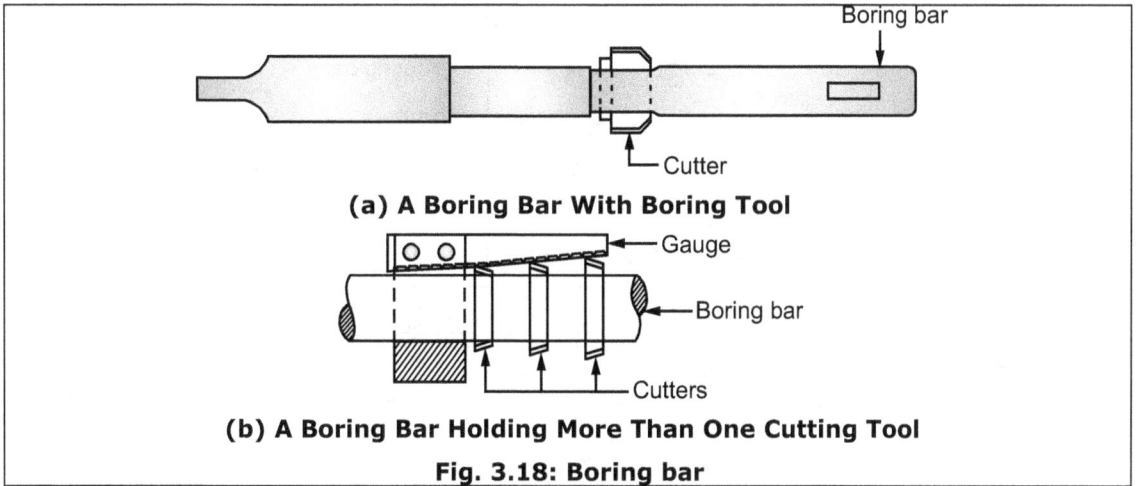

(a) A Boring Bar With Boring Tool

(b) A Boring Bar Holding More Than One Cutting Tool

Fig. 3.18: Boring bar

3.32 BORING HEADS

- The boring head is a more rigid boring tool holder than a boring bar. Use of a boring head becomes necessary in the following circumstances.
  - (a) If there is a large difference, in the diameter of the boring bar and diameter of the hole. To avoid the excessive overhang of the cutter, boring head is mounted on the boring bar.
  - (b) When the position of the cutter or cutters along the bar is to be changed frequently during the operation.
- Types of boring head
  - (a) Simple boring head
  - (b) Trailing cut boring head

3.32.1 Simple Boring Head

- Fig. 3.19 shows a simple boring head. It consists of a circular body. Two or three slots are made radially in the body in which cutters are fitted. A micrometer dial is provided for the precision adjustment of the tool if required.
- Boring head can be keyed at any desired position on the boring bar it supports the tool. A boring head may have number of cutters.
- The advantage of having several cutters is metal removal rate is high, hence machining time is reduced. Boring heads are always provided with two sets of cutters. One set is being used for roughing and other for finishing.

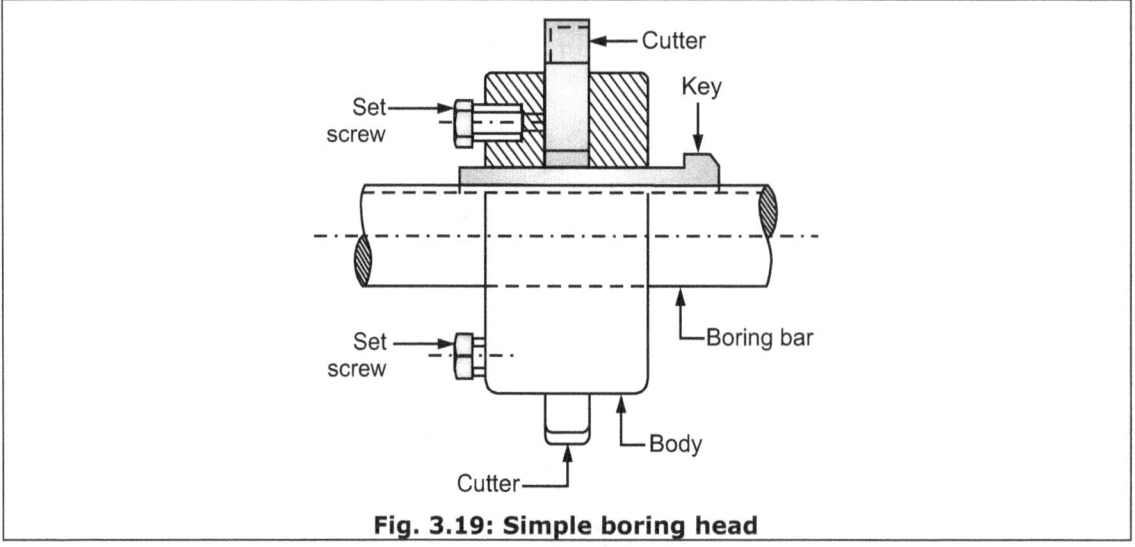

Fig. 3.19: Simple boring head

3.32.2 Trailing Cut Boring Head

- The training cut boring head is shown in Fig. 3.20.
- It consists of a body which is clamped to the boring bar with the clamping screw C.
- The boring head can slide in the slot along the length of the boring bar and clamped in the desired position.
- The body carries arrangement for mounting of two boring tools.
- The tools are held firmly in position by means of sets screws. The tool can be fed into the work piece by the adjusting screw A.

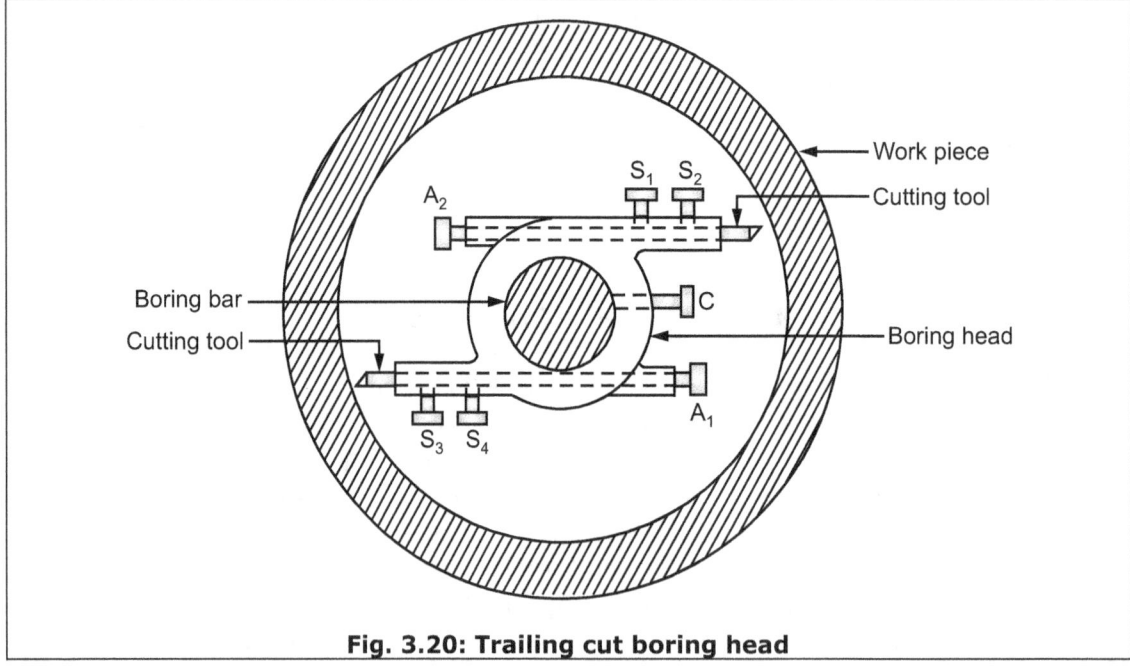

Fig. 3.20: Trailing cut boring head

Important Points

Broaching

- Broaching is the process of removing metal with a tool called as broach
- Broaching is used to produce both internal and external features
- Production rates are high and tolerances of +/– 0.01 mm are possible
- Broaching is similar to planning, competes with milling and boring, and gives turning and grinding stiff competition

Advantages of Broaching

- The process can be done for both internal and external machining
- It is simple operation, hence does not require highly skilled operator
- As loading and unloading is rapid, the rate of production is high
- Broaching is faster than any other machining process
- High accuracy and higher surface finish can be obtained

Disadvantages of broaching

- It is a single purpose tool
- In some cases, it is not suited for low production rates
- Surface to be broached must be accessible
- Blind holes cannot be easily produced
- Tool sharpening is difficult and expensive process

Applications of broaching

- Machining of bearing caps
- For machining of gears
- For machining of aircraft engine parts
- For machining of turbine blades
- For producing variety of shapes

Capstan and Turret lathe

- A capstan lathe or a turret lathe is a production lathe used to manufacture any number of identical pieces in the minimum time.
- Special characteristics of a capstan or turret lathe enable it to perform a series of operations to produce a large number of identical pieces in a minimum time.
- In Capstan and turret lathes the tailstock is replaced by an indexable multi-station tool head called the capstan or turret respectively.

Principle parts of Capstan lathe

- The cross slide is mounted on a saddle which has a transverse movement.
- Capstan head is hexagonal or circular in shape and can hold 6 tools in shank through the centre of each hexagonal face.
- The turret is mounted on an auxiliary slide which slides on the guideways provided on the top surface of the saddle.
- A star wheel provides the movement of the turret towards the head stock.

Principle parts of Turret lathe

- The cross slide is mounted on a saddle which has a transverse movement.
- Turret head is square, hexagonal or octagonal in shape.
- It can hold 4, 6 or 8 tools in shank through the centre of each hexagonal face.
- The turret can be indexed to bring the required tool in position.
- The turret slide and the saddle is fed by a star wheel towards the head stock.

Important features of Capstan and Turret lathe

- They are semiautomatic.
- They hold large number of cutting tools.
- They are costlier the centre lathes.
- They are more suitable and economical for batch production.
- They require more setting time but have less cycle time.

Advantages of Capstan and Turret lathe

- Less skilled operators are required as compared with engine lathe.
- No need to change tools or more the tool to other machines.
- Provides the level of accuracy required for interchangeable production.
- Threads are usually cut by taps and dies, making the operation easier.

Disadvantages of Capstan and Turret lathe

- Initial investment cost is high.
- Initial setting time is very high.
- Not suitable for small number of jobs.

Specifications of Capstan and Turret lathe

- Distance between spindle nose and turret face.
- Bore diameter in turret.
- Speed range.
- Feed range.
- Power of the main motor.
- Floor space area required.

Boring Machines

- Boring is the process of enlarging the already existing hole. This existing hole can be due to casting, forging, drilling or punching.
- Boring can also be used for trueing and finishing the previously drilled holes.
- The machine used for performing the boring operation is called as boring machine.

Principle features of Horizontal Boring Machine

- Heavy and strong bed.
- Two vertical columns.
- Head stock.
- Horizontal table.
- Horizontal spindle.
- Bar holder.

Specification of the Horizontal Boring Machine

- Type of machine.
- Maximum spindle travel.
- Maximum travel of table in longitudinal direction.
- Maximum travel of table in cross direction.
- Spindle speeds and feeds.
- Floor space area required.
- Size of the table.

Boring Bars

- The boring bar is the simplest boring tool holder in which cutter is held in a crossed slot on the boring bar.
- The length of the tool from the centre of the boring bar can be adjusted by a set screw.
- The boring bar serves to transmit the power from boring machine spindle to the cutter.

Practice Questions

1.	Define broaching.	(Refer Section 3.1)
2.	Give the classification of Broaching machines.	(Refer Section 3.2)
3.	Explain the nomenclature of broaching tool.	(Refer Section 3.3)
4.	Give the comparison between pull and push broach.	(Refer Section 3.4)
5.	Explain the basic parts of horizontal broaching machine.	(Refer Section 3.5)
6.	Give advantages of broaching.	(Refer Section 3.6)
7.	Give disadvantages of broaching.	(Refer Section 3.7)
8.	Give applications of broaching.	(Refer Section 3.8)
9.	Explain the Capstan and Turret lathe.	(Refer Section 3.10)
10.	Explain the principle parts of capstan lathe.	(Refer Section 3.11)
11.	Explain the principle parts of turret lathe.	(Refer Section 3.12)
12.	Explain the important features of capstan lathe.	(Refer Section 3.13)
13.	Give the comparison between centre and capstan lathe.	(Refer Section 3.14)
14.	Give the comparison between turret and capstan lathe.	(Refer Section 3.15)
15.	Give advantages of capstan and turret lathe.	(Refer Section 3.16)
16.	Give disadvantages of capstan and turret lathe.	(Refer Section 3.17)
17.	Give specifications of capstan and turret lathe.	(Refer Section 3.18)
18.	Explain the construction of Planomiller.	(Refer Section 3.19)
19.	Define boring.	(Refer Section 3.20)
20.	Explain types of boring machines.	(Refer Section 3.21)
21.	Describe the principle features of horizontal boring machine.	(Refer Section 3.22)
22.	Give the specifications of horizontal boring machine.	(Refer Section 3.23)
23.	Describe the Table type horizontal boring machine with neat sketch.	Refer Section 3.24)

24. Describe the standard vertical boring mill with neat sketch.   **(Refer Section 3.25)**

25. Describe the vertical turret lathe machine with neat sketch.   **(Refer Section 3.26)**

26. Give the specification of the vertical boring machine.   **(Refer Section 3.27)**

27. Describe the jig boring machine with neat sketch.   **(Refer Section 3.28)**

28. Give specifications of jig boring machine.   **(Refer Section 3.29)**

29. Sketch any two boring tools.   **(Refer Section 3.30)**

30. What are boring bars?   **(Refer Section 3.31)**

31. What are boring heads? When is its use recommended?   **(Refer Section 3.32)**

32. Sketch any two types of boring head.   **(Refer Section 3.32)**

33. Explain the working of a trailing cut boring head with neat sketch.   **(Refer Section 3.32)**

MSBTE Questions & Answers as Per 'G' Scheme

Winter 2014

1. Give the classification of broaching machine.   **(4 M)**

Ans. Refer Section 3.2.

2. Compare Capstan and Turret lathe.   **(4 M)**

Ans. Refer Section 3.15.

3. Explain the construction of planomiller.   **(4 M)**

Ans. Refer Section 3.19.

4. Differentiate between pull and push broach.   **(4 M)**

Ans. Refer Section 3.4.

5. Draw a neat labelled sketch of horizontal broaching machine.   **(4 M)**

Ans. Refer Section 3.5.

6. Give specifications of horizontal boring machine.   **(4 M)**

Ans. Refer Section 3.23.

Summer 2015

1. State advantages and applications of broaching machines.   **(4 M)**

Ans. Refer Sections 3.5.2 and 3.5.3.

2. Give classification of broaching machines.   **(4 M)**

Ans. Refer Section 3.2.

3. List parts of horizontal broaching machine and state functions of any four parts.   **(4 M)**

Ans. Refer Sections 3.5.1 and 3.5.

4. Sketch any two boring tools.   **(4 M)**

Ans. Refer Section 3.24 and 3.25, Pages 3.18, 3.19, 3.20.

5. Distinguish between Capstan and Turret lathe.   **(6 M)**

Ans. Refer Section 3.15.

Winter 2015

1. Compare pull broach with push broach.   (4 M)
Ans. Refer Section 3.4.
2. Draw labelled sketch of horizontal broaching machine and state function of any four parts.   (4 M)
Ans. Refer Fig. 3.2, Section 3.5.1.
3. List parts of boring tools and explain.   (4 M)
Ans. Refer Section 3.30
4. State applications of broaching.   (4 M)
Ans. Refer Section 3.8.
5. Compare between planar and plano-miller.   (6 M)
Ans. Refer Section 3.19.1.

Summer 2016

1. Sketch any four shapes that can be machined by broaching process.   (4 M)
Ans.

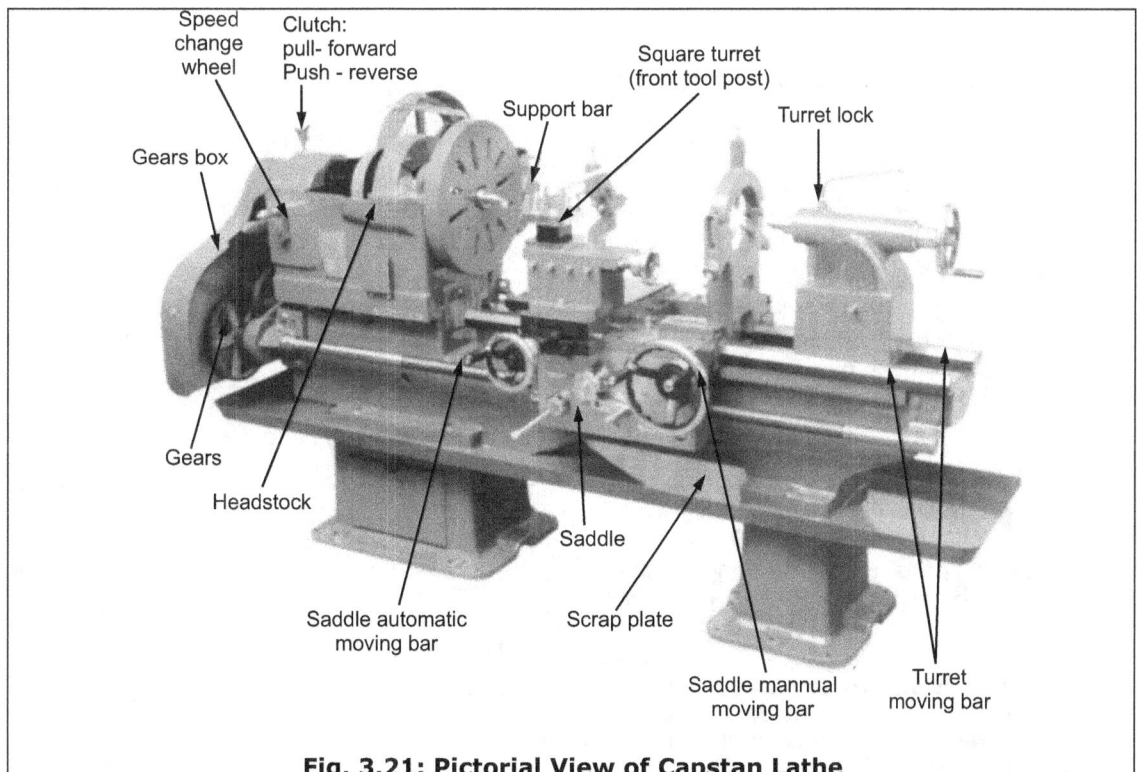

Fig. 3.21: Pictorial View of Capstan Lathe

2. Differentiate between pull and push broad.   (4 M)
Ans. Refer Section 3.4.
3. Explain salient features of capstan and turret lathe.   (4 M)
Ans. Refer Section 3.13.
4. Sketch a planer and explain its working.   (4 M)
Ans. Refer Section 3.19.
5. What is boring operation? Give the specifications of vertical boring machine. (4 M)
Ans. Refer Sections 3.20 and 3.27.

1. Sketch any two broaching tools.   **(4 M)**

Ans. **Types of Broach:**

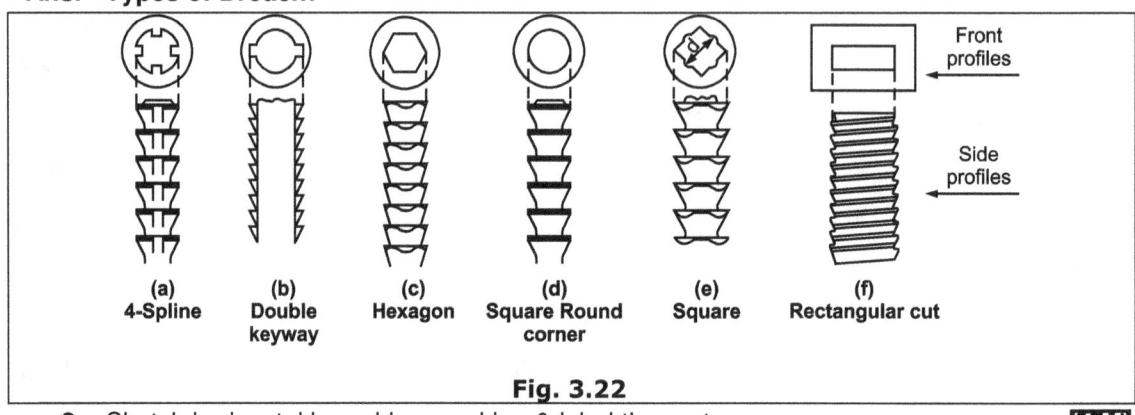

| (a)
4-Spline | (b)
Double
keyway | (c)
Hexagon | (d)
Square Round
corner | (e)
Square | (f)
Rectangular cut |

Fig. 3.22

2. Sketch horizontal broaching machine & label the parts.   **(4 M)**

Ans. Refer Fig. 3.5.

3. Differentiate between broaching & burnishing.   **(4 M)**

Ans.

Sr. No.	Broaching	Burnishing
1.	Broaching is material removing and finishing process by using multi point broach tool.	It is a process of super finishing, in which mirror like surface is produced.
2.	Tools have small and multiple teeths.	Smooth rollers/balls act as tool.
3.	Pulling or pushing force is required to remove the material.	Pressure is required to press the balls or rollers.
4.	Broaching components are - Bearing caps, cylinder blocks, connecting rods etc.	Burnishing components are: Cam and followers, matting parts of engine, aesthetical components etc.

4. Sketch a planomiller with labels.   **(4 M)**

Ans. Refer Fig. 3.8.

5. Explain construction of boring machine.   **(4 M)**

Ans. Refer Sections 3.22 and 3.24 with Fig. 3.10.

1. State advantages and applications of broaching machines.

Ans. Refer Sections 3.6 and 3.8.

2. Differentiate between planer and planomiller.

Ans. Refer Section 3.19.1

3. Compare capstan and turret lathe.

Ans. Refer Section 3.15.

4. Define boring. State its types.

Ans. Refer Sections 3.20 and 3.21.

5. Draw neat sketch of any two boring tools.

Ans. Refer Section 3.30.

6. Compare pull broach and push broach.

Ans. Refer Section 3.4.

Chapter 4

MILLING AND GEAR CUTTING

At the end of this chapter students will be able to:

- Identify different type of Milling Machine and their main parts
- Describe different type of Milling Operations
- Categorization various Milling Cutters
- Understand Indexing, Different methods of Indexing

4.1 INTRODUCTION TO MILLING

- Milling is a machining process in which metal is removed by a rotary multi-point tool called as milling cutter.

- With each revolution of the spindle a small amount of material is removed by each tooth.

- The cutter has multiple cutting edges and so it removes metal at a very fast rate.

- As both the cutter and work piece can be moved in more than one direction at the same time, the surfaces having almost any orientation can be machined.

- The principal differences between milling and other machining processes are:

  o The interruptions in cutting that occur as the teeth of the milling cutter alternatively engage and leave the workpiece.

  o The relatively small size of the chips in milling.

  o The variation in thickness within each chip.

  o Chip thickness varies during the cut-off any individual tooth because feed is measured in the direction of table motion (workpiece moving into cutter), while chip thickness is measured along the radius of the cutter.

- A milling machine is a machine tool that removes metal as the work is fed against a rotating multipoint cutter. The cutter rotates at high speed.

- The milling machine is widely used in production work, as it can hold one or more number of cutters at a time.

- The accuracy and surface finish obtained by milling machine is superior to any other machine.

- The complicated jobs like gear, cam, helix can be done on milling machine.

- In many applications, due to its high accuracy and higher machining rates, milling machines has replaced shapers and slotters.

4.2 WORKING PRINCIPLE OF MILLING

- The working principle used in milling is shown in figure 4.1. The work piece is rigidly clamped on the table with the help of bolts and T-slots.

- The milling cutter is mounted on the arbor or a spindle. The cutter rotates at a high speed and the work is fed slowly against the cutter.

- The metal is removed by a series of cutting edges. The metal removed is in the form of discontinuous chips.

- The work can be fed in longitudinal, vertical and crosswise direction. As the cutter advances, the metal is removed from the work surface to obtain the desired shape.

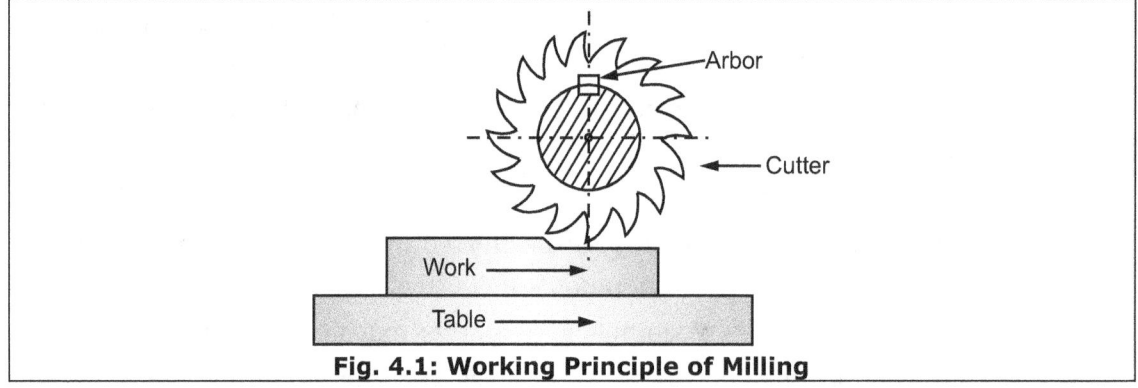

Fig. 4.1: Working Principle of Milling

4.3 CLASSIFICATION OF MILLING MACHINES

- Milling machines can be classified into different categories depending upon their construction, specification and operations.

- The choice of any particular machine is primarily determined by nature of the work to be done, its size, geometry and operations to be performed.

- The typical classification of milling machines on the basis of its construction is given below.

- Column and knee type milling machines
  - Plain milling machine
  - Vertical milling machine
  - Universal milling machine

- Fixed bed type milling machine
  - Simplex milling machine
  - Duplex milling machine
  - Triplex milling machine
  - Rise and fall type milling machine
- Production milling machine
  - Rotary table milling machine
  - Drum type milling machine
  - Tracer controlled milling machine
- Planer milling machine
- Special milling machine
  - Planetory milling machine
  - Thread milling machine
  - Profile milling machine
  - Gear milling machine
  - Cam milling machine
  - Double end milling machine
  - Spar milling machine

4.4 BASIC PARTS OF COLUMN & KNEE TYPE MILLING MACHINE

- A general column and knee type milling machine is shown in Fig. 4.2.
- Any column and knee type milling consist of the following basic parts:
  - **Base:** It is a heavy cast iron casing at the bottom of the machine. It carries a column at its one end. It also serves as reservoir for the coolant.
  - **Column:** A vertical column mounted on base carriers accurately machined guideways on its front face. A spindle is mounted on the front face of column. Guideways are machined on its front face.
  - **Knee:** A knee is mounted on the front face of column and can slide in vertical direction on the guideways. The knee can be operated by the elevating screw provided below the knee. Machined guideways are provided on the top surface of the knee.
  - **Saddle:** It is mounted on the knee and can move over it in cross-direction. Accurately machined grideways are provided on top of saddle.
  - **Table:** The table is mounted on saddle and can be moved in longitudinal direction. The table is provided with T-slots to hold the workpiece. Also the cutting fluid can be drained back to the reservoir through these slots.

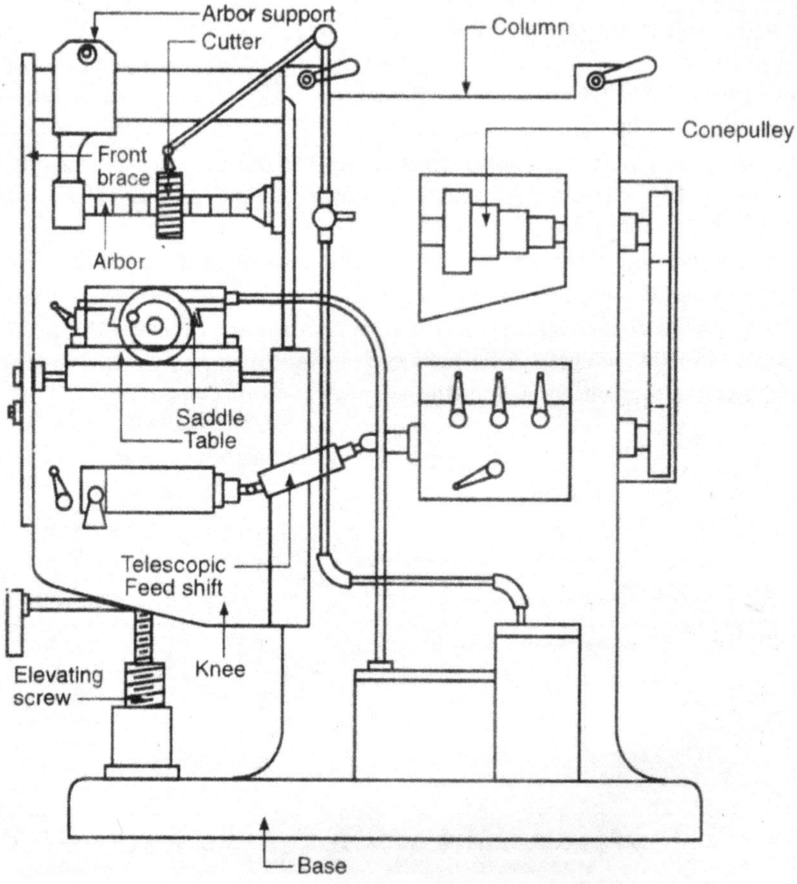

Fig. 4.2: Column and knee type milling Machine

4.4.1 Functions of Basic Parts of Column and Keen Type Milling

1. **Base:** To support all the parts of milling machine.
2. **Column:** To support Spindle and drive mechanism.
3. **Knee:** Can be moved vertically up and down on column by using elevating screw.
4. **Over-arm:** To support other end of the arbor.
5. Saddle: To move horizontally towards the column and away from column.
6. **Table:** To move towards the left and right of operator and to clamp the work-piece with T-slots on it.
7. **Spindle:** To hold rotary milling cutter.

4.5 VARIOUS COLUMN & KNEE TYPE MILLING MACHINE

• The important column and knee milling machines are explained below:

4.5.1 Plain Milling Machine   [W-14]

• The plain milling machine is rigid and sturdy machine and can accommodate heavy work piece.
• It is used for producing grooves, slots on bolt head, keyways and other simple operations.

- The plain milling machine is shown in Fig. 4.3. and its construction is explained below:
  - **Base:** It is a heavy cast iron casing at the bottom of the machine. It carries a column at its one end. It also serves as reservoir for the coolant.
  - **Column:** A vertical column mounted on base carriers accurately machined guideways on its front face. A spindle is mounted on the front face of column. Guideways are machined on its front face.
  - **Knee:** A knee is mounted on the front face of column and can slide in vertical direction on the guideways. The knee can be operated by the elevating screw provided below the knee. Machined guideways are provided on the top surface of the fence.
  - **Saddle:** It is mounted on the knee and can move over it in cross-direction. Accurately machined grideways are provided on top of saddle.
  - **Table:** The table is mounted on saddle and can be moved in longitudinal direction. The table is provided with T-slots to hold the workpiece. Also the cutting fluid can be drain back to the reservoir through these slots.
  - **Overarm:** The overarm is mounted on the top of the column. It supports the overhanging arbor through yoke.
  - **Arbor:** It is the extension of spindle over which milling cutters can be mounted. The distance between cutter can be adjusted by using spacing collars.

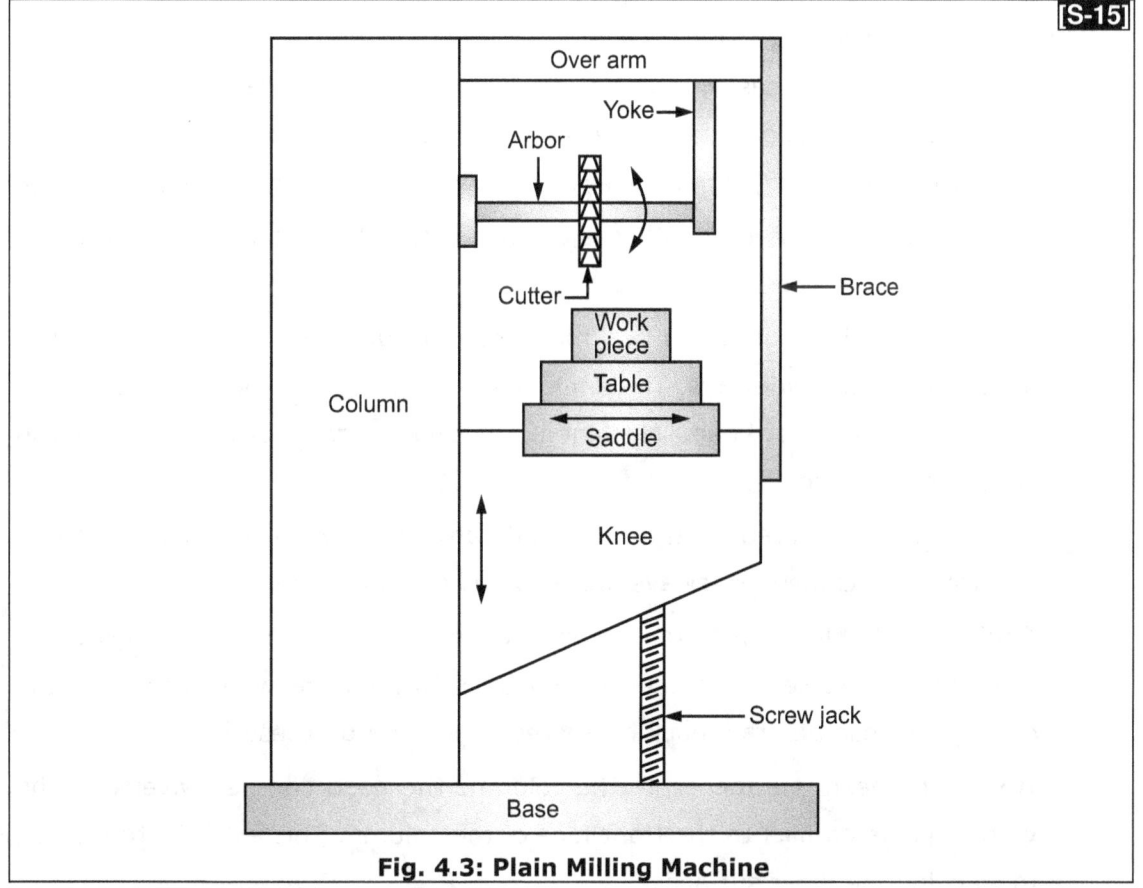

[S-15]

Fig. 4.3: Plain Milling Machine

Working:

- The work piece is mounted on the table and can be moved in three directions. Vertical by moving the knee, longitudinal by moving the table and cross-wise by moving the saddle.

- A milling cutter is mounted on the arbor and rotates about the horizontal axis at a high speed.

- The work piece is first made to touch the cutter by moving the table and then machining takes place.

4.5.2 Vertical Milling Machine

- As the name suggests the spindle of vertical milling machine is vertical.

- The cutter is mounted in the spindle.

- It is generally used for slotting, grooving, drilling, boring of holes etc.

- The commonly used vertical milling machine is shown in figure 4.4. and its construction is explained below:

  o **Base:** It is a heavy cast iron casing at the bottom of the machine. It carries a column at its one end. It also serves as reservoir for the coolant.

  o **Column:** A vertical column is mounted on the base. The overarm of the machine is made integral with the column. The column carries a head at its front which carries a vertical spindle.

  o **Knee:** A knee is mounted on the front face of column and can slide in vertical direction on the guideways. The knee can be operated by the elevating screw provided below the knee. Machined guideways are provided on the top surface of the fence.

  o **Saddle:** It is mounted on the knee and can move over it in cross-direction. Accurately machined grideways are provided on top of saddle.

  o **Cable:** The table is mounted on saddle and can be moved in longitudinal direction. The table is provided with T-slots to hold the workpiece. Also the cutting fluid can be drain back to the reservoir through these slots.

  o **Head:** The head is attached to the column. The head can be swiveled in the vertical plane parallel to the front face of the column. This extra feature helps to machine the taper surfaces.

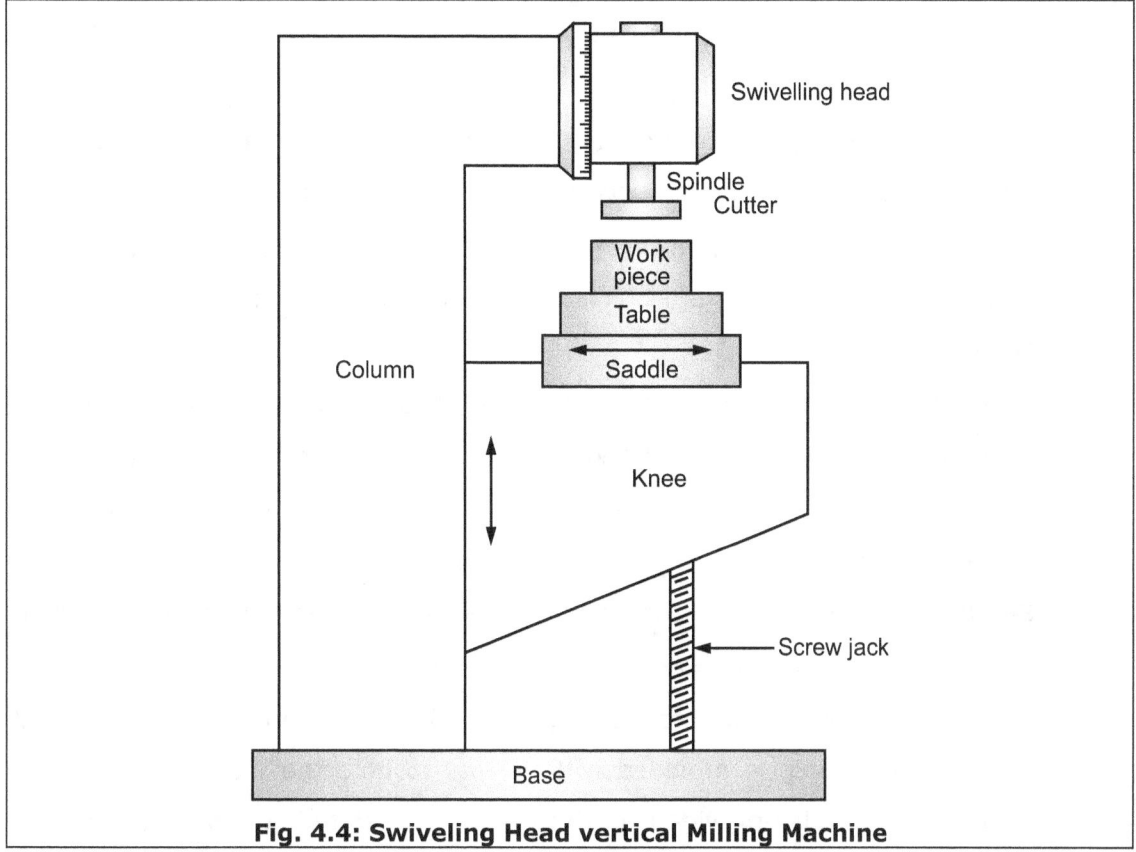

Fig. 4.4: Swiveling Head vertical Milling Machine

Working:

- The work piece is mounted on the table and can be moved in three directions. Vertical by moving the knee, longitudinal by moving the table and cross-wise by moving the saddle.

- A milling cutter is mounted on the vertical spindle and rotates about the vertical axis at a high speed.

- The work piece is first made to touch the cutter by moving the table and then machining takes place.

4.5.3 Universal Milling Machine

- The universal milling machine is most rigid and sturdy milling machine and can accommodate heavy work piece.

- It can be used for a wide range of milling operations and almost eliminates the need of drilling, shaper, slotter etc.

- It is a modification of plain milling machine with an additional table movement.

- It is used for producing spur, spiral, bevel gears, drills, reamers etc.

- The universal milling machine is shown in figure 4.5. and its construction is explained below:

  o **Base:** It is a heavy cast iron casing at the bottom of the machine. It carries a column at its one end. It also serves as reservoir for the coolant.

  o **Column:** A vertical column is mounted on the base and carries accurately machined guideways on its front face. A spindle is mounted on the front face of column.

  o **Knee:** A knee is mounted on the front face of column and can slide in vertical direction on the guideways. The knee can be operated by the elevating screw provided below the knee. Machined guideways are provided on the top surface of the knee.

  o **Saddle:** It is mounted on the knee and can move over it in cross-direction. Accurately machined guideways are provided on top of saddle.

  o **Table:** The table is mounted on saddle and can be moved in longitudinal direction. The table is provided with T-slots to hold the workpiece. Circular guide ways are also provided on the top surface of saddle, so that the table can be swiveled in horizontal plane about 45° on both sides.

  o **Overarm:** The overarm is mounted on the top of the column. It supports the overhanging arbor through yoke.

  o **Arbor:** It is the extension of spindle over which milling cutters can be mounted. The distance between cutter can be adjusted by using spacing collars.

  o **Brace:** Front base is used to adjust the relative position of knee and overhanging arm. It is also an extra support fixed between the knee and overhanging arm for rigidity.

  o **Spindle:** Spindle is projected from the column face and provided with a tapered hole to accommodate the arbor.

- Performance of a milling machine depends on the accuracy, strength and rigidity of the spindle. Spindle also transfer the motive power to arbor through belt or gear from column.

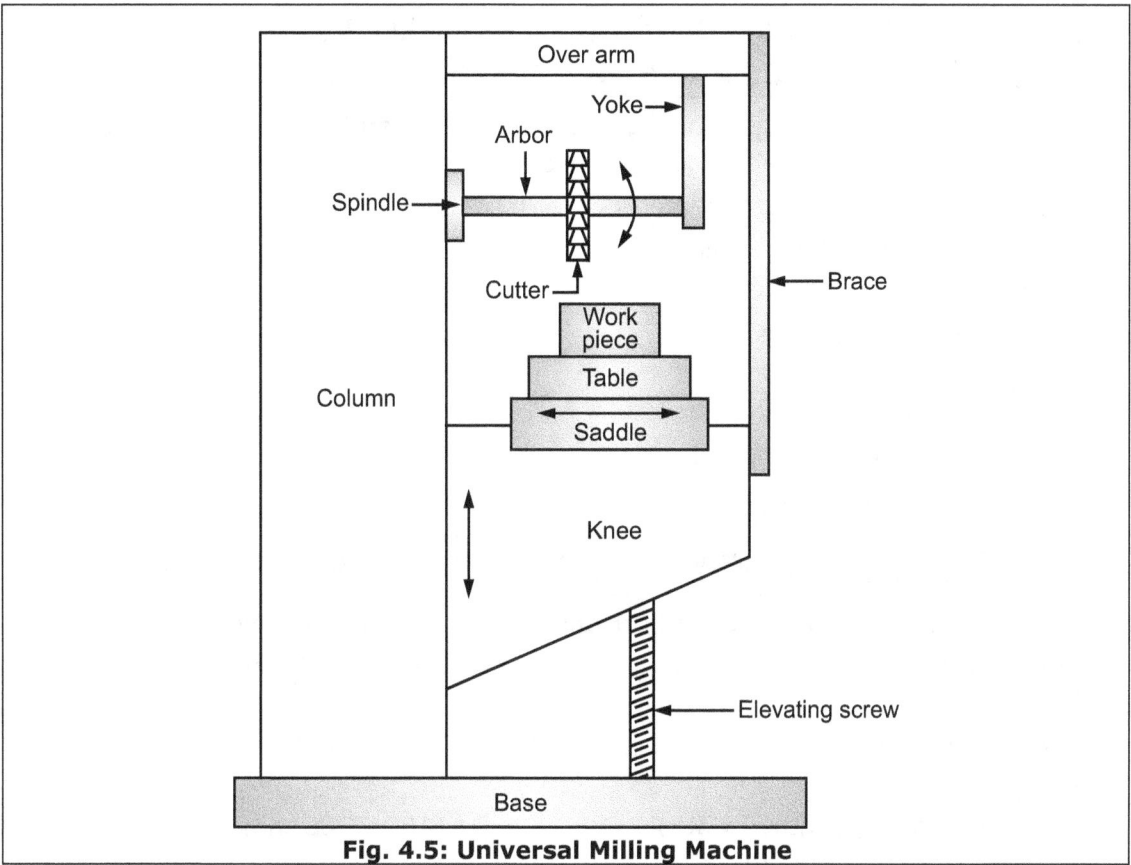

Fig. 4.5: Universal Milling Machine

Working:

- The work piece is mounted on the table and can be moved in four ways. Vertical by moving the knee, longitudinal by moving the table, cross-wise by moving the saddle and swiveling of table.

- A milling cutter is mounted on the arbor and rotates about the horizontal axis at a high speed.

- The work piece is first made to touch the cutter by moving the table and then machining takes place.

4.5.4 Omniversal Milling Machine

- This is an improved for of milling machine. The table is provided with all the movements of universal milling machine. In addition to that, it can be tilted in a vertical plane by providing a swivel arrangement at the knee.

- Also the entire knee assembly is mounted in such a way that it may be fed in a longitudinal direction horizontally. The addition swivelling arrangement of the table enables it to machine taper spiral grooves in reamers, bevel gears etc.

- Omniversal milling machine is a tool room and experimental shop machine.

4.6 SPECIFICATION OF A COLUMN AND KNEE TYPE MILLING MACHINE

- A column and knee type milling machine is generally specified by its table dimensions, table travel and distance between the cutter and work piece.
- Apart from this the other parameters that matters are
  - Number of spindle speeds
  - Number of feeds
  - Total power available.
  - Spindle nose taper.
  - Horse Power of the motor
  - Approximate weight of the machine
  - Floor space area required

4.6.1 Specification of a Horizontal Milling Machine

- The specification of a particular horizontal milling machine is given below.
- The size and specification of a milling machine means the dimensions of the main parts.
- The specifications for a typical horizontal knee type of milling machine is given below:

1. Size of table (length × width)   = 1100×300 mm
2. Longitudinal travel of table   = 650 mm
3. Cross travel of table   = 225 mm
4. Vertical travel of table   = 420 mm
5. Number of spindle speeds   = 9
6. Range of spindle speeds   = 45 to 730 rpm
7. Power of the spindle motor   = 40 H.P.
8. Net approximate weight of the machine = 1500 kg
9. Floor space area required   = 3 m^2

4.7 DIFFERENCE BETWEEN PLAIN AND UNIVERSAL MILLING MACHINE   [W-15]

Plain Milling Machine	Universal Milling Machine
1. The table of plain milling machine has three movements cross, longitudinal and vertical.	1. The table of universal milling machine has 4 movements i.e. cross, longitudinal vertical and swiveling.

contd. ...

2. Helical milling cannot be performed without using a spiral milling attachment.	2. No such attachments is required.
3. It is more rigid and heavier in construction.	3. It is less rigid and light in construction.
4. Its overarm is fixed.	4. Its overarm can be pushed back or removed and a vertical milling head can be fitted in place of the arbor to use it as a universal milling machine.
5. It is particularly adopted for manufacturing operations.	5. It is mostly intended for tool room work.
6. No auxiliaries are provided.	6. Various auxiliaries are provided.

4.8 MILLING CUTTERS

- Milling cutters are cutting tools typically used in milling machines to perform milling operations.

- They remove material by their movement within the machine or directly from the cutter's shape.

- Milling cutter can be defined as, "A rotary tool-steel cutting tool with peripheral teeth, used in a milling machine to remove material from the work piece through the relative motion of work piece and cutter".

4.8.1 Classification Of Milling Cutter

- The milling cutter are generally classified as follows:
    1. Plain milling cutter
        (a) Light duty plain milling cutter
        (b) Heavy duty plain milling cutter
        (c) Helical plain milling cutter
    2. Side milling cutter
        (a) Plain side milling cutter
        (b) Half side milling cutter
        (c) Staggered teeth side milling cutter
        (d) Interlocking teeth side milling cutter
    3. End milling cutter
        (a) Solid end milling cutter
        (b) Shell end milling cutter

4. Metal slitting milling cutter
   (a) Plain metal slitting cutter
   (b) Staggered teeth metal slitting cutter
5. Angle milling cutter
   (a) Single angle milling cutter
   (b) Double angle milling cutter
6. Formed milling cutter
   (a) Convex form milling cutter
   (b) Concave form milling cutter
   (c) Corner rounding form milling cutter
   (d) Formed gear cutter
7. Slot milling cutter
   (a) T-slot milling cutter
   (b) Dovetail slot milling cutter
8. Thread milling cutter
9. Fly milling cutter

4.9 TYPES OF MILLING CUTTER [S-16, 17]

- The important types of milling cutter are explained below:

4.9.1 Plain Milling Cutters

- These cutters are cylindrical in shape having teeth on their periphery.
- The teeth are generally parallel to the axis of the cutter.
- Such cutters are mounted on the machine arbor between the spacing collars.
- These are used to produce flat surfaces parallel to axis of rotation.
- Plain milling cutter is shown in Fg. 4.6. Depending upon the size and applications plain milling cutters are categorized as light duty, heavy duty and helical plain milling cutters.
- A plain milling cutter with a larger width is called as slab mill shown in Fig. 4.7. To remove more material and from harder surface a coarser teeth slab mill is used. Whereas to remove less material a fine teeth slab mill is used.

Fig. 4.6: Plain Milling Cutter　　　　**Fig. 4.7: Slab Mill**

4.9.2 Side Milling Cutters

- Side milling cutters are used to remove metals from the side of work piece.
- Peripheral teeth do the actual cutting of metal while side teeth do the finishing work.
- The teeth may be parallel to the axis of the cutter or helical.
- These cutters have teeth on the periphery and on its sides as shown in Fig. 4.8.
- These are further categorized as plain side milling cutters having straight circumferential teeth. Staggered teeth side milling cutters having alternate teeth with opposite helix angle providing more chip space. Half side milling cutters have straight or helical teeth on its circumference and on its one side only.
- Interlocking side milling cutter has teeth of two half side milling cutter which are made to interlock to form one unit.

Fig. 4.8: Side Milling Cutter

4.9.3 End Mill

- End mills are used for cutting slots, pockets, small holes, keyways and light milling operations.
- These cutters have teeth on their end as well as an periphery as shown in Fig. 4.9.
- They are so named because they have teeth at one end only and the other end acts as a shank similar to a drill.
- The cutting teeth may be straight or helical. Such cutters are mostly used on vertical milling machine.
- Depending upon the shape of their shank, these are categorized as discussed below.
- **Taper Shank Mill:** Taper shank mill have tapered shank.
- **Straight Shank Mill:** Straight shank mill having straight shank.
- **Shell End Mills:** These are normally used for face milling operation. Cutters of different sizes can be accommodated on a single common shank.

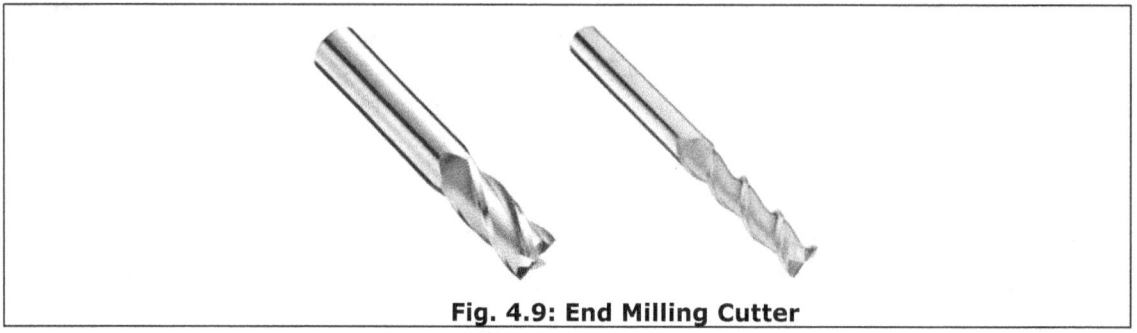

Fig. 4.9: End Milling Cutter

4.9.4 Metal Slitting Saw

- These cutters are like plain or side milling cutters having very small width upto 5 mm as shown in Fig. 4.10.
- These are used for parting off, milling deep slots or narrow slots.
- It has more teeth per unit of diameter as compared to ordinary plain milling cutter.
- Metal slitting saw is shown in Figure 4.10. The teeth of this cutter may be straight as in plain milling cutter or staggered like staggered teeth side milling cutter.

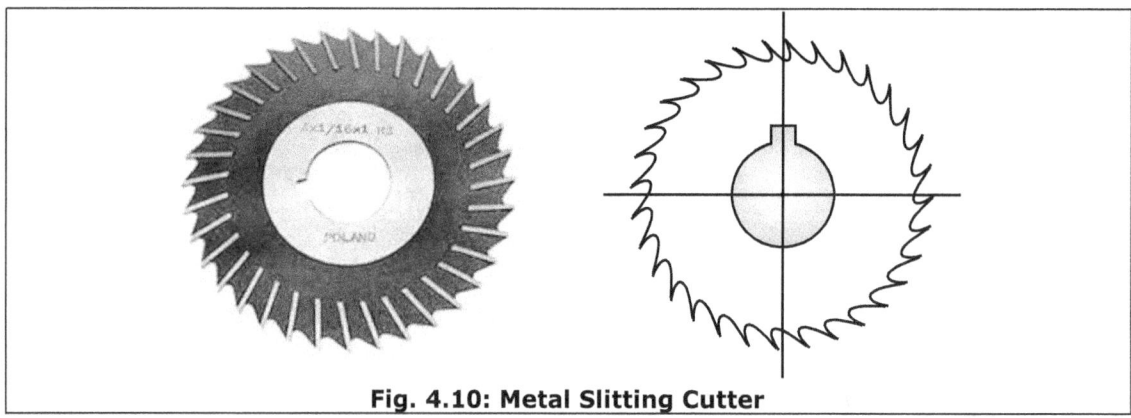

Fig. 4.10: Metal Slitting Cutter

4.9.5 Angle Milling Cutter

- These cutters are used to cut angles in the work piece and are shown in Fig. 4.11.
- These cutters have conical surfaces with cutting edges over them.
- These are used to machine angles other than 90°.
- Two types of angle milling cutters are available single angle milling cutter and double angle milling cutter.
- Single angle milling cutters have one conical surface and are used for milling dovetail surfaces. The cutter angle is generally 45° or 60°.
- Double angle milling cutters have teeth on two conical surface and are used for machining V-grooves. The included cutter angle is generally 45°, 60° or 90°.

(a) Single Angle   **(b) Double Angle**
Fig. 4.11: Angle Milling Cutter

4.9.6 Formed Cutters

- Formed cutters may have different types of profile on their cutting edges which can generate different types of profile on the work pieces.
- Depending upon tooth profile and their capabilities some of the formed cutters are explained below and shown in figure 4.12.
- **Convex Milling Cutters**
  - These cutters have profile outwards at their circumference.
  - They are used to generate concave semicircular surface on the work piece.
- **Concave Milling Cutters**
  - These milling cutters have teeth profile curve in words on their circumference.
  - These are used to generate convex semicircular surfaces.
- **Corner Rounding Milling Cutters**
  - These cutters have teeth curved inwards.
  - These milling cutters are used to form contours of quarter circle. These are main used in making round corners and round edges of the work piece.
- **Gear Cutter**
  - These cutters are used in making gears on milling machine.
  - Gear cutting is an operation which cannot be done otherwise.
  - These cutter have tooth profile which are to be reproduced on the gear blank.

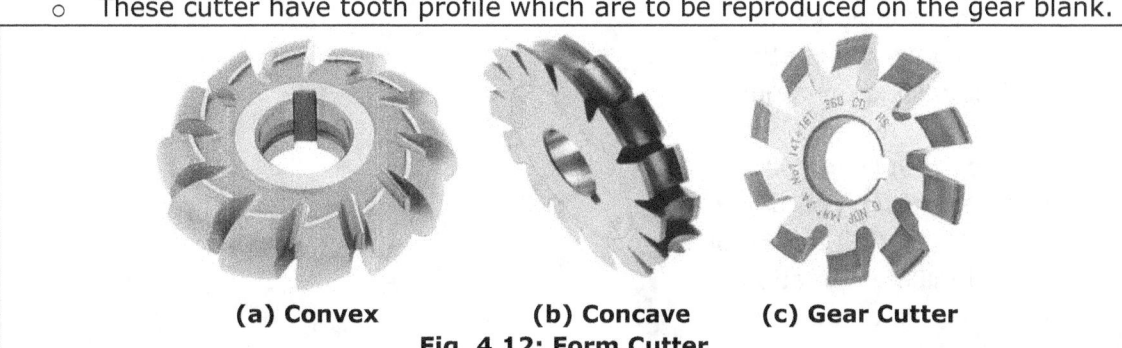

(a) Convex   **(b) Concave**   **(c) Gear Cutter**
Fig. 4.12: Form Cutter

4.9.7 'T' Slot Milling Cutters

- These are the special form of milling cutters used to produce "T" shaped slots in the work piece.
- These have cutting edges on their periphery and both sides.
- They have integral shank which can be hold in the machine spindle.
- A typical T-slot milling cutter is shown in Fig. 4.13.

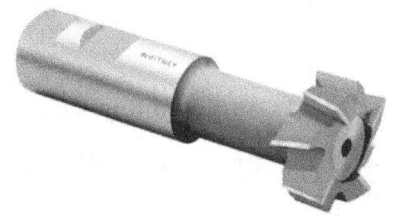

Fig. 4.13: T-slot cutter

4.10 MILLING CUTTER MATERIAL

- The following properties are desired in the milling cutter material:
  - o The cutting edge should be able to retain its hardness even at elevated temperatures. This property is called as red hardness.
  - o The cutting edges should not wear out quickly due to abrasive nature of the material. This property is called as high abrasive resistance.
  - o The cutting edge should not readily break due to heavy load or inhomogeneous material of the work piece.
- Considering the above properties, milling cutter are generally made-up of the following three materials:
  - o HSS for general purpose
  - o Cemented carbide for long production runs and heavy cuts
  - o Cast alloys for high speed
  - o Inserted tooth type cutters are more common now-a-days as they reduce the cutter cost.

4.11 MILLING MACHINE OPERATIONS

- Following different operations can be performed on a milling machine:
  - (a) Plain milling operation
  - (b) Face milling operation
  - (c) Side milling operation
  - (d) Straddle milling operation
  - (e) Angular milling operation
  - (f) Gang milling operation
  - (g) Form (Profile) milling operation
  - (h) End milling operation
  - (i) Saw milling operation
  - (j) T-Slot milling operation

4.11.1 Plain Milling

- Plain milling is operation of producing plain, flat, horizontal surface parallel to axis of rotation of plain milling cutter. It is shown in Fig. 4.14

- For this operation, the work piece surface is mounted parallel to the surface of the milling machine table.

- The milling cutter is mounted on a milling machine arbor and is rotated at high speed.

- The arbor is well supported in a horizontal plane between the milling machine spindle and one or more arbor supports.

- The depth of cut is adjusted by rotating the cross feed screw of the table.

- If large quantities of metal are to be removed, a coarse tooth cutter should be used. Such operation is also known as '*slab milling*', shown in Fig. 4.15.

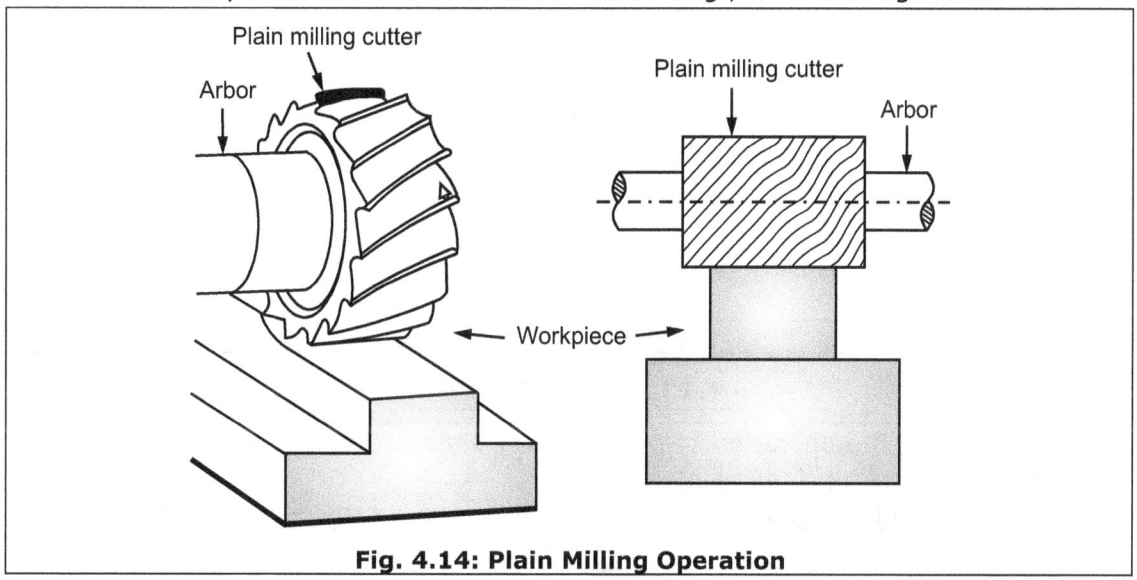

Fig. 4.14: Plain Milling Operation

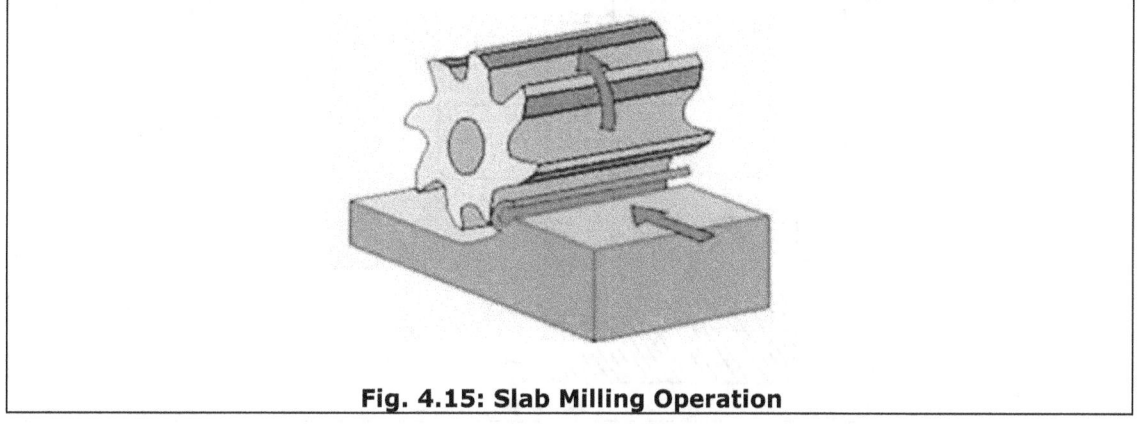

Fig. 4.15: Slab Milling Operation

4.11.2 Face Milling

- Face milling is the milling of surfaces that are perpendicular to the cutter axis.
- Face milling produces flat surfaces.
- This operation is performed by face milling cutter mounted on stub arbor of milling machine as shown in Fig. 4.16
- The peripheral cutting edges of the cutter do the actual cutting, while face cutting edges finish up the work surface by removing a very small amount of material.
- In face milling, the feed can be either horizontal or vertical.
- The depth of cut is adjusted by rotating the cross fed screw of the table.
- Large surfaces are generally face milled on a vertical milling machine with the work piece clamped directly to the milling machine table to simplify handling and clamping operations.

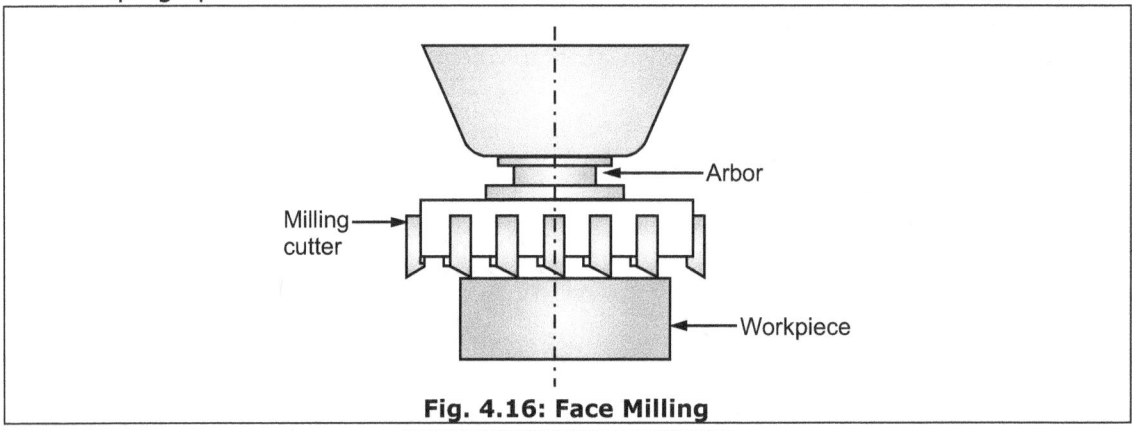

Fig. 4.16: Face Milling

4.11.3 Side Milling

- Side milling is the operation of production of flat vertical surface on the sides of work piece by using side milling cutter.
- The depth of cutter is adjusted by vertical feed screw provided on table.

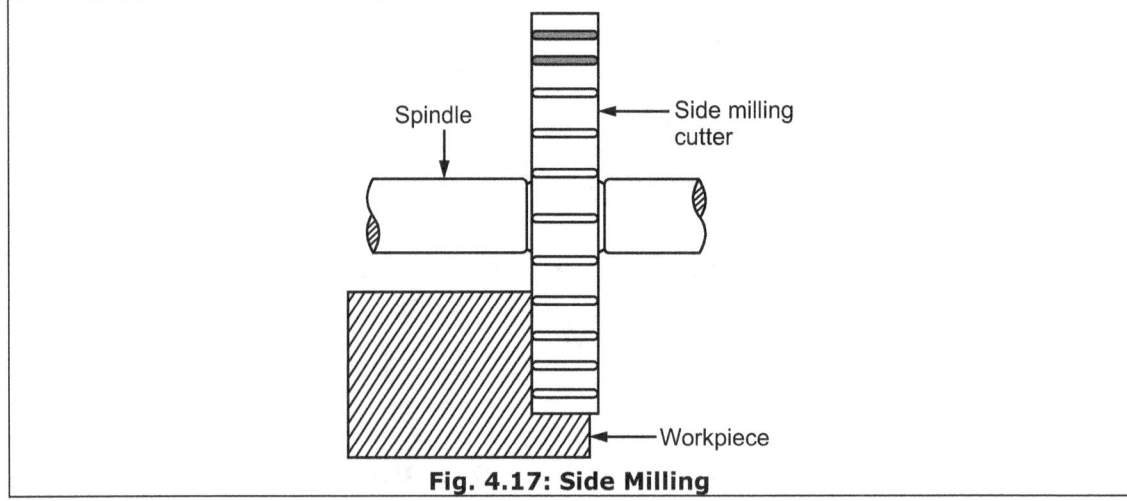

Fig. 4.17: Side Milling

4.11.4 Straddle Milling Operation [S-15, 17, W-15]

- This is a type of side milling operation shown in Fig. 4.18.

- When two parallel vertical surfaces are machined simultaneously by two side milling cutters mounted on the same arbor the operation is called straddle milling.

- Distance between the cutters is so adjusted that both sides of the work piece can be milled simultaneously.

- The two side milling cutters are separated by spacers, washers, and shims so that the distance between the cutting teeth of the cutters is exactly equal to the width of the work piece area required.

- Usually two half side milling cutters are used so that they straddle the work piece.

- The work piece is usually mounted between centers in the indexing fixture, or mounted vertically in a swivel vise.

- When cutting a hexagonal head of a bolt, two opposite sides of the head are cut, then the spindle of the indexing fixture or the swivel vise is rotated 60° and other two sides of the work piece are straddle milled, then the spindle is again rotated 60° and remaining two sides of the work piece are straddle milled.

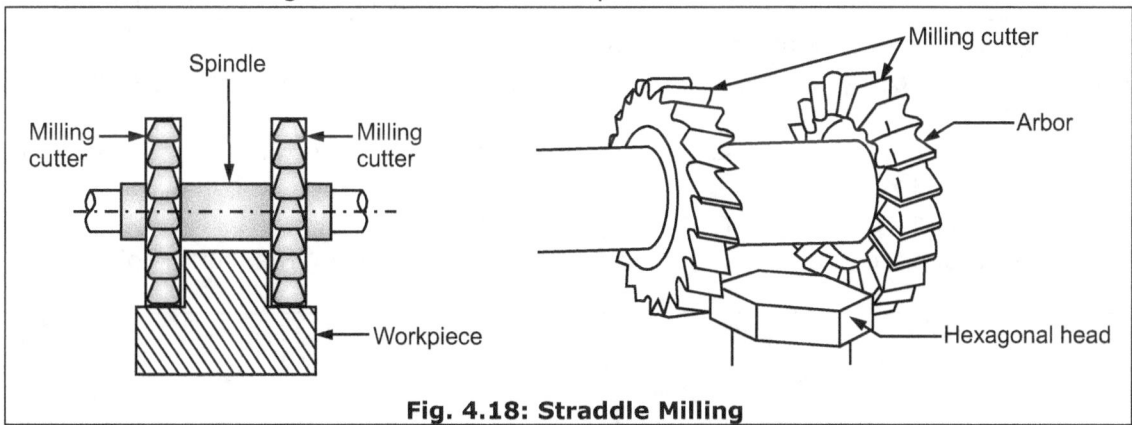

Fig. 4.18: Straddle Milling

4.11.5 Angular Milling Operation

- Angular milling is milling of flat surfaces which are neither parallel nor perpendicular to the axis of the milling cutter.

- A single-angle or double-angle milling cutter is used for this operation.

- A double-angle milling cutter is shown in figure 4.19.

- Milling dovetails, "V" shaped groove is the example of angular milling operation.

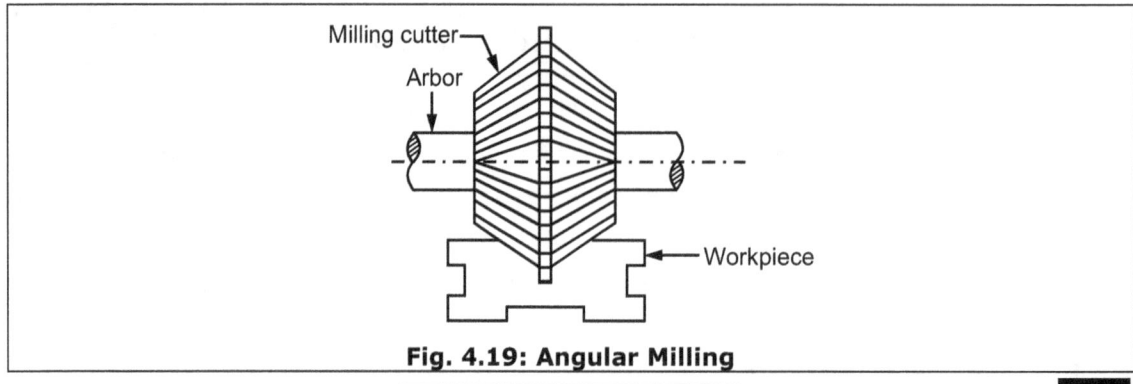

Fig. 4.19: Angular Milling

4.11.6 Gang Milling [S-17]

- Gang milling is the term applied to an operation in which two or more milling cutters are used together on one arbor for machining number of horizontal surfaces of a job.

- All cutters may perform the same type of operation or each cutter may perform a different type of operation.

- The diameter of cutters may be same or different.

- The cutters are mounted on arbor of plain milling machine. The distance between cutters is correctly adjusted by means of spacing collars.

- For example, several workplaces need a slot, a flat surface, and an angular groove.

- The usual method is to mount two or more milling cutters of different diameters, shapes and/or widths on an arbor as shown in figure.

- The possible cutter combinations are unlimited and are determined in each case by the nature of the job.

- The rate of production is high since numbers of surfaces are machined simultaneously.

- The duplicate parts can be made with accuracy.

- Cutting speed of gang milling cutter is calculated from the cutter of largest diameter.

[W-16]

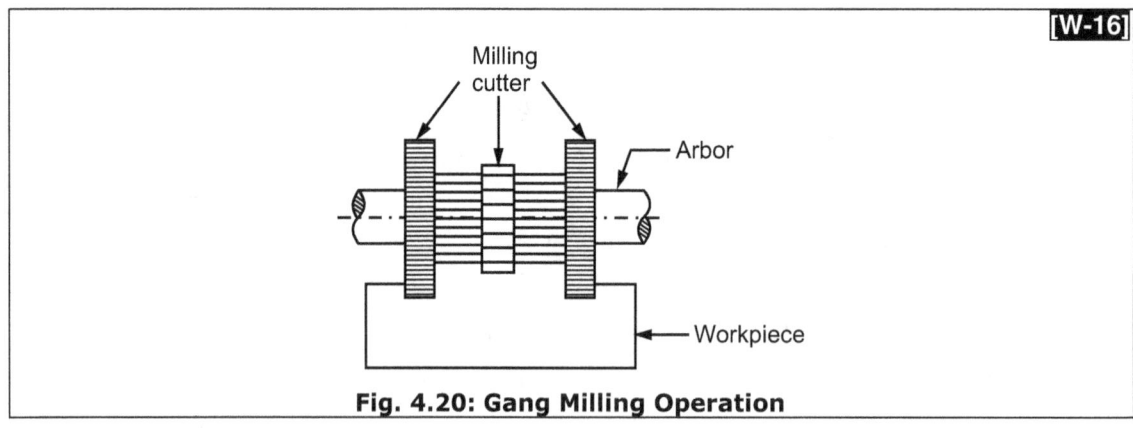

Fig. 4.20: Gang Milling Operation

4.11.7 Form Milling

- Form milling is operation of producing irregular surfaces by using form cutter as shown in Fig. 4.21.

- It is a process of machining special contours composed of curves and straight lines, or entirely of curves, at a single cut.

- This is done with formed milling cutters, shaped to the contour to be cut.

- Depending on the shape of the surface to be produced, the form of cutter is chosen. The irregular surface may be convex, concave, or any other shape.

- Other jobs for formed milling cutters include milling intricate patterns on workplaces and milling several complex surfaces in a single cut such as are produced by gang milling.

- Cutting gears on a milling machine is a common application of form milling.

- This operation is done comparatively at very low cutter speed than plain milling operation.

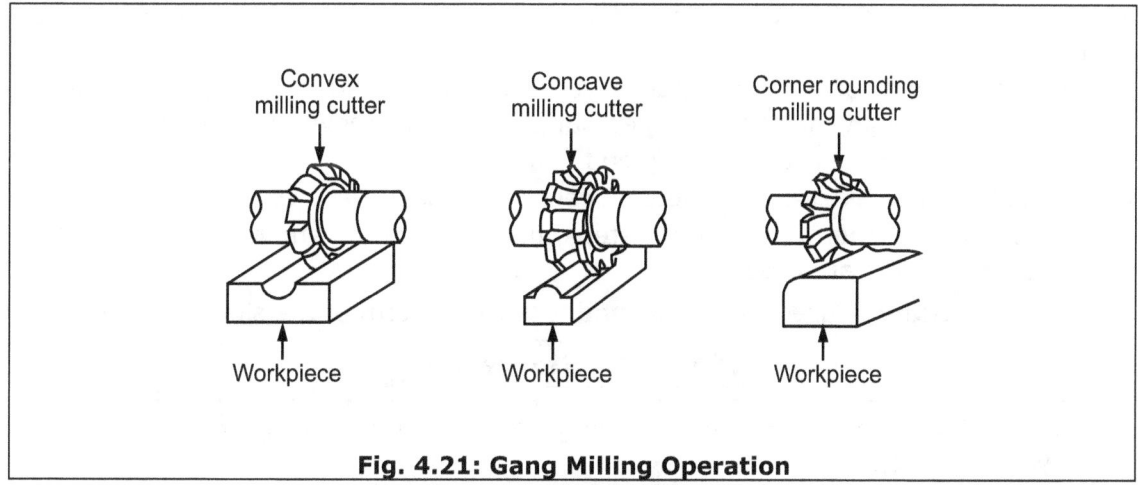

Fig. 4.21: Gang Milling Operation

4.11.8 End Milling

- End milling is the operation of producing a flat surface which may be vertical, horizontal or at an angle.

- The cutter used is an end mill. The end mill cutters are also used for producing slots, grooves or keyways.

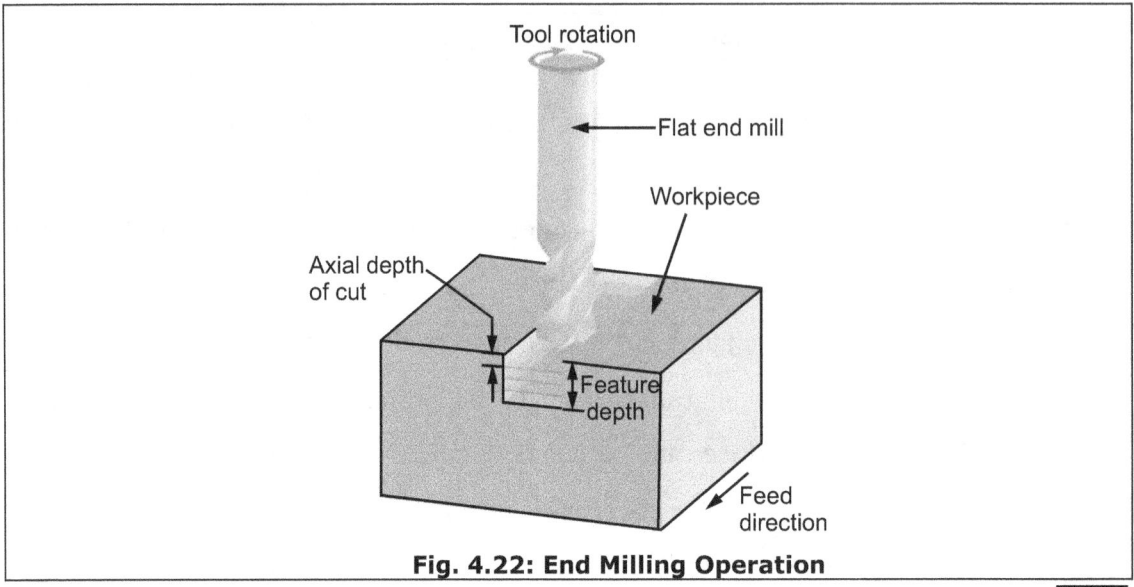

Fig. 4.22: End Milling Operation

4.11.9 Slot Milling

- The operation of producing keyways, grooves, slots of varying shapes and sizes is called slot milling operation.
- Slot milling operation can use any type of milling cutter like plain milling cutter, metal slitting saw or side milling cutter.
- Selection of a cutter depends upon type and size of slot or groove to be produced.
- Right placement of milling cutter is very important in this operation as axis of cutter should be at the middle of geometry of slot or groove to be produced.
- The closed slots are used by using end mill cutter.
- For milling dovetail slots or T slots a special type of cutter is used.
- This operation is performed in two steps, first by using an end mill or plain milling cutter, plain slots are produced.
- The T slot cutter is used to enlarge and face the bottom of the slots.

4.11.10 T- Slot Milling

- Cutting T-slots in a work piece holding device is a typical milling operation as shown in Fig. 4.23.
- The size of the T-slots depends upon the size of the T-slot bolts which will be used. Dimensions of T-slots and T-slot bolts are standardized for specific bolt diameters.
- Two milling cutters are required for milling T-slots, a T-slot milling cutter and either a side milling cutter or an end milling cutter.
- The side milling cutter or the end milling cutter is first used to cut a slot in the work piece equal in width to the throat width of the T-slot.

- Position the T-slot milling cutter over the edge of the work piece and align it with the previously cut groove.

- The T-slot milling cutter is then used to cut the head space to the prescribed dimensions.

- Feed the table longitudinally to make the cut.

- Use good amount of cutting oil between the cutter and work piece during this operation.

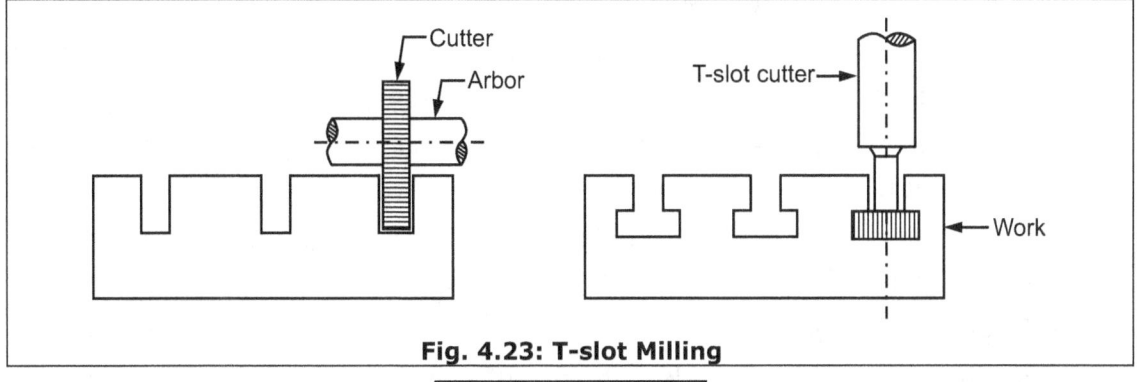

Fig. 4.23: T-slot Milling

4.11.11 Slitting

- Saw milling operation produces narrow slots or grooves into the workpiece using saw milling cutter.

- This operation is also used to cut the work piece into two equal or unequal pieces which cut is also known as "parting-off".

- In case of parting-off operation cutter and work piece are set in a manner so that the cutter is directly placed over one of the "T-slot" of the worktable as illustrated in Fig. 4.24.

- It is the operation of parting-off a solid work piece into two parts, or cutting a narrow slots and grooves. The work piece is required to be rigidly held in work holding device for slitting operation. Slitting saw is used for slitting operation.

Fig. 4.24: Slitting

4.12 NOMENCLATURE OF A PLAIN MILLING CUTTER

- It is also called as elements of plain milling cutter or terminology of plain milling cutter.

- The elements of a plain milling cutter are explained below and are shown in Fig. 4.25.

- **Body of cutter:** The part of the cutter left after exclusion of the teeth and the portions to which the teeth are attached.

- **Cutting edge:** Edge formed by the intersection of the face and the circular land or the surface left by the provision of primary clearance.

- **Face:** The portion of the gash, adjacent to the cutting edge on which the clip impinges as it is cut from the work.

- **Fillet:** Curved surface at the bottom of the gash which forms the face of one tooth to the back of the tooth immediately ahead.

- **Gash:** Chip space between the back of one tooth and the face of the next tooth.

- **Land:** The portion of the back of tooth adjacent to the cutting edge which is relieved to avoid interference between the surface being machined and the cutter.

- **Lead:** Axial advance of the helix of the cutting edge in one complete revolution of the cutter.

- **Outside diameter:** Diameter of the circle passing through the peripheral cutting edge.

- **Root diameter:** Diameter of the circuit passing through the bottom of fillet.

- **Arbor:** The shaft on which the milling cutter is mounted and driven.

- **Rake angle:** The angle measured in the diameteral place between the face of the tooth and a radial line passing through the tooth cutting edge. The rake angles can be positive, negative or zero.

- **Clearance angle:** Angles formed by primary or secondary clearance and the tangent to the periphery of the cutter at the cutting edge. They are called the primary and secondary clearance angles, respectively.

- **Lip angle:** Included angle between the land and the face of the tooth or alternatively the angle between the tangent to the back at the cutting edge and the face of the tooth.

- **Helix angle:** The cutting edge angle which a helical cutting edge makes with a plane containing the axis of the cylinder cutter.

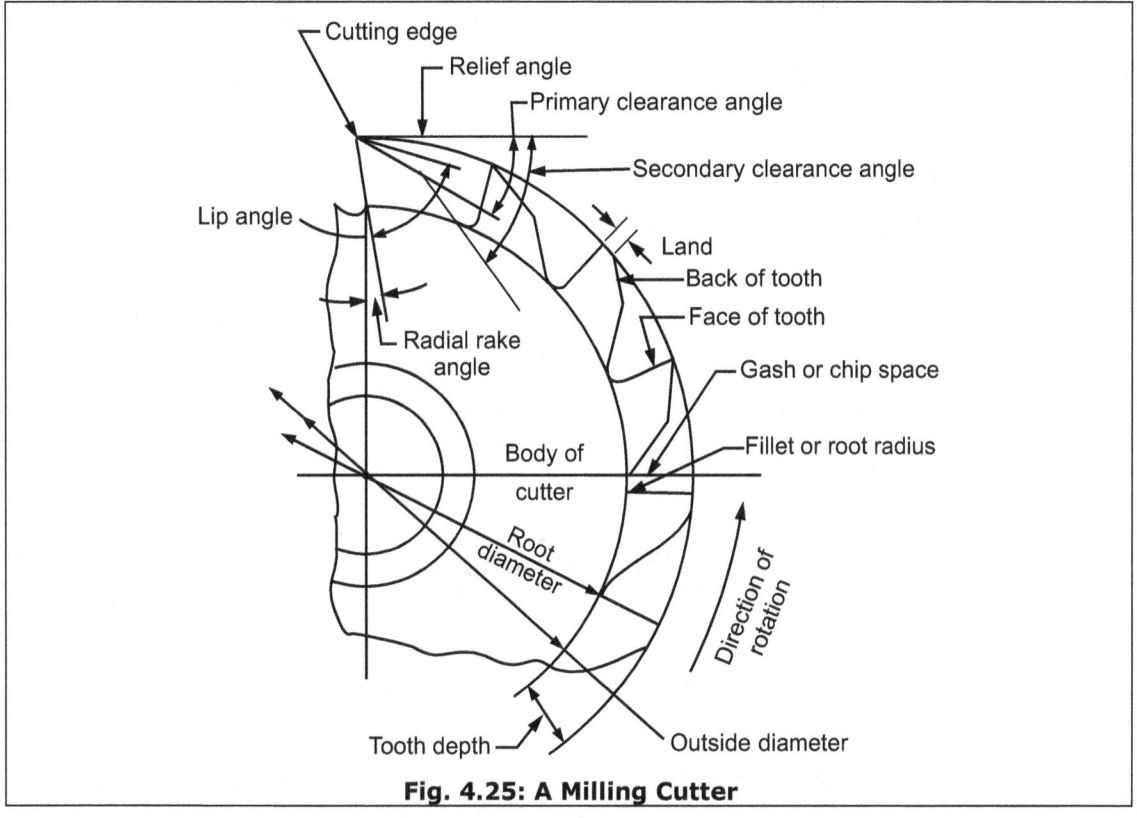

Fig. 4.25: A Milling Cutter

4.13 METHODS OF FEEDING THE WORKPIECE

- The methods of feeding a work piece can be categories as up milling and down milling. The methods are explained below and sketch in Fig. 4.26.

4.13.1 Down Milling   [W-14, S-16]

- It is also called as climb milling.
- In this process, the cutter is rotated in same direction as that of the travel of workpiece.
- The cutter tooth starts removing metal as soon as it reaches the work surface without sliding.
- The chip thickness is maximum at the start of cut and it reaches to minimum at the end of cut.
- The cutting force is maximum when tooth begins to cut and reduces to minimum when tooth leaves the work.
- In down milling, the cutting force tends to seat the work firmly in the work holding devices.
- Hence, the fixture design becomes easier.

- The chips are disposed off easily and do not interfere with the cutting.

- The coolant can be directly poured on the cutting zone where cutting force is maximum.

- This gives better surface finish.

- Also, the heat generated is diminished.

- In spite of above advantages of down milling, if there is backlash error present between feed screw of table and nut, it causes the work to be pulled below the current when the cut begins and leaves the work free at the end of cut.

- This causes vibrations and damages the work surface.

- So, down milling operation should not be performed on old machines and rigid machines should be used.

4.13.2 Up Milling

- It is the conventional milling process.

- In this process, the cutter is rotated in a direction opposite to direction of travel of work.

- The cutter does not start cutting metal as soon as it comes in contact with workpiece.

- The thickness of chip in up milling is minimum at the beginning of the cut and reaches to maximum at the end of cut.

- The chip thickness per tooth is not uniform.

- So the surface machined in up milling appears to be slightly wavy.

- The cutting force is minimum at the beginning and reaches to maximum at the end of cut.

- The cutting force is directed upwards and tends to lift the job from the fixtures.

- So, design of fixture is difficult in up milling.

- Also, due to typical nature of cut, it is difficult to pour coolant at the point where chip beings.

- As the cutter progresses, the chips accumulate and may spoil the work surface.

- As compared to down milling, the maximum undeformed chip thickness is slightly smaller and chip length larger.

- The up milling process being safe is still commonly used, in spite of so many disadvantages.

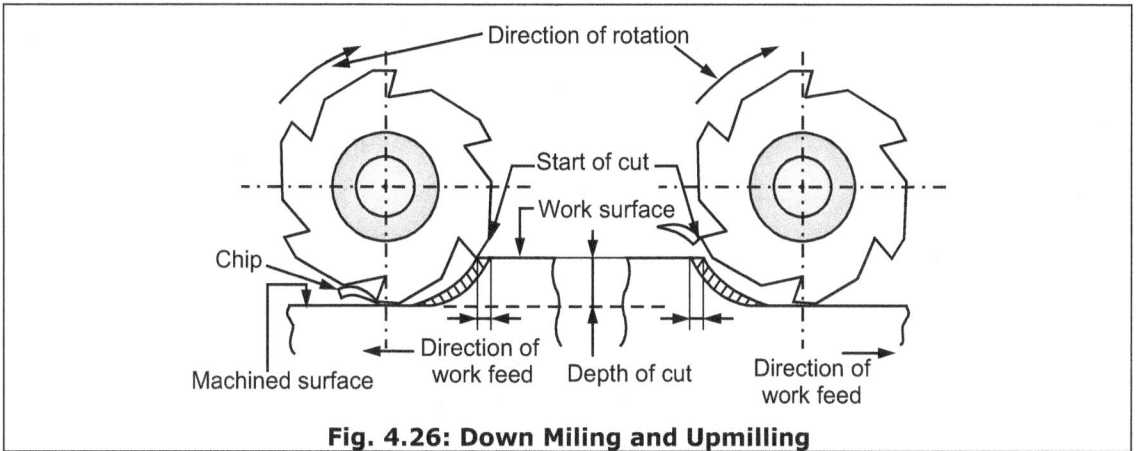

Fig. 4.26: Down Miling and Upmilling

4.13.3 Comparison between Up Milling And Down Milling [S-15]

Conventional Milling	Climb Milling
1. In conventional milling the cutter rotates in a direction opposite to that in which the work is fed.	1. In climb milling, the cutter rotates in the same direction to which the work is fed.
2. The chip thickness progresses gradually from start to cut to end of cut (i.e. chip thickness is minimum at the beginning of cut and maximum at end of the cut).	2. The chip thickness is maximum at the beginning of cut and minimum at end of the cut.
3. The cutting force tends to lift the w/p away from the fixture.	3. The cutting force tends to seat the w/p into the fixture.
4. It is difficult to pour coolant at the point of machining.	4. It is easy to pour coolant at the point of machining.
5. It is difficult to design the fixture.	5. Fixture designer is easy.
6. Wavy type of surface finish is obtained.	6. Better surface finish is obtained.
7. The cutter does not start cutting metal as soon as it comes in contact with the workpiece.	7. The cutter starts cutting metal as soon as it contacts the w/p.
8. The cutting force is ↓ at beginning and reaches to ↑ at the end of the cut.	8. The cutting force is ↑ at beginning of cut and reaches to ↓ at the end of the cut.

4.14 CUTTING PARAMETERS   [W-14, S-16]

4.14.1 Cutting Speed

- The cutting speed of milling cutter is its peripheral linear speed resulting from rotation. It is expressed in m/min. The cutting speed is calculated as,

$$\text{Cutting speed (v)} = \frac{\pi \times d \times N}{1000} \text{ m/min.}$$

Where,

v = Cutting speed in m/min

d = Diameter of cutter in mm

N = Speed of cutter in RPM

4.14.2 Feed

- The feed in milling machine is defined as 'the rate with which the work piece advances under the cutter'. The feed can be defined in following ways,
  1. **Feed per tooth**: It is defined as 'the distance the work advances in a time between engagements by the two successive teeth'. It is expressed in mm/tooth of cutter.
  2. **Feed per cutter revolution**: It is 'the distance the work advances in the time when the cutter turns through one complete revolution'. It is expressed in mm/revolution of cutter.
  3. **Feed per minute**: It is defined as 'the distance the work advances in one minute'. It is expressed in mm/min.

4.14.3 Depth of Cut

- It is the thickness of material removed in one pass of the work under the cutter. It is a perpendicular distance measured between the original and final surface of the work piece, measured in mm.

4.15 MACHINING TIME CALCULATION   [W-14]

- The time required for machining on milling machine is calculated as,

$$\text{Machining time (T)} = \frac{L}{F \times Z \times N} \text{ min}$$

Where,

L = Length of milling slot in metre

T = Machining Time in min

F = Feed per tooth in mm

Z = Number of teeth on milling cutter

N = Speed of cutter in RPM

4.16 INTRODUCTION TO GEAR CUTTING [S-17]

- Gear is one of the important machine tool elements which is an integral and inevitable part of power transmission system.

- A gear is a round blank having teeth along its periphery. A gear is defined as a toothed wheel which when meshed with other gears transmits motion from one part of mechanism to another.

- Gears transmits power or torque as well as rotary motion from one shaft to another. Along with the transmission of power gears also transfer the accurate velocity ratio between two shafts.

- Gears may be internal as well as external. Gears are vastly used to form mechanism for transferring power from prime mover to the place where other parts in the machine is to effect change in speed, torque or both.

- Speeds of two different parts in a machine can also be maintained relatively and precisely.

- Different types of gears are used for this purpose.

- Selection of a particular type of gear depends on so many factors such as relative position of two shafts, power and velocity ratio to be transferred, space limitation, percentage reduction of velocity, running conditions, accuracy of transmission.

- Gear can be manufactured by various methods like casting, stamping, powder metallurgy, machining etc.

- Because of their capability for transmitting motion and power, gears are among the most important of all machine elements.

- Special attention is paid to gear manufacturing because of the specific requirements to the gears.

- Power is normally transferred with the help of pair of gears in mesh together, each of these two are mount on driven shaft and driver shaft.

- The gear mounted on the driver shaft is called driver gear and another gear mounted on the driven shaft is called driven gear.

- Driver gear and driven gear both constitute a pair of mating gears, these gears are identical with reference to all parameters except their diameters and number of teeth.

4.17 GEAR MATERIALS

- The material used for the manufacture of gears depends upon the strength, Ease of manufacture, service conditions (like wear, noise, temperature, vibration etc), Overall cost of material and manufacture

- The gear materials used for transmitting torque and speed should be strong in shear and bending, sufficiently tough and resistant to wear, fatigue and chemical degradation.

- The materials generally used for making gears are:

(a) Metallic materials

Ferrous metals – for high loads

  o Cast iron is used when large gears are to be produced and when stresses are not high.
  o When gears are difficult to fabricate and when stresses on gears are high, then cast steel is used.
  o Medium and high carbon steels are extensively used in industrial gears.
  o Alloy steel is used when low tooth wear is required.

  Non-ferrous metals – for light load

  o Aluminium is used for light weight gears, gears in toys, instruments.
  o Bronze is used in order to reduce wear.

(b) Non-metallic materials

  o Non-metallic gears are widely used for light load, non-precision and noiseless operation.
  o Wood, plastic or fiber are used as non-metallic material.
  o These gears are light in weight having noiseless operation and are oil resistant.
  o Such gears cannot be used to transmit heavy power.

4.17.1 Selection of Gear Material

- The proper selection of gear material depends on
  o Amount of power to be transmitted.
  o Size and weight of the gear.
  o Service period of the gear.
  o Continuous or intermittent mode of drive.
  o Method of manufacture to be used.
  o Servise requirement – noiseless drive, light/heavy drive.
  o Degree of accuracy required.

4.18 GEAR MANUFACTURING METHOD   [W-14, S-16, 17]

- The different methods of manufacturing gear are classified below:

Casting   Stamping   Rolling   Powder metallurgy technique   Extrusion   Plastic moulding   Machining

Machining:
- Forming method
  - On a shaping/Planning machine
  - On milling machine
  - On broaching machine
- Template method
- Generating method
  - Gear shaping
  - Gear hobbing
  - Gear planning
  - Bevel gear generation

4.18.1 Casting

- It is the cheapest method of producing gear where economy is the main criteria.
- This method of producing gears is the same as that used for casting other products.
- Usually heavy gears are made by this process.
- These gears are relatively weak and slightly inaccurate.
- They are not efficient in transmitting power.
- They are generally used for slow speed drive.
- The casted gears cannot be very fine, these are rough, low strength, and with some inaccuracies in operation.
- For casting of gears sand moulds or permanent moulds are prepared, then molten metal is poured into the mold cavity to get the required gear.
- Cast iron gears are made by this method comfortably.

4.18.2 Stamping

- This process is widely used for mass production of small and their gears.
- The method is used for metal sheets upto a thickness of 3 mm.
- Stamping is done by punch and die with the help of power press.
- It give high accuracy and surface finish.
- Gears used in toys, watches, clocks etc. are produce by this method.

4.18.3 Rolling

- Both hot and cold rolling process are used to make gears.
- In hot rolling, gear blank is rolled against a master gear (hardened steel gear) to produce desired teeth on its periphery. Both are rolled together till the force between them makes the metal to flow to obtain the shape and size of the teeth of the master gear. The teeths are finally finished by machining.
- The cold rolling process is similar to hot rolling but requires high pressure.

4.18.4 Powder Metallurgy

- Small size high quality external or internal spur, bevel or spiral gears are also produced by powder metallurgy process.
- Large size gears are rolled after briquetting and sintering for more strength and life.
- Powder metallurgically produced gears hardly require any further finishing work.

4.18.5 Extrusion

- It is well suitable for production of small size gears from material like AC, brass, bronze.
- In this process are heated gear blank is placed inside the cylinder and pressed from one end with a ram.
- The other end carries a die similar to the shape of the required gear.
- On processing, the gear comes out of the die.
- It is then finished to size.
- The method is used for mass production.

4.18.6 Plastic Moulding

- In plastic moulding, gears of plastic material can be manufactured by using injection moulding or compression moulding.
- These are the very light duties gears used for transmission of very low amount of power but maintains velocity ratio accurately.
- Non-ferrous metals can also be used as raw material for gear making by plastic moulding methods.

4.18.7 Machining

- This is most widely used method for manufacturing of gear. It is also the most accurate method of gear manufacturing.
- Gear blank of accurate size and shape is first prepared by cutting it from metal stock. The gear blank can also be the metal casting.
- Gear is prepared by cutting one-by-one tooth in the gear blank of desired shape and size along it periphery.
- In this method the metal is removed in the form of chips.

4.19 SELECTION OF GEAR MANUFACTURING METHOD

- Machining or gear cutting is the most common and accurate method of gear manufacturing.
- The Type of Gear Manufacturing Method depends on:
  - Type of gear.
  - Size of gear.
  - Quantity required.
  - Accuracy desired.
  - Cost and availability of equipment.

4.20 GEAR CUTTING ON MILLING MACHINE

- On milling machine, the gear cutting operation is performed by using formed milling cutter. Gear form milling cutter may be used for this purpose.
- The cutter profile corresponds exactly with the tooth space of the gear.
- The cutter is mounted on arbour of the milling machine. The gear blank is mounted on dividing head spindle.
- The cutter is first adjusted so that its center line is truly radial with respect to blank.
- The cutter is lowered till the required depth of cut is obtained.
- Feed mechanism is then engaged to make the blank to traverse past the cutter.
- When the spindle starts to rotate, one tooth space is cut by the cutter, as the feed is given by the longitudinal movement of the table.
- Then blank is withdrawn and indexing is done by the universal dividing head so that next tooth space can be cut.
- This forms one tooth and the process is repeated till all the teeth are formed.
- The gear cutting on milling machine is shown in Fig. 4.27.

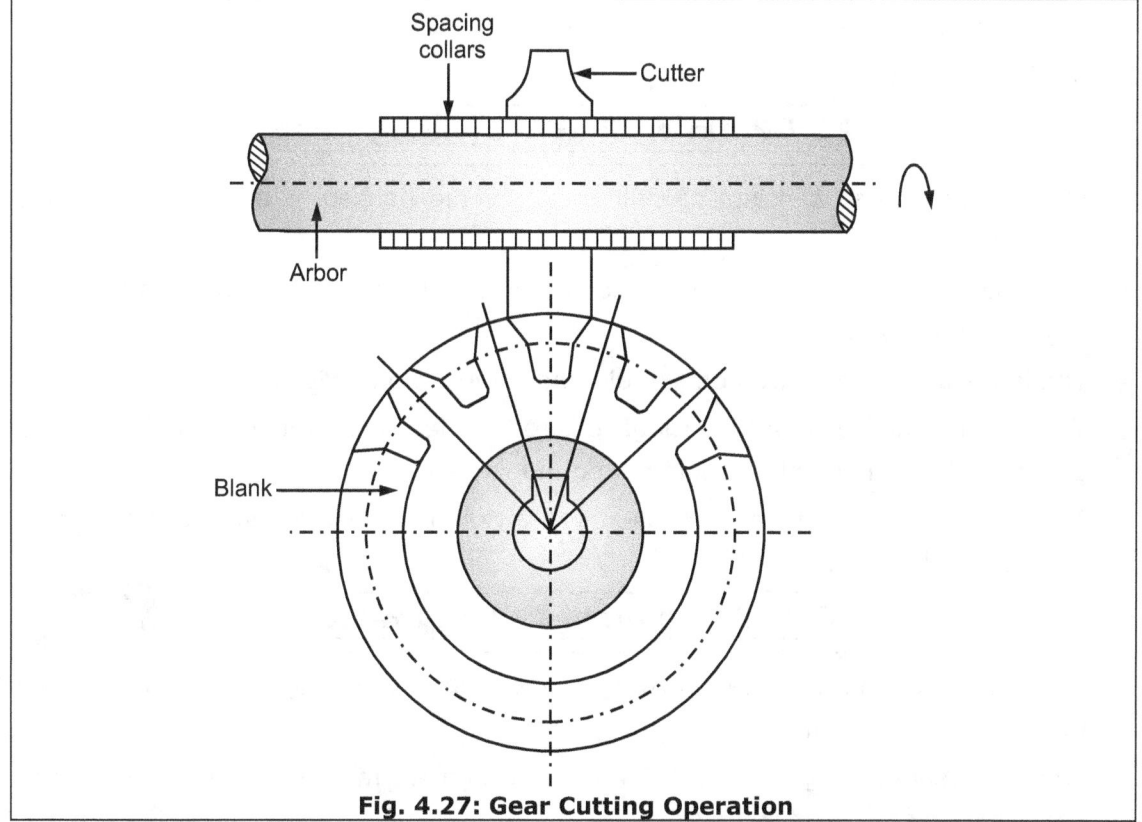

Fig. 4.27: Gear Cutting Operation

4.21 INDEXING

- The indexing is the process of dividing the periphery of work piece into any number of equal parts.

- In cutting spur gear, equal spacing of teeth on the gear blank is performed by indexing. Suppose it is desired to cut 20 teeth on gear, then it is necessary to divide the periphery of gear blank in 20 equal parts.

- This means, after one teeth has been cut it is necessary to rotate the work through 1/20 of revolution or 18° for cutting next teeth and so on.

- The indexing is done by using special attachment known as 'dividing head' or 'index head'.

- The indexing method is used to cut teeth on gear, cut splines on shaft, flutes on drill etc.

4.22 DIVIDING HEAD   [S-16]

- The dividing head is of three types:
    1. Plain or Simple dividing head.
    2. Universal dividing head.
    3. Optical dividing head.

4.22.1 Plain or Simple Dividing Head

- Plain dividing head consists of cylindrical spindle housed in a frame, and base bolted to table.

- Index crank is connected to tail end of spindle directly. The crank and spindle rotates as one unit.

- The index plate is mounted on spindle and rotates along with it.

- The spindle can be rotated through desired angle and clamped by inserting the clamping lever in one of the hole cut on index plate.

- This type of indexing head is used for dividing the work periphery by small number of divisions.

4.22.2 Universal Dividing Head   [W-16, S-17]

- It is the most common type of arrangement used in work shop which can be used for all forms of indexing.

- The universal dividing head consist of worm and worm gear, index plate, sector arm, change gears and spindles.

* The external view of universal dividing head is shown in Fig. 4.28.

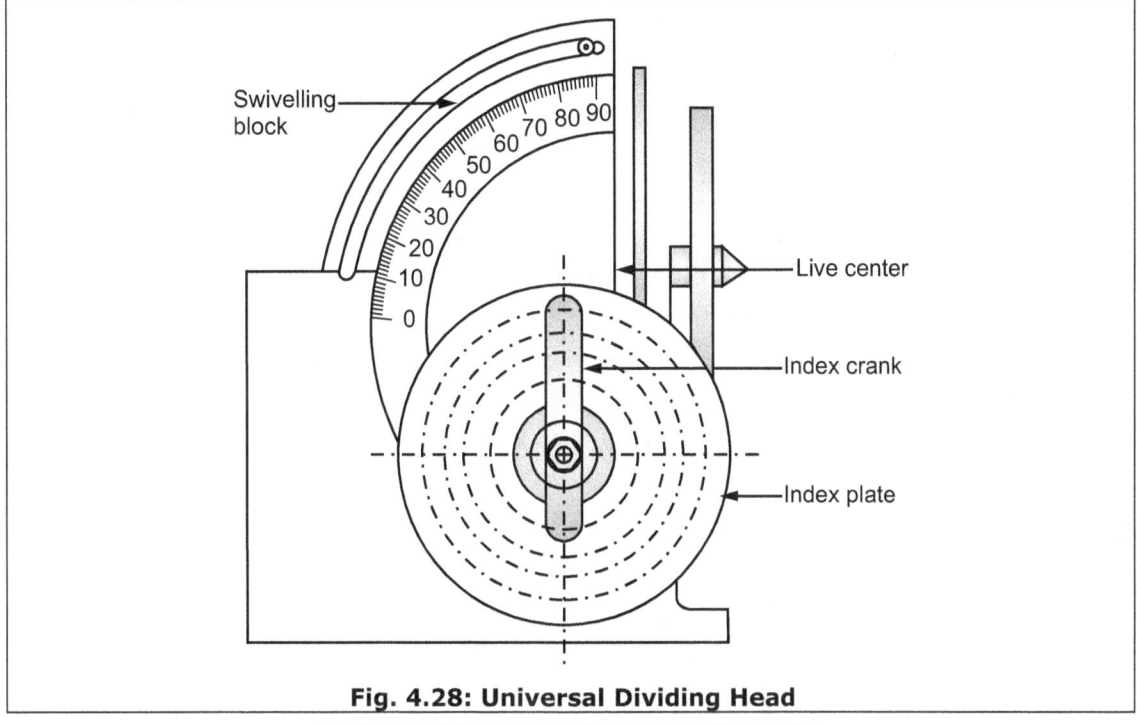

Fig. 4.28: Universal Dividing Head

4.22.3 Optical Dividing Head

* Optical dividing head is used for precise angular indexing and for checking accuracy of various angular surfaces.
* The mechanism consists of worm gear keyed to the spindle.
* A circular glass scale graduated in 1° division is rigidly mounted on worm wheel.
* Any movement of spindle is read-off by means of microscope fitted on dividing head body.
* The eye piece has a scale having 60 divisions and each division is equivalent to 1 movement of the circular scale.
* Thus, with type of arrangement precise index movement can be done.

4.23 INTERNAL MECHANISM OF UNIVERSAL DIVIDING HEAD

* The universal dividing head is a robust body containing the following parts:
    1. **Worm and worm wheel:** The worm wheel is mounted on the spindle. In general the worm wheel has 40 teeths. It mesh with a worm which is single threaded.
    2. **Worm shaft:** The work is mounted on the worm shaft.

3. The index plate is mounted on a sleeve which in turn is mounted on the worm shaft. Index plate is a circular steel plate having several concentric rows of holes which are equidistant in each separate row.

4. **Crank:** The crank is mounted on the worm shaft. A slot is provided radially on the crank.

5. **Plunger and plunger pin:** The plunger is mounted on the crank. It can slide along the slot in the crank and can be adjusted along the desired hole circle on the index plate. The plunger is spring loaded and can fit into the index plate hole by means of plunger pin.

6. **Spindle:** The spindle is provided with a job carrier and a centre at its front end to hold the workpiece.

7. **Sector arm:** It is provided on the index plate. It can be set a desired angle with no one another.

Working:

- As shown in the Fig. 4.29.

- The plunger is pulled out and rotated in one direction. This rotates the crank. As the crank is mounted over the shaft, the shaft rotates. The worm rotates as it is formed on the shaft. The worm wheel is in the mesh with worm, so the wheel rotates. This rotates the spindle and ultimately the work piece.

- One rotation of crank rotates the work by 1/4 revolutions.

- Or we can say when the crank is rotated by 40 turns, the main spindle and hence work will rotate through one turn.

- To rotate the crank through fraction of turn, index plate is used.

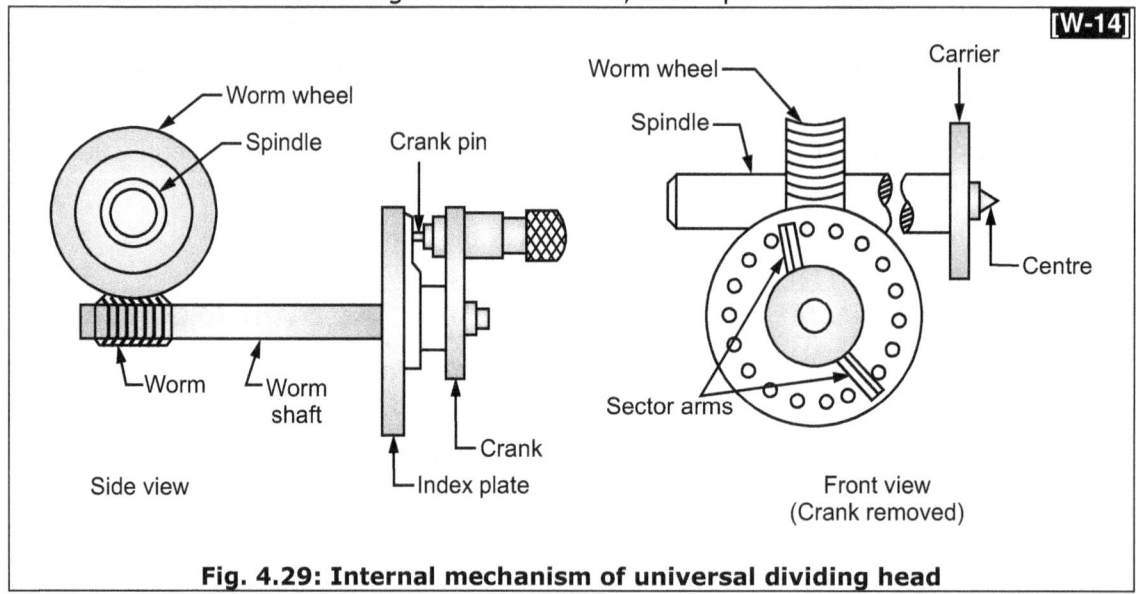

Fig. 4.29: Internal mechanism of universal dividing head

4.23.1 Functions of Universal Dividing Head   [W-14, S-17]

- Universal dividing head is used to perform various operations.
- The Functions of universal dividing head are explained below:
  - It sets the workpiece in a desired position in relation to the machine table [i.e. horizontal, vertical or inclined]
  - After each cut, it rotates the job through a desired angle and thus indexes the workpiece.
  - It provides a continuous rotary motion to the job during milling of helical grooves.
  - It acts both as holding and supporting device for the workpiece during operation (along with tailstock).

4.24 INDEXING METHOD   [W-16]

- There are various methods of indexing.
- The type of method used depends on number of divisions required and type of dividing head used.
- The different methods of Indexing are:
  - Direct or Rapid indexing.
  - Plain or Simple indexing.
  - Compound indexing.
  - Differential indexing.
  - Angular indexing.

4.25 DIRECT OR RAPID INDEXING

- For direct indexing the worm and worm wheel of index head is disengaged.
- Index plate having 24, 30 and 36 hole circle is then fitted to the front end of the spindle nose.
- A spring loaded pin can be pushed into any one hole to lock the spindle with frame.
- While indexing, the pin is first taken out and then the spindle is rotated by hand.
- After required position is reached, index pin is once again locked with frame.
- With 24 hole plate we can divide the periphery of work into 2, 4, 6, 8, 12 and 24 equal divisions.
- Direct indexing is used for milling of square, hexagonal nut and bolts on milling machine.
- **Example:** To divide the work periphery in 8 divisions with the help of 24 hole plate. The index movement is 24 / 8 = 3. Thus, we should move the pin by 3 holes after each teeth is cut.

4.26 PLAIN OR SIMPLE INDEXING   [S-15]

- Plain or simple indexing involves the use of universal dividing head.
- Referring to Fig. 4.29, when the plunger is pulled outward the plunger pin comes out of the index plate hole.
- When the plunger is rotated for the calculated turn, the crank rotates.
- The crank rotates the worm shaft and ultimately the spindle through the worm and wheel arrangement.
- The index plates with circles of holes patented by 'Brown and Sharpe Manufacturing Company':

   Plate No. 1: 15, 16, 17, 18, 19, 20

   Plate No. 2: 21, 23, 27, 29, 31, 33

   Plate No. 3: 37, 39, 41, 43, 47, 49
- These plates have been accepted as standard by the Indian Machine Tool manufacturers.
- In simple indexing, the index plate remain fixed by means of lock pin connected to the frame of dividing head.
- Index crank movement is given as,
- Index crank movement = $\dfrac{40}{N}$,

   where N = Number of divisions required on work.
- If the index crank movement calculated from the above formula is whole number, the index crank is rotated through that complete number of turns.
- And if the index crank movement obtained is whole number and fraction, the numerator and denominator of the fraction after simplifying are multiplied by suitable common number, which will make the denominator equal to the number of holes plate used and numerator will denote number of holes to be moved.

Ex. 4.1: *Find the index movement for cutting 25 teeth on spur gear blank.*

Sol.: Index crank movement = $\dfrac{40}{N}$.

where   N = Number of divisions required on work

$$= \frac{40}{25} = 1\frac{3}{5} = 1\frac{3 \times 3}{5 \times 3} = 1\frac{9}{15}$$

Thus, index movement will be one complete turn of the index crank and 9 holes on a 15 holes index plate.

Ex. 4.2: *Find the index movement for cutting 28 teeth on spur gear blank.*

Sol.: Index crank movement = $\dfrac{40}{N}$,

where   N = Number of divisions required on work

$$= \frac{40}{28} = 1\frac{3}{7} = 1\frac{3 \times 3}{7 \times 3} = 1\frac{9}{21}$$

Thus, index movement will be one complete turn of the index crank and 9 holes on a 21 holes index plate.

4.27 COMPOUND INDEXING

- Compound indexing is used when the available capacity of the index plates is not sufficient for the given indexing job.

- In other words when the work piece periphery cannot be divided by simple indexing method, compound indexing is used.

- It is trial and error method. The method consists of two basic operations.

  1. First operation is to turn the index crank through a required amount as it is done in case of simple indexing.

  2. Second operation involves turning the index plate and crank both either in same or reverse directions, thus adding or subtracting the further movement, from that obtained in the first operation.

$$\text{Index crank movement} = \frac{40}{N} = \frac{n_1}{N_1} \pm \frac{n_2}{N_2}$$

where, N = Number of divisions required.

N_1 = Hole circle used by crank pin.

N_2 = Hole circle used by lock pin.

n_1 = Holes moved by crank pin in N_1 hole circle plate.

n_2 = Holes moved by plate and crank pin in N_2 hole circle.

4.27.1 Steps for Compound Indexing

- The procedure adopted for compound indexing a number which is easily factorized is as follows:

  1. Resolve into factors the number of divisions required.

  2. Choose at random two hole circles.

  3. Subtract the hole number of one circle from other.

  4. Factor the difference.

  5. Place the factors of division required and factors of difference above horizontal line.

     Factor the number of turns of crank required for one revolution of spindle (40) and factors of two hole circles below the horizontal line.

  6. Cancel the common factors above and below the line. If all the factors above horizontal line are cancelled by those below the line, the two hole circle chosen can be used for indexing. And if factors above line do not get cancelled, then go for another combination by trial.

  7. The factors which will remain un-cancelled below the line, should be multiplied to obtain the number of holes in hole circle plate to be moved by two indexing movement.

Ex. 4.3: *Explain procedure for indexing 69 divisions by compound indexing.*

Sol.: For compound indexing,

$$\text{Index crank movement} = \frac{40}{N} = \frac{n_1}{N_1} \pm \frac{n_2}{N_2}$$

Where,
$\quad N$ = Number of divisions required.

$\quad N_1$ = Hole circle used by crank pin.

$\quad N_2$ = Hole circle used by lock pin.

$\quad n_1$ = Holes moved by crank pin in N_1 hole circle plate.

$\quad n_2$ = Holes moved by plate and crank pin in N_2 hole circle.

$$\text{Index crank movement} = \frac{40}{69} = \frac{n_1}{N_1} \pm \frac{n_2}{N_2}$$

1. $69 = 23 \times 3$

2. Index circle 23 and 33 are chosen.

3. $33 - 23 = 10$

4. $10 = 2 \times 5$

5. $69 = 23 \times 3$

    $10 = 2 \times 5$

    $$\frac{23 \times 3 \times 2 \times 5}{2 \times 2 \times 2 \times 5 \times 23 \times 1 \times 11 \times 3}$$

    $40 = 2 \times 2 \times 2 \times 5$

    $23 = 23 \times 1$

    $33 = 3 \times 11$

6. $$\frac{\cancel{23} \times \cancel{3} \times \cancel{2} \times \cancel{5}}{\cancel{2} \times 2 \times 2 \times \cancel{5} \times \cancel{23} \times 1 \times 11 \times \cancel{3}}$$

    All the factors above line are cancelled, hence plate circle 23 and 33 can be used for indexing. Thus $N_1 = 23$ and $N_2 = 33$

7. The factors which remain un-cancelled below the line are,

    $2 \times 2 \times 11 = 44$, Therefore 44 is the number of holes moved for indexing.

8. $\dfrac{40}{69} = \dfrac{44}{23} - \dfrac{44}{33} = 1\dfrac{21}{23} - 1\dfrac{11}{33} = \dfrac{21}{23} - \dfrac{11}{33}$

    (Use less number of hole plate first, and use trial error method of addition and subtraction to maintain $\dfrac{40}{69}$).

Thus, for indexing 69 divisions, the index crank should be moved by 21 holes in 23 hole circle in forward direction and then plate and crank together are moved by 11 holes in 33 hole circle in backward direction.

Ex. 4.4: *Explain procedure for indexing 51 divisions by compound indexing.*

Sol.: For compound indexing,

$$\text{Index crank movement} = \frac{40}{N} = \frac{n_1}{N_1} \pm \frac{n_2}{N_2}$$

Where, N = Number of divisions required.

N_1 = Hole circle used by crank pin.

N_2 = Hole circle used by lock pin.

n_1 = Holes moved by crank pin in N_1 hole circle plate.

n_2 = Holes moved by plate and crank pin in N_2 hole circle.

$$\text{Index crank movement} = \frac{40}{51} = \frac{n_1}{N_1} \pm \frac{n_2}{N_2}$$

1. $51 = 17 \times 3$

2. Index circle 27 and 17 are chosen.

3. $27 - 17 = 10$

4. $10 = 2 \times 5$

5. $51 = 17 \times 3$

    $10 = 2 \times 5$

$$\frac{17 \times 3 \times 2 \times 5}{2 \times 2 \times 2 \times 5 \times 9 \times 3 \times 17 \times 1}$$

    $40 = 2 \times 2 \times 2 \times 5$

    $27 = 9 \times 3$

    $17 = 17 \times 1$

6. $$\frac{\cancel{17} \times \cancel{3} \times \cancel{2} \times \cancel{5}}{\cancel{2} \times 2 \times 2 \times \cancel{5} \times 9 \times \cancel{3} \times \cancel{17} \times 1}$$

    All the factors above line are cancelled, hence plate circle 27 and 17 can be used for indexing. Thus $N_1 = 17$ and $N_2 = 27$

7. $2 \times 2 \times 9 = 36$, Therefore 36 is the number of holes moved for indexing.

8. $$\frac{40}{51} = \frac{36}{17} - \frac{36}{27} = 2\frac{2}{17} - 1\frac{9}{27}$$

    (Use less number of hole plate first, and use trial error method of addition and subtraction to maintain $\frac{49}{51}$).

    Thus, for indexing 51 divisions, the index crank should be moved by 2 revolutions and 2 holes in 17 hole circle plate in forward direction and then crank is moved by 1 revolution and 9 holes in 27 hole circle in backward direction.

Ex. 4.5: *Explain Procedure for indexing 87 divisions on the periphery of a blank by compound indexing.*

Sol.: For compound indexing,

$$\text{Index crank movement} = \frac{40}{N} = \frac{n_1}{N_1} \pm \frac{n_2}{N_2}$$

Where, N = Number of divisions required.

N_1 = Hole circle used by crank pin.

N_2 = Hole circle used by lock pin.

n_1 = Holes moved by crank pin in N_1 hole circle plate.

n_2 = Holes moved by plate and crank pin in N_2 hole circle.

$$\text{Index crank movement} = \frac{40}{87} = \frac{n_1}{N_1} \pm \frac{n_2}{N_2}$$

1. $87 = 29 \times 3$
2. Index circle 29 and 39 are chosen.
3. $39 - 29 = 10$
4. $10 = 2 \times 5$
5. $87 = 29 \times 3$

    $10 = 2 \times 5$

    $$\frac{29 \times 3 \times 2 \times 5}{2 \times 2 \times 2 \times 5 \times 29 \times 1 \times 3 \times 13}$$

    $40 = 2 \times 2 \times 2 \times 5$

    $29 = 29 \times 1$

    $39 = 3 \times 13$

6. $$\frac{\cancel{29} \times \cancel{3} \times \cancel{2} \times \cancel{5}}{\cancel{2} \times 2 \times 2 \times \cancel{5} \times \cancel{29} \times 1 \times \cancel{3} \times 13}$$

    All the factors above line are cancelled, hence plate circle 29 and 39 can be used for indexing. Thus, $N_1 = 29$ and $N_2 = 39$.

7. All the factors above line are cancelled, hence plate circle 29 and 39 can be used for indexing. Thus, $N_1 = 29$ and $N_2 = 39$.

8. $2 \times 2 \times 13 = 52$, Therefore, 52 is the number of holes moved for indexing.

9. $$\frac{40}{87} = \frac{52}{29} - \frac{52}{39} = 1\frac{23}{29} - 1\frac{13}{39} = \frac{23}{29} - \frac{13}{39}$$

    (Use less number of hole plate first, and use trial error method of addition and subtraction to maintain $\frac{40}{87}$).

    Thus, for indexing 87 divisions, the index crank should be moved by 23 holes in 29 hole circle in forward direction and then plate and crank together are moved by 13 holes in 39 hole circle in backward direction.

4.28 DIFFERENTIAL INDEXING

- In this method, the required divisions are obtained by the combination of two movements.

  1. The movement of index crank similar to simple indexing.

  2. The simultaneous movement of index plate when the crank is turned.

- The index plate is free to rotate in differential indexing.

- One gear of the gear train is connected at the back end of dividing head spindle and other is mounted on a shaft and also connected to the shaft of the index plate through bevel gears.

- After rotating the index crank the motion is communicated to the work piece spindle.

- When the chosen index is less than required index, the index plate rotate in same direction, to add an additional motion.

- If it is more, the plate will move in opposite direction.

- The index plate may rotate in same direction as that of crank or in opposite direction as may be required.

- The result is that at every time the actual movement of crank is automatically increased or decreased giving required indexing movement to the spindle and hence the work.

- Because of this differential indexing may be considered as an automatic method of performing compound indexing.

- The direction of rotation of the index plate to that of crank will depend upon the gearing.

- The universal dividing heads are supplied with change gears having 24, 28,32, 40, 44, 48, 56, 64, 72, 86 and 100 teeth.

- We can index any number of divisions from 1 to 382 with the help of these gears and three set of standard index plates.

4.28.1 Working of Differential Indexing

- The working of differential indexing is illustrated in figure 4.30.

- The lock pin (1) is first disengaged with the index plate (16) which is screwed to a sleeve (14).

- A mitre gear (14) is fastened to the end of the sleeve. This mitre gear meshes with another mitre on the driven shaft (13).

- The driven shaft and the driving shaft are connected through a gear train (12).

- The driving shaft (4) is connected to the spindle (7) through a stud (11).

- The worm (5) is mounted on the worm shaft (4). The worm meshes with the worm wheel (6) which is mounted on the spindle (7).

- When the crank (3) is rotated, the worm shaft (4) rotates. The worm (5) is formed on the worm shaft. The worm is in mesh with the worm wheel (6). The worm wheel is mounted on the spindle (7). The carrier (8) rotates with the spindle. The carrier is connected to the mandrel (9), which also rotates with the spindle. Ultimately the work piece (10) also rotates.

- At the other end as the spindle (7) rotates, the stud (11) also rotates, which in turn also moves the gear train (12). The driven shaft (13) is driven by the gears. The other end of shaft has bevel gear (14). It meshes with the mitre (14) formed on the sleeve (15). Finally the index plate (16) which is mounted on the sleeve also rotates.

- Thus when the crank is rotated, the actual movement is the movement of the work piece due to crank plus/minus the movement of the index plate.

- The work piece movement due to crank rotation is 3 – 4- 5 – 6 – 7 – 8 – 9 – 10.

- The index plate movement is 3 – 4 – 5 – 6 – 7 – 11 – 12 – 13 – 14 – 15 – 16.

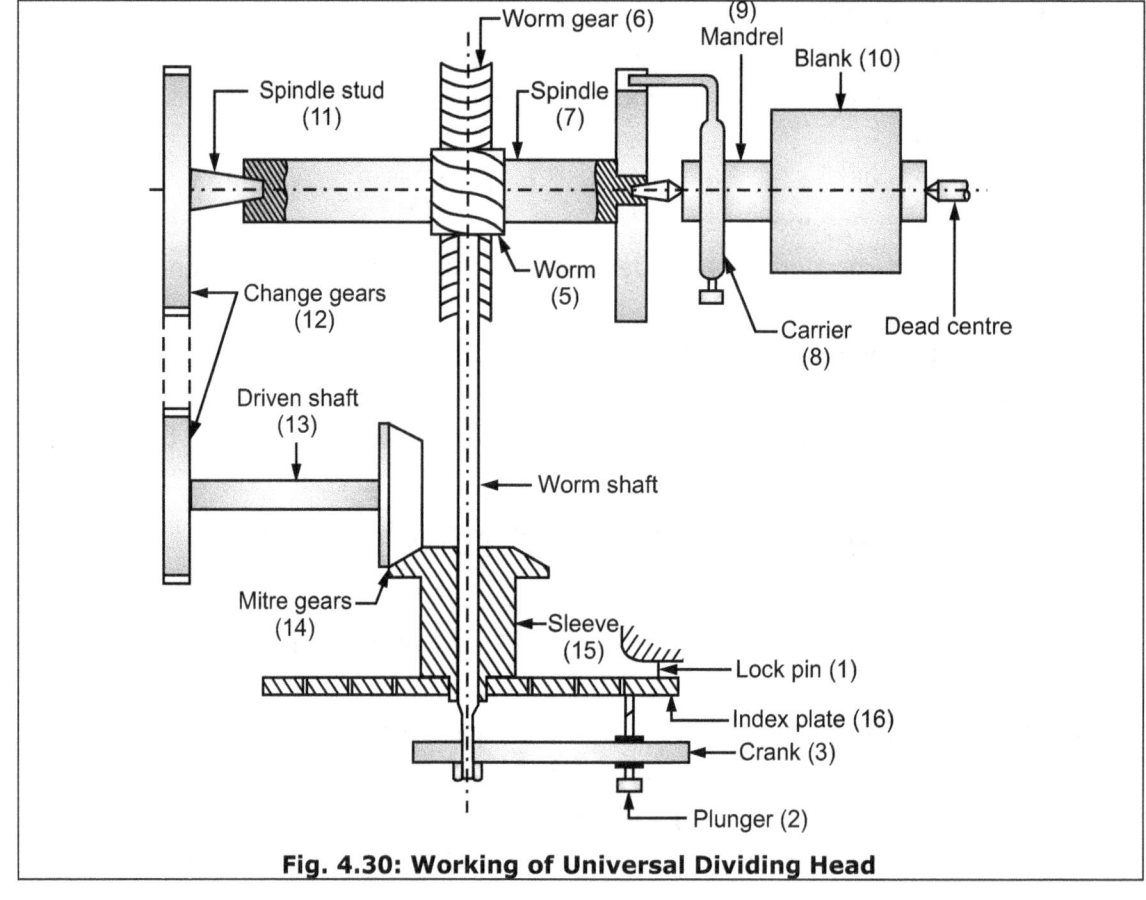

Fig. 4.30: Working of Universal Dividing Head

4.28.2 Rule for Differential Indexing

1. Gear ratio $= \dfrac{(A - N)\,40}{A}$ where, A is any number closer to required division N.

2. Index crank movement $= \dfrac{40}{A}$.

   - When the division required is a prime number which cannot be simplified then differential indexing method is employed.
     (a) First we select a number which is closer to N and is divisible.
     (b) Then by gear ratio formula we obtain the number of teeth on driver and driven gear.
     (c) Thus obtained gears are selected from the set and then driver gear is mounted on the spindle axis, and driven gear is mounted on the axis of meter gear.
     (d) We obtain the index crank movement = 40/A
     (e) As we rotate the crank and engage the index pin the index plate which is made free to rotate from back side also rotates slightly in the same direction or reverse direction. Thus, this movement of plate compensate the approximately selected number A.

Ex. 4.6: *How 83 divisions are indexed by differential indexing method.*

Sol.: (a) Gear ratio $\dfrac{(A - N)\,40}{A}$

where, A is any number closer to required division N.

Thus, N = 83 assume A = 86 (generally select higher no.)

$$\text{Gear ratio} = \frac{(A - N)\,40}{A}$$

$$= \frac{(86 - 83)\,40}{86}$$

$$= 3 \times \frac{40}{86}$$

$$= \frac{3 \times 24}{24} \times \frac{40}{86}$$

$$= \frac{72}{24} \times \frac{40}{86}$$

(b)   Driver gear = 72, 40

(c)   Driven gear = 24, 86

(d)   Index movement $= \dfrac{40}{86} = \dfrac{20}{43}$

For indexing the index crank will have to be moved by 20 holes in 43 hole circle.

(e) The gear ratio is compound.

(f) No. of idler gear = A − N = 86 − 83 = 3.

But as the gear ratio is compound, no idler is required.

4.29 ANGULAR INDEXING

- Angular indexing is the process of dividing the periphery of work in angular measurement and not by number of divisions. The 360° of circle is equivalent to 40 revolutions of index crank. Thus, one complete turn of crank will cause work to rotate through 360 / 40 = 9°.

Ex. 4.7: *A gear blank has to be indexed through an angle of 17°40'. Find the indexing movement required.*

Sol.: Angular indexing: 40 turns of the crank will rotate the work through one revolution i.e. through 360°. Therefore, one complete turn of crank will cause the spindle and hence the work to rotate through 360/40 = 9°.

$$\therefore \qquad \text{Index crank movement} = \frac{\text{Angular displacement of work in degree}}{9}$$

$$= \frac{17\frac{40}{60}}{9} = \frac{17\frac{2}{3}}{9}$$

$$= \frac{53}{27} = 1\frac{26}{27}$$

i.e. One complete turn and 26 holes in 27 hole circle.

4.30 DIFFERENCE BETWEEN SIMPLE AND DIFFERENTIAL INDEXING

Sr. No.	Simple indexing	Differential indexing
1.	Lock pin need not be disengaged before indexing.	Lock pin must be disengaged before indexing.
2.	Calculations to obtain crank movement are simple	Calculations to obtain crank movement are complex.
3.	Gear train is not needed.	Gear train is needed to obtain the final movement of the index plate.
4.	Index plate is stationary or not moved.	Index plate movement is obtained.
5.	Total movement of work piece is obtained by the movement of crank only.	Total movement of work piece is obtained by the movement of crank and index plate both.
6.	Any number of division cannot be indexed.	Any number of division can be indexed.

4.31 GEAR HOBBING

- 'Gear hobbing' is a process of generating gear teeth by means of a rotating cutter known as 'Hob' that revolves and cuts like a milling cutter.

- The hob is similar to worm equipped with proper clearance for cutting action.

- Flutes are cut across the threads forming racked shaped cutting teeth.

- The thread (start) may be left or right handed and flutes may be straight or helical.

- A hob may have one, two or more threads. Single threaded hob cuts one teeth and double threaded hob cuts two teeth simultaneously.

- The number of teeth depend on the ratio of the revolutions of hob to revolutions of gear blank.

- Hobs are made with any desired pitch and can be used to manufacture the gear of that pitch.

- Any number of teeth can be cut on gear blank.

- It is continuous process.

4.31.1 Principle of Operation

- Gear hobbing is a machining process in which gear teeth are progressively generated by a series of cuts with a helical cutting tool (*hob*).

- All motions in hobbing are rotary, and the hob and gear blank rotate continuously as in two gears meshing until all teeth are cut.

- For hobbing the spur gear, the hob and gear blank are connected by means of proper change gears.

- The gear blank is first moved in towards the rotating hob until the proper depth is reached.

- As soon as the proper depth is reached, the hob cutter is fed across the face of the gear blank until the tooth is completely cut.

- During cutting operation both gear blank as well as hob (tool) rotates simultaneously during the entire process.

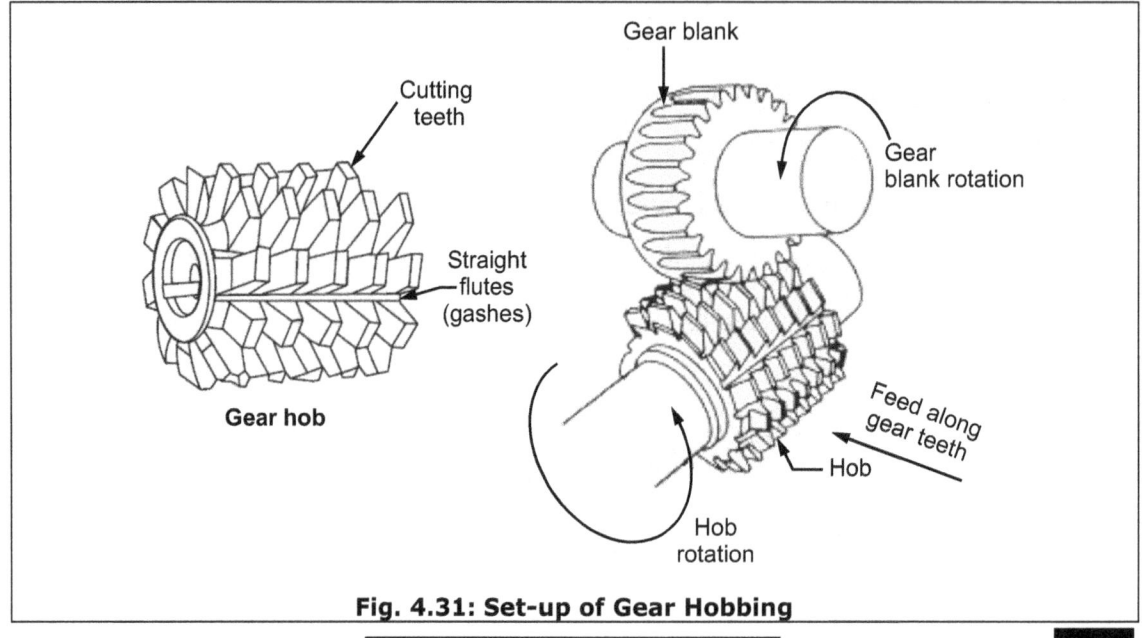

Fig. 4.31: Set-up of Gear Hobbing

4.31.2 Hobbing Process   [W-14]

- The process of hobbing is shown in Fig. 4.32.
- In this process the hob and gear blank are mounted on the shafts that are at right angles to each other. The hob axis may be either horizontal or vertical.
- For machining of spur gears, the hob must be tilted through its helix angle to result in the involute profile.
- The hob and blank are rotated about their axes with different speeds.
- The blank is then moved towards the hob until proper depth is reached.
- The hob is then fed into the gear blank.
- As soon as the proper depth is achieved, the hob is fed in a direction parallel to the axis of rotation of the gear blank.
- This enables the teeth to be gradually cut over the full face of the gear blank.
- Both the hob and blank are rotated as if they are in mesh with each other.
- The speeds of two are so adjusted that the blank rotates through one pitch distance for each complete revolution of the hob.
- This results in generation of teeth on the blank periphery.
- The operation is a continuous one with no break in between.
- Thus the gear cutting with hob involves three basic motions, all of them occurring at the same time.
  - ○ The rotation of hob.
  - ○ The rotation of blank.
  - ○ The axial advancement (feed) of the hob.

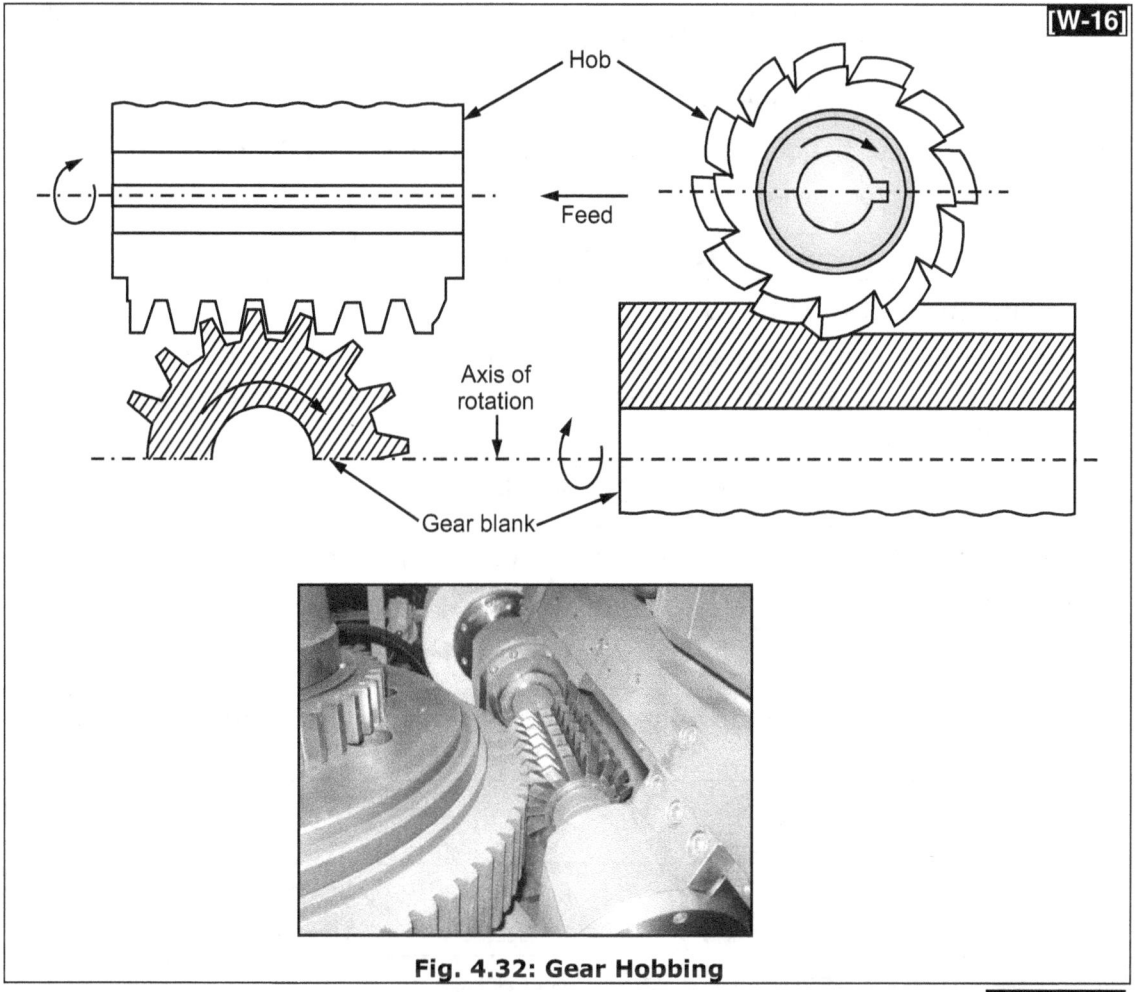

Fig. 4.32: Gear Hobbing

4.31.3 Advantages of Gear Hobbing [S-15, S-16]

1. It is faster and continuous process.

2. Rate of production is high as it cuts several teeth simultaneously.

3. Hobbing machine set-up is simple and quick.

4. High accuracy can be obtained.

5. Many gears of same size can be cut simultaneously.

6. It can cut spur gear, helical gear, worm gear, sprockets, splines etc.

7. Gap type herringbone gears can be generated only through this process.

8. Long shafts and splines can be easily accommodated on hobbing machine.

9. The heat generated during the process is evenly distributed over gear blank and hob therefore excessive heating of both is avoided.

10. Irrespective of number of teeth, same hob can be used for same module of gear.

4.31.4 Limitations of Gear Hobbing

1. It can not generate internal gears.

2. It can not cut the gears which are having shoulders and flanges.

3. It can not produce unsymmetrical shapes.

4.32 HOBBING TECHNIQUES

Climb and Conventional Hobbing

- The axial feed method is used for cutting spur and helical gears. It involves the moving of the hob towards the gear blank or gear blank towards the hob to bring the two in relative position.

4.32.1 Climb Hobbing

- The climb hobbing is done by feeding the hob from bottom of gear blank to top of gear blank.

4.32.2 Conventional Hobbing

- When feed is given from top of gear blank to bottom of gear blank, it is known as conventional hobbing.

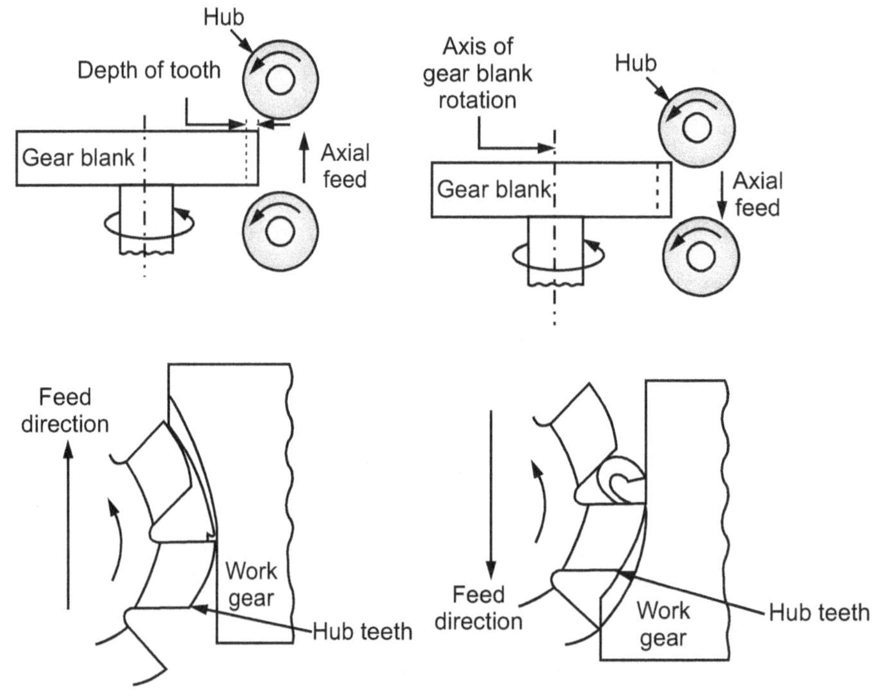

(a) Climb Hobbing   **(b) Conventional Hobbing**

Fig. 4.33

4.32.3 Advantages of Climb Hobbing

- Higher cutting parameters are used and so the productivity is higher.
- One-cut hobbing will be sufficient when the conventional hobbing may require two cuts for similar results with same cutting parameters.

4.32.4 Limitations of Climb Hobbing

- Poor surface finish.
- The machine requires good maintenance with minimum play in moving parts and feed mechanism.

4.32.5 Selection of a Particular Hobbing process

- Actual application decides the method of hobbing - climb, conventional, or a combination of both in two cut method.
- For high helix work gear, the conventional hobbing is superior because of better hob entrance conditions.
- Rough cutting by climb hobbing results frequently in higher lead error and poorer surface finish.
- A roughing cut by conventional method may follow a finishing operation by climb hobbing to produce the desired quality on the gear being cut.
- For very coarse pitch gears, the conventional hobbing is preferred because of less tendency of chatter.
- In conventional hobbing of spur gear, entrance angle is small.
- In climb hobbing, entrance angle is larger. All the cutting edges cut into the surface of outer circle.
- Hob life is better in conventional hobbing.
- Naturally, material, amount of stock, helix angle, setup and machine condition decide the method.

4.33 GEAR SHAPING

- Gear shaping is a gear generating process. It is adopted because of its high speed and versatility. Gear shaping process is of two types:
  1. Pinion cutter generating process.
  2. Rack cutter generating process.

4.33.1 Principle of Operation

- The cutter is mounted with its axis vertical and is reciprocated up and down by sliding the spindle head along vertical ways of machine.
- In addition to reciprocating motion, the cutter and gear blank both are rotated slowly about their own axis.
- Relative speed of rotation of the two is the same as the gear to be cut.

- It is accomplished by providing a gear train between the cutter spindle and the work spindle.
- The cutter in its rotation generates the tooth profile on the gear blank.
- In this process, one rack or pinion cutter having given pitch can be used to cut any number of teeth on gear blank with same pitch.
- Thus for different pitch, different cutters are used.
- The principle motions involved in rotary gear shaper cutting are:
  1. **Cutting stroke:** The downward linear motion of the cutter spindle together with the cutter.
  2. **Return stroke:** Upward linear travel of the spindle and cutter to withdraw the later to its starting position.
  3. **Indexing motion:** Against each rotation of cutter the gear blank revolves through n/N revolutions, where n = number of teeth on cutter, N = number of teeth to be cut on gear blank.

4.33.2 Pinion Cutter Gear Shaping Process

- In this method instead of rack cutter a pinion cutter having formed similar to gear to be produced is used.
- The pinion cutter reciprocates along vertical plane. Gear blank is mounted on a vertical shaft and rotates very slowly.
- The depth of cut is given during the cutting stroke (Downward stroke) and during return stroke work is relieved and cleared from cutter.
- During the process the cutter is fed radially to the gear blank to obtain required tooth depth.
- The use of pinion makes the process continuous and rate of production is more.

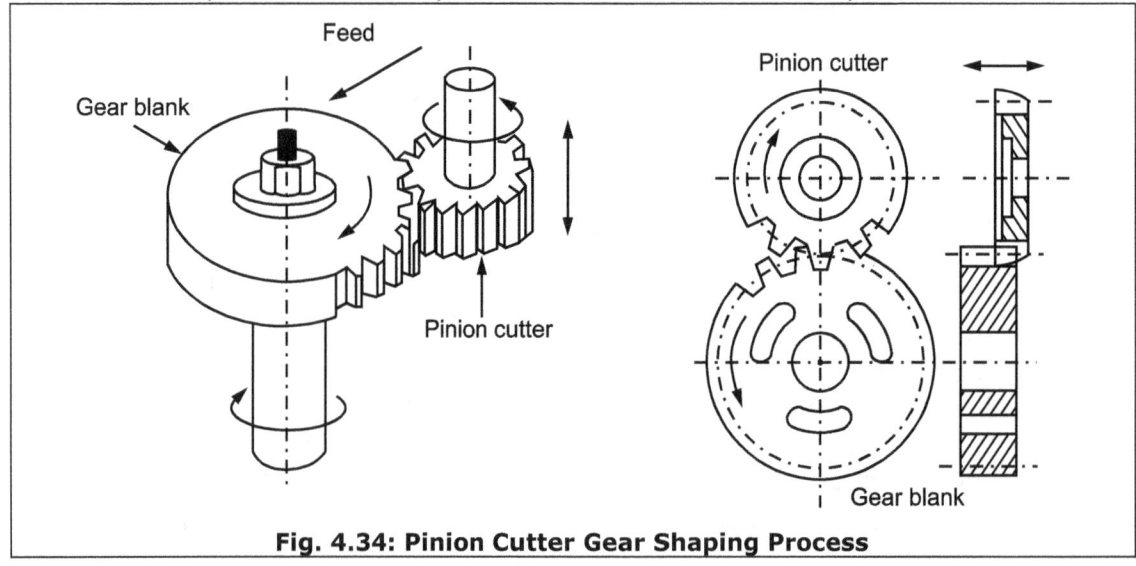

Fig. 4.34: Pinion Cutter Gear Shaping Process

4.33.3 Rack Cutter Gear Shaping Process

- In this method, the cutter has a rack form for the gear to be generated.

- The gear blank is rotated slowly and uniformly about the vertical axis.

- The rack cutter reciprocates with the required cutting speed to remove the material from the gear blank.

- The cutter is radically fed to obtain the correct teeth depth by means of cam.

- The cutter removes the material only during cutting stroke and relieved during return stroke.

- Thus, because of reciprocating motion of cutter and angular relative motion of gear blank, gear teeth is generated on the gear blank.

- The main limitation of this method is that once the full length of rack is utilized the cutting operation is required to be stopped.

- In such case the blank is indexed next and the cut started as usual.

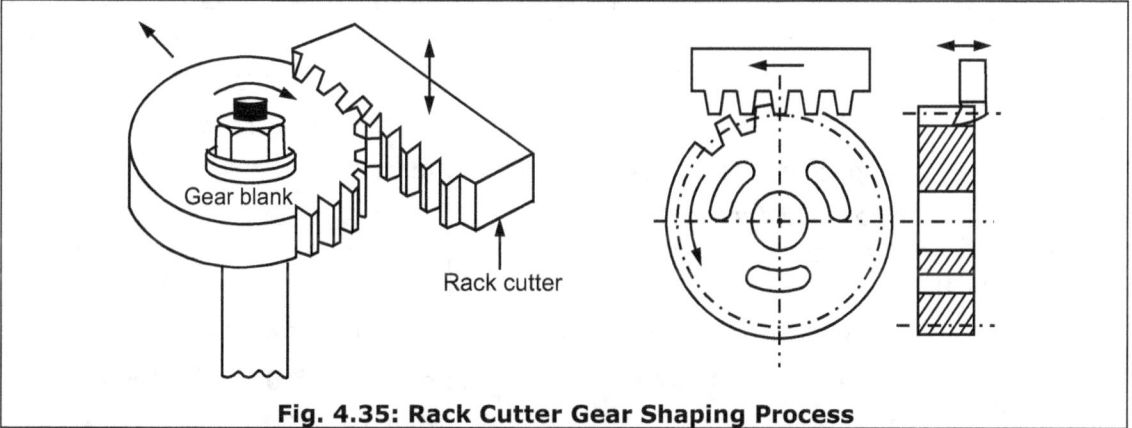

Fig. 4.35: Rack Cutter Gear Shaping Process

4.33.4 Comparison between Rack and Pinion Cutter Process

Sr. No.	Rack cutter Process	Pinion cutter Process
1.	The process needs to be stopped to retract the rack.	It is a continuous process.
2.	It takes more time compared to pinion cutter process.	It is a faster process.
3.	Cannot cut internal gears.	It can cut internal gears.

4.33.5 Advantages of Gear Shaping

1. It is fast process suitable for medium and large size batch production.
2. Most of the gears like spur gears, racks, double helical gears, herringbone gears, sprockets can be generated by this process.
3. Teeth very close to shoulder can also be cut.
4. Gears cut have good profile.
5. For same pitch same cutter can be used.
6. Both external as well as internal gears can be cut (for pinion cutter process).

4.33.6 Limitations of Gear Shaping

1. For cutting helical gears special guide called as helical guide is required.
2. Worm and worm wheels cannot be produced by this method.
3. Cutting takes place only in forward stroke (for rack planning) and return stroke is idle, so time is wasted.

4.34 COMPARISON BETWEEN HOBBING AND SHAPING PROCESS

Features	Hobbing	Shaping
Accuracy	Better with respect to tooth spacing and runout. Equal so far lead accuracy is required.	Better with respect to tooth form.
Surface finish	Hobbing produces a series of radial flats based on feed rate of hob across the work.	Shaping produces a series of straight lines parallel to the axis of the gear. Surface finish may be better.
Versatility	Can not be used for internal gears.	Can be used for internal gears
Limitation	Faster for gears with larger face width.	Time cycle will be 2-3 times of hobbing for wider gears.
Production rate	Stacking can make hobbing faster than shaping even for gears with narrow face widths.	With high speed stroking, narrow width job can be finished in lesser time than by hobbing.

4.35 GEAR FINISHING PROCESSES   [W-15, S-16]

- The surface of gear teeth produced through gear generating process is not very accurate and properly finished. Such surface results in lot of noise, excessive wear, play or backlash while meshing teeth or some times may cause ultimate failure.

4.36 NEED OF GEAR FINISHING   [W-15, 16]

1. For smooth running, good performance and long service life, the gears need
2. To achieve be accurate in dimensions and forms.
3. To achieve high surface finish.
4. To be hard and wear resistive at their tooth flanks.
5. To remove inaccuracies produced through gear generating process.

- Gear teeth finishing work after near accurate performing and machining can be achieved by finishing processes. Gear finishing is a process of removing or clearing out the irregularities from the flank of the gear, where the teeth came in contact with each other during machinery.
- Such operations make the gears quite dependable and smooth running.
- The commonly used finishing operations are:
  1. Gear shaving.
  2. Gear grinding.
  3. Gear burnishing.
  4. Gear lapping.
  5. Gear honing.
  6. Roll finishing.

4.35.1 Gear Shaving   [W-14; S-15]

- In gear shaving process, very thin chips are removed from the gear tooth surface by the cutting edge of gear shaving cutter.
- Gear shaving is employed to remove the material on the teeth in the form of very fine chips of sizes 0.005 mm to 0.1 mm from the gear tooth.
- The cutter has narrow grooves or serrations on the tooth flanks. These teeth form the cutting edges of the shaving cutter.
- It is process of finishing gear teeth by running the gear at high speed in mesh with gear shaving tool, which is in the form of rack or pinion.
- The teeth of shaving tool are hardened, accurately ground and their faces are provided with serrations.
- These serrations form the cutting edges which actually provide a scraping operation on the mating faces of gear teeth to be finished.
- The gear is pressed in contact with rotating shaving tool. The gear rotates in mesh with shaving tool and is also reciprocated simultaneously.
- This prevents jamming of two and relative motion between shaving tool and gear results in high surface finish on gear.

- A typical gear shaving tool is shown in Fig. 4.36

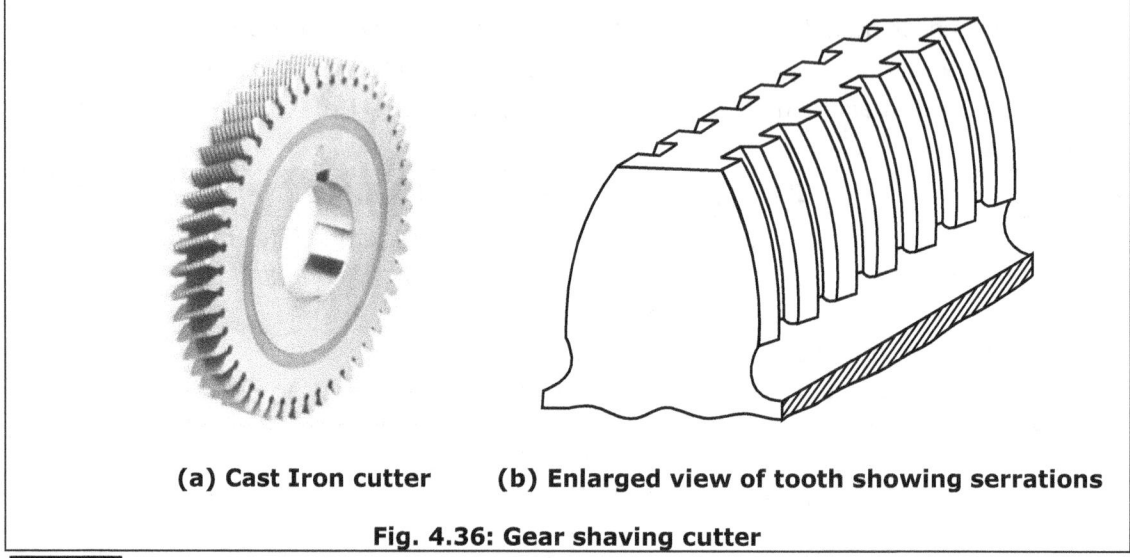

(a) Cast Iron cutter   **(b) Enlarged view of tooth showing serrations**

Fig. 4.36: Gear shaving cutter

4.35.1.1 Disadvantages of Gear Shaving

1. Initial cost of gear shaving cutters is very high.

2. Skilled operators required since the process is complicated.

3. Cannot be used for very high rate of production.

4.35.2 Gear Grinding

- Gear operating at high speeds and high loads are always hardened and there is distortion in gear flank.

- In order to remove this distortion and to have accurate profile on gear teeth, for smooth running gear grinding is done.

- Grinding is a very accurate method and is, though relatively expensive, more widely used for finishing teeth of different type and size of gears of hard material or hardened surfaces.

- The properly formed and dressed wheel finishes the gear teeth flanks by fine machining or abrading action of the fine abrasives.

- The grinding tool is formed by trueing the grinding wheel to the shaped and size of gear tooth to be finished.

- The gear is mounted on indexed head and grinding wheel is fed to required depth. The gear is then withdrawn and indexed for next teeth.

- A typical gear grinding tool is shown in Fig. 4.37.

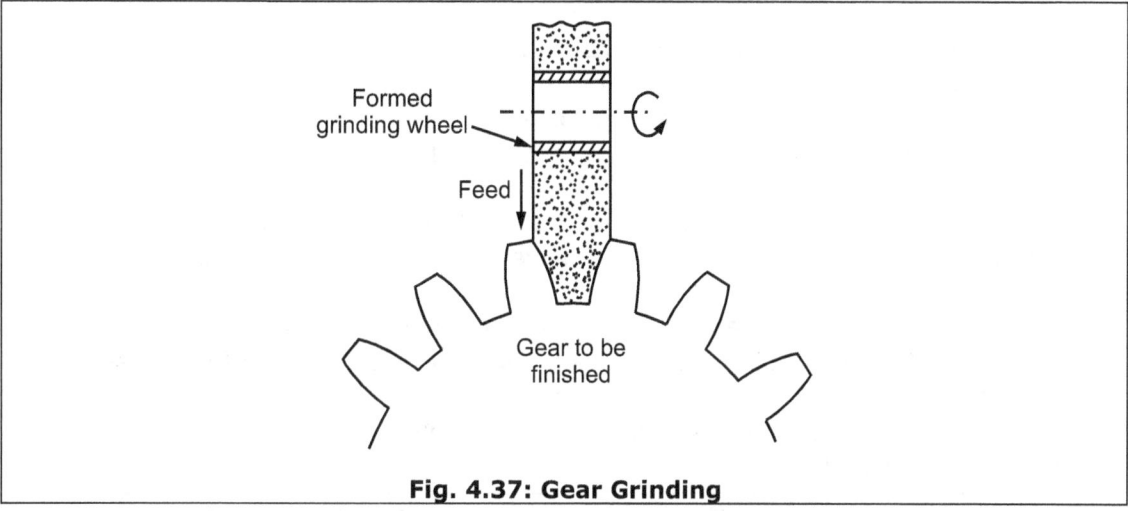

Fig. 4.37: Gear Grinding

4.35.3 Gear Burnishing

- Gear burnishing is the cold finishing process of gear teeth and used for gears after cutting but before hardening to improve the surface finish and uniformity.

- The gear is mounted on a vertical reciprocating shaft in mesh with three hardened and ground burnishing gears.

- These gears are power driven and are fed into the cut gear and rotated through a few turns in both directions.

- This makes the gear surface smooth and also imparts little hardness on it.

- The load is provided by means of pneumatic, hydraulic or electric means.

4.35.4 Gear Lapping

- The gears which are finish machined or shaved and then heat treated and finally lapped to remove scale, improve surface finish on teeth and rectify small errors due to distortion during the hardening process.

- In this process, the gears to be lapped are run under load in mesh with one or more cast iron toothed laps.

- Either abrasive paste is introduced between the teeth or fine abrasive powder, mixed in oil and is made to flow through the teeth during running.

- A negligible amount of metal is removed during this process.

- Gear lapping helps in improving surface finish.

4.35.5 Gear Honing

- It is a gear finishing process for hardened gears. It improves the surface fininsh of the tooth profile. It also reduces the noise of spur and helical gears after heat treatment and corrects heat treatment errors.
- Gear tooth honing is generally carried out with a constant pressure between teeth of the gear and honing tool.
- On a machine tool resembling the gear shaving machine, gear honing is performed. Gear tooth hone is an abrasive imbedded plastic helical gear shaped tool.
- The grain size of the abrasive is selected between 0.025 to 0.05 mm which is suitable for the honing allowances as well as requirements of surface finish.
- The honing tool and the work gear are meshed in a crossed axis relationship.
- When the work gear traverse back and forth parallel with the work gear axis honing tool drives it.

4.35.6 Compare Gear Burnishing with Gear Grinding

Sr. No.	Gear Burnishing	Gear Grinding
1.	The workpiece gear is mounted on a vertical reciprocating shaft in contact and under pressure with three hardened burnishing gears.	The workpiece gear is mounted on indexing head in contact with the formed and dressed grinding wheel/wheels.
2.	No. of teeth are finished at a time.	Teeth are finished one-by-one.
3.	Quicker process.	Slower process.
4.	New method of gear finishing.	Old method of gear finishing.
5.	It is process of finishing gear, before hardening.	It is process of finishing gear, after hardening.
6.	Less accurate.	High accurate.
7.	Cheaper than gear grinding.	Costlier than gear burnishing.
8.	After burnishing gear surface have smear metal.	After grinding fear surface have small scratches.

Important Points

Milling

- Milling is a machining process in which metal is removed by a rotary multi-point tool called as milling cutter.
- The cutter has multiple cutting edges and so it removes metal at a very fast rate.
- A milling machine is a machine tool that removes metal as the work is fed against a rotating multipoint cutter. The cutter rotates at high speed.

Working Principle of Milling:

- The work piece is clamped on the table and the milling cutter is mounted on the arbor.
- The cutter rotates the metal is removed by a series of cutting edges.
- The work can be fed in longitudinal, vertical and crosswise direction.

Specification of a Column and Knee type Milling Machine

- A column and knee type milling machine is generally specified by its table dimensions, table travel and distance between the cutter and work piece.
- Other parameters that matters are spindle speeds, feeds, power , weight of the machine, Floor space area required.

Milling Cutters

- Milling cutters are cutting tools typically used in milling machines to perform milling operations.
- They remove material by their movement within the machine or directly from the cutter's shape.
- Milling cutter can be defined as, "A rotary tool-steel cutting tool with peripheral teeth, used in a milling machine to remove material from the work piece through the relative motion of work piece and cutter".

Plain milling cutters

- These cutters are cylindrical in shape having teeth on their periphery.
- The teeth are generally parallel to the axis of the cutter.
- These are used to produce flat surfaces parallel to axis of rotation.

Side Milling Cutters

- These cutters have teeth on the periphery and on its sides
- Side milling cutters are used to remove metals from the side of work piece.
- Peripheral teeth do the actual cutting of metal while side teeth do the finishing work.
- The teeth may be parallel to the axis of the cutter or helical.

End Mill

- End mills are used for cutting slots, pockets, small holes, keyways and light milling operations.
- These cutters have teeth on their end as well as an periphery
- They are so named because they have teeth at one end only

Metal Slitting Saw

- These cutters are like plain or side milling cutters having very small width upto 5 mm
- These are used for parting off, milling deep slots or narrow slots.
- It has more teeth per unit of diameter as compared to ordinary plain milling cutter.

Angle Milling Cutter

- These cutters are used to cut angles in the work piece.
- These cutters have conical surfaces with cutting edges over them.
- These are used to machine angles other than 90°.

Formed Cutters

- Formed cutters may have different types of profile on their cutting edges which can generate different types of profile on the work pieces.

'T' Slot Milling Cutters

- These are the special form of milling cutters used to produce "T" shaped slots.
- These have cutting edges on their periphery and both sides.

Milling Cutter Material

- HSS for general purpose
- Cemented carbide for long production runs and heavy cuts
- Cast alloys for high speed

Plain Milling

- Plain milling is operation of producing plain, flat, horizontal surface parallel to axis of rotation of plain milling cutter.
- For this operation, the work piece surface is mounted parallel to the surface of the milling machine table.

Face Milling

- Face milling is the milling of surfaces that are perpendicular to the cutter axis.
- The peripheral cutting edges of the cutter do the actual cutting, while face cutting edges finish up the work surface

Side Milling

- Side milling is the operation of production of flat vertical surface on the sides of work piece by using side milling cutter.

Straddle Milling Operation

- When two parallel vertical surfaces are machined simultaneously by two side milling cutters mounted on the same arbor the operation is called straddle milling.
- Distance between the cutters is adjusted by spacers so that the distance between the cutting teeth of the cutters is exactly equal to the width of the work piece area required.

Angular Milling Operation

- Angular milling is milling of flat surfaces which are neither parallel nor perpendicular to the axis of the milling cutter.

Gang Milling

- Gang milling is the term applied to an operation in which two or more milling cutters are used together on one arbor for machining number of horizontal surfaces of a job.

Form Milling

- Form milling is operation of producing irregular surfaces.
- It is a process of machining special contours on the work piece.

End Milling

- End milling is the operation of producing a flat surface which may be vertical, horizontal or at an angle.

Slot Milling

- The operation of producing keyways, grooves, slots of varying shapes and sizes is called slot milling operation.

T- Slot Milling

- The side milling cutter or the end milling cutter is first used to cut a slot in the work piece equal in width to the throat width of the T-slot.
- The T-slot milling cutter is then used to cut the head space to the prescribed dimensions.

Slitting

- Saw milling operation produces narrow slots or grooves into the workpiece using saw milling cutter.
- This operation is also used to cut the work piece into two equal or unequal pieces which cut is also known as "parting off".

Cutting Speed

- The cutting speed of milling cutter is its peripheral linear speed resulting from rotation. It is expressed in m/min.

Feed:

- The feed in milling machine is defined as 'the rate with which the work piece advances under the cutter'.

Depth of Cut

- It is a perpendicular distance measured between the original and final surface of the

Gear cutting on Milling Machine

- On milling machine, the gear cutting operation is performed by using formed milling cutter mounted on arbour of the milling machine.
- The gear blank is mounted on dividing head spindle.
- When the spindle starts to rotate, one tooth space is cut by the cutter, as the feed is given by the longitudinal movement of the table.
- Then blank is then withdrawn and indexing is done by the universal dividing head so that next tooth space can be cut.
- This forms one tooth and the process is repeated till all the teeth are formed.

Indexing

- The indexing is the process of dividing the periphery of work piece into any number of equal parts.
- The indexing method is used to cut teeth on gear, cut splines on shaft, flutes on drill etc.

Universal Dividing Head

- It is the most common type of arrangement used in work shop which can be used for all forms of indexing.
- The universal dividing head consist of worm and worm gear, index plate, sector arm, change gears and spindles.

Functions of universal dividing head

- Universal dividing head is used to perform various operations.
- The Functions of universal dividing head are explained below:
  - The U.D.H. performs the following functions of operations.
    - It sets the workpiece in a desired position in relation to the machine table [i.e. horizontal, vertical or inclined]
    - After each cut, it rotates the job through a desired angle and thus indexes the workpiece.
    - It provides a continuous rotary motion to the job during milling of helical grooves.
    - It acts both as holding and supporting device for the workpiece during operation (along with tailstock).

Plain or Simple Indexing

- When the plunger is pulled outward and rotated for the calculated turn, the crank rotates.
- The crank rotates the worm shaft and ultimately the spindle through the worm and wheel arrangement.
- Index crank movement = $\dfrac{40}{N}$.

Compound Indexing

- Compound indexing is used when the work piece periphery cannot be divided by simple indexing method, compound indexing is used.
- The first operation is to turn the index crank through a required amount as it is done in case of simple indexing.
- Second operation involves turning the index plate and crank both either in same or reverse directions, thus adding or subtracting the further movement, from that obtained in the first operation.

Differential Indexing

- In this method, the required divisions are obtained by the combination of two movements.
  - The movement of index crank similar to simple indexing.
  - The simultaneous movement of index plate when the crank is turned.
- The index plate is free to rotate in differential indexing.

Angular Indexing

- Angular indexing is the process of dividing the periphery of work in angular measurement and not by number of divisions.

Gear Hobbing

- 'Gear hobbing' is a process of generating gear teeth by means of a rotating cutter known as 'Hob' that revolves and cuts like a milling cutter.

Hobbing Process

- The gear cutting with hob involves three basic motions, all of them occurring at the same time.
  - The rotation of hob.
  - The rotation of blank.
  - The axial advancement (feed) of the hob.

Gear Shaping

- Gear shaping is a gear generating process. It is adopted because of its high speed and versatility. Gear shaping process is of two types:
  - Pinion cutter generating process.
  - Rack cutter generating process.

Principle of Operation

- The cutter is mounted with its axis vertical and is reciprocated up and down by sliding the spindle head along vertical ways of machine.
- In addition to reciprocating motion, the cutter and gear blank both are rotated slowly about their own axis.
- The principle motions involved in rotary gear shaper cutting are:
  - The downward linear motion of the cutter spindle together with the cutter.
  - Upward linear travel of the spindle and cutter to withdraw the later to its starting position.
  - Indexing

Gear Finishing Processes

- The surface of gear teeth produced through gear generating process is not very accurate and properly finished.
- Such surface results in lot of noise, excessive wear, play or backlash while meshing teeth or some times may cause ultimate failure.
- For smooth running, good performance and long service life gear teeth finishing operations are needed.

Gear Shaving

- In gear shaving process, very thin chips are removed from the gear tooth surface by the cutting edge of gear shaving cutter.
- It is process of finishing gear teeth by running the gear at high speed in mesh with gear shaving tool, which is in the form of rack or pinion.
- This prevents jamming of two and relative motion between shaving tool and

Gear Grinding

- Gear operating at high speeds and high loads are always hardened and there is distortion in gear flank.
- In order to remove this distortion and to have accurate profile on gear teeth, for smooth running gear grinding is done.

Gear Burnishing

- Gear burnishing is the cold finishing process of gear teeth and used for gears after cutting but before hardening to improve the surface finish and uniformity.

Gear Lapping

- The gears which are finish machined or shaved and then heat treated and finally lapped to remove scale, improve surface finish on teeth and rectify small errors due to distortion during the hardening process.

Gear Honing

- It is a gear finishing process for hardened gears. It improves the surface fininsh of the tooth profile. It also reduces the noise of spur and helical gears after heat treatment and corrects heat treatment errors.

Practice Questions

1. State the difference between milling and other machining processes. **(Refer Section 4.1)**
2. Explain working principle of milling with neat sketch. **(Refer Section 4.2)**
3. Give the classification of milling machines. **(Refer Section 4.3)**
4. Describe the basic parts of column and knee type milling machine. **(Refer Section 4.4)**
5. Describe the construction and working of plain milling machine with suitable sketch.
(Refer Section 4.5.1)
6. Describe the construction and working of vertical milling machine with suitable block diagram. **(Refer Section 4.5.2)**
7. Describe the construction and working of universal milling machine with block diagram.
(Refer Section 4.5.3)
8. What parameters are needed to specify a column and knee type milling machine.
(Refer Section 4.6)
9. Compare between plain and universal milling machine. **(Refer Section 4.7)**
10. Define milling cutter. **(Refer Section 4.8)**
11. Give the classification of milling cutter. **(Refer Section 4.8.1)**
12. Enlist the milling machine operations. **(Refer Section 4.11)**
13. Explain plain milling with neat sketch. **(Refer Section 4.11.1)**
14. Explain face milling with neat sketch. **(Refer Section 4.11.2)**
15. Explain straddle milling with neat sketch. **(Refer Section 4.11.4)**
16. Explain angular milling with neat sketch. **(Refer Section 4.11.5)**
17. Explain gang milling with neat sketch. **(Refer Section 4.11.6)**
18. Explain form milling with neat sketch. **(Refer Section 4.11.7)**
19. Explain slot milling with neat sketch. **(Refer Section 4.11.9)**
20. Explain T-slot milling with neat sketch. **(Refer Section 4.11.10)**
21. Describe with a sketch, the nomenclature of a plain milling cutter. **(Refer Section 4.12)**
22. Describe up milling with suitable sketch. **(Refer Section 4.13.2)**
23. Describe down milling with suitable sketch. **(Refer Section 4.13.1)**
24. Compare between up milling and down milling. **(Refer Section 4.13.3)**
25. Explain various cutting parameters in milling. **(Refer Section 4.14)**
26. What is meant by gear cutting. **(Refer Section 4.16)**
27. What are the various gear materials. **(Refer Section 4.17)**
28. Which factors decides the selection of gear material. **(Refer Section 4.17.1)**
29. What are the various methods of manufacturing gears. **(Refer Section 4.18)**
30. Which factors decides the selection of gear manufacturing method. **(Refer Section 4.19)**
31. Explain gear cutting on milling machine with suitable sketch. **(Refer Section 4.20)**
32. Define indexing. **(Refer Section 4.21)**
33. Describe internal mechanical of UDH. **(Refer Section 4.23)**
34. What are the functions of UDH. **(Refer Section 4.23.1)**
35. What are the methods of indexing. **(Refer Section 4.24)**
36. What is simple indexing. **(Refer Section 4.26)**
37. What is compound indexing. **(Refer Section 4.27)**
38. What are the various steps for compound indexing. **(Refer Section 4.27.1)**
39. What is differential indexing. **(Refer Section 4.28)**
40. Explain the working of differential indexing with sketch. **(Refer Section 4.28.1)**

41. What are the working rules for differential indexing. **(Refer Section 4.28.2)**
42. Define angular indexing. **(Refer Section 4.29)**
43. Compare between simple and differential indexing. **(Refer Section 4.30)**
44. What is gear hobbing. **(Refer Section 4.31)**
45. Explain the principle of gear hobbing. **(Refer Section 4.31.1)**
46. Explain gear hobbing process with sketch. **(Refer Section 4.31.2)**
47. Give advantages of gear hobbling. **(Refer Section 4.31.3)**
48. Give limitations of gear hobbing. **(Refer Section 4.31.4)**
49. Explain various hobbing technique. **(Refer Section 4.32)**
50. How is a particular hobbing process selecting. **(Refer Section 4.32.5)**
51. Explain the principle of operation of gear shaping. **(Refer Section 4.33.1)**
52. Describe pinion cutter generating process. **(Refer Section 4.33.2)**
53. Describe rack cutter generating process. **(Refer Section 4.33.3)**
54. Compare rack and pinion cutter process. **(Refer Section 4.33.4)**
55. Give advantages of gear shaping. **(Refer Section 4.33.5)**
56. Give limitations of gear shaping. **(Refer Section 4.33.6)**
57. Compare between gear hobbing and gear shaping process. **(Refer Section 4.34)**
58. What is gear finishing? Enlist its types. **(Refer Section 4.35)**
59. Explain gear shaving. **(Refer Section 4.35.1)**
60. What are the disadvantages of gear shaving. **(Refer Section 4.35.1.1)**
61. Explain gear grinding as a finishing process. **(Refer Section 4.35.2)**
62. Explain gear burnishing. **(Refer Section 4.35.3)**
63. Explain gear honing. **(Refer Section 4.35.5)**

MSBTE Questions & Answers as Per 'G' Scheme

Winter 2014

1. Explain the cutting parameters in milling. How is the machining time calculated on a milling machine? **(8 M)**
Ans. Refer Section 4.14 and 4.15.
2. Explain with sketches upmilling and down milling. **(4 M)**
Ans. Refer Section 4.13.1 and 4.13.2.
3. Describe the construction and working of plain milling machine with a neat sketch. **(4 M)**
Ans. Refer Section 4.5.1.
4. What is the function of dividing head. Sketch the internal mechanism of universal dividing head. **(4 M)**
Ans. Refer Fig. 4.29 and Section 4.23.1.
5. What are the different methods of manufacturing gears. **(4 M)**
Ans. Refer Section 4.18.
6. Explain gear hobbing process with a neat sketch. **(4 M)**
Ans. Refer Section 4.31.2.
7. Why gear shaving process is employed? Explain the process. **(4 M)**
Ans. Refer Section 4.35.1.

Summer 2015

1. State advantages of gear hobbing. **(4 M)**
Ans. Refer Section 4.31.3.
2. Explain with neat sketch straddle milling. **(4 M)**
Ans. Refer Section 4.11.4.

3. Compare between up milling and down milling.   **(6 M)**
Ans. Refer Section 4.13.3.
4. Draw neat labelled diagram of knee type milling machine.   **(4 M)**
Ans. Refer Fig. 4.3.
5. Explain plain indexing.   **(4 M)**
Ans. Refer Section 4.26.
6. With neat sketch explain Rach cutter gear generating process.   **(4 M)**
Ans. Refer Section 4.33.3.
7. Explain gear shaving.   **(4 M)**
Ans. Refer Section 4.35.1.

Winter 2015

1. Compare plain milling machine with universal Mμ.   **(4 M)**
Ans. Refer Section 4.7.
2. Explain with neat sketch pinion cutter gear shaping process.   **(4 M)**
Ans. Refer Section 4.33.2.
3. With suitable example, explain the steps of compound indexing.   **(8 M)**
Ans. Refer Section 4.27.1.
4. Draw sketches and state use of slab milling cutter and T-slot milling cutter.   **(4 M)**
Ans. Refer Section 4.9.7 and 4.11.1.
5. How gear manufacturing process are classified?   **(4 M)**
Ans. Refer Section 4.18.
6. 83 divisions are to be index by differential indexing method. Calculate: (i) Gear ratio, (ii) no. of idler gear, (iii) Index crank movement, (iv) Sketch of gear train.   **(4 M)**
Ans. Refer Example 4.6.
7. How hexagonal head of a bolt is prepared by using straddle milling operation?   **(6 M)**
Ans. Refer Section 4.11.4.
8. What is gear finishing? State the need of gear finishing.   **(4 M)**
Ans. Refer Sections 4.35 and 4.36.
9. Compare gear burnishing with gear grinding.   **(4 M)**
Ans. Refer Section 4.35.6.
10. List basic parts of C&K type of milling machine. State function of any four.   **(4 M)**
Ans. Refer Section 4.4.1.

Summer 2015

1. Explain down milling with a neat sketch.   **(4 M)**
Ans. Refer Section 4.13.1.
2. List gear finishing methods and explain any one in detail.   **(4 M)**
Ans. Refer Section 4.35.
3. Draw and state the use of any two standard milling cutters.   **(4 M)**
Ans. Refer Section 4.9.
4. What is a dividing head in gear cutting process with a neat sketch explain the construction of any one dividing head.   **(4 M)**
Ans. Refer Section 4.2.2.
5. Give the cutting parameters of milling operation.   **(4 M)**
Ans. Refer Section 4.14.
6. Give the advantages and disadvantages of gear holding process.   **(4 M)**
Ans. Refer Sections 4.31.3 and 4.31.4.
7. Name the methods by which gears are produced by machining. Explain any one method.   **(6 M)**
Ans. Refer Section 4.18.

Winter 2016

1. Classify indexing methods in gear cutting. **(4 M)**
Ans. Refer Section 4.24.

2. State advantages & disadvantages of gear shaping process. **(4 M)**
Ans. **Advantages:** Refer Section 4.33.5.
Disadvantages: Refer Section 4.33.6.

3. Sketch milling cutters for followings: (i) side milling (ii) facing and (iii) plain milling. **(4 M)**
Ans. (i) Side milling: Refer Section 4.9.2.
(ii) Facing: Refer Section 4.11.2.
(iii) Plain milling: Refer Section 4.19.1.

4. Sketch slitting & gang milling operation. **(4 M)**
Ans. **Sketch of slitting:**

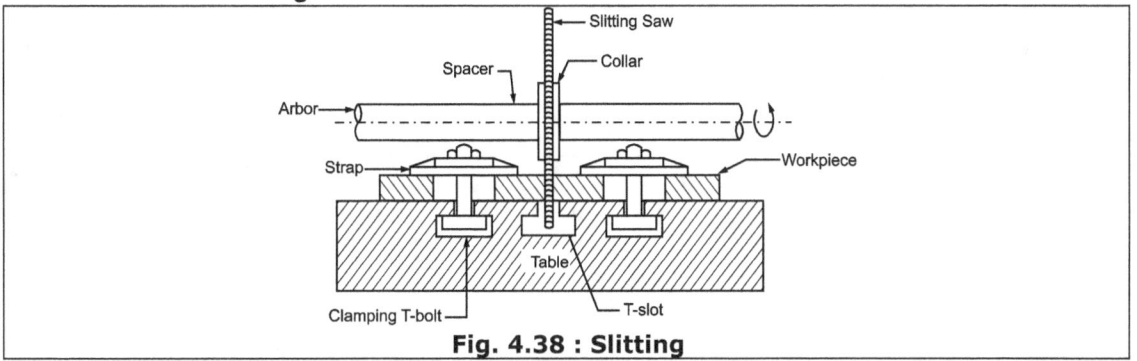

Fig. 4.38 : Slitting

Sketch of gang milling: Refer Fig. 4.20.

5. Differentiate between end milling & facing operation. **(4 M)**
Ans.

Sr. No.	End Milling	Facing Operation
1.	In this process End Milling cutters are used to produce slotting, recessing and small facing operations.	In this milling operation number of flat surfaces are machined which are right angles to the axis of rotating cutter.
2.	Cutter used here is End mill cutters. Like shell end mill cutter and solid end mill cutter. Single cutter is used at a time.	Cutter used here is side and face mill cutter. Number of cutters are different diameter can be used at a time.
3.	This process is used when machining area is large.	Used for small machining area.
4.	Single face is machined at a time.	Number of parallel or perpendicular face can be machined simultaneously.
5.	Used for simple geometry jobs.	Used for complicated geometry jobs.

6. Explain universal indexing mechanism. **(4 M)**
Ans. Refer Section 4.22.2.

7. Sketch gear hobbing process. **(4 M)**
Ans. Refer Fig. 4.32.

8. List gear finishing processes. **(4 M)**
Ans. Refer Section 4.36.

Summer 2017

1. Define gear cutting. State gear manufacturing methods.   (4 M)
Ans. Refer Sections 4.16 and 4.18.

2. With suitable example, explain the steps for compound indexing.   (4 M)
Ans. Refer similar problem to 4.27.

3. Sketch milling cutters for following:
   1. Side milling, 2. Facing, 3. Plain milling   (4 M)
Ans. Refer Section 4.9.

4. Explain how grinding wheels are specified with suitable example.   (4 M)
Ans. Refer Section 4.18.

5. How hexagonal head of a bolt is prepared by using straddle milling operation.   (4 M)
Ans. Refer Section 4.11.4.

6. Explain gang milling.   (4 M)
Ans. Refer Section 4.11.6.

7. What is universal dividing head? State its function.   (4 M)
Ans. Refer Sections 4.22.2 and 4.23.1.

8. Explain slot milling.   (4 M)
Ans. Refer Section 4.11.9.

■■■

Chapter **5**

SURFACE FINISHING

About This Chapter

At the end of this chapter students will be able to:

- ⊃ Understand the difference between other machines and Grinding Machines
- ⊃ Designate a grinding wheel.
- ⊃ Identify defects in grinding wheel
- ⊃ Able to understand Surface finishing operations.

5.1 GRINDING

- Grinding can be defined as a metal cutting operation performed on the work piece by means of a rotating abrasive wheel called as grinding wheel.

- Grinding is performed to bring the work piece to the required shape and size.

- But grinding is a slow process. First the work is brought close to its final stage by using machining methods (turning, milling, shaping etc.) and then grinding is done to achieve desired finish.

- It is much of a finishing operation than machining operation used for producing close dimensional accuracies and desired smooth surface finish.

- Grinding is process of removing the material in the form of small chips by the mechanical action of abrasive particles bonded together in the grinding wheel.

- The grinding wheel has thousands of cutting edges formed out of these abrasive grains projecting from its surface which acts as tiny cutting edges.

- The principle of grinding is shown in Fig. 5.1.

- The metal removing rate in grinding operation is less as compared to other machining processes, usually 0.25 mm to 0.50 mm.

- The dimensional accuracy can be of 0.025 mm.

- Grinding machines are generally manufactured with rigid frames, heavy power and accurate spindles to produce parts with close dimensional tolerances as they are used for precision work.

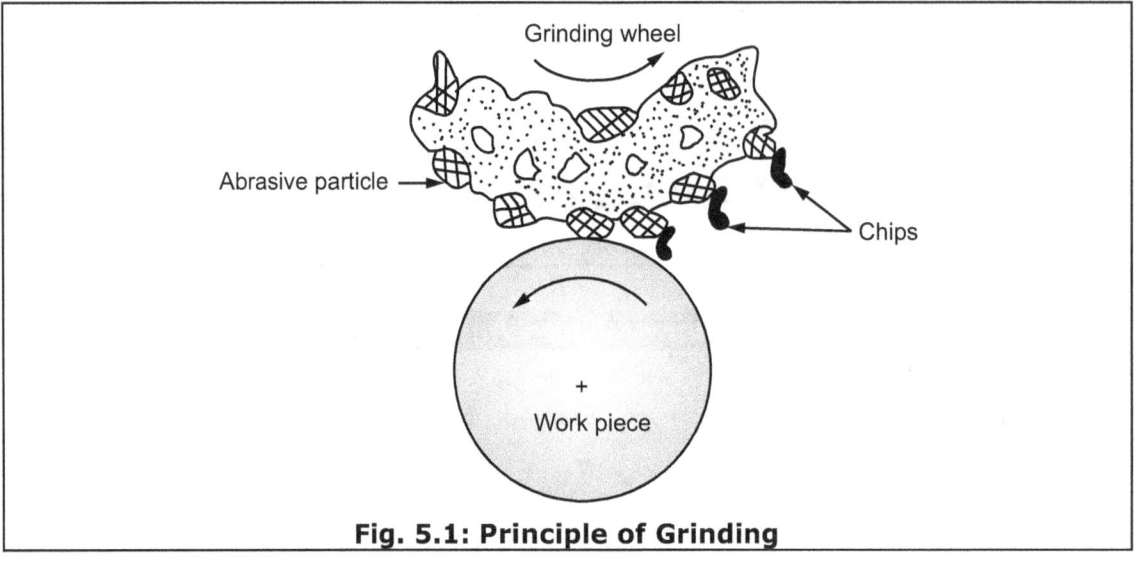

Fig. 5.1: Principle of Grinding

5.2 COMPARISON BETWEEN GRINDING AND OTHER MACHINING PROCESSES

Grinding	Other Machining Processes
1. It is a slow process.	1. These are faster process.
2. The grinding wheel has no orientation.	2. The cutting tools has a specific orientation.
3. It has thousands of cutting edges.	3. It has limited number of cutting edges.
4. Mainly used to remove little material from the workpiece.	4. It removes most of the material from the workpiece.
5. Grinding wheel rotates at a high speed of about 2000 rpm.	5. Speed of cutting tool is in hundreds only.

5.3 NEED OF GRINDING

- Grinding is mainly used for the following purpose:
    1. To remove a very small amount of metal continuously from the work piece to bring its dimensions within very close tolerance, after all the rough working and heat treatment operations have been carried out.
    2. It is sometimes used to obtain better finish on the surface.
    3. For machining those hard surface which are otherwise difficult to be machined by the high speed steel tools or carbide cutters.
    4. Used for sharpening the cutting tools.
    5. Used for grinding threads in order to have close tolerances and better finish.

5.4 ADVANTAGES OF GRINDING PROCESS

* Grinding process has the following advantages over other cutting processes:
  1. Grinding is the only method of cutting hardened steel etc.
  2. Extremely smooth finish desirable at contact and bearing surfaces can be produced due to large number of cutting edges on the grinding wheel.
  3. No marks as a result of feeding are there, as the wheel has considerable width.
  4. Very accurate dimensions can be achieved in short span of time.
  5. Very little pressure is required in this process, so permitting its use on very light work that would otherwise tend to spring away from the tool.

5.5 CLASSIFICATION OF GRINDING MACHINES [S-15, 16]

* Grinding is basically classified in to rough and precision grinding.
* Grinding machines are classified according to the quality of surface finish produced in the above two types.

5.5.1 Rough Grinders

* The main purpose of rough grinder is to remove excess material from castings, forgings and weldments.
* The accuracy and surface finish obtained is of secondary importance.
* Rough grinding is performed at a slower work speed and a fast traverse.
* Generally used rough grinders are:
  o Floor stand and bench grinders.
  o Portable and flexible shaft grinders.
  o Swing frame grinders.
  o Abrasive belt grinders.

5.5.2 Precision Grinders [W-14]

* Precision grinders are used to remove a small amount of material from the work piece.
* The main purpose of precision grinders is to finish part to very accurate dimension and at close tolerance.
* The surface finish and high degree of accuracy is main function of precision grinder.
* Thus precision grinders are those that finish the components to a very accurate dimension and with good surface finish.
* According to the type of surface generated, precision grinders are classified as:
  o Cylindrical grinders
    ▪ Centre type (Plain)
    ▪ Centre type (Universal)

- o Centre-less grinders
- o Internal grinders
  - Plain
  - Universal
  - Planetory
  - Centre-less
- o Surface grinders.
  - Horizontal spindle, reciprocating table
  - Vertical spindle, reciprocating table
  - Horizontal spindle, rotary table
  - Vertical spindle, rotary table
- o Special grinding machines
  - Roll grinding machines
  - Thread grinding machines
  - Cam grinding machines
  - Crank pin grinding machines
- o Tool and cutter grinders

5.6 FLOOR STAND AND BENCH GRINDERS

- It is mounted on stand, bench or floor.
- It is rough grinder used to remove excess stock from the surface.
- It is generally used for grinding cutting tools on shop floor.
- It is also used for polishing work by mounting polishing wheel on it.

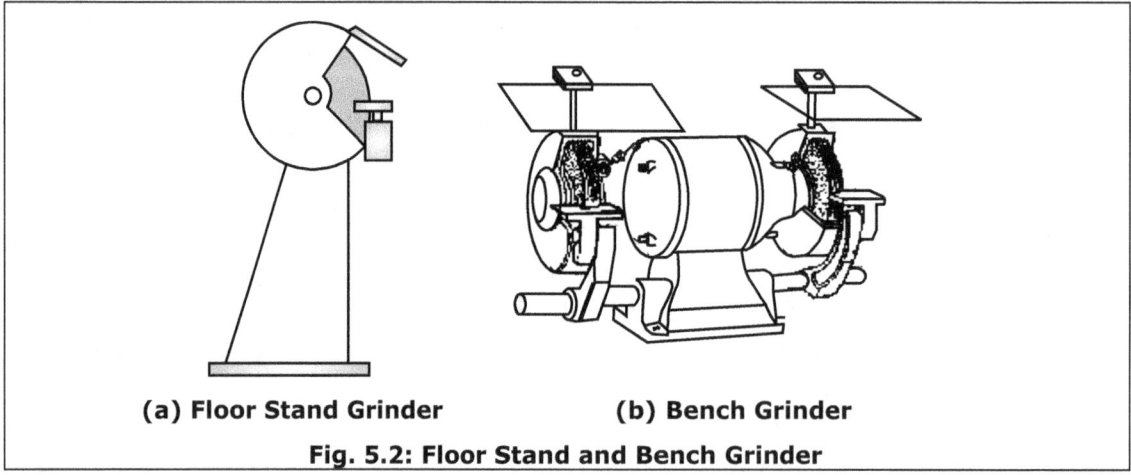

(a) Floor Stand Grinder (b) Bench Grinder

Fig. 5.2: Floor Stand and Bench Grinder

5.7 PORTABLE AND FLEXIBLE SHAFT GRINDERS

- It is portable grinder similar to portable electric drilling machine with a grinding wheel mounted on spindle instead of drill chuck.

- Flexible shaft grinder consists of a long flexible shaft on which grinding wheel is mounted. The shaft is drawn by motor.

- It is generally used to remove the excess material from heavier work piece like castings, forgings, welded structures etc.

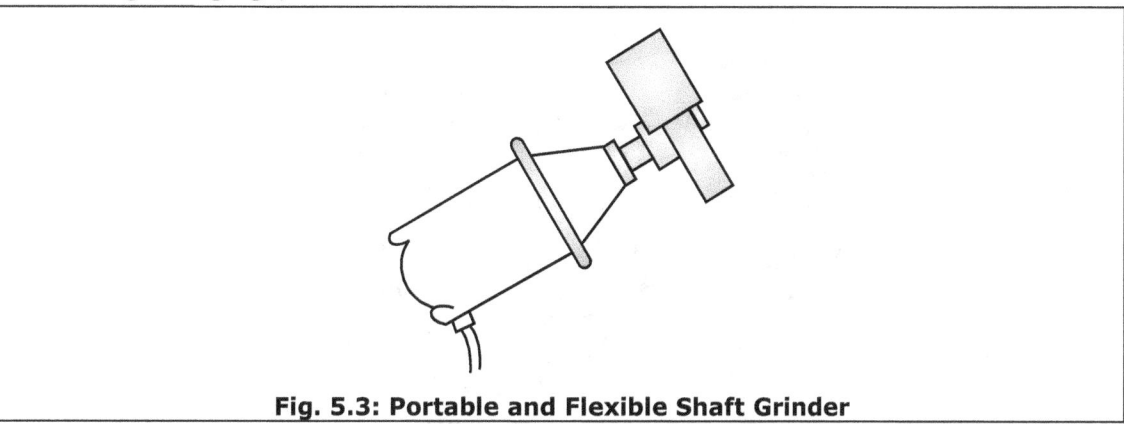

Fig. 5.3: Portable and Flexible Shaft Grinder

5.8 SWING FRAME GRINDERS

- In swing frame grinder horizontal frame (2 to 3 m long) grinder wheel is mounted at one end and motor at another end.

- It is generally used for snagging of large castings and forgings.

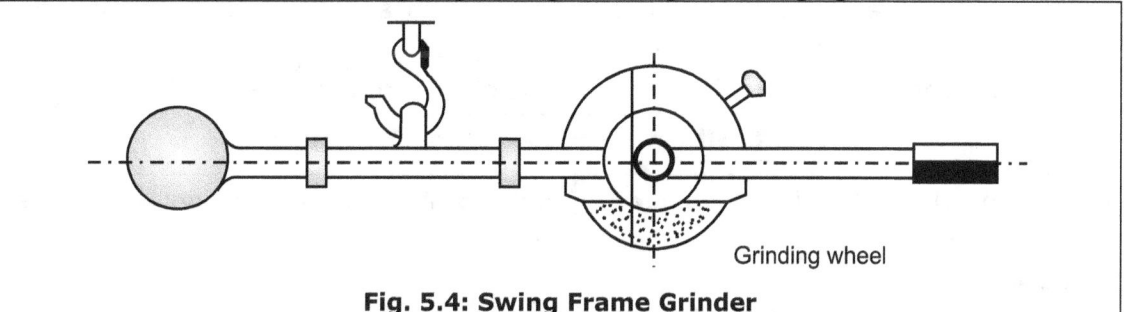

Grinding wheel

Fig. 5.4: Swing Frame Grinder

5.9 ABRASIVE BELT GRINDERS

- In this type of grinder, a continuous abrasive tensioned belt is used over two pulleys.

- The linear speed of belt is controlled between 75 to 1800 m/min.

- The work comes in contact with moving abrasive belt to remove stock.

- The work can be mounted on table with rotary or reciprocating machine.

- The abrasive belt grinder is used for removal of stock, finishing and polishing operations.

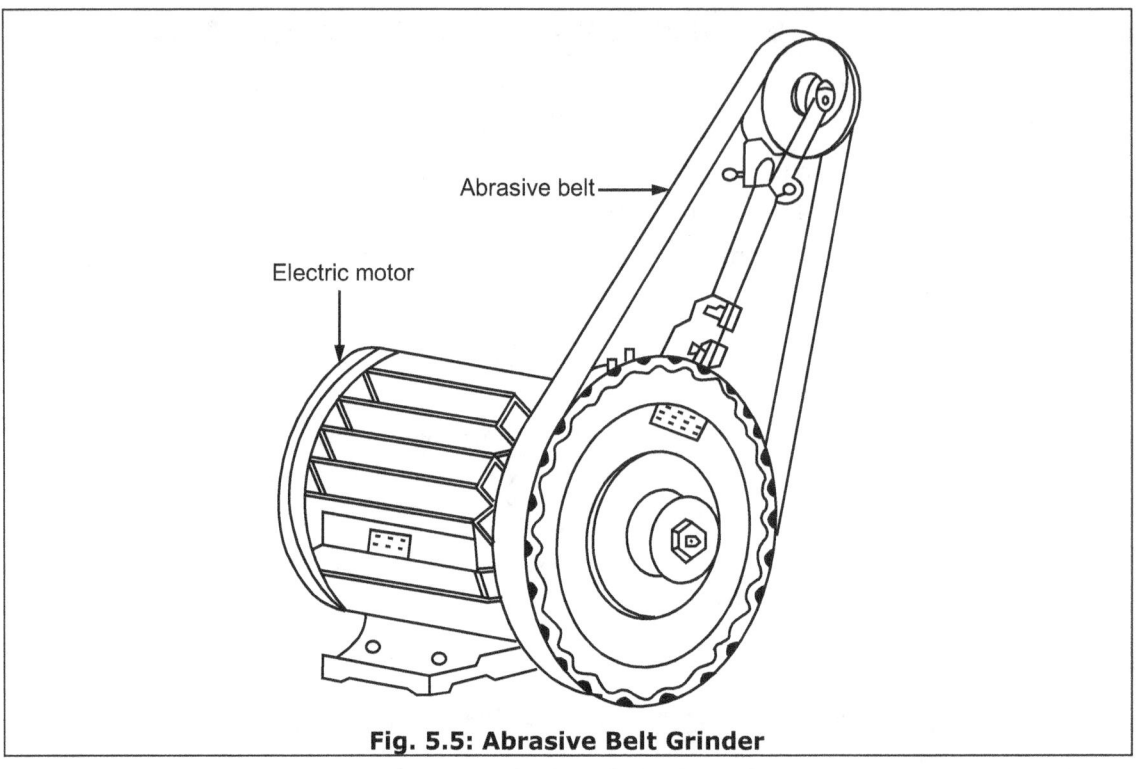

Fig. 5.5: Abrasive Belt Grinder

5.10 CYLINDRICAL CENTRE TYPE GRINDERS

- Cylindrical grinders are used to produce cylindrical or conical shapes on a work piece.
- The work piece is mounted between the centres and the face of the grinding wheel passes over the external surface of work piece.
- The cylindrical centre type grinders may be of plain or universal or type.

5.10.1 Plain Centre Type Grinders

- A plain cylindrical grinder is shown in Fig. 5.6 and the construction is explained below.
- **Bed:**
  - It is a heavy CI casting that rest on floor and supports the entire machine.
  - The top surface of the bed carries machined horizontal guideways.
- **Table:**
  - The machine carries two tables. The upper table and the lower table.
  - Lower table is mounted on longitudinal guide ways of bed and moves in longitudinal direction.
  - The upper table is mounted on the top surface of lower table and swivels about a vertical axis in the horizontal plane at around 10° on either side to accommodate taper surface.

- **Head stock and tail stock:**
  - o Head stock and tail stock are mounted above the upper table.
  - o The head stock is fixed and supports the work piece through a centre.
  - o The tailstock can be moved along the table and clamped at any desired position to accommodate work piece of different lengths.
- **Grinding wheel head:**
  - o A grinding wheel head consists of grinding wheel, spindle and motor.
  - o It is mounted on the cross guide ways provided on the bed which are perpendicular to longitudinal guide ways.
  - o This movement of the spindle is known as the infeed.
- **Working:**
  - o The work piece is usually held between centres of headstock and tailstock.
  - o Head stock hold support and rotate the work piece. Tail stock gives support at dead centre.
  - o The rotating work is traversed across the face of rotating grinding wheel.
  - o Grinding wheel is fed crosswise to obtain the depth of cut and lower table is reciprocated to finish entire length of work piece.
  - o Plain cylindrical grinders are used for heavy, repetitive simple type of external grinding operations on plain or stepped surfaces, cylinders, taper surface etc.
  - o These machines produce cylinders, tapers, concave or convex radii on the surface, undercuts etc.

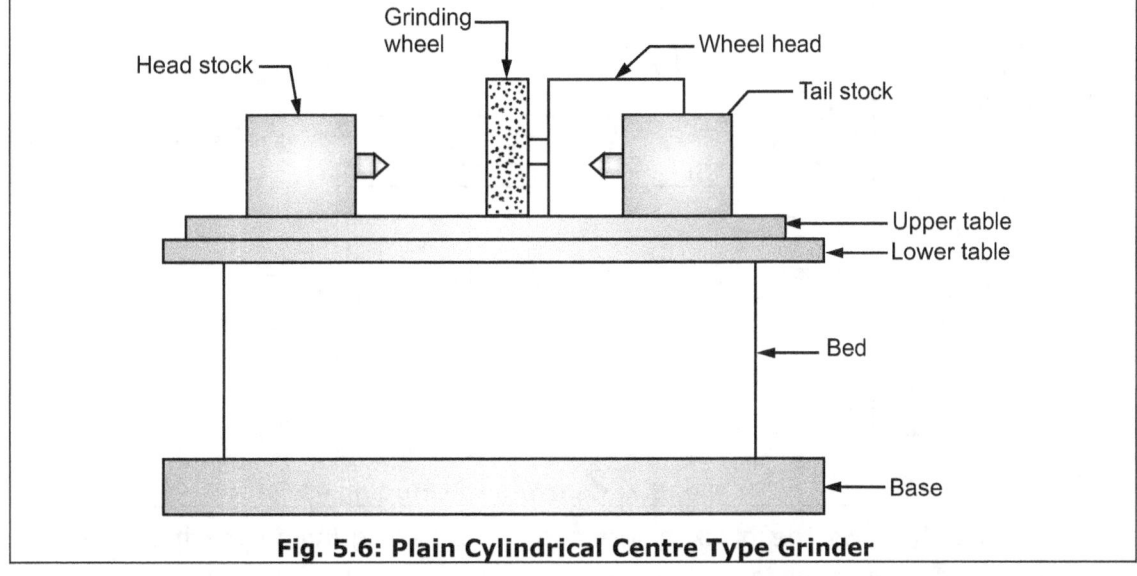

Fig. 5.6: Plain Cylindrical Centre Type Grinder

5.10.2 Universal Centre Type Grinders

- Universal centre type grinders have added features like:
  - Head stock can be made to carry live or dead centre as desired.
  - Head stock can be swiveled in a horizontal plane.
  - Wheel can be raised or lowered and can also be swiveled to 90° to grind taper surfaces having large taper angle.
  - With the facility of hydraulic drive for wheel head approach and feed, table traverse and elimination of backlash in the feed gives greater versatility to this machine.
  - This makes possible on it surface grinding, taper grinding, and cylindrical grinding.

5.11 CENTRE-LESS TYPE GRINDERS   [W-14, 15, S-17]

- In centre-less grinding, work is not held between the centers as in cylindrical grinding.
- Here the work piece is held by a combination of two rotating wheels a regulating wheel and also on a work rest blade.
- This eliminates the use of work holding devices. Also there is no need to centre the work piece.

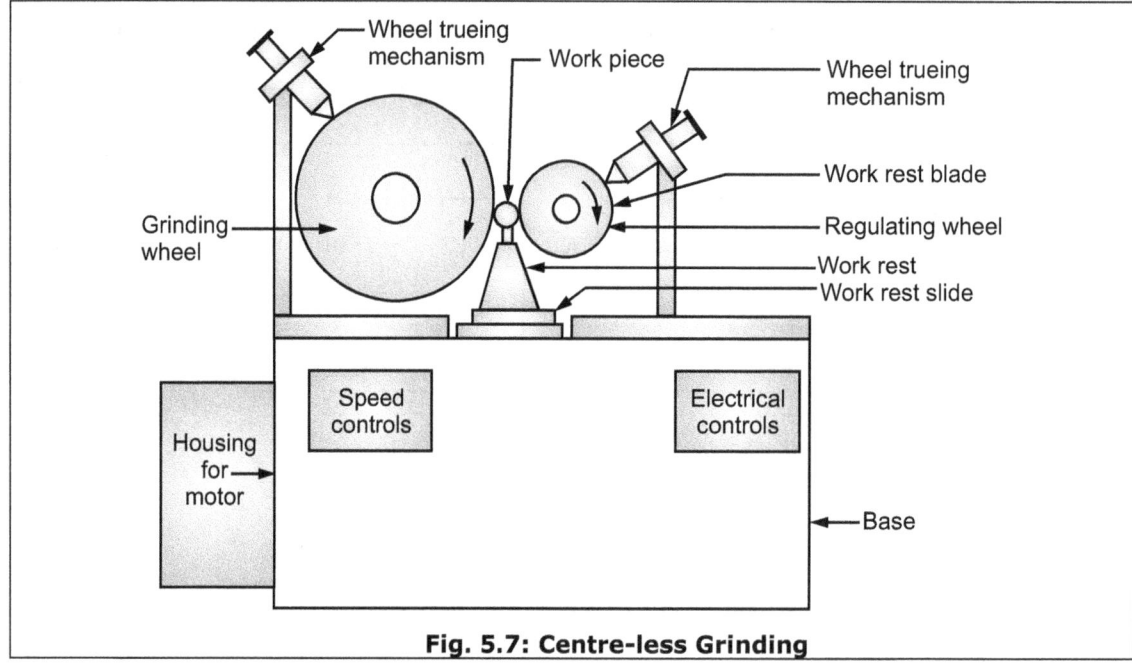

Fig. 5.7: Centre-less Grinding

- The Fig. 5.7 shows the block diagram of centreless grinding machine and the various parts are explained below.

Base:

- It carries a heavy base which is a CI casting and hollow from inside.
- The base carries speed control panel and electrical control panel.

Grinding wheel:

- The machine carries a grinding wheel at one end mounted on the wheel head.

Regulating wheel:

- A regulating wheel, smaller in size than the grinding wheel is mounted on the outer end of the machine.
- The wheel carries a rubber bond and helps in the rotation of work piece, apart from giving support to it.
- It also controls the speed of rotation of the work piece.

Work rest blade:

- The work rest is mounted on the work rest slide on the base of the machine.
- A blade is provided on the top of the work rest, which supports the work piece.

Control Panels:

- A speed control panel and electric control panels provided on the front face of the machine.
- The speed panel controls the speed adjustment of the two trueing mechanisms and the infeed grinding mechanism.
- The other panel carries control for hydraulic mechanism, speed adjusting of regulating wheel etc.

Working:

- During working the work piece is held and rotated by two wheels and supported by work rest blade.
- Both the wheels rotates in same direction.
- The feed in centre-less grinding is given to the work piece in one of following methods:
  1. Through feed grinding
  2. In feed grinding
  3. End feed grinding
- Fig. 5.8 shows the methods of feed in centreless grinding.

1. Through Feed Grinding:

  - o It is the simplest method used for straight cylindrical work such as rollers, pins and straight long bars.
  - o In this case the regulating wheel and grinding wheel is adjusted equal to the desired diameter of the work piece and the job is fed and passed through the wheels.
  - o The work piece is given axial feed. For this the axis of the regulating wheel is inclined at 2° to 10° with the vertical.

2. In Feed Grinding:

o It is used for grinding headed, stepped and tapered parts.

o This method is similar to through feed and there is no relative axial movement between work and grinding wheel, as the length of grinding has to be controlled.

o Here both the grinding wheel and regulating wheel are more in width than the work piece length to the ground.

o To control the length of grinding, work piece is placed on work rest against an end stop and regulating wheel is advanced to grinding wheel by lever arrangement until the work piece is reduced to the desired diameter.

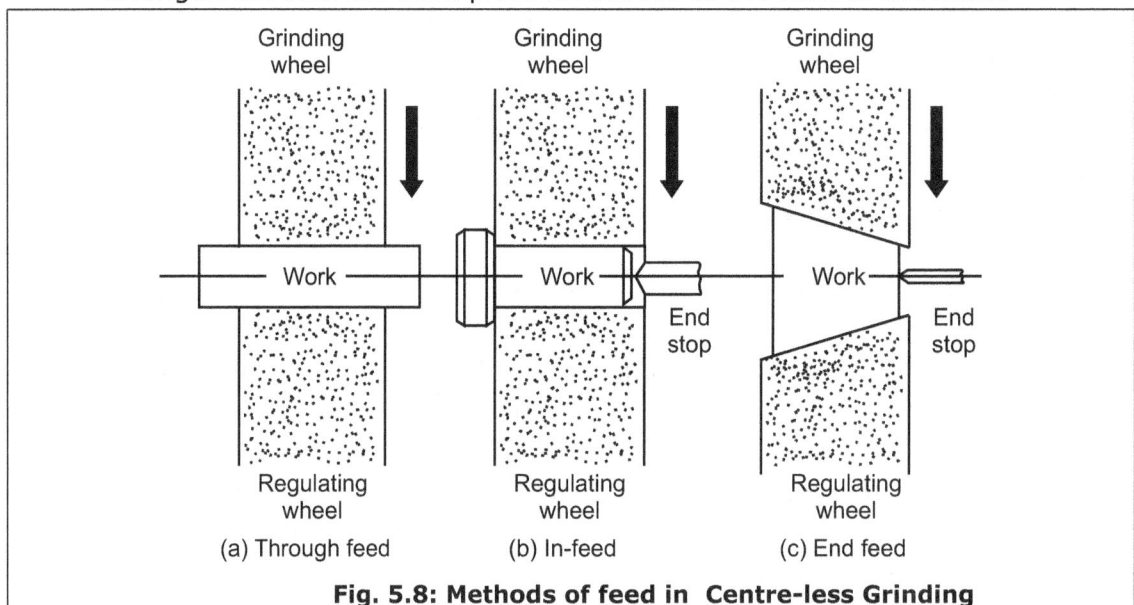

Fig. 5.8: Methods of feed in Centre-less Grinding

3. End Feed Grinding:

o It is used for short tapers. Here both the wheels have the form corresponding to the shape of the work piece.

o The work piece is fed longitudinally from the side of the wheels.

o As it advances between the revolving wheels, its surface is ground till its farther end touches the end stop.

5.11.1 Advantages of Centre-less Grinding

• The advantages of external centreless grinding are given below:

o The rate of production is much higher in centre-less grinding than cylindrical grinding. Hence, cost of production is less.

o As true floating condition exists during the grinding process no need of holding the work piece between the centres. Hence, axial thrust is absent.

- o The work piece is rigidly supported along the entire length, hence better stability.

- o Large grinding wheels can be used. Wheel wear and tear is less and hence less maintenance.

- o The work is supported throughout its length and there is no deflection, therefore long slender workpiece can be ground easily.

- o The process is continuous and can be used for production work.

- o Size of work is easily controlled.

- o Semi-skilled operator can perform operation.

5.11.2 Disadvantages of Centre-less Grinding

- The disadvantages of external centreless grinding are given below:

  - o The work piece having multiple diameters of steps and shoulders cannot be handled.

  - o The work piece having flat surfaces and key ways can be ground.

  - o In case of hollow work piece, shape may change.

5.11.3 Applications of Centre-less Grinding

- The applications of external centreless grinding are given below:

  - o Centre-less grinding is used for exterior cylindrical, tapered and formed surfaces on work piece that are not held and rotated on centres.

  - o Through feed grinder is used for grinding long and slender shafts or bars.

  - o In feed grinder is used for form grinding and to grind shoulders.

  - o End feed grinder is used for grinding tapered surface.

  - o Internal centre-less grinder is used to finish internal surface of any hollow work piece.

5.12 INTERNAL GRINDER

- Internal grinders are used mainly for finishing round holes.

- It is also used for finishing internal bores and tubes having more than one diameter.

- Internal grinders may be of plain type, universal type, planetary type or centre-less type.

5.12.1 Planetory Internal Grinder

- The working principle of planetary internal grinder is shown in Fig. 5.9. In planetary grinder, a work is held stationary and mounted on table of machine.

- The grinding wheel has three motions

  (a) It rotates about its axis.

  (b) It travels along a circular path around the axis of the hole in the work piece.

  (c) It travels longitudinally inside the work piece.

- The longitudinal travel can be obtained by

  (a) Reciprocating movements of the grinding wheel or,

  (b) By moving the slide along with the work piece.

- The grinding wheel is given a radial infeed (into the work piece) after each planetary circle is completed. This gives the depth of cut.

- It is possible to grind large holes of varying diameter depending upon how much the wheel spindle is made to run eccentric.

- This machine is used only for bore grinding of heavy or irregular shape work, which is difficult to rotate.

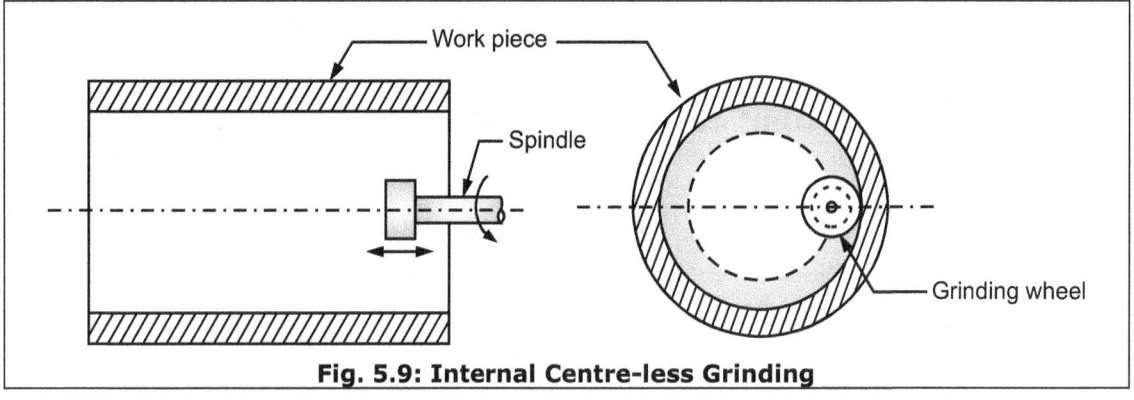

Fig. 5.9: Internal Centre-less Grinding

5.12.2 Centre-less Internal Grinder

- In centre-less grinding the workpiece is supported between the three rolls. The rolls are pressure roll, supporting roll and a regulating roll (grinding wheel).

- All the three rolls rotates in the same direction and rotates the workpiece with them.

- The workpiece and grinding wheel rotates in the same direction.

- The direction of rotation of the three rolls and workpiece is opposite.

- The grinding wheel always contacts the workpiece at the horizontal centerline of the regulating wheel.

- This ensures uniform wall thickness of the workpiece and also ensures concentricity of the bore with the external surface of the workpiece.

- To load or unload the workpiece, the pressure roll can be swung away.

- The grinding wheel is given infeed so as to obtain the required depth of cut.

- This type of machine is used for work having repetitive nature.

- It has advantages similar to external centre-less grinding.

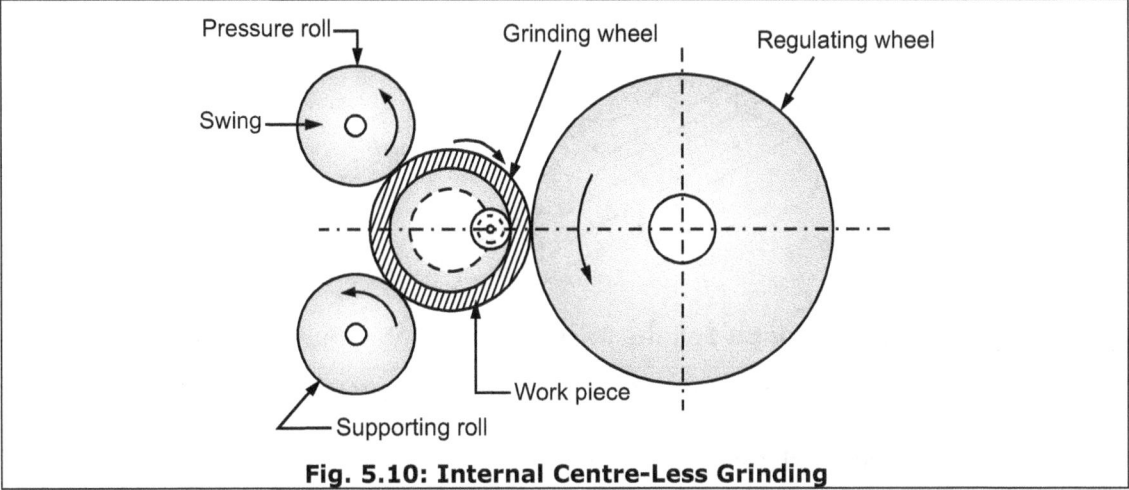

Fig. 5.10: Internal Centre-Less Grinding

5.13 SURFACE GRINDERS   [S-15]

- Surface grinder is used to finish the surface produced by milling, shaper and planer.

- It is intended to grind flat surface. However curved or irregular surfaces can also be ground by using special fixtures.

- Surface grinder may be of reciprocating or rotary table type. The spindle may be vertical or horizontal.

5.13.1 Horizontal Spindle Reciprocating Table Surface Grinder

- It consists of horizontal spindle carrying a straight grinding wheel.

- Work piece is clamped on magnetic table.

- During operation the table reciprocates under the rotary grinding wheel.

- The reciprocating motion of the table provides longitudinal feed and cross feed is provided by the spindle.

- For taking depth of cut grinding wheel can be fed downwards. This is called as infeed.

- The amount of feed is very small about 0.005 to 0.15 mm.

- The grinding area is small and the speed is uniform over the grinding surface.

- It is used for tool room for light work.

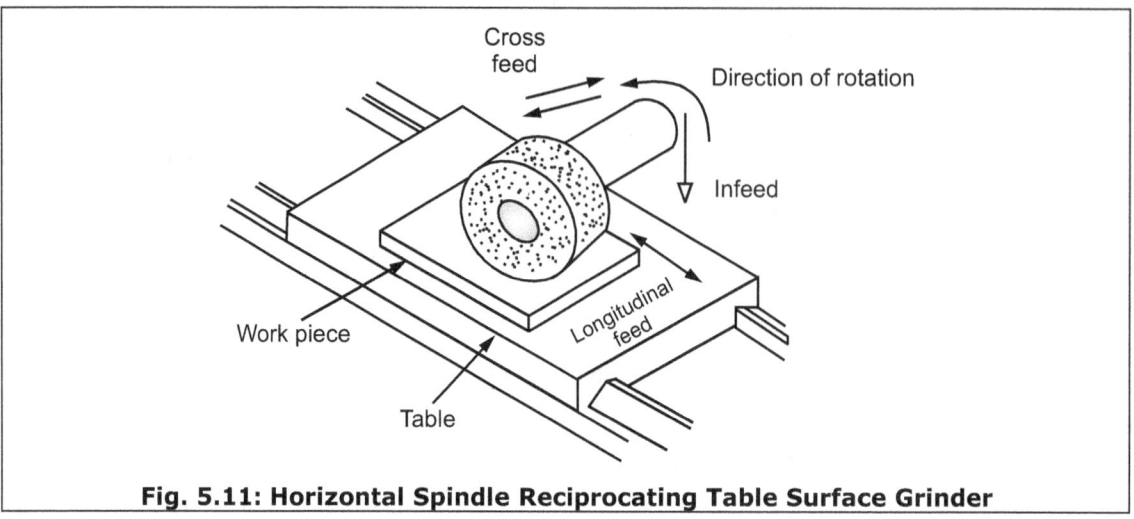

Fig. 5.11: Horizontal Spindle Reciprocating Table Surface Grinder

5.13.2 Horizontal Spindle Rotary Table Surface Grinder

- It is used for facing circular work and narrow rings. Work is clamped on rotary table and grinding wheel is mounted on horizontal spindle.

- Work pieces are normally arranged in a circular fashion, concentric with the circular magnetic chuck.

- The table is made to rotate in a direction opposite to that of the rotation of the grinding wheel.

- The vertical feed is given by moving the wheel head along a column and the cross feed by the horizontal movement of wheel spindle.

- The work table can be lowered or raised to accommodate different height work pieces.

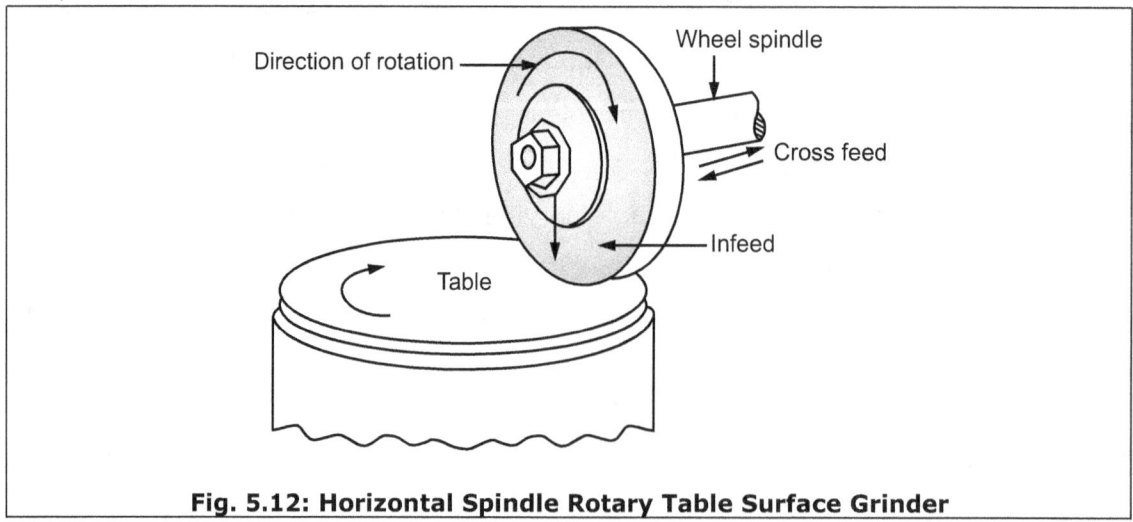

Fig. 5.12: Horizontal Spindle Rotary Table Surface Grinder

5.13.3 Vertical Spindle Reciprocating Table Surface Grinder

- In this type of machine, grinding wheel spindle is vertical.
- Work is clamped on table which reciprocates under rotary grinding wheel. Grinding is performed by face of the wheel.
- Infeed and cross feed is given by movement of spindle.
- In this type of machines cuped, cylindrical or segmental grinding wheels are used.
- The grinding area is large and large quantity of stock is removed.

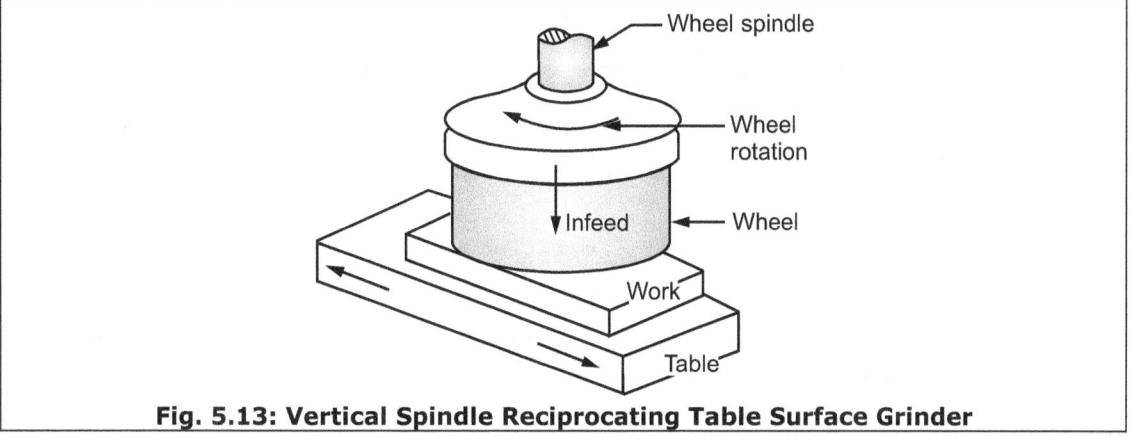

Fig. 5.13: Vertical Spindle Reciprocating Table Surface Grinder

5.13.4 Vertical Spindle Rotary Table Surface Grinder

- In this type of machine, grinding wheel is mounted on vertical spindle.
- The work is mounted on magnetic chuck which rotates with the table.
- Cuped shaped, cylindrical or segmental grinding wheels are used on the vertical spindle.
- The table rotates in opposite direction to that of wheel.
- Infeed and cross feed is given by movement of spindle.
- This type of machine gives higher production rates so comparatively surface finish is not good.

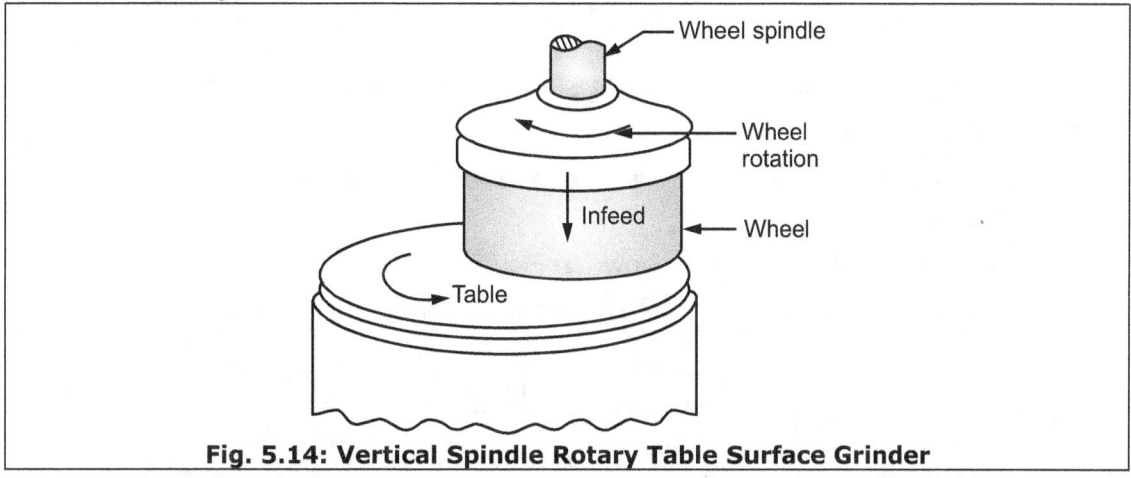

Fig. 5.14: Vertical Spindle Rotary Table Surface Grinder

5.14 GRINDING WHEEL COMPOSITION

- Grinding wheel is multi-tooth cutter made-up of many hard particles known as abrasive.

- Abrasive grains are mixed with suitable bond which hold the particles when wheel is in use.

- The wheel consists of one piece or made of segments joined together.

- The properties of grinding wheel depends on type of Abrasive, type of bond, Grit or Grain size, Grade of the wheel and Structure of the wheel.

5.15 SHAPE OF GRINDING WHEEL

- Depending upon the type of grinding machine and class of work, grinding wheels are made in number of standard shapes and sizes to meet a wide range of work requirements.

- The shape of the wheel must be such that there will be proper contact between the wheel and the surface of the work.

- The grinding wheel is a multipoint cutting tool. The cutting points of grinding wheels are irregularly shaped and randomly distributed over the active face of the wheel.

- It does not have a fixed orientation.

- The most common shapes used are:

1. **Straight Grinding Wheel:**

    o   It is used for cylindrical grinding, centreless grinding and internal grinding.

    o   A straight grinding wheel is shown in Fig. 5.15.

    o   It may have recess on one side or on both sides.

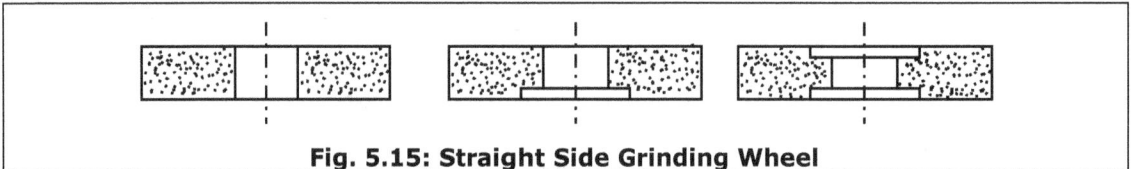

Fig. 5.15: Straight Side Grinding Wheel

2. **Tapered Grinding Wheel:**

    o   It is used for thread grinding or gear tooth grinding or machining tapered surfaces.

    o   A tapered grinding wheel is shown in Fig. 5.16.

    o   The taper may also conform to the required shape of the work piece.

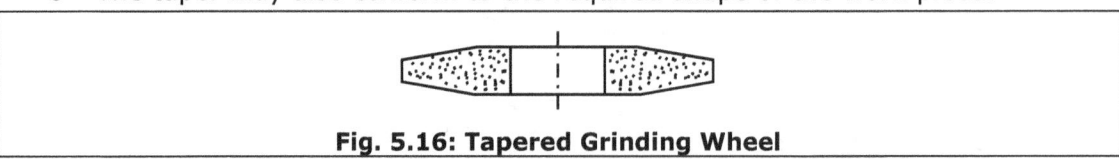

Fig. 5.16: Tapered Grinding Wheel

3. Straight Cup Grinding Wheel:

- o It is used for grinding plain surfaces.
- o A tapered grinding wheel is shown in Fig. 5.17.
- o It is generally used on surface grinders.

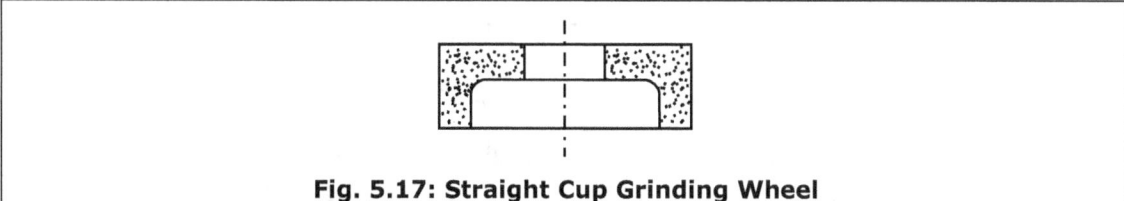

Fig. 5.17: Straight Cup Grinding Wheel

4. Flared Cup Grinding Wheel

- o It is used for precision grinding of plain surfaces.
- o A tapered grinding wheel is shown in Fig. 5.18.
- o It is generally used on surface grinders.

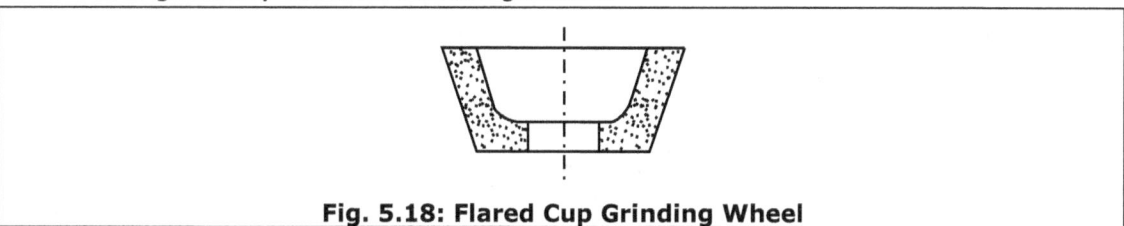

Fig. 5.18: Flared Cup Grinding Wheel

5. Saucer Grinding Wheel:

- o It is used for precision grinding.
- o A tapered grinding wheel is shown in Fig. 5.19.
- o It is generally used to sharpen the saws.

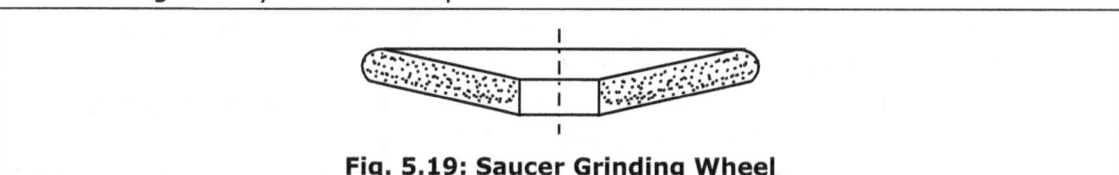

Fig. 5.19: Saucer Grinding Wheel

6. Dish type Grinding Wheel:

- o It is used to grind teeth of milling cutter, broach etc.
- o A dish shaped grinding wheel is shown in Fig. 5.20.
- o It is mounted on tool and cutter grinder.

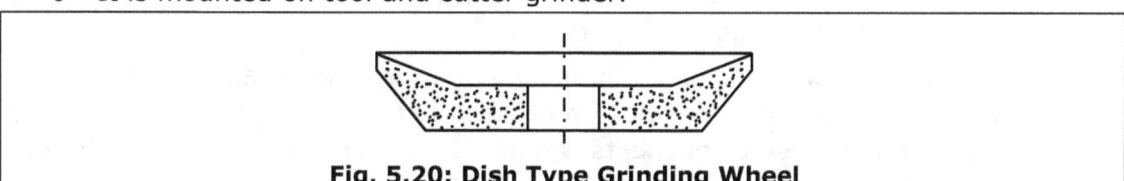

Fig. 5.20: Dish Type Grinding Wheel

7. Cylindrical Grinding Wheel:

- o   It is used for grinding of plain surfaces.
- o   A cylindrical grinding wheel is shown in Fig. 5.21.
- o   It can be used on horizontal as well as vertical surface grinders.

Fig. 5.21: Cylindrical Grinding Wheel

5.16 ELEMENTS OF GRINDING WHEEL

- •   The various elements of grinding wheel are as mentioned below.
- •   It influence the properties of grinding wheels.
  - o   Abrasive.
  - o   Bond
  - o   Grit or Grain size.
  - o   Grade of the wheel.
  - o   Structure of the wheel.

5.16.1 Abrasive

- •   An abrasive is an hard and tough material. It has many sharp edges and can be used to cut or wear away the other materials. Abrasive particles used for the grinding wheels are of two types:

1. Natural abrasives
2. Artificial abrasives

1. **Natural abrasives:** Natural abrasives are obtained from the nature. Natural abrasive includes minerals, diamond, corundum, emery, sand stone or quartz. The main element of corundum and emery is natural alumina (Al_2O_3). The natural abrasive contains certain type of impurities which reduce the cutting abilities and create non-uniformities in abrasive wheel. For example, emery contains 50 to 65% abrasive material and 35% impurities. These impurities not only make difficulties in cutting action but also create non-uniformity in the wheel. Hence for most of the purposes, natural abrasives are not used. Diamond is supported to be hardest natural substance, known in its crystalline form. It is used in grinding wheels for grinding materials like cemented carbides, glass, stone etc.

2. **Artificial abrasives:** The artificial abrasives are man-made, manufactured abrasives. These are manufactured electro-chemically. The qualities and composition of these components can be easily controlled and their efficiency is better than natural abrasives.

The main groups of artificial abrasives are aluminium oxide (Al_2O_3) and silicon carbide (SiC).

Aluminum oxide is denoted by English alphabet 'A'.

Silicon Carbide is denoted by English alphabet 'S'.

5.16.2 Bond

- The bond is the substance which when mixed with the abrasive grains, holds them together enabling the mixture to be shaped to form grinding wheel.
- The Bonding material should have the following properties:
  - It should withstand the grinding temperature.
  - It should withstand the spindle speed without disintegration.
  - It should be capable of retaining the abrasive grain during cutting operation.
  - Bond should be rigid to enable the grit to penetrate and cut the work.
- There are several type of bonding materials as given below:

1. Vitrified Bond (V):
  - Vitrified bond is used for making vitrified grinding wheel.
  - It is made by bonding clay melted to a glass like consistency with abrasive grains.
  - The clay and abrasive grains are thoroughly mixed together with sufficient water to make the mixture uniform.
  - The mixture is moulded to desired shape and dried to a point where it can be handled.
  - It is then heated in a klin about 1200°C temperature for about one week to vitrify the bond.
  - Vitrified bond gives good strength. Wheel can be made dense or porous; therefore 75 % of grinding wheels are with vitrified bond.
  - The only disadvantage of vitrified bond is that, it is brittle and sensitive to impact.
  - Vitrified bond is designated by letter 'V'.

2. Silicate Bond (S):
  - Silicate bond is used for making Silicate wheels.
  - The silicate bond is made by mixing abrasive grains with sodium silicate, pressed in mould to give required shape, dried and backed in furnace at a temperature of 260°C for several days.
  - Silicate wheels are water proof.

- o Silicate bonded wheels has limited applications as it is soft, comparatively weak and has low production capacities.
- o Silicate bond is used for making wheels of large diameters above 90 cm.
- o Silicate bond wheel is designated by letter 'S'.

3. Shellac Bond (E):

- o Shellac bond is used for making elastic wheels.
- o In this process, the abrasive and shellac are mixed in heated containers and then rolled or pressed in heated moulds.
- o Later the shapes are backed a few hours at a temperature of 150°C.
- o The elasticity of this bond is greater than any other type and has considerable strength.
- o It is not intended for heavy duty work and used for finishing chilled iron, cast iron and steel rolls, hardened steel cams and aluminium pistons, cam shaft grinding, scissors and cutlery.
- o Shellac bond wheels are made in small size upto 3 mm.
- o Shellac bond is designated by letter 'E'.

4. Resinoid Bond (B):

- o The resinoid bond is used for making resinoid wheels.
- o The resinoid wheels are manufactured by mixing abrasive grain with synthetic resin and other compound.
- o The mixture is placed in moulds and heated at about 200°C.
- o At this temperature, the resin sets to hold the abrasive grains in wheel form.
- o Wheels bonded with the synthetic resin, such as bakelite are used for application, which demand strong and high speed wheels, which can remove stock very rapidly.
- o It is used for precision grinding cams and rolls requiring high finish.
- o The resinoid bonded wheel is denoted by letter 'B'.

5. Rubber Bond (R):

- o Rubber bond is used for manufacturing vulcanized wheels.
- o It is made by mixing abrasive grains with pure rubber and sulphur.
- o The mixture rolled into sheets, and wheels are punched out of the sheets on a punch press and finally wheels are vulcanized.
- o The rubber bonded wheels are more resilient, less heat resistant and more dense than resinoid wheels.
- o It is used where good surface finish is primary requirement.
- o They are strong and tough enough to make extremely thin wheels.
- o Rubber bonded wheels are designated by letter 'R'.

Type of Bond	Symbol
Vitrified bond	V
Silicate Bond	S
Shellac bond	E
Resinoid bond	B
Rubber bond	R

5.16.3 Grit or Grain Size

- The grit or grain number indicates the size of abrasive used for making a grinding wheel. These sized particles are called grains or grits.
- The choice of grain size is determined by
  - Nature of grinding operation.
  - Material to be ground.
  - Material removal rate.
  - Surface finish desired.
- The size of grains are expressed by the size of screen opening at a time of sorting after crushing as shown in Fig. 5.22.
- The grain size 30 means there are 30 opening per square inch in a screen which is used for sorting.
- The grain size is designated by number from 6 to 1200.
- Number 6 being courser and 1200 being finer.
- The grain size may be classified as:
  - Coarse.
  - Medium.
  - Fine.
  - Very fine.
- Various abrasive grain sizes commonly used from course to very fine are:

Grit Designation	Grain size or Grit
Coarse	6, 7, 8, 10, 12, 14, 16, 20, 24
Medium	30, 36, 46, 54, 60
Fine	70, 80, 90, 100, 120, 150, 180
Very fine	220, 240, 280, 320, 360, 400, 600, 800, 1000, 1200

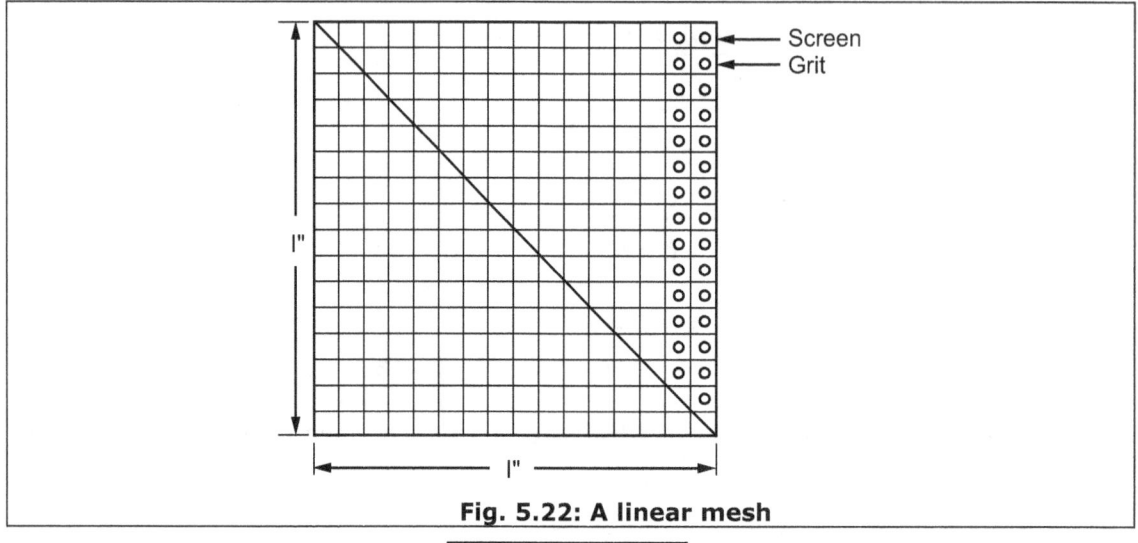

Fig. 5.22: A linear mesh

5.16.4 Grade

- The grade means degree of hardness of the wheel means the hardness with which the bond holds the cutting points or abrasive grains in a place.

- It does not refer to the hardness of the abrasive grain.

- The hardness of a grinding wheel depends on:
  - Hardness of the material being ground.
  - Arc of contact.
  - Wheel and work speed.
  - Condition of grinding machine.

- Hard wheels are recommended for soft material and soft wheels are recommended for hard work materials.

- The words 'hard' and 'soft' refer to the holding power or strength of the bond.

- The grade shall be indicated in all bonds and processes by a letter of the English alphabet.

- 'A' denotes the softest and 'Z' denotes the hardest grade.

- Grades can be classified as:
  - Soft
  - Medium
  - Hard

Grade Scale		
Soft	**Medium**	**Hard**
A ,B, C, D, E, F, G, H	I, J, K, L, M, N, O, P	Q, R, S, T, U, V, W, X, Y, Z

5.16.5 Structure

- Abrasive grains are not packed in the wheel but are distributed through the bond.
- The structure of grinding wheel depends on the grain spacing. i.e. the manner in which the abrasive grains are distributed throughout the wheel.
- The relative spacing is referred to as the structure and denoted by the number of cutting edges per unit area of structure and denoted by the number of cutting edges per unit area of wheel face as well as by number and size of void spaces between grains.
- The primary purpose of structure is to provide chip clearance and may be open or dense.
- Wheel structures commonly used are indicated by numbers varying from 1 to 15 or higher, 1 being the closest and 15 being the most open.
- The structure of grinding wheel is shown in Fig. 5.23.

Dense	1	2	3	4	5	6	7	8
Open	9	10	11	12	13	14	15	or higher

- The structure of grinding wheel depends on:
  - Hardness of material being ground.
  - Surface finish desired.
  - Nature of grinding operation.
- Soft and ductile material and heavy cuts requires open structure.
- Hard brittle and finishing cut requires a dense structure.

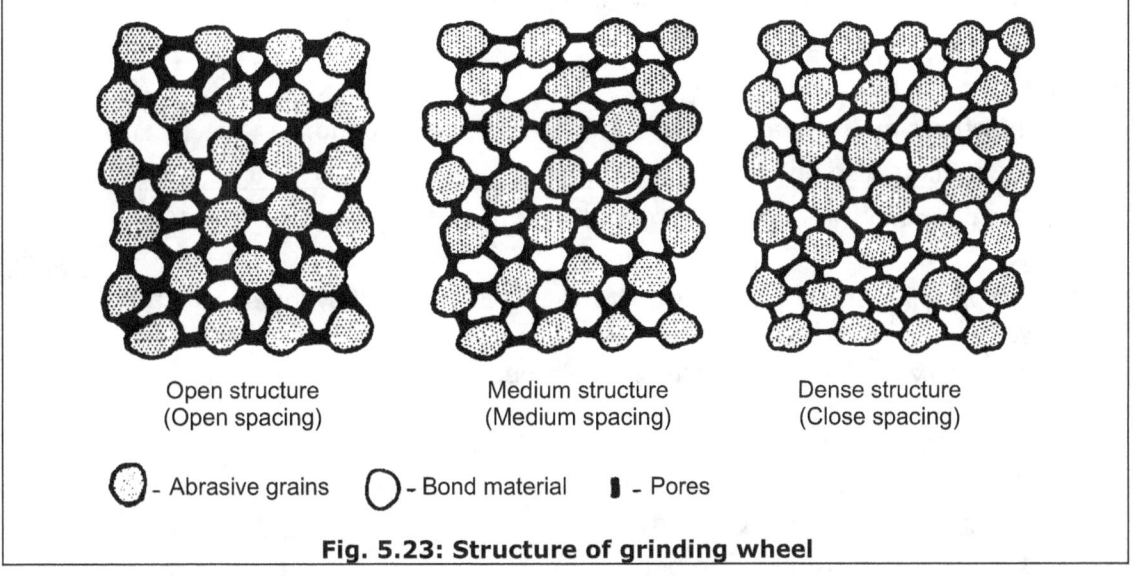

Open structure   Medium structure   Dense structure
(Open spacing)   (Medium spacing)   (Close spacing)

- Abrasive grains   - Bond material   - Pores

Fig. 5.23: Structure of grinding wheel

5.17 SIZE OF THE GRINDING WHEEL

- The size of the grinding wheel is specified by the following parameters in the given sequence.
  - o Diameter of the wheel.
  - o Thickness or face width of the wheel.
  - o Diameter of the central bore of the wheel.
- For example, 300 × 25 × 20 means
  - 300 = Diameter of the wheel.
  - 25 = Thickness of the wheel.
  - 20 = Diameter of the central bore of the wheel.

5.18 DESIGNATION OF GRINDING WHEEL [W-14]

- It is also referred as specification of the grinding wheel or marking scheme of grinding wheel.
- Method of grinding wheel specification differ with the manufacturer and country, in order to bring the uniformity, Bureau of Indian Standards has suggested the marking scheme consisting of following six characters in sequence.
- This codification is as per Bureau Of Indian Standard Code IS 551: 1989.

0	1	2	3	4	5	6
Prefix	Abrasive Type	Abrasive Grains	Grade	Structure (Use Optional)	Nature of Bond	Manufacturer's Symbol (Type of Bond)

Prefix:

- Manufacturer may use a suitable prefix preceding the type of abrasive notation to indicate his own trade brand of the abrasive used.
- Use of prefix is optional.

Manufacturer's symbol:

- Manufacturer may use a suitable suffix to the type of bond.
- Use of suffix is also optional.

Ex. 5.1: Explain the meaning of Grinding Wheel designated as W A 46 K 5 V 17.

[W-15]

Sol.: A wheel marked as **W A 46 K 5 V 17** will have following specifications:

- W : Manufacturer's prefix
- A : Type of abrasive (Aluminium oxide)
- 46 : Grain size (medium)
- K : Grade (Medium)
- 5 : Wheel structure (Dense)
- V : Type of bond (Vitrified)
- 17 : Manufacturer's number.

Ex. 5.2: Explain the meaning of Grinding Wheel designated as W A 46 H 8 V 15.

Sol.: A wheel marked as **W A 46 H 8 V 15** will have following specifications:

W : manufacturer's prefix

A : Type of abrasive (Aluminium oxide)

46 : Grain size (medium)

H : Grade (soft)

8 : Wheel structure (Dense)

V : Type of bond (Vitrified)

15 : Manufacturer's number.

Ex. 5.3: Explain the meaning of Grinding Wheel designated as 51 A 36 L 5 V 23.

Sol.: A wheel marked as 51 A 36 L 5 V 23 will have following specifications:

51 : Manufacturer's symbol.

A : Abrasive type (Aluminium oxide.)

36 : Grain size (Medium.)

L : Grade (Soft.)

5 : Structure (Dense.)

V : Type of Bond (Vitrified.)

23 : Manufacturer's marking.

Ex. 5.4: Explain each term of grinding wheel designation.   [S-15]

200 × 15 × 20 WA 46 K 5 V 17.

Sol.: A grinding wheel marked as 200 × 15 × 20 W A 46 K 5V 17 will have meaning as specified.

200 : Diameter of wheel

15 : Thickness of wheel

20 : Bore diameter

W : Manufacturers prefix for abrasive

A : Abrasive type (Aluminum oxide)

46 : Grain size (Medium)

K : Grade (Medium)

5 : Wheel Structure (Dense)

V : Type of bond (Vertified)

17 : Manufacturer's suffix for bond

5.19 FACTORS CONSIDERED FOR SELECTION OF GRINDING WHEEL [S-15]

- Important factors considered for selection of grinding wheel are as follows.

1. **Constant Factors:**

   (a) **Work-piece Material:** Work-piece material affects the choice of abrasive grain, its size, grade, structure and bond. For hard work material, soft grinding wheel and for soft work material, hard grinding wheel is selected.

   (b) **Amount of Stock to be Removed:** Amount of stock to be removed affects grain size and bond. Coarse grains are used for rough grinding and fine grains are used for finish cut.

   (c) **Area of Contact:** For smaller area of contact, hard and fine grinding wheel is used and for large area of contact, coarse and soft grinding wheel is used.

   (d) **Type of Grinding Machine Used:** Heavy rigid machines demand softer grade of wheel.

2. **Variable Factors:**

   (a) **Wheel Speed:** Depending upon grade and bond, maximum recommended speed is used.

   (b) **Work Speed:** For high speed of workpiece, hard grade grinding wheel is used.

   (c) **Condition and Capacity of Machine:** New and rigid machine can be mounted with softer grade wheel, and old machines are mounted with hard wheel.

   (d) **Personal Factor:** Skilled operator can handle softer wheel carefully and give better and economic production.

- For smaller area of contact, hard and fine grinding wheel is used and for large area of contact, coarse and soft grinding wheel is used.

5.20 BALANCING OF GRINDING WHEEL

- In order to obtain a good surface finish, prevent vibration and chatter and undue wear of machine parts, it is necessary that grinding wheel has good balance.
- Thus, the grinding wheel should be properly tested for balance before use.
- If the wheel becomes out of balance through wear it should be balanced by removing from the machine.
- The wheel should be trued before balancing.
- Balancing can be done by three ways:

   (a) **By filling the lead:** Small wheels may be balanced by milling a short recession the inside of the flange and filling it with lead.

(b) By stucking weights: The wheel is mounted at the centre of a perfectly straight and round spindle, the assembly is them rested on a know edge balancing stand. Any out of balance will result in the wheel coming to test with the heavy side underneath. Correct weight can be then struck on the opposite side to balance the wheel.

It is shown in Fig. 5.24.

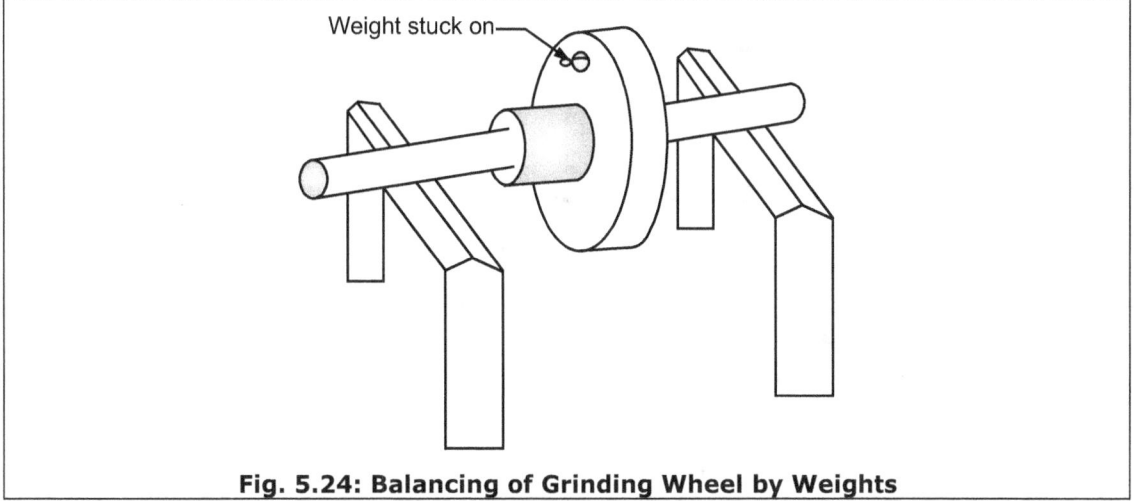

Fig. 5.24: Balancing of Grinding Wheel by Weights

(c) By using a recessed flanged: The wheel inbalance is tested as in above methods. A recersed flange is used and the weights can be moved over it along the recess to balance the large wheels.

5.21 DEFECTS IN GRINDING WHEEL

- The two common operating faults which occurs with the grinding wheels are:
  (a) Loading
  (b) Glazing

(a) Loading:

- The cut particles of the work-material may get adhere to the face of the grinding wheel.

- These particles occupy the open space between the cutting points.

- Due to this, the sharpness of the cutting paint is lost.

- The face becomes smooth and looses its cutting ability.

- This phenomenon is called as loading of wheel and the wheel is called as loaded wheel.

(b) Glazing:

- Due to continuous use of the grinding wheel the cutting points of the abrasive grains the comes dull.
- The loose their cutting ability and sharpness.
- Thus the wheel face becomes smooth.
- The wheel instead of biting into the wash material, provides a sort of rubbing action only.
- Thus the wheel becomes useless.
- This phenomenon is called as glazing of wheel and the wheel is called as glazed wheel.

5.22 CAUSES AND REMEDIES: LOADING AND GLAZING

Causes of Loading:

- Wheel carrying a hard bond.
- Taking very deep cuts.
- Grinding a soft material.
- Running the wheel slowly.
- By not using the right cutting fluid.

Remedy for loading:

- Increase the speed of the wheel.
- Use of soft wheel.

Cause of Glazing:

- Wheels carrying a hard bond.
- Wheel speed very high.
- Work speed very low.

Remedy for Glazing:

- Increase the workspeed.
- Decrease the wheel speed.

5.23 METHODS TO REMOVE DEFECTS IN GRINDING

5.23.1 Trueing

- It is the process of making the wheel face perfectly true, to ensure that its circumference is perfectly concentric with the spindle on which it is revolving.
- It removes glazing defect.
- It is carried out with a diamond tool.

- For trueing the grinding wheel is rotated and a diamond tool is held against the wheel.

- The tool is reciprocated over the wheel to cover the complete width of the wheel.

- The process of trueing is shown in Fig. 5.25

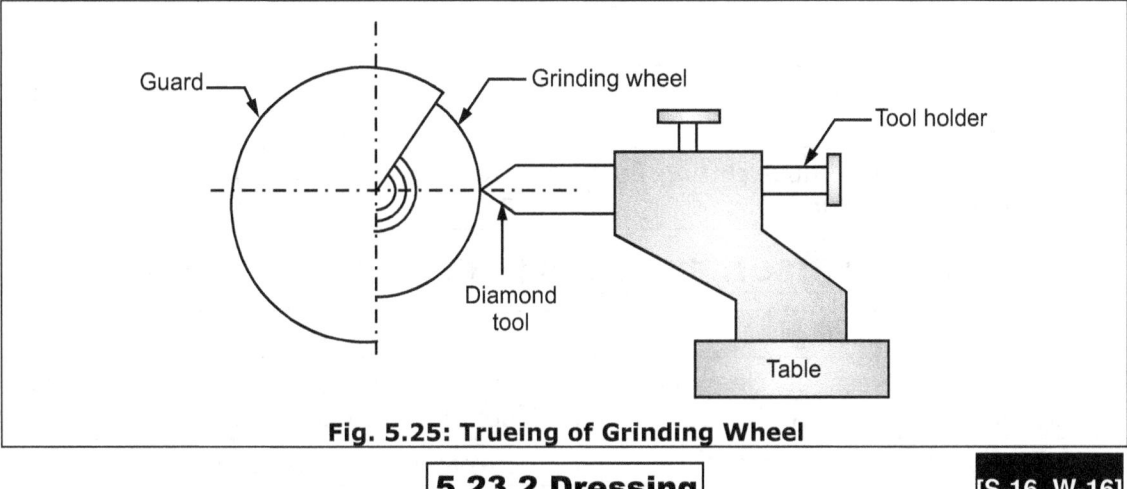

Fig. 5.25: Trueing of Grinding Wheel

5.23.2 Dressing   [S-16, W-16]

- It is the process of cleaning and opening up of the face of the wheel.

- It removes warm out grains from the wheel face and the sharp abrasive particles are again presented to the work.

- It removes loading defect.

- It is carried out by a start wheel dresser.

- A dresser consists of a number of hardened steel wheels with point on their periphery. The dresser is held against the face of the revolving wheel and moved across the face to dress the wheel surface.

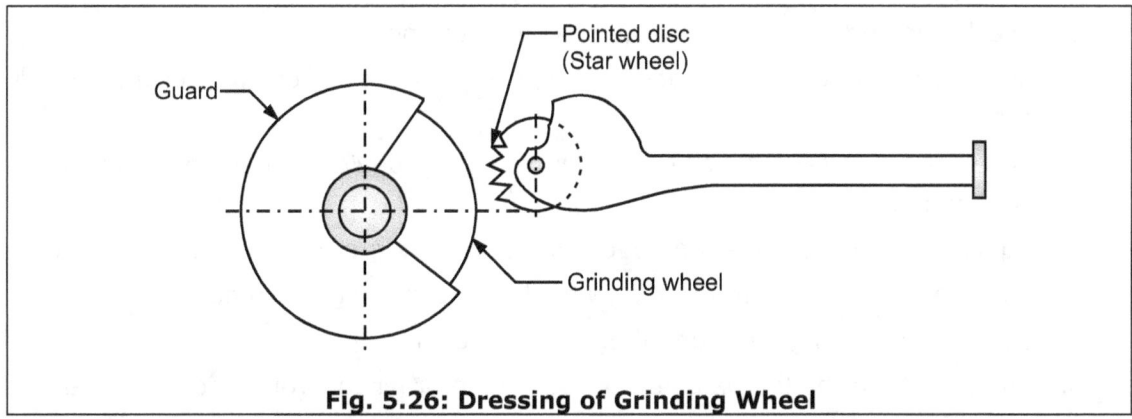

Fig. 5.26: Dressing of Grinding Wheel

5.24 COMPARISON BETWEEN LOADING AND GLAZING

Loading	Glazing
1. The cut particles occupy the open space between the abrasives.	1. The abrasives wears out and looses its ability.
2. This defect is corrected by dressing.	2. This defect can be corrected by trueing.
3. It is caused by running the wheel slowly.	3. It is caused by running the wheel at a higher speed.
4. Very deep cuts without cutting fluid gives rise to loading.	4. Working continuously without cutting fluid gives rise to glazing.

5.25 COMPARISON BETWEEN DRESSING AND TRUEING

Dressing	Trueing
1. It is the process of cleaning and opening the face of the wheel.	1. It is the process making the periphery concentric to bore dia.
2. It removes loading defect.	2. It removes glazing defect.
3. It is done with a start wheel dresser.	3. It is done with a diamond tool.
4. Profiles cannot be obtained.	4. Profiles can be obtained on the wheel face.
5. It is done to recover proper cutting action of the wheel.	5. It is done to recover the lost shape of the face.

5.26 SAFETY PRECAUTIONS IN GRINDING   [S-17]

- Grinding machines are used daily in a machine shop. To avoid injuries follow the safety precautions listed below:

  1. Wear goggles for all grinding machine operations.

  2. Check grinding wheels for cracks before mounting.

  3. Never operate grinding wheels at speeds in excess of the recommended speed.

  4. Never adjust the workpiece or work mounting devices when the machine is operating

  5. Do not exceed recommended depth of cut for the grinding wheel or machine.

  6. Remove workpiece from grinding wheel before turning machine off.

  7. Use proper wheel guards on all grinding machines.

  8. Do not tighten the flange bolts excessively in order to avoid crack in wheel.

5.27 INTRODUCTION TO SURFACE FINISH

- Various basic metal machining operations like turning, boring, milling, shaping, drilling etc. produces fairly accurate surface in size.
- But they do not produce high degree of surface finish.
- In many cases such parts do not readily suit the service, they are intended for and are subjected to one or further operations to obtain desired surface finish on them.
- Surface finish has influence on properties like wear, friction and corrosion resistance.

5.28 NEED OF SURFACE FINISH

- Surface Finish is essential for the following purposes:
  - To reduce the friction between two mating parts having a relative motion.
  - For controlling wear.
  - To achieve dimensional and geometrical accuracies.
  - To increase fatigue strength.
  - To machine quite operation of machine parts.
  - For good appearance.

5.29 HONING [S-17]

- Honing is a surface finishing operation based on abrasive action performed by a set of bonded abrasive stones called hones.
- Honing is primarily used to correct out of roundness, taper, tool marks and axial distortion.
- Mostly honing is done on internal cylindrical surfaces, such as automobile cylinder walls.
- It is generally used to finish bores of cylinders of IC engine, hydraulic cylinders, gas barrels, bearings etc.
- It can reduce the level of surface roughness below 32 µm.
- It produces a characteristics surface pattern as cross hatched which is a fit case to retain lubrication layer to facilitate motion to moving parts such as in IC engine.

5.29.1 Honing Stone [W-16]

- Honing stones are made from common abrasive and bonding materials, often impregnated with sulphur, resin or wax to improve cutting action and lengthen tool life.
- The set of honing stone is shown in Fig. 5.27.
- The various abrasives used to make honing stones are silicon carbide, aluminium oxide, diamond or cubic boron nitride.
- Silicon carbide is used for honing cast iron and non-ferrous materials, where as aluminium oxide is used to hone steel parts.

- Diamond is also used as an abrasive to hone parts made of ceramics or hard carbides.
- The abrasive grain size ranges from 80 to 600 grit. Almost every material can be efficiently honed.
- Materials of all varieties, cast iron, aluminium, magnesium, brass, bronze, glass, ceramics, hard rubber, graphite and silver are the examples of honed material.

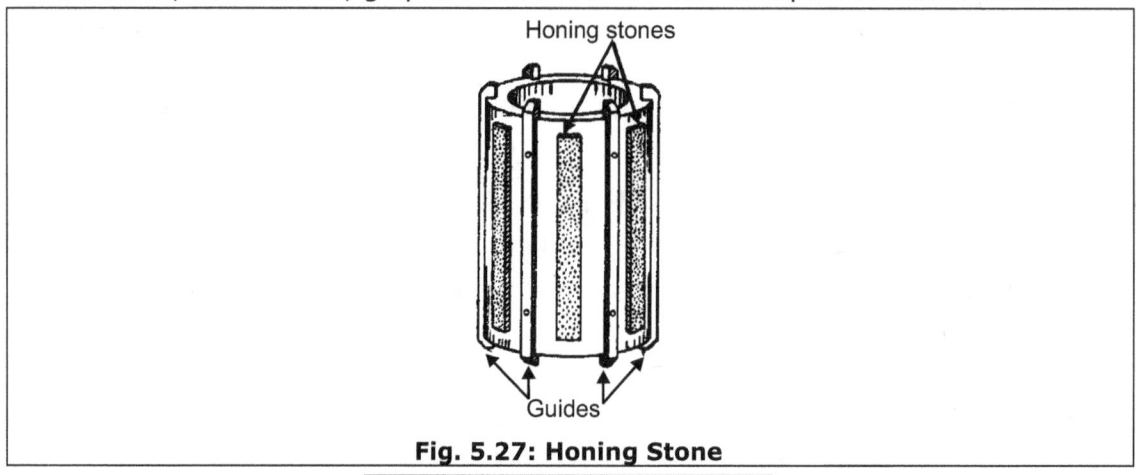

Fig. 5.27: Honing Stone

5.29.2 Honing Principle

- When honing is done manually, the honing tool is rotated and work piece is passed back and forth over the tool.
- Length of motion is such that the stones extend beyond the work piece surface at the end of each stroke.
- For precision honing, the work is usually held in the fixture and the tool is given a slow reciprocating motion as it rotates.
- The stones are thus given a complex motion as rotation is combined with oscillatory axial motion.
- These two motions combine to give a resulting cross hatch lay pattern.

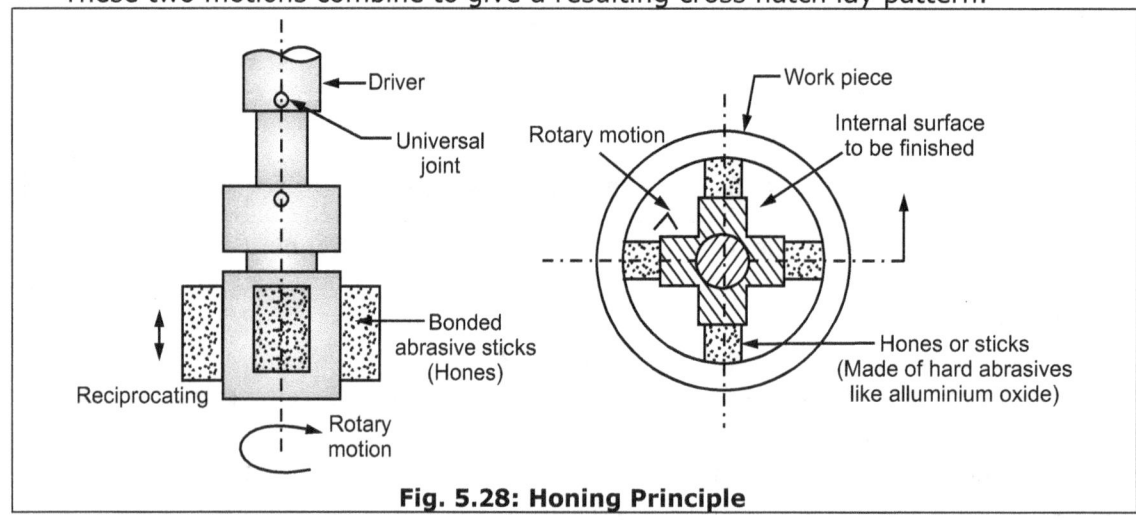

Fig. 5.28: Honing Principle

5.29.3 Honing Set-up

- Honing stones may be held in the honing head by cementing them to metal shells, which are clamped into holder or they are cemented directly into holders.

- During honing operation, the spindle of the honing machine rotates the hone and simultaneously reciprocates it in a work piece.

- The spindle speed is generally 2 m/sec for rotation and 0.5 m/sec for reciprocating motion.

- Coolants are essential to the operation of this process, to flush away small chips and to keep temperatures uniform.

- Sulphurized mineral oil or lard oil is generally used for this purpose.

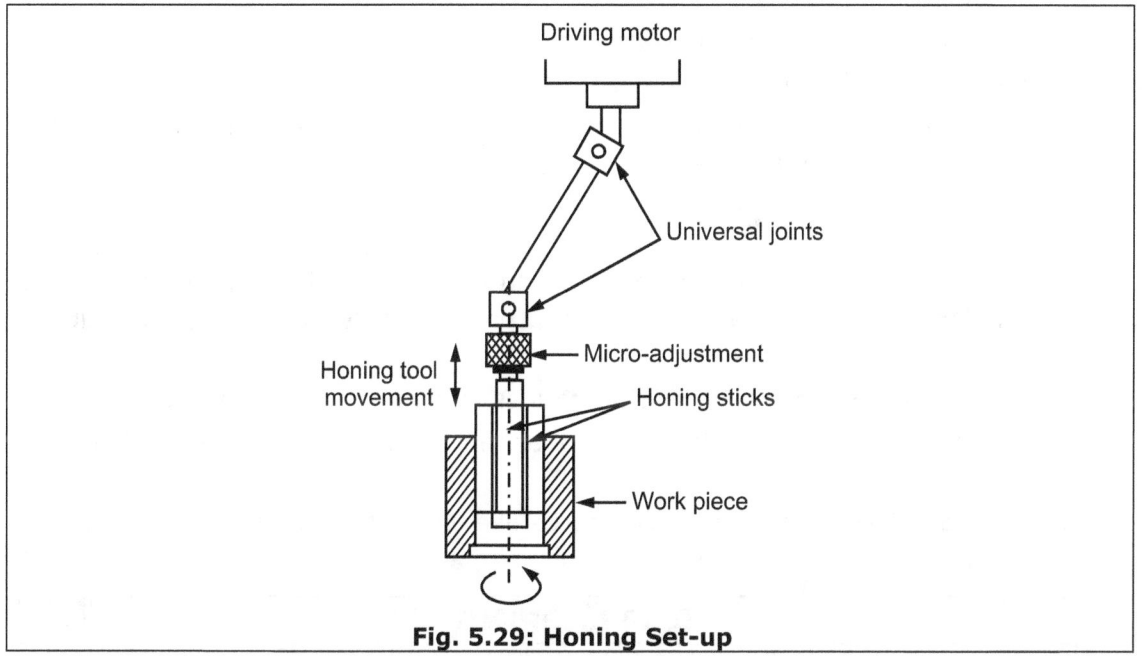

Fig. 5.29: Honing Set-up

5.29.4 Uses of Honing

1. It is used to correct some out of roundness.

2. It is used to superfinish internal bore or holes.

3. It is used to correct axial distortion.

4. It is used to remove tool marks and scratches.

5. It is used to reduce friction between mating parts by increasing surface finish.

6. To obtain better fit on mating parts.

5.29.5 Advantages of Honing

1. The honing process enables highly accurate holes, as the possibility of vibration is very less.

2. Many holes can be honed simultaneously on multiple spindle machines.

3. Holes of any dimension can be honed.

4. The size can be controlled easily.

5. As compared to other hole finishing methods, high productivity at low cost is obtained.

6. Minimum of heat and distortion of work material.

5.29.6 Disadvantages of Honing

1. It is impossible to improve lack of straightness in holes.

2. Horizontal boring creates oval holes.

3. Honing stone wear out fast.

4. It is difficult to hone tough non-ferrous metals due to glazing or clogging of the pores of the abrasive stick.

5.29.7 Applications of Honing

1. Honing is mostly performed for finishing cylindrical holes like in gun barrels, cylinders of I.C. Engine, hydraulic and pneumatic cylinder bore, long tubular parts.

2. Internal finishing of bearings, ring gauges, ends of connecting rod.

3. For finishing external surfaces like gear teeth, valve seat, recess of balls and roller bearings.

4. External finishing of cylindrical parts like piston rods, piston pins, spindle shaft.

5.30 LAPPING

- Lapping is also one of the abrasive processes used to produce finished (smoothly accurate) surfaces.

- Lapping is a precision finishing process done on precision tools, gauges, valves where resistance to wear of moving parts, better sealing characteristic are important.

- It gives a very high degree of accuracy and smoothness so it is used in production of optical lenses, metallic bearing surfaces, measuring gauges, surface plates and other measuring instruments.

- All the metal parts that are subjected to fatigue loading or those surfaces that must be used to establish a seal with a mating part are often lapped.

- The process of lapping uses a bonded abrasive tool and a fluid suspension having very small sized abrasive particles vibrating between the work piece and the lapping tool.

- A thin layer of metal around 0.005 to 0.01 mm usually removed by lapping.

- Thus, lapping is an abrading process employed for improving the surface finish by reducing roughness, waviness and other irregularities on surface.

- The basic purpose of lapping is to minimize the extremely minute irregularities left on work piece after machining.

5.30.1 Principle of Lapping

- The process of lapping is shown in Fig. 5.30. The fluid with abrasive particles is referred as lapping compound. It appears as a chalky paste.

- Normally the fluid used in lapping compound is oil or kerosene. The fluid should have slightly lubricating properties to make the action of abrasive mild in nature.

- Abrasives used in lapping compound are aluminium oxide and silicon carbide. Their girt size is kept 300 to 600 μm.

- It is hypothesized that two alternative cutting mechanisms are working in the process of lapping.

- In first mechanism the abrasive particles roll and slide between the lapping tool and workpiece. These particles produce small cuts on both surfaces.

- Another mechanism suppose to work in lapping is that the abrasives become imbedded in the lap surface to give cutting action like in case of grinding.

- It is assumed that lapping is due to the combination of these two above mentioned mechanism.

- Lapping can be done manually but use of lapping machine makes the process accurate, consistent and efficient.

- Lapping is an abrasive rubbing process in which loose abrasive with vehicles functions as cutting points taking momentary support of the lap.

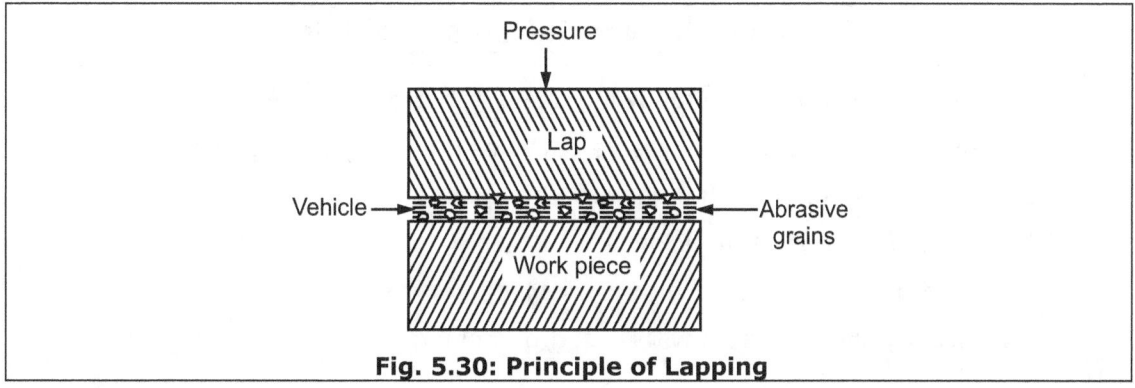

Fig. 5.30: Principle of Lapping

5.30.2 Lap Material

- The lap material should be softer than work piece, so that abrasive gets embedded in the lap until it fractures from the pressure of lapping action.

- Cast iron is the best lap material. But brass, bronze, lead and soft steel can also be used.

5.30.3 Abrasives used in Lapping

- In lapping process natural as well as artificial abrasives are used.

- For harder work piece hard abrasive and for softer work piece soft abrasives are used.

- Aluminium oxide is used for lapping soft ferrous and non-ferrous metals. Silicon carbide and corundum is used for hardened steel parts.

- Diamond is the hardest material and is used for lapping cemented carbides and precious stones.

- For lapping small components, diamond dust or boron carbide in the finest grain size gives better results.

- For obtaining highly reflective surface without any significant material removal softer abrasive such as emery is used.

5.30.4 Vehicle used in Lapping

- Lubricant to hold and retain the abrasive grains during lapping is known as vehicle.

- The purpose of vehicle is to suspend abrasive and keep grains separated as well as lubricate the work.

- The general vehicle used is machine oil, water soluble oil, vegetable or olive oil, mineral oil, petroleum jelly and grease.

5.30.5 Characteristics of Vehicle

- The vehicle used should have following characteristics:
  - It should able to hold the abrasive particles uniformly during operation.
  - Its viscosity should not change with change in temperature.
  - It should not evaporate quickly.
  - It should be non-corrosive with work piece.
  - Its viscosity should match with speed of lapping.

5.30.6 Lapping Speed and Pressure

- For soft material 0.07 to 0.2 Kg/cm^2 and for hard material pressure upto 0.7 Kg/cm^2 is applied.
- And normal speed used for lapping is between 1.5 m/s to 4 m/s.

5.30.7 Set up of Lapping

- The lapping process is shown in Fig. 5.31.
- Typical vertical spindle lapping machine consists of two circular plates, one over another.
- The lower plate has continuously rotating rings or cages, in which work with loose abrasive grain and vehicle is placed.
- The bottom plate is in rotary motion.
- These two motions provide the gyratory motion to work piece.
- The pressure is applied on top plate and bottom.

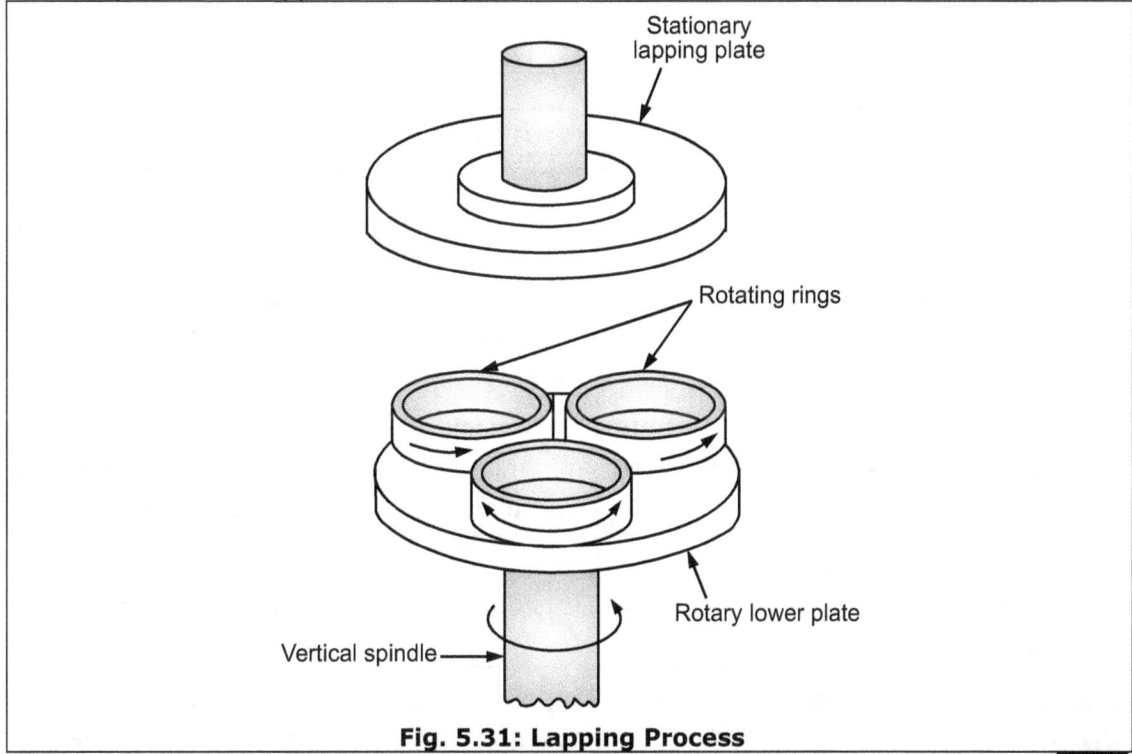

Fig. 5.31: Lapping Process

5.30.8 Advantages of Lapping   [S-15]

1. Any material hard or soft can be lapped.
2. There is no warping of lapped components.
3. It provides liquid and gas tight seals without using gaskets and piston rings.
4. It removes the errors in gears and make transmission noise less.
5. Provides superfine surface finish, greater uniformity and optical flatness.

5.30.9 Limitations of Lapping

1. It requires experience and skilled operator.
2. Trial and error may be needed to get uniform result.

5.30.10 Applications of Lapping   [S-15]

1. Press work dies.
2. Moulds for casting.
3. Limit gauges.
4. Surface plate.
5. Engine valve and valve seat.
6. Races of ball and roller bearings.
7. Piston rings.
8. Slip gauges.
9. Crank shaft.

5.30.11 Difference between Honing and Lapping   [w-14]

Honing	Lapping
Honing is an abrading process used mainly for finishing round holes	Lapping is an abrading process employed for improving the surface finish by reducing roughness, waviness and other irregularities on surface.
Honing is primarily used to correct out of roundness, taper, tool marks and axial distortion.	The basic purpose of lapping is to minimize the extremely minute irregularities left on work piece after machining.
It is done by means of bonded abrasive stones called hones.	It is done by means of Cast iron laps.
Mostly honing is done on internal cylindrical surfaces, such as automobile cylinder walls.	Lapping is a precision finishing process done on parts where resistance to wear of moving parts is important.

5.31 POLISHING

- Polishing is carried out with the help of above mentioned polishing wheels.
- Abrasive grains are bonded by gluing to the outside periphery of the wheel.

- After the abrasives have been worn down and used up, the wheel is replenished with new grits.

- Polishing is done to make metal surface smoother and to produce a more uniform surface by removing deep scratches, nicks, discolouration and other surface imperfections occurring due to grinding.

- It is generally used as intermediate operation done after grinding and before buffing.

5.31.1 Principle of Polishing

- An abrasive belt (endless) with very fine grade abrasive rotates continuously on two rollers.

- The work piece to be polished is hand held over this rotating belt.

- In this way a very thin layer is removed from the work piece.

- Sometimes polishing is performed to obtain a tolerance value of 0.025 mm or less.

5.31.2 Applications of Polishing

- Polishing is done for internal work on tools, dies, parts of fountain pens, parts of bicycle, turbine blades of jet engine, sole plates of electric iron etc.

- It is also used for small hand tools like axes, hatches, screw drivers, hammer heads etc.

- Internal work on tools and dies.

5.31.3 Difference between Lapping and Polishing

Polishing	Lapping
Polishing produce a shiny surface.	Lapping does not produce bright shiny surface.
Polishing removes negligible amount of metal.	Lapping removes metal from the surface to be finished.
Polishing consists of producing a kind of plastic flow of the surface crystals so that the high spots are made to fill the low spots.	Lapping involves cutting action.

5.32 BUFFING [S-16, 17]

- Buffing is a finishing operation which is usually performed after polishing.
- It provides much higher lustrous and reflective surface finish or glossy finish that cannot be obtained by polishing.
- Buffing is like a polishing operation in which the work piece is brought in contact with a revolving cloth buffing wheel that usually has been charged with a very find abrasive.
- Buffing is different from polishing due to the fact that polishing is an abrasive operation used for metal removal, whereas buffing involves gentle plastic deformation of a surface to give bright smooth finish.
- Buffing status is somewhere in between polishing and lapping.
- A minor cutting action with microchip is done in case of buffing. Buffing wheels are made of discs of liners, cotton, broad cloth and canvas.
- These are made more or less firm by the amount of stitching used to fasten the layers of the cloth together.
- Buffing tools are enough flexible to polish upto interior of intricate cavities.

5.32.1 Set-up of Buffing

- The work pieces are held in fixtures on a suitable rotating worktable so as to move the buffing wheels.
- The buffing wheel is rotated with high speed and work piece to be buffed is made to rub against the charged wheel.
- The abrasives are bided to the wheel with the help of grease, kerosene or paraffin like binders.
- The abrasives removes the minute amount of metal from the work piece, eliminate fine scratches and gives high reflective surface finish.
- The set-up of buffing process is shown in Fig. 5.32.
- Buffing wheels are made of discs of linen, cotton, broad cloth or canvas that are made firm by stitching, to fasten the layers of cloth together.

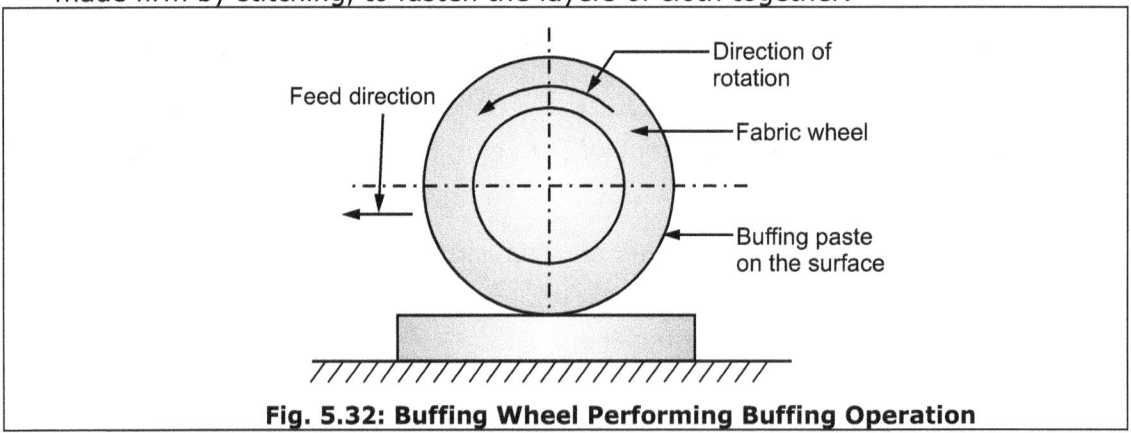

Fig. 5.32: Buffing Wheel Performing Buffing Operation

5.32.2 Applications of Buffing

- It is used for finishing of automobile parts, motor cycle parts, bicycles.
- For mirror like finish in sport items, tools, furniture, fixtures.
- To provide aesthetic finish to home appliances and house hold utensils etc.
- For finish in commercial and residential hardware.

5.32.3 Difference between Polishing and Buffing

Polishing	Buffing
Polishing is done to make metal surface smoother and to produce a more uniform surface.	Buffing is a finishing operation which provide much higher lustrous and reflective surface finish that can not be obtained by polishing.
It is done by removing deep scratches, nicks, discolouration and other surface imperfections occurring due to grinding.	It is done by rotating wheel with high speed and work piece to be buffed is made to rub against the charged wheel.
It is generally used as intermediate operation done after grinding and before buffing.	Buffing is a finishing operation which is usually performed after polishing.

5.33 BURNISHING   [W-14; S-15, 17]

- Burnishing is a cold working process, by which improvement in surface finish, dimensional accuracy and work hardening can be obtained without removing the metal.
- Burnishing is a non-cutting operation and uses no abrasives.
- It is a process of producing bright, shining and smooth surface on metals.
- It is a finishing operation and is normally done on parts which are turned, bored, reamed or ground. Any ductile or malleable material with hardness less than 49 HRC can be successfully burnished.
- Burnishing is done as supplementary process after metal cutting operations like turning, milling, shaping operations.
- Lapping and Honing is eliminated with burnishing.
- Burnishing is a metal finishing process that involves physical displacement of surface irregularities rather than cutting or grinding.
- The process involves moving a set or hardened rollers or balls against the metal surface under pressure, thereby causing microscopic blemishes in the metal surface to flatten for a perfect, mirror surface.

- In addition to the fine finish achieved with roller burnishing, a metal part is also work hardened during the process, thereby leaving its surface better able to withstand wear and corrosion.
- Both internal and external surfaces can be burnished using an appropriate tool.
- The burnishing pressure to be applied depends upon factors like ductility, tensile strength, diameter, shape of the rolls etc.

5.33.1 Burnishing Principle

- In this process fine surface finish is produced by the planetary rotation of hardened rollers over a bored or turned metal surface.
- All the machined surfaces consist of a series of peaks and valleys (surface irregularities) of irregular height and spacing. The plastic deformation created by burnishing is a displacement of the material from the peaks which cold flows under pressure into the valleys.
- There is rubbing and peening action on work surface by smooth but hard tool, spreading minute surface irregularities into flat surface.
- This helps to flatten the high spots by allowing plastic flow of the metal. The edges of the metal can be smoothened by pushing it through a die that will smooth out the burrs and the blanked edge caused by the die break.
- The result is a mirror-like finish with a tough, work hardened, wear and corrosion resistant surface.
- The principle of burnishing is shown in Fig. 5.33.

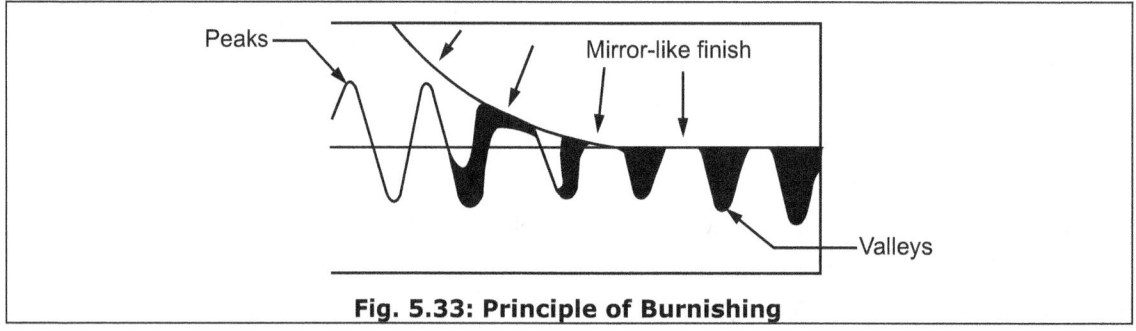

Fig. 5.33: Principle of Burnishing

5.33.2 Burnishing Tool

- A roller burnishing tool is shown in figure 5.34.
- Burnishing tools are generally made of high Speed Steel or Carbide material that is positioned in slots along with a retaining cage.
- It has a number of tapered and polished precision rollers. An inversely tapered mandrel is used for rotating the rollers.

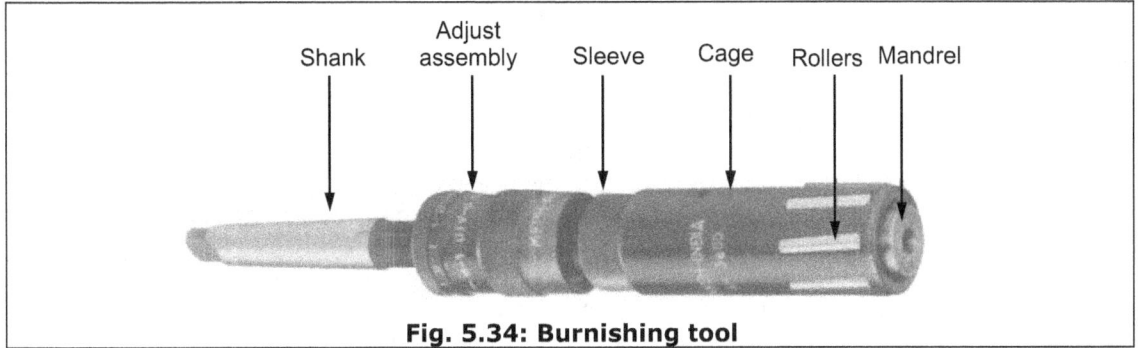

Shank   Adjust assembly   Sleeve   Cage   Rollers   Mandrel

Fig. 5.34: Burnishing tool

5.33.3 Advantages of Burnishing Process   [W-14]

- Internal and external surfaces can be burnished.
- Improves surface hardness and fatigue strength.
- Long Tool Life, No Operator Skill Required, Low Torque & Power Requirements.
- It also eliminates the Lapping and Honing processes.
- Produces mirror finish in One Pass with accurate sizing and close tolerances.
- No Additional Machine Investment is required as the tool can be attached to any Standard Machine Tool available in the Shop
- Assembly problems are totally eliminated since part dimensions are maintained within tolerances.

5.33.4 Disadvantages of Burnishing Process

- It is very important to wear eye protection when burnishing.
- Polishing has to be performed is an important first step in the burnishing process.
- It is costly process to obtain high surface finish and tolerance.
- Skilled operator is required to perform the process.

5.33.5 Comparison between Burnishing and Polishing   [S-15]

Polishing	Burnishing
1. It produces a smooth finish, but not a hard one.	1. It produces a smooth as well as hard finish.
2. Polishing is more about removing material to obtain the desired finish.	2. Burnishing is a stretching and hardening with minimal material loss.
3. It will be necessary to use magnification when polishing in order to see the fine details of the surface being polished.	3. Such thing is not needed.
4. Polishing can be done with any kind of abrasive or sandpaper or stones are common polishing agents.	4. It is done by balls or rollers made of metal.
5. Less expensive	5. Comparatively expensive.

Important Points

Grinding

- It can be defined as a metal cutting operation performed on the work piece by means of a rotating abrasive wheel called as grinding wheel.
- The grinding wheel has thousands of cutting edges formed out of these abrasive grains projecting from its surface which acts as tiny cutting edges.
- The metal removing rate in grinding operation is comparatively less as compared to other machining processes.

Need of grinding

- To obtain very close tolerance on the work piece.
- For machining hard surface which are difficult to be machined
- Used for sharpening the cutting tools.

Advantages of grinding

- Grinding is the only method of cutting hardened steel etc.
- Extremely smooth finish desirable at surfaces can be produced
- No marks as a result of feeding.

Cylindrical centre type grinders

- Cylindrical grinders are used to produce cylindrical or conical shapes on a work piece.
- The work piece is mounted between the centres and the face of the grinding wheel passes over the external surface of work piece.
- The cylindrical centre type grinders may be of plain or universal or type.

Centre-less type grinders

- In centre-less grinding, work is not held between the centers as in cylindrical grinding.
- Work piece is held by a combination of wheels and a work rest blade.
- This eliminates the use of work holding devices. Also there is no need to centre the work piece.

Internal grinders

- Internal grinders are used mainly for finishing round holes.
- It is also used for finishing internal bores and tubes having more than one diameter.

Surface grinders

- Surface grinder is used to finish the surface produced by milling, shaper and planer.
- It is intended to grind flat surface.
- Surface grinder may be of reciprocating or rotary table type. The spindle may be vertical or horizontal.

Grinding wheel composition

- Grinding wheel is multi-tooth cutter made-up of many hard particles known as abrasive.
- Abrasive grains are mixed with suitable bond which hold the particles when wheel is in use.
- The wheel consists of one piece or made of segments joined together.
- The properties of grinding wheel depends on type of Abrasive, type of bond, Grit or Grain size, Grade of the wheel and Structure of the wheel.

Elements of grinding wheel

- The various elements of grinding wheel are Abrasive, Bond, Grit ,Grade and Structure

Size of the grinding wheel

- The size of the grinding wheel is specified by the following parameters in the given sequence.
- Diameter of the wheel.
- Thickness or face width of the wheel.
- Diameter of the central bore of the wheel.

Designation of Grinding Wheel
- It is also referred as specification of the grinding wheel or marking scheme of grinding wheel in the following sequence.

Abrasive Type	Abrasive Grains	Grade	Structure (Use Optional)	Nature of Bond	Manufacturer's Symbol (Type of Bond)

Need of Surface Finish
- To reduce the friction between two mating parts having a relative motion.
- To achieve dimensional and geometrical accuracies.
- For good appearance.

Honing
- Honing is a surface finishing operation based on abrasive action performed by a set of bonded abrasive stones called hones.
- Honing is primarily used to correct out of roundness, taper, tool marks and axial distortion.

Lapping
- Lapping is also one of the abrasive processes used to produce finished (smoothly accurate) surfaces.
- Lapping is a precision finishing process done on precision tools, gauges, valves where resistance to wear of moving parts, better sealing characteristic are important.

Polishing
- Polishing is carried out with the help of above mentioned polishing wheels.
- Polishing is done to make metal surface smoother and to produce a more uniform surface by removing deep scratches, nicks, discolouration and other surface imperfections occurring due to grinding.

Buffing
- Buffing is a finishing operation which is usually performed after polishing.
- It provides much higher lustrous and reflective surface finish or glossy finish that cannot be obtained by polishing.

Burnishing
- Burnishing is a cold working process, by which improvement in surface finish, dimensional accuracy and work hardening can be obtained without removing the metal.
- Burnishing is done as supplementary process after metal cutting operations like turning, milling, shaping operations.

Practice Questions

1. Define grinding.   [Refer Section 5.1]
2. Explain the principle of grinding.   [Refer Section 5.1]
3. Compare between grinding and other machining process.   [Refer Section 5.2]
4. State the need of grinding.   [Refer Section 5.3]
5. State the advantages of grinding process.   [Refer Section 5.4]
6. Give classification of grinding machines.   [Refer Section 5.5]
7. Explain the construction and working of plain centre typical cylindrical grinding machine with neat sketch.   [Refer Section 5.10.1]
8. Explain the construction and working of centreless type grinder with suitable sketch.
                                                                       [Refer Section 5.11]
9. State the advantages of centreless grinding.   [Refer Section 5.11.1]
10. State the disadvantages of centreless grinding.   [Refer Section 5.11.2]
11. State the applications of centreless grinder.   [Refer Section 5.11.3]
12. Explain the principle of planetary internal grinders with neat sketch.
                                                                       [Refer Section 5.12.1]

13. Explain centreless internal grinder with suitable sketch. **[Refer Section 5.12.1]**
14. Explain the principle of horizontal spindle reciprocating table surface grinder with suitable sketch. **[Refer Section 5.13.1]**
15. Explain the principle of horizontal spindle rotary table surface grinder with suitable sketch. **[Refer Section 5.13.2]**
16. Explain the working principle of vertical spindle reciprocating table surface grinding machine with suitable sketch. **[Refer Section 5.13.3]**
17. Explain the working principle of vertical spindle rotary table surface grinder with neat sketch. **[Refer Section 5.13.4]**
18. Draw the various shapes of grinding wheel. **[Refer Section 5.15]**
19. Explain various grinding wheel with suitable sketch. **[Refer Section 5.15]**
20. Describe the various elements of grinding wheel. **[Refer Section 5.16]**
21. Define abrasive and explain types of abrasives. **[Refer Section 5.16.1]**
22. Define bond. What are its types. Explain any one type of bond. **[Refer Section 5.16.2]**
23. What is meant by grain size or grit? **[Refer Section 5.16.3]**
24. What is grade of grinding wheel? **[Refer Section 5.16.4]**
25. Define structure. **[Refer Section 5.16.5]**
26. How is the size of grinding wheel specified? **[Refer Section 5.17]**
27. How is a grinding wheel designated. **[Refer Section 5.18]**
28. Explain the factors considered for selection of grinding wheel. **[Refer Section 5.19]**
29. Describe balancing of grinding wheel. **[Refer Section 5.20]**
30. Explain defects in grinding wheel. **[Refer Section 5.21]**
31. What are the causes and remedies for loading and glazing. **[Refer Section 5.22]**
32. What are the methods to remove defects in grinding. **[Refer Section 5.23]**
33. Explain trueing and dressing. **[Refer Section 5.23]**
34. Compare between loading and glazing. **[Refer Section 5.24]**
35. Compare between trueing and dressing. **[Refer Section 5.25]**
36. State the need of surface finish. **[Refer Section 5.28]**
37. Define honing. **[Refer Section 5.29]**
38. Explain having principle. **[Refer Section 5.29.2]**
39. Explain the honing setup with sketch. **[Refer Section 5.29.3]**
40. State uses of honing. **[Refer Section 5.29.4]**
41. State advantages of honing. **[Refer Section 5.29.5]**
42. State disadvantages of honing. **[Refer Section 5.29.6]**
43. Give applications of honing. **[Refer Section 5.29.7]**
44. Define lapping. **[Refer Section 5.30]**
45. Explain the principal of lapping. **[Refer Section 5.30.1]**
46. State the characteristics of lapping. **[Refer Section 5.30.5]**
47. State advantages of lapping. **[Refer Section 5.30.8]**
48. Give applications of lapping. **[Refer Section 5.30.10]**
49. Compare between honing and lapping. **[Refer Section 5.30.11]**
50. Define polishing. **[Refer Section 5.31]**
51. Give the applications of polishing. **[Refer Section 5.31.2]**
52. Differentiate between lapping and polishing. **[Refer Section 5.31.3]**
53. Define buffing. **[Refer Section 5.32]**
54. Explain the set-up of buffing. **[Refer Section 5.32.1]**
55. Give the applications of buffing. **[Refer Section 5.32.2]**
56. Compare between polishing and buffing. **[Refer Section 5.32.3]**
57. Define Burnishing. **[Refer Section 5.33]**
58. Explain burnishing principle. **[Refer Section 5.33.1]**
59. Give advantages of burnishing process. **[Refer Section 5.33.3]**
60. Give disadvantages of burnishing process. **[Refer Section 5.33.4]**
61. Compare between burnishing and polishing. **[Refer Section 5.33.5]**

MSBTE Questions & Answers as Per 'G' Scheme

Winter 2014

1. What are precision grinders? Explain with a neat sketch the working of centreless grinding machine. **(6 M)**
Ans. Refer Sections 5.5.2 and 5.11.
2. How grinding wheel is designated? **(4 M)**
Ans. Refer Sections 5.18 and 5.16.
3. What are safety precautions to be observed while using grinding machines? **(4 M)**
Ans. Refer Section 5.26.
4. Differentiate between honing and lapping. **(4 M)**
Ans. Refer Section 5.29.11.
5. What is purnishing? What are its advantages? **(4 M)**
Ans. Refer Section 5.32 and 5.32.3.

Summer 2015

1. Explain what is burnishing. **(4 M)**
Ans. Refer Section 5.32.
2. Compare between burnishing and polishing. **(4 M)**
Ans. Refer Section 5.32.5.
3. State advantages and applications of lapping. **(4 M)**
Ans. Refer Sections 5.29.8 and 5.29.10.
4. What is criteria for solution of grinding wheel? **(4 M)**
Ans. Refer Section 5.19.
5. State classification of grinding machines. **(4 M)**
Ans. Refer Section 5.5.
6. Explain each term of grinding wheel designated as $200 \times 15 \times 20$ WA 46 K 5 V 17. **(4 M)**
Ans. Refer Example 5.4 in Section 5.18.

Winter 2015

1. Write safety precautions to be taken during grinding process. **(4 M)**
Ans. Refer Section 5.26.
2. What is centreless grinding? Explain the methods of feed in centreless grinding. **(6 M)**
Ans. Refer Section 5.11.
3. Explain each term of grinding wheel designation WA46K5V17.
Ans. Refer Example 5.1.

Summer 2016

1. Explain grinding wheel dressing. **(4 M)**
Ans. Refer Section 5.23.2.
2. Give the classification of grinding machines. **(4 M)**
Ans. Refer Section 5.5.
3. Sketch surface grinding machine and explain its working. **(4 M)**
Ans. Refer Section 5.13.
4. What are the advantages and disadvantages of honing process. **(4 M)**
Ans. Refer Sections 5.28.5 and 5.28.6.
5. Explain buffing operation. State its advantages. **(4 M)**
Ans. Refer Section 5.31.
6. Explain with a neat sketch machine lapping process. **(4 M)**
Ans. Refer Section 5.29.1.

Winter 2016

1. Explain with sketch honing process. **(4 M)**

Ans. Refer Sections 5.29 and 5.29.1.

2. Explain how grinding wheel is designated. **(4 M)**

Ans. **Grinding wheel is designated by six symbols representing following properties of grinding wheel.**

- It is also referred as specification of the grinding wheel or marking scheme of grinding wheel.
- Method of grinding wheel specification differ with the manufacturer and country, in order to bring the uniformity, Bureau of Indian Standards has suggested the marking scheme consisting of following six characters in sequence.
- This codification is as per Bureau Of Indian Standard Code IS 551: 1989.

0	1	2	3	4	5	6
Prefix	Abrasive Type	Abrasive Grains	Grade	Structure (Use Optional)	Nature of Bond	Manufacturer's Symbol (Type of Bond)

Prefix:

- Manufacturer may use a suitable prefix preceding the type of abrasive notation to indicate his own trade brand of the abrasive used.
- Use of prefix is optional.

Manufacturer's symbol:

- Manufacturer may use a suitable suffix to the type of bond.
- Use of suffix is also optional.

3. Explain centreless grinding with sketch. **(4 M)**

Ans. Refer Section 5.11.

4. Discuss grinding wheel dressing and trueing. **(4 M)**

Ans. Refer Section 5.23.2.

Summer 2017

1. Draw neat labelled sketch of centreless grinding. Explain its working.

Ans. Refer Section 5.11.

2. Explain: (i) Honing, (ii) Lapping.

Ans. **(i) Honing:** Refer Section 5.29.

(ii) Lapping: Refer Section 5.30.

3. Explain in short: (i) Burnishing, (ii) Buffing

Ans. Refer Sections 5.32 and 5.33.

4. State safety precautions in grinding.

Ans. Refer Section 5.26.

■■■

Chapter 6

MAINTENANCE OF MACHINE TOOLS

About This Chapter

At the end of this chapter students will be able to:

➲ Differentiate between the various types of maintenance.

➲ Use and understand the maintenance manual.

➲ Keep record of the types of maintenance used.

➲ Analyse repair cycle for any machine.

6.1 INTRODUCTION

- The dictionary defines maintenance as follows: "the work of keeping something in proper condition". This means that maintenance is action taken to prevent a device or component from failing or to repair normal equipment to keep it in proper working order.

- Maintenance is defined as the actions intended to retain an item in, or restore it to, a state in which it can perform a required function.

- Maintenance can also be defined as a set of organised activities that are carried out in order to keep an item in its best operational condition with minimum cost acquired.

- The older concept of maintenance was to repair a machine only when the breakdown occurs. Therefore, in the earlier stages of industrial development, a very little attention was paid to maintenance of machine. It was carried out only when the machine breakdowns. The failure in machine may occur very early in its life due to a material fault or much latter due to wear and fatigue. This may result in loss of production. So maintenance should be planned at regular intervals to prevent uncalled breakdown.

- With the advancement of technology and industrial growth, the maintenance of machine tool is gaining importance. Research made in this field has proved that preventive maintenance of equipment not only increases its life but also results in fewer breakdowns, resulting in huge savings.

6.2 OBJECTIVES OF MACHINE TOOL MAINTENANCE [S-13]

- The maintenance of machine tool is an important part of the total productive effort. It is necessary to serve the following objectives:

  (i) To minimize the number of breakdown.

  (ii) To keep plant in good working condition at the lowest possible cost.

  (iii) To minimize the hindrance and interruption of work.

  (iv) To carry out the work of all the machines smoothly.

  (v) Minimizing the loss of production because of equipment failure.

  (vi) Prolonging the life of capital assets by minimizing the rate of wear and tear.

  (vii) To minimize accidents through regular inspection and repair of safety devices.

  (viii) To improve the quality of products and to improve productivity.

6.3 CAUSES OF BREAKDOWN [W-13]

- If proper attention is not given to the machine tool then it will fail. But sometimes instead of regular check-ups there could be breakdown because of the following reasons:

  (i) Excessive friction between the parts. (insufficient/improper/lack of lubrication).

  (ii) Failure to replace parts that are known to wear.

  (iii) Indifferent attitude towards minor faults. (For example, vibrations, temperature).

  (iv) Improper and neglected cooling system.

  (v) Poor foundation, excessive vibrations, unusual sounds.

  (vi) External factors like excessive/low voltage, wrong fuel etc.

  (vii) Overloading of machine, wrong fuel, faults in some items of equipment.

  (viii) Improper handling of the machine by the operator (Lack of knowledge).

6.4 NEED FOR MACHINE TOOL MAINTENANCE

- As every person requires maintenance, machine tool also requires maintenance to keep it in proper working condition. The need for machine tool maintenance is:

  (i) Its accuracy does not deteriorate.

  (ii) It manufactures the components most economically.

  (iii) It remains in working condition at all the times.

For this, machine tools are inspected periodically against

(a) Dust, heat and humidity.

(b) Vibration and Chatter.

(c) Use of wrong or inadequate lubrication.

(d) Wrong use and overloading of the machine tools.

(e) Wear of slideways, bearings and other components.

(f) Corrosion of some parts due to the use of wrong lubricants etc.

6.5 BENEFITS OF MAINTENANCE

(i) It increases the efficiency and speed of the equipment.

(ii) It helps to avoid the replacing of the parts of the equipment before the scheduled time.

(iii) It reduces the cost when the work done is faster and the machine doesn't break down in the middle of the work schedule.

(iv) It is better because it saves from spending too much when the machine breaks down completely and requires a big time repair or a replacement.

(v) It helps to save money since maintenance would cost lesser than repairs and replacement.

(vi) It also ensures the safety of the person who is working with the machine since if the machine is not in a proper condition it might also lead to a major accident which is not desirable at all.

6.6 IMPACT OF POOR MAINTENANCE

• Maintenance operations include all efforts to keep production facilities and equipments in an acceptable operating condition.

• Failure or malfunctioning of machines and equipments in manufacturing and service industries have a direct impact on the following:

(i) Production capacity:

  o Machines idled by breakdowns cannot produce, thus the capacity of the system is reduced.

(ii) Production costs:

  o Labour costs per unit rise because of idle labour due to machine breakdowns.

  o When machine malfunctions result in scrap, unit labour and material costs increase.

  o Besides, cost of maintenance which includes such costs as costs of providing repair facilities, repair crews, preventive maintenance inspections, spare parts and stand by machines will increase as machines break down frequently.

(iii) Product and service quality:

- o Poorly maintained equipments produce low quality products.
- o Equipments that have not been properly maintained have frequent break downs and cannot provide adequate service to customers.

(iv) Employee or customer safety:

- o Worn-out equipment is likely to fail at any moment and these failures can cause injuries to the workers, working on those equipments.

(v) Customer satisfaction:

- o When production equipments break own, products often cannot be produced according to the master production schedules, due to work stoppages.
- o This will lead to delayed deliveries of products to the customers.

6.7 IMPORTANCE OF MAINTENANCE ACTIVITY   [W-14]

(i) Quality of product

- o Inconsistencies in equipments lead to variability in product characteristics.
- o It may also result in defective parts that fail to meet the established specifications.
- o Beyond just preventing break downs, it is necessary to keep equipments operating within specifications (i.e. process capability) that will produce high level of quality.

(ii) Cost control

- o Good maintenance management is important for the company's cost control.
- o As companies go in for automation to become more competitive, they increasingly rely on equipments to produce a greater percentage of their output.
- o It becomes more important that, equipments operate reliably within specifications.
- o The cost of idle time is higher as equipment becomes more high-tech and expensive For example, CNC, FMS and robots.

(iii) Customer service

- o Dependability of service is one of the performance measures by which a company can distinguish itself from others.
- o To establish a competitive edge and to provide good customer service, companies must have reliable equipments that will respond to customer demands when needed.

- o Equipments must be kept in reliable condition without costly work stoppage and down time due to repairs, if the company is to remain productive and competitive.

(iv) Market reputation

- o Many manufacturing organizations, particularly those with JIT programs are operating with inventories so low that, they offer no protection in the event of a lengthy equipment failure.
- o Beyond the cost of idle equipment, idle labour, and lost ales that can result from a breakdown, there is a danger of permanently losing market shares to companies that are more reliable.
- o Maintenance function can help prevent such as occurrence.

(v) Cost of investment

- o Organizations like airlines and oil refineries have huge investments in the equipment.
- o Equipment failure will be disastrous for such companies.
- o They need proper maintenance to keep the equipment in good condition.

6.8 RESPONSIBILITY OF MAINTENANCE ENGINEER

- The maintenance Engineer has to perform the following duties in general:
  - o Maintain and service all machinery.
  - o Troubleshoot faults with mechanical, electrical, hydraulic and pneumatic systems in a wide variety of situations.
  - o Monitor and execute Planned Preventative Maintenance on various systems.
  - o Analysis of repetitive equipment failures.
  - o Estimation of maintenance costs and evaluation of alternatives.
  - o Forecasting of spare parts.
  - o Assessing and reporting safety hazards associated with maintenance of equipment.

6.9 TYPES OF MAINTENANCE   [W-12, 16, S-13]

- The following are the types of maintenance followed in general:
  - (i)   Preventive maintenance.
  - (ii) Predictive maintenance.
  - (iii) Breakdown maintenance.
  - (iv) Corrective maintenance.
  - (v)   Scheduled maintenance.

6.10 PREVENTIVE MAINTENANCE   [S-12, 15; W-13]

- It is the planned maintenance of machine tools at regular intervals in order to prevent or minimize breakdown.

- The primary goal of preventive maintenance is to prevent the failure of equipment before it actually occurs.

- After preventive maintenance repairs, the equipment's health is restored back nearly to the equipment's original condition.

- Preventive maintenance covers vast area like routine inspection, minor repairs, lubrication, cleaning, replacement of consumables like belts, gaskets etc. and overhauling and reconditioning.

- In addition, workers can record equipment deterioration so they know to replace or repair worn parts before they cause system failure.

- Maintenance work should be carried out by properly trained workers, to ensure rapid work at minimum cost.

- Preventive maintenance is actually an investment to protect and prevent emergency and major breakdown from occurring.

- The frequency of preventive maintenance is planned earlier and it is carried out at fixed time interval.

- The interval is decided mainly keeping in view, the complexity of the machine tool and the amount of its usage.

- The actual duration of preventive maintenance schedule is derived from manufacturer's recommendations, by past experience of similar machines or by monitoring the conditions.

- The preventive maintenance schedule should be decided correctly otherwise preventive maintenance may lead to preventing production rather than to preventing breakdowns.

- A tailor made programme for preventive maintenance is not practicable and the frequency should be improved over time.

6.10.1 Functions of Preventive Maintenance   [W-12]

- The various functions of preventive maintenance are:
  (i)   To prevent the failure of equipment before it actually occurs.
  (ii) To protect and prevent an occurring of emergency and major breakdown.
  (iii) To record equipment deterioration, so as to know when to repair or replace the worn parts.
  (iv) To minimize the loss of production by preventing breakdown.
  (v)   To keep the maintenance cost and time less than repair after failure occurs.

(vi) To provide safety to the operator and workers.

(vii) To minimize the possibility of production interruptions by tracing out any condition that may lead to it.

(viii) To maintain the optimum productive efficiency and to maintain operational accuracy of the equipment.

(ix) To ensure the availability of equipment and ready for use.

6.10.2 Advantages of Preventive Maintenance [S-12, W-13]

(i)   Flexibility allows for the adjustment of maintenance periodicity.

(ii)   Reduced equipment or process failure and increased equipment life.

(iii) Reduced breakdown and connected downtime.

(iv)   Greater safety for workers.

(v)   Fewer large scale and repetitive repairs.

(vi)   Identification of equipments requiring high maintenance cost.

(vii) Reduced down time as the machine work smoothly.

(viii) Minimized loss of production due to breakdown.

(ix)   Greater control and supervision can be obtained.

(x)   Inventory of standard spare parts of the machine is reduced.

6.10.3 Disadvantages of Preventive Maintenance

(i)   Catastrophic failures still likely to occur.

(ii)   Labour intensive. (A group of labour is required).

(iii) Includes performance of unneeded maintenance (maintenance is carried out of those parts also which does not required maintenance).

(iv)   Reduction of output as machine is called off for maintenance (closed for maintenance).

(v)   Direct loss of profit.

6.11 PREDICTIVE MAINTENANCE [S-12]

* The name suggests that predictive maintenance means predicting the failure before it occurs.

* It includes identifying the root causes for failure symptoms and eliminating those causes before they result in extensive damage to the machine tool.

* In predictive maintenance, equipment conditions are measured periodically (at short intervals) or on a continuous basis.

- The predictive maintenance encompasses the following three distinct stages:

  (i) Detection: During this stage, the 'initialization of defect' is detected through changed symptoms.

  For example, unusual sounds coming out of a rotating equipment, an excessively hot electric cable etc.

  (ii) Analysis: This stage is for analysis to find out main causes responsible to generate the detected defects.

  (iii) Correction: During this stage, the main causes analysed in earlier stages are eliminated by conducting necessary repairs.

- All the above three stages are important and should be practiced properly and in sequence.

- Cost of predictive maintenance is justified by prolonging the time interval between shutdowns or repairs or overhauls.

- **For example**, most people change the oil in their vehicles every 3,000 to 5,000 miles travelled. This is based on the oil change need of equipment run time. No concern is given to the actual condition and performance capability of the oil. It is changed because it is time. This methodology would be analogous to a preventive maintenance task.

- If, on the other hand, if the operator of the car analyse the oil to determine its actual condition and lubrication properties then he/she may be able to extend the oil change until the vehicle had travelled 10,000 miles or can change the oil after 2000 miles if it is not suitable. This approach is similar to predictive maintenance.

- This is the fundamental difference between predictive maintenance and preventive maintenance.

6.11.1 Advantages of Predictive Maintenance [S-12]

(i)   Increased component operational life/availability.

(ii)   Decrease in equipment or process downtime.

(iii) Decrease in costs for parts and labour.

(iv)   Better quality of product.

(v)   Improved worker and environmental safety.

(vi)   Improved worker moral.

(vii) Estimated 8% to 12% cost savings over preventive maintenance program.

(viii) Eliminate catastrophic equipment failures.

(ix)   Inventory can be minimized to support the maintenance needs.

6.11.2 Disadvantages of Predictive Maintenance [S-12]

(i)   Increased investment in diagnostic equipments.

(ii)   Increased investment in staff training to detect root cause.

(iii)   Savings potential not readily seen by management.

(iv)   Maintenance has to be carried out as early as possible when the defect is detected (depending on the nature of defect).

6.12 BREAKDOWN MAINTENANCE

- As the name suggest in the breakdown maintenance, repair is undertaken only after the failure of the equipment.

- For example, a belt is broken, gear tooth broken, motor does not start.

- The routine inspection is not carried out in breakdown maintenance expect some necessary activities like lubrication, pressure control etc.

- The machine is not considered for maintenance until it fails to perform the desired function.

- After removing the fault, the maintenance department does not attend the machine tool until another breakdown occurs.

- This type of maintenance may be quite justified in small factories where following problems arises:

(i)   No specialized maintenance staff.

(ii) Maintenance is done by persons who operate the machine.

(iii) Have less demand in excess of normal operating capacity.

(iv) Downtime cost is less.

(v) Unpredictable equipment operation.

- In case of big industry having large number of machines, this breakdown maintenance system cannot work.

6.12.1 Advantages of Breakdown Maintenance

(i)   Low cost as maintenance is not done frequently.

(ii)   Less staff required in maintenance department.

(iii)   No loss of production for other types of maintenance.

6.12.2 Disadvantages of Breakdown Maintenance

(i)   Increased labour cost, especially if overtime is needed.

(ii)   Cost involved with repair or replacement of equipment.

(iii)   Possible secondary equipment or process damage from equipment failure.

(iv) Inefficient use of staff resources.

(v) Greater risk of unexpected failures with consequent loss of production.

(vi) High risk of damage to plant and machinery.

(vii) Increased chances of accidents and less safety to both workers and machines.

(viii) Breakdowns generally occur at importunate times. This leads to poor, hurried maintenance and excessive delays in production.

(ix) Faster plant deterioration.

6.12.3 Advantages of Preventive Maintenance Over Breakdown Maintenance

[W-11, W-12, S-13]

- Preventive maintenance is better than the breakdown maintenance for the following reasons:

  (i) It prevents occurring of breakdown.

  (ii) It can be done at the pre-scheduled time without distributing the production.

  (iii) It prevents the equipment from a large failure.

  (iv) It provides safety to operator.

  (v) It is less costly over a large period of time.

  (vi) Less standby or reserve equipment and spare parts.

6.13 CORRECTIVE MAINTENANCE

- Corrective maintenance is defined as maintenance work that involves the repair or replacement of components that are about to fail or have failed or broken down.

- Corrective maintenance is the result of a regular inspection that identifies the failure in time.

- Different sensors are connected to every machine in the workshop, to detect any change in the various parameters when they run out of the normal performance or a shutdown is produced.

- The objective of this maintenance is to take action before a failure occurs because the machine is still capable of producing satisfactory work.

- Therefore the maintenance work can be arranged at a time to meet the convenience of both production and the maintenance department.

- But such action should be taken as quickly as possible.

- When corrective maintenance is done, the equipment should be inspected to identify the reason for the failure and to allow action to be taken to eliminate or reduce the frequency of future similar failures.

- Corrective breakdown actions can either be taken after breakdown to restore an equipment to a satisfactory condition or they can be planned action.
- **A good example** is the failure of packing in a process pump. Packing can be monitored by checking leakage, so repacking should not normally be a fixed-time maintenance task. It should be done at frequencies that depend on the operating context.

6.14 SCHEDULED MAINTENANCE [W-13]

- Scheduled maintenance is aimed at avoiding breakdowns.
- It follows the very old principle of "a stitch in time saves nine".
- Breakdowns can be dangerous to life and as far as possible should be minimized.
- Scheduled maintenance utilizes a previously developed maintenance schedule for each machine tool.
- It incorporates inspection, lubrication, repair and overhaul of certain equipments which if neglected can result in breakdown.
- The scheduled maintenance may take place too soon, while the machine still operates well thereby reducing the chances of breakdown.
- It is required to schedule the maintenance early because in some cases, the machine may still be running but producing unacceptable parts.
- Scheduled maintenance can be considered a part of preventive maintenance known as fixed-time maintenance (FTM).

6.15 DIFFERENCES BETWEEN TYPES OF MAINTENANCE

6.15.1 Predictive and Preventive Maintenance

Sr. No.	Predictive Maintenance	Preventive Maintenance
1.	Predictive Maintenance is carried out as the machines are running in their normal production modes (when failure is detected).	Preventive Maintenance tasks are completed when the machines are shut down (during weekly-off).
2.	It is done when any part of the machine tool require maintenance.	It is done at the preset schedule.
3.	It is requirement based.	It is time based.
4.	Concern is given to the actual condition and performance capability of the machine.	Actual condition and performance capability of the machine has no concern.

contd. ...

5.	Predictive Maintenance jobs are less repetitive in nature.	Preventive Maintenance jobs are more repetitive in nature.
6.	It is more suitable for heavy, costly and very critical equipments where overhauling requires excessive downtime.	It is more suitable for industries where large number of similar or nearly similar machines are available.
7.	For example, turbines, wind mill, furnaces of steel mill.	For example, machine tools of machine shop, pumps, compressor, motors etc.
8.	The predictive maintenance is done on the basis of condition monitoring.	The preventive maintenance is done on the basis of manufacturer's recommendation, past experience and judgement.

6.15.2 Breakdown and Preventive Maintenance   [S-12, W-14]

Sr. No.	Preventive Maintenance	Breakdown Maintenance
1.	For preventive maintenance tasks, the machines are shut down.	Breakdown maintenance is done when machine gets shut down.
2.	It is done at the preset schedule.	It is done when the need occurs.
3.	It is time based.	It is need based.
4.	Even if the performance capability of machine is good, the maintenance is done on schedule.	Actual condition of the machine is not concerned at all, whether good or bad, maintenance is done only at breakdown.
5.	In early life of machine preventive maintenance jobs are comparatively more in nature.	In early life of machine breakdown maintenance is very rare.
6.	It is more suitable for industries where large number of similar or nearly similar machines are available.	It is suitable for small industries only having less number of machines. It is not suitable in big industries having more number of machines.

6.15.3 Breakdown and Corrective Maintenance [W-13]

Sr. No.	Corrective Maintenance	Breakdown Maintenance
1.	It involves the repair or replacement of components that are about to fail.	It involves the repair or replacement of components that have failed.
2.	Corrective maintenance is the result of a regular inspection that identifies the failure in time.	There is no regular inspection to identify failure in breakdown maintenance.
3.	It prevents the component from failure and thus reduces chances of heavy loss.	It does not take any action to prevent the component from failure and thus increases chances of heavy loss.
4.	Maintenance work can be planned as per the convenience.	Maintenance work has to be done at a time when breakdown occurs.
5.	Even after removing the fault, regular inspection is carried out.	After removing fault, the machine tool is unattended until another breakdown occurs.
6.	Downtime is less as breakdown is planned.	Downtime is more as breakdown is unplanned.
7.	Equipment cost is required for diagnosis of fault.	Equipment cost for diagnosis of fault is not required.

6.16 REPAIR CYCLE ANALYSIS [W-11, S-12, S-13, 17]

- Preventive maintenance involves carrying out inspection, repair and complete overhaul of the machine. [S-15]

- The inspection and repair activities are carried out on the machine tool in a particular sequence.

- This sequence is determined forehand in the early life of the machine.

- Thus the cycle of I, R (small or medium repair) and C (complete overhaul) is repeated till three or four overhauling.

- The cycle of inspection, small repair and medium repair between two complete overhauls is called as repair cycle.

- **OR** The cycle from machine commissioning to first complete overhaul is called as repair cycle.

- For example,

    (i) I_1 - S_1 - I_2 - S_2 - I_3 - M_1 - I_4 - S_3 - I_5 - S_4 - I_6 - M_2 - I_7 - S_5 - I_8 - S_6 - I_9 - C   is a repair cycle for a particular grinding machine. After every inspections, small repair is carried out. However, after every three inspections, medium repair is carried out and after two medium repairs, complete overhauling is carried out.

    (ii) C - I_1 - I_2 - I_3 - S_1 - I_4 - I_5 - I_6 - M_1 - I_7 - I_8 - I_9 - S_2 - I_{10} - I_{11} - I_{12} - C is a repair cycle for an elevator which consists of one medium repair, two small repairs and twelve inspections between two overhauls.

6.16.1 Need of Repair Cycle Analysis [S-12, W-12]

- The need of repair cycle analysis in maintenance of machine tools is:

    (i) To carrying out inspection, repair and complete overhaul of the machine.

    (ii) To know when the inspection or repair turn comes.

    (iii) To determine Number of maintenance personnel required.

    (iv) To determine Quantity of spare parts required.

    (v) To determine List of the material required for the maintenance work.

    (vi) To Estimate the annual repair cost of the machine tool.

    (vii) To determine Number of times the breakdown may occur.

6.17 STAGES OF PREVENTIVE MAINTENANCE [S-13]

- The four stages of preventive maintenance are:
    (i) Inspection
    (ii) Small repair
    (iii) Medium repair
    (iv) Complete overhaul

6.17.1 Inspection

- Inspection of machine tool is the first stage of maintenance. It involves the following operations:

    (i) To inspect all the mechanism at all the available speeds and feeds.

    (ii) To replace the used oil and to set it to the required level.

    (iii) To tighten all nuts and bolts.

    (iv) To clean the oil filter, lubricators, guides, mating parts etc.

    (v) To properly adjust the clutches, bearings, couplings, cams, brake tension etc.

    (vi) To regulate smooth sliding of tables, slides, saddles, carriages etc.

    (vii) To check and regulate springs tension.

6.17.2 Small Repairs

- It obviously involves all the operations of inspection. It also includes the following operations:
  (i)   To carry out repairs of lubricating and coolant system.
  (ii)   To clean scratches and damages on friction surfaces of bed guides, carriages, columns etc.
  (iii) To replace worn-out parts of tool holder, clamping plate, wedge etc.
  (iv)   To clean the spindle surface by removing it from the spindle shank.
  (v)   To replace the worn out bearings and other parts which may not last till the next repairs.
  (vi)   To replace the belts.
  (vii) To eliminate leakages through pipes, joints and cocks and to carry out minor repairs of pumps and fittings.

6.17.3 Medium Repairs

- It involves repairs of more number of components beside the operations in small repair. It includes the following:
  (i)   To wash the parts of disassembled unit to wipe out the complete machine.
  (ii)   To repair the tool post, tail stock, head stock.
  (iii) To paint the external un-machined surfaces of the machine.
  (iv)   To restore accuracy of lead screws by machining its threads.
  (v)   To check for noise by running the machine at no load at all speeds and feeds.
  (vi)   To replace the bushes, gears, fasteners etc.

6.17.4 Complete Overhauling

- It involves inspection and repair of all the parts. This stage contains disassembly of each and every unit. The worn out parts are replaced by the new ones. The following operations are included in complete overhauling:
  (i)   To check for accuracy before disassembly.
  (ii)   To completely disassemble the machine and all its parts.
  (iii) To replace or repair the worn out parts.
  (iv)   To wash and wipe out all the parts.
  (v)   To check and repair the lubricating system and to replace the oil.
  (vi)   To assemble all the units of the machine and to run the machine at no load at all the speeds and feeds.
  (vii) To paint all the interior and exterior unmachined surfaces of the machine tool.

6.18 REPAIR COMPLEXITY [S-11, 16, 17, W-11, 12, 14]

- It indicates the complexity of a machine tool. (i.e. it tells about how complex a machine is to repair.)
- Repair complexity cannot be measured by any absolute means, but can be decided from relative figures of similar machines.
- It is a relative index to give a comparative idea of the complexity of a machine.
- It takes into account the mechanical gearings, hydraulics and pneumatic unit, guide surfaces and other transmission units incorporated in the machine.
- Repair complexity is indicated by figures.
- Repair complexity plays a very important part in the machine tool maintenance.
- It helps in deciding the duration between the individual repair and in turn the repair cycle.
- Also, the cost of repair, manpower required, spares required etc. depends upon the complexity of the machine tool.
- For example,

  (i) Repair complexity for a centre lathe of small size is 5.

  (ii) Repair complexity for a medium duty milling machine is between 11 to 15.
- The Repair complexity for a machine changes with the change in specification.
- Its value increases with increase in capacity of the machine.

6.18.1 Need of Repair Complexity [S-12]

- The repair complexity concept is used to determine the following:

  (i)   Number of maintenance personnel required.

  (ii) Quantity of spare parts required.

  (iii) List of the material required for the maintenance work.

  (iv) Estimate the annual repair cost of the machine tool.

  (v)   Number of times the breakdown may occur.

6.18.2 Importance of Repair Complexity [S-16]

  (i)   Tells about requirement of material for maintenance.

  (ii) Tells about requirement of time for maintenance.

  (iii) Tells to buy components required for maintenance.

  (iv) Tells about material, labour and overall cost.

6.19 MAINTENANCE MANUAL   [W-13, 16, S-16]

- The maintenance activity of a machine tool is carried out by maintenance department.
- Each maintenance personnel has his own way of doing the maintenance job.
- If proper procedure is not followed, then it can create problem in the machine during operation.
- Therefore, in order to standardize the maintenance procedure and to do the maintenance as per the norms designed by the manufacturer, the maintenance manual is supplied with the machine tool.

6.19.1 How To Use Maintenance Manual   [W-11, S-13]

- If you have a maintenance manual, using it to make repairs or do maintenance on machine can be much simpler and efficient.
- Most manuals are self-explanatory, but here are some tips on getting more out of yours.
  (i)   Make sure you are reading the right manual.
  (ii) Look for specific sections detailing the type of service or repair you are going to perform. For example, lubrication, inspection, repairs etc.
  (iii) Read the "Table of Contents" to search for the topics that you are looking for. For example, In a lathe machine the topics may be chuck, spindle, carriage, tool post etc. The table of contents will give you the page number of the required information.
  (iv) Look in the "Index" for keywords or phrases related to the specific task you intend to perform, if it is not covered in a section or table of contents.
  (v)   Read the section (mentioned in step iii) that describes the task you are undertaking to understand all of the steps you must complete to finish the job.
  (vi) Look in the "Abbreviation" to get the complete meaning of the acronym.
  (vii) Look for specific warnings if any.
  (viii)Find any reference to specific tools, gauges, or other specialized equipment that is required to perform your maintenance or repair.
  (ix) Follow instructions when performing the maintenance carefully, until you are familiar with the procedure. Recheck your work, and test it if possible.
  (x)   Put a "Tab" or "Bookmark" on pages that you refer to frequently.

6.19.2 Need of Maintenance Manual   [W-11, S-12]

- The maintenance manual is necessary:
  (i)   To provides with the information necessary to maintain the system effectively.
  (ii) To know how long a job will take, when all resources are available.
  (iii) To determine inspection dates that will fulfill the future requirement.
  (iv) To provides the regular activities essential for the support and maintenance.

6.20 CONTENTS OF A MAINTENANCE MANUAL

[W-13, 15, S-16, 17]

- The contents of a maintenance manual vary from machine to machine.
- But in general the maintenance manual contains the following chapters:
  - (i)   Maintenance procedure.
  - (ii)   Maintenance requirement.
  - (iii)   Safety Precautions.
  - (iv)   General notes on handling.
  - (v)   Troubleshooting.
  - (vi)   Limitations to Warranty.
  - (vii)   Abbreviations.
  - (viii) Index.

6.20.1 Maintenance Procedure

- This chapter contains the detailed step-by-step procedure to repair, remove and replace the worn out parts.
- As an example the steps to adjust the belt tension of the head stock belt in a lathe machine is given below:
- **To adjust the drive belt:**
  - (i)   Unplug the power cord.
  - (ii)   Remove the motor cover from the back of the lathe.
  - (iii)   Remove the change gear cover.
  - (iv)   Remove the control box from the front of the lathe, but do not disconnect any wires.
  - (v)   Loosen all the lock nuts on the front of the lathe.
  - (vi)   Back-off the top and bottom set screws for a couple of turns.
  - (vii)   Make sure that nothing will get into the change gear drive.
  - (viii) Make sure the control box is in a safe but accessible position.
  - (ix)   Plug in the power cord.
  - (x)   Reach around to the back of the lathe and hold the motor.
  - (xi)   Turn the motor on at slow speed.
  - (xii)   While the motor is running, move the motor to a position where the belt has sufficient tension and does not rub either side of the pulley.
  - (xiii) Tighten the nuts on the two studs that are aligned horizontally.
  - (xiv) Snug the set screws that are aligned vertically.
  - (xv)   Turn-off the motor.

(xvi) Tighten the lock nuts.

(xvii) Replace the control box.

(xviii) Replace the change gear cover.

(xix) Replace the motor cover.

6.20.2 Maintenance Requirement   [W-11, S-12]

* This chapter gives the information about the type of maintenance required for the machine.

* It also provides the schedule for the maintenance.

* For example,

  (i) Coolant of a machine tool to be replaced after 300 hours of running.

  (ii) Belt of a lathe machine to be replaced after 01 year or 2500 hours whichever is earlier.

6.20.3 Safety Precautions

* All the maintenance operators must know the safety hazards that are associated with the machine during maintenance.

* They must be aware of all the safety precautions to avoid accidents and injuries. Carelessness and ignorance are two great menaces to personal safety.

* Other hazards can be mechanically related to working with the machine, such as proper machine maintenance and set-up.

* All the machines require special care to be taken during maintenance.

* The common safety precautions to be taken are given below:

  (i)   The very first step is to remove the cutting tool from the machine before maintenance process starts.

  (ii) When installing or removing the cutting tool, always hold it with a rag to prevent cutting your hands.

  (iii) Loose or torn clothing should not be worn when operating the machine.

  (iv) Do not attempt to tighten arbor nuts when machine is running.

  (v)   Never adjust the workpiece or work-mounting devices when the machine is operating.

  (vi) When using a cutting oil, prevent splashing by use of appropriate splash pans. Cutting oil on the floor can cause a slippery condition that could result in injury to the operator or other machinists.

  (vii) In case of a milling machine, never operate a cutter backwards, it may result in cutter breakage.

(viii) New tools received from stock are usually wrapped in oil paper which should not be removed until the tools are used.

(ix) Take care to operate the machine at the proper speed for the tool being used, as excessive speed will cause the tool to wear rapidly from overheating.

(x) Take care to prevent the tool from striking the hard jaws of the vise, chuck, clamping bolts, or nuts.

(xi) Oil and grease the machine regularly with the lubricant recommended.

6.20.4 General Notes on Handling

- This chapter provides general information regarding the maintenance operation.
  (i) Vibrations and shocks more severe than allowed will cause fatal damage to the device, so be very careful.
  (ii) Do not leave the running machine unattended.
  (iii) Use only those tools and equipments which are specified in the operating manual.
  (iv) Place removed screws and other parts where they will not get lost or damaged.
  (v) Keep a record of all maintenance work.
  (vi) Tighten screws securely but not excessively.
  (vii) Ensure that all electric connections are removed before carrying out any maintenance.
  (viii) Wear appropriate safety equipments when performing maintenance activities, including goggles, hearing protection, gloves and respirator.

6.20.5 Troubleshooting

- Most maintenance manuals have a chapter covering "Troubleshooting tips", which are helpful tips in diagnosing mechanical problems in almost any machine.
- If the operator feels that the machine is not working properly, he should first check some of the things before calling the technician.
- This checklist of possible causes is given in a column to the right as given below:

Problem	Checklist/remedy
Machine not running at all.	(a) Check for power cut-off. (b) Is the power cord connected properly?
Abnormal noise during running.	(a) Check for any part touching the machine. (b) Check-up and provide lubrication.
Guides require high force to move.	(a) Require lubricant. (b) Check for chips between the guiding parts.
Clutch does not engage.	(a) Check for wear of disc and grind if required. (b) Replace the disc.

6.20.6 Limitations to Warranty

- It lists down the various factors when the warranty does not apply.
- Some of the points covered under this chapter are as follows:
  (i) This warranty does not apply if;
    - Damage is caused by accident, improper handling or neglect in following the instructions given in the manual.
    - Damage is caused by defective electric supply.
    - Maintenance is done by an unauthorized person.
  (ii) The terms of warranty will not be varied.
  (iii) Under the terms of warranty free service will be provided only within the "Municipal Limits". Free service outside the Municipal Limits will be provided after charging the travelling and other incidental charges.
  (iv) The company is not liable to carry out replacement within any specified period of time.
  (v) The warranty will automatically terminate after the period specified in the warranty card.

6.20.7 Abbreviations

- This section lists the abbreviated terms and their full words used in this manual.

6.20.8 Index

- This section provides the easy assess to the information of the required section.

6.21 MAINTENANCE RECORD   [W-14, S-12, 15, 17]

- Maintenance records are the part of maintenance documentation that contains failures, faults, and maintenance information related to the part.
- It is written notes that provide documentation about the upkeep of a certain piece of equipment. These records are particularly useful in maintenance management because they help businesses ensure their equipment is kept in good condition. In addition, they provide businesses with a way to manage and track repair and preventative upkeep expenses.
- These records can help make sure that any appropriate equipment maintenance or plant maintenance has been completed so that plant operations will run smoothly.
- The maintenance department keeps a full record of the maintenance activity of every machine on a chart called as maintenance record.
- The maintenance activity is carried as per the instructions given in the manual.
- The record of every single maintenance is maintained in a log book of the respective department.
- The data in the maintenance record differs with the types of maintenance.

- However some common information in the maintenance record is given below:

  (i)   Name of the company.

  (ii) Name of the department.

  (iii) Name of the machine.

  (iv) Type of maintenance.

  (v) Nature of fault.

  (vi) Repair action taken.

  (vii) Total downtime of the machine (Time required for maintenance).

  (viii) Date of maintenance.

  (ix) Name and signature of the maintenance personnel and authorities.

6.21.1 Record for Preventive Maintenance [S-12, 15, 17]

- The maintenance record used during preventive maintenance of any machine will have a format similar to what is shown in Fig. 6.1.

COMPANY LOGO	NAME OF THE COMPANY			ISO _____
MAINTENANCE RECORD OF PREVENTIVE MAINTENANCE				
DEPARTMENT	SCHEDULED DATE:	REMARK:	MAINTENANCE STAFF	
NAME OF MACHINE:	ACTUAL DATE:	TOTAL DOWNTIME:	1. _____ 2. _____ 3. _____	
S.N.	CHECK DETAILS	REQUIRED STATUS	OBSERVED STATUS	REMARK / WORK DONE
1.	Scrool plate:			
	(a) Check OD of the plate	215 mm	214 mm	
	(b) Depth of groove	5.8 mm	5.8 mm	--------------------
2.	Jaw:			
MAINTENANCE ATTENDED BY NAME : _____ SIGN : _____ DATE : _____	CHECKED BY _____ _____ _____		APPROVED BY _____ _____ _____	
Fig. 6.1: Maintenance Record of Preventive Maintenance				

6.21.2 Record for Breakdown Maintenance

- The maintenance record used during breakdown maintenance of any machine will have a format similar to what is shown in Fig. 6.2.

COMPANY LOGO	NAME OF THE COMPANY								ISO _____	
MAINTENANCE RECORD OF BREAKDOWN MAINTENANCE										
DEPARTMENT:	DATE OF COMMISSIONING:						MAINTENANCE STAFF 1. _____ 2. _____ 3. _____ 4. _____			
NAME OF MACHINE:	MONTH AND YEAR:									

Sr. No	NAME OF THE DEFECTIVE PART	DETAILS OF REPAIR DONE	REPAIR DETAILS			BREAKDOWN				
			PART NAME	PART NO.	QTY.	FROM		TO		IDLE HRS
						DATE	TIME	DATE	TIME	
1.	Belt	Replaced	V-Belt	B030	01					
2.	Bushes	Replaced	Rub-ber Bush	R193	02					
3.										
4.										

MAINTENANCE ATTENDED BY   CHECKED BY   APPROVED BY

NAME   : _____   _____   _____

SIGN   : _____   _____   _____

DATE   : _____   _____   _____

Fig. 6.2: Maintenance Record of Breakdown Maintenance

6.22 BASIC MAINTENANCE PRACTICE

6.22.1 Basic Maintenance Practice for Bearing [W-14, 15]

- Bearing may fail before its expected life, if its proper care and maintenance is not taken. Many bearings require periodic maintenance to prevent premature failure, although some such as fluid or magnetic bearings may require little maintenance.
- Most bearings in high cycle operations need periodic lubrication and cleaning and may require adjustment to minimize the effects of wear.

- Bearing life is often much better when the bearing is kept clean and well lubricated.
- The following care is required to increase the life of bearing.
  - Keep the bearings dirt-free, moisture free, and lubricated.
  - Water will rust the bearings and dirt will destroy the smoothness of the super finish on your bearing races, increasing friction.
  - Clean the bearings when they become dirty or noisy with the most environmentally friendly cleaner.
  - Do not add oil to dirty bearings. It will not clean the bearing, but merely flush the existing dirt further into the bearing.
  - Clean the bearings before re-lubricating them.
  - Additional supply of grease should be given to the newly procured bearings before they are started running, or to the bearings that have stopped running for more than 2 months before they are re-started for running.
  - The discharged grease should be removed timely.

6.22.2 Basic Maintenance Practices for Coupling [S-16, W-16]

- Gasket should be placed in the female coupling to make the connection water tight. Gasket should be checked every time a connection is made and should be replaced if there is an indication of wear cut etc.
- To facilitate making and breaking connections, couplings are furnished with rocker lugs. Rocker lugs are located on all male and female couplings with the exception of couplings found on booster hose.
- All couplings are attached to the hose jacket by an expansion ring. This expansion ring is pressed outward, securing the hose jacket to the coupling.
- The lug portion, the locks and the race way of the coupling should be lubricated.
- Do not lubricate the gasket or seals. Replace the gasket periodically.
- Following practice should be followed for bearing:
  - Coupling maintenance is generally a simple matter, requiring a regularly scheduled inspection of each coupling.
  - It consists of performing visual inspections, checking for signs of wear or fatigue, and cleaning couplings regularly.
  - Checking and changing lubricant regularly if the coupling is lubricated.
  - This maintenance is required annually for most couplings and more frequently for couplings in adverse environments or in demanding operating conditions.
  - Documenting the maintenance performed on each coupling, along with the date.

6.22.3 Causes of Failure of Coupling   [S-13]

- Even with proper maintenance, however, couplings can fail. Underlying reasons for failure, other than maintenance, include:
  - Improper lubrication.
  - Improper installation.
  - Poor coupling selection due to improper hub size selection.
  - Improper coupling alignment.
  - Operation beyond design capabilities (for excessive torque).
- The only way to improve coupling life is to understand what caused the failure and to correct it prior to installing a new coupling.
- Some external signs that indicate potential coupling failure include:
  - Abnormal noise, such as screeching, squealing or chattering.
  - Excessive vibration or wobbling that can loosen belt.
  - Failed seals indicated by lubricant leakage or contamination.
- They are eliminated by adopting following maintenance activities:
  - (i)   Regular scheduled inspection.
  - (ii) Visual inspection of each element.
  - (iii) Proper lubrication.
  - (iv) Documenting the maintenance performed on each coupling.

6.22.4 Basic Maintenance Practices for Shaft and pulley

- Shaft misalignment is responsible for up to 50% of breakdowns in rotating machinery. Those breakdown cause increased machine downtime, which translates directly into higher costs. Additionally, incorrect alignment places a greater load on machine components, resulting in increased wear and tear.
- As in the case of shaft alignment, belt alignment or pulley alignment is an important maintenance task. When carried out correctly, it can prevent breakdowns and save considerable costs. Belt alignment and pulley alignment are synonymous, as the process of belt alignment hinges on the correct alignment of the pulleys on which the belt runs. For the sake of clarity, however, we will speak of belt alignment.
- Belt alignment concerns aligning the belts in a manner that results in the least wear on the belts and lowest energy loss for the machine or driver unit. In practice this means that the grooves of the pulleys are in line with one another.
- A shaft drive system will have multiple bearings supporting the shafts. If the bearings are worn out, it will accelerate the wear of the rest of the system. Many

times, replacing the bearings in a shaft drive system will require special tools. Consult the service manual for the model in question to have special holders, locknut wrenches, bearing pullers and drivers ready for the job at hand.

- Lubrication is the most basic maintenance item for shaft drive systems. The final drive unit requires periodic oil changes. When draining the oil, check for signs of metal shavings as this could be a sign of damage to the gears.

- The maximum center to center distance of pulleys should be around 15 times that of the pitch of the smallest pulley and should not exceed 20 times the pitch of this pulley. Greater distances than this require tight control of belt tension because a small amount of sketch will cause a large drop in belt tension, creating slippage and reducing power transmission efficiency.

6.22.5 Basic Maintenance Practices for Chains

[W-14, 15; S-15, 17]

- Following practice should be followed for chains :
  - Periodic examination is required at least every 6 months.
  - Clean the chain thoroughly.
  - Lubricate the chain regularly and properly.
  - Every chain sling should have an identification tag which states the safe working load (SWL) or Working Load Limit (WLL) of the sling.
  - Lay the chain on a clean surface or hang it up in a well lit area.
  - Every chain link should be individually inspected for any signs of wear, twisting, stretching, nicks, gouging and any worn link measured to determine the degree of wear using vernier calipers.
  - 10% maximum loss of cross section is permissible
  - Accessories - Lifting hooks must be replaced when the opening of the mouth is deformed more than 10% or if hook looks worn more than 5% or Shows signs of deep notches
  - Support the chain to prevent uncontrolled movement of chain and parts.

6.22.6 Basic Maintenance Practices for machine belts [S-16, 17]

- Following practice should be followed for belts:
  - Keep the belt groove clean and in good condition.
  - Check the alignment of belt drive before it is put to use.
  - Preserve the belt from conditions injurious to rubber.
  - Belt should not be operated close to furnaces, radiators, steam pipes or where they may get heated.
  - Never use idler on the top side of a V-belt.
  - The belt should not be too tight or else it will wear out quickly.
  - It should not be too loose or else it will slip out of the pulley.

6.22.7 Basic Maintenance Practices for gears [W-15, S-17]

- Following practice should be followed for gears:
  - Check all bolting and retighten if necessary.
  - Check oil level while unit is not running.
  - Remove inspection cover and examine gear teeth for undue wear.
  - With unit running, observe shaft extensions for axial or radial runout.
  - Inspect unit for oil leaks.
  - Check for any noise while in operation.
  - Check operating temperature.
  - Check oil viscosity.
  - High oil temperatures are not harmful to the metal of the gears, bearings, and housings, but could be hazardous to the life of oil seals as well as to the oil itself.

6.23 SAMPLE HISTORY CARD FOR MILLING MACHINE [W-15]

Machine History Card	
Logo of Company	**Name of Company**
Department / Shop: Machine Soap	**P. O. No./Date:**
	Machine Cost:

Make: HMT			**Machine No.:** ML 01		
Date	**Details of Fault**	**Action**	**Time Taken**	**Remark**	**Sign**
01.12.2015	Lack of Lubrication	Oiling	20 Min.	Ok	
10.12.2015	Belt Broken	Replaced	01 Hr.	Ok	

Checked By, Name: _____ Sign: Date:	Approved by, Name: _____ Sign: Date: _____

Importance of Machine History Card: This card gives you the detailed information about the previous maintenance done on the machine with respect to date of repair etc.

Important Points

Introduction to Maintenance

- Maintenance should be planned at regular intervals to prevent uncalled breakdown.
- If proper attention is not given to the machine tool then it will fail.
- The maintenance of machine tool is needed to keep them in working condition at all the times.
- The maintenance of machine tool is important to minimize the hindrance and interruption of work.

Causes of Machine Tool Breakdown

- Excessive friction between the parts.
- Failure to replace parts that are known to wear.
- Improper and neglected cooling system.
- Poor foundation, excessive vibrations, unusual sounds.
- Improper handling of the machine by the operator.

Need For Machine Tool Maintenance

- Its accuracy does not deteriorate.
- It manufacture the components most economically.
- It remain in working condition at all the times.

Benefits of Maintenance

- It increases the efficiency and speed of the equipment.
- It helps to avoid the replacing of the parts.
- It is better because it saves from spending too much.
- It also ensures the safety of the person.

Importance of Maintenance Activity

- Quality of product
- Cost control
- Customer service
- Market reputation
- Cost of investment

Types of Maintenance

- Preventive maintenance.
- Predictive maintenance.
- Breakdown maintenance.
- Corrective maintenance.
- Scheduled maintenance.

Preventive Maintenance

- It is the planned maintenance of machine tools at regular intervals.
- The primary goal of preventive maintenance is to prevent the failure of equipment.
- After preventive maintenance repairs, the equipment's health is restored back.
- It minimises loss of production due to breakdown.

Predictive Maintenance

- Predictive maintenance means predicting the failure before it occurs and preventing it.
- In predictive maintenance, equipment conditions are measured periodically.
- The predictive maintenance encompasses the three stages of detection, analysis and correction.
- Predictive maintenance eliminates catastrophic equipment failures.
- The disadvantage is that, it increases investment in diagnostic equipments.

Breakdown Maintenance
- It is the maintenance only after the failure of the equipment takes place.
- The routine inspection is absent in breakdown maintenance.
- Low cost and less staff is required as maintenance is not done frequently.
- It involves greater risk of unexpected failures with consequent loss of production.

Corrective Maintenance
- It involves the repair or replacement of components that are about to fail or have failed or broken down.
- Corrective maintenance is the result of a regular inspection that identifies the failure in time.
- Maintenance work can be arranged as per the convenience of production and maintenance department.
- Downtime is less as breakdown is planned.

Scheduled Maintenance
- It is based on the principle of "a stitch in time saves nine".
- Scheduled maintenance utilizes a previously developed maintenance schedule for each machine tool.
- Scheduled maintenance can be considered a part of preventive maintenance.

Repair Cycle Analysis
- The cycle of inspection, small repair, medium repair and complete overhaul is called as repair cycle.
- Inspection of machine tool is the first stage of maintenance.
- Small repair carry out repairs of coolant system, replace of belts, tool holder, pumps etc.
- Medium repair involves the activities like wash the parts, paint the surfaces, repair the assemblies etc.
- Complete overhauling includes disassembly, repair, replace, paint and assembly of each unit.

Repair Complexity
- Repair complexity is indicated by a number.
- It tells about how complex a machine is to repair.
- Repair complexity cannot be measured.
- It can be decided from relative figures of similar machines.

Maintenance Manual
- Maintenance manual is supplied with the machine tool to do maintenance as per the instructions given by the manufacturer.
- Maintenance manual contains the information like maintenance procedure, maintenance requirement, safety precautions, general notes, troubleshooting, limitations to warranty, abbreviations, index.

Maintenance Record
- The maintenance data is recorded on a chart called as maintenance record.
- The maintenance activity is carried as per the instructions given in the manual.
- The common information provided in the maintenance record contains name of the company, machine and department, type of maintenance, nature of fault, repair action taken, time required for maintenance etc.

Practice Questions

1. What are the objectives of machine tool maintenance? **(Refer Section 6.2)**
2. What are the causes of machine breakdown? **(Refer Section 6.3)**
3. What is the need for machine tool maintenance? **(Refer Section 6.4)**
4. What are the benefits of maintenance? **(Refer Section 6.5)**
5. State the impact of poor maintenance. **(Refer Section 6.6)**
6. State the importance of maintenance activity. **(Refer Section 6.7)**
7. Explain the basic maintenance practices for bearing. **(Refer Section 6.8.1)**
8. Explain the basic maintenance practices for coupling. **(Refer Section 6.8.2)**
9. What are the types of maintenance? **(Refer Section 6.9)**
10. Explain what is meant by preventive maintenance. **(Refer Section 6.10)**
11. State functions of preventive maintenance. **(Refer Section 6.10.1)**
12. Give advantages of preventive maintenance. **(Refer Section 6.10.2)**
13. Give disadvantages of preventive maintenance. **(Refer Section 6.10.3)**
14. What is predictive maintenance? What are the stages in it? **(Refer Section 6.11)**
15. What are the advantages of predictive maintenance? **(Refer Section 6.11.1)**
16. What are the disadvantages of predictive maintenance? **(Refer Section 6.11.2)**
17. What is breakdown maintenance? Give its advantages and limitations.
 (Refer Section 6.12)
18. Explain corrective maintenance with an example. **(Refer Section 6.13)**
19. Explain scheduled maintenance. **(Refer Section 6.14)**
20. Difference between predictive and preventive maintenance. **(Refer Section 6.15.1)**
21. Difference between breakdown and preventive maintenance. **(Refer Section 6.15.2)**
22. Difference between breakdown and corrective maintenance. **(Refer Section 6.15.3)**
23. Explain repair cycle analysis. **(Refer Section 6.16)**
24. State the need of repair cycle analysis. **(Refer Section 6.16.1)**
25. What are the stages of preventive maintenance? **(Refer Section 6.17)**
26. Explain the stages in a repair cycle. **(Refer Section 6.17)**
27. What work is carried out in each stage of repair cycle **(Refer Section 6.17)**
28. What is repair complexity? **(Refer Section 6.18)**
29. What is the need of repair complexity? **(Refer Section 6.18.1)**
30. What is the importance of repair complexity? **(Refer Section 6.18.2)**
31. What is maintenance manual? What are its content? **(Refer Section 6.19)**
32. What are the important points while referring to maintenance manual?
 (Refer Section 6.19.1)
33. Explain in brief the various contents of a maintenance manual. **(Refer Section 6.20)**
34. What safety precautions should be followed during maintenance of a machine tool?
 (Refer Section 6.20.3)
35. What is maintenance record? What are its contents? **(Refer Section 6.21)**
36. Draw a blank format of maintenance record used for preventive maintenance.
 (Refer Section 6.21.1)
37. Draw a blank format of maintenance record used for breakdown maintenance.
 (Refer Section 6.21.2)

MSBTE Questions & Answers as Per 'G' Scheme

Winter 2014

1. Write the importance of maintenance. Differentiate between breakdown and preventive maintenance. **(6 M)**

Ans. Refer Sections 6.7 and 6.12.

2. Give the maintenance practice for bearing and chains of a machine. **(4 M)**

Ans. Refer Sections 6.22.1 and 6.22.5.

3. What is maintenance record? What are contents of maintenance record? **(4 M)**

Ans. Refer Section 6.21.

4. Explain repair complexity. **(4 M)**

Ans. Refer Section 6.16.

Summer 2015

1. Explain preventive maintenance. **(4 M)**

Ans. Refer Section 6.10.

2. Explain what is repair cycle analysis. **(4 M)**

Ans. Refer Section 6.16.

3. State basic maintenance practices for chains in chain drives. **(4 M)**

Ans. Refer Section 6.22.5.

4. What is maintenance record? Prepare typical maintenance sheet for preventive maintenance. **(4 M)**

Ans. Refer Sections 6.21 and 6.21.1.

Winter 2015

1. Describe contents of maintenance manual. **(4 M)**

Ans. Refer Section 6.20.

2. Describe the maintenance practices for gears. **(4 M)**

Ans. Refer Section 6.22.7.

3. Give the maintenance practice for bearings and chains of machine. **(4 M)**

Ans. Refer Sections 6.22.1 and 6.22.5.

4. Prepare a sample history card for the milling machine. State its importance. **(4 M)**

Ans. Refer Section 6.23.

Summer 2016

1. List the types of maintenance and explain any one of them. **(4 M)**

Ans. Refer Section 6.9.

2. Explain the maintenance practice for couplings and machine belts. **(4 M)**

Ans. Refer Sections 6.22.2 and 6.22.6.

3. What is repair complexity? How is it useful to the maintenance team? **(4 M)**

Ans. Refer Sections 6.18 and 6.18.2.

4. What is maintenance manual? What are its constants? **(4 M)**

Ans. Refer Sections 6.19 and 6.20.

Winter 2016

1. State the types of maintenance of machine tools.   (4 M)
Ans. Refer Section 6.9.
2. Explain the 'Maintenance Manual'.   (4 M)
Ans. Refer Sections 6.19 and 6.20.
3. Discuss maintenance practice for coupling.   (4 M)
Ans. Refer Section 6.22.2.
4. State the need of maintenance record. Explain with example.   (4 M)
Ans. Need of maintenance record: Records are indispensable for smooth, systematic and successful working of an industry or manufacturing plant. The need of maintenance records is as below-

1. Any industry has to maintain certain maintenance records of the machine tools to meet legal requirements. Sometimes court maters require accurate information about the plant, machine tools, workers, supervisors if any accident happens.
2. It is also important from administrative point of view. Planning & scheduling of various production & inspection related activities are to be based on records. It is also clear from the records available that how much time a machine tool requires to get repaired after breakdown.
3. It is also needed to meet certain financial needs such as preparation of budget for maintenance & repair work for various machine tools for upcoming year and records provides the expenditure.
4. It provides a clear picture and up to date information regarding machine tools & their conditions which will be helpful for purchase department for procurement of some new equipments & tools well in advance to avoid delay if any.

For example maintenance chart for milling machine is given below:

Kinds of maintenance work	Interval
1. Cleaning of guideways	Daily
2. Inspection of oil level (sight glasses)	Daily
3. Lubrication as per lubrication chart	As per instructions on lubrication chart
4. Oil renewal	Semi-annually/annually
5. Inspection and, if necessary, refilling of coolant tank	Weekly
6. Thorough cleaning of the machine	Weekly
7. Inspection of slackness of bearings	Annually
8. Inspection of electrics (contractors, limit switches, cable connections)	Every 3 months
9. Inspection of lubrication pump	Semi-annually
10. Coolant renewal	Semi-annually

Summer 2017

1. Define: (1) maintenance manual, (2) maintenance records. State the types of maintenance.
Ans. **(1) Maintenance manual:** Refer Section 6.19.
   (2) Maintenance records: Refer Sections 6.21 and 6.9.
2. Explain the concept of: (i) Repair cycle analysis, (ii) Repair complexity.
Ans. **(i) Repair cycle analysis:** Refer Section 6.16.
   (ii) Repair complexity: Refer Section 6.18.
3. Give the maintenance practice for bearings and chains in machine.
Ans. Refer Sections 6.22.1 and 6.22.5.
4. State how maintenance of gears and machine belts are done.
Ans. Refer Sections 6.22.6 and 6.22.7.